The Dog
Who Saved Me
&
A Man of
His Own

Also by Susan Wilson

What a Dog Knows

The Dog I Loved

Two Good Dogs

The Dog Who Danced

One Good Dog

Summer Harbor

The Fortune Teller's Daughter

Cameo Lake

Hawke's Cove

Beauty

The Dog
Who Saved Me
&
A Man
of His Own

SUSAN WILSON

ST. MARTIN'S GRIFFIN
NEW YORK

Published in the United States by St. Martin's Griffin, an imprint of St. Martin's Publishing Group

THE DOG WHO SAVED ME. Copyright © 2015 by Susan Wilson. A MAN OF HIS OWN. Copyright © 2013 by Susan Wilson. All rights reserved. Printed in the United States of America. For information, address St. Martin's Publishing Group, 120 Broadway, New York, NY 10271.

www.stmartins.com

The Library of Congress Cataloging-in-Publication Data is available upon request.

ISBN 978-1-250-84238-1 (trade paperback)

Our books may be purchased in bulk for promotional, educational, or business use. Please contact your local bookseller or the Macmillan Corporate and Premium Sales Department at 1-800-221-7945, extension 5442, or by email at MacmillanSpecialMarkets@macmillan.com.

First Edition: 2021

10 9 8 7 6 5 4 3 2 1

The
Dog Who
Saved Me

To my daughters, Elizabeth and Alison.
You are still my best creations.

Prologue

When Lev Parker, Harmony Farms' chief of police, called me the first time about the job as animal control officer, I was insulted—there was no way I was going to return to Harmony Farms, and certainly not to wear the uniform of a dog officer. I'd escaped from there long ago. The first in my family to go to college, I'd lived in an overcrowded and rowdy apartment, attending a community college with a tuition I could afford on my own with the help of a part-time job that filled every hour I wasn't in class or studying. I majored in criminal justice. That path led to acceptance in the Police Academy and, finally, the fulfillment of a dream, a position on the Boston police force. I'd found my place, my niche, a purpose. I wore that blue uniform with pride. I had outgrown my past, my family history. On my rare trips back to Harmony Farms, I imagined that now people looked at me with a new respect.

Three times Lev called with the offer, each time modifying it with pot sweetening—a little more money squeezed out of the finance committee, an almost new town vehicle, an assistant. I'd be a dynamic part of his team.

Lev's clumsy "I need a good man" bullshit made it sound like I was the only ex-cop who could possibly do justice to the job of animal control officer. I felt like I was a little kid getting picked last for the basketball team. Or, worse, that what he was offering to me was a handout—a pity play. I knew I wasn't fit for duty, at least not for any real police duty; even though my own physical injuries had begun to heal, my psychic injuries had festered. Maybe that's all I was good for, scraping up roadkill, getting cats out of trees. At least no one gets killed in a job like that; nobody expects you to be brave. I would have no emotional attachment to the animals I encountered. Even at six months, I wasn't at a distant-enough remove to believe that I could ever attach myself to another dog. The idea of partnering again with a canine was out of the question. *Is* out of the question, I still tell myself.

I know Lev didn't look at it that way—that he was tossing me a bone—at least I don't think he did. His point of view was that he had an opening and, clearly, I needed a job. I'd quit the force, tendering my resignation with relief. Maybe *relief* isn't the right word; more like *capitulation*. I'd given in to the overwhelming consequences of my loss. I was incapable of climbing out of the pit of despair that I had been blown into on that night in January.

"Cooper, with your experience, you'd be a real asset to me."

"I was part of a K-9 unit, not a dogcatcher."

"But you know dogs."

"I knew one dog." Argos. My German shepherd. No, the Boston PD's shepherd. My partner. For months, I'd been mourning his loss, and my inability to put what had happened into its proper compartment and get on with my life had made me vulnerable to losing control of everything else in my life.

The animal control job was a one-year contract. Temporary, a stopgap, Lev said, while I got better. Even so, I resisted the urge to hang up on the man who had once been a good friend, resenting both the suggestion that I might be interested in such a job and the barely disguised pity with which it was offered. "I know this is hard for you, Coop, but I really do need a good man in the position. The applicant pool around here is pretty shallow. The only other guy is a preppy grad student our first selectman is pushing on me. I thought of you because—"

I cut him off. I didn't want to hear his justifications. "You, of all people, know why I don't want to come back."

"It's history, man. Ancient history. There are so many new people around here, they don't even know who Bull is. "

"It's not just Bull, and you know it. I've spent two decades on the other side of the law from my brother. We Harrisons don't have a sterling reputation in this town."

"Harrison is pretty common name, and Jimmy's not around anyway. Hasn't been for years." As well I knew. My older brother was incarcerated in the prison at Walpole—in the eleventh year of his twelve-year sentence for drug trafficking.

Lev's words might, once again, have fallen on my—literally—deaf ear, but they came just when my wife, Gayle, had had enough. It was when Gayle broke it to me that she wanted me out of the house—she couldn't take what she called my "moods" anymore—that I finally listened to what my old basketball teammate had to say.

Gayle rested her fingers on the open mouth of the fifth of bourbon, which had become my drink of choice. "I'm going to the gym. Why don't you come with me?" She picked up the cap and screwed it back on.

I watched her slowly twist the cap, a casual motion. No recriminations, just a maternal "That's enough for you," acted out with a tightened bottle cap.

"No thanks. I'm fine. You go ahead."

It's a conversation we'd had over and over, and I could tell that she was growing impatient with me. No, *impatient* isn't the word. Worried, concerned. Maybe even bored. Tired of me and my inconsolable grief. She'd held my hand; she'd held my head when I'd gone too far with the bourbon. She'd held her tongue.

"Really, I'm just fine. Kind of tired. So you go." I had my eye on that bottle, wondering if she'd notice if another inch was missing when she got home from the gym. She disappeared into the bedroom, then reappeared, kitted out in flattering Spandex. "Hey, Gayle," I said.

The hostility in her eyes was liquid. There is a sheen to the human eye when anger and frustration sheath it in dammed tears.

"You look great." It was my clumsy attempt at a mollifying compliment, but she wasn't buying it.

"How would you know? When was the last time?" She didn't have to say anything more. Along with everything else I'd once held dear, our marital relations had suffered with my descent into the black hole of despair.

She knew I was lying. Gayle didn't look fine. She looked pinched and angry, and I knew it was my fault. But you can't stop being sad just because some shrink says that you should be "moving on."

Midnight and I was still awake, the ringing in my ear singing to me in the quiet of a lonely man's vigil. It sang of self-doubt, of regret. It sang of another night, deeply cold, stars so bright, they could make you believe in God.

I stood on the balcony, which was the real estate company's primary sales feature of the condo. Look, a view of the city, cheap at the price. Behind me was the closed sliding door that kept my wife from hearing the sound of the bottle repeatedly touching the rim of my glass. In the near distance, with my good ear, I could hear the barking of a dog. A throaty, "mean it," kind of bark. A warning. I was dwelling on my loss, maybe even wallowing in it. The good news for me was that I knew that's what I was doing. The bad news: It had become a comfortable place, but one that didn't really allow for anyone else. Gayle just didn't get my failure to get over Argos's loss.

I had Argos, my police dog, long before I knew Gayle. You don't get many dogs like Argos. Full-on police dog when tracking down felons, total puppy when playing in the backyard. His bark was deep, his bite crushing, but his love for me was unmistakable. Gayle had claimed to love Argos, as much as she could love something that was as devoted to me as he was. Her love was simply a normal affection for an animal, and why not? She didn't work with him, depend on him for professional success. He was the big dog taking up a lot of space in our condo. He wasn't her first love. He was mine.

It was a buddy of mine who got me interested in going for the K-9 unit. He'd been a dog handler in Afghanistan and couldn't say enough about the rewards of having a canine partner. I'm not going to say that meeting Argos for the first time was like love at first sight, more like a bromance. Unlike human partners, we didn't say good night at the end of a shift; we went home together. We spent holidays together. We played a lot of catch together. We had boundaries, like any good friends. He slept in his kennel at night. He didn't beg at the table. Argos never questioned my authority and I never questioned his dedication to the job.

When Gayle came into our lives, Argos accepted my sudden distraction with grace, placing her under his protection. Of course, he was not a pet. He was, for all intents and purposes, a tool. I was trained to use that tool. Affection and camaraderie were allowable, but not to the point of undermining the dog's purpose. Argos wasn't a therapy dog; he was a weapon. Tell that to the human heart. To me, he was the whole package.

"I'm done." That's what she said. She'd come back from the gym and I was exactly where she'd left me—slouched on the couch, still in the same sweats I'd started out in the day before, the bottle of bourbon down another four inches. "I can't take this drinking, this self-pity, this refusal to try." And then she said the killing words: "You're becoming just like your father."

So when Lev had called earlier that evening, instead of saying no, I'd offered to think about it. "I'm not promising, you understand, but maybe it wouldn't be a bad thing to get away for a while."

Lev shot the last arrow in his quiver—I could rent the old hunting camp on Bartlett's Pond. I knew what he was offering, even if he didn't. Solitude. Time and place to lick the wounds that had been inflicted on me.

"Come see me."

"Okay." I stood in the middle of the kitchen, my phone still in my hand. I placed it facedown on the granite countertop. I told myself that I hadn't said yes, but somehow it felt like I had made a decision. Gayle, holed up now in the bedroom, sleeping, or pretending to sleep, had made it abundantly clear that she didn't want me around anymore. She'd had enough.

So as dawn crept up over the horizon, I called Lev back and told him I'd take the job.

Part One

1

My quarry is intelligent, experienced, elusive. I make a slow turn off the main road and head into a development, easing my government-issue vehicle over the numerous speed bumps designed to keep the rate of speed through the neighborhood down to fifteen miles per hour. I'm craning to see if my fugitive is skulking somewhere behind the cultivated shrubbery or hidden deep in the landscape architect–designed three-acre parcels of this, the most exclusive of all of Harmony Farms' neighborhoods. This isn't the first time I've had to collect this particular miscreant. He has a taste for the good life, a sense of entitlement that frequently brings him here to this covenant-restricted monument to suburban living.

I throw the vehicle into park, sit for a moment, collecting myself, running a hand over my military-short brush of hair. This is the most likely place. It is also where I need to be on foot. It's time to roll. I settle my cap on my head and gather up my equipment. I shut the driver's door very carefully so as not to alert my fugitive. Unlike me, my quarry has extraordinary hearing. The element of surprise is the only weapon at my disposal and the only one that gives me any advantage. The good news is, it's still early in the day, the better not to have interference in the proceedings. Once the neighborhood residents are up and about, my chances of capturing the escapee are pretty well shot. Nothing worse than a posse of vigilante home owners in pursuit of a trespasser.

Despite the similarities of tracking down an enemy or a felon or a missing person and tracking down this miserable runaway, there is no sense of danger, of imperative in this situation. Which, given my nightmares and panic attacks at the thought of returning to my former profession, is a good thing.

I shoulder the coil of rope and squat to examine a print in the dust, depending only on my eyes to tell me the whereabouts of my target. Back in the day, I would have depended less on my vision than upon my canine partner's acute sense of smell to determine the direction of our quarry, his acute hearing to detect the slightest sound. This entire hunt would have been a snap with Argos by my side. I could have been blind and deaf and it wouldn't have mattered. Now I'm just deaf.

It's a pretty morning. The rising sun breaks rosy above the lake that is this town's chief attraction—the view of which is the Upper Lake Estates at Harmony Farms' chief selling point. The bucolic name of Harmony Farms belies the discordant undertones that have developed in the three decades since urban flight brought an influx of newcomers to the village. It was once simply a farming community, carved out of New England soil, etched into hillsides with dry-stone walls, its pastures grappled from the stingy fists of old-growth timber, itself then committed to use as fence posts, firewood, and farmhouses. Lake Harmony is still its centerpiece, a ten-acre, pristine jewel in the crown, complemented by the half dozen spring-fed ponds that punctuate the terrain between gentle hills. Much of the shoreline is privately owned now, but the conservation people have carved out a nice public beach on the Lake Shore Drive side, the less pretty side, my side. It's where we swam when I was a kid, and where ice fishermen would slide their ice shacks out to the middle of the lake back in the day when it froze solid.

Old-timers like Deke Wilkins, whose family was one of the five original families given the charter for Harmony Farms back in the 1600s, have been pitted against the "new people," who arrived back in the glory days of the 1980s. People like the first selectman, Cynthia Mann, who leads the charge for quality-of-life improvements to the roads, the school, and the gentrification of Main Street. Or her husband, Donald Boykin, who sits on the land-use committee and likes to write big checks as "lead gifts" for a variety of big-ticket charities here and elsewhere. Theirs are the names you see on the top of donor lists, the ones who know how to throw a party.

But with influence come accommodations. A few of the niceties. In other words, bring all of the things we like best about city life to this hamlet where we fled to avoid the pitfalls of city life. And besides, twenty miles is too far to go to get a decent cup of coffee. Deke Wilkins likes the sludge that Elvin sells at the Country Market. He doesn't need any high-priced beverage too highfalutin to call itself small, medium, or large. *Grande.* He hoots when he says the word. At Elvin's, he can get a small coffee, and that's just fine with him. "Gimme a *petit*, will ya?"

I jog along a meticulously groomed driveway, following a scattering of prints pressed into the sprinkler-moist edge until I reach a gap in a determinedly trimmed hedge. On the other side, there's a depression in the grass that might be a print; a little farther into the property, I find another. I spot the best indicator that my quarry has passed this way, a small pile of manure. And there he is, happily grazing upon the expansive flower beds of Harmony Farms' wealthiest resident, Cutie-Pie, the miniature donkey, who has made a career out of escaping from his owners' inadequately fenced-in yard.

I pull a carrot out of my back pocket. Cutie-Pie eyes me with suspicion, gives me a wink, and goes back to eating the no doubt expensive and probably imported late-summer flowers. His little brushy tail twitches in derision. The thing with these miniature equines is that they don't think like real equines. They are independent thinkers. A horse will allow itself to be led. A miniature donkey will plant four feet and become an immovable object. A statue of a donkey. I swear that it's Eddie Murphy's voice coming out of Cutie-Pie. *Say what? Yours truly get in that truck? I don't think so. You're jokin', right?* Cutie-Pie is only the size of a large dog. Not even as tall as Argos was.

Right now, my goal is to get a lead line attached to this animal. I hold out the carrot. Cutie-Pie, without moving his legs, stretches his neck to its full length, reaching with his prehensile lips for the carrot. I keep it just out of reach, making the donkey choose: Flowers? Carrot? Cutie-Pie finally takes a step, then another. As soon as the donkey is within reach, I snag his halter, snapping the lead line to it. At least I've finally convinced the Bollens to keep the halter on at all times, even if I haven't convinced them to fix the freakin' fence. Nice couple, one tick away from doddery. They treat this out-of-control equine like a baby. Mrs. Bollen was my third-grade teacher, so it's pretty much impossible for me to threaten them with fines or confiscation. Besides, I really don't want a donkey at the limited facility my part-time assistant, Jenny Bright, refers to as the "Bowwow Inn." It's barely adequate for the canine inmates. I mean, it's better than it was when I arrived on the scene, but still pretty primitive.

Before I got here, there was no shelter, just the pound, which was nothing more than a wire run attached to the outside of the town barn. At least now the impounds have a proper kennel, proper care. Even if this isn't a job I want, I still have the integrity of purpose to make sure my animals are safe and rehomed. No animal on my watch will be put down unless critically injured or unequivocally dangerous, and I haven't encountered either of those circumstances to date, a third of the way into my twelve-month contract. I do that in memory of Argos. Argos, who could interpret what I was thinking even before I thought it. A pure white shepherd, his eyes deep brown, he was big for his breed, and maybe too pretty, but his magnificent nose was what made him the best of the best. Acute and never wrong. Not once. I shake off the thought. My shrink wants me to develop a mechanism to switch off those thoughts, develop what he calls "coping" mechanisms; adopt something that will bring me out of the past and back into the moment.

Half a bag of carrots later, I have the donkey crammed into the backseat of the town's white Suburban, a cast-off vehicle from the building inspector's department. Although I hope that Cutie-Pie doesn't let loose in the ten minutes it'll take to drive him home, I've set yesterday's *Boston Globe* under his back end. I've really got to lay the law down with the Bollens. Armand Percy isn't going to be too pleased to see his million-dollar gardens destroyed by a miniature donkey. Armand Percy isn't exactly a warm and fuzzy kind of guy. We assume he's some sort of venture capitalist who managed to survive the downturn. No one really knows what he does, just that he was one of the very first of the very wealthy to arrive in Harmony Farms thirty years ago.

What's certain is, Percy isn't likely to be the sort of fellow to overlook the destruction of his gardens. He's more likely to be the sort of fellow who will demand restitution. In all the years that Percy has lived in Harmony Farms, there isn't anyone who can claim to have seen him. Still, he keeps a cadre of housecleaners, yardmen, gardeners, and window washers employed year-round, most of whom come from the same side of the tracks as I did. Not the fancy side with the homes with a view of Lake Harmony and two bathrooms, but the rough side, where getting through high school was an accomplishment and home was often subsidized housing or one cheap rental after another, like the places we'd end up each time my mother left my father, dragging us boys with her.

Tina Bollen rushes up to meet me as I pull into the driveway. "I knew you'd find him!"

"Mrs. Bollen, this can't keep happening."

"I know." She says she knows, but I don't think she really gets it.

To her, and to her husband, Cutie-Pie is just a mischievous child. A bad little boy, which is exactly what she says as I extricate the donkey from the backseat.

"Oh, Cutie-Pie, what a bad little boy you are." She makes kissy noises and scratches his forehead, as if he's done something cute. This attitude puzzles me, given Mrs. Bollen's strict authority in the third-grade classroom. Oh, how times have changed.

"Some one of these days, a home owner is going to sue you if he finds Cutie-Pie munching on his flowers." I throw that out in the hope that the threat of litigation will bring her into reality. "That's if he doesn't keep a rifle." If litigation doesn't work, how about the threat of plain old violence?

But Mrs. Bollen just smiles. "I don't think so." There's a little of the old Mrs. Bollen in that remark, and something in her tone reminds me of the time she had me facing the blackboard, hands behind my back, all my pals outside at recess. Mrs. Bollen was sitting there at her desk, humming softly, as I anguished over being kept in, the sounds of school yard play in my ears. My friends were playing dodgeball, and every hollow bounce of the flaccid ball felt like a slap. I don't remember what it was I did wrong to merit so unfair a punishment. Unlike my older brother, Jimmy, I wasn't a bad kid, never intentionally fresh or into destructive mischief. I was probably caught chewing gum. Mrs. Bollen was a bug on gum chewing. To this day, I never put a stick of Doublemint in my mouth without feeling like I'm committing a misdemeanor. "Will you call someone to come build you a proper fence?"

Mrs. Bollen takes the donkey's lead line out of my hand. She doesn't look at me, just makes kissy sounds at Cutie-Pie. I look around, noting the flaking paint on the house and the poor condition of the roof.

"Look, if you can manage materials, I'll do it for you. I just can't keep chasing him down."

The Mrs. Bollen of my childhood was tall and imperious, her

steel gray hair disciplined into a crown of curls. This woman barely comes up to my shoulder, and her white hair is loosely gathered into a relaxed bun. She reaches up and pats my cheek, as if I'm still eight, not thirty-eight. I see a glint of that pity she once showed me, as if I haven't outgrown the need for it.

Mrs. Bollen was my teacher when my father was thrown in jail for drunk driving. Maybe she punished me that day because she wanted to keep me away from the other kids, the ones who knew what was going on. The ones who had heard from their parents that Bull Harrison had driven up Main Street in broad daylight, knocking down parking meters like toothpicks with his '68 Nova, until finally plowing through the plate-glass window of the Cumberland Farms. He climbed out of the truck, shook his head, bits of glass falling out of his beard, grabbed a half gallon of milk, and dug out his wallet. He looked at the shaken clerk. "Sorry about that." Three little words that became the town joke. No one was killed, thank God, and miraculously no one hurt, but Bull was—once again—the laughingstock of the village of Harmony Farms. Town drunk. Town joke. My father. *Sorry about that.*

Mr. Bollen has arrived on the scene, as bent over and plump as his wife is straight and thin. He gives Cutie-Pie a fond scratch on the neck. "That would be great, Cooper. If you'll buy the materials, we'll reimburse you. And for your time."

"No, no need for that. Maybe a plate of that lasagna Mrs. Bollen is so famous for." Somehow, I know that I'll be using my own account at the lumberyard for the fencing and that I may never have the chutzpah to hand Mr. Bollen the bill. But it'll be worth it to have that miserable little faux equine corralled permanently.

This is my life.

The dog waits patiently as the man who has kept him locked in the crate stands with two other men, a third man standing at a distance.

The dog can smell the sweet scent of fresh air all around him. The birds at this early hour have begun their chittering, and a new sun tinges the pond water pink.

The men are leaning against the big car, smoking cigars and passing a bottle from one to the next, pouring something into paper cups that smells sharp to the Labrador's clever nose. Unpleasant, as is the smoke drifting out of their mouths. The fourth man says something to the trio, and the man who seems to be in possession of the dog finally drops his cigar, stamps his foot on it, and snatches up the dog's leash. "*Come on, dog.*" The dog tags along happily enough. The others follow. Like the man who holds his leash, they all cradle shotguns in their arms.

The walk is a pleasant one as they follow the fourth man, who moves quickly and quietly in the lead. They come to the pond, and a roofless structure, into which they go. Sunlight dapples the stamped-down riparian grasses under their feet. There's some talk, and then the three men all face the water. The fourth man walks away. The dog is uninterested in the absent man; it's enough to try to befriend the one in charge of him.

The dog doesn't know what they're waiting for, if indeed that's what's happening. He senses a general restlessness as the men, leaning through the open space above the low wall, shift on their booted feet and begin to mutter. Finally, a duck quacks, twice. The dog's ears perk up at the sound.

The explosion over his head launches the dog into a frenzy of panicked barking. Once, twice, three times the guns blast two feet over his head. It's only the grip the man has on the dog's leash that prevents him from running away. He's hauled back close to the man's legs, close to the discharged and stinking weapons, their heat and odor burning fear into the dog's mind.

He's given an order, but not with words he's ever heard before. It's a human-language mystery, what this man wants of him. He's pushed toward the water. "*Go, go, go. Get the goddamn, duck, you expen-*

sive goddamn piece of . . . " The dog is shaking, trembling, and the rage and frustration in the man brings the dog down to his belly; he rolls over, utterly submissive, quaking. The two other men stalk away, guns broken open, leaving the man and the dog alone on the edge of the pond.

The first kick hurts. The second kick breaks a rib. The blow with the stock of the shotgun cracks but does not shatter his skull. The dog scrambles to his feet, pulls against the leash, sets his feet against the constriction of the web collar, struggles, and finally slips free to bolt.

"Get back here, you mutt."

The man raises his shotgun, one barrel still loaded. Fires.

2

When I drop into Country Market to pick up a deli sandwich for lunch, Deke Wilkins is there, as he always is at this time of day, elbow resting on the meat case, that petit cup of coffee in his other hand. Jawing about who knows what with Elvin. The old man has been a constant in my life, and I can't think of a time when Deke wasn't in that exact spot, wearing those same overalls, his wiry gray hair sticking up like boar's bristles, and the nicotine of his pack-and-a-half habit staining the work-worn fingers of his right hand. Whenever my mother sent me into the market for a loaf of bread or a dollar's worth of bologna, there was Deke. On an ordinary day, he might have acknowledged me with a "Hey, kid." But when Bull was in trouble, as he often was, the old man sometimes stuck a packet of Twizzlers or pack of Doublemint into my pocket. When I'd mumble an embarrassed thanks, Deke might say, "Share with your brother. Come help me with my stone wall sometime. I could use a big boy like you."

Yeah, right. Share with Jimmy. More like, if Jimmy saw that I had a treat, my older brother would whack me in the back of the head and confiscate it.

Two little boys on a walk with their father. One boy is tall for his age, although compact, his jeans a little big, puddling over his worn Keds. The other boy still has that puppyish roundness to his face, a little boy's belly poking above the jeans he's already begun to outgrow. Like them, their father holds a fishing pole. In his rucksack is a plastic box of hooks and sinkers. The boys know what else is in his rucksack besides lunch and two bottles of Coke. Three cans of beer. Maybe a nip or two. Or three.

Their father has promised them he's going to teach them how to fish. The various NO FISHING and NO TRESPASSING and PRIVATE PROPERTY signs that they've pushed past indicate that, once again, Dad is following his own devices. At six, the younger boy, Cooper, is old enough to read, and he has made a point of mentioning signs. Bull tells him to keep quiet. Mind himself. He knows what he's doing. "Trust me, boys."

Eventually, they make their way to Lake Harmony, the eastern side of the lake, deep within the riparian territory of Upper Lake Estates. Home ownership there comes with waterfront access and the guarantee that no one else is allowed to fish at this particular spot. The exact spot where, for centuries, the best trout have congregated. Although there are only, at this time, three homes established in the development, all the amenities of curvilinear drives and new lush plantings, a boat ramp, and a brand-new pier are visual enticements for those urbanites considering relocating to the rustic—but sophisticated—Harmony Farms.

"Dad, I don't think we're supposed to be here." Cooper again. Fretting about signage.

"I fished here all my life. No newcomer is going to tell me otherwise." Bull snatches the pole out of Jimmy's hand and fumbles around in the rucksack to find the small tackle box.

Cooper hears the clinking of bottle against bottle as Bull finally locates what he's looking for—a chiming sound that he, at six, already associates with trouble. Sure enough, as soon as he's finished with the hooks, Bull sits down on the edge of the new pier and pulls out a nip and a can of beer. "Drop your lines, boys. Get me a fish."

Anyone looking at them might think that their trio looks like a family in a Rockwell painting. Two boys and a dad, poles twitching at their tips as false hope convinces them they've caught something. A bright orange life ring hanging from a peg is the brightest dash of color. Rockwell wouldn't have painted the ruddy flush darkening Bull's face as the hours pass and the nips go down. Sometimes Bull is a jolly drunk. Sometimes he's not. Cooper keeps his line in the water and his back to his father. He'd already figured out that it's best just to keep quiet.

They sit for hours, waiting for Bull to decide they've had enough, that the fish aren't biting, that occupying the private and forbidden pier hasn't brought them any luck. After the third or fourth nip, Bull lies back on the decking of the new pier and falls instantly to sleep, the sound of his snoring mimicking the sound of a distant motorboat. The sun has scorched the back of their necks and it becomes painful to look up. The creel beside them is empty, their sandwiches long since eaten, the Cokes gone, and there is nothing else for them to drink. Cooper nudges his brother and mouths, "I want to go home."

Jimmy reels in his line. Nods. Cooper reels in his. Bull's vigorous snores vibrate against the planking and they can feel it in the soles of their feet.

"Dad?" Louder. "Dad?" Jimmy steps a little closer to his father.

The snoring stops, but Bull's eyes remain closed. They wait for a moment. "Dad? Can we go now?"

Quick as a darting snake, Bull's hand grasps Jimmy's ankle and, with one smooth movement, he flips the boy off his feet. Jimmy's head nearly smacks the decking. "You catch any fish yet?"

Jimmy isn't crying; he's that stunned.

Cooper runs up to his father. "No. We tried. We tried." He's pushed aside, nearly falls off the pier. He catches himself, windmilling his arms to regain balance.

"Know what happens to boys who won't fish?" Laughing, Bull hauls Jimmy to his feet and tosses him off the pier, as if he's a too small fish. He's forgotten that Jimmy can't swim, that Jimmy is terrified of water.

Cooper screams and then runs, afraid that he, too, will end up drowning in the lake, the cold water taking him in and under, filling his lungs.

"Stand up, you pussy. That water isn't over your head." Bull is roaring with laughter. He pulls the orange life ring off the hanger. "You want I throw you this?"

Jimmy is thrashing, but finally he finds his feet. Bull drops the life ring, reaches down, and brings him up. Hands him his cap. "Time you learned to swim, boy."

Cooper is off the pier, standing on the shore, watching and ready to run for his life, but things seem to have simmered down. Bull unsnaps the useless hooks off their poles and shoves the plastic box back in his now-empty rucksack. He and Jimmy come off the pier, father and soaking-wet son. Bull strides past Cooper, confident that the boys are on his heels. Jimmy isn't crying anymore; he's wiped the tears and lake water off his face. As they fall in behind their father, Cooper reaches over and takes Jimmy's hand. Jimmy snatches his hand away from his little brother and runs to catch up with Bull.

What kept waking Cooper up at night after that wasn't nightmares about drowning, but the look in his brother's clear, cold gray eye. As if the Jimmy who had been his big brother had been utterly changed by his baptism in the lake and now was someone else entirely.

"Hey, Deke."

"Afternoon, Coop."

These days, Deke no longer buys me licorice or gum. These days, Bull Harrison is on the wagon and keeping his nose clean, and Jimmy is in Walpole, serving out his sentence for drug distribution. He was lucky that the value of the heroin found in the trunk of his car wasn't enough to get him sent away for longer. That he didn't plea-bargain himself down a couple of years only suggested to me that his contact is a very scary guy.

My way of dealing with my father is to avoid him. The first night that I was back in town, he spotted me in the market and enfolded me in one of his signature bear hugs. I extricated myself, maybe a little more roughly than necessary. He hadn't changed much since the last time I'd laid eyes on him. Still slovenly, still clueless.

"Hey, good to have you back, son. Put down those groceries and come have dinner with me." I hadn't told him I was coming back, but I wasn't surprised that he knew I had. Not at all. Not in this town.

"That's okay, Bull. I have a bunch of stuff to do. Another time." Another time in a pig's eye, I thought. I backed away as fast as I could, and the embarrassment that I'd left behind me so long ago worked its way up my face and I thought exactly like my younger self: Dear God, I hope no one saw me with him. My promise to myself in this reluctant return to Harmony Farms is that I have arrived as a stranger, not a native son.

"So, Cooper, I hear that Polly Schaeffer got another kitten." Deke settles his elbow back on the meat case. "Isn't she about over her limit?"

"Somewhat." The cop version of me keeps me from gossiping about my work, despite the juicy stories I could be telling. Polly, the local animal hoarder, being one such topic. Sweet, misguided, delusional, she's seeking something that her family, her onetime friends, her community simply can't provide. Maybe I should get Cynthia Mann to drum up interest in a mental-health clinic to serve the community, as she did with the new community yoga center. Never underestimate the power of a woman with money and time on her hands, coupled with a civic conscience that extends primarily to young upscale families. Maybe her hubby, Donald, can float the starter funding. No, on second thought, a mental-health clinic would disturb the equipoise between the fantasy Harmony Farms and the reality. These people came here to escape the touted evils of the city—poverty and drugs and abuse—and then they find themselves having to turn a blind eye to the rural poverty and spousal abuse and drug use, so that they can believe that they have bettered their lives.

"Can't her kids do something about her?" This from Elvin, who slaps a pair of neatly trimmed pork chops onto the scale.

"I'll go out. Talk to her again." I grab a bag of kitty litter and a flat of canned cat food.

Polly Schaeffer gave me the only other dog I had before my partnership with Argos. Back then, she was like any woman running a household. Back then, she had a husband, two kids, only two cats and one dog, a beagle bitch who'd wandered off in pursuit of a rabbit and come back *enceinte*. Polly, over some objections from my mother, and with Bull's grudging okay, gave me one of the puppies. Snoopy, I called him, even though he looked more pit bull than beagle. He was a good puppy, a perfect pal for a five-year-old boy living in the sticks.

I had to give up Snoopy when my mother left my father the first time, when I was six. Jimmy was eight. I begged her, if we couldn't have him, to let Bull keep the dog, but she said no. She said she didn't trust him with any living creature. Six weeks later, she moved us back into the ramshackle house on Poor Farm Road, but Snoopy didn't come back. I don't know what happened to him. Mom just said he had a new family, no one from around here. When I was a little kid, that sounded like he had a choice. When I was older, I envied him.

"You know what happened to that mutt?" Jimmy pushes Cooper's face into the mud at the edge of the lake. They've been fighting, squabbling over possession of a fishing pole. "They had him shot. That's what. Ha. You're stupid, thinking that poor old Snoopy is in some nice rich boy's home." Jimmy flips Cooper onto his back and shoves a handful of mud into his brother's mouth. "That pole's mine."

Polly took pity on me, let me walk Snoopy's mother, take her to the lake, play fetch with her. She never said anything bad about my mother's decision to get rid of my dog; she just kept her opinion to herself and was nice to me. Some years ago, after her husband died and her kids moved away, Polly Schaeffer began rounding up stray cats. What started as a noble gesture soon elevated to an obsession. But no matter how many times I've been out to talk Polly out of collecting more animals, I still think of her kindness and it makes my job all the harder to do.

I heft the bag of litter and flat of cat food out of my truck. I've swapped the town vehicle for my personal pickup truck because I'm here as an old friend. I never come in guns blazing with Polly. It's a matter of tact and finesse to get her to even open the door anymore. Over the years, as her hoarding has grown more pronounced, Polly has stopped letting her cats outside at all, fearful that someone will steal them, so I'm greeted with the eye-watering stink of too many cats in one tiny house. Cats are on the couch, the windowsill, and the television set, which blares with some talk show. Others weave themselves through and around my legs as I come in; a calico hisses and threatens me with polydactyl paws.

"Shut the door!" Polly stomps toward me, a kitten clutched to her pillowy breast. "You'll let them out."

"It's all right, Polly. No one escaped."

"How do you know? Now I have to count them again."

"And how many do you think you have?"

Polly throws me a coy look. "If I say, you're going to get mad."

"Why would I get mad?"

"I know you're not here just to say hi."

"That the new kitten?"

"Maybe."

"Not from one of your litters?" The one thing I've been able to do about Polly since I took the job is get all of her cats neutered. It's taken half my medical budget, but at least my pal Max Philbine, DVM, gives me a multiple cat discount. So, if she's adding to her collection through theft, at least the pride isn't increasing by uncontrolled breeding.

"Maybe not."

"You can't." I stop myself. "You should leave some kittens for other people."

"No one takes care of them like I do."

I have to push into the house to set my peace offerings down on the kitchen table, which is, predictably, layered with cats, cat hair, bowls of rancid milk, and something that may or may not be cat vomit. I have worked the mean streets of a major city, but this pretty much turns my stomach. When Lev Parker talked about my taking on the dog officer role in Harmony Farms, he left out the part about Polly Schaeffer's proclivities. I've chalked up a number of successes in this job—for example, rehoming seven stray dogs and an equal number of cats—but Polly stands out as my key failure to do my job. In my book, that failure has far more weight than the successes.

"Where'd you get the kitten, Polly?" I try to sound casual, simply interested.

"Found her."

"Okay, fair enough. Where did you find her?"

"I didn't steal her, if that's what you're suggesting."

I imagine putting Polly in an interrogation room and getting Lev to play bad cop so that I can be good cop, but here I've got to play both sides. "No. You didn't steal her, but is it remotely possible that she wasn't lost?" I don't allow myself to finger air quotes around the word *lost*, although I want to.

"She wasn't in a house."

"So, this kitten, which, if you ask me, looks half-grown, was just out wandering around?"

"Yes."

"And, if I call my office, Jenny Bright isn't going to tell me that someone has reported a lost kitten. Let's see, what is it? Gray and white, yellow eyes. Answers to the name of . . . "

"They let it out."

"Who, Polly?"

"I don't know. How should I know?"

A good policeman doesn't show frustration or impatience. But I'm not a cop anymore. "I'm calling Jenny."

"Okay. I found her wandering around in a yard near the old Callahan place."

"Near or *on* the Callahan property?" Despite how they speak of it, the place is no longer the Callahan family's landmark eighteenth-century homestead, but a completely remodeled version of the antique farmhouse with all the amenities, including pool house and five-bay garage.

"On." Polly is defeated, but only momentarily. "They're summer people. Probably left her behind when they went back home. People do that, you know."

"Yes. Occasionally, some summer person thinks that his or her impulsive vacation adoptee will survive on the charity of others. If no one answers the door, I'll entertain that notion." I hold out my hands. "Let me take her home, Polly."

"If no one's home, you'll bring her back, won't you?"

And this is where a lie is as good as a promise. If no one is home, or no one claims this kitty, my assistant will be tasked with finding her a new home. One, preferably, where there aren't already a dozen or more felines taking up space. So I lie. "Of course I will. You'll have first refusal."

I box the kitten and snug the crate behind my seat. As soon as the truck engine starts, the kitten sets up a pitiable yowling, as if she's being torn from the bosom of her family. I take care not to look up to see Polly's expression. I know that she knows that I've lied to her.

As I drive away from Polly's, I give Jenny Bright a call, and, sure enough, there has been a report of a missing gray cat. Not just a cat, but a rather expensive pedigreed Himalayan. Now, I know nothing about cats, and less about cat breeds, but it's pretty certain that this fluff ball is the missing feline. It seems easier simply to take the critter home than to have the family come get her. At the old Callahan property, I follow the new cobblestone driveway to the back of the house. No sign of life except for the faint scent of a Bounce dryer sheet wafting in the air. A woman in a gray uniform answers my knock. "Miss Mousy, where have you been?" She has an accent; I'm guessing Bulgarian. "I thought a dog got her. The missus would kill me if she knew she'd gotten out."

"So, you don't let her out normally?"

"No. Never. I think the pool man did it. I let him use the bathroom. Never again."

"Okay. Good to hear." It's good to think that Polly actually had found the kitten and not stolen it. It makes me feel a little better, knowing that at least she's not stealing other people's pets, that she hasn't gotten that bad. Yet.

I swing by the package store on my way home. I've given up the bourbon because I'm too often called to work in the middle of the night. But I haven't forsworn beer, and I open the cold case for a six-pack of Sam Adams. That and a couple of slices of yesterday's pizza are all I need. I head home, hoping that tonight I can enjoy a full night's sleep, uninterrupted by calls from the communications center reporting raccoons in trash cans or skunks holding dog walkers hostage. A night in my isolated cabin with just the radio tuned to NPR, loud.

Home is a former hunting camp on Bartlett's Pond, a bare-bones cabin with just enough insulation to call it winterized and just close enough to the main road to have electricity. My morning wake-up call is the sun easing itself up over the rim of the pond and the raucous sound of birds on the pond and in the woods. Lately, it's the honking of migratory geese and the sharp *come-to-tea* of the towhee that penetrates through the ringing in my ear. The red-winged blackbirds and their rusty-spring calls are gone. Chickadees chitter and complain and demand I fill the bird feeders *right now*. The rustic peace is shattered now and then by the early-morning blast of shotguns obliterating some game bird—a sound that has the power to make my hands shake.

In the evening, as the light from the setting sun filters through the single window on the western side of the cabin, I can't tell if the silence is mine or if the birds have settled in. If I lived closer to town, I might go to the Lakeside Tavern every night instead of once in a while. I might find myself keeping upright on a bar stool, drowning my silence in a bath of noise from the old-fashioned jukebox and the cacophony that places like the tavern encourage. Instead, I turn on the radio and sit with my good ear closest to the sound of other voices talking about things that have nothing to do with me—things like war and famine and the state of health care.

Eventually, I will make myself go to bed, where I'll close my eyes and hope that I might enjoy a dreamless sleep.

Dusk comes so early these days. It's barely six-thirty, but I have my headlights on as I turn off the main road leading out of Harmony Farms. A few miles later, my headlights pick out the reflector nailed into a single fence post that marks the turnoff for my camp, a two-track driveway that meanders a half mile into the woods. A song I really hate comes on the radio and I reach for the off button. When I bring my eyes back to the narrow, rutted lane, something moves in the periphery of my vision. A shape, a suggestion. I'm tired enough to think that whatever it was moved like a ghost—dog-shaped.

It isn't so much the explosion as the exquisite silence preceding it that haunts Cooper's dreams. That awful silence like the air has been sucked into a vacuum. No air in his lungs. No way to scream. No way to stop the inevitable.

3

B arton "Bull" Harrison is a lumbering shaggy dog of a man. Built for strength, not speed. In a small town of increasing affluence, where the de rigueur Saturday uniform is Gap or Diesel, he stands out with his shock of gray-streaked hair and shaggy Fu Manchu mustache, sagging Wrangler blue jeans, and a flannel shirt no matter what the weather. He's most often seen pedaling his three-speed Raleigh on his way to his job at the lumberyard, where he ties two-by-fours or decorative lattice onto the roof racks of Land Rovers and Escalades or hefts six-by-six beams into the backs of carpenters' work vehicles. He's well liked at the lumberyard. Good for a laugh. Drinks Mountain Dew out of a can all day long. They say about him that he wouldn't hurt a fly. Some remember him from his bad old days, but most just know him as the affable guy at the lumberyard. One or two of the women who come in to shop for decorative molding or new drawer pulls remember him when he was a handsome young man. *Oh that Bull Harrison, you wouldn't believe it now, but he attracted the girls like flies. Shame about how he's turned out. Drugs, you know. Booze. Vietnam. Those kids. His wife.*

He's pretty happy about having his younger son back in town. It's been years since Cooper left town, getting away as fast as he could. Bull isn't ignorant about the whys and wherefores of Cooper's flight. It's pretty hard to grow up in a little town that witnesses your every movement. Because he, too, grew up in Harmony Farms, Bull remembers that sense of never having any privacy. Anytime he'd do something, well, let's be honest, stupid, the story would meet him at his own front door. Small-town fame is what it was. He was famous for trying, on a cow-tipping dare, to tip a bull over—hence his nickname—or for being the kid who could never resist a dumb challenge like driving his father's ancient and beloved '52 Ford truck across the ice of Lake Harmony from the boat landing to the opposite shore. Only he never quite got there. Pop was sure pissed off about that. Even today, when he tells the story, as he is given to do with the first sign of ice, Bull gets to laughing about the look on his father's face. He never mentions the whipping his old man gave him.

Ah, but Cooper is a different kettle of fish. Bull doesn't remember giving that kid a whipping very often; he kept his nose clean and hid in his room whenever Bull had to mete out punishment to his much more lively older brother. The things Cooper was famous for were, when you think of it, pretty good things—like good grades, like being a good basketball and hockey player.

It was hard on Cooper when Mona died. You would have thought that Jimmy would have been sorrier, but Cooper never quite got over it. Bull had tried, he really had, to be a good father, but back then he just couldn't keep clean. When you think about it, he couldn't keep clean when Mona was around; it's why she kept leaving. Then he'd straighten out, show her he was reliable, and she'd come back. Mona had very little faith in him but was eternally hopeful.

"Yeah, Coop fled the coop,"—that is what Bull likes to say whenever anyone asks him about his prodigal son. Took up a profession on the other side of the law from his brother, that's for damn sure. Jimmy, well, he's also a different kettle of fish, more like a barracuda. And from what Bull hears, that son, too, is on his way home.

Lenny Haynes stands in front of the bins of screws and nails.

"Getcha anything, Len?" Bull rocks back on his heels, takes a slug of his Mountain Dew.

"No. I got it." He grabs a paper bag from the stack and starts to fill it with roofing nails.

"Got a project going?"

"Maybe."

Bull doesn't take offense. This is the kind of conversation he and Lenny have been having all their lives. Lenny and his brother Bob live up in the hinterlands of Harmony Farms. About as prickly a pair as two porcupines in heat, as Bull likes to say. The kind of folks who protect their privacy with a barricade of NO TRESPASSING signs and hold the Second Amendment as sacred, convinced that every visitor is a potential invader, a threat to their sovereignty. Only the UPS man is welcome on their property. They are of the self-sufficient pioneer stock who make one trip to town a month. But Bull has known them forever and doesn't take their politics or their rudeness to heart.

"Got a sale on hammers. Buy one, get another for half price."

"What would I want with two hammers? Can't break 'em. Don't go bad. That's just bull crap and you know it."

Bull laughs. This is Len's humor. "I dunno. Maybe get that brother of yours to bang a few nails with you."

Len doesn't say anything, just drops the bag of nails onto the scale, waits while Bull writes him a slip.

There's a rangy yellow-colored dog in the back of Len's Ford truck. A short chain keeps it from jumping out of the bed. Bull walks over to give it a pat, but the dog snarls with an impressive show of teeth. Bull jumps back. Figure a Haynes to have a vicious dog.

"Watch it, Bull." Len makes no apology for his dog's behavior; in fact, Bull thinks that there's maybe a slight smile of pleasure in Len's face, a satisfaction. At his master's approach, the dog goes to his belly, his ears flattened back. His tail beats feebly against the metal of the truck bed. The dog looks anything but vicious; he looks defeated, and Bull kind of feels sorry for him.

4

Another day in paradise and I'm slowly driving up Main Street, looking for a loose dog that's been spotted by some concerned do-gooder. I'm of the persuasion that most wandering dogs make their way back home eventually. If I find it and it doesn't have a tag, then I've got to go through the hassle of locating its owner and, until I do, keeping it fed, and right now I don't have space in my shelter to house it, what with all three kennels occupied. Jenny Bright is exceptionally good at finding lost owners and has displayed an extraordinary capacity for knowing individual dogs as they come in. But she's off today. Getting another tattoo, no doubt. Or shacking up with her no-count boyfriend. Or reapplying the boot polish black to her chopped hair. For a girl named Bright, she's plenty dark, a small-town version of Goth.

I'm grouchy. It was a bad night last night. Even though the com-munications center left me alone, I was more restless than usual and unable to fall sleep. Some nights are like that. With no one else in my house, I'm free to get up and pace around, let my thoughts stream undammed and undeterred by the presence of another human being. That was the biggest reason for taking this cabin. I disturb no one with my pacing, my sighs, not even a neighbor who might be drinking a midnight glass of water and staring out his back window, idly wondering why his neighbor is up and every light in the house on. It's part of what drove Gayle out of her mind. She wanted me to take the damned Ambien, quit the bourbon. Well, she doesn't have to suffer my neuroses anymore.

Seeing the apparition that flowed past in my peripheral vision last night wasn't the first time that I've seen something like that. Easily explained away—fox, coyote, swamp gas, rising mist—but I'd rather wallow in the rather adolescent desire for the supernatural; think that, benignly, I'm being haunted by the ghost of my dog. There have been times when I was running and I had the unmistakable sense of being accompanied. I've seen his ghost in the blaze of rising sun on the pond—in the shape of a shadow. Heard his breath in the rustle of cattails as I pass by. I've heard him bark with such clarity that it wakes me from my sleep, and that's when I get up and pace and think.

I keep telling myself that if I *think* about it long enough, hard enough, I'll figure out how to accept Argos's violent death. Everyone kept telling me to *forget* about it, saying that was the only cure. It isn't just coping with the grief, although that's the part I understand. It's the fear, the liquefying fear that it will happen again. Every sudden noise sends jolts of anxiety through me. I couldn't bear to go to the Fourth of July fireworks. I jump out of my skin when the mechanic drops his wrench on the cement. Thunder makes me hold my hands over my half-deaf ears. With the start of duck-hunting season, every morning is torture, the erratic shotgun blasts ruining my place of refuge. The sound puts my teeth on edge and I have to leave long before I'm due at work, then stand at the door of the Country Market, waiting for Elvin to open at six, or burn expensive gas driving

around Lake Harmony. I'm gun-shy. Worse, considering it wasn't a
bullet that has caused this spiral, but, rather, my failure to use my
weapon.

I am afraid to go back out there. There is a darkness, a hole, where
my self-confidence used to be.

I spot my father as I turn the corner onto Maple Street. The old man
is pedaling slowly, keeping neatly to the side of the road, so it will be
impossible not to pass him. My Suburban wears the town seal on its
side and he'll know it's me, maybe wonder why I'm passing without
stopping.

*It's the last game of the regular season and Cooper Harrison is on the bench,
swiping a towel over his face and head, sucking in the fuggy, overheated air of
the gymnasium. He's just hit a three-pointer. Lev is on the court now. In the
way of best friends, he knows that Lev's hoping to best his three points and bring
the exceptionally close game to a successful conclusion. There's a minute left on
the clock. It's close, 81–83, but Cooper's pretty certain that the points that he
and Lev have scored will hand the Harmony Farms Patriots a win and a spot
in the play-offs. It's up to defense now.*

*Above the frenzied sound of screaming fans and bellowing coaches, the re-
lentless chanting of cheerleaders, and the squeaking of basketball sneakers on
polished hardwood, there is the awful sound of one man falling off the bleachers.
Not a slip, a misstep, a thump, but a complete drunken tumble. The crowd's
attention shifts from the game to the man. He gets up, shakes off helping hands,
and purposefully strides right across the basketball court as if he's walking across
the street, right through the ten boys scrambling for last points. Bull is so inebri-
ated that he's forgotten where he is. The other team, grateful for the momentary
distraction, scores before the ref can halt the game. The buzzer sounds, rude and
final. The Harmony Farms Patriots have lost a heartbreaker.*

"Your father has shit for brains, Harrison." Not quite playfully, Lev shoves Cooper aside as they head for the locker room.

I slow down, keeping well behind my father, who's pumping the Raleigh slowly up the rise. And then there he is, the runaway dog. I pull the Suburban over, wait a couple of beats until I'm sure Bull is out of sight, then get out to retrieve the dog.

Lucky for me the dog, Ralph, is a repeat offender and I know where to take him. Ralph's owner works over at the small medical center as a receptionist. She's a single mom, transplanted to Harmony Farms and then abandoned by her husband, who had the bad grace to die of a massive heart attack. She's a little dumpling of a woman, and her dog is the least of her problems. I haven't got the heart to fine her. She reminds me too much of my mother. Not the dumpling part, but the struggle to manage two boys with limited resources. She reminds me of the mother who moved her boys from one shithouse rental to another and then back to Bull's house when he showed signs of remorse and recovery. Brenda Connors works for the same practice my mother once worked for, which isn't odd, given that Harmony Farms has only one medical practice. It's bigger than it was when my mother worked there, but it's still in the same place.

I haul Ralph out of the Suburban and into Brenda's house. As is the case with most homes in Harmony Farms, the back door is unlocked, which is obviously how Ralph got out. I run a fresh bowl of water for the dog, then write a note. *Brenda, Ralph got out again. I think that the trouble is either your back door latch or your kids. Please get your latch fixed and remind your boys that someday Ralph may not come home. C. Harrison, ACO.* I tear the sheet from my notepad and stick it on her fridge with a magnet shaped like Cape Cod.

Scattered around the small, very messy kitchen is the detritus of active boys: remote controls and PlayStation handsets, mismatched athletic shoes, a sock. Ralph flops down on his bed, which is jammed into a corner, sighs, and closes his eyes, as if his wandering adventure was exhausting. Some dogs just love to wander; others never leave home. Maybe Ralph was just looking for his boys.

The very first assignment Argos and I were given right out of training was a search and rescue mission to find an autistic child. This was a city hunt, not a wilderness one, and exceedingly challenging. We went up and down city blocks, into alleyways, scaring druggies shooting up, but keeping to the mission. The frantic mother was pleading with me to find her child. What I remember most about that day is the moment that Argos hit the boy's scent—the way his tail wagged, the joy for him in completing the game. The dog was so clear in his surety that we'd found our man that it was as if there were a conversation between us. Argos said, *he's in there.* I replied, "Good boy."

The mother knelt in front of Argos. Her inexpressible joy over her son's return was almost painful to watch, and it was more painful to have to stand tall and pretend it was all in a day's work, to maintain the facade of dignified policeman. Argos didn't feel any such restrictions on his dignity. He licked the boy's face, making him laugh, and let the mom hug him, his tail beating from side to side with the pleasure of it.

I always looked on that as the moment when I fell in love with my dog. I'd loved him from the get-go, sure. Who wouldn't have? But the heroic accomplishment of finding that child, which this animal did with joy, transformed the mere affection of a man for his working dog to something I can only call passion—a pride-stoked passion. Maybe that's how normal parents feel about their children—that no matter what, there will always be love.

When I was a kid, the police were fairly regular visitors to our house on Poor Farm Road. Part of this was due to the number of times

Bull was brought home half in the bag rather than being dumped in the drunk tank, thanks to the kindness of one or the other of the town's two officers who had gone to school with him, one of them Lev Parker's father. Other times, especially as we got older, it had more to do with Jimmy being suspected of something—vandalism, theft. I would stand in the corner of the kitchen, unobserved, quiet, just in awe of the blue uniform, the duty belts with their serious hardware, how the officers exuded an authority like no one else I knew. It was the way that they were so in control, so confident, that put the idea of becoming a policeman in my head. I would grow up to be just like them.

5

I start my day, as I almost always do, with a five-kilometer run around the perimeter of Bartlett's Pond. Against the advice of my audiologist, I plug my earbuds into my ears, jack up the volume on my iPhone, and absorb the beats. It's cooler these mornings when I start off, but by the time I've made my first lap, I'm sweating and I yank my venerable Police Academy T-shirt off and drop it behind me, to be retrieved on my cool-down lap. The relentless music camouflages the ringing in my left ear and fills my head with enough noise that I can run without thinking. So I don't plan my day. I don't actually have to, as my days are pretty routine. I don't intentionally think about Argos. It's more the lack of a presence which brings that presence to mind. Does that make sense? Probably not, but that's the danger of the solitary life. You get away with random musings. Not all that long ago, Argos would have been attached to my side, and I deeply miss the sense of the dog beside me. Of course, if Argos were still alive, I wouldn't be running around this particular pond. Our favorite run was along the Charles River, on the Cambridge side. The tall military-looking man and the stunning white German shepherd garnered a lot of admiring looks. Argos ran with his nose at my knees, his elegant gliding stride matching his partner's pace beat for beat. He'd be panting a little, but not out of breath. It was more like encouragement. *Ha ha ha. Keep moving man, keep moving.*

At the end of however many kilometers I wanted to do, we looked for our reward, jogging over the Longfellow Bridge and up Charles Street to our favorite café. The owner had good cause to be happy to see me and Argos; we were the K-9 unit who had run down the man who had robbed him at gunpoint one foul November night. Despite the washed-down sidewalk, Argos had pinpointed the man's hiding place within minutes. I always left the equivalent of my "on the house" snack in tips. Argos graciously took the proffered gluten-free cookie, paying for it in his high five–raised paw before crunching the peanut butter–flavored treat.

It's a particularly pretty early fall day, trees a couple of cold nights away from blasting color, the tall grasses and bushes doing their own seasonal change of costume. The sky's a cloudless blue. As I trace the border around the pond, a turtle plops into the water. There are deer tracks in the soft mud at the edge of the pond. Soon enough, the pastoral quiet around here will be threatened by the groups of hunters that find Bartlett's Pond a fine place to bag pheasant, deer, and rabbit. Duck hunters have already been around, and the migratory water fowl that move out deeper into the pond as I pass by might end up duck soup soon enough.

I increase my pace with the change of tune in my carefully selected running music, going from a slow four beats to a rapid six-eight. Warm-up done, I sprint now. The soft burn of full-bore running reminds me that I haven't entirely erased the months of inactivity after what we all call "the incident," for lack of a better word. Other words have been auditioned—for instance, *event, trauma, horror, cri-*

sis, depression. And there's the always popular *self-pity,* the one that
Gayle likes best. Or at least that's the one she chose as her default
word to describe my rendering our marital life null and void.

I claim I can't think and hear music at the same time, but obviously, that's not quite true.

Another lap and I've hit the two-mile mark. I've calculated that
five laps around the fairly large kettle-hole pond is about five kilometers. On bad days, I'll run it twice. I want to believe that actual
running helps and isn't just running away. On good days . . . well,
there aren't that many of those. Today, however, I have time for only
one 5K.

My cool-down lap is the sixth and I slow to a moderate walk,
letting the oxygen work its way back into my starved lungs, hunting
for my discarded shirt. When I finally find it, some dog has planted
one big muddy paw print on the front of my white Academy T-shirt.
And no, I don't immediately think this is a message from beyond
from Argos. I'm not quite that delusional. However, I haven't seen
any dogs on my run.

We have three dogs in residence today. I picked up two of them together, a pair of nice-looking beagles. They've got tags, and we're
just waiting for their owner to show up. Like many beagles, once
these picked up the scent, they got too far away from their owner
and didn't have the sense to turn around. The third is a solemn-
looking mutt I brought in yesterday afternoon, probably a pit bull
or some kind of AmStaff mix. Who knows where she came from.
Maybe somebody failed in an attempt at a second chance for her in
a country setting. Like the beagles, this girl is healthy and friendly.
Jenny has her posted on social-media sites and has been running
down leads. I can never figure out why people don't automatically
call the shelter when their dogs go missing, instead of making us do
the heavy lifting and spend taxpayers' money on classified ads.

Jenny and I go through the door that leads to the small indoor kennel area. All three kennels are empty, the inmates clearly in the outside runs, taking the air. The outside door sticks a little and I have to give it a shove with my shoulder. Two dogs behind wire enclosures look up at me with quintessentially beagle expressions of silly expectation. *A walk! Food!*

"Did someone collect the pit bull?" I ask.

"No." Jenny looks back indoors, as if the pit bull could be playing some sort of game of hide-and-seek with us.

It has been three-quarters of a year since I was a real cop, but the certainty that a crime has been committed is a liquid sense that flows through my brain, and I can feel myself tense with the muscle memory of being a cop. The runs don't have outside doors; the only access is through the shelter. The main door of the shelter is locked at night. The kennels are on cement slabs so that no dog can dig its way out. I gently back Jenny away from the area around the outside kennels. I'm looking for footprints, anything that will set me on the right course for solving this puzzle. The wire walls are over six feet high. There's no way a dog could jump that fence, nor a sixty-something overweight woman who prefers caftans climb up it. Polly Schaeffer is the first suspect to come to mind, although I well know from long law-enforcement experience that you can't always assume the obvious suspect is, in fact, the actual perpetrator. However, there is the theory of Occam's razor, that the most obvious answer is usually the correct one. Polly Schaeffer certainly fills the "obvious" bill with her recent proclivity for rescuing animals not in need of rescue. And unless I'm way off the mark, there's a size-six depression in the soft dirt, one that looks like it might have been made by a Ked, not by one of Jenny's honking Doc Martens.

"Looks like an inside job." Jenny can barely keep the smile off her lips.

"What do you mean?"

"Just joking. I mean, who else besides me is inside?"

"Right. And you had nothing to do with this?"

Jenny delivers me a cutting look. "As if."

"You were off yesterday."

"Yeah. And you were on."

"Right."

She stops smiling. "Coop, the back door wasn't bolted this morning. Just now. Neither of us had to unlock it."

I could swear that I locked the front door. I did; I distinctly recall locking it with the key that catches a little as you insert it. But did I bolt the back door? That I can't quite remember.

Mistakes come out of complacency, out of carelessness. Or out of distraction. I have little patience for mistakes like this. But I can only blame myself for failing to lock up properly last night. I remember now. The phone rang as I was getting ready to leave, someone with a complaint about a dog rooting in the garbage. A skinny yellow dog, a stray the person didn't recognize. There has been a rash of raided trash barrels in the past few weeks, and two other good citizens have called with similar sightings. In each case, as with this most recent sighting, the skinny yellow dog has been described as limping badly but fast enough on three legs to bolt as soon as he's discovered.

I can tell myself all day that a missing pit bull isn't a life-or-death situation, but this kind of mistake suggests that maybe I'm better off as an animal control officer in my former home town than being responsible for other people's lives.

I send Jenny out on a call about a missing bunny. I'm just not in the mood to be a comfort to someone who's idea of a pet is a caged rabbit. The beagles' owner has finally returned my call and is on his way in to collect his runaways. As if inflicting punishment on myself, I clean the empty run, vaguely hoping that it will give up the mystery of who took the missing pit bull. I've got to go to the town hall anyway, so I'll stop in and check with the town clerk to see if anyone has recently registered a bully type. Maybe the owner made an off-hours call and figured he could just liberate his dog and skip the ticket. But just in case, I'll casually drop by Polly's to see if she's acquired a dog. Although her preferred collectible is feline, she's fond enough of dogs, and a little loony, so my hunch that she made the heist is not exactly far-out.

I'm outside when a Range Rover pulls into the visitors' parking space. A stout man climbs out, two leashes in his hand and a disgruntled look on his face. "Got my dogs?"

"I believe that I do. Let's see and then do a little paperwork."

"How much?"

I name the fine, times two because of the double trouble.

The expression of annoyance on the man's face quickly dissolves into relief at the sight of his less than contrite hounds. *"Bad boys, bad boys,"* he says, but he hugs them and lets them lick his face in a rapture of reunion. I was wrong: He's not a hunter, but a middle-aged dog lover.

"Beagles are tricky. Best to have them on long lines when you're out walking."

"I will." The man offers his hand to me. "Thanks.

The gratitude coming from this guy makes me smile. Sometimes it feels good to be recognized for doing your job. Not exactly like the commendations Argos and I earned for bravery, but nice all the same. Mostly, with this job, the public regards me with something between disdain and annoyance. Despite the fact I'm working under the umbrella of the police department, the public really doesn't look at me as a cop. Barely an authority.

The beagle man shakes my hand vigorously. "I'd just die if anything ever happened to these guys."

Which pretty much sums up why I will never have another dog. Not a pet. Not a partner.

No sooner has the beagle man left than Doc Philbine pulls up.

"I was passing by, thought I'd stop in."

"I can give you a cup of coffee, maybe find a doughnut to go with it."

Max Philbine has the movie star good looks of a man more suited to a life in a power suit, not rubber boots and, during bovine breeding season, a plastic glove with a sleeve up to his armpit. But he's the son of a veterinarian who was the son of a veterinarian and he doesn't recall ever wanting to be anything else. Unlike his father and grandfather, though, Max can't make a living by being paid in eggs and pie, and the high cost of medical equipment and the sheer magnitude of laboratory tests and procedures never imagined by his forebears has Max wondering out loud to me if that teaching position at Tufts isn't worth considering.

"What, throw over all this glory for a three-day-a-week teaching load and a sports jacket?" I hand Max the sugar.

"And benefits and maybe a car that doesn't have to double as a portable office."

"Haven't classes started already?"

"The job would start in January."

The coffee in my mug is bitter, dregs left over from the first pot Jenny put on at seven-thirty, so I toss it into the sink. "Not to influence your decision, but you do know that you'd be leaving this town without veterinary care. You're all right with that?"

"I'd sell the practice. Actually, I'm pretty close to selling the practice anyway. Looking for a starry-eyed recent vet school grad hoping to become the next James Herriot."

I give him a blank look.

"*All Creatures Great and Small*? Books? Television series?" He shakes his head. "Never mind."

"You've made up your mind." I know that I sound like I'm interrogating a miscreant and so I busy myself with making a new pot of coffee. We really should invest in one of those single-cup dispenser things. Too much wasted coffee. The line item for office supplies, where I hide the coffee, is going over budget.

"What about you?"

Such an open question. Max knows my contract goes only to June 30. He thinks, like everyone else, that once my hearing improves, I'll be ready to go back to active police duty. He thinks that it's just a matter of decibels. He has no idea about the overpowering anxiety that squeezes my guts at the thought of taking on another K-9 partner. I can't lose another dog. And policing without one is out of the question. "We'll see."

"I'm heading out. You want to grab a bite at the tavern Friday?" Max rinses his mug, setting it into the little sink.

"Sure." It's become something of a regular thing for us, this Friday-night burger at Harmony Farms's local pub. It's my one concession to social activity. Otherwise, it's just me in my splendid isolation.

Max heads off on his rounds, which makes me think about starting on the annual farm visits as soon as Jenny comes back from her rabbit hunt. As my official title is Officer of Animal Control and Inspector of Animals, part of my job is to visit the local farms, count the livestock, and make sure that nothing inhumane is going on. I'll start with Second Hope Farm, the equine rescue on the other side of the pond from my cabin. But first, I'll pay Polly a visit.

"Nobody understands these dogs." Polly Schaeffer keeps one hand on the boxy head of the "rescued" pit bull. "They do terrible things to them." The pit bull is sporting a rhinestone collar and pink leash. She looks like a hooker. I think *that's* a pretty terrible thing to do to a dog.

"Polly, she's somebody's pet. Not a scar on her. She's friendly. She needs to go back to her people." I casually reach for the leash, but Polly jerks it away.

"She can stay here till you find her people."

"That's not possible." Once again, I feel like I'm in hostage negotiations. This time, I've arrived without litter or food, nothing to negotiate with. I've got nothing but the law on my side, and I'm tired and annoyed and pretty ready to use it against my old friend. "Polly, give me the leash."

Polly heaves a great sigh. "What if no one claims her? I know what you do to the unclaimed dogs."

"Polly, when I took this job, it was with the caveat that we find homes for the homeless. Or we place them with breed-specific rescues. I'll find her owner, or get her a new one. I promise."

"Or she comes back to me." Polly keeps the hand holding the leash behind her so that if I'm going to get to it, I'm almost going to have to knock her over. It's a far better thing simply to lie to her once again. "Fine. She comes back to you."

Polly gives me a girlish smile, coy and teasing. But then offers me the end of the leash. I replace Polly's blinged-out leash and collar with a nylon slip-knot leash.

"Just tell me one thing. How did you even know she was in there, and what made you think the door would be unlocked"

"You said one thing; that's two. It's pretty simple. Jenny posted her on Facebook, and I didn't know the door was unlocked. That was just dumb luck."

"My mistake."

"Oh, by the way, I saw your brother the other day, at the market."

"Jimmy?" I ask this as if there's another brother in my life. Jimmy. A white kid named for Jimi Hendrix. Born during my parents' brief hippie phase, which I figure was less about peace, love and rock 'n' roll than it was about drugs. I wrap the leash around my hand and give the pit bull a little tug to get her to follow me to the Suburban.

"This was definitely Jimmy. He greeted me like I was a long-lost relative. Kissed me on both cheeks, very Continental. I can't think that he learned that in the big house." Polly touches her plump cheek with the back of her hand, as if still feeling the smarmy lips of my ex-con brother. But she's smiling like a girl. Jimmy always did have that kind of dark attraction for women. That whole James Dean bad-boy look. What do they call it in the insurance business? "An attractive nuisance." The fun never stops here in Harmony Farms.

Lev Parker won't be pleased to know that Jimmy Harrison is back in town. Even if he's cleaned up his act and is now a model citizen, his history certainly means that Lev will keep his eye on him. When we were little kids, maybe seven, eight, Lev and I both looked at Jimmy as if he were some kind of god. Two years older, always on the cutting edge of adventure, he tormented the life out of us. He'd set us up for practical jokes, and just being victimized by his antics made us feel sophisticated and included. We thought it was cool and that it meant he liked us. Deluded little kids. By the time Lev and I were in fifth grade, and Jimmy was in junior high, the practical jokes and antics had evolved to serious mischief and an attraction for the illicit. My mother, Mona, couldn't cope with the seemingly endless round of trouble this kid was in, and Bull didn't care what Jimmy did as long as he didn't steal the beer money. Vandalism became petty theft, which became prescription-drug theft, which became hard-core drug dealing.

When my teachers saw my name on the class list, the automatic response was to look at me and tense their mouths. *Oh, here's another Harrison boy. Here comes trouble.* I spent a lot of time and effort trying to prove them wrong.

I might give Lev a call, just to let him know that Jimmy is back; but, on reflection, I figure that the chief of police has probably already heard that bit of news. Lev is a good cop, a good small-town cop. Looking at the well-tended gardens and high-end homes, the clean main street with its planters filled with seasonal flowers, and the cheerful banners suspended from the new Beaux-Arts–style lampposts proclaiming HARMONY FARMS WELCOMES YOU!, most people would assume that the worst crime in the area would be bad fashion sense. The darker secret is that the best customers for the drugs that men like Jimmy provide are the people who sit on the beautification committee and live in those megamansions that have taken over the old pastures and orchards of bygone days. Maybe they're not interested in heroin, but they have a hunger for prescription pills—oxycodone and Percocet—habits formed by the pain of living an active life, the wages of a good golf game or a face-lift, the upset of an occasional car crash. Or their kids party with the enhancements of whatever pills are available. It will be very hard for a man who has no moral compass to stay clean in a place that provides such an easy market.

As I don't have the heart to do it, instead of crating the pit bull and putting her in the back of the truck, I invite her onto the back seat of the Suburban. She immediately leaps over the seat to sit next to me like a date. I pet her, something I rarely do with these dogs temporarily in my custody.

When Gayle realized that I meant it, that I was going to take the job in Harmony Farms, be the dog officer in my old community, the first thing she said to me was that I wasn't going to be able to do the job because under my stiff exterior beat the heart of a pushover. She didn't mean it kindly. "You're too animal-soft. You'll never be able to keep an emotional distance." Which, on the face of it, was an odd thing to say for a woman who was making me move out of our home because she claimed I was emotionally distant from her. What she didn't seem to understand was that all of my "softness" for animals had been focused on my own dog. I am perfectly capable, even determined, not to engage with any of the animals in my care. I treat them well; I just don't get to know them. Sort of how I treated prisoners when I had occasion to transport them. Like I treat Bull and, now, how I'll treat my brother. Distant. No deliberate engagement.

No. I'm sure that Lev already knows that Jimmy's here. I can relax and add my brother to the list of people I'm trying to avoid. Contact with Jimmy is a lot like that old racist folktale about Uncle

Remus and the Tar-Baby. Getting anywhere near Jimmy is a bad idea, especially for someone who has worked for so long in the law-enforcement profession. There is nothing I liked more than bringing down dealers. Buyers were one thing, but these dealer guys were predators, benefiting from the weaknesses of others. Jimmy had skimmed along the edge of using, but he found a career in distributing.

My cell phone sounds off with the office ringtone, a series of barks. Jenny's idea. I push the Bluetooth button. "Coop."

"Did you find the pit bull?"

"Yeah. Polly had her."

"Good, cuz I've got her frantic owner on the phone."

"I'm on the road. Give me the address and I'll drop her off."

Second Hope Farm, Bates Road, third mailbox on the right."

Ah, the very place I intended to begin my farm calls. I love the old "kill two birds with one stone" theory of efficiency. I signal for a quick left turn and pat the pit bull on the head.

6

~⦦~

Jimmy's being home is a mixed blessing for Bull Harrison.
Jimmy has a driver's license and a used—or what he calls a
"pre-owned"—Honda that he babies, so sometimes Bull can sweet-
talk Jimmy into giving him a lift to work on those days when he
can't bring himself to mount his old Raleigh, like on rainy days and
those days when every abuse he's ever heaped on himself reminds
Bull of his age. However, with Jimmy, everything comes at a price.
Bull remembers back to the days when he and the boys were batch-
ing it, as Bull called it, trying to make living without Mona sound
better than it was. Father and sons in the house on Poor Farm Road.
With no feminine influence, standards slipped. They ate dinner in
front of the TV and their housekeeping was pretty rudimentary.
No one shouted at the boys about homework or bedtime. Clean laundry was optional and sheets were replaced with more convenient
sleeping bags. The boys did their own thing, and he did his. Bull
liked calling the three Harrisons "free spirits." It felt as close to
being roommates as could be. In that spirit, Bull stepped further

back from parental duties than he already had done with Jimmy, giving the boy carte blanche to run wild. Routinely, Bull ignored summonses to the school to discuss Jimmy's failing grades or misbehavior. He might say, "Hey, try keepin' your nose clean for a while" as he dropped a slice of pepperoni pizza in front of Jimmy, but mostly he just shrugged off the reports of bullying or fights. He overlooked the accusations of stealing wallets out of teachers' purses. Nobody had proof. Boys will be boys.

The truth was that Bull was a little afraid of Jimmy, of the way his cold gray eyes would harden like stone in his face whenever Bull tried a little authority with him.

The price he's paying now for the convenience of an occasional lift into town is Jimmy's taking over of the house. As much as he doesn't take care of it to any effective degree, Bull still likes his home, which he's owned since his parents passed it on to him. It's the house he's always lived in, except for the years he was in the army; the house he brought Mona home to and where he and she conceived the kids, in the same bedroom he'd always slept in and is still sleeping in. And now this old place feels invaded by the very kid, grown man now, who was one of those babies. Doors that never had locks are locked. He needs a freakin' key to get into his own house, and how hard it is to remember to take it with him? Jimmy gets mad when he has to cut his phone calls short to go let his old man in. "Wear it around your neck, for God's sake."

Bull touches his neck to make sure that the gimp lanyard one of the boys made in some day camp is there, the house key dangling from it. Jimmy is off somewhere and didn't want to wait around to give him a lift to work this morning. Jimmy goes for days at a time, driving off in the black Honda to parts unknown. Bull never, ever asks where he's been. He knows better. You don't ask Jimmy questions.

So he's got one son who is living back in the old homestead and the other one, who won't stop and give his old man the time of day.

Deke Wilkins has given Cooper a pair of Rhode Island Reds as a birthday present. He'd had the sense to ask Mona if that was okay, and she'd shrugged, figured that fresh eggs might be a good thing to have. Sometimes gifts just boomerang on you. First thing, Bull has to build a coop for them. "Coop's coop," he calls it. Six-by-six pen, five feet of chicken wire. Deke was clear on his instructions: "Stretch chicken wire over the top; keep the hawks out." Except that Bull runs out of chicken wire. "I'll pick some up." A promise forgotten almost as soon as spoken.

Cooper's stricken little face when he goes to feed his chickens and finds nothing but feathers and a foot. He doesn't cry, Bull will give him that. He gathers the feathers, putting them in a paper bag, like he was gathering the eggs that the two hens had produced only once or twice, careful, respectful. Bull watches as his younger son wanders off the property, heading toward Deke's place on foot. He should go get him, promise him another pair of birds, a better coop, but he doesn't.

7

I drive into the yard of Second Hope Farm and see right away that this isn't some dilettante's version of a horse farm. No miles of white fences, no massive barn with an artsy weather vane and imported wood and ironwork stalls. Nope. This is very much a working farm, plain old electric fencing, a dull red barn crying out for a coat of fresh paint. Various equines are distributed among the small dirt paddocks. The only grassy pasture contains a skinny horse, standing with one hind leg cocked under him, dozing in the warm fall sunshine.

A woman comes out of the barn at a run. "You have Betty? Oh my God, I was so upset." Even before I can climb out of the truck, she wrenches open the passenger door and the dog called Betty jumps out into her arms and nearly knocks her over. "I was freaked-out when I got home and found out that my house sitter had let her out. I couldn't believe that she didn't call and let me know right away that Betty had disappeared. I won't use her again, I can promise you that. The whole idea of a sitter is to take care of the animals. I'll just never go away again. Poor, poor Betty."

"We had her overnight, Ms. . . . ?" I need to get back on the official track here.

"Everett, Natalie Everett." She sticks out her hand as if we are standing at a cocktail party. Her grip is no nonsense and I can feel in the toughness of her skin the hard work that she's putting into the place.

"Cooper Harrison." I give her hand a firm shake.

"Well, thank you for bringing her home. Do I owe any fines or boarding fees?"

"We'll bill you."

"You have my address." She sounds a little like she is expecting me to say, "Aw shucks, ma'am, you don't owe the town anything for taking your dog off the streets."

One of the horses stamps, whinnies to a more distant pal, drops his nose into his hay.

I haven't forgotten that this is a two-part visit. "You weren't in operation last year, were you?"

"No. Last year was the dreaming year; this year is the action year." When she says this, Natalie takes a deep breath and waves a hand at the aggregate of animals and fencing, the shelters, and the hills that cradle the whole. "I chucked it all and bought a farm. Pretty insane, huh?"

"I guess that would depend on what it was you chucked." I think, Job? Boyfriend?

"Wall Street, Ann Taylor suits and three-inch heels."

Okay, a chucked career.

"Now it's Carhartts and muck boots."

"And this is a rescue, right? Not a boarding facility."

"Rescue and rehab. I give a few lessons on my two steady Eddies to supplement the income. Let me introduce you to the gang." Natalie smiles at me, the lovely sunshiny smile of someone pleased as Punch to be doing what she's doing.

"I just need to know how many equines and what other livestock you might have here. As long as I'm here, I'll do my annual farm inspection." I reach back into the truck and pull out my clipboard.

The sunshiny smile fades, quickly replaced by the face she must have most worn as a bond trader. All business. "Five horses, two ponies, one dog, and three guinea hens. And a useless cat."

"Cats aren't livestock." I write on the multipart form, then look up. "I need to inspect for water source, safe fences."

"Believe me, they've got water. And I'm doing the best I can with fences."

"Can I please inspect?"

Natalie hasn't given me back the leash I had on Betty, and she walks off, dog at her side, expecting me to follow. I'm wearing my cop face, I know. Straight man. It's my default expression. There is no need for such formality on a call like this, but I can't help myself, even in the face of a pretty woman whose only attachments seem to be to animals. Once a cop, always a cop. Sometimes I forget that I'm not an officer of the law, but a dog officer. A different man would chat her up, ask her questions intended to ease her mind, let her know that he's not an adversary, but—potentially—an advocate. Instead, I march alongside her in silence. For a small woman, she's got a quick pace. I check off a box on my form. "How many acres do you have?"

Natalie answers, and I can tell she doesn't know if this is a trick question or not.

"And you have seven equines?"

"Yes." She doesn't blink. Natalie knows exactly how many animals she can have on a property this size, but I see that she's expecting me to make her squirm.

"Zoning allows you to have up to ten."

"That may be, but prudence keeps me at seven. Once that off-the-track Thoroughbred puts on some weight and gets over his injury, he'll be adopted out. And, yes, I have all the licensing to do that legally." She points to the farthest paddock. "Shall we?"

"Hey, I don't need to see each and every bucket. Obviously, you're doing a fine job here."

"I guess I should say thank you." She's got the kind of blue eyes that echo the sky as it is today, bright blue, set deep.

"But I will need to see your instructor's license."

"Right." I follow her into the barn, where she has a corkboard with her license prominently displayed. "There it is, Officer."

We're standing in the aisle of the small barn. There's a bay horse in residence, her head leaning over the door to her stall. She reaches toward me, putting her warm, soft nose against my cheek, and I can feel her breath on my skin. "Hey there." I pat her neck.

"That's Moxie. She's my beginner horse."

"A beginner horse?"

"Sorry. A horse that teaches beginning riders."

I scrawl my signature on the bottom of the multipart form and tear away the pink sheet, handing it to her. "Looks fine. See you next year."

"I'm sure I'll see you before then. We do live in a small town." Her sunshiny smile has come back, although it's little more restrained. "Hey, thanks for bringing Betty back. She's a rescue, too, and hasn't quite figured out that she's safe."

"No problem." Stupid remark. I try again. "I mean, it's my job." Worse.

"And you're doing a fine job, too."

I point in the direction of the pond. "Do you ride around Bartlett's Pond?"

"Yeah. Why?"

"I've seen hoofprints."

"We hack the old schoolies. Keeps them fit." Natalie opens the door to Moxie's stall, slips a halter over the horse's head, and brings her out. "Do you ride?"

For the first time since arriving at Second Hope Farm, I give up a smile. "No, ma'am."

"Didn't think so."

"I run. Around the pond. Maybe I'll see you there sometime."

"Maybe." Natalie clips a line to either side of the horse's halter. She hands me a carrot, instructing me to break it into smaller pieces, then walks away to gather a saddle and bridle.

Her dog, Betty, is nosing along the length of the short aisle. Who knows what she's looking for.

"Betty doesn't go with you, does she?" Gingerly, I feed Moxie a piece of the carrot, amazed at how gently she takes it off my palm.

"No, she's not made for keeping up with horses. Why? Is there a law against that?"

"No. Well, technically a leash law, but I'm never going to enforce it on dogs away from town. It's just that some dog left paw prints on my shirt when I dropped it on my run."

She is obviously trying to treat this complaint as serious. "No, sir. Not my dog."

"Okay, then." I let Moxie have the rest of the carrot as Natalie tacks her up.

Natalie leads the mare outside, snaps her fingers to get the dog's attention. Two grays are engaging in a little horseplay, running and kicking up their heels, pretending to fight. A teenage girl I hadn't realized was there suddenly appears, takes the reins out of Natalie's hand, and leads the mare into the riding ring. I guess there's nothing left to say. Even before I climb into the Suburban, Natalie walks into the ring, into her chosen new life.

As I pull out of Natalie's barnyard, I'm thinking about how I should try to lighten up a little with these farm calls, take the authoritarian bit down a notch. Sometimes, when I got home from a long day of work, Gayle would have to remind me to drop the stiff, still, deliberately macho authoritarian demeanor of my job. "Take the dog out for a walk and pretend that he's just a pet." It's funny, but everyone hereabouts assumes that I, as a dog officer, would have a dog. When I tell them no, I don't, I get this look, like there's something wrong with me. Especially the fosterers. They just can't figure me out. Why wouldn't I have a dog? Might humanize me. I just won't, that's why.

It's a beautiful evening and I take advantage of it by lighting a fire in the fire pit, setting my wobbly camp chair in front of it, a beer in one hand and only the sound of late-season crickets suggesting that winter is coming. My thoughts circulate, undistracted by radio or phone or anything beyond the stunning purity of the sky overhead and the whispered, to me, sound of wind in the grasses and the occasional rustle of a creature making its way through the dead leaves that blanket the ground around this one-man camp. Exhausted, I doze off in the chair like an old man in front of the television, the animation of the yellow flames of my campfire, colored now with the umber and green of improperly dried wood, mesmerizing me into a lulled state that might be sleep, or might be deep meditation. In my dream state, there appears on the other side of the snapping fire—something. A wraithlike form, indistinct behind the curtain of flame. White. Like Argos. Vaguely dog-shaped, immobile. Watching me. A ghost of a dog. Argos. Standing in the flames. He looks at me with wolfish eyes, his long tongue lolling, laughing. I reach to take him out of the flames.

The fire pops like a gunshot, startling me awake, and the ghost vanishes. I am left with a hard-beating heart, knocking so loudly in my chest that I almost can't breathe. The adrenaline of panic forces me out of my wobbly chair to pace around the dying fire, manic with fear. It's what I can't conquer, no matter how many sessions with a psychiatrist, no matter how many times I push the memories back. I am afraid.

8

〰

It's been a hard day. I went out to Deke's to inspect his farm and ended up spending three hours splitting and stacking two cords of wood for him. He's got to be in his eighties, and the idea of him still stacking wood is just wrong, so I volunteered and, for once, the old man didn't demur and send me packing. Which, in and of itself, is a little sad. When I was a kid, I hung around Deke's farm a lot. He had everything a boy could want—a pony, two or more cows, a small flock of sheep, chickens and ducks, and occasionally a pig; a fishing hole and acres of pasture and woods that were just perfect for a kid who enjoyed solitary wandering and secret fort building. He'd give me chores in exchange for a buck or two. Just like today, I'd stack firewood, or pull shingles off his chicken house. As when he used to give me Twizzlers or Doublemint, he'd be most generous on those occasions when I'd fled to his place to escape what was going on in my own, giving me the consolation of physical labor and a five-dollar bill.

His current dog followed me from woodpile to woodshed, her amber eyes fixed on keeping me in line. As long as I've known him,

Deke has kept a series of Border collies to work with the sheep. This one looked to be middle aged, and it struck me that this might be the last dog of his life. Which made me wonder what will happen to his place when he goes. I've never heard him speak of a relative, and he's pretty much outlived his friends. No doubt some rapacious developer will descend on it, unless Deke has made some arrangement. I could ask him, I suppose. But I won't.

His chief complaint today was that something had been bothering his chickens a day or so ago. Deke's old-school, keeps a shotgun at his back door. He may be in his eighties, but his hearing is damn good. The other night, he heard the squawking and leapt out of his bed to grab the gun. His hearing may be good, but his eyes aren't as reliable as they once were, so he missed the critter skulking around the pen. Because his first thought was that it was a coyote, he kept his old dog in. But the creature that ran away didn't run like a coyote. He said, "Think it might be a dog." Which is a bad thing. Chicken-killing dogs are trouble in a place like ours, where it's become fashionable to have free-range chickens. "Whatever it was, Coop, it was limping, dragging a hind leg."

"You should have called me."

"Hardly an emergency, and the shotgun scared it off. Haven't been troubled by it since."

It might not have qualified as a reason to get the ACO out of bed, but with the series of garbage can–tossing incidents and now this, it's pretty clear to me that I've got a problem dog on my hands.

Bad enough that I was knackered from the unaccustomed labor, but even before I could get back to the shelter, I got a call about the Bollens' freakin' donkey, gone again. This time, the little wretch gave me a good crack in the knee as I shoved him into the SUV. I swear, I'm building them a proper paddock, whether they like it or not.

The last straw was when I pulled up beside my cabin and saw

my single trash barrel rolled all the way to the pond. I was more pissed than curious. Already done in by the wood chopping, I had to retrieve the soggy paper towels and scoop up the mélange of garbage deemed inedible by whatever had tossed the barrel and gotten the bungee cord off it. It was too dark to see what kind of prints might be there, and I really didn't have the time or the interest in playing Tracker John. Because all of the other dog-in-the-garbage calls have been closer to town, I only considered for a moment that this might have been the same dog. More likely it was a raccoon. I don't think a dog could get the shock cord off. You need hands for that.

Max Philbine is already at the Lakeside Tavern when I get there, freshly showered and out of my work clothes and into clean jeans and a dark blue polo shirt. Max hands me a menu. "Hard day?"

"You could say that." I open the menu, although I know exactly what I want. We come often enough that I've got the limited menu memorized, and it's just for show that I even bother to open it. "Crazy day, and then I got home and found my trash barrel in the pond. That's twenty feet. I guess either some very determined raccoon gave it his best shot or we've got a bear in the neighborhood."

We both order beers and the house specialty—bacon cheeseburgers with sweet potato fries—making no excuses about the cholesterol therein, and toast each other with our first pints. We knock around sports and the current foibles of Congress before our burgers arrive, then sit in agreeable silence as we devour them. The server arrives with our second beers, at which point Max and I are ready to explore topics closer to home: his wooing by the university, my firm belief that he'll miss his practice if he gives in.

I don't know why I'm so upset by Max's temptation to leave Harmony Farms behind. After all, I'm not planning on staying here, so why should anyone else? This is a place easily left behind. At least it was for me. Max is as generationally rooted here as I am, except that his family has always been highly respected. Max doesn't have the stigma of a family's bad reputation hanging over his head, coloring everyone's opinion.

Maybe it's just that he's pretty much the only friend I have in town. The guys I hung out with in my youth are mostly living in faraway places, their parents still here, looking forward to the holiday visits from sons and grandchildren. One of the guys I knew was killed in Afghanistan. Another married his boyfriend last year but didn't invite any of us to his wedding. In adulthood, my friends have been my colleagues on the job. And now I'm no longer part of that culture, and that's made an unavoidable difference in our relationship. I represent the second worst-case scenario: unrecoverable trauma. We've lost touch.

I see her before Max does. Sitting at the antique oaken bar is Natalie Everett, a wineglass in her hand, out of her Levi's and now wearing jeans with a little bejeweled swoop on the back pockets. Her dark brown hair is loose and she keeps tucking it behind her ear as she laughs at whatever it is her companion is saying. Laugh, tuck, laugh. I find the unconscious motion unbelievably endearing. And am shocked at the thought. I don't even know her.

Natalie spins herself off the bar stool and, as she heads toward the rest rooms, passes our way.

"Hi, Natalie." Max calls out to her, waving as she passes. She seems not to notice me there at the same small table, and then does.

"Hi, Doc. Officer Harrison." She smiles at us and keeps moving.

"Nice view." Max raises his glass to his lips.

"I guess."

"Dead from the waist down, man?"

"What are you, twelve?"

"Sometimes. When it suits me." Max is a veteran of the marriage wars, and that's one of the reasons that he and I have become pals.

I say that it's because misery loves company, but Max says it's safety in numbers.

"Yes, she's attractive. But I don't think I'm her type."

"What type would that be?"

"A horse."

"That's no horse sitting next to her at the bar." We lean so that we can see the companion Natalie has just rejoined.

"Not from around heah."

"You're right. Not a rube."

"City boy for sure. Got Wall Street smeared all over him." I'm done with my pint and signal to our server for another round. To hell with my self-imposed two-beer limit. It's Friday, I've worked my tail off, and I'm a little weary of self-discipline. Despite what Gayle said, I'm not my father. I can handle myself.

Natalie and her companion are long gone by the time we're ready to split the check and head out. The temperature has risen since early evening, an early-fall warm front moving through, making Max conjecture if the latest tropical storm forecast to miss our area might not be moving in our direction after all. I can only repeat what I heard on the weather forecast this afternoon, possible thunderstorms passing through, followed by a cold front. It never fails to amaze me how much we New Englanders love to talk weather. It's like our comfort zone. What do people in temperate areas talk about during those last minutes of a late-night date or the awkward moments of waiting in a line at the post office with a stranger whose face is familiar but whose name you don't know?

We stand outside the tavern, staring at a blank canvas of sky. A bat fritters over our heads and we both duck, then laugh. A drop of rain. The first rumble of thunder and we say good night, running for our trucks.

My body aches, as if I've been lifting weights, and I regret that third beer a little. I'm not drunk, but it's a little hard to stay focused on the road. I'm really glad to see the reflector announcing the safe and solitary track to my cabin. It would not do at all to get stopped by one of Lev's real cops for a suspected DUI. I can just hear it, the "Like father, like son" condemnation. The storm is nearing and I'm gripping my steering wheel with each flash and boom.

A close flash of lightning. There it is again, a white wraith, a ghost of a creature, illuminated for a nanosecond. I can't explain why this *apparition,* for lack of a better word, makes my heart beat faster or why I call out: "Argos!" I shake off the feeling. Laugh out loud at myself. But I hurry down the dirt road, just in case there is a big white dog waiting for me at the cabin.

9

~≈~

I wake with a jolt, sitting up, throwing off the sheet, and landing on my feet. It takes me a moment to collect myself, to remind myself that I'm in the old hunting cabin, that I'm fine, and that it's nothing but a lousy thunderstorm that has revved my imagination into nightmare. The lightning illuminates my room for an instant, my clothes on hooks, the single bed, the cheap nightstand with my books piled on it. Another flash so bright and I can pick out the colors of the braided rug under my feet. Like a little kid, I cover my ears to block out the thunder that follows. It percusses against my bare chest. This storm is sitting right on top of me. I sit up, cup my eyes in the heels of my hands to stop the flow of nightmare-induced tears. It just doesn't get any better. I have had this nightmare before. Some of my bad dreams have everything to do with inchoate fear. Objects and sounds represent terror—a solid wall, a tumbling rock, a cawing crow. My dream self sees the imagery and knows that it's the embodiment of danger.

Tonight, the thunder has evoked a more exact reenactment of

the explosion that has unraveled my life. Once again, I am the helpless witness in Argos's death.

In that split second after waking, I feel the relief of knowing it was just a dream, and in the next moment, I know that the real nightmare won't go away. The loss is still there. The fear. In the daylight, I'll be able to shrug off this nightmare. Make it disappear. I rub my face, a gesture that has become habitual. As I feel the night's growth of beard beneath my fingers, I realize that the electricity is out, ergo the pump, and so I head outdoors to pee. It's raining too hard to venture off the porch, so I act like a little boy and aim my stream into the downpour. Finished, I breathe in the sodden air, admire the distant light show as the storm moves away, a bolt or two thrown in retreat, halfhearted. One Mississippi, two Mississippi, three Mississippi. It takes six counts before the thunder reaches me. As the storm slides off, heading for the city, where it will die, the rain slows, lessens, and is done. In the sudden quiet, I hear something scrabble against the wet surface of the small porch, the unmistakable sound of claws against wood. I really wish that I'd brought a flashlight outside. What kind of wild beastie is taking advantage of the protection of the porch? Not under the porch, but on it. I turn my head so that my good ear is able to follow the animal's movement across the rough boards of the porch, hoping to interpret by sound what kind of trespasser I have. I don't think it can be a skunk, but, nonetheless, I stay very, very still. A raccoon is a strong possibility, especially with the trash can incident yesterday, and that's a little scary, as it's also possible that such a bold creature could be rabid. Two towns over, they've had a case of rabies in a raccoon. Puts everyone on edge.

I'm getting cold, standing outside in my underwear. The storm has heralded the forecasted cold front and the air has gone from muggy to chill. I shiver and whisper, "Hey, critter, move on. I want to go back to bed." A flash of lightning and I see it. A dog. At least

I think it's a dog. A dog-shaped thing is huddled against the stack of firewood. As the animal is revealed in the brief flare of distant lightning, I can see that, whatever it is, it's wholly consumed by terror. Finally convinced that it really is a dog, I step closer, squat, snap my fingers. Ten seconds and the thunder finally reaches our ears and the dog bolts. I'm not sure if he's running from me or from the sound. The thing is, he is definitely on three legs.

"Hey, fella!" I know that shouting after a frightened dog is a recipe for failure, but I do it anyway. "Here, boy!"

I think that this must be my phantom, and I have to confess, I'm a little disappointed at the reasonable explanation.

I'm shivering and the cold forces my retreat into my chilled cabin. I pull an extra blanket off the shelf, find a pair of sweatpants to pull on. The temperature drop is quite astounding. It's as if fall has arrived at the flip of a switch. I climb back into bed, but sleep is elusive after that excitement, and it's just as the first birds announce the new freshly washed day that I finally fall into a deep sleep.

The power is still out, which kind of proves that I didn't dream the weirdness of last night's stormy encounter with the terrified dog. There are paw prints in the mud around the base of the porch, a skid mark where the dog must have slipped as he leapt off in his panic to get away from me. The storm has stripped some foliage from the trees, most of which are only beginning to color up. The thinned-out canopy lets in so much more light and makes the whole camp look more cheerful. I heat up some old coffee on the gas stove and sit on the porch to admire my new cleared view to the pond. A flat-bottomed boat drifts toward the middle of the large pond—duck hunters out before dawn, their Labrador in the prow like an ebony figurehead. Argos had a couple of Labs in his graduating class, great dogs for drug sniffing. They lacked the gravitas of the more serious-looking Belgian Malinois or the other German shepherds who came up in that class, but there was a lot to like about them. Half the pet dogs in this town are Lab or Lab crosses. Want to give away a dog, tell them it's part Lab. Jenny Bright isn't above doing that if we have a particularly unattractive inmate in need of a home. "Oh, yeah, he's part Lab for sure." Jenny's Goth looks are diametrically opposed to her persuasive appeal over the phone.

I'll set up the big Havahart trap I have at the shelter, bait it with a bowl of meat scraps, and I should have this phantom garbage-raiding, chicken-scaring dog caught within a day or two. That will be the easy part. The hard part will be to figure out what rabbit hunter went home without his dog, or what idiot thought dropping off an unwanted dog in the country would ensure its finding a nice new home. And then getting Jenny Bright to make sure that it actually does get a good home.

The lumberyard is Saturday busy and it takes a lap before I can find a parking place close enough to the fencing materials that I don't have to get a cart. I'm here to fulfill my promise to the Bollens to build them a fence that even Cutie-Pie can't breach. I'm here on a Saturday, on my own time, because, as far as I know, Bull doesn't work on Saturdays. A million times a week I pass by Crane and Sons Lumber, and on any one of those passes I could have pulled the town's SUV into the lot and gotten what I need to do the job. Fortunately, my own vehicle is more than sufficient to hold the posts and rolls of thick narrow-gauge wire I'm going to use. Gayle got the Jetta; I've got the Ford F-150 crew-cab four-by-four pickup with the United States Police Canine Association decal on the back window.

Crane's Lumber is like my own backyard; I know exactly where to find what I'm looking for, as I've been coming to Crane's all my life. Even when I lived in Boston, when I had occasion to need a lumberyard, this was the one I came to. The business is over a hundred years old, and there are no longer any Cranes, sons or otherwise, by that name still alive, but the sense of its still being a mom-and-pop operation persists.

I pull a crumpled piece of paper out of my pocket to check my estimated measurements against the size of the rolls and the height of the posts. I'll need a posthole digger, and I can rent one here. There is little that Crane's doesn't offer the DIYer or helpful neighbor or former student doing an old teacher a favor. One of the better things Cynthia Mann and her exurban cronies have done is to prevent the encroachment of big-box stores within the borders of Harmony Farms. On the outside, yes. Over the edge into the less pretty, less prosperous, less desirable areas, sure. Plenty of Harmony Farms residents take their business over the line, but I'm not usually one of them. I just don't patronize Crane's on weekdays, when Bull might be there. Any encounter with my father inevitably makes me feel bad. Bad because I can't look at the guy without cringing, what with his outdated Fu Manchu mustache, crumpled-paper-bag face, sick bloodhound eyes, pale and always looking a little wet, his shock of defiant gray hair, and his mostly toothless grin, every time he sees me, his younger son. Bull is a wreck of a man, and I would feel sorry for him, except my father did it to himself. Every helping hand, Bull managed to slap away.

As a city policeman, I saw plenty of human train wrecks—the druggies and the prostitutes, the lost souls who found themselves in trouble with the law out of stupidity or bad judgment, or poverty or mental illness, not necessarily anything as straightforward as malfeasance. Some were even quite likable, almost sublimely ignorant of what was wrong with taking a few bucks for a blow job or selling an ounce of weed to a college student. Each one, in some way, reminded me of Bull. And as was the case with a lot of those jerks, everyone likes Bull Harrison.

"Hey, son. Whatcha buyin'?"

Bull. I'm guessing that he's working overtime. 'Tis the season when home owners and caretakers get started on those projects that have been waiting for the cooler weather.

"Bull, how are you?" I have long since stopped calling my father by anything other than the nickname he earned long before I was a glint in his eye.

"Sittin' up, takin' nourishment. You're lookin' good."

"I'm all right. Can't complain." My God, this could be a bit of bad dialogue in a bad sitcom set in Rubesville USA. "I need fencing for the Bollens' donkey." In other words, this is business, not a social call.

"Right over here." Even though I really don't need an escort, Bull tags along beside me, chatting away about nothing. Ignoring him, I slide a metal fence post out of the pile. "I want to build a twenty-by-thirty pen. What heights have you got for wire fencing? I need something at least four feet high."

"With that mule, I'd go five feet."

He's right. I choose a taller post.

Pulling the stub of a pencil out from behind his ear, Bull does a couple of calculations on a scrap of paper, figures out how many posts and how much fencing, and hands me the results. "Take that in and pay for it. I'll throw the stuff in your truck."

I pay, then carefully fold the cash register receipt and put it in my wallet. I'm still not sure I'll hand it to Mr. Bollen, but this is a pretty expensive good deed if I don't. I head outside to where my father has neatly stacked the poles and rolls of fencing in the back of the truck. If this was the other yard guy, I might hand him a five and tell him to go get a cup of coffee and a doughnut on me, but it's not, and the best I can do it clap Bull on his meaty shoulder and say thanks.

"Don't be a stranger, Coop." Bull runs fingers down the length of his tobacco-stained Fu Manchu mustache, then spits.

Bull's tired phrase reminds me and I say, "Hey, I hear Jimmy's back."

Bull repeats the grooming and spitting. "Yeah. Got sprung a week or so ago."

"Where is he living?" I know I sound more investigatory than curious.

"With me."

"Watch out for him. Don't get involved. . . ." This is not good news.

"I know. Don't worry about us. He's clean. I'm clean."

"This isn't about *clean*. It's about keeping out of jail."

"Been there, done that. Don't intend to do it again. Neither does Jimmy. He's reformed."

I have enough self-control to refrain from saying "Yeah, I've heard that before." I don't say anything else to the old man; there's no point in it. I'll just get frustrated. I have no doubt that Jimmy is holing up till his next opportunity to make a buck outside of the law. He's a recidivist, not capable of true reformation, real change. Just thinking about him makes me mad.

I walked out of our house the day after high school graduation. Bull was somewhere, probably at a bar, and Jimmy was sitting on the couch in his boxers, smoking a joint. He took a hit, holding on to it like a little kid holding his breath. His hazed-over eyes studied me until he let the stream out. "Where you goin'?"

"Away." Far, far away from being the *other* Harrison boy, the boy people thought I must be, given my family history. No one ever again would know about my wreck of a father, or my having a brother like Jimmy.

"Where?"

"To the rest of my life." The sudden notion of freedom swept through me, making me laugh out loud with the joy of it.

That was twenty years ago, and, kind of like Jimmy, I have proven to be a recidivist, returning to the place I once fled and to the people I thought I was done with.

I slam the truck door and drive away from my father. I don't mean

to, but I glance in the rearview mirror. Bull is there, waving good-
bye to me.

Mrs. Bollen has sent me home with a rectangular Pyrex dish of her
signature lasagna and instructions on how to heat it up. There's
enough here to feed a family of four, and that's great, except I'm not
certain if my electricity is back on, and I'd hate to lose this national
treasure because there's no way to keep the leftovers cold.

Natalie Everett is in the Country Market when I stop in to pick
up the makings of a salad and get some scrap meat from Elvin for
the Havahart trap. I'm behind her in line and can't help but notice
that three bags of carrots and a Lean Cuisine box are the sum total
of the contents of her basket. What I also can't help noticing is that
she really doesn't need to be eating Lean Cuisine.

It isn't my style, and I wouldn't have said anything, but Natalie
happens to glance back and catches me looking at her groceries, so I
make a weak joke and say. "You can tell a lot about a woman by the
items on her grocery list."

"Officer Harrison, hello. Yes, I spend more on carrots than on
anything else in the market."

I point at the Lean Cuisine box. "That's hardly a fit dinner for
a woman who does physical labor all day."

"Cheap, nourishing, and fast. Three qualities I require."

I think of the lasagna sitting on the seat in my truck. "Are you
vegetarian?"

She smiles, as if she thinks that she should be, given her chosen
vocation. "No. An unrepentant meat eater."

"I have incredible homemade lasagna in my possession and there's
no way I can eat it all by myself. Would you like some?"

"Oh, I couldn't."

We dance around the idea in a conversational two-step as I insist and she demurs. After several more rounds of this, I insist one

more time for emphasis and, as she pays for her groceries, I realize that I've inadvertently arranged a date with Natalie Everett. I give her directions and my phone number just in case she thinks better of this impromptu dinner.

"See you at six." She hefts her cloth grocery bag of carrots over her shoulder. "I think I can find it, but if not, keep your phone handy."

I throw my package of meat, the head of lettuce, the two small tomatoes, and the single cucumber back in my basket and back out of the line. I'm going to need more stuff. And I hope to God that the electricity is back on. Dinner by candlelight would be way too predatory.

Then I think, Hey, it's just shared lasagna, no big deal. From what I saw at the tavern last night, she's got a boyfriend—a thought that doesn't make me feel any less awkward. Grow up. This is just neighborly breaking bread together. A chance to show that I'm not really an asshole.

Cooper is almost surprised that Celia said yes, that she agreed to go to the prom with him. They've casually dated since midwinter, a movie, a ride to the lake. Made out a little bit. But the prom is a big deal. It's the kind of event where you have to invite your date over to meet your parents, have pictures taken. Celia's parents don't know that they're dating. She's never suggested that he have dinner at her house; she's never let him pick her up at home. Cooper is no fool; he knows that her parents will flip at the idea of their college-bound daughter mingling with a Harrison boy. The fact of his prowess on the basketball court or the ice is nullified by his family history.

He's nervous as he arrives at Celia's house on Sunset Lane, the rented tux making him feel ludicrous instead of suave. He nearly drops the plastic box with the corsage in it. The front door opens and Celia comes out in a rush. Her face looks flushed, and he realizes she's been crying.

Behind her come the parents. No one looks happy. Cooper recognizes family discord and moves to disarm it with an outthrust hand and a smile on his face.

"Mr. and Mrs. Laughton, so nice to meet you. Celia, you look beautiful." It's as if he's taken his lines from Leave It to Beaver, *but it works and the parents stand down. Mrs. Laughton has the pair of them pose against the open front door and takes one picture. Cooper doesn't think she gave them time enough to smile. It's going to look like a double mug shot.*

"Home by eleven." Mr. Laughton doesn't say this with a wink. Cooper will have Celia home by ten-thirty. A day later and she says she thinks that they should take a break. After all, she's leaving for college in eight weeks. Long-distance romances really don't work. Cooper doesn't even try to argue her out of it. He understands the power of parental disapproval.

Natalie and I sit in the harsh light of my two camping lanterns, one on the small kitchen table and the other on the counter. The lasagna, reheated in the gas oven, has been invaded and still half of it remains. I'll insist that she take it home, making the case that I'm not being polite but that I have no way of keeping it cold. In the old days, the camp had a propane generator, but that's long gone, the advent of reliable electricity making it pointless, unless you have a situation like this. I could have lighted candles, kept the glare of the battery-powered Coleman lanterns out of our eyes, but I thought better of it. I keep telling myself that this isn't a date, that she's only here for the meal. She's got a boyfriend. So I use the lanterns.

We've chatted about the weather, finally seasonal; the high cost of grain, climbing every time she buys a bag. She asks a polite question about my job, so I entertain her with the antics of the Bollens' mischievous miniature donkey. Conversation lags a little. It's only seven-thirty, and already dark, and to two people who have been up since dawn, it feels like the middle of the night. My restless night, and the effort of building a donkey-proof fence for the Bollens, and her own physically demanding job of stall mucking, hay bucking, and saddle time have worn us both out. Natalie apologizes for yawning, so I suggest a breath of fresh air. "It's not too cold; let's sit out on the porch."

I grab the bottle of pinot noir that Natalie, arriving a little late and wearing those dressy jeans, handed me upon arrival, then open the door for her as she shrugs on her jacket. It is so dark and so quiet here on this little piece of paradise. Even the crickets have quieted down. Natalie stands on the edge of the porch, leaning out to look at the stars now crowding the sky above the pond. "I get a pretty spectacular view of the night sky over my place, but not quite like this—too many neighbors living around me." She takes the refilled wineglass. "I suppose your neighbors are without electricity, too. Makes it look like it must have looked a hundred or so years ago."

"No neighbors to speak of, although I do get a glow in the sky from all the streetlights in Harmony Farms. Come over here." We step off the porch and move to the side of the small cabin. I stand behind her, directing her to look toward the northwest, where the sky is indeed more pale. "Clear nights, it's harder to see, but on over-cast nights, the lights bounce right off the cloud cover and it looks like the end of days." Her hair smells nice. I lean in a little, then pull myself back. Not a date.

"Speaking of the end of days, I'd better call it a night. Early chores." She's still got her back to me, inches away from my chest. She finishes off her wine.

"Me, too." I take a backward step. "Hey, you've got to take the rest of the lasagna."

She turns around, shakes her head. "Only because you don't have electricity. You know, you should have picked up bags of ice at the market. That would have held you."

"I did, but my cooler is only big enough to hold milk, beer, and dog meat."

"I didn't see a dog. Of course you'd have dog. Where is he?"

"I don't." *Not anymore.* "The meat is for a feral dog that I have to trap."

"Trap?" The way Natalie says the word, I might be some fur trapper about to commit an atrocity.

"Havahart. No harm will come to him. That's assuming he gets to the meat before the rest of the critters out there find it. Trap's too big to prevent a skunk or raccoon from getting there first, snatching the bait, and scurrying away."

"Feral, huh? Should I be worried?"

"No. I think it's just a dumped dog. He'll come in from the cold with a little encouragement."

We go back into the cabin to wrap up the remainder of the lasagna. Suddenly, the electricity flares on and the refrigerator rumbles to life. "Take it anyway." I put the Pyrex pan in her hands. "Just drop the pan off at the shelter and I'll return it to Mrs. Bollen."

"It's just me; I can't eat all this."

"Freeze it, then. You'll have it when your boyfriend comes."

"Boyfriend?"

"Fiancé, then? The fellow you were with at the tavern last night."

"My brother?"

"Even the best detective in the world couldn't have deduced that by observation."

"We look alike."

"Can't say I saw the resemblance. So, next time your brother comes, you've got something to feed him."

"Okay, I'm not going to keep playing pass the lasagna with you. I'll take it, but then you've got a meal owed." She takes the pan out of my hands with a little jerk.

"Thanks for coming. And for the wine."

"Thank you for asking. Neighborly, right?"

Why do I feel wrong-footed? "I'll walk you out to your car, fend off the skunks." I grab my flashlight, the big serious one that I use when trying to locate kittens or bunnies or snakes stuck in odd, dark places. Given that I now know that she's single, there is a whole new matzo ball hanging out there. Should I kiss her good night? A cheek kiss? Both cheeks? Something Continental? Boy, am I out of practice.

"See you. Thanks again." She's in her car, keys in hand, lasagna pan on the seat beside her, but her door is still open. "Hey, good luck with that dog."

Screw it. I lean in and give Natalie a gentle kiss on the cheek. Nothing overtly meaningful, just a friendly, neighborly peck on the cheek.

The way she smiles at me, I know that I may have blown the evening but that I've gotten that just right.

It was getting harder to get around. At first, the wound had been exquisitely painful, but after days of licking at it and lying in the soothing mud at the edge of the pond, the dog had managed to adapt to the constant ache of the pellets embedded in his hip. He was more hungry than hurting after a week. Instinct and experience kept him away from humans, but not from human habitation. As his mobility briefly improved, his ability to focus on finding food also improved. A visual learner by nature, he observed the raccoons, which tolerated his presence, neither threatened by him nor very interested. But he was interested in their habits, their routes into the neighborhoods that grew out of the woods and fields. He watched as their clever paws lifted trash-can lids and they hoisted themselves inside. The mouth-watering scent of offal and rotted vegetables encouraged him to limp closer. A flash of wisdom and he chased off the raccoons, taking the contents of the trash barrel for himself.

Other creatures, crows and skunks, led him to compost heaps. He attempted to chase a skunk away from its feast only once. Ignoring the pain in his hip, the dog fled, stopping every few yards to try to roll the stinging, stinking spray out of his eyes and off his skin.

It was the clever coyote who led him to the chickens. He followed her at a distance, upwind, so that she wouldn't know he was there.

They'd met only through scent marking, hers distinctive from the older, potent male who owned this territory, but the dog knew her the moment her rangy gray form slipped out from between the dense trees and glided silently down the hill toward the house and barn. He stayed behind, keeping to the trees, aware that there was a dog somewhere on the property. He watched as the coyote bitch circled the quiet pen, poking a paw here or there to see if there was an opening. Suddenly, she raised her head and looked right at him. There was no challenge in the look. The dog licked his lips, yawned. Nervous, tempted.

He took her invitation and in an awkward three-legged trot came down the hill, his clumsy noise alerting the sleeping hens. At the first squawk, the coyote was gone. The back door of the house slammed open and the yard lights burst on. Fighting the weakness in his leg, the dog bolted for higher ground, the double shotgun blast reminding him of the treachery—the danger—of humans.

As the weeks have passed, it's grown harder and harder to travel any distance away from his makeshift den. Not only has his hip wound festered but every bone in his body screams with a feverish ache that makes even sitting painful. He's been living mostly on crickets and what frogs he can catch, and the cold penetrates his now-fleshless body.

His dinner of crickets has not satisfied him by any means. He's spent all day limping along, sniffing every likely hiding place for some edible and catchable creature, with limited success. Grass and water are all that he can depend on. It's too much now to venture as far as the houses that have trash barrels. He's tucked into his den, exhausted. His acute ears hear the man who approaches at a run. The scent of fresh meat is somehow attached to him. The dog gets up and moves gingerly through the tall grass to where he can observe.

He watches as the man sets up the crate in the middle of the path that he runs along every day. He pulls the meat-scented package out of his pocket and opens it up. The overpowering scent of raw meat fills the air, bringing saliva to the dog's mouth. He swallows, yawns. Keeps his eyes on the man as he places chunks of the meat inside the crate, the bright cone of battery-powered illumination casting the man into shadow but the meat into the spotlight.

Now satisfied with the arrangement of the meat and the openness of the crate door, the man gets to his feet. He stands over the crate, walks around it, examining the ground with the sweep of his light. The dog is fixated on the scent of the meat within the crate but is unwilling to reveal himself. He waits, patient as a statue, for the man to go away. Finally, he does, striding quickly along, following the beam of his flashlight. The dog hunkers down in the tall grass, unaware that if the man's flashlight should sweep his way, his wide open eyes would give him away.

The man is gone, and the dog hears the cabin door shut, the sound of windows being cranked back in. He hears the man's human sounds without paying them any attention. His eyes and nose are on the meat. And he understands the price to be paid for getting it. He remembers the crate he was placed in by humans. He remembers how the door was shut and latched and how he was lifted into the back of a truck. He remembers only pain and torment after that.

The meat has attracted others. A red fox tiptoes out of the cattails, his brush outstretched and proud. The fox is startled off by the sudden advent of a larger predator. The adolescent female coyote sniffs the air but doesn't come close to the meat-baited box. The dog understands. There is too much human scent lingering around it. Of the three members of the Canidae family, only he has had true contact with these two-legged creatures. But she makes no move to leave, and the dog sees that this tantalizing offering is subject to loss. He may be afraid to retrieve it, but he doesn't want anyone else to have it. Even as emaciated as he is, he's still bigger than this adolescent coyote. He emerges from his cover and walks toward her. He growls. She lowers her head, waggles it, then bolts.

Alone now with the crate and the untouched meat, the dog lies down in the path, his nose pressed up against the mesh of the cage. He breathes in the odor of the fat, the bones, and the stringy red flesh. He sticks his tongue in, stretching it as far as he can against the obstruction of the wire mesh, and is rewarded by a taste. He struggles to his feet and circles the crate, standing for a long time in the obvious entrance. Some deeper caution prevents him from entering. The meat is a full body length away from the opening, too far to commit to trying to get at it. He settles down beside it once again, protecting from others that which he cannot, will not, get for himself.

Then another, stronger scent of coyote comes to him. This isn't the young female. This is the coyote who has left the scent marks defining his territory, his range. The dog has been aware of living within that range, and the inherent danger of it. And now this big male will demand that meat. The dog struggles to his feet. Once upright, he lowers his head, pulls his lips into a snarl, vocalizes his possession.

The male coyote, bigger than the dog, heavier and healthy, stiff-legs toward him, his hackles up, his yellow eyes fixed and hostile.

10

E ven before the lazy sun fully lights up the pond, I'm up and
dressed and tying on my venerable L.L. Bean boots. I'll run
later, if I run at all. Right now, I want to get out and see if the dog
is in the trap. I've got a catch pole and a second Baggie of food and
every expectation that a dog, no matter how feral it's become, won't
have been able to resist the smorgasbord of meat products I baited
the trap with last night. I'm less certain about what I may have
captured—whether it will be a domestic dog or something I'll have
to call the Wildlife Service to come deal with.

I check my messages as I walk out the door. Nothing this early
from the communications center. Good. A voice-mail message from
Max, wondering if I want to come over for the game. Better. And a
text from Natalie saying she enjoyed herself last night and asking if
I'd like to take a riding lesson sometime. Best. I text a quick yes to
Max, saying I'll bring the beer, and, before I can overthink my response, text a yes to Natalie.

There is something that appeals to me about the idea of having
an activity in place of an awkward reciprocal dinner. I do much bet-

ter when I'm doing things, rather than just making conversation. Gayle and I spent the first few months of our courtship hiking and biking and river rafting. It was a long time before I realized that conversation with her was no longer contrived, but natural. And it was even longer before I realized that we both saw silence as a welcome thing. And then my silence went from a comfortable manifestation of our relationship to being withdrawn and guarded and maybe even hostile. No wonder she found a new guy.

Knock it off. Enough with the thoughts of that which is no longer in my control—*id* freakin' *est*, my marriage.

The October morning is lemon-colored, and I tilt the bill of my hat as I head due east toward the location of the trap, catch pole over my shoulder like a kid going fishing. I swing left along the path, and when the trap is only a few yards away, I start talking, alerting the animal, should he be incarcerated, of my approach, and my non-threatening intentions. "Hey, boy. Good fella. Did you enjoy your meal?" I whistle, a dog-calling "Come to me" whistle like the one I used for long-gone Snoopy and the one I used to call Argos back from his dog park free time. A towhee mocks me with its own sharp two-note upbeat whistle. *Tow Hee!*

The trap is in shadow, but I can see right away that not only is it empty but it's overturned; the trap's door is sprung and the bait is gone. I wish I was enough of a tracker, a hunter, to thoroughly assess the clues. There are definitely paw prints, but of a size to be the dog's? Maybe. Maybe not. It's also possible that there are two sets of prints. There's definitely fur. I pick up a silvery tuft. I need forensics out here. There's something very dark brown spattered on the pounded-down grass beside the trap. Another hunk of fur, this one with a little skin attached. More pale yellow than silver.

Max hands me a bowl of popcorn and a beer.

I set the bowl down on the coffee table and flop onto Max's ancient leather couch. I've been telling him about my failed attempt at capturing the feral dog. "He's not the first fugitive I've had to pursue using a couple of different methods." I take a swallow of beer. "I may have to track him and see if I can get him with a tranquilizer gun."

"If that's what you want to do, let me know and I'll give you the right dosage."

I don't mention that my tracking skills are nonexistent. Despite a couple of years in the Boy Scouts, I never earned a merit badge for tracking. Even when Bull offered to take me hunting, teach me how to find rabbits, I declined. Not out of any squeamishness, but because I didn't want to be anywhere near Bull and a gun. Later, professionally, my tracking was all done via canine nose.

We settle to watch the Patriots beat up on the opposition, and the conversation is essentially nothing more weighty than cheers, second-guessing referee calls, and epithets. By halftime, the Patriots are well ahead and Rocco's, the one pizza place in town that delivers, has brought us dinner.

"Maybe you shouldn't try trapping him. Maybe something a little less aggressive would work better with a dog like that."

"What do you mean?"

"He needs to be brought back into the fold, so to speak. The human fold. If he is a runaway, or a lost dog who's figured out how to survive without humans, he needs to be reminded that people are okay."

"How do I do that?"

"Don't try to trap him."

"I should just invite him into the house?"

"Something like that. Be around. Get him used to you."

The game is back on and that's it for conversation.

Jenny Bright isn't at the shelter when I get to work on Monday morning. I know that she'll pull in any minute now, and, because it's Monday, she'll be carrying a bag of what she calls her "go-to-work-on-Monday incentive." Harmony Farms, so far, has avoided any chain doughnut shops, and what those shops offer cannot be classed in the same genus as what she brings from Darlene's Bakery. Homemade, still warm, not quite perfectly ovoid, tantalizing doughnuts in a waxed white bag, wafting out of which is the scent I believe heaven might smell like.

My job is to get the coffee started. That set, I do something I should have done far earlier—pull out my logbook and review all the lost, missing, misplaced dogs over the past few weeks. Dogs wander, dogs get lost, but usually they find a human and turn themselves in. It's also possible that whoever lost this dog never thought to alert the dog officer. Some folks in this town are still unaware that they even have a dog officer. Still, my finely honed animal control officer instincts tell me that this is an abandonment case. His avoidance of humans is suggestive of human-caused trauma. Something I understand.

There's nothing logged that remotely resembles a missing midsize yellow dog with a limp. I look at the reports of garbage tossing, plus Deke's chicken harassing, add in my own sightings, and there develops a territory of sorts where this stray dog is hanging out. My cabin's in the dead center.

I slap the book shut. Jenny has arrived and the sweet scent of freshly made doughnuts preceding her makes all else unimportant.

"Is that coffee ready?" she asks.

I get us both mugs from the chipped collection as Jenny divvies up the contents of the bakery bag. The first time Jenny brought doughnuts to the office, she made some remark about cops and doughnuts. Nothing particularly witty. I gave her a deadpan lecture on profiling and how making assumptions most often leads to personal offense. She blanched even whiter than she normally is under her Goth makeup and fell all over herself apologizing before I laughed and made a cop and doughnut joke myself. Jenny is the daughter of the golden couple of my first year in high school. Mark Bright and Olivia something. The homecoming king and queen, the couple all the other couples wanted to be. I know the story, but I'd never say anything to Jenny, who is the daughter of their teenage passion. College scholarships lost, the golden aura tarnished. Mark is in his father's business, plumbing, and Olivia works as a bookkeeper somewhere. Good people. Raised a quirky, if nice, kid. Their only child.

"I take it you didn't catch that dog, the one you took the big Havahart for?" Against her Goth-blackened lips, the white sugar of her powdered doughnut makes an interesting contrast until she licks it off.

"I'll get him. I was just checking to see if we had any reports on a lost dog in that vicinity, but the only unaccounted-for missing dog is that Lhasa apso that went missing a year ago."

"Coyote, my guess." Jenny breaks off another piece of doughnut and dips it into her black coffee.

"Probably."

Jenny pops the last of her doughnut into her mouth. "Poor family. It's tough not knowing."

"They're telling themselves that some well-meaning but misguided Samaritan picked it up and took it home. Home being a penthouse overlooking the Charles in Boston."

"You have to tell yourself whatever you must to gain acceptance of the unanswerable."

"Wisdom from a chick with seventeen piercings and a tattoo of Cookie Monster on her bicep."

"Yes, my son." Jenny crumples the paper bag and tosses it, then heads to the rest room.

I brush the crumbs from my glazed doughnut into my palm and then, with an eye to the closed rest room door, lick them off. Jenny's offhand pseudophilosophic remark floats in the air. Maybe she's right, and I wonder what I'm telling myself to get through my own unanswerable questions.

I pull into the uphill driveway of the Haynes brothers homestead, ignoring the array of NO TRESPASSING signs nailed to the stockade fence, as well as various other signs, all variations on the same theme: *Stay out.* BEWARE OF DOG. NEVER MIND DOG, BEWARE OF OWNER, PROTECTED BY MAGNUM. Sweet boys, Len and Bob. I'm here because I've gotten a call from an anonymous whistle-blower reporting animal cruelty. Anonymous because no one wants to be on the wrong side of the Haynes boys, but I'm pretty sure it's the electric company's meter reader.

Behind the stockade fence, the Haynes property makes Bull's shabby Poor Farm Road house look pristine. Blue tarp on the roof, random piles of salvaged wood, roofing shingles, rocks. A rusted-out John Deere sits cattywumpus against the side of a tilted outhouse. It's not deer season, but there's a carcass hanging from an oak tree, gutted and bled out. At least I think it's a deer. The Haynes are meat-on-the-table hunters, not sportsmen. Some speckled hens scrape at the dirt. So far, no one has called out to warn me off the property. But my instincts tell me that I'm being observed. The big Suburban with the town seal is announcement enough of who I am, and probably why I'm here. I climb out of the SUV, stand tall and bold as I take a quick survey of the yard. And there they are, three mongrels attached to short chains, which are fixed to a bare wheel rim from some kind of big vehicle. They fan out like spokes on a wheel and their chains are so short, they can't reach one another. No water. No food. No shelter. Feces everywhere.

They are on their feet, big dogs, hounds, by the look of them. They growl and then, at the approach of the two men, grovel.

"You got a warrant?"

"Hey, Bob. Len." I want to keep this on an even keel, but I know my job. "I don't need one. But you've got to provide shelter for these dogs. Basic needs."

"They're fine."

"No, they're not. And you want to keep them, you provide shelter, food, and water."

"You and what army going to take them away from us?" This is Len, the elder.

"You don't want to know." I hate bullies, especially the ones that have no original material.

"Get back in your town vehicle and get off the property."

"Neither one of you wants real trouble, so just move the dogs into that crappy shed, or lose 'em."

Len takes a step closer to me. "I said get off my property."

Although my voice is steady, there is a terrible roiling in my blood right now. I can hear the pulse in my ears, overriding the tinnitus. I don't want to lose my temper, my professionalism. I fall back on my training. "Please step away, sir." *Sir*, the default method of address for the irrational. Respect but no fear.

The dogs are back on their feet now, ears pinned, tongues popping against lips, nervous, anxious dogs. I decide that I should take a closer look. I shoulder myself past the barricade of Len and Bob. "Hey, pups. Good boys." I don't try to touch them; I'm only looking for signs of starvation or injury. They bark at me, but the look on their faces is pure fear aggression. They look well-enough fed. No obvious signs of injury. I notice a fourth chain, a collar still attached to the clip. I face the Haynes brothers. "I'll be back in a few days. See that they're sheltered properly."

I climb back into the SUV, back out slowly, implying that they haven't chased me away.

It's a beautiful, cool early October night and I'm camping out. I've got my sleeping bag and my camping lantern, a book, and a pot of stew simmering on my camp stove. I've chosen a spot where the feral dog can't miss my presence in the woods. There was enough daylight when I got home from work for me to scope out where the dog might most likely be living. It's not unlike hunting, or chasing felons. It just takes thinking and observation, measurements, and luck. I've chosen a flat, more or less comfortable site just inside the woods, a few feet from the path, twenty-five yards from the driveway. This is where I'll eat and sleep until the dog grows used to my nightly presence. If Muhammad won't come to the mountain . . . Fill in the rest for yourself.

I scoop some lukewarm stew out of the pot for myself, then ladle a second helping into a dog dish. This I set out ten feet from where I sit with my back against a scrub oak. I whistle twice and then settle in for what I know may be a very long wait. It could take days, maybe even weeks. I'm not sure I have the stamina—or interest—to do this for long, but, for now, it's a beautiful fall night and it isn't the worst place I've ever slept.

Two little boys, too young really to be out at night on their own. Lugging He-Man sleeping bags never meant for outdoor use. They set up camp on the imported sand of the small public beach at the edge of the lake, ignorant of the fact that the nylon bags will soak up the moisture from the ground, leaving them both soggy and shivering in the morning. Cooper thinks it's worth it, this discomfort, to have the benign attention of his older brother. He spends most of the night shivering and trying not to think about how badly he needs to pee, but he's afraid to climb out of the bag, afraid that some creature of the night might get him. The night birds and the bullfrogs sound so ominous when you're lying awake and cold and desperate to pee.

"I've got to go take a piss," Jimmy says.

Cooper didn't know his brother was also awake. "Me, too."

They crawl out of their damp sleeping bags to stand side by side as they urinate against a tilted tree. A screech owl cries out across the lake, making Cooper shiver.

"It's just a bird, stupid."

"I know." But it's good to have confirmation.

I wake from a surprisingly dreamless night. The sky is just beginning to turn gray and it is light enough that I know I won't be going back to sleep. Far from being cold or sore from a night on the ground, I feel, for the first time in a very long time, refreshed. Instead of awaking to my collection of stressful thoughts, I think immediately of my canine quarry. I struggle out of my sleeping bag to check the dog dish. Untouched. Disappointed but not surprised, I leave it, break camp, and head home for a shower. I'm a patient man. I can do this every night if I have to. Maybe there is even something pleasurable in the quest. It's been a long time since I've had a challenge that engages both my intellect and my competitive nature.

11

⁘

I think this one will fit you." Natalie pulls a riding helmet off a shelf, hands it to me. "Buckle the strap. Make sure the harness is tight."

She's giving me that promised riding lesson today and I'm feeling like a new recruit trying not to piss off a drill sergeant. I take the helmet, put it on, buckle the chin strap as directed. She's told me to wear the most worn jeans I own and sturdy boots with a heel. If I like riding, I can invest in the right gear later.

Nat's already kitted out in riding pants, paddock boots, and half chaps. In a graceful, practiced motion, she gathers her hair into a knot and puts her black-and-brown riding helmet over it. If I survive the lesson, she'll take me out for a quick trail ride, so two horses are tacked up. I'll be on the bay mare that kissed my cheek the other day, and she'll be on the big chestnut, a rescued "off-the-track" Thoroughbred she's rehabbing for a new career in dressage. This, it seems, is her specialty, buying broken-down racehorses and retooling them.

I always admire people who know what they're doing, whether it's hammering shingles, directing traffic, or tracking felons. Natalie exudes the confidence of someone who is completely at home in her job. I can't imagine that she was ever a bond trader. I can't picture her in a suit, with high heels, a briefcase. She couldn't look any more attractive than she does right now, leading her horse out of the barn, every contour of her very well defined posterior perfect in mouse gray breeches. I pull myself back into the moment. Right now I'm with an attractive woman and about to climb aboard a horse for the first time since Deke let me swing a leg over his elderly pony when I was a kid.

It's one of those mid-October days that sparkle and make you squint against the angle of the sun as it grazes the tops of trees dressed in flaming red and orange leaves. The faded red of the barn somehow compliments the foliage, and the pasture grass has greened up again after a long, hot summer. The rustic charm of Natalie's Second Hope Farm is picture-perfect.

"Use the mounting block." Natalie holds the mare as I mount. "Have you ever ridden before?"

I mention the pony rides.

"Okay." And, with that, Natalie takes my left leg and positions my foot in the stirrup, telling me to do the same with the other leg, hands me the reins and shows me how to hold them properly, steps down from the mounting block, and walks to the middle of the ring. "Squeeze with your legs."

The mare moves toward the middle of the ring with a shuffling walk, her ears twitching from side to side. She ends up standing next to Natalie.

"Around the ring, not in the middle. Look where you want to go."

I look, squeeze, and the mare, reluctantly, shuffles off to the perimeter of the riding ring.

"Squeeze harder; make her move."

I do, and suddenly I'm riding. A walk, to be sure, but I have the horse moving forward and, with Natalie's order to "shorten" my reins, I have the feel of her between my hands and legs. I feel pretty good, pretty accomplished for a first-timer. This isn't so hard. We change direction, make some circles. I'm feeling pretty good.

"Want to try a trot?"

Half an hour later, I understand very well the location of what Natalie calls my "seat bones." I'm pretty sure that I will recognize them every time I sit down for the next week. My lesson is declared over; she's up on her chestnut, and even a first-timer like me can see the world of difference between my riding skills and hers. On his long dancer's legs, the horse appears to be floating above the ground as she trots him around the ring. I think of the hours of practice Argos and I put in, drills designed to make action into reaction. Hours of practice takedowns, searches, refinements to our skills. What Natalie and the chestnut are doing is more like a ballet lesson. I am seated on my mare in the middle of the ring, watching Natalie's face as she concentrates on moving her horse in gliding lateral moves. I know that kind of concentration, the kind that blanks out the rest of the world. When Argos and I were on patrol, the only thing on my mind was the task at hand. Not hunger or thirst, or weariness, for either of us. A goal was set, to find a missing person. Or to take down and hold a criminal until backup arrived. Nothing could distract us from that goal.

"Get 'em, boy."

Argos is a streak of white motion, accompanied by the throaty music of his trademark growl. More than a growl, a roar, a fearsome vocalization guaranteed to frighten the most aggressive criminals.

"Get him off me! Get him off me!" The perpetrator rolls on the ground beneath the big dog's savage advance.

"Argos, all done." Cooper has his handcuffs out, and the perp is almost glad to have him snap them on. He hauls the guy to his feet. "You have the right . . . "

Argos fairly dances beside the pair, cop and collar, his amber eyes fixed on the man in Cooper's grip, silently reminding the captive that he, Argos, is still on the job and he'd better not try anything.

This collar is the twenty-first for Cooper and Argos and it gets the attention of the papers, and the local news station does a little story on it, on Argos, which makes Cooper feel like a proud parent.

Natalie's goal is a little more obscure, but I think it involves perfection in movement. I stroke the silky neck of the mare, Moxie, and feel her relax under me, dropping her head, her thick black tail casually swishing behind me. She blows air gently through her nostrils, the horsey equivalent of sighing. A peaceful, contented sound.

"Got enough energy left in you? Want to go out for a hack?" Natalie is walking her horse, his neck stretched out fully, his ears drooping with relaxation.

"I do." I may never walk again, but I've got enough energy for a trail ride. As instructed, I "gather" my reins, which gets Moxie's attention and she perks up.

We leave the paddocks behind, moving slowly toward the hillside bordering Natalie's pastures, on the other side of which is Bartlett's Pond. My mare takes the lead without my express say-so, but Natalie just says that's who she is. The big chestnut docilely follows along, putting his trust in the smaller mare to save him from scary things. Or to be eaten first. Warm from my riding-lesson exertions, I've left my jacket behind, and the cool October air feels good. The movement of horse hooves through the dry fallen leaves is a cheerful sound, like crunching bran flakes. Once in a while, I hear Natalie's voice behind me, but I can't catch what she's saying over the rustling of the leaves. I haven't mentioned my hearing loss, although she must have wondered about me, as I wasn't quick to respond to her instructions as I tracked to the left in the ring. She had to repeat herself enough that she must have thought me a student with very poor retention; after all, I'd done so well going clockwise.

Very quickly we are at the pond and begin to circumnavigate my running path side by side, which makes conversation a lot easier.

There's a gathering of Canada geese on the bank, muttering to themselves as the horses pass by. They glide out into the water, complaining of the intrusion.

"Did you ever catch that dog you were after?"

"No. He's savvy enough about traps to keep out of them. I've been trying to get him to know me by dropping some meat as I run, leaving my dirty shirt where he can smell it, that sort of thing."

"Tame him?"

"I guess you could say that, although I don't think he was born feral. But clearly something happened to him, and I'm afraid that if I don't get him pretty soon, before the real cold settles in, I'm just going to find a corpse one day. No dog deserves that kind of end."

"I know. That's how I feel about the horses I rescue. You wouldn't believe the conditions some animals are kept in. By well-meaning idiots mostly, people who have no idea what it takes to keep a horse healthy. They get one for their kids, keep it in a backyard in a six-by-six pen. Or find out they can't afford to feed it and let it loose. Or race it at age two with damaged ligaments masked by drugs." Natalie is getting wound up.

"But we can't save them all."

"But you're going to save this one. I just know it."

We veer off the trail around the pond, following a narrower path.

"Max told me you were a cop before you were an animal control officer."

"That's right. K-9 unit."

"That must have been pretty exciting work." Subtext: So how come you're a lowly ACO in a Podunk town.

"It had its moments." I'm not going to be sucked into a conversation I haven't had with anyone. "Bond trading must have had some heart-stopping moments, too."

"There were days, sure. But I didn't quit because it was too exciting."

"I assume you quit to follow a dream."

"Second Hope?"

"Isn't it? Your dream, I mean."

"It's more than a name, Second Hope. More than a dream. It saved my life." She doesn't look at me when she says this, and I know that she, too, has a story she'd rather not get into. She strokes her horse's neck. We pause at the edge of a small field that I recognize as Deke's back pasture. "Want to try a canter?"

It's just like in the cowboy movies; the wind in my face, my eyes watering, and the sense that I'm either going to fly or fall hard keeps me smiling. I'm just beginning to relax into the rocking horse rhythm of this mare when Natalie brings her horse down to a trot and my mare suddenly follows suit, almost unseating me with the abrupt change of rhythm.

"How was that?" Natalie has dropped her reins, her horse completely ready to head home without guidance.

"Amazing." I give my mare a pat on her neck and a little scratch. "Where do I get the right gear?"

It has been a very long time since a woman looked at me with approval, and I bask in the radiance of Natalie's smile. She's got dimples I haven't noticed before. I've always liked dimples.

We make our way back to Second Hope at a walk, side by side.

12

Roger Schaeffer is a pudgy, balding, colorless man dressed in the überbland colors of beige and taupe. In the harsh fluorescent overhead lights of the animal control office, his skin is as mushroom-colored as his pants and his eyelashes are so pale that his watery blue eyes appear bald. He is the polar opposite of his florid, caftan-wearing, overblown mother, Polly. And it's his mother he's come to see me about. About her animals.

"I guess you could say that we're staging an intervention. We'll get her out of the house; you collect the animals and get them out of there."

"And where am I supposed to take them?" I point to the three-dog kennel and the short stack of cat cages, two of which are occupied by cats, and the third contains a black-and-white rabbit. "I don't have the room."

"She can't go on like this. I'm afraid that the Health Department is going to come in."

"Look, Roger." I sit forward in my office chair, put on my

authority face. "I'm keeping tabs on her and she's got a lot of cats, yes, but she's not breaking any laws."

"She's a crazy cat lady." To my surprise, Roger is on the verge of tears. "How would you like it if everyone made fun of your mother?"

Don't you remember what folks said about my family? I think. My mother may not have been made fun of, but she sure was an object of pity. *What does Mona see in him? Why does she keep going back to that drunk?* Funny what a kid overhears. Some adults think that a child who appears to be focused on his Legos isn't aware of their conversation—teachers, baby-sitters, neighbors—that a little kid doesn't understand that his mother is gossip fodder; that he isn't listening.

"No one is making fun of her." I get it now, Roger's distress. It's no laughing matter to have a parent who is out of control, or a danger to society, or an embarrassment to you as you grow up and you have to distance yourself from their foibles. "Have you ever gotten her help? I mean, you know, a psychiatric evaluation? If there was a diagnosis, maybe something could be done."

"We've tried, my sister and I. At first, we thought, Great, she's got an interest, and something to keep her company because neither one of us lives here. That was for the first three cats. Now I can't take my kids to see their grandmother."

"She's a good soul, Roger." I could mention the puppy that she gave me, but I am squeamish about reminding Roger, who has about fifteen years on me, about that grubby little poor-side-of-town kid who would show up at his house to play with his dog. I want Roger to know that his mother has friends. "Folks like her. She's active at church." But I don't tell him that no one will go to her house to visit. I also don't tell Polly's son that sometimes I have to remove her "rescued" animals and return them to their rightful owners

Roger knuckles away a tear, sniffs. "We'd just appreciate anything you can do. Maybe even just take a couple of the cats? Even that would help."

I slide my rolling chair to my office door. "Hey, Jenny, can you come in?"

Jenny Bright has a file folder with the names of local residents who have been willing to foster some of the inmates of the Bowwow Inn. She works with a variety of rescue organizations to place the unclaimed dogs that occasionally languish in the kennel here. If a dog fits a breed type, Jenny has the capacity to sweet-talk even the most reluctant of program directors to take a chance on the animal.

I ask if she can come up with a few animal lovers willing to foster a cat or two.

"I don't know, Coop. There aren't a lot of feline fosterers around. Not quite as glam as dog fostering." She squeezes one of her multiple ear studs in more securely, the movement showing to advantage the red-and-green lizard tattoo crawling along her forearm.

"Work your magic."

"I'll see what I can do, but no promises."

Roger is staring after Jenny as she walks out of my office, his round face a pale mask of doubt.

"Don't worry. She's very good at what she does."

I walk Roger Schaeffer out of the building and to his, unsurprisingly, beige car. "Give me a call in a couple of days, and I'll let you know if we've got places for some of the cats." I'm not about to empty Polly's house out. I can't do that to her. But, as Roger says, she's a crazy cat lady and I need to do something.

As he drives away, it occurs to me that he has no idea that I'm one of *those* Harrisons. What a pleasant thought. Maybe Lev was right when he said no one would remember me.

It's been almost a week, but I'm still feeling my first horseback ride in my thighs. It's kind of a good pain, a reminder of an enjoyable experience and something that is beginning to feel like a new friendship. Tonight, Friday, I'm taking her out properly, to the Lakeside Tavern. The tavern is perfect because it's so local, so unassuming, we can be perfectly relaxed and not look like a couple out on the shakedown cruise of a first date. Besides, it isn't a first date, not technically. We've already broken bread together—which reminds me that I still have Mrs. Bollen's lasagna dish in my truck—and shared an outdoor experience. So, to be accurate, this is the third date, practically routine. Still, I'll go home and shower before driving to her place to pick her up. Maybe take her one of those ten-dollar bouquets from the Country Market.

Max Philbine is the only one who knows that I'm testing the dating waters with Natalie, and that's only because Friday is usually the night he and I hit the tavern ourselves. I felt a little like a playground fink, breaking a date with a pal to go out with a girl. Max laughed and forgave me. "Hey, she's a great girl. Go have fun. I've got other friends, you know."

"Max?"

"What?"

"Why haven't you asked her out?"

"I did." Max waits a beat. "Kidding."

"Seriously, why not?"

"Coop, old man, I've been down the marriage path twice and have foresworn ever becoming entangled in that again."

"I'm not talking engagement here, but a date, you know, two people of the opposite sex talking over a plate of linguini."

I certainly have no ulterior motive, no desire at all to go down that path Max referred to, not at all. It's just a date. Besides, Natalie's made it fairly clear that she's glad of a date but not looking for a lifestyle change any more than I am. Phrases clutter her conversation—"I'm so busy," "I'm so focused on my work, I can't think of anything else"—in a pretty obvious deflection of unwanted intentions. I'm not courting, or seducing, and I think that suits us both.

I'm only buying her a meal to say thank you for introducing me to a new sport. That's all. Really. It's what friends do.

Before I can turn my attention to the pleasures of my upcoming evening, I have to go check on the Haynes's dogs. It's must be the Puritan in me, do the hard thing first so that you can enjoy the fun thing later. I keep my fingers crossed that not only will the brothers be away from the property, which would make my inspection a lot more pleasant, but that they have heeded my warnings. I'm one for two when I pull into the yard. No dogs in sight. This is encouraging, but then I don't hear them, either, and I think that I would. Len comes out of the house. I get out of the truck. We meet like the sheriff and the gunslinger, halfway. "Len, where are the dogs?"

He doesn't say anything; neither does he meet my eyes. He blows his nose into a red bandanna, stuffs it into his overall pocket. "When you were here last time, I didn't know you were Bull's boy. Thought you were a newcomer."

Bull's boy. "Right. Cooper Harrison."

By virtue of knowing my family, of my being determined a native, as it were, I am suddenly okay in Len's book.

"I'll show you." Len leads me around the tilted shed to a flat shaded area where he's erected a proper kennel, not luxury living by any means, but each dog now has its own doghouse and run. There are still only three dogs, but he's built a fourth kennel.

"You didn't happen to lose a dog recently, did you? I've got a stray I'm tracking."

"Nope. Had one die."

"How?" I have to ask.

"Bone got stuck in his throat." Len turns away from me. Our conversation is ended.

As it turns out, I don't have time to run by the market and buy flowers for Natalie. The truth is, I kind of chickened out. Flowers just seem too suggestive of intentions she isn't interested in. I may not have had time to buy flowers, but I have built in time to take a two-lap run around the pond and drop some stew beef as I go, feeding the dog and making inroads against his distrust of me. When I get back tonight, I will fill the bowl with meat, add a couple of dog biscuits, and set it, as I always do, ten feet from my sleeping bag. Far enough away that the dog knows he can't be grabbed, close enough that he will identify me with the food. This morning, I was over-joyed to see that, for the first time, the food was gone. Of course, without having actually seen the animal that took it, I can only hope that it was my target dog, not some sneaky woodland creature un-afraid of humans. One of these nights, I should really try to stay awake, watching for the glitter of animal eyes in the dying flames.

It's already dark by the time I pull into the yard at Second Hope Farm. The barn lights are on, the doors wide open, and the effect is warm and welcoming. Natalie's dog comes out to greet me, as if wondering where I have been all her life. I squat to pat her, stand up, to see Natalie coming toward me, the lights of the barn illuminating her way.

The water is the only thing that feels good against his wounds. It was only the looseness of the skin around his neck that saved the dog from the fangs of the male coyote, suffering punctures but not a broken neck. His forelegs bear the gashes inflicted by the bigger canine. The punctures and the gashes are filled with pus and the stink has attracted flies, which torment the dog.

Every day, he awaits the sound of the man running along the path. Only then, after the man passes, does he rouse himself from the shelter of the reeds and pick up what the man has carelessly left behind. Chunks of meat. Because it's daylight, and the man scent lingers, there is no competition for it. The dog swallows the cubes whole.

The dog closes his eyes, almost as desirous of sleep as he is of food and water. Even for a young dog, not even a yearling, this constant discomfort is wearing, and he could be an old dog just at the end of his life for the amount of will left in him.

13

The meeting had been a good one. Someone had brought seasonally decorated doughnuts, and the coffee was a little less acidic than usual. Maybe whoever brought the orange-and-black sprinkled goodies had plumped for Dunkin' Donuts coffee. Couple of new guys, shy first-timers mumbling through the introductions. Bull didn't usually speak at these things; he was happy to sit in the back and listen to others relate how many days it'd been since their last drink or what extraordinary efforts they were making toward sobriety. Or why they were starting over again at day one. He'd had a lot of day ones. The novelty of sobriety would wear off and things would happen. Right now, he was clinging to day 753. But, hey, who was really counting?

Jimmy's got stuff locked away. But Bull knows where it is. For the first few days that Jimmy was at the house, he'd done what a lot of guys do when they get out—gone on a drunk. It was as if he didn't know that Bull was on the wagon, that he'd gone over two years without a drink or a hit. But Jimmy was a man coming off the desert, so he brought a boxful of liquor into the house, setting it on the banged-up kitchen table. "Oh, yeah, right. You're off the sauce, right, old man?"

"Seven hundred and thirty-six and counting." Bull was proud to tell his boy this. The last time he'd seen Jimmy, Bull'd been sober, too, but only since dawn, which was when Deke picked him up to drive him to Walpole for a visit with his elder son. It was a long ride and a longer day, being without the anesthesia of alcohol. Made the visiting room all the more depressing.

"You keep a calendar?" Jimmy asked.

"I have to."

"Well, I hope you don't mind, but I'm indulging. I counted days, too, and by my calculations, I'm at day four thousand and something." Jimmy opened a cabinet and pulled out an old jelly glass with the cartoon images of Fred Flintstone and Barney Rubble decorating it. Jimmy filled the glass to the top of Fred's head with the whiskey and raised it to Bull. "What should I toast?"

"Freedom?" Bull takes a Coke out of the refrigerator, pops the top. The sizzle of carbonation tickles his mouth. "Good health?"

Jimmy studies Fred's face on the glass. "To old friends and new endeavors." He throws back a deep swallow, winces, bangs the tabletop with an open hand. "Good stuff."

Jimmy keeps the booze in his room, the same room that he slept in all those years ago when the whole family was living on Poor Farm Road. Back in the day when Mona was here and things were better. Not good, but better. She was so beautiful. At least until the lines began to develop and deepen around her eyes and in her cheeks, and eventually there was a hardness to her eyes that wasn't there back in their early years. Even then, defeated by the life she'd gotten, Mona was beautiful in Bull's eyes.

A singularly golden spring evening, two kids about to fall in love. Bull in his leather jacket, Mona, a fragile-looking seventeen, in a miniskirt. The sweetness of that first kiss, the feel of her breast under his hand. There is an urgency, more than just desire; in a month, maybe two, Bull knows that he'll be drafted. He's been dealt a lousy number, and he's not college material. That's okay. It means that he and Mona can get married all the sooner. It's all he wants, to give her his name and have her back home waiting for him. She's smitten by his hasty proposal. There is a certain romance to the idea of being a war bride. Like her own mother had been. No one tells Mona "Marry in haste, repent at leisure." She's known Bull all her life but has loved him only since that first kiss, the smoky taste of passion.

He looks so handsome in his uniform; she looks so beautiful in her wedding dress. Two kids, stars in their eyes. They have no idea that Bull will never be the same man as he is in this moment. All of the optimism and happy expectations of building a better life will have been replaced by inertia. A new conviction: What's the use?

"How you doing, Bull?" One of the newer guys had clapped a hand on Bull's shoulder. He was new to the group, but not to Bull's acquaintance. He was one of the Highway Department guys Bull used to work with back in the day. He was a kid back then, fresh out of high school and delighted to be on the crew, a family sinecure. Now he'd risen to department head, just like his dad and his grandfather before him.

"Hey, Tom. Good enough. You bring these?" Bull stuffed a doughnut into his mouth, tongued the sprinkles off his lips.

"Yeah. My turn."

"Rite of passage. There are enough of us, you won't have to do it too often."

"Hear that Jimmy's back."

"That's right." In another man, a red flag might have snapped to attention, but Bull wasn't suspicious. Tommy was here, in a meeting. He couldn't have been looking for trouble. He'd just told thirty sweaty men how he'd been sober so many days and clinging to his

Higher Power. Then again, Jimmy never dealt in alcohol. Bull knew all too well the rationalizations an addict can conjure. But, as far as he knew, Tommy was a run-of-the-mill, too many G&Ts after work kind of alcoholic, there at the meeting because Lev Parker had nailed his ass doing fifty in a twenty-mile-an-hour zone and had given him the choice of AA or thirty days. "He's doing okay," Bull said, referring to Jimmy.

"He got a job yet?"

"No." At least not one he clocks in for, Bull thought. As part of Jimmy's probation he had to at least appear to be making an effort to job-hunt.

"Tell him come to me if he's interested."

Near as Bull could figure, his boy had no marketable skills. He had no CDL license or experience on a factory floor. He'd never had so much as an after-school job. Unless they'd taught him some trade in Walpole, Jimmy's résumé only boasted selling illegal drugs. "Jimmy's not the pick and shovel type, if you get my meaning."

"Naw, nothing like that. No heavy lifting." Tommy laughed, reached for a glazed doughnut. "I could use someone in the office to do scheduling, that sort of thing. Detail stuff."

"Okay. I'll mention it." Bull didn't think that Jimmy would be interested, but he hated to discourage people. Besides, it was nice of Tommy to make this offer. He was a stand-up guy. Not too many employers around there were going to want an ex-con on the payroll. "Thanks."

Tommy clapped Bull on the shoulder again, the gesture both empathetic and patronizing.

14

The bar is three-deep when we arrive at the Lakeside Tavern. There's a twenty-five minute wait for a table, so we join the throng at the bar and order a drink. For a relative newcomer, Natalie seems to know half the people here and she air-kisses and nods to faces that I don't recognize or have a name to put to. I know the bartender, Guy, simply because Guy has been behind the oak bar since I used to come in here to pull my father out. I see a couple of folks whose dogs I've nabbed, the woman who runs the natural-foods store, where I occasionally shop.

In an unusual show of rubbing shoulders with the proletariat, the town's power couple, Cynthia Mann and her husband, Donald Boykin, are here. I know Cynthia a little, Donald not at all, and yet they wave to me in a friendly manner. I almost walk over, then realize that they're gesturing to the person behind me.

Max is at the corner table next to the fireplace, which is glowing now with the first fire of the season. He's got a guy with him, no one I've ever seen before, and I wonder if this is someone from Tufts here to further seduce our town's only veterinarian.

The Irish music trio is warming up, and the whole scene seems so cozy, so cinematic. The jolly neighborhood tavern, gathering place. Maybe I should have suggested getting out of town, going someplace more sophisticated, a place where we might have had to wear something other than jeans. A place where we would have to pay attention to each other, without the comfort of the familiar, the buffer of other acquaintances keeping us safe.

"Marla's flagging us."

Of course Natalie would know the hostess.

"She's a student. Decent rider. She rides the mare you rode."

Marla seats us at the table opposite Max's, flanking the other side of the fireplace. Natalie greets Max with a peck on the cheek. Max does introductions. His tablemate is not from the university, but another vet. I get it: Max is vetting—no pun intended—a potential replacement for himself.

That bit of civility done, Natalie chooses the chair at our round table that puts her back to them. Behind her, Max nods to me, then lifts his glass in a little mocking salute. Natalie's eyes are on me, or I might have good-naturedly flipped Max the bird.

On the ride over, we covered the easy topics of my sore ass and her crazy, busy day. As we have already dealt with the obvious elements in our current lives—her farm, my job—now, we both know, it is the time in our acquaintance to begin to burrow underneath the known surface. We've touched upon the observable, and if we are to become friends, we need to pry a little into each other's lives.

Fortunately, our server arrives just in time.

The special sounds good enough for Natalie, and I fall back on my usual cheeseburger. We order a shared appetizer and new beers. The Irish trio are in full volley and it's impossible for me to hear anything that Natalie is saying over the relentless fiddle and tabor. I keep leaning in, finally shifting my seat over so that my good ear is near her. "I can't hear." I point to my left ear. "It's damaged, and this doesn't help."

Natalie leans in close, so close, I feel her breath on my cheek. I slide an arm around her to keep her there, to hear her.

"How? How was it damaged?"

"Bomb." I take a sip of beer, think about it for a second, then add, "It's when my K-9 partner was killed."

And, as simply as that, I have finally neutralized what happened. Not diminished or defined, or with any less grief, but honed down into a sentence that informs, without killing me by saying it out loud.

The tabor player's mallet beats out a frantic pulse and the fiddle screeches with the same six bars in manic repetition until, at last, the reel comes to a merciful end and I hear Natalie's response clearly. "I'm so sorry." She touches the back of my hand, one finger gently pressing on my knuckles. "Is that why you're here?"

Slowly, I take my arm from around her shoulders, smile up at the server bearing our appetizer of baked Brie and warm bread. A lock of Natalie's dark hair has tangled itself around the button of my shirt cuff and I'm a little stuck. I untangle myself without pulling a strand out.

"Is it?"

"Yes." I stab the Brie with the knife and the warm cheese oozes out over the white plate through the split. I have said enough. I'm not going to reveal to this relative stranger the core disease of my heart, the depth of my grief, the chasm of my fear.

Natalie takes the bread and cheese I hold out to her, rolls her eyes heavenward at the taste. I can see her watching me, waiting for more from me. And then comes the glimmer of understanding. "Okay. Another time."

"Fair enough. Now I'll ask you one, and you can duck it. Why Harmony Farms?"

"You mean, with no connection, no family, no reason to choose this rural location rather than one closer to my origins?"

"Yes. Exactly."

"For exactly those reasons."

"You needed to get out of Dodge?"

She laughs, the first full-throated laugh I've heard from her. "Yes. Something like that."

"As a former law-enforcement officer, I have to advise you that anything you say can only make me curiouser."

"Like Louis Carroll's Cheshire cat?"

"I thought it was Alice who first used the term."

"With you, Mr. Harrison, I suspect that things do get curiouser and curiouser."

The Brie is gone, the white plate nearly licked clean, and our server has appeared with our main courses. Natalie orders a glass of white wine to go with her swordfish and I switch to root beer. "Designated driver."

"How nice for me."

The trio has started up again, this time with a set of sweet ballads. It's easier to talk, but we don't. The silence is comfortable and the food good. Max and his potential replacement have left—Max slapping me on the shoulder in a good-old-boy manner on the way out—and the crowd has been winnowed down to the point that their table remains empty after having been cleared by the busser.

Even a nondate like this needs a second half. Dinner is the first part; a movie or a concert or a couple of strings at the bowling alley, if Harmony Farms had a bowling alley, would make up the remainder of an evening between people not ready for a third act. I am so out of the dating scene that I haven't given any thought to what we might do as a postprandial activity.

As if there had been no pause, Natalie says, "I came to Harmony Farms because the property was for sale and I could afford it. The reason I could afford it was because I was awarded a fairly large sum in a lawsuit. Ugly, but that's the truth. It's when I knew that I had to do something different from what I'd been doing. This was a God-given opportunity."

"I'm going to assume you won't tell me what kind of lawsuit."

Natalie touches the bowl of her glass, stroking away the moisture glistening there. "Wrongful death."

"I'm sorry." There are so many varieties of wrongful death—parent, child, spouse. Medical malpractice, car accident. Shooting. The dead child on the street, caught in the cross fire.

Like me, she's not quite willing to give up her story. I stifle the urge to interrogate her, suppress my curiosity. Whatever her story is, I'll let her keep it to herself until she's ready to tell me. It's a comfortable thought, this idea that there will be other times.

Natalie excuses herself for a moment, leaving me to decide if we should stay for a last drink or take off now, find somewhere else to go for a nightcap. I'm sober, and I can certainly indulge in a glass of wine at that new wine bar on Main Street, the place that took over the space once occupied by Marie's Yarn Shop. Then again, maybe we aren't dressed appropriately for something called a wine bar.

When she gets back from the ladies' room, Natalie decides for us. "I have about an hour left on my internal clock before I crash and burn. Would you like to get out of here and finish up with pie and coffee at my place?"

Yes, please.

Timing in life is everything. A minute less in the ladies' room, a server quicker to bring the check, one less minute in the Lakeside Tavern and I could have avoided my father and brother. It might even have been possible if only they hadn't made a beeline for the empty table for two vacated by Max and his friend. There they are, Bull grinning at me and Jimmy looking at Natalie with his cold gray eyes.

"Hey, Cooper, how they hangin'?" Bull wraps a meaty hand

around my neck, shakes me like a cat with a mouse in her mouth. "You treating this girl all right? He treatin' you right, ma'am? You tell me he's not and I'll kick his teeth in."

"Oh, he's a perfect gentleman." Natalie steps back, her booted foot stepping on mine, her head against my shoulder.

I am blocked against the table by my family. There is no escape. Natalie's body against mine is like a shield, and I think of captors and hostages. I notice that the pint glass in Bull's hand is clear, a wedge of lemon floating against the ice.

"So, we don't get an introduction?" Jimmy has changed since the last time I saw him. He's put on jail weight; he looks more like Bull, less like me. He looks like what he is, a middle-aged ex-con. Unlike his still-on-the-wagon father, Jimmy holds a glass of dark beer; a thin creamy head tilts slightly as he maneuvers closer to Natalie.

I can feel the skin of my face tighten with anger. I will not lose control of myself. I will not let them get the better of me. "Natalie, this is Bull, and Jimmy." Do I deliberately leave out the common factor of our last name? Maybe, but Bull chimes right in.

"Bull Harrison, pleased to meet you." Bull smiles at Natalie with what amounts to a toothless smile, yet, like a baby's, somehow charming.

Jimmy snatches her hand, gives it a little shake. "Natalie, you want to have fun, you call me. My brother's never been much fun."

"You bet." Natalie extricates her hand from his grip, shoulders her handbag and, with the coolness I've seen her use in the paddock when walking between fractious sixteen-hand horses, pushes through the wall that Bull and Jimmy create.

I feel a deep need to apologize for my family, but I don't really have cause. After all, except for being who *I* know they are, for being crude, they hadn't committed any egregious crimes. Besides, the less said about Bull and Jimmy the better.

So instead of opening up a can of worms with my apology, I

open the passenger door for her and ask, "What kind of pie are you offering?"

"I only know how to make one kind, apple. Hope that's all right."

"My favorite."

The yard light comes on as we pull into the parking spaces by the barn. Moisture shows in the cone of light. The air has grown colder, more in line with the time of year than previously, and for the first time I'm not looking forward to sleeping outside. My sleeping bag is rated for twenty degrees, and it's well above that, but, still, the idea of a warm bed after a pleasant evening is a sweet one. And no, I wasn't thinking of hers. Not exactly.

I follow Natalie as she does her late-night barn check. The barn smells of warm animals and hay, shavings and manure. The horses chuckle, used to having their naps interrupted, expecting treats. Natalie hands me some carrots and I find Moxie and feed her snapped-off pieces. I love the touch of her muzzle against the palm of my hand.

We're done in the barn and head to the house, where the pit bull, Betty, greets us as returning heroes. Of course, Natalie has brought some leftover swordfish back, so, in fact, she is a hero. I'm comfortable at the kitchen table. Natalie's got one of those single-cup coffeemakers and a carousel with varieties of coffee in small containers. "I've got to fall asleep outside in the cold, so you'd better give me decaf." I hope that doesn't sound like a bad play for an overnight stay with her.

"Still trying to lure your dog in?"

"Yeah. He's not cooperating. Max said if I showed kindness that he'd be enticed into capture. So far, not so much."

The pie is good, the coffee hot, and the evening's energy is spent. I don't hesitate this time to kiss her good night and am rewarded with a second kiss. "Hey, take the rest of this fish; maybe your ghost dog would like a change from meat." She hands me the ecofriendly cardboard box. "Betty can share."

The wind has picked up by the time I get out to the campsite. I'm too tired to get fancy, so I open the cardboard container for the dog, whistle twice so that if he's around, he'll know I'm there, and climb into my goose-down bag. The ground feels particularly hard tonight. With the colder air, the sky has dried out and the stars are amplified against a jet black sky. No moon. No fire. Just the light from my lantern before I shut it off. I stare up at the sky and wait for sleep. There is Sirius, the dog star, faithful companion of Orion. Mythical dogs. My dog, Argos, was named for the faithful hound of Odysseus, who recognized his master first upon his return. Legendary dogs.

Argos wouldn't recognize me now.

The dog waits for the man to come back. It has become a habit by now, this expectation that the human will join him for the night. The food that he drops, the sound of another animal's breathing, vocalizations, movement—these have become something the dog has accepted. But the night grows colder and darker and there is no sign of the man. He waits, sniffing the air, hearing his own vocalizations, an interrogatory rumble in the back of his throat: *Where are you?* It could easily become a whimper.

The dog hears in the distance the sound of the truck that he identifies with the man. The headlights glance through the trees and vanish. With his acute hearing, the dog follows the man's path from truck to porch to house. He merges with the thick brush, waits until the man appears bearing the sweet scent of cooked food. The dog, shivering, licks his dewlaps, pants with widened mouth, trying to gather in more of the sublime odor.

He hears it, the whistle, the man's voice. The words *come* and *boy*. He can't yet bring himself to be seen by the man, so he stays where he is until his fellow night creature climbs into his nest, and only then does the dog venture close enough. At first sniff, the man is the same, his scent as it always is, an amalgam of sweat and laundry soap, and the debris of skin cells that offer so much detail to a dog. But, tonight, there is an overlay, a sexual tinge to his odor, a loosening of pheromones and anxiety that brings a new texture to the information the dog has been garnering about this man. The man makes soft noises in his sleep, utterly confident that, as a human, no harm can come to him out here in the dark woods.

The yellow dog limps over to the open box, carelessly left on the ground by this very careless man. Inside, there is a new treat, the sweet, salty scent announcing something he's never had before. He wolfs it down, his eyes at all times on the form of the sleeping man. The fish and vegetables are gone, but their odor clings to the textured interior of the cardboard box. Eyes still on the man, the dog deftly picks up the box; the flavorful, ecofriendly cardboard box will help to fill his belly.

The dog comes closer to the man. Still hungry, always, but tonight his curiosity has brought him as close to this person as he has ever dared before. Confident that this human is completely unaware and won't suddenly leap up in a startled reflex, the dog stretches his neck out, the better to breathe in the scent wafting up from the only exposed part of him, the top of his head. He is almost leisurely as he sniffs, loosening his dewlaps to gather in the scent molecules that drift out of the warm-scented sleeping bag. The idea of warmth is beginning to grow in importance, along with finding food. With none of the fat that his breed normally carries, this dog feels the cold in his scant flesh. He lacks the layers that will let him survive the coming winter. Even this early in the waning season, he feels the cold seep into his bones as he burrows into his place beneath the fallen tree. Even if he can manage to find enough to eat to keep alive, instinctively the dog knows that it will still be hard to survive once winter sets in.

The man rolls over, dragging the sleeping bag over his head. The dog backs up, a movement that pains his hip. The hip wound has opened up again, and he's spent hours licking the place, tasting the rot within. The dog positions himself behind the form of the sleeping man. He should retreat to his nest, to his safe place, to the hollowed-out protection against the rising wind. He listens carefully to the exhalations of the man, watches his restless motion inside the cocoon of the bag, which makes it wriggle, as if a butterfly is about to emerge.

The flavorful box is gone and the dog rests his chin on his paws, his eyes on the man. Simply being there, in the presence of a sleeping human, gives the dog an oddly contented feeling. As long as the man remains asleep, the dog is going to enjoy this temporary companionship.

15

⤜⤛

I awaken in that last moment before dawn, when the suggestion that
night is over is confirmed by the first note of the first bird, close
enough and loud enough that even I can hear it. My neck is stiff and
it feels like I've been sleeping on rocks. The wind has died down,
but the cold front that was pushing it has arrived and I can see my
breath in the predawn gray. Okay, I've had enough. This is the last
night for me on the ground in this Ahabesque quest. I lie there, gathering up the courage to emerge from my warm chrysalis into the
cold day. In my good ear, I hear a sound, so faint that it might be a
leaf scraping stubbornly against a branch, a leaf that is particularly
rhythmic. I know that sound, a hind foot motoring against ribs in
an ecstasy of scratching. Unbelievably, my quarry is right behind
me. I don't dare move, but I need to see for myself what my good
ear is telling me.

I am so excited at the prospect of finally seeing my elusive ghost
dog that I can hear my heart's systole in both ears. Slowly, millimeter by millimeter, I roll my head toward the noise. In some foolish

notion that I can convince the dog that I'm still innocently asleep, still harmless, I keep my eyes closed.

Argos always knew when I was awake, never falling for a pretend sleep, or a desperate attempt to regain sleep, but nosing me under the arm as soon as my eyes had flickered open, as if he was waiting just patiently enough to hear the sound of my blink before bounding into action.

Maybe that was the time when I loved that dog the most: his pesky insistence that I get out of bed, start his day, go for a walk, go to work, take advantage of being together, partners, pals. Argos, bearing little resemblance to the all-serious working K-9 that he would become the moment I opened the door to the cruiser, would prance and play-bow and carry on like any dog who loved his human unconditionally.

Once we'd moved into the condo, I'd broken a lot of the rules, no longer making Argos sleep in his kennel, blaming it on the condo board for prohibiting an outdoor kennel. But the truth is that I'd stopped treating him like a weapon that needed locking up. I'd started treating him like a member of the family. A pet.

The scratching has stopped, so I'm certain the dog has bolted. I open my eyes and I'm not wrong. With nothing to lose now, I softly say, "Hey, boy. Come on, fella. I'm not going to hurt you. You're all right. Come on over." I keep my voice gentle, nonthreatening. I whistle, the same two-note whistle I use when I run and drop the food along the path. For the first time since I started this quest, I feel encouraged. The dog, it would seem, has made contact.

I crawl out into the cold. My jeans and jacket are stowed in the bottom of the bag and I dump them out, dressing quickly. I roll up the sleeping bag, think about maybe one more night, one more try, now that I'm coming so close to making headway with the dog. But the idea of another night on the hard ground reminds me that I'm closer to forty than twenty.

Back at the cabin, I light the first fire of the season in the wood-stove, hoping that the flue will draw and the chimney is clean enough that I won't start a chimney fire. As part of my incredibly cheap rent, I have all of the responsibilities of a caretaker, and some of the expenses of an owner. Like gas for the stove, and electricity, a wood-stove is a utility. I've been stockpiling wood all summer, but my kindling pile is a bit small. Along with making a note to call the chimney-cleaning people, I jot down a reminder to stop by the lumberyard and pick up some broken shingles and a bucket of two-by-four trim ends. I can do that on my way to the tack shop Natalie told me about, where I'll buy my own helmet and half chaps. It's Jenny's weekend to tend the inmates, so I indulge in a long hot shower, give myself a fresh buzz cut, and settle down with yesterday's newspaper.

My cell phone barks twice and my quiet, well-planned Saturday is out the window.

There's been a dog-versus-car incident out on Route 114. The spot is closer to my cabin than to the shelter, so I don't bother to stop and swap my personal vehicle for the town's SUV. When I arrive, there's a cruiser with all lights flashing and a Subaru Forester tipped nose-down in the gully. I set my flashers and climb out of my truck with a black trash bag in my hand. The rumble of a Jerr-Dan tow truck announces its arrival to haul the unfortunate Forester out of the hole. I walk over to the visibly shaken driver, who is standing with one of Lev's officers. I don't yet see the body, but in my heart of hearts, I just know that this is the dog I've been pursuing.

"Ma'am. Officer Taylor. Where's the . . . " I hesitate to use the word that I should, *carcass*. In my previous life, I would have said "the victim."

"He ran off. But I hit him, I know I did. He was just standing in the middle of the road as I came around the curve. It was horrible.

I tried to miss, but . . . " Her voice trails off. She's confirmed my worst fear and I have to look away. It sucks. It would have been better to have had a clean kill. Now an already-compromised dog is more damaged, and this ups the ante on the game of luring him in. "Which direction?"

She points across the road. I start tracking, following nothing more than her pointing finger, because there are no prints on the pavement, no blood, which I allow is a little encouraging.

I trained myself to not be sensitive. Sensitivity in my line of work—my real line of work—is useless and boneheaded. That notwithstanding, I remember the pressure of those times when something or someone got under my skin and close to my heart. The lost child found—or not. The child caught in the cross fire. The stranger tying a necktie tourniquet around the leg of a homeless man hit by a car. I wouldn't be human if those kinds of things didn't affect me; but I wouldn't have been a good cop, a successful policeman, if I had let it show. Only some nights, after dinner was done and Gayle and I were doing the dishes, I might have mentioned the child or the stranger, and been content that my wife understood that I needed to tell these stories not out of hubris or self-importance, but so I could sort out the emotions that had gathered in my chest. Gayle might have said nothing at all, simply lain the palm of her hand against my cheek. Even Argos, who had been with me when I was searching for the missing child, or chasing the shooter who had killed the bystander in the street, or watching me taking over for the stranger with the necktie tourniquet, couldn't quite relieve my unwanted emotions as effectively as the touch of my wife's hand.

Now it's more than I can bear, the idea of coping with things of this nature. There is no sense to the cruelty that put this dog into this situation. The idea of one abused dog's life ending under the wheels of a car eats at me and I no longer have the comfort of my old dispassion. Nonetheless, in front of my fellow officer and this lady, I must put on a mask of occupational indifference. But inside, I wonder, can

I ever protect myself again with the armor of true bravery, of stoicism? My professional reserve has become jellied.

If a dog's endangerment affects me this way, how can I ever return to a profession where I encounter human suffering on a regular basis? This is why I can never have another dog, K-9 partner or otherwise. I can never put myself in this vulnerable position ever again.

I keep walking, swiping away tall grass and sweetbriar until my hands are dotted with spots of blood. I call for him. Ludicrous, I know, a nameless dog that has never but that once—this morning—come close to me is hardly likely to respond. He'll be in shock. Dragging himself off to his death.

I've been stupid, listening to Max's Buddhist idea of seducing a dog. I should have been out hunting him like I might a deer, a felon. Getting a dose of tranquilizer into him three weeks ago instead of believing that this Zen approach would somehow work. I'm a marksman. Shooting him outright rather than prolonging his suffering would have been the kinder thing. But I'm not that brave.

Cooper holds his weapon in both hands as he has been taught, as he has practiced for years. Safety off. Finger on the trigger. He has only to squeeze the round off and put an end to this. But he doesn't. He hesitates. In all the years he's been a cop, Cooper has never fired a weapon at a human target before. Has never had to. Argos has always sufficed. But this time, it's different.

There is no sign of the wounded dog. I've circled back to my truck. The Forester, the cruiser, and the tow truck are all gone. Only a streak of tire marks on the state road suggests that anything untoward has happened here. And then I see it, hidden in plain sight. There's a rocky apron around a storm drain at the foot of the sloping verge. The car strike sent the dog into the rocks and its coat color has camouflaged it. I unfold my black plastic bag and carefully retrieve the body of a speckled spaniel I'm pretty sure belongs to Cynthia Mann.

She's waiting for me as I pull around the circular drive fronting her Georgian-style home. I've called, so she knows why I'm here. For all her lofty position and relevance to the life of the village, Cynthia is still a grief-stricken pet owner, and I feel for her. I know what it's like to lose a beloved animal to violence.

I take up my burden and present the bagged body of her beloved pet to Cynthia with the same heartfelt words of condolence I all too often had to use in my former life when speaking to parents of lost children, to the grandmother of a murdered drug dealer who had raised him, to the wives of men lost in the line of duty. I tell Cynthia, "I am so sorry for your loss." The adverb is my own, and off-script: *So* sorry.

Donald Boykin brings his Land Rover to a halt behind the Suburban, rushes over to his wife, who is still cradling the black-shrouded body of their dog. "Honey, how did this happen?" He looks at me with a look of puzzled contempt. As if I'm the one who hit the dog that shouldn't have been loose in the first place. "Who did this?"

That's the question I was pretty certain he'd want an answer to. Donald Boykin doesn't strike me as a man who thinks unanswered questions are acceptable.

"I'm not at liberty to say." I actually don't know and I'm leaving any repercussions regarding that poor woman to the discretion of the local police. "Purely an accident; your dog ran out in front of the car No way to avoid it."

Boykin wraps an arm around his wife, who is obviously suppressing tears while I'm still there. "I want the name. I want it now."

"Why don't you contact Chief Parker." I'm not getting any vibe of grief from this man, only anger that something of his has been devalued. Maybe I'm being unfair, but that's what I think.

"What's your name?"

I know this tack. The "I'll put you in your place" tack beloved of the powerful, of those who seldom don't get their way.

"Harrison." I don't touch my forelock, shuffle my feet. I pull my shoulders back. "Once again, my condolences."

"Officer Harrison." Cynthia adjusts the inert bundle in her arms. "Thank you. It's been a bad year for dogs for us."

As the first heavy drops of rain begin to fall, I sit at the drop-leaf kitchen table, the radio on but not much company, the newspaper spread out in front of me, although I'm not reading it. The woodstove pops as the heat builds up; a slightly damp log sizzles. The rain spits against the skylight with a cold sound, and I am glad that I'm inside, a proper bed waiting for me, for the moment when I think that I might be able to fall asleep.

I'm glad I'm inside, but I can't help but think of the feral dog. I'm a little ashamed by the relief I felt in discovering that the victim of the car strike wasn't the yellow dog. But maybe it would have been better. This dog, this ghost of a dog, cannot survive a night like this, when the rain beats down and the temperature drops. I get up and pace around the living area of the cabin, straightening a faded photograph on the wall depicting long-ago hunters with their old-fashioned rifles against their shoulders and their game bags full, dogs sitting patiently at their sides.

"Cooper, there's plenty of time to make that decision. You get better, then come talk to me." Lieutenant Carter hands Cooper back the resignation letter he's carefully written, printed out on smooth ecru stationery.

The gathering has been as close to a funeral as possible without disrespecting the memory of fallen humans. Cooper's brothers in arms, his fellow K-9 officers and their dogs, have shown the fallen K-9 Argos every honor due his name.

Glasses have been raised and toasts made. Moments of silence. Inclusion in news-paper reports and Facebook postings and Web-site memorials. Hero. Brave.

It's almost impossible for Cooper to look at the other dogs, the way they keep to their handlers' sides, the way they look at their human partners, the way it's assumed that he's going to partner with another K-9 just as soon as his hearing is better, when his back heals. He keeps his mouth tightly clamped, gritting his teeth.

Lieutenant Carter is correct. It is too soon to make a career-altering decision, life-altering. But that doesn't stop Cooper. There's no way he can ever endure this kind of pain again. It's like a sickness, a cancer growing in his psyche.

The rain is coming from the southwest, smacking against the windows on the unprotected side of the cabin. I flip on the porch light. The rain drips in attenuated lines from the overhang like a beaded curtain, but the porch itself is bone-dry. I empty the large wicker basket filled with split logs. I stack the logs and then get my sleeping bag. Out on the porch, I set the basket against the wall of the cabin, slide the sleeping bag out of its nylon carry bag, unfurl it, and layer it carefully inside the concavity of the basket. I go back in and bring out a bowl of dog meat and a water bowl. Something will find this and eat it; something might even poke a hole in the sleeping bag and take out the lovely goose down for its own nest. But maybe, just maybe, the dog will accept this humble offer of shelter for the night. As I always do when dropping the meat as I run, or leaving the bowl filled with dog food, I whistle, two notes, sharp and consistent. Then call, "Come on, boy. Come on get your dinner." I whistle again. I can hear nothing except the sound of the rain beating down on the porch roof.

16

The ambulance blows past Bull as he pedals his bike to work, rocking him in the backwash. Seems like there's an ambulance roaring down the main street or Route 114 every fifteen minutes lately. Just another symptom of an expanding population in a small town. Jimmy keeps talking about it, how all these rich people living here in those big houses just means more money being spent on infrastructure. You'd think he paid the property taxes. Funny the stuff he takes issue with. Still, he's good for a meal now and then, like the other night at the tavern. Funny, too, seeing Cooper there with that little horse lady who comes into Crane's for stuff. Weird having both boys back in town after so many years. Bull knows that he should feel lucky; lots of parents never see their kids. Polly Schaeffer is always moaning about the fact her kids won't visit her. But when you think of it, the Harrisons don't really enjoy a warm and fuzzy Hallmark card kind of relationship. Any family gathering is a contest with those boys.

Jimmy was in a good mood that night, flashing a wad of cash, telling Bull to order anything he wanted off the menu. Just seeing that much cash fanned out in Jimmy's well-manicured hand put Bull off of mentioning Tommy's offer of a desk job for Jimmy. Clearly, Jimmy wasn't in need of an eighteen-dollar-an-hour handout.

Jimmy flirted aggressively with their waitress, a cute kid Bull remembers used to work in the Cumberland Farms store. Way too young for the likes of Jimmy, but that didn't stop Jimmy from hitting on her. Bull admits that it was a little uncomfortable when Jimmy wouldn't stop flirting. When his hand grabbed hers as she reached for the check holder, stuffed as it was with more than the cost of the meal and a huge tip, it made Bull feel more than a little awkward. "Come on, Jimmy, let the girl do her job." The look Jimmy gave him could have frozen water, but Bull laughed, wanting the girl to understand that Jimmy was only kidding. That Bull was in her corner, that Jimmy really meant no harm. That Jimmy would never do her harm.

Guy, the bartender, had his eye on them. Bull waved, a careless, "Everything's fine" kind of wave, and then put his hand on Jimmy's arm. A silent caution: Don't make an issue of this. You don't want trouble.

"Next time, sweetheart." Jimmy shoved his chair back, nearly toppling it against the people behind them. "I'll see you around."

The waitress had the cojones to snark back at him as she marched back to the kitchen, "Not if I see you first."

"I won't overtip her again."

"Come on, Jimmy. She's too young for you."

"Can't fault a man for wanting to get laid."

There was an ugliness to Jimmy's turn of phrase. That girl was only a couple of years away from being jailbait.

As they worked their way around the collection of tables to the exit, Guy kept his eye on them, and the look on his meaty face was clear: They would not be welcomed back. Which kind of sucks, as Bull really enjoys the Lakeside. It's the one place he was welcomed back into once he was firmly established in the program. The other bars still won't let him in, even if his drink these days is only seltzer and lemon.

But that's Jimmy for you. Tough guy, full of himself. Doesn't give a rat's ass about what other people think. Never did, even as a kid. Bull can't think of one person Jimmy ever deferred to. Not a teacher, a parent, or even a cop. He would stand there, that flinty look in his eye, just daring whoever it was to carry out their threatened punishment. Wouldn't even plea-bargain for a reduced sentence. Took the whole stretch—less a few months for good behavior, what a joke— keeping his mouth shut and his loyalties solid. Now he's reaping the benefit of that sacrifice. "It's only time," he'd said. "Just time."

Jimmy is still young enough to believe that he has unlimited time.

17

〜

Waking up on this rainy Sunday, I think first of the dog, surely dead by now, my impulsive gesture of last night a pretty foolish one. I'm so convinced that this quest is over that I don't even take a peek out the window to see if he has actually taken me up on my offer of a warm bed. The one thing I've never done is allow myself foolish hope. Not now. Not ever. Not even when I regained consciousness after the blast; I knew even before I opened my eyes that Argos was dead. So there is no subterfuge in my clumping around the cabin, adding wood to the fire and getting the coffeemaker going.

The coffee is ready, the fire cheerfully crackling in the Jøtul; my bed, in military fashion, is made up tight. Unlike what I do on a workday, I'm letting myself enjoy a first cup of coffee while still in my pajama bottoms and T-shirt. Maybe I'll get really lax and skip shaving. Except for Elvin at the market, where I'll pick up a paper and possibly one of those lemon squares that sit temptingly in a clear case above the paper rack, it's unlikely that there will be anyone today who will see my unshaven face. The Patriots are on this afternoon, and I don't know if I'll listen to the game on the radio or if Max will invite me over to watch the game at his house. The truth is, I'd really rather stay put and listen to the game by myself. I'm not in the mood for company.

Thinking that I've got another chance to have a quiet day at home, I duck outside to the porch to bring in more split quarters to dry by the fire.

Because I have no expectation that the dog took advantage of my hospitality, I am completely shocked to see him curled up in the basket. Shocked and then alarmed as the dog, doesn't even raise his head. It's only the slow rise and fall of the animal's emaciated rib cage that tells me he is still alive. As if I've cornered a wanted man, I take my time assessing the situation. The first thing that I see is the festering wound on the dog's hip. I can see it, and can smell the putrefaction oozing out of it. Gunshot, I'm pretty sure. It bears the hallmarks of an old unhealed wound. What looks like dark fur is actually filth scored into the yellow. What toenails I get a glimpse of are broken off, shattered into frayed remnants. But mostly what I see are ribs, and a spine with each and every vertebrae detailed beneath the loose skin. With no muscle, the skin looks like it belongs to a larger dog. There is nothing to this animal but skin and bones and patchy, filthy fur.

The animal is so still that at first I think the dog has come up onto my porch and died. But with each slight rise and fall of his rib cage, I understand that, in his weakened condition, the comfort of the goose-down sleeping bag has lured the dog into a deep sleep. Every instinct that has helped this dog survive in the wild has been subverted by the simple warmth of a sleeping bag.

I don't move. I deliberately soften my muscles, relax my breathing, as if I'm meditating or practicing that yoga my first shrink recommended I do to try to alleviate my "tension," as he called it. The ringing in my left ear increases, as if my blood is gushing into it with every pumping heartbeat. What I hear is my uncertainty, the chiming of indecision. I simply don't know what to do with this turn of events. I need my catch pole, or another handful of meat to keep the dog's attention when he comes awake and realizes he's compromised his freedom. And then it hits me: Maybe the dog has volunteered his freedom. Maybe that's why he's so sound asleep. I've seen this in captured fugitives, this sudden exhaustion, as if capture has broken the strain of trying to stay free. They take to the narrow mattress of the holding cell and sleep the sleep of the dead.

The water bowl is empty, the dog dish licked clean, so at least I'm confident that dog is hydrated and his hunger assuaged for the moment. In a very literal sense, I'm getting cold feet. I stepped out here barefoot and this wet October Sunday morning feels more like a November day. The rain has finally let up and the sun is breaking without warmth through the sooty cloud bank malingering over Bartlett's Pond. A duck calls to a mate, twice, and I think that it's a man-made duck call, that there must be hunters out on the pond this morning. It always strikes me as funny: If I'm not fooled, why are the ducks? I turn my good ear toward the pond, and when I turn back, the dog is sitting up, looking at me.

"Hey, fella," I whisper, trying to find the right pitch. "Hey, boy. Good boy. You want some breakfast? I've got some in the cabin. I won't hurt you. I'm here to help." As long as the dog doesn't move, I natter on like a nervous suitor, hoping that the sound of my voice is soothing, not frightening; cajoling and harmless. "Good boy. I can help you. You just gotta trust me." I take a step closer. This dog is so weak, I know that if I can just grab the loose skin around his neck, I'll be able to hang on to him.

The dog pushes himself more upright, cocks his head, listening to my voice, deciding. His eyes are runny; mucus whitens the lids. Fully engorged deer ticks cling to his ears, his cheeks, little pale brown dollops of disease. I wonder if the dog is so weakened that he actually *can't* stand up. I move about a foot closer. Now the dog does get to his feet, if only three of them. The right hind leg dangles, as if he's lost the use of it. I take another cautious step, putting myself close enough that if he will simply step out of the basket, I can maybe grab the skin around his neck. First one front leg, then the other, and the working hind leg hops over the edge of the shallow sleeping bag–filled nest. Close enough. I take a step backward. The first sign of a good negotiator is to know when to step back. Let the opposition relax a little. The dog lowers his head, sniffs the air, taking in my scent. I'm hoping he reads that I mean him no harm. I'm hoping that he associates me with the food I've left him, the nest I built for him. I whisper reassurances: "You're okay. You're okay."

I kneel on the decking, bringing my eyes down to the dog's eye level. He looks left and right, as if assessing an escape route. I make a kissy noise and the dog cocks his head again, interested. He's got wrinkles above his eyes, and I think that this wreck of a dog could actually be a Labrador. Slowly, very slowly, the dog takes a step closer, his eyes on mine, begging for kindness.

Just as the dog finally, cautiously, comes close enough that I should be able to put a hand on him, a shotgun blast rends the quiet, followed by a second blast and then another. He yelps as he scrambles to jump off the porch, landing in a three-legged heap. He yelps again as a second volley brings him to his feet, and in seconds the terrified dog is gone. For such a physically compromised animal, he moves incredibly fast in his panic. Although I leap, I have no chance of grabbing him. I end up on all fours, staring at the porch floor. "Shit." Freakin' hunters have chosen this delicate moment to fire. I jump to my feet and off the porch, stupidly chasing after the animal in bare feet, a clumsy predator after a terrified dog.

Two more shotgun blasts. This poor dog is probably in the next county by now. I pull up from my foolish pursuit. So much for the quiet Sunday. So much for getting the paper. Probably so much for the football game. I have no choice, I'm going after the dog, and this time I'm going to find him. But first I have to head into the shelter to pick up the tranquilizer gun. The options for bringing this dog in have been whittled down to one. I have to shoot a dog that is clearly terrified of guns.

It felt like the sound of the gunshot was inside his head, hollowing out his brain, echoing through his skull, and blinding him to anything but movement. Even the agony in his hip was obliterated by the sheer terror caused by that sound. And it came again, over and over. Volley after volley blasting away in astounding cacophony. The dog kept moving, dragging the useless leg, his aching forelegs pulling, his good hind leg pushing him over the ground, through the grass, and into the deeper woods and beyond. Running, he makes an anguished crying, a primal sound of expected death. The memory of his original terror at having a gun fired over his head keeps him moving even after the firing ceases; he can smell the sharp, mean scent of fired gunpowder and hot metal lingering in the air, drifting over the place where he's denned, tainting it.

He is past his den; he is traveling far away from the familiar pond side. He is distancing himself from the cabin and the man there who offered him food. As long as there is that sound reverberating in the air, there is no place safe for him.

It had felt so good, that soft, warm, comforting circle of basket and bag. It hadn't felt like danger or capitulation to take advantage of it. For so long now, the running man had been a part of the dog's daily experience, it was becoming harder to stay away from him than it was to actively avoid him. The forgotten food, the quiet solace of sleeping within proximity. The memory of better things influenced his slow loss of caution. How wrong he had been.

The dog can run no farther. His lungs are burning and his whole body is trembling, all energy spent. Even the fear can't keep him on his feet, and he crumples to the ground, his sides heaving with oxygen starvation. His tongue lolls out of his wide-open mouth and he tastes the dirt.

A red-tailed hawk soars above the prone body of the dog, limning slow arabesques in the overcast sky. Behind it, bullying it, a pair of crows defend their territory. The hawk isn't particularly bothered by the crows, and it continues its slow wending. It screeks once, rises higher than the crows care about, and departs to hunt live game elsewhere. The crows then turn their attention to the dog. They land and pompously stride over to see if this inert form is already carrion, or if they must wait until more time has passed before they begin to peck away at the soft parts.

The dog lifts his lip and growls. The birds back off, consult with each other, and then elevate to a pair of low branches to patiently wait out the inevitable.

18

❧

"Max, can you set me up with the right dose of tranquilizer?" I'm trying to keep the frantic out of my voice, but I'm sure that Max got a hint of it. I don't panic, ever, but sometimes my voice hits a decibel that suggests I'm in a hurry. "I don't want to kill him."

"I'm just on my way to Second Hope. Meet me there."

"What's going on?" I don't know a lot about horses, but I know that they have a tendency toward fatal bellyaches. I immediately think of my little quarter horse mare, Moxie, and have a moment of concern before Max tells me what's happened.

"One of her horses stepped on a nail. Puncture wound."

At least it's not a life-threatening incident. "I'm on my way to grab the dart gun. I'll see you there."

I'm out of the truck and into the shelter, unlocking the cabinet that contains the dart gun. I also grab the catch pole. Jenny, there to feed the inmates, hands me one of the donated blankets and a couple of bath towels off the shelf. I don't know if I'll find the dog; if I do, it's more than a safe bet that I'll be coming back with its lifeless body wrapped in the towels.

"You'll find him, Cooper. I know it." Jenny gives me a smile, but I see the doubt in her eyes. If I haven't been successful yet, what makes me think I'm going to be now?

I wish that I had a siren on the town's Suburban. I really miss those things at times like these when I'm in a hurry and every freakin' Grampa Goosie is out on the road and oblivious to my flashing red lights. I can't help it, I feel like there's a ticking time bomb about to go off and every second counts. Even heading out to Second Hope is going to cost me time in what I know is likely a losing race. That dog isn't going to survive the night. It's amazing that he even survived last night, and the weather forecast predicts that the temperature tonight is going to fall off to below freezing. But even if I get going in record time, I still have to find him. It might not be a needle in a haystack, but it's acres of conservation land. *If only I had a dog.* A tracking dog. Argos. But if I still had Argos, we'd both be working and it wouldn't be trying to find a feral dog, but feral humans. The circular nature of that logic is enough to make me laugh out loud in what Gayle used to call my "humorless laugh," the one I'd employ when I was in a bad mood, which became all too often after the last night of my career.

By the time I pull into the yard at Second Hope, Max is there in the barn aisle, tending the horse with the nail puncture. Nat's student Marla is holding the horse steady. Max is bent over the horse's left front hoof. In a neat motion and without setting the foot down, Max reaches into his vest pocket and pulls out a vial of tranquilizer.

"Thanks, Max."

"What are you going to do?" Natalie comes around the other side of the horse. As anxious as I am to get this party started, I take in her worried frown and the way she keeps one hand on the horse.

"Hopefully, find him alive. I had him this close." I demonstrate with thumb and forefinger a quarter of an inch apart. "Some asshole duck hunter fired his gun and that dog took off like his tail was on fire."

"Do you have any idea where he might be?"

I motion toward the wooded hillside between our places, dull now with the fading glory of late October. "He could be anywhere out there. He bolted in this direction, but I can't imagine that he made a straight line."

Max sets the wounded hoof into a bucket of water and Epsom salts, straightens up as if he's fighting a bad back. A lot of his work requires awkward bending. "Good job not pulling that nail out, Natalie. You do that and you end up introducing bacteria into the puncture. He'll just need a little soaking twice a day, and I'll leave antibiotics." Max gives the horse a pat on the neck.

Natalie fingers a carrot chunk into the horse's mouth. "Cooper, I've got an idea."

A precious half hour later, I'm mounted on Moxie and Natalie is leading her favorite gelding out of the barn. I'm torn between thinking that I'm wasting time when I should start looking for the dog closer to my place and grateful that there will be two of us on the hunt. I'm waiting on the patient mare for Natalie to adjust her girth, when Max closes the hatch of his Jeep and walks over. "As soon as you find that dog, you call me. I'll meet you at the office."

"I will. And, hey, thanks for making it sound like I'm not on a fool's errand."

"I didn't say that." Max gives the mare a pat on the neck. "Ride safe."

So here I am, mounted and riding beside Natalie along the trails wending through the conservation land surrounding Bartlett's Pond and along the fence lines of the last remaining working farms of Harmony Farms, including Deke Wilkins's place, an area deeply familiar to me from my youthful adventures when I would stay with

"Uncle" Deke. Although it has stopped raining, the air is chilly and I wish that I'd dressed in warmer clothes. We ride through an orchard of untended and gnarled apple trees, along the ridge with views that open up, revealing the pewter surface of distant Lake Harmony. Here and there, a curl of smoke rises in the still, damp air, marking the place where one of those big houses lurks, hidden in the landscape.

And all the time we ride through this scenic countryside, I am searching for the dog and seeing nothing but ground. We ride in silence. Even the sound of hoofbeats is muffled in the deep, wet leaf mold beneath us. We should be bushwhacking, pushing our horses through the briars and low-hanging pine boughs, because the dog is certainly not going to be handily waiting for us on the main trail. As we descend the ridge, we come to a fork in the trail. One way leads to Bartlett's Pond; the other will take us to the open field the conservation group has cleared to encourage certain kinds of birds to choose Harmony Farms as their seasonal home. It's a place popular with dog walkers, as their dogs can run free, and I often stop by just to see what's going on, who's out there with what dogs, and generally just to offer a friendly face. It's a good policy, in police work—and in animal control—to know your population by name.

Natalie pulls up her gelding. "What do you want to do?"

One way leads back to my place and to the area around the pond where the dog has apparently been living. But it also leads toward the place where the hunters were, where the firing of their guns had freaked the dog out and sent him running. The question is, How far could the dog have gotten before he had to stop? Was he scared out of his usual haunts and even now holing up in some new hideout? How easily my thoughts revert to the lexicon of my past: *holed up, hideout.*

"Let's head to the field. I doubt he could get that far, but we can eliminate it as a possibility pretty quickly."

Natalie gathers her reins and pushes her gelding forward. We follow at a safe distance. The field opens up in front of us as we emerge from the woods, four or five acres of grass and empty bluebird boxes surrounded by a perimeter of bramble and pine, juniper and scrub oak. The rain has kept the dog walkers away, which is good, I think. We ride a slow circuit around the edges, but I wonder if the dog, if he's there, will be visible against the grasses, which are nearly as yellow as he. "We should split up and ride through the field itself. If he's there, he's camouflaged."

I like how Natalie doesn't spend time revising my plan, even though she also doesn't say "Good idea." We ride to the center of the field and then set off in opposite directions, making loops so that more ground is covered visually than in a straight line. I am about halfway down my section of the field when I notice the crows.

I've only been on a horse twice now, but that doesn't stop me as I charge across that field like I'm some kind of cowboy running down a calf. It doesn't even occur to me that I might not be in control. All I know is that where there is a murder of crows, there's carrion, and I think it has to be the dog. I'm moving so fast that I barely hear Natalie bellowing out instructions, probably thinking that I'm being run away with.

The crows reluctantly move aside, but I don't know if it's the full-bore approach of the mare or my hollering that convinces them they need to get to safety. I pull back on the reins with an awkward elbows-flying grab. The mare drops into a teeth-jarring trot and I nearly bounce off of her, but by the grace of God, I don't. I stay on and manage to slow her to a walk before leaping off her back as I see the body of the dog nestled in the tall grass. If it hadn't been for the crows, even with my careful survey, I might not have seen him, he matches the yellow grass so perfectly.

Then Natalie is there, and she takes the reins from me as I squat next to the dog. His eyes are open, but do I see a flicker of life left in them, or just the dull reflection of the overcast sky? I reach out, wave my hand close to his face, and am relieved to see the blink impulse still there. "Hey, fella. We're going to get you some help. Just stick with me, okay?"

The fear is still in his eyes, but there is something else there, as well. I'm a human being, and I want to think that maybe, just maybe, there's some hope there, too. Do dogs hope? I don't know. If Argos could show enjoyment and anticipation, why can't this wreck of a dog feel hope?

Natalie is on her phone, calling for her student Marla to bring her truck to the field parking lot. I like her initiative. I hadn't considered how I was going to transport the dog if we were on horseback. I pull the bath towel out of the saddlebag attached behind my saddle. I place it on the ground and, together, Natalie and I lift the dog onto it. He's long, but he weighs nothing, and I can see the horror in Natalie's eyes.

"At least I didn't have to try to dart him. I expect that even a little tranquilizer would likely have killed him."

"Probably. You dodged that bullet."

"Ha."

"Sorry, bad choice of words." She gently folds the ends of the towel over the dog, packaging him like a burrito. Thin lines of red seep through the worn terry-cloth; his skin is sliced into ribbons from his mad dash through the vicious briars that grow in the underbrush. "You take my truck. Marla and I will take the horses home." I am absurdly grateful to her. There doesn't seem to be anything else to say as we wait for Marla, the horses happily grazing the meadow for the last green of the year.

When the truck shows up, I gather up the dog in my arms, trying not to think of how little he weighs, or how much this feels like it must when you carry a sleeping child. My other failing. I didn't fail at the idea of having kids; I failed at trying to make it happen. I tell myself that it's probably for the best. I don't think that I would make a good father. You have to have a model for that.

The dog moans with a surprisingly human sound as I bundle him into the truck. "Hang on, pal. You can do it."

As he promised, Max is waiting for me at his office. He's changed out of his farm-visit clothes and is wearing scrubs, as if he's betting that he's going to be doing surgery on this dog. I set the dog down on the examining table and step back as I would once the EMTs had arrived on the scene, respectfully letting the professional assess the situation. But I watch his face and know exactly what he's going to say. Max won't be telling me anything I don't already know.

Part Two

19

Bull Harrison is pedaling his beat-up old bike along Route 114. Despite its designation as a state highway, Route 114 is a quiet country road that attaches Harmony Farms village to the far-flung world like a frayed string on a yo-yo. No longer the main route from here to there, it serves as the quickest way to get to the main north-south highway and thence to the civilization of Starbucks, Pottery Barn, and Wal-Mart. The road follows the contours of the metes and bounds of long-gone farms, the farmers' names recalled now only in the signs that fingerpoint up narrow, unlined roads: roads called Barnaby, Fletcher, and Winkler. Others bear the names of their past purposes: Mill and Orchard, Quarry and Church. Bull pushes hard against the pedals to gain the top of the rise to the turn off to Poor Farm Road. His road.

Poor Farm Road has the distinction of having once housed the indigent of Harmony Farms, where they were put to work in the fields in exchange for a roof and meals. Farmers who had lost their farms due to bad yields or bad management or bad health might have ended up there. Others who made up its workforce might have been the unemployables, or the men who were drinkers and had no homes to go to.

The actual poor farm is featured prominently in the historical society's pictorial display of old Harmony Farms, but no one still living remembers it in operation. The buildings are long gone, the fields turned into Harmony Farms' cash crop, housing estates. Bull has lived on Poor Farm Road all of his life. His is the eyesore that has the real estate brokers take prospective clients onto Poor Farm Road from the other end. That way, they can fall in love with the pristine model homes on their three acres of meticulously kept lawns without ever seeing Bull's place, with its sagging porch and algae green roof, the wheel-less Nova moldering out front and the row of trash cans filled with empty Coke cans that line the driveway, Bull's savings account.

Bull is just the most recent Harrison to live in the house. He got it from his parents, and they got it from his paternal grandparents and so on, back to 1849, when the original Barton Harrison bought it and a hundred acres of stony topsoil-deprived hillside. It has always been Bull's intention that his sons would follow him in home ownership. For a man who seems not to be in control of his life, Bull is surprisingly efficient. He had a will made out, years ago, even before he went on the wagon, and divided up the property between his sons equitably. The fact that Cooper has no interest in the house or, to be truthful, in him doesn't mean that he'll just give Jimmy the whole enchilada, even if Jimmy seems intent on making the place his own. Bull thought that he'd like the company, but Jimmy isn't the same kid who used to be fun to be around, getting into mischief, sure, but still willing to hang out with the old man, especially when Bull was willing to provide a little liquid refreshment for Jimmy and his underage buddies. Nowadays, he's moody, secretive. He yelled at Bull just yesterday for opening up a cupboard. As if he had every right to lock a cupboard in Bull's own house, Jimmy went out and came back with a hasp and padlock, which he screwed to the cupboard, then snapped the padlock shut and glared at Bull as he ostentatiously dropped the key into his shirt pocket. "You stay out of my business. Okay?"

"I don't care about your goddamn business."

"Keep it that way, and you'll be better off."

Bull thought that Jimmy's threats sounded like something out of a B movie—Cagney menacing some weak-chinned underling. He wasn't spying on Jimmy, hell no. All he had been looking for was a jacket that he'd been missing. He couldn't remember where he put it, and he was looking everywhere. And everywhere included that cupboard under the stairs. Even though he's been dry for a long time, there are times when his memory of doing things is completely shot— like sticking a winter coat in that cupboard, or arriving at the market with no idea why he's there. Or, worse, arriving at the market with no recollection of how he got there. Senior moments. That's what he calls them, even though the holes in his memory are a titch more unnerving than a momentary lapse. He can't recall going to his father's funeral. He knows that he must have, but his dad passed so close to Bull's return from Vietnam that the funeral, along with a lot of other things, just never stuck in his memory. Those first months stateside remain a long blur. It sometimes seems like he only woke up on the day that Jimmy was born.

Jimmy is out in the yard when Bull gets home. It's nice having a working car in the yard, and Jimmy's is pretty decent. If Jimmy is in a good mood, maybe he'll ask his son to drive him down to the Wal-Mart to stock up on paper goods and Coke. He's going through a lot of stuff, having a permanent houseguest now. Jimmy's been back for several weeks and hasn't even hinted at when he might find himself a place of his own. He can't enjoy being a grown man living with his dad, but the rent is cheap—that is, free. Guess you can't beat that when you are first getting back on your feet after incarceration.

Bull remembers the days after he'd been sprung from his little sojourn in the county jail. It was hard, really hard, to find work, especially with a permanently revoked driver's license and a long history of walking-off the job for no reason. Well, not exactly for no reason, but his chief reason for wandering away from a job site was to get a drink. The county jail's program of locking inmates away from the nearest source had gotten Bull on the right road for a while. But, within a few months of his release, he was at it again, helpless without the county's oversight and daily AA meetings. Instead of finding a meeting to help him stay out of trouble on the outside, Bull had exchanged the bottle for something a little more efficient. The best part was, except for his dealer, he hadn't had to efface himself to get his fix, like he did when he was in the liquor store every day, handing over crumpled dollar bills for a few nips and a six-pack. Then everyone who saw him go in or out of Ray's Bottle Shop knew that Bull Harrison was feeding his need.

In those days, Jimmy's easy access to drugs was a poorly kept secret. With his son's ready supply of relatively cheap stock, Bull realized that he could hold his head up as he walked past Ray's and pretend he was in recovery. Of course, that had ended when Jimmy's first business associate was busted. Jimmy himself disappeared for a while after that, and Bull was back at Ray's, keeping his eyes down as he pocketed the nips.

All water under the bridge now. Bull leans his bike against the porch, pulls a pack of Camels out of his shirt pocket, and joins Jimmy, who's standing beside his car. He offers his eldest a smoke, but Jimmy waves him off.

"I quit. You know that." He's got that impatient, the-old-man's-acting-senile-again tone to his voice.

"Good, just checking." In fact, he has forgotten that Jimmy arrived fresh from the state pen a reformed smoker. You can say this about Jimmy: He keeps himself pretty clean. No tobacco smoking. Back in the day, once he'd started selling drugs, Jimmy had stopped using, preferring to pocket the dough rather than enjoy the high.

No free samples, he says. Bull is no dope; he knows what Jimmy's keeping in that locked closet. Sometimes it makes him want some, just a taste, just a little reminder of what painlessness feels like. It's only knowing that it's so close at hand that reminds him of the need; he wouldn't think of it otherwise. He also knows that his son would kill him if he stole anything.

Bull doesn't want to get back on that merry-go-round. He likes his job at the lumberyard. He likes that now some people actually say hi to him when he pedals by. "Hi, Bull. How's it going, Bull?" Sometimes he even feels like a regular guy, someone who is an upstanding citizen of this town. No longer the town clown.

Jimmy is cleaning out his car, stuffing a plastic grocery bag with receipts, used tissues, paper coffee cups, and soda cans. He looks maybe too busy to ask for a lift to Wal-Mart. Maybe he should give Cooper a call, see if he's available sometime for a paper-towel run. Bull drags on his cigarette and blows the idea out of his mind with the exhale of smoke. Nah. Bad idea. Cooper's made it plenty clear that he's not looking to renew any family ties.

Bull drops the cigarette on the ground. "You wanna head over to Wally World?" He presses the heel of his boot onto the smoldering butt. "I'll buy you a Big Mac on the way."

Jimmy neatly ties the grocery bag's handles together. Grins at his old man. "You still think that's appealing? Like when we were kids?"

"It's cheap, tastes good."

"Funny, but the first few years I was in, all I wanted was a Big Mac. Don't ask me why, I never ate that many of them. Then once, for some reason, you brought me one. Remember? I couldn't eat it. It was cold and the grease was tasteless. After that, I don't know. Guess I lost the taste. Guess I grew out of them."

Bull doesn't like it when Jimmy reminds him of where he's been the past dozen years. That an entire decade of his life has passed mostly out of Bull's sight. "So does this mean you won't take me?"

"No. I can't. Sorry." Jimmy slam dunks his makeshift trash bag into the barrel.

The four of them pile out of the Nova, the boys running ahead, heedless of the cars in the drive-up line. Usually, they get their McDonald's to go, but tonight they're there to eat in, as if this Friday night is special. Happy Meals for two. Mona and Bull get Big Macs and share a box of fries. Milk shakes so thick, they give Bull brain freeze.

Who knows what starts the fight. They have reached a point in their marriage when anything and everything provides a trigger point for an argument. Maybe Bull got greedy with the fries; maybe Mona got snarky about something. Then Jimmy did something to Cooper. Probably took his Happy Meal prize. So Mona's mad, and Cooper's screaming at Jimmy to give it back. Jimmy's running around the restaurant, rolling the purloined plastic toy over the backs of seats and benches, even those occupied. Mona's yelling at him to stop.

Bull gets up, walks out. He's left the keys to the Nova on the table and has ten bucks left in his pocket from what he spent on dinner. It's not much, but enough. He's not thinking at all about how he's going to get back to Harmony Farms from here; he's only interested in the VFW-post bar he knows is on the next block.

20

I'm in the tiny lab-cum-drug closet of Max's office. I left the exam room and the dog to Max's ministrations, using the privacy to call Natalie and let her know that I am at Max's and that when I'm done here, I'll return her truck and pick up mine. Instead, she offered to meet me here, so I'm looking through the blind slats at the three parking spaces in front of Max's storefront practice. The cop in me is thinking that he really shouldn't have his drugs in a room so close to a plate-glass window when he comes into the room to deliver his pronouncement.

"Cooper, I think that a merciful euthanasia is the right thing to do."

"Euthanasia?" I don't know why I am shocked by Max's all-too-reasonable suggestion.

According to Max, the dog is near death; the infection has traveled deep and the wounds on his legs and neck are from another dog, or, worse, a coyote, which suggests rabies. Stupidly, I ask if he can do a test to find out, and Max tells me that the only test for rabies is postmortem.

Even if I had the budget to take care of him, it wouldn't be hu-
mane to put him through the trauma of surgery and what would
likely be an unsuccessful recovery—in effect, prolonging the inevitable. Why would I do that? It makes no sense. So why am I so upset at this verdict? Nothing Max has said comes as a surprise. All I
have to do is say 'Okay.' Not exactly the executioner, but certainly
the judge and jury. But I can't say the word. I've worked too goddamn hard to bring this dog in. How many nights of sleeping out?
How many attempts to lure him in? How much time have I spent
thinking about this miserable beast?

It reminds me of something. Like the memory of a dream. The
quest had a purpose, and maybe I've inflated its importance. But
here he is at last, my quarry. A wounded and traumatized dog. I
think what it reminds me of is that moment when a job is done, when
it's time to stand down.

"Are you sure?" I feel a little foolish saying this. Of course Max
is certain. He's too fine a vet to suggest euthanasia out of laziness. If
he thought there was hope, he'd be in the OR right now. I sigh, let
the decision settle in. It just seems wrong to reward this dog's fight
to survive with death.

"Right. Look, I'll go in with you. He shouldn't be alone." I want
this over with by the time Natalie arrives. I don't want her looking
at me with the disapproving eyes of a professional rescuer.

Max reaches for the barbiturates and I leave him to it, going into
the exam room, where the dog is as still as if he's already gone.

But he's not, and he raises his head as I come in. Looks me in
the eye. Looks at me with Argos's eyes.

No two dogs are exactly alike, not even dogs of the same breed.
Dark brown eyes reflecting from a white face aren't the same as
these pained and equally dark brown eyes buried in the yellow
mask of this dog. Argos's eyes were never troubled, never anything
but alert and game. This yellow dog's eyes tell me that he is deeply
afraid.

I hear Max come in, the squeak of his trainers against the worn linoleum of the exam room floor.

"Max, don't. Let's just try. Okay? Give him a couple of days."

"Cooper, you really want to put this stray dog through that?" He's holding two hypodermic syringes, both capped with plastic guards.

"I do." As I say it, Natalie comes into the exam room.

Max looks at me, then at Natalie. He shakes his head and sets the lethal injections down on the counter. "Your call."

"Yeah, I know. Probably the wrong one, but I think we should give him one more chance. He's hung on this long."

"I've never known you to be sentimental."

"It's not sentiment. At least I don't think it is." Natalie moves into the room to stand beside me. She reaches over and gently runs her hand over the dog's skull. The very tip of his tail flutters into the semblance of a wag. "It's common decency."

Max shrugs with an elegant capitulation that says he thinks I'm nuts but that he'll humor me. He shoos us out of the room, and for a brief, distrustful second I wonder if he'll do it anyway and claim the dog died on the table. The two hypodermics are on the counter, and Max sees me glance at them. "Put these in the med room, will you?" I'm embarrassed at my obvious skepticism. Max deserves better than that from me.

There is something, something in the way this dog has led me on a merry chase, something in the singular fact of his having survived against the odds clearly stacked against him. He's tougher than he looks. And right now he's looking at me with Argos's eyes, saying, *Give me a chance.*

It's only one o'clock, although it feels like I've put in a whole day. I'm exhausted and, frankly, sore from my morning on horseback. I don't want to sit in the waiting room, watching a clock hand move minute by painful minute, but I don't want to go home, either.

Then I feel Natalie's hand on my back. "Let's go. Max will call when he's done." Natalie has stepped up in a quintessentially female way to assess and act. It is so comforting, like having a mother say, "Time for bed," or "Eat your peas." We leave the office and I suggest that she doesn't have to spend who knows how long waiting for me.

"Look, I'm starving. Why don't we get lunch first? Besides, the Patriots versus Jets game is on at the tavern."

When we get to the tavern, we're able to squeeze in by the bar. We order sandwiches and root beer. I check to make sure that my cell phone is not only on with the loudest ring but also on vibrate; then I place it on the bar in front of me so that I have a visual. In a noisy football crowd, the chances of my hearing my phone decrease drastically. Natalie doesn't waste her breath mouthing platitudes like "He'll be fine," or "It's in God's hands." It's almost like having a buddy as she turns her attention to the screen with the closed captioning and devours her fries one after the other.

Second quarter, eighteen seconds left on the clock. I'm studying the time display on my phone, trying to calculate how long Max has been working on the dog. It seems to me that the longer he takes, the worse the news. He said that he wouldn't attempt a surgical fix to the hip wound until the dog was stabilized. I understood the words, if not the specificity of them. Fluids, antibiotics?

Natalie nudges me out of my thoughts. "I have to go. I've got to soak that hoof again." She's had the good grace to wait until halftime. Bless her heart. After a small scuffle, I pay the tab; then she drives back to Second Hope Farm and I go back to Max's, fully expecting the worse.

21

"It'd be a good idea if you made yourself scarce." Jimmy slathers a gob of mayonnaise on the sandwich he's making. "Just for an hour or two." He picks three slices of ham off the pound that Bull has brought home and lays them on the bread, adds cheese, a swath of mustard. "You got someplace you can go?"

Where's he going to go? Library's closed on Mondays. In the bad old days, this needing a place to hang out wouldn't have been a problem, and Bull smiles reflexively at the thought of a couple hours spent like any other joker, belly up to a bar, soaking up the suds, laughing with perfect strangers. He sighs, waits for his son to recall that his father has only a bicycle for transportation. Maybe he should take in a movie. That'd be fine. He hasn't been to a movie in years, but that would mean getting Jimmy to take him out of town to the mall. "It's raining, Jimmy. I'll just stay in my bedroom. You'll never know I'm here."

"No. I need a little privacy. Trust me, Bull. You don't want to be anywhere near this house a couple of times a week. That's all I'm saying. Make yourself scarce."

"Then make your arrangements for when I'm at work." Bull pulls a slice of the ham off the pound, folds it into his mouth.

"I serve at the pleasure of my clients."

"Yeah. Right. Clients."

"Shut up, old man." Jimmy isn't smiling, isn't kidding when he says this, and this is what's beginning to get on Bull's nerves—his son's disrespect. Worse than disrespect, downright meanness. There is something dead in Jimmy's eyes, like whatever he experienced in the state pen killed the last bit of the boy he'd once been, the boy quick to laugh. Quicker, sure, to bully, that laughter generally at the expense of someone weaker, vulnerable.

"Jimmy, you in trouble?"

Jimmy chews his sandwich, says nothing. Then he meets Bull's eyes. "What if I was? What could you do about it?" He shoves the rest of his sandwich into his mouth. "Just be out of here for an hour or two."

"It's raining, Jimmy. I don't want to get wet."

Jimmy doesn't respond, he's making himself another sandwich. Annoyed, Bull pretends he's just had a great idea: "I know. I'll call Cooper, see if he can pick me up. He hasn't been by since you got here."

"Not on your life. I don't want you to bring him here under any circumstances. Especially when I got company coming. Got it?" He seems to swell up as he takes a hostile step toward Bull. His chest expands and the belly that he grew in prison widens, draping over his belt. Cherries of color dot his pallid cheeks. The pale water gray of his eyes darkens perceptibly.

"Calm down. I was just trying to figure something out."

Jimmy shrinks back to size, steps away. "All right. All right, I'll drop you off someplace."

"And pick me up."

"Get your jacket." Jimmy walks away from the ham and cheese

on the counter, the open jars of mayonnaise and mustard, the loaf of bread.

They don't speak as Jimmy drives to the village. Bull can see the tension in his son's softened jaw, how the muscle in his cheek keeps working with his very private thoughts. He's hatless and there's more skin at his temples than he had before he went away. Bull is surprised to find himself the father of a middle-aged man. One not aging particularly well. Even though he's been out for weeks, Jimmy hasn't lost the tallowy look of a man who has spent years with less than an hour of sunshine a day. Sometimes that gray pallor never really goes away, as if the lighting of the prison has entered your pores.

Why does Jimmy treat him like a pain in the ass even as he has come back to the Poor Farm Road house of his own volition, holing up with his old man while trying to get his life back on track. He should be grateful for a free roof over his head, not ordering his father around like a servant, or, worse, like Bull's an annoying child. This business of being put out of his own house rankles; he can't deny it.

Beyond the irritation, there lies a subtext of worry. Jimmy is up to no good, not even giving it six months of good behavior before falling into recidivism. Bull knows that word all too well. *Recidivism.* A word so often applied to himself during the bad old days. A week, a month, a half year in the county jail and they'd pour good sense down his throat, warning him off becoming a recidivist. Like Jimmy, Bull couldn't make it stick the first few times; he reverted to type within hours of release. But that was just being a drunk, a drug addict. What Jimmy's into is certainly far worse. The temper. The secretiveness. The lock on his bedroom door.

Jimmy drops Bull off at the intersection of Route 114 and Main Street. It's pouring, and Bull pulls up the collar of his ancient army-surplus jacket, puts a soggy Camel between his lips. "Don't forget to come back and get me."

Jimmy pulls away even before Bull slams the Honda's door, and Bull wonders if he's been abandoned.

In Harmony Farms, all the stores close at six o'clock. The only place open on Main Street is Cumberland Farms, so Bull goes in, buys a pack of smokes, lingers at the magazine rack. Bull knows that the kid behind the counter has his froggy eyes on him. He buys a coffee, then spends a long time leaning against the counter, sipping it until it cools to tepid, tasteless. He throws it out. Bull uses the bathroom, then buys another coffee. The kid openly stares now, as if the tractor beam of his gaze will move Bull out of the store before he has to ask him to leave. The NO LOITERING sign is outside, not inside. Ha. Take that, Frog Eyes.

No one who comes into the Cumberland Farms greets him. He doesn't know anyone. It's like he's been dropped into a foreign land, a place that is unfriendly to strangers. He was born and raised here, so how can it be that no one is familiar? He's not so old that all his peers are dead. At least not the peers with whom he grew up. He has lots of dead peers, dead in a foreign land, a land unfriendly to the strangers sent to win their war. Ducky and Marvin, Whip and Del. Names now. Just names.

Knee-deep in a rice paddy, wearing blackface like some old-fashioned minstrels. Every flicker of movement brings a jolt to the gut, a griping like cramps, pure fear. An ugly cow stands in the middle of the paddy; the dull moonlight glints off her curved horns. A woman wearing the ubiquitous conical hat stands on the edge, staring at them; her hands are down, flattened palms against her skinny legs. She calls out, but none of the men—boys—speaks a word of the language. To them, it's gobbledygook. Gook. They don't know if she's warning them that the Vietcong are ahead, or if she's alerting the VC to their presence. Maybe she's just yelling at them to get out of her paddy. No one has any idea, and that makes her dangerous. Bull doesn't know who gives the order, or even if an order has been given—a critical distinction.

With one shot, the woman crumples to the ground, her hat rolling down the slope to the rice paddy, a loose wheel. When he walks past the body, Bull can see that by Vietnamese standards, she is an old woman. Maybe fifty. Her vacant eyes look right at him.

The platoon moves on, wading deeper into the paddy. The ugly cow lowers its head and makes a moaning, lowing sound. The conical hat floats in front of Bull. He picks it up, drains the water out of it. Breaking away from the line, he trudges through the underwater growth to place the hat over the woman's face.

Bull walks out of the Cumberland Farms, trying to walk away from the thoughts that burn at him. Nearly fifty freakin' years, and yet the suddenness with which the war memories rise up still has the power to bring on the shakes. If he can keep his memories at bay, he can keep the thirst, the cravings, at bay. It's as simple as that. Stop thinking.

The rain has leveled off to a cold drizzle that glitters in the streetlights. A car approaches, and Bull hopes that it's Jimmy, but it keeps moving, its high-tech sodium headlights like the eyes of some prowling animal, washing the street with sharp white light. Bull begins walking; he'll stick his thumb out and catch a ride with someone. Anyone.

22

I see him, caught in the headlights of the car in front of me. I'm on my way back to the cabin after work, and when I see the figure on the side of the road, I can't immediately tell if it's man or beast. In the dusk Bull's bulk is bear-shaped.

Lying on his good side, recumbent upon the flipped-down rear seat, in my custody and my care, is the yellow dog. Max confirmed what I suspected, that this is a Labrador retriever, although he's such a bag of bones, it's hard to imagine that he could ever weigh eighty pounds. Because Max doesn't have a twenty-four-hour presence in his office, the dog had to go home with me. So I've shoved painkill-ers and antibiotics down his throat and applied the veterinary ver-sion of Neosporin into his wounds. The ticks are gone, but Max didn't want to bathe him until he's recovered enough to take the soaking. So he stinks. And he's afraid. Really afraid. He shakes like he's got the d.t.'s when I approach him, no matter how softly I try, how Mother Teresa I try to make myself. I've had him in an empty ken-nel all day, but I can't leave him at the shelter, where he belongs, because he needs meds every six hours. I feel like a new parent, fussing over timing and warmth and food, coddling an infant. Except that every time I stood by the cage, even just to make sure he was still breathing, he struggled to withdraw deeper into it, like I was going to haul him out and beat him. Whoever had this dog has some dues to pay. In the drama of trying to save him, neither Max nor I thought about wanding him, see if he's chipped. He's got a recheck in a few days; I'll get it done then.

I realize that it's Bull standing by the side of the road in the drizzle, and I immediately think that he's been out drinking. He's going to get hit by a car. When he's drunk, he has no sense of self-preservation. I don't want to, but I pull over. "Get in the truck."

"Good to see you, too, son."

He climbs in, and I feel myself recoiling, anticipating the scent of alcohol fumes coming from him, but there are none, just the benign odor of coffee. I don't ask him why he's out in the rain on a Monday night. I don't really care. Bull is a world unto himself and there is very little about it I'm interested in. Actually, there's nothing about Bull's life that interests me. The solid wall of indifference is how I am maintaining this separation of my childhood self from my adult one. I have come back to Harmony Farms a different man from the one who left twenty years before. I have had the satisfaction of people asking me where I'm from, never connecting this Harrison with that one, who is, at this moment, looking over his shoulder at the recumbent dog. I always say I'm from Boston. I pull away from the side of the road a little fast. Gravel spits out from beneath the rear tires.

"Layin' rubber?" Bull chuckles, like I'm trying to entertain him.

"I assume I'm taking you home."

Bull doesn't answer, letting me take that as a yes. Then, ursine, he shakes his head. "No. I don't think so."

"You have someplace to be?"

"Not really. Where you going?"

"I'm taking you home. You need groceries or something?"

"I'm good. Just drop me at the Lakeside."

"I'm not going to do that."

"You think I drink anymore?" He pulls this magnificently of-fended face. "I'm strictly on fizzy water and lime these days. My tele-vision doesn't work. I want to watch the game."

"There's no game tonight."

"Okay, you caught me. *Dancing with the Stars.* I like watching the ladies in those naked-looking costumes."

This is almost plausible. But, however diminished I am, I am still, at heart, a cop. "Why don't you want to go home? What's Jimmy up to?"

Bull doesn't answer, he's looking again at the dog on the rear seat. "What's with this dog? Is he yours?"

"No. He's been injured and I'm taking care of him until I can either find the owner or get him fostered out."

"Poor guy. He looks pretty bad off. Lab?"

"Yeah." I think about it for a second. "He look like one of the Haynes's dogs to you?"

"Possible, though I think they keep hounds."

He's done it, distracted me from my question, so I repeat it. "Where's Jimmy?"

"Home."

"And you don't want to be there with him?"

"Coop, I told you, I want to watch TV."

I wonder if the dog behind me is listening to this conversation. I wonder if he understands the subtle tone of a born liar. Argos was like a polygraph machine when it came to liars. It was like he could smell dishonesty coming out of their pores. This dog just sighs, a sound even I can hear in the silence of the cab. It's a deep, cleans-ing sigh, and I worry for a moment that it is the sigh of death. That he has, after all our efforts, breathed his last. At the next stop sign, I turn around in my seat and flip on the overhead light. The dog's head is still on the seat, but his much brighter eye is open, and he is looking at Bull.

I flip off the light and take my turn through the last village intersection. Three miles up the road and I'll take the right onto Poor Farm Road.

"Coop, Jimmy just needs a little time alone. Without his old man hanging around. You get what I mean." Bull gives me the old wink, wink, nudge, nudge, implying that my pasty-faced, overweight excon older brother is entertaining a woman.

I'm taking Bull home out of decency, but mostly I'm going to see if Jimmy is there, alone. I don't know why it should matter, why it's got my hackles up that he's sent Bull out in the rain and told him to keep away. There can only be one reason, and I don't think for a minute it's because he's got a girl in the house. I have no authority, no warrant. No reason to get involved. But I do.

"What's Jimmy up to, Bull? And don't tell me he isn't up to anything."

"The God's honest truth is that I don't know."

"He's making sure that you don't."

"Yes. It's better that way."

"Is he dealing? I mean, do you think that he might be? Take an educated guess."

"Cooper, if I did, and I don't, why would I tell you that? I'm *his* father, too. I wouldn't turn on you, and I won't turn on him."

"I'm not asking you to; I'm just putting it out there. Bull, you don't want to have the kind of trouble that comes with Jimmy."

"I only know that you're both my sons and I'm no snitch. Especially with no what you lawmen like to call *evidence*." He waits a beat, maybe two. "And you'd be some kind of asshole to turn your own brother in, specially without any proof. You go be a cop in Boston; don't try to be a cop here.

"In case you haven't noticed, I'm not a cop anymore." I mean this as a way to make him understand that I don't have any real intention—at the moment—of doing anything about Jimmy, but even to my sorry ears it sounds petulant.

The dog behind me sighs again. Bull turns around and speaks to him with a soft garble of baby talk. I can hear the thumping of his tail on the backseat, a little heartbeat of a sound in my good right ear.

"Why don't you drop me at the end of the road? Better for both of us."

Hey, what would I prove if Jimmy is at the house, that maybe he has company? That maybe Bull isn't, well, bulling me and Jimmy is just entertaining a woman? Can I just let this go for now? It's not raining anymore, and Bull can use the exercise. I pull over at the bottom of Poor Farm Road. A Lexus goes around us, high beams undimmed. Bull gets out, but before he closes the door, he reaches in to pet the dog, who is still lying on his side, as if the motion of the truck is soothing him. He doesn't growl, doesn't make any sound at all as my father gives him a gentle pat. "Take care of this guy. He looks like he could be a nice dog."

"I will." I am more puzzled than jealous; the dog still cringes in fear at the sight and touch of me, but for this wreck of a man who has blown every chance he ever had at a normal life, he thumps his tail.

23

Bull Harrison stands by the side of the road, his younger son's taillights moving away from him at a clip a little too fast for the road, as if he can't get far enough away from his father fast enough. Well, Cooper's always been like that, always had a bug up his ass. What are you going to do? Bull accepts the fact that he might have been a better father, but, hell, the boy isn't a kid anymore; he's a grown man. Get over it! Bull trudges along Poor Farm Road, nursing his indignation.

A little too close for comfort, a car zips by Bull, and a fine spray of runoff hits him at knee level. Bull waves a fist, but he moves to the other side of the dark country road to face oncoming cars. Now his pants are wet, and after that last cup of coffee, he needs to pee. Home is a quarter of a mile away, and he has no idea if Jimmy will welcome him back or not. Sometimes it just seems like life sucks. The ornate sign announcing Poor Farm Estates—does no one but Bull see the irony in that?—is one of those artfully carved hand-painted gated-community signs gracefully illuminated by up-lights, situated on its own little island of grass, with twin entrances bifurcated to either side of it. Six-row cobblestone aprons demarcate the entrances to the development from the road. The fine drizzle sparkles in the soft beams like fairy dust. Bull steps beside the sign, unzips, and waters the well-trimmed burning bush shrubs that embrace the entrance. Now he can make it the rest of the way home.

The house is dark, no welcoming porch light turned on for his benefit, which may be due more to the fact that the light hasn't worked in donkey's years than any malintent on Jimmy's part. It's actually been kind of nice, coming home from work most evenings to a light in the parlor, the clutter of another person's belongings. Jimmy may not be easy, but it's kind of nice to have someone to watch TV with of an evening.

The kitchen is at the back of the house, and if Jimmy is home, he's probably in there. Bull checks for any other cars in the driveway, but there's only Jimmy's Honda and his own up-on-blocks '68 Nova. Now, there was a car. Bull had many a night in that automobile he'd love to relive. Runs out to the lake with Mona, who was at her hottest back in those days, a six-pack and a handle of Jack in the trunk. Wearing that aged leather jacket he eventually lost somewhere in the last quarter century. Bull runs his hand along the old car as he works his way in the dark around to the back door of the house. Sure enough, there's a light in the kitchen. Jimmy is framed by the curtainless window like he's a piece of art. A piece of work, more like. He's on his phone and gesturing, as if his caller can see him, punching the air with his forefinger. Bull recognizes the gesture as one of his own. The emphatic forefinger. You. Will. Do. What. I. Say. Yeah, half the time his kids would flip him the bird and do what they damn well pleased. Looking at the expression on Jimmy's face, though, Bull thinks that no one is going to disrespect this guy. It is a look of smoldering anger. Dangerous anger. Bull turns around and climbs into the front seat of the Nova. The bench seat is pushed way back, so he stretches his long legs into the well on the passenger side. He folds his arms across his chest against the chill night air. He'll give Jimmy a few minutes, then go in. It's his house, damn it. He won't be kept out of it. Bull feels the pull of gravity against his eyelids. He closes his eyes, just to rest them; another minute and he'll go in. He nods off.

Bull has no idea where he is when he is startled awake by the blast of high beams sweeping through the Nova's windows. Oh, right. Stuck out here in the car while Jimmy's on the phone. The high beams belong to a car Bull doesn't recognize, and instinct makes him hunker down lower in the front seat. He doesn't know how long he's been asleep—a few minutes or an hour—but it's no longer raining and the stars have finally broken through the three days of heavy clouds.

The car is a late-model bullet-shaped thing. Black, wire rims. Nice. The man who gets out of it pauses to get his bearings. Without a porch light, the yard is dark, and Bull sees doubt in the way the guy keeps one hand on the handle of his fancy car. Maybe not doubt. Wariness. He'll bolt if he thinks he's in the wrong place or that maybe something isn't kosher. But the front door opens, a box of light with Jimmy in the middle. The man trots into the house and the door closes with a thump.

Now he'll have to stay put until this visitor leaves. Bull is savvy enough to know that whatever Jimmy planned, did not happen at the appointed hour and that things are pretty tense. Jimmy wants to keep him in the dark about his "client" and Cooper wants him to blab about Jimmy's dealings. Jekyll and Hyde. No, these boys aren't two halves of any whole. More like those biblical brothers, Cain and Abel. Bull shivers as the cold front that has pushed away the clouds settles in. No, that doesn't sound right, either. Cooper and Jimmy are just a pair of dissimilar men. Same upbringing, different results. Well, he's no fool, and he's not about to let Jimmy think that he saw this car or that man, and he's not going to breathe a word to Cooper about his brother's nighttime visitor. Bull's just glad he had the sense to hole up in the Nova. And then he thinks, What an awful thing it is to be afraid of your own son.

Bull doesn't have time to nod off again before the visitor emerges from the house. Jimmy doesn't linger in the open door, shutting it even before the stranger has reached his fancy car. Even after the car leaves the yard, Bull stays in the Nova for a little while, giving Jimmy a grace period, giving himself enough time that there will be no question but that he hasn't witnessed any comings or goings. The trouble with deception is that you have to think of every contingency. What if Jimmy, business conducted, suddenly remembers he has to go fetch his father and then doesn't find him? It's been five, six minutes. Bull cracks open the rusted car door, pulls himself out. His pants are dry now.

"Shit, Bull. I'm sorry. Things went long and I forgot." Jimmy seems genuinely contrite. "I'd of remembered in a couple of minutes. You should have stayed put."

"S'okay. I hitched." Bull heads to the bathroom, noticing as he goes, that the padlocked understairs closet is open.

"Who picked you up?"

"No one you know." This is, kind of, the truth.

24

Come on, boy, take it." It's been three weeks and the dog and I are still in the hostage/guard mind-set. Apparently, I'm the guard and he feels like he's a prisoner. I'm hopeful that we'll achieve some sort of Stockholm syndrome soon and that he'll begin to look to me for friendship and validation. I have yet to get his tail to wag even in the slightest. At least he's no longer pressing himself against the bars of his kennel to get as far away from me as he can. And at night, in the cabin, I've actually been able to walk past him in his basket to the bathroom without his scrambling behind the couch. Small steps. Natalie has been invaluable to me as I try to socialize this animal. "Rescues have such baggage," she says. I say, "This isn't a rescue"—and I finger air quotes around the word—"I may have rescued him from the wild, but I'm not a rescue operation." She always gives me this look, like she's hearing what I'm saying but not giving it much credence. I don't think she knows exactly how serious I am about keeping this enforced companionship with the dog all business.

Frankly, he should be kept in the shelter, but until the course of antibiotics is done, he's got to have me near. With all those ticks that had been clinging to him, in addition to the infection in his hip, he's also got Lyme disease and—drum roll, please—ehrlichiosis. Max says it's just dumb luck that he hasn't got the other tick-borne illnesses available to mammals, or heartworm. So a normal course of antibiotics for the infection was extended to sixty days. The fun part is, of course, to pill a dog who is terrified of me.

In order to not traumatize the dog further by shoving the capsule down his throat while I have him in a headlock, I've been opening up the cap of doxycycline and mixing it in with a potage of rice and hamburger. Soft foods, Max says. Easy on the tummy against the ravages of the doxy. Still he looks at me like he believes I'm poisoning him. I've never seen a dog eat with such an expression of fatalism. It's as if he's saying, *I know you're trying to kill me, but I'll eat it on the off chance you're not.* He makes me miss Argos in the strangest ways. Argos, who would take his dinner bowl in his teeth and present it to me if he thought he should have seconds. Argos, who would lick the bowl until there was no point in putting it in the dishwasher. We worked hard and we deserved good meals. Argos frequently inspired me to break the cardinal rules instilled in us in training. I fed him the ends of my sandwiches, the crusts from my morning toast. I even cooked us bacon and eggs. Hearty breakfasts to keep us strong.

I crouch down, place the plastic bowl next to the basket containing the yellow dog. "Hey, fella, you should eat this. I made it for you with special rice and special hamburger. The expensive stuff from the Country Market. Elvin is a highway robber when it comes to meat, but it's worth every penny. Eat up. Come on." I am cajoling and wonder if I sound like a daddy playing "One for the airplane, one for the baby." It's not hot, although I've poured the grease from the frying pan over it to give it even more flavor and more needed calories.

The dog gets to his feet, climbs over the edge of the basket like a deposed king mounting the guillotine. The good news is that he's bearing weight on the bad leg. Last week, Max finally chanced anesthesia and removed the pellets, confirming my belief that some asshole duck hunter shot his own dog—whether intentionally or accidentally is irrelevant to me—and then drove off without him. I asked Max to wand the dog, but the microchip reader came up blank, which means either the dog isn't chipped or that it's the type of chip that requires a different reader. Max will try to get one on loan.

I sit down on the floor beside him and he turns to look back at his safe place. "If you don't eat it, I will." He knows that threat is toothless. He sits. I push the bowl closer. He definitely looks better than he did, now that he's all cleaned up and his eyes are much brighter. He's gained some weight, but it's an uphill battle. Maybe he's anorexic. Can dogs be anorexic? I give up and get off the floor to see about my own breakfast. I push the bowl under his front legs. As soon as I turn my back, he goes at the food, inhaling it in three gulps. Now I get it. He won't take it if I'm looking, as if he expects me to snatch it away from him. I can see my shrink nodding with a grim expression and declaring, "Trust issues." Guess this dog and I are well matched. We both have issues.

My phone rings just as I set down my own plate of bacon and eggs. It's not the barking ringtone, so I know that it's not work-related. It takes me a minute to locate the phone, which has fallen between the nightstand and the bed. The number displayed isn't one I recognize and I'm tempted to let it go to voice mail, but it's a local number, so I don't. In the end, I'm glad that I didn't, as the caller is Polly Schaeffer. In some moment of weakness that I don't remember, I must have given her my personal number. Or maybe she spotted it on the board at the shelter during her little B and E attempt. Whichever the case, she's bawling like a baby and can hardly get the words out.

"Polly, settle down. Tell me what's the matter."

"They took them. They took them all."

"Who took what?" I'm asking only to get her to take a deep breath. I know goddamn well what she's talking about and I'm furious. I told Roger Schaeffer I'd deal with it. I have dealt with it. Jenny found nice permanent homes for a couple of the cats and Polly let them go more or less willingly. And she found four foster homes for up to six of Polly's collection. These things take time, as I told Roger, and to strip the old lady of all of her pets is simply cruel. If I thought for one blessed moment that any of Polly's cats was in any way suffering from an excess of companions, I would have had no compunction against taking them all. But, despite the rank odor of too many cats in too small a house, they are all clean, fat, neutered, and, according to Max, up-to-date on their vaccines. There's just no law against it as long as everyone is healthy.

"Roger took my babies. He said that the Health Department was going to arrest me."

"Jesus, Polly." I really don't know if he can do that, or even if the Health Department has the authority to arrest anybody. I think of them more as a fine-imposing department. I think Roger has played a mean trick on his mother. "Give me an hour; I'll stop by."

I thumb off the phone and go back to my breakfast, which is gone.

The dog is back in his basket and the slow stroke of his pink tongue along his lips incriminates him. Not only is my cooked breakfast licked off my plate but the half pound of bacon left on the counter and the two raw eggs sitting in their cardboard cradle are gone, too. Shells and all. The only thing untouched on the table is my mug of coffee.

"What's the matter? You don't like my coffee?"

The dog just looks at me with those sad, innocent brown eyes.

"You're a thief, aren't you? Won't take what's offered. You prefer to steal it? Okay, if that's how it's going to be. So be it." At least I know now how to get food into him. Just turn my back or leave it on the table. Bingo. It's going to be hard to adopt out a dog who steals off a table, so that habit has got to be broken pretty quickly. But, I know, first I have to get him to relax around people. Nobody wants a cowardly dog, a dog that shrinks from every human touch, casts craven, pleading eyes at the friendliest of folks..

What am I thinking? I need Jenny to find this boy a foster home ASAP. As I have said to Jenny and Natalie and anyone else who thinks I should be rehabbing this mutt, I have neither the time nor the inclination to retrain a dog I have no intention of keeping.

I guess the silver lining to Polly's lament is now that Roger has removed all of his mother's cats, Jenny can focus on finding this boy a home. Not me. We've got forty-five more days of meds and then off he goes. I just have to be more diligent about where I put my food. It's like having a bear in the house.

The man is patrolling the room, clearly aware of the theft of the food, which is sitting rather heavily in the dog's belly right now, having followed the large amount of just slightly off-tasting meat and rice. He's not yelling, which is good. But he's not sitting still, and that means he's a threat.

Although this is a pleasant sort of captivity, it is still captivity. The interior scents are fully human—the sweetish odor of soaps, the fulsome odor of food hidden most of the time behind impenetrable doors. And there's the odor of the man himself, tainted perhaps by the soap smells, but still clearly identifiable, different from that of any other person this dog may ever encounter. He is attached to a leash when the man carries him outside to relieve himself. He is behind a closed door otherwise—in the basket, with the soft man-smelling sleeping bag, subjected to pills being shoved down his throat, but then rewarded with bowls of room-temperature meat, fresh water. Wary and worried, the dog keeps his eyes on the man until he retires to his own bed. The man's touch isn't unkind, but it lacks the meaning that would finally put this dog at ease. It is the touch of business, not affection. There's the awkward demand to open his mouth and have things forced down his gullet, always followed by a voiced "Good boy." It's confusing. Still, he can't trust that this man won't one day hurt him, and so every time the man brings him food, or takes him outside, or makes him swallow the pill, the dog cowers in his corner, shrinking himself down to as small a target as he can reasonably become. *Don't touch. Don't touch. Don't hurt me.*

During the day, they go to that place with the other captives. The cage is not quite as comfortable as this place, but his aches are beginning to lessen and the foam rubber pad is good to stretch out on. There is no fire to lie beside, but the place is warm enough. Certainly far warmer than the nest he had under the fallen tree. Even a dog knows when there have been improvements in his living situation. The only time the dog can truly relax is when he's got the two other dogs beside him in an adjoining kennel; only then can the dog drop his guard long enough to sleep, leaving the watching to his comrades.

The other two dogs are friendly enough, poking curious noses through the diamond-shaped spaces of the wire that separates him from them when they are outside. It is clear to him that this pair has a family bond. Littermates certainly. They carry their tails at exactly the same plane and they move as one unit, patrolling the limited space of their run, communicating effortlessly as they mark and remark the same four posts. The yellow dog envies them. He'd like to be a part of their pack, but the wire prevents him from testing their openness to a third party. Still, it's nice to have company. He can sense that their lives have been disrupted, that this isn't their normal place any more than it's his. They whine sometimes, a soft, plaintive sound that speaks to his own distress. Unlike him, however, whenever the man or the chatty woman comes in, they wriggle and yap and leap in the air like they expect kindness. They get excited about these humans, and not just for the food that is offered. It's like they are excited to see these captors. He is simply worried. The woman will snap leashes to their collars and take them outside, beyond the confines of the run, to sniff and mark and even chase balls. There is something about that little sphere that keeps his attention. A vague notion of how it tastes, a desire for it.

The yellow dog stands in his isolation, watching, panting with anxiety, pacing from side to side until the aching in his hip starts up and he crumples to the ground, a low and involuntary whine coming out of him.

"Easy, fella. No ball playing for you till you get better. Doctor's orders."

The dog has no idea what the man is saying. One ear turns back toward the man, listening, analyzing, parsing out of human language the man's intent. He's recognized a few words from his early life: *boy, fella,* and the one the woman uses often—*sweetie.* Some words are becoming familiar from hearing them over and over: *easy easy it's okay okay okay.* Then the man barks loud human words and any fleeting sense of safety flies away.

He simply doesn't understand what the man wants of him.

25

Polly is sitting in a lawn chair in her front yard. Her voluminous caftan is mottled shades of pink and lime, a curious but unidentifiable pattern smeared across her body. Her reddened eyes clash with the pink. Her beehive hairdo is tilted slightly to one side. As I climb out of my truck, she pushes herself out of the chair and stomps over to me, apprehending me before I set a foot on her property. One finger points at me. "How could you?"

"Simmer down, Polly, I didn't—"

"You colluded."

She's got me on that one. "I talked with Roger, sure. But I told him we wouldn't—"

"Give them back."

"Polly, I don't have them."

Her mouth begins to quiver, a word I'd heard but never before actually seen happen. As the realization dawns on her that her cats are long gone, she begins to make disjointed utterances, and I worry that she's having some kind of seizure or stroke. Then she pulls herself back from the brink. "Why, Cooper? Why did he take all of them?"

Somewhere in my training, there must be a protocol for this. But if there is, I don't recall it. I reach out and pat her shoulder, a pat that becomes a full body hug as she throws herself against me. Her weeping is dampening the front of my uniform.

"I want to press charges."

"For what?"

"Catnapping."

I literally bite my tongue against an inappropriate chuckle. "Let's call it feline theft."

"Purr-loined." I can feel her laughter against my chest. A laughter that evaporates pretty quickly. Roger is a shit.

"Make me a cup of tea, will you, Polly?"

The yellow dog is sitting in the backseat. His head is framed by the window; he is looking at us with a curious expression of concern. As he's regained his body mass, the wrinkles around his face have become expressive instead of simply too loose skin.

"That the dog you rescued from the woods?"

"Yeah. He look at all familiar to you?" I ask everyone I meet this question.

"Maybe. Lots of yellow Labs in Harmony Farms."

"What about the Haynes?" Polly is one of those rare people whom the Haynes brothers seem to like. She's hired them for years to do her odd jobs.

"I don't think they go in for purebreds, but maybe. If somebody gave it to them, say. Why don't you go ask them?"

Oh, I will.

The dog in the back of my truck is not just a mystery; he's a crime. Or, rather, a crime victim. If he were a human being, the cops would be all over this, trying to find the perpetrator and bring him to justice. To me, it's obvious that someone abused this animal, certainly left him for dead, even may have actively tried to kill him, and here I am, treating him like a regular old lost dog, albeit one who needs more care than most, and, as with the rest of the unclaimed freight languishing in my kennel, I think that my main job is to find a new home for him. I've missed the big picture. Just because the victim is a dog, there is still a bad guy out there needing punishment. This line of thinking gets my juices flowing. I'll deal with this. I'll figure it out, and breathe a little life into my job.

With no tag and apparently no chip—Max hasn't picked up the other reader from his colleague, too busy with his plans, I guess—I'm going to have to figure out another way to find this dog's owner. Jenny's done the social-media posts and we've looked at registrations to see if any yellow Labs about this guy's age have been licensed in the past year. I have a list that is a starting point, but my gut tells me that anyone who would do something like this isn't going to have been inclined to register his dog. And that surely smacks of Haynes.

It gives me a nostalgic feeling to think that, as a dog officer, I am still, in some small way, an enforcer of the law. It's all I ever wanted to be. From earliest childhood, I wanted to be a cop. Every consecutive Halloween until high school, when I hung out with a group that inclined toward dressing like thugs, I dressed up as a policeman. Squirreled away in some shoe box that I've carried around since forever is a snapshot of me in my miniature uniform, plastic badge pinned on my chest, hat positioned perfectly on my crew-cut head. Unsmiling, like a true officer of the law. All business. Thinking about investigating this crime reminds me of all those make-believe games I played as a kid. The sweetness of pretend because you were always successful. Fearless and successful. Bad guys didn't try to blow you up in those days. You never failed to pull the trigger.

"What do you say, fella? Want me to bring your assailant to justice?"

The dog, typically, says nothing. Not even a whimper. Not even the comforting sound of his tail thumping on the car seat.

Well past Halloween, a little boy dressed in a well-loved policeman's costume comes into the kitchen, the scent of peach pie imbuing the room with a sweet warmth. The ancient wood and kerosene range is fired up, and his mother is lifting pies out of the deep and mysterious cavern of the oven. The man they have always called Uncle Deke is at the kitchen table, a cup of coffee already in front of him, his fingertips splayed against the mug.

"You ever need anything, you or the boys, you come to me." The old farmer reaches out and takes Cooper's mother's right hand, shaking it so that she meets his eye. "Hear me?" Cooper is a little scared by the force of Uncle Deke's quietly spoken words, the fact that he's grasping Mona's hand. He can't fathom what their old friend means. If they needed milk? A ride someplace? Cooper needs new shoes, and he wonders if Uncle Deke is offering to buy him new ones. He's done things like that before, arriving with groceries and saying that he over-bought, that he'd take it as a favor if Mona would take some of the extra cans and jars, these gifts coinciding most times with Bull's absence. When Cooper's mother would cry in her bedroom when she thought the boys were outside.

"You don't have to put up with this. His parents may have been my dearest friends, but I don't mind saying . . . "

"I can take care of myself, Deke Wilkins. But I appreciate your kindness." Cooper's mother sets a piece of too-hot peach pie in front of Deke and the filling slides out from under the crust, coloring the white plate. "I'm not going to be here, me and the boys, when he gets out."

"I've got room, Mona. It's a big house for one old man."

"No. But thank you. It wouldn't be right to put you in that position, you being like Bull's own family."

At that moment, Jimmy comes through the back door, bringing in with him the cold late-afternoon air; a finger of breeze chills the back of Cooper's neck a moment before Jimmy knocks the toy policeman's cap off his head.

"Yeah, Deke. It's Cooper. Thought I might come by this afternoon." I know that I'm shouting into my phone, but the old farmer has grown increasingly deaf. "You need anything? I haven't seen you around much."

"No. I'm fine."

I hope that this is true. Deke's of the old-school Yankee mentality. Wouldn't ask for a Band-Aid if he was bleeding to death.

"See you soon." I sign off and decide to ignore Deke's assertion that he doesn't need anything. I'll take over a few supplies. Maybe get him a peach pie. It'll help assuage the flicker of guilt that I have regarding my real reason for paying this call. I need to make sure that Deke's aim wasn't better than what he admits to and that he didn't, in fact, hit the dog that he chased away from his chickens.

Jenny is back in with a pair of setters that I've taken custody of recently. Sad case. Their elderly owner dropped dead and the dogs were left alone until some neighbor realized he hadn't see the old man for days. They'd stood guard over him, loyal to the end.

Working with a setter rescue, she's lined up a potential foster home for them. I am amazed at Jenny's network and how she seems to have the confidence of every breed-specific rescue group within a three-hundred-mile radius. This potential foster couple are an hour away and Jenny has volunteered to check them out for the rescue group. I have to note that she's volunteering her time, but it's during regular work hours, and as she's worked hard to find the right situation for these orphaned dogs, I've signed off on this junket as being part of the job.

I go into the kennel room to fish the yellow dog out of his cage.

Just once I wish he'd not look at me as if I'm the Grim Reaper, shrinking against the wall, tail tucked. I have to confess that I'm getting a little impatient. If you could have two thoroughly opposite dogs, it would be my magnificent and brave Argos and this, well, yellow, dog. One inspiring, the other despairing.

Argos never lacked for courage. It was as if he were a structure built around a solid core of bravery. I'll tell you what: There were moments in our career when I was the one who was afraid. You might say, yeah, sure, he didn't know that there was an AK-47 behind one of those hollow-core doors, or that he didn't have the intellect to be worried. You'd be wrong. But his courage under fire, or his determination to track down his man, would often fire up my own rectal fortitude and persistence. I never wanted to let that dog down. I knew that, like a human partner, maybe even more than a human partner, he had my back. A human partner can disappoint; a canine cannot. A human partner can make the wrong call. A human partner can fail.

I finally manage to get my patient out of his cage and into my truck. Because of his wound and his stubborn reluctance, I have to lift him onto the backseat, and his reaction is always like I'm about to throw him over a bridge. Ensconced on the rear seat, he heaves a great sigh and settles down. At least he's not the kind of truck dog that hangs his head out the window and barks at everything. I'll give him that. It's actually almost easy to forget that he's back there.

In exchange for the junket on company time, Jenny's agreed to do the night check for me. I'm driving away, thinking that I'm a free man, my evening is my own, and that I intend to pull one of those "Hey, I have a thought" pseudoimpulsive calls on Natalie. I'm hungry, she's hungry, and it's two-for-one night at the Lakeside. What'd you say? Not a date. Definitely not a date. I continue to be of the opinion that Natalie would prefer that to a standard date. Just sayin'. She's an interesting mix of hot and cold. Totally wonderful and then doesn't return texts. I'm not looking for anything big and scary, but a little encouragement might be nice.

A fresh, still warm peach pie is beside me as I arrive at Deke's. His place has that early-November look about it, russet leaves on the ground from the line of ancient oaks that border his drystone wall, the big pasture a mix of wheat-colored tall grass and short emerald green last-of-the-year growth. His pair of milk cows are recumbent, idly chewing their cuds, contemplating whatever it is that cows think about. Deke's chickens are behind bars 24/7 ever since the advent of coyotes in the area, and I kid him about no longer being able to sell his birds as free-range ones.

It is a quintessentially pastoral scene, up to and including the wisp of smoke that is rising from the foursquare center chimney of Deke's eighteenth-century house. Except for the 2011 Nissan truck in his driveway, it could be a scene from two hundred years ago. It makes you think about why folks like Deke and Elvin, and maybe even me, get frustrated with the influx of newcomers bent on taking the bucolic nature of Harmony Farms and making it suit their needs. Deke's been making a subsistence living on this land all his life, and his family before him, back to the first influx of newcomers, who, admittedly, pushed the original inhabitants into a war. I guess that's just the way of the world. No one much likes the imposition of change.

Deke comes out of his barn, followed by his old dog, adding to the sense that I've driven back in time, this time only as far back as the mid-1950s. Trucker cap, heavy green duck-cloth coat, jeans so faded and stained that only a trace of their original blue shows, knee-high black rubber boots. Scowl. It's like I've come home. "Hey, Deke."

"Hey yourself. That a pie?"

"Peach."

"I won't say you shouldn't have. Come in. I'll fix some coffee."

I fall in behind him, and I can't help but notice the rocking side-to-side gait that suggests the old man's hips or knees or back are slowing him down. Once again, it occurs to me that, with no kids and no help, he's going to be forced into a hard decision sooner rather than later. My grandparents would be in their late eighties if cancer hadn't gotten my grandmother and heart disease my granddad. Deke and my grandparents were in eighth grade together, which was as much education as they were offered in Harmony Farms in those days, so I know that he's very definitely in his eighties, maybe even in his nineties, so I guess you could say that he's not doing so bad. Still bucking hay bales and shoveling manure. Riding his tractor into the fields and planting corn. I kind of hope that he simply drops dead in his barn or out in his pasture before he's faced with having to sell up because he physically can't cope with the farm anymore. Too bad there's no one to leave this chunk of paradise to, a thought that really saddens me.

Deke may be an octogenarian farmer, but he's got a fancy single-cup coffeemaker and plants a cup of high test in front of me within a minute of my coming into the house. He makes his, sits down, and says: "What's on your mind, son?"

"Just paying a call." I fork a hunk of pie into my mouth.

"Right. And the queen of England is on my social calendar for bridge."

"I just wanted to see how you're doing out here."

"Same as always. Sitting up and taking nourishment."

"Haven't seen you at Elvin's."

"I been there." He takes a bite of pie, admits, "Maybe sticking a little closer to home. Most of the old crowd are gone. Dead or gone to assisted-living hellholes. Even Elvin's gone to Florida."

"Since when?"

"You're not a very observant officer of the law. He's been gone since last month."

"Hey, I'm just the dogcatcher here. And, speaking of dogs, come out with me and take a look at the one I've got in the back of my truck." Nice segue, Cooper.

Like a good guest, I take my plate to the sink, swallow the last of my coffee, and wait for Deke to shrug back into his ancient jacket. He gives his sleeping collie the command to stay. I'm not sure she is even aware of our leaving.

We stand in front of the open truck door, staring at the dog, who has pushed himself upright. In his eyes is the seemingly permanent look of worry at the approach of two men, one of whom has been attending to his every need for weeks. The dog's brown eyes won't meet ours; he turns his head sideways, as if to pretend we aren't there.

"Any chance you've seen this dog before?"

"Nope. Never. Ones like him, but not this one."

"Might have been a lot bigger; he's been feral for a while, down to skin and bones when I captured him."

"Nope. Can't say I've ever seen him."

"Okay. "

"Why are you asking me?"

"What about that dog you saw poking around the chicken coop. You fired at him, didn't you?"

"I told you before, I didn't hit him. And that dog, well, I still don't know if it was a dog. Too dark to see and he moved too fast."

"Okay. Just had to ask."

Deke nods his head, then juts his whiskery chin in the direction of the dog. "Looks like a nice dog, though. Skinny, but nice."

"He's better than he was." Who am I kidding? The dog has tried very hard to become one with the backseat, shrinking himself as best he can against the opposite back door.

I close the door and follow the old man back into the house, where the sleeping dog rouses herself enough to wag her tail. Given that Deke's place was a sanctuary of sorts for me when I was a kid, I haven't spent near enough time here since I came back. I'm hungry for another piece of pie and I think that Deke is hungry for the company. Or maybe that's me.

At any rate, I've given myself the rest of the day off and he's grateful for an extra hand with the cows.

It's a two-edged sword, having someone know you for your entire life. On the one hand, there are no mysteries. It's all just hanging out there. On the other, there's no shield against probing personal questions.

"How come you're still here, Coop?"

"Don't feel like going home." I dump the bucket of feed into the trough in front of his dry cows. They're old girls, living out their natural lives in this small paradise of Deke Wilkins's farm.

"That's not what I mean, and you know it. I mean, why aren't you back to work, your real work?"

"I still have ringing in my ears."

"They don't have any desk jobs on that force?"

"I don't want a desk job."

"So, when the ringing stops, you'll go back?"

He means go back to the K-9 unit. Deke was enthusiastically supportive of my decision to join that unit after several years as a patrolman. He told me it was a natural fit. He even came to our graduation, beaming like a real grandfather as Argos and I received our commission.

I don't answer, as if, due to this oft-cited tinnitus, I can't hear his question.

"You were a good cop, Cooper. It was your dream, wasn't it? Why'd you give it up so easy?"

"It wasn't easy."

"You fell off your horse. Get back on."

"No sir." He's not the first to use that shopworn adage. I didn't fall off a horse; I was blown apart.

Deke pats his knee and his collie moseys over. I don't want to be angry with Deke, but he's got me pretty riled. So I say something that's really none of my business, but I want to let him know that we all have things we give up.

"You weren't always a bachelor, were you?"

"Never married. That's a bachelor."

"But you were engaged. I remember hearing about it. My mother was talking to someone about it."

"Then you know what happened."

"She died, didn't she?"

"Don't. It's not the same, and don't you dishonor her by comparing Isabel's death with that of a dog."

Argos wasn't just any dog. "I'm just saying that sometimes the pain of loss becomes fear. The fear of loss."

But Deke's gone, his old Border collie trailing along behind him.

I should go in, apologize, but I don't. I climb into my truck and drive away.

26

Since Jimmy is apparently uninterested in getting his own place, it seems to Bull like it might be kind of nice to have some Christmas decorations up at the old place. It's been donkey's years since he did so much as hang a wreath on the door, much less drag some unfortunate balsam out of the woods and prop it up against the living room wall. It's been just him here, alone on Poor Farm Road, the scratching of the mice in the walls keeping him from being entirely by himself as he watches marathons of *It's A Wonderful Life* or *A Christmas Story*.

Even when Jimmy and Coop were still kids, they didn't do much in the way of celebrating the holidays. Bull would give Jimmy a few bucks in an envelope. The kid might buy him a pack of smokes; well, maybe not *buy* exactly, but would hand him a crisp pack on Christmas morning. And Cooper, jeez, that kid. He was the kind of kid who wanted to believe in Santa and, all evidence to the contrary, never quite got over the hope that some Christmas morning, that spindly tree in the living room might have that new bike under it. And that line of thinking gets Bull to chuckling. He did manage to get a bike under the tree one year, one that he "found" in the open garage of one of those new houses down the street. Nice BMX. Sweet ride. Jeez, the look on Cooper's face when the cops took it back.

Crane's sells trees and wreaths. Maybe he can get a good discount on a little one. Dress it up with popcorn and spray-painted pinecones. Bull has a vague memory of construction paper chains by the yard, projects both boys did when they were real little. Before things got really bad, before his demons stole the life he had hoped to live back in the day when he and Mona were courting and the draft was the only threat to their happiness.

Aw, Mona. My beautiful Mona. She dazzled the eye. She dazzled his eyes. Tall and slender, a body made for the low-slung bell-bottoms and flower-power shirts. Blond hair as perfectly straight and long as a model's. It swished every time she turned her head, and Bull teased her into turning her head just so he could hear the sound. Her hair smelled of lemons; she smelled of Jean Naté. She had those clear gray eyes that her sons would inherit. Bull had admired Mona from afar all his life, from kindergarten, where she was the popular girl, the one that all little kids gravitated around for games. In middle school, where she was the first girl most of the boys had a crush on, and where she was the fashion arbiter for the rest of the girls in their class. To high school, where, miraculously, she noticed him and pulled him to his feet at the homecoming dance. Not that Bull hadn't enjoyed a certain amount of popularity himself. Big, strong, athletic, and funny, he had never lacked for friends or girlfriends. The girls told him he was handsome, and, well, maybe he was. Thick hair the color of oak, fashioned into an earnest rendition of Elvis's pompadour, the strong square-cut jaw that would be his legacy to his sons. Together, he and Mona cut a swath through the high school.

Bull misses that Mona, the one who looked at him with happy eyes. Not the one who she became, sad and defeated.

"You can't keep doing this." Mona stands in the doorway of the house on Poor Farm Road. He can see Jimmy behind her; Cooper is hitched to her hip. She looks like that Depression-era picture, the woman who looks old but probably isn't, sitting in front of her tumbledown house, kids with hungry faces around her, worry working ugliness on her face. He'd quit his job again. Plenty of good reasons, but he knows that Mona will say the biggest reason is the drink. Which isn't true, not this time. She's wrong. Nonetheless, he knows it is possible that she will finally make good on her threat to leave him if he loses another job. But, technically, he hasn't lost the job; he gave it up—before he got fired. Bull might be working his way through every low-level job in town, but he has his dignity, so it doesn't matter to him that the job, sanitation worker, had come with the first health benefits he had ever brought home as part of a job. First time his wife could take the kids to the doctor for any minor sniffle and be proud to hand over that insurance card like anyone else. Well, shit, he'll find another job with benefits. That was the benefit, pun intended, of quitting before getting fired. His terms. All the way home Bull had thought about what he was going to tell Mona, what spin he was going to put on the tale of high dudgeon and dignified resignation.

"Just tell me that they gave you a reference." Mona shifts Cooper to her other hip.

"Hey, we'll be all right. The Highway Department has an opening."

"Not for a quitter. For someone who maybe applies for it, for a department transfer maybe. I just don't understand you, Bull. I just can't keep doing this."

"It was their fault." Bull wants to launch into his grievances, shift out of the role of screwup to that of aggrieved victim, but Mona won't hear it. She shuts the door of his own house in his face. He doesn't carry a key, so he's left banging on his own front door, pleading with his wife to let him in. It's cold out. It's going to rain. He doesn't deserve this. He's the man of the house. In moments, the door opens and Mona, dragging a black trash bag behind her, shoving the two boys ahead of her, walks out of his house without a word.

"Where you going, Mona?"

She doesn't answer, just shoves the bag into the backseat of the Nova and hurries the boys along with a frantic gesture, as if she's afraid Bull will chase them. Cooper is crying, upset at a situation he cannot begin to understand. But Jimmy, who's maybe four years old, stares at Bull with those hard crystal eyes. Without a word, Mona slams the door and guns the Nova out of the yard. Jimmy is kneeling on the backseat, looking at his father through the rear window. As Mona pauses long enough to let a passing car go by before she peels out of their driveway, Bull can see his elder son, his childish fist raised in an eloquent gesture of disdain, a single middle finger extended.

It wasn't so many years ago when he and Mona had made that kid in the back of that car. Back when he was first home from Vietnam, back when the only thing in the world Bull wanted was a good night's sleep and to be held in the arms of this beautiful woman.

Funny how just thinking about Christmas trees can bring the early days to mind. There's a lot Bull has forgotten, or maybe stored away in some unreachable corner of his mind. Or forgotten because he was so blind drunk that he never stored the memories like a normal person. She came back that time, and he thought that she always would, once she got over her mad; once she discovered that even a bad husband was better than no husband. Not crawling back, though. It was never like that. She'd just show up, the kids a month or two older, she a little calmer, standing in his kitchen like she'd never left. He'd go back to meetings and she'd let him sleep with her. They even tried having another kid, like that would fix what was wrong, but it never happened. But it was good, those times when Mona came back, to sleep beside the one person he couldn't live without. To have someone there to wake him from his nightmares and not ask him to talk about them.

Bull sets his Raleigh against the back of the lumber shed and pulls on his deerskin gloves. He goes over to where the Christmas trees are displayed, studies them for a moment, and then picks out a skinny six-footer, gives it a little shake, watches the needles rain down. It'll do. He walks the tree back to his bike without wondering how he's going to get a six-foot tree home by bicycle.

Jimmy is at the house when Bull finally gets home. It was a long, awkward walk from work to home with a bicycle and a Christmas tree, and any number of times Bull thought about abandoning one or the other along the road. He called Jimmy about every quarter mile to see if his son was around and could come get the tree. Jimmy never answered the phone, and Bull figured that he must have forgotten to charge it, or had it off. Neither excuse held water, but Bull always prefers to give folks the benefit of the doubt. Jimmy is pretty much attached to that phone, like he was to his security blanket back in the day. Bull remembers throwing the filthy thing into the fireplace to burn it. The kid threw a fit, screaming and crying and carrying on. Well, now he's got a new toy, and no one would dare separate him from it. "It's my office," he told Bull. "My workplace."

"Hey, you got that thing off?" Bull drags the tree in by the stump, sprinkling pine needles behind him. "I been calling you."

Jimmy holds the phone up, waggles it. It's a different phone. Bull can see the difference between the fancy phone Jimmy usually uses and this one. And even Bull knows what Jimmy has in his hand is what they call on TV "a burner." Disposable. Untraceable.

Bull sets the tree, sticky with pine pitch, against the wall. It's going to take Lestoil to get the pine tar off his hands, and he has no idea if he has any. In the meantime, he has to remember not to touch anything, lest it stick to him.

After supper Bull goes up to the attic to try to find some ornaments for the tree.

"What are you doing?" Jimmy's sudden appearance startles Bull from his attic search. All he can see is Jimmy's head; the rest of him is on the rickety foldout attic steps.

"Looking for the ornaments." He's been through the two upstairs rooms, rummaging through boxes and trunks that have been up there since he himself was a kid, finding nothing remotely ornament-like.

Jimmy laughs like the Grinch. "Right. And I'll just get the mulled cider going. Ornaments. Anything we ever had as kids is long gone. Used to keep them in the shed out back and, don't you remember, one year you decided that we'd been so bad, you'd just use 'em for target practice?"

Bull doesn't remember doing that. He does remember Jimmy being so angry one day that the kid went into the shed and smashed everything in it with his baseball bat. He doesn't even bother wondering why Jimmy has a completely different memory. As a kid, even a little kid, Jimmy liked to break things, and sometimes after smashing a pal's radio-controlled car or Cooper's rabbit cage—who knows what happened to the two rabbits—Jimmy would have no idea he'd done it. He wasn't faking it; the kid really did black out some of these violent acts. Not all of them, though. He'd own up to one or two a year, like the time he took a baseball bat to the principal's headlights. He'd owned up to that one because it made him a hero in his pals' eyes, but mostly he'd deny any wrongdoing. He'd look at Bull with those clear gray eyes and say, "No sir, I have no idea what happened." He was a cute kid, almost pretty, and it was painful to believe he was capable of such anger. Of course, after Mona died, he stopped being pretty. And his behavior went from delinquent to criminal.

"Guess I'll have to go to the Dollar Store and see what I can get," Bull says.

"You do that. Why not buy a big inflatable Santa while you're at it." Jimmy's laughter is infectious, and Bull laughs, too, but it doesn't feel jolly.

It was a busy night last night, two customers tapping on the front door. Furtivelike. Tap, uh, tap. On his way to the front door, Jimmy told Bull to go to his room, like he was the kid and Jimmy was the dad. "Stay there," he said. "Don't come out and turn up your TV loud. This is private."

"Bullshit." That's what Bull said, and left his room to amble down the hallway to the bathroom, right past the kitchen. Jimmy had said he was on Weight Watchers. That's why he'd gotten the scale. Right. And Bull was born yesterday. Skinny guy arrived first, dressed in nice clothes, shiny shoes, with only a thin ridge of mud on them from the front yard. Second guy wasn't a guy. Bull didn't need to go to the bathroom when she arrived, but she was so nervous that her voice carried, a high-pitched, nervous voice trying to sound not nervous, but experienced. Jimmy's quick, "We don't need any conversation" silenced her. Jimmy always said he was having a client stop by. Jimmy, Bull knew, was back in business.

It would be easy to blame Mona for the way Jimmy turned out. What kid might not be forgiven for going bad when his mother upped and died on him when he was at such a vulnerable age; what was he, thirteen? But the fact is, Jimmy was always a difficult child. From birth, if you want to believe it. Defiantly refusing to sleep, using his baby toys as weapons, smacking his parents with rattles and teething rings, yanking the cat's tail not like some normal kid, but really wanting to pull that tail out by the roots. Biting anyone and anything that got in his way.

"So, you want me to take you to get some decorations? I could use a run to the mall."

"That would be great. Yeah." Bull grins at the unexpected offer. You just never know with Jimmy. That's what makes him dangerous.

27

"Any luck with that list of dog licenses?" Natalie hands me two flakes of hay. "Toss those to Silky."

I get a kick out of how Natalie seems to think I know the names of all these horses. I don't, but I have noticed that every stall has a dry-erase board with names and instructions, so I find the right one and toss in the hay. It's lovely to be in the animal-fueled warmth of the barn. They're all sporting blankets, plaids and solid blues or reds. Dignified black for the handsome gelding Natalie rides. The mare I ride—Moxie—is dressed in girlie pink. Frankly, if she was my horse, I'd get her one of those plaid blankets. It's such a silly thought that I have to smile at myself. I've never thought about dressing animals. Weird. Except for his bulletproof vest, Argos was au naturel at all times.

"Not much." Actually, none at all. I've called everyone on the list who had a male yellow Labrador registered in the last year, and although I've had a lot of pleasant conversations, no one has a missing animal. At least no one has admitted to it. "Next step is that I'll start with a couple of assumptions and then move on. Assumption number one: This is a hunting dog and his owner was hunting; ergo, there should be a permit. With a little digging, I might come up with a few names to look at."

"That sounds a little like a needle in a haystack to me."

"Perhaps. A lot of police work falls under that category. It's not all guns blazing and heroic rescues. Assumption number two is that there is a microchip between those shoulders and assumption number one can be vacated."

Natalie hands me another pile of hay. "I'm not going to ask why you're numbering your assumptions in such a strange order. But I will ask why Max hasn't already checked to see if the dog has a chip."

"When the dog was first brought in, we were too concerned with fixing him to remember to do it. And then, when we did, we found out that Max's reader pings only on a certain kind of chip. He borrowed one from another practice, and that one was broken. Now he's so wrapped up in getting ready for his new job, he's hardly around. He's basically closed the practice until the new vet arrives."

"It makes me so nervous not having a vet close by. I just hope that the new vet is good with horses. Not every veterinarian deals with large animals."

"I can't imagine that Max would ever hand his practice over to someone who handles only small animals. Half his practice is equine and bovine." I take the armful of hay and drop it into Moxie's stall.

I'm here to pick Natalie up for dinner. The weather has been better and I've had a few more riding lessons, a couple more casual dinners at the tavern. I feel like we're slowly sculpting the definition of our relationship. Sometimes she's my instructor; sometimes she's my friend.

We've gotten a little exotic and are heading an hour down the highway to Boston to a North End restaurant, so we're wearing actual dress-up clothes. This time, we both agree it's a real date. She's in black silk pants and I'm in my chinos, and now we're littered with hay. I pluck a stem out of her hair; she brushes chaff off the sleeve of my blue jacket—a possessive gesture.

I've cleaned up my truck for the occasion so that we don't have to worry about dog hair on our nice clothes. The yellow dog is in my cabin, with a bowl of water and a warm bed, and he's been medicated for the night. I'm sure that he'll be fine alone for the very first time. Shoot, he'll probably finally relax. I'll be home, if this date goes south, by ten. If it turns into a good night, I'll be home around midnight, and I'm sure he can hang on till then. At the very least, he's definitely housebroken. A tiny little bell rings in my head and I think that might be my tinnitus: *Put him in the shelter. No,* I say to the little voice in my head, *he'll be fine.*

The best way to get from Natalie's farm to the main highway is by taking Poor Farm Road. I won't point out the family homestead, but I do slow as we go by; this is where the road narrows, and for some reason deer like to play roadside roulette at this point in the route. In the house, the overhead living room light is on and there is a bulky form in the window. It takes me a second to realize it's a tree. An undecorated, unlit Christmas tree. In the yard is a car I assume is Jimmy's. Behind it is a black Lexus, angled in such a way you know that the driver isn't planning on staying but for a minute. I can't help it: I slow even more, as if I expect that the backup lights are going to go on at that moment. It's just a lucky guess, but they do, and I let the Lexus back out of the driveway, as if I'm a good neighbor. Then I think about following it. Natalie seems unaware of my little game. She's still chatting about her success with some arcane movement with her gelding. Renvers? I am surprised, however, when the Lexus makes the next right-hand turn into Poor Farm Estates. Hmm.

Bull's isn't the kind of place anyone would choose to stop by to get directions, and in this day and age of GPS and navigational devices, there's no chance that anyone would mistake the muddy driveway of 179 Poor Farm Road as the entrance to Poor Farm Estates. Too late for trick or treat, and too dark for Jehovah's Witnesses. In my overactive but police-trained imagination, it's way more likely that it's one of Jimmy's buyers or suppliers come to call. Someone who lives nearby.

I must have hmm'd out loud, because Natalie says, "What?"

"Nothing." Nothing at all. I really should stop this nonsense.

Villa Rosa is one of those Italian restaurants that is unprepossessing on the outside, a basic storefront with philodendron plants filling the window, but when you're inside it's like being in a neighbor's dining room, if one's neighborhood was in northern Italy. I've been going there since I was introduced to the Villa Rosa by a classmate in the Police Academy whose parents were friends with the owners. Villa Rosa is small enough to be intimate, which is a good thing, unless you happen to be seated very close to someone you'd rather not be near. The hostess leads us to our reserved table for two right beside my ex-wife and her boyfriend.

My first and probably best instinct is to back up, tell Natalie that I've changed my mind, that we should eat French, not Italian, but the moment comes upon us too quickly and the space is too tight for a graceful exit.

She is seated facing us; her gentleman friend has his back to me. "Cooper. Hello." The moment she says my name, Rudy gets to his feet. He's about my height, but not in good shape. I could take him if I had to. He's one of those pale types, thinning sandy hair, blue eyes, no definition to his jaw, a little saggy but not bad-looking. We've met before—at our divorce hearing, Gayle's and mine. Rudy was being "supportive."

There is that drawing-room-drama moment of how to introduce everyone. What are we to one another? Gayle and me. Natalie and me. Rudy and me.

Natalie takes over by offering Gayle a hand. "Natalie Everett." She's ingeniously vague about who she is in my life.

"Gayle." A two-beat pause. "O'Neal." That's not going to clarify things. "This is Rudy Verdick." I notice she doesn't give Rudy a
playing position. These women are two very good chess players.

"I'm a little surprised to see you here," I say. I'm looking around
to get the hostess's attention. There's no way I'm spending my first
actual date with Natalie almost knee-to-knee with my ex-wife.

"I don't know why you should be. Unless you've forgotten that
it's my favorite place."

I bite back some smart remark about who got custody of this place
and every other restaurant we both liked.

Natalie pulls out her own chair, sits down side by side with Gayle.
I'm pretty sure she's figured out who Gayle is. She immediately flashes
Rudy a big smile, both of them costars in this marital play.

"Hey, Nat, let's go someplace else." I'm not sitting down next to
Rudy on a bet.

"No need. We're done here." Gayle stands up, swivels her way
out from behind the round table with just enough motion in the swivel
to remind me of what I've left behind. Maybe *forfeited* is a better word.

Rudy hasn't said a word. He offers a tepid handshake, goes off
in pursuit of their coats.

Gayle lingers. "So, tell me, Cooper, are you enjoying your job as
a dogcatcher?"

"I prefer the term *animal control officer.*"

"Of course you do."

Rudy returns with her coat, holds it open like a proper gentleman. Gayle slips her arms into the sleeves. "Natalie, so nice to meet
you."

"It's been very nice meeting you." Natalie wears the delighted
look of a woman about to interrogate a man.

I sit down as soon as they vacate the space. "I am so sorry."

"What did you ever do to her?" Natalie takes up her menu.

"I failed her as a husband."

"Oh. I had no idea that's who . . . " By the way that she flushes,

I don't entirely believe that Natalie hadn't figured out who Gayle is. I know that Natalie wants more. I'd certainly want more of the story if I were her.

"Good evening, folks. May I interest you in a glass of wine?" Our server has arrived, setting the house specialty of warm crusty bread and olive oil to dip it in on the table.

I am very grateful for the performance-art quality of our server, a handsome young man who might be a son of the owner or an Emerson student working his way through college. He distracts what is an awkward silence with his rendition of the specials, rolling the Italian off his tongue as if tasting the food himself. Playing for a little more time to recover from my shock at seeing Gayle, I ask him to repeat them with more detail.

When he leaves, I hand Natalie the basket of bread. "He should be wearing a pencil-thin mustache."

"And a pinkie ring."

I laugh harder than the weak joke deserves, but I am relieved to have hurdled the moment.

Natalie dips her piece of bread in the dish of oil, swirling it in a pretty gesture that spreads the darker balsamic into the oil. "Cooper, I won't pry into the whys and wherefores of your divorce, trust me. It's not that I'm not curious; of course I am. It's that I really hate being asked probing personal questions, so I won't ask any." She takes a strong bite of her bread. "However, I wouldn't mind hearing your public version."

"Irreconcilable differences. I stopped being the man she married. I have been, since Argos, I've been . . . " This is not easy. I've never used the word before out loud other than in a clinical setting. "I've suffered from depression. It kind of runs in the family." I'm not sure that's true, but, having endured the black dog, I think that it's likely that my mother also did. "But I'm better now. I think."

"Argos. Nice name for a dog."

This from Natalie makes me smile. "From Odysseus."

"You were supposed to get over it."

"Yes."

"I get that." She keeps her eyes down. "We're really allowed to grieve for only a little while nowadays. We don't go from black to lavender like the Victorians. We're expected to compartmentalize, not to offend or disturb others with our unbearable grief."

I reach across the table and take her hand, squeeze it gently, release it. "I won't ask you anything, either. But I am a good listener."

Our plates arrive and I pour us a second glass of the outstanding red.

It's not late when we head back to Harmony Farms. We've had a good meal, walked around and admired the city's holiday lights, held hands. I think that we've had a good time; at least I did after I settled down from having run into Gayle.

Natalie is such a hard read. The silent moment had given way to the set piece of two people enjoying a fine meal, and it wasn't until we were in that satisfied stasis of postprandial and precheck when she finally told me her story. I listened, knowing that, with Natalie, commentary and bluster and a sympathetic show wasn't necessary to prove my interest. She didn't want outrage on her behalf; she only wanted me to know what had pushed her from Wall Street to Harmony Farms.

"I was married." She immediately paused, and I wondered if that was all she was going to say, the past tense enough of a clue that I could make my own conjectures, the most obvious a bad divorce. A beat or two and she went on. "He was killed."

"How?" I gently prompted her, afraid that she wouldn't push herself to give me the story. I figured she'd back out. She was a little like that lazy ex-school horse rehab project of hers, if she didn't give him a little encouragement with her crop, he wouldn't move. Natalie, too, needed a little encouragement.

"Shot to death. By a frightened home owner." She gestured toward her glass and I poured more of the very good red wine into it. "He made the mistake of being black in a white neighborhood. A flat tire and a forgotten cell phone and little option but to knock on a door in broad daylight and hope that he'd be met with human kindness. Instead, he was met with panic and fear and prejudice and a legally owned handgun."

"I am so sorry." I'd heard this story, or stories like it, all too often. "A case of stand your ground?"

"No. Fortunately, this wasn't Florida. I mean, if there can be a fortunate side to it. My husband was dressed in a business suit and not a hoodie, a pair of expensive shoes and a rep tie from his prep school, and was clearly no threat. The shooter was a known hothead; he'd been arrested twice before for threatening neighborhood children. Between the criminal trial and the civil suit that followed, he'll never threaten anyone ever again.

"But the point here is that when I went back to work that first day after my allowable bereavement leave was over, it was business as usual. Forget your personal drama and jump right back into the important drama of buying and selling money, making money. Put your loss behind you, Nat, and let's read some prospectuses. I went into the ladies' room and threw up, then wrote a resignation letter out by hand. I didn't take anything but my photo of Marcus. I walked out."

I hesitated a moment before I reached across the table to take her hand for the second time that evening. I wasn't sure if she'd let me, or if she'd pull it away in a show of whatever the female equivalent of machismo is. She let me take it, squeeze it gently, even though she works too hard for her hand to be soft and fragile, as it must have been back when she was on Wall Street. "How did you get from walking out to owning Second Hope?"

I was rewarded with a genuine smile. "It's more a case of how I ended up on Wall Street when a place like Second Hope had been a dream of mine since I was a little girl in braids riding a fat pony."

She fingered the rim of her glass and I split the remainder of the bottle between us.

On the way home, I again take the shortcut through Poor Farm Road and again I slow as we pass by Bull's house. It's before eleven on a weekend so yet another strange car in the driveway shouldn't be suggestive of anything going on. Except my father has no friends and my brother is hardly likely to be entertaining. No porch light, no lights on at all in the front of the house. No lights on that Christmas tree.

Natalie invites me in. For us it's late, but neither one of us remarks on the time. She lets Betty out and I give the yellow dog a brief thought, quickly deciding that he can hang on another few minutes. I hope so at least. She offers me another glass of wine, but I decline. She offers a cappuccino instead and that sounds good. We are standing in her small kitchen, where traces of her previous life show up in the expensive-looking cappuccino maker. She hands me the tiny cup and we move into the living room, sitting side by side in the embrace of her ultrasoft microfiber-covered sofa, a fabric, she says, that is her second favorite, after polar fleece, being both dog hair– and horsehair-resistant.

My cappuccino is gone in a sip. I set my cup down on the glass and wood coffee table and she does the same. I take her cheek in my palm and she presses her hand against the back of my hand. She feels warm, her cheek and her palm. I lean in to kiss her and her mouth is warm, too, and tastes wonderful.

It's the first time he's been left alone since the man brought him inside. The novelty of it is quite invigorating. Now that the pain is mostly gone from his hip and his other more internal aches and pains are all gone, the dog moves quite ably through the small cabin, sniffing luxuriously at the man's objects—the bed, the clothes dropped on the floor, the shoes. The shoes. He picks up one shoe and mouths it like a puppy does a soft toy. The mouthing is comforting and quickly becomes chewing. The relief of using his jaws is intoxicating, equally entertainment and relaxing.

Midway through the shoe, the dog feels hungry; the chewing has gotten his juices flowing. He drops the shoe and heads into the kitchen area of the cabin, laps water from his bowl and licks the empty dinner dish. He'd been fed, but he doesn't remember when. In his mind, nothing is certain; one meal may have happened, but another may not. Still, the scent of food fills this room, his good nose telling him that behind those doors lies paradise. The man may never come back. Or he may come back and not put food in the bowl. Or he may be replaced by another man. Life's uncertain. Get those cupboard doors open. He scratches at the under-the-counter cupboards, leaving long claw marks. He throws himself against them, and the force of his body blow bounces the door to one of the cupboards open. Ha, ha, ha. Therein lies the bag of kibble that the man has begun to mix into his moist food. He takes the top of the bag in his teeth and pulls. It falls open with a satisfactory thump, scattering the kibble from one end of the room to the other. The yellow dog begins to vacuum up the spill.

Enough with the kibble. There are far more interesting things to investigate. The dog lifts himself up on his hind legs and taps the hanging cupboards with a paw. Like the body blow he dealt the lower cabinets, the force of his big paw bounces the weak magnet keeping the door shut and it pops open. He's got the door open, but he can't reach inside the cupboard for the few items that aren't in cans and unassailable, things like cookies and a box of cereal, another of crackers. The dog stands on the floor on all fours, contemplating the largesse just out of reach. With a grunt and a surge of desire overcoming waning disability, he jumps onto the counter, knocking off a can of coffee and a bowl of sugar. Utensils drying on a dish towel scatter into the sink and onto the floor in a twangy cascade of sound.

A few hours later, back in his basket bed, sated and working now on the other shoe, as happy as he's been in a year, the dog hears the man's truck coming down the track. It doesn't occur to him that he's done anything wrong. He's a survivor, and that's what he's ensured for himself while alone here in this place, his survival.

"Oh my God." The man stands in the open door, his hand still on the light switch. "What have you done?"

The dog shrinks deeper into the protection of his basket. He can sense the change in scent even as the man walks gingerly through the debris field of his cabin. He came in smelling of food and contentment, and a certain kind of animal satisfaction, but that olfactory story has quickly changed to the sharp scent the dog most associates with escalating human anger. He makes himself smaller, hoping that the man won't take out his anger on him. He doesn't know why the man might go from content to angry in a split second, but he's not going to provide a target. He's had that experience before and he's not about to make the mistake of nosing up to an angry man.

"Guess I shouldn't have left you alone."

And then the man makes a sound that the dog hasn't heard come out of him before.

The man laughs.

28

My first thought was that my solitary cabin had been tossed. The scene looked exactly like a botched burglary or a hate crime. Funny how professional experience overrides common sense. Claw marks on the cabinet doors and paper trash strewn all over pointed a pretty convincing finger at my houseguest. I was so tired, so content, I just left the mess and went to bed. It isn't till I get up this morning that I notice my only pair of running shoes have been destroyed. I find one in the bedroom, the other peeking out from under the dog's heavy head, like he's trying to hide the evidence from me. They have been systematically chewed into pulp; the only thing that makes them recognizable as footwear are the soles. I've put a lot of miles on those Nikes and they had a lot of miles left in them. A new pair isn't exactly a budgeted line item in my personal finances for this month.

At least he had the good grace to look ashamed when I came in last night and took in the magnitude of my mistake in assuming that he wouldn't take advantage of being left alone to wreak such havoc on my possessions, ignoring that little voice telling me to put him in the shelter. I guess I didn't think that this dog had it in him. I'd never had a dog that willfully destroyed property before. Then again, except for the brief time Polly let me have Snoopy, I'd only ever had Argos. And my belongings were sacrosanct to him. Another good reason to stay dog-free.

The sugar is gritty and sticky on the wooden cabin floor and there isn't enough ground coffee left in the can to make a cup. I'm not a good candidate for caffeine withdrawal. The kibble is all gone, and if it hadn't been impossible for the dog to get the refrigerator door open, he wouldn't have any breakfast, either. I warm up the rest of the hamburger and rice mix, dump in the contents of his last two capsules of medication, and smile. He's finally done with the meds. I can take him back to the shelter and get him out of my house. Monday. Jenny's on this weekend and I have no interest in going to the shelter even to rid my tossed cabin of the tosser.

"Okay, no running today. But we're going to have to go find coffee." I don't know why I'm telling the yellow dog this; it's not something I've been doing, talking to him, but he is listening to me from a distance, those soulful, guilty eyes not meeting mine. Submission, I know. A dog who meets your eye is challenging you, or trusts you. I suppose submission is a good thing, but I'd love it if, just once, he'd look at me without looking like he expects me to beat him. Jimmy used to smack me because he said he didn't like the look on my face. All I wanted was for him not to hit me.

I clip a leash to the new flat collar the dog is sporting, an impulse buy when I was in the hardware store, and we go out to the truck. I'm still lifting him into the backseat, but now I wonder if I haven't just inadvertently trained him to expect to be lifted. Next time, I'll invite him to jump up. Surely he knows how to do that. After all, he most likely got out here in a truck, a thought that renews my determination to find out who this dog belongs to. As Natalie says, sifting through the Massachusetts Division of Fish and Game's computer records to find someone who might theoretically fit my mental description of the asshole who might have shot his own dog, and assuming my lone contact in that department is willing to give me access, is pretty much a long shot. Like winning that lottery my father insisted would change our lives. There was a time when he substituted the lottery for drinking. I'm not sure we were any better off; the money was still spent. So, I'll leave a message for Max to see if he's finally gotten a working microchip reader. Another gamble, another chance at the lottery.

I lift the yellow dog into the backseat of my truck and race off in pursuit of caffeine. And, having found coffee and lemon squares at the Country Market, I buy two and drive over to Natalie's.

Despite the cold, Natalie is out in her ring, schooling the off-the-track Thoroughbred she calls Lew. He looks like a fire-breathing dragon as jets of frozen breath plume out of his nostrils as she asks him to collect. I can see her breath, too, as she talks to him in both spoken language and the language of seat and hands. Her dog, Betty, greets me, and after a minute's internal debate, I decide to let the yellow dog out to have a little fellowship with his own species. His tail beats from side to side, and I'm surprised at the thrill I get out of seeing it wag. They perform the customary canine greeting, taking turns putting nose to anus, checking out whatever it is dogs check out. Salutations done, Betty gets playful, and the yellow dog goes into a play bow. Against my better judgment, I decide to let him off the leash. I figure either I have half a chance that he'll run off again, which is sort of seeing things glass half-empty, or I'll be pleasantly surprised if he doesn't. I have a moment's trepidation before getting it—Betty will keep him close. And, sure enough, he happily follows Betty as she heads into the relative warmth of the barn.

"I'll be done in a minute; I just want to repeat that movement. He's coming along so well once I get past his stubborn streak." Natalie puts the horse into a canter and I lean on the top rail of the fence. I'm not at all sure what's she's asking for, but all at once she smiles and transitions to a trot, then a walk. She drops the reins, Lew drops his head, and they make a slow circuit, slow enough that I hand her the rapidly cooling paper cup of coffee and she sips it as she cools out a horse in twenty-degree weather. By the time Natalie decides that the horse can stop moving, my feet are numb from standing in one place. She pulls up and dangles her own feet. "The hardest part is getting off once my toes are dead. The rest of me is plenty warm enough."

"I'll catch you." So I do, in a fairly awkward and silly attempt to prevent her from having to hit the ground with frozen feet. I have her in my arms and that feels pretty good, and she lets me kiss her. Then she pulls away to grab the soft, fuzzy blanket hanging over the fence and drape it over the horse, commencing to walk him around and around the ring. We walk together, and I'm holding the hand that isn't holding the horse's reins.

We head into the barn and I greet Moxie, who dangles her head over her stall door. She nuzzles my palm, hoping for treats. Lucky for her, I know where Natalie keeps the mints. I feed her a few, and my hands are warmed by the soft feathers of her breath. The tack room is heated, and I retreat into it to get my own frozen feet thawed while Nat pots around untacking and blanketing the horse. In the time that I've been hanging around Second Hope Farm, it seems to me that horses are mostly about dressing and undressing. Finally, Natalie joins me and we sit enjoying the warmth of the tack room, eating our lemon squares. The room is decorated by the saddles on their wall racks and the collection of bridles dangling from hooks. An umbrella stand shaped like a Chinese vase holds an assortment of crops and whips. The room smells like leather dressing, not a scent I can describe, but one that I associate with things well cared for.

The temperature has dropped further and the early-morning blue has paled to a cottony white. As we head back to the house, I can taste snow in the air. Maybe the weather guy has it right this time; they're predicting the season's first real snowfall tonight.

I realize that I don't see either dog, and Natalie tells me that while

I was thawing out in the tack room, she's put Betty and the yellow dog in the house. "He was a little skeptical about it, but he was cold enough that he finally agreed to go in with her."

"Wait till I tell you what he did." I make the story a lot funnier than it was, make myself out a lot more forgiving than I am. "I hope that Betty is a good-enough chaperone that he hasn't tackled your pantry."

The two dogs meet us at the back door, tails wagging. I take a quick survey of the kitchen, but the only thing out of order is the sloppy-dog ring of water surrounding the water bowl. "Looks like you're safe."

"You really should have known better than to leave a dog with issues alone in the house."

"I know that now and I sure won't make that mistake again. Trouble is, it's going to make his a hard adoption. People don't want destructive dogs. Dogs with *issues*."

"So you are going to adopt him out?" She leans a little on the word *are*. Like she's been entertaining some storybook notion of my keeping the animal.

"Of course."

"Oh."

"Why?"

"I just thought that, well, because of how hard you fought to rescue him, and then keep him alive, that you'd want him."

"No." That sounds so abrupt. I don't really have the words to express why I can't bring myself to ever have another dog. So I fall on the simplest explanation. "I've had my dog."

"So, what does that mean? There's some rule that says you can't have another?"

"I don't want another."

"That I understand. Sort of. But, really, you've devoted such good care to this guy, how can you not be attached?"

"Just doin' my job, ma'am. Doin' my job."

She doesn't smile.

I change the subject posthaste. "I think it's going to snow. What would you say if I suggested we hang out, watch it snow?"

"It's not snowing yet and, as much as I'd love to hang out, I've got things to do."

"How about tonight? I could bring over some of my famous chili."

"I didn't know you were famous for chili."

"Oh, there's lots you don't know about me."

"I'll bet." She's smiling at me, and then she stops smiling, as if she's been caught doing something wrong. She turns away from me, puts one hand up like a traffic cop. "Cooper, this is good, but I need to slow down a little."

"I thought that men are supposed to say that." I want it to sound funny, but it sounds petulant.

"You, too. I mean, we both need to take this a little slower."

Slower? In my view, we've been taking this—whatever it is—pretty damn slow already. "Hey, Nat, it's not rebound; it's been too long, for me, for it to be anything but really liking you. Wanting to be around you."

"Cooper. It isn't rebound for me. It's grief."

I'm put in my place. "Right. I'm sorry. I've been hasty." I get it. Despite what we talked about last night, I know that unless she gives herself permission to get on with her life, her love life, she's never going to be happy again. Or maybe I'm just not the guy to do it.

"Coop, I'm sorry."

"It's okay." To prove it, I hug her and am saddened by her sigh, not of relief, but of something deep within her. It's time for me to go.

It takes a few minutes to get the leash on the yellow dog. As usual, he shrinks away from me, which is embarrassing in front of a woman who rescues animals. I assure Natalie that despite the dog's implication, I really don't eat dogs. This dog is falsely accusing me with his tucked tail. I make a joke of it and am rewarded with her laughter. Finally, just to heap more embarrassment on me, she puts her hand out and the dog goes to her. She hands me the leash. "You really must stop beating him."

"Righto. I'll try to remember that."

"Seriously, you've got to at least make an effort to befriend him. It's clearly not enough to feed and medicate and keep him safe. He's got to learn to trust you. Do you think that mare you ride was always such a love? No way. She came to me so head-shy and nervous that she was a danger to ride. It took me months to earn her trust, and now, here you are, a rank amateur, completely confident on her back."

"I'll do my best." I zip my jacket, pull open the back door. The dog balks at the doorway. Fighting the urge to yank his leash, I say gently, "Come on, fella, time to go. Say bye-bye."

"You know, training exercises are a nice way to bond."

"I'll keep that in mind."

Training exercises. A few rounds of "Sit, stay, heel" are kindergarten compared to the kinds of things Argos and I did together. I don't think she'd toss that out so casually if Natalie really had a clear understanding of the kind of work I did before. She knows the basics—that I was a cop, that I was a dog handler. But she can have no concept of the complexity of partnership I enjoyed with Argos. He wasn't a pet, or even, to use the more politically correct term, my companion; he was my partner, my backup, my wingman. And, yeah, my companion. It's not something that I can talk about. Not now. Maybe not ever. Argos was my one and only. And then I think: Kind of like Natalie and her murdered husband.

The yellow dog traipses behind me, as if using every inch of the six-foot leash to keep his distance. He's not pulling back, or resisting, just keeping distance between us. I open the back door, point. "Up."

He gives me a hangdog look. His root beer–colored eyes, clear now and brighter, are cast down and, despite the frigid temp, he pants, yawns. I speak enough dog to recognize that he's having one of his panicky moments. "Okay. No new tricks today." I heft him into the backseat. I turn around to make a joke of it with Natalie, but her door is closed.

When their mother died, Bull's reaction was to go on the bender of all benders. That was hardly a surprise; he went on benders at the drop of a hat—when the Sox lost the pennant or when things simply got a little tougher than usual, like coping with a rainy day. This time, a single day after the funeral, he gets tossed into the drunk tank, and Jimmy and Cooper pretend that they have an uncle living with them so that they don't get shipped to foster care. They're lucky; in a way, they do have an uncle. Deke Wilkins parks his seldom-used Oldsmobile Cutlass in the front yard of 179 Poor Farm Road to make it look like someone is living with the two boys. Jimmy point-blank refuses Deke's offer of staying with him at his place. They are thirteen and eleven, and Jimmy says that they will be fine alone. That they want to be alone. The boys will wait out Bull's episode, living off food dropped off by neighbors like Polly Schaeffer and the third-grade teacher, Mrs. Bollen. They have food, a roof over their heads. The one thing that no one offers, though, is an explanation of how to live with the loss. Cooper cries for a couple of days, until Jimmy smacks him and tells him to grow up. Cooper never sees Jimmy cry about their mother's death. Even the sudden death of his mother fails to penetrate the hardened heart of that boy. He fends off all attempts at consolation with sharp elbows and by disappearing for hours. As a result, everyone leaves Cooper alone, too.

I do understand Natalie's need to pull back. Grief, after all, is a mercurial element, shape-shifting and breaking off to bury itself in different regions of the heart. Sometimes you just want to go back to normal, stop being the kid everyone feels sorry for. And sometimes you need to crawl into the bedroom closet and cry.

29

They're never going to get here in time. We are completely alone. The big white dog is following me at heel like a shadow. We have tracked down the perp. He is our quarry. Where the fuck is backup? It's dark now, and on this dead-end street, there are no streetlights, so the stars embedded in the night sky are visible, glittering in the cold air. It's so cold, but so beautiful. A night when you might believe in God if you weren't standing outside a crack house, pretty certain that there is someone pointing a weapon in your direction, and your backup wasn't taking forever to arrive. Argos growls. His sharp ears have heard the sound of the back door opening. Our shooter is going to make a break for it.

I swallow the taste of bile. I have no idea what the population is inside that house. The perp could have dashed in for protection, or he's got a posse sitting there, guns drawn. There could be women and children in there, potential hostages, or nothing but rats.

I speak into my radio, keeping my voice low and in control, but I can't hear my own words. They are garbled, as if my tongue is stuck to the roof of my mouth. What I want to say is, "We have the shooter." But what comes out of my own mouth is gibberish. I can't form the words. There is nothing, not even static, to suggest that I am connected. The darkness feels like someone has put a blindfold *over my eyes. I reach out to touch my dog but can't find him. The darkness is liquid; the silence is a weight. But I know that he's there; he's still with me. Finally, the brush of a cold nose touches my hand.*

Something's keeping my reinforcements from getting here. It's just me and my dog. And that's enough. I won't wait; I won't take a chance that this mad man gets away. Argos is backup enough. "Let's go."

In my blindness, deafness, I stumble up stairs and am in a large empty room brightly lighted, bringing sight back to me. It looks like a gymnasium. Mats hang from the walls and ropes dangle from the ceiling. There is a trampoline in one corner and a small child bounces and flips, bounces and flips.

The large form of a man materializes, bulky, misshapen. His face is obscured, blurry, inhuman. I feel a building terror. Argos barks twice. I try to tell him to stay, but again, nothing comes out of my mouth. Without the order to stand down, Argos flies away from me, intent on his man.

With a slow, graceful gesture, the bulky man, bear-shaped and faceless, pulls the detonator.

I wake up screaming, screaming and screaming until I feel a warm, wet nose pressed against my cheek. I clutch the dog around his neck, press my face into his fur, breathe in his wonderful animal smell, and weep with relief. It was all a dream. It was just a terrible dream.

And then, fully awake, I realize that the yellow dog is the dog in my arms, not Argos.

It was the sound that brought the yellow dog into the man's room. Whimpers and moans, meaningless words in his tongue language that weren't meaningless to the dog in their timbre. The man was making the sounds that the dog heard himself make. Usually when the man made noises, the dog sought out his bed, his safe place, and stayed there, head down, tail tucked. But this night, when it was almost no longer night, but graying toward a new morning, there was something in the man's cries that reached into the dog's own experience, and he rose from his basket and stood in the doorway, breathing in the scent of the man's dreams, pungent, sour with distress.

When the man called out in his sleep, his arms reaching out to grasp something that wasn't there, the word he used, the *name* he called—Argos—meant nothing to the dog, except that he knew that it was a name in the way that the man said it, with deep fear, with deeper love. It was like he was being called, although that wasn't his name. Was the man calling him? He'd talked before, but never asked him to *come*. It was a word he knew.

His almost-healed hip creaked a little as the yellow dog tentatively took a step toward the recumbent man. One step, then another. If the man had awakened, looked at him with wide-awake eyes, the dog would have bolted. He aligned himself against the side of the narrow bed, sniffed at the man's sweaty neck, took a careful taste with the tip of his tongue. The man said the name again—Argos— this time with a reverence, a softness in his voice that the dog had never heard him use before. The dog knew that the man wasn't calling him by that word, that name, but it didn't matter. There was enough kindness in that tone that the yellow dog's self-protective fear eased even when the man, in his sleep, flung an arm over his back. The touch was not gentle, his arm in sleep heavy, but the face buried against the yellow dog's neck was warm and wet and harmless. The dog sighed and let himself be hugged, and he found a great comfort in that creature-to-creature touch.

Even when the man woke, the dog remained as he was, pressed into the man's arms, not struggling.

"Come on by the house. I got something for you."

I'm gassing up my truck as Bull comes out of the Cumberland Farms. It's Christmas Eve, a day that pretty much feels like any other

day of the week to me. Not a creature is stirring. The setters are nestled into their new home and for once we don't have any stray cats in
residence, so I've given Jenny the afternoon off. I've been mostly just
hanging around the shelter, catching up on paperwork, basically
dogging it. Too many cups of coffee and a little too much time doing
playful Internet searches on random topics like the weather in Ta-
hiti and what a one-way ticket would cost. Too much is the answer.

"You got plans for the holiday?" Bull is persistent; I'll give him
that.

"Yeah, I do." I don't, but my nonexistent plans don't involve a
family gathering at the Harrison homestead.

"That's good. But come by when you can anyway."

"I will." I hang up the hose and plug in the gas cap. I don't see
Bull's bike and I wonder if he's on foot. I will say this: He's looking
better, and by better I mean a little thinner and a little less unkempt.
His clothes are clean and he's clean-shaven around his mustache.
Guess he's still keeping sober. He's trying. And I know that I will
probably drop by the house, if only for a minute, and that I should
go get some little thing to give him for Christmas.

"That's good. That's good. So, see you later?" He's grinning that
big baby grin of his.

I go into the store to get some milk and bread, and when I come
out, he's leaning into the backseat, petting the dog.

"You got a name for this dog?"

"Nope. His new owners will get to name him."

The truth is, I'm still a little shaken up from finding the dog in
my arms this morning and by how much that gesture of comfort has
touched me. I have no explanation for what happened, only that it
did. I guess you could call it "creature comfort." I almost tell Bull
about it, but I don't. I remember those times, when I was a kid, hearing him crying out in his sleep, wild, anguished sounds that frightened me. Mona would wake him up. I'd hear their voices through
the wall as she kept telling him it was just a dream, just a dream.

I don't want to talk about nightmares; that might just lead to talking about fears. I've had that nightmare before, or ones similar to it—subconscious reenactments of painful memory decorated by random images.

The dog is sitting up, for once not shrinking back against the opposite door. Bull strokes his bony head with his big spatula of a hand. "That's good; he'll be a good dog for someone."

He will. Bull's right about that. With the right family, people understanding of his shyness and shoe-chewing quirks, he'll enjoy a long, happy life. Jenny's in discussions with two potential Labrador rescue outfits. I should let go of the idea of bringing his assailant to justice and just get the poor animal into the adoption pipeline. I would, but that seems so, I don't know . . . unfinished.

Max called me a little while ago to say that he's got another microchip reader and that if I've got a minute, I should drop by, see if the dog is chipped. I'm really hoping that he is. I've struck out with tracking down a hunting license. My one contact at Mass Fish and Game practically laughed me off the phone at my suggestion that their computers could locate, out of all the license holders, one random hunter who might have been in Harmony Farms over the last year. Who did I think they were, CSI Boston? If the microchip doesn't pan out, after the holidays I'll check with the Conservation Commission, which hands out written permission to carefully selected hunters who want to hunt on some of their properties. The odds with that are only a little more in my favor. I could be cold-calling fifty hunters to ask if they'd lost a dog. This is one reason I was never interested in moving up to detective—too many phone calls.

Max isn't alone when we get there. He's got his replacement with him. I am prepared to be nice, but I want her to understand that she's got some big shoes to fill. It's not all kittens and puppies around here. I think of Natalie's remark about not all vets working with large animals. Horses. Max makes the introductions. She's Amanda Davios, DVM. He rattles off her credentials as she takes the dog's leash out of my hands and drags him into the exam room. For some reason, I think of the Cloris Leachman character in *Young Franken-stein*. What was it? Frau Blücher? I expect to hear horses neigh. Like minions, we follow.

"He's looking pretty good. Eyes are much brighter. We'll weigh him before you leave, but he definitely looks less ribby to me. Keep up what you're doing, Coop." Max hands Dr. Davios the new reader.

As she waves it over the dog's shoulders, I feel an excited thumping in my chest. It's like it's tomorrow, Christmas morning, and all I want is to know who shot and dumped this dog.

"Bingo." Dr. Davios is actually pretty when she smiles. "I've got a number."

All I have to do now is call the microchip company and see who's registered to it.

God bless us every one.

The village of Harmony Farms looks pretty, dressed as it is in holiday finery. The planters that in summer are filled with pansies each contain a small Christmas tree, little red-and-gold bows providing daytime interest and, at night, glittering on the verge of tawdry, with tiny white lights. We have learned how to celebrate a secular Christmas, no crèches on the lawn of the town hall, but loads of trees and swags of greens and HAPPY HOLIDAYS! posted everywhere. Even Max's storefront window boasts a massive wreath, eight tiny reindeer climbing diagonally across the center.

I couldn't get a parking space in front of the office, so the yellow dog and I have to walk a half block to reach my truck. He's anxious, panting in the cold December air, but there's no avoiding this short walk down a sidewalk crowded with last-minute shoppers. He's not a tugger; he's more a lag behinder. "Come on, dog. Pick up the pace a little. I've got things to do." Top of the list, call the dog-finder company. He suddenly goes belly-down, literally trying to crawl away from oncoming foot traffic. I haul him to his feet.

I'm embarrassed to be seen by Donald Boykin, embarrassed to look like a dog officer without patience, and am relieved when he walks into the next store he comes to. Lucky Cynthia. Her husband has just gone into Harmony Farms' version of Victoria's Secret: Mandy's House of Lingerie. Funny, Cynthia doesn't look like a garter belt kind of girl. I've heard it said that Mandy's caters to a, shall I say, *Fifty Shades* kind of client.

Finally, the yellow dog agrees with me that moving toward the truck is the better idea, and he pulls me along with a new strength. I have to wait for Bob Haynes to climb into the passenger side of his truck before I can open my door and lift the dog in. He nods to me. For a Haynes, that's tantamount to a conversation. I nod back. Once in the backseat, the dog squeezes himself into the right-side foot well.

The dog tethered in the bed of the Haynes's truck growls at me as they pull out of their parking space.

The scent had come to him, barely filtered by the tangle of humans crowding him, the one other scent he recognizes from among the myriad human scents. A scent that sends his sensitive nerves into a frenzy. The scent of pain. Of violence. Panic closes in on him; he drops and crawls away from it, instinctively making himself less of a target. And the man holding the leash continues to insist on heading toward the scent, not away from it. But then, there, safety: the open truck door.

I want to make this call on a landline. The ringing in my left ear is definitely letting up, but it's still better to use a landline than jack up the volume on my cell phone. I head back to the office, leaving the dog in the truck, where he's comfortably curled up on the seat, and fish the paper with the number on it out of my wallet. As I dial the microchip registry, I'm thinking that I will have to put on my best officer of the law voice. The voice on the other end of the phone is male. The man identifies himself as Dan and I identify myself as Officer Harrison, Harmony Farms. He takes the number, says he'll make the call and give the owner my contact information. I start to insist that I be the one to make the call to the owner, but Dan is adamant, saying that's not the way it's done. I could pull the officer of the law card, but I figure, What's the point? Unless I don't hear from the owner; then I can get assertive with Dan the microchip man. I wouldn't want some guy on the other end of my headset bullying me out of doing my job correctly.

I hang up and sit by the phone like an idiot or a teenage girl waiting for a boy to call. Just as I shove my rolling chair away from my desk, the phone rings. I'm startled to my feet. It's Dan from the registry and he lets me know that I don't have the final answer to the conundrum of the yellow dog. The number is for a kennel, Barkwell Kennels, Labradors and Golden Retrievers. He doesn't want to linger on this problem anymore than I do; it's Christmas Eve, after all, so he gives me the information and wishes me well. I call the number and, like Dan, get an answering machine wishing me Merry Christmas and Happy New Year from Bob and Donna Stinson. According to their message, the Stinsons are enjoying a rare vacation in Hawaii. My policeman reaction is to think, You idiots! Never leave a message like that unless you plan to invite mayhem.

My dog officer reaction is, frankly, a little bitter. Now I'm going to have to stick it out until they get back. I really wanted to get this solved now. It's been weeks. Almost three months if you count the time I spent trying to lure the dog in. It's the holidays, the shelter is finally empty, and Jenny's off, so I can't simply leave the mutt in the shelter like I would a normal impound unless I want to be driving back and forth three times on Christmas Day. Then again, that would be a good excuse to duck going to Bull's.

When I climb back in the truck, the yellow dog sits up and gives himself a healthy shake from nose to tail. He puts his head over the back of my seat, breathes in my good ear. I reach back and give his head a pat. He doesn't immediately shrink away, a first for us. "You want to spend Christmas with me?"

He shakes his head again, ears flapping. I take that as a yes.

It's late, and I really should do that bit of last-minute shopping, find a present for Bull, and, what the hell, one for Jimmy. Go to the Stop & Shop and pick up something to take tomorrow for lunch, because I'm pretty certain that Bull won't have thought about a Christmas meal. One of those preroasted chickens would be good. "What do you say, fella? Let's go shopping?" I'm talking to the dog again.

The yellow dog apparently doesn't disagree, so I head out of town.

30

"You did what?" Jimmy shoots out of his chair like a Roman candle on the Fourth of July. "Tell me you didn't invite Cooper over here."

"Hey, I did. So what? It's freakin' Christmas and he's my son, too." Bull grips the can of Coke so hard, he can feel it dent.

"What did I tell you? How we can never have Cooper over here. He's a nosy cop."

"He's not. He's the dog officer."

"Bull. Get real. Once a cop, always a cop. Okay. Damage done. What time is he coming?"

"Don't know exactly. Kind of open-ended."

"Christ." Jimmy sits back down, takes out the most recent of his cheap cell phones, and starts thumbing through contacts. "Get out of here for a little while. I got to make a couple personal calls."

"You've got business on freakin' Christmas? What are you, a doctor or something?"

Jimmy grins at his father. "Something like that. Now, get out of here."

Bull lingers, defiant.

Jimmy gives him the stink eye and presses the burner phone to his ear. "Hey, yeah, it's me. Change of plans."

Bull tosses the empty Coke can into the sink. The clatter of hollow can against stainless steel follows him as he walks out of the kitchen.

"Personal calls"—that's what Jimmy calls them. Calls to one or two of the guys he's been dealing with since his last trip to juvenile hall. Used to call them classmates, like he'd been to prep school instead of incarcerated. Type attracts type. The last time Jimmy was sent to juvie was for breaking and entering and theft of more than five hundred dollars' worth of electronics. Just like with the first time he went, everyone—counselors, teachers, lawyers—hoped that yet another turn in reform school would finally straighten him out. Feelgood programs hadn't. Counseling hadn't. It hadn't been his first B and E. But it was his first time charged with assault, which was the main reason the judge decided that Jimmy Harrison wasn't going to get anything out of a few months of doing community service. Lucky for Jimmy, he was under seventeen, barely, and didn't get sent up to an adult facility, where, with his pretty-boy looks, he might have been made some guy's girlfriend. On the other hand, he met these two characters in juvie. What he didn't already know about trouble, they were happy to teach him. Guys with such ordinary names, Mike and Dave. Sound more like furniture salesmen than hard-core drug dealers. Come on down to Mike and Dave's Furniture Emporium and drug shop. Bull remembers them coming to the house, holing up in Jimmy's room, smoking dope, laughing. They didn't look like teenagers then, and he supposes that they haven't changed much.

What got lost in all that business was the reason Jimmy broke into the Slaters' house and beat the crap out of the Slaters' kid. The kid had bought an ounce from Jimmy and didn't pay him. And the guy that Jimmy owed for the weed wasn't happy about that and gave Jimmy his orders. So in effect, the Slaters' kid brought it on himself. He didn't do any time for having bought the weed; that part got swept under the rug, and Bull has never been able to forgive the little shit for the injustice. Now that kid is a partner in the town's oldest law firm. Funny, huh? Funnier still, Jimmy never ratted on the dealer, even though he could have avoided jail time by turning him in. Even at seventeen, that kid had cojones.

Bull really doesn't want to know what Jimmy is up to, but it's hard not to imagine that whatever credit he earned by not succumbing to a plea bargain this last go round has earned him a higher rung on the ladder in his field. Jimmy likely made some pretty good contacts at Walpole, and, along with his old friends Mike and Dave, he's clearly been elevated into the big time. Maybe not cartel level, but definitely involved in something bigger than selling nickel bags to kids on the street. It just sucks that he's decided to use the homestead for his base of operations. Makes day-to-day living with him a challenge. And Cooper, there's no figuring him out. Bull's got enemies who treat him more cordially.

"Come on, Bull. You've had enough." Cooper is skinny, too skinny even for a high school junior. Like no one ever feeds him, which isn't true. He's a ravenous eater; it just doesn't show. "Now." Cooper slides a hand under his father's elbow, knowing that he'll have a hard time finding his balance once he vacates the bar stool. Bull's a sailor finding his land legs.

"I'm fine. You go home, boy."

"They want you out of here, Bull." The bartender nods in agreement. Fink. Rat fink. Isn't his money as good as anyone else's around here? "I'm not making no trouble. Why can't I stay till last call?"

"It was last call half an hour ago, Bull." The bartender takes the glass locked in Bull's fist, tugs it free.

"You should be in bed, Coop. You got school tomorrow."

"Yeah. I do." Cooper reaches to take Bull's other arm; like assisting an in-

valid, or teaching a toddler how to walk, he guides his father to his feet. "I have the AP English test in the morning."

Bull isn't sure what an AP test is, except that it's something Cooper is doing that separates him from his dropout brother. And probably something he should be getting a full night's rest to do.

Bull sleeps all the way home. Roused to get out of the car, he stumbles through the doorway, finds his bed, and flops facedown.

Cooper fills a glass with water, lays out four aspirin on Bull's nightstand, then falls into his own bed but does not go back to sleep.

Bull shuts his bedroom door and turns on his television. There's a Christmas special on. He'll wrap the presents he got for the boys and watch it. Pretend like he's got normal kids.

31

It's Christmas morning, although I don't remember that until I turn on the radio and get a blast of prepackaged seasonal music on our local radio station. It's six o'clock in the morning and they're playing the whole of Handel's *Messiah*. I can live with that. I peek at the outside thermometer and decide that, even with the new running shoes that I got yesterday at a last-minute shopper's extreme discount, I'll give myself the day off from running. "That okay with you, pal?"

The yellow dog is sitting in the exact middle of the ancient braided rug that serves less as decor and more as a dirt catcher. His tail twitches from side to side, and he bobs his head. I can't tell if he's agreeing with me or trying to talk me into running around the pond at eighteen degrees Fahrenheit.

I'm not that much of a masochist. "Give me a break. It's Christmas, or have you forgotten?"

The dog steps into his basket, shakes, turns three times counter-clockwise, and tucks himself in.

I have to admit that I'm a little surprised at myself, talking like this with this dog. Now, with Argos, conversation was a given. We had a great back-and-forth. I'd ask hypothetical questions like "Think we should tell Gayle we want pizza for dinner?" Argos would tell me with wise eyes that Gayle would not be pleased with pizza; that it was my night to cook and cook I should, not bail out on my responsibilities. He was tough on me.

I'm still in my T-shirt and pajama bottoms, the woodstove cranked up to sultry, a messy pile of breakfast dishes on the counter—except for the egg-smeared plate that I've put on the floor for the dog to prewash for me. I've got the latest Carl Hiaasen and I'm deep into the fantasy life of a disgraced but lovable detective when my cell phone goes off. It's not the bark ringtone, so I don't flinch. It's Natalie.

We haven't been in touch much. At all. I've been "giving her space." "Hey, Nat. Merry Christmas."

"Same to you. Having a good one?"

"Actually, very peaceful." I look at the yellow dog, tucked in his basket like a cashew. "Just me and the dog."

"Still no owner?

I give her a brief synopsis of my thwarted investigation.

"I think he's growing on you."

"Like a wart. What are you up to?" It crosses my mind that maybe I can duck going to Bull's and spend the rest of the day in her company. No implications, just a little time spent together. I've got that chicken in the fridge.

"Stuffing a turkey. My in-laws are coming for dinner. It's the first time they've seen the place."

"You nervous?"

"Kind of. I mean, if Marcus, if it hadn't happened . . . "

"Hey, they'll be impressed with the place. They'll be happy to see you happy."

"Thanks. I hope so."

"Who wouldn't be?"

"Coop, I wish I could invite you, but I . . . "

"Nat, don't. Besides, I'm expected at my father's."

"That's good. It's a good day to be with family."

Right. Family. Always a good thing.

"I'm glad you called, Nat. Merry Christmas."

"I'm glad I called, too."

I sit for a long time, my phone still in my hand. The radio station has switched to secular Christmas songs, bouncy and all holly jolly. The fire in the woodstove has burned down and I feel a cold draft against my neck. I need to add some wood, get dressed, take the dog out. But I just sit here. Smiling.

As much as I understand Natalie's cold feet, her putting the brakes on what could be a developing relationship, or nothing, I've missed her. I like her company.

I've put off going to Bull's as long as I can. In the old days, I would have taken him a bottle of Jack and a carton of cigarettes. Now I'm just aiding his nicotine habit with a carton of Camels that I picked up at a gas station convenience store where I never shop. I've added a pair of thick work gloves and a knit cap to replace the one he wears, which stinks. I mean literally stinks—of unwashed hair and cigarettes. For Jimmy, the perfect gift that says, *I'm just being polite*, a box of Russell Stover candies. The wrapping paper cost more than the chocolates. I've got the cooked chicken as my edible contribution to the family reunion. I put the chicken and the candy into one carry bag, grab the gift bag with the hat and gloves, pull on my Carhartt jacket, and hunt around for my own hat and gloves. I'm the only person living here, and yet there are times when I swear gremlins have moved my stuff. It's really just an example of how far I've come from the structure that ruled my life, where my bed was made tight and my possessions were put where they belonged. My scalp was visible beneath a buzz cut and I never went a day without shaving. I run a hand over the three days' stubble on my face right now and tell myself that, at last, I've become fashionable.

Now all I have to do is figure out what to do about the dog. I suppose that I can lock him in the bedroom, as long as I'm careful to put all my footwear out of reach. I don't dare leave him alone in this rental cabin otherwise. But when I call him to follow me into the tiny bedroom, he balks, as if he's being asked to take a perp walk. He retreats to his basket and turns his back to me.

"Hey, come on. You can sleep on the bed." I try to make it sound like I'm offering him a Caribbean vacation; instead, I sound like a huckster selling swampland to retirees. "It's great, soft and warm. You'll be fine. Besides, I won't be long."

Nothing except a great sigh.

Short of dragging the dog by his collar into the bedroom, an act that would surely set him back to whimpering in the corner, I'm out of ideas. I gather the bag with the presents and the chicken in its plastic sarcophagus and call to him. "Okay. But you're going to have to stay in the truck. Come on." I open the cabin door and walk outside, pause on the porch. The yellow dog emerges from his basket, stretches fore and aft, and walks out of the cabin as if he's expected this all along. His tail isn't wagging, but it's not tucked, either. For once, he jumps into the backseat under his own power.

The afternoon is nearly over as I head toward Poor Farm Road, taking the longer Lake Shore Drive route as much for the scenery as for procrastination. The sky is that dull shade of gray that defines a winter sky in our minds when we think of winter. The dark days of winter. Gloomy and threatening.

I might take a run by Deke's on my way home from Bull's. I feel bad about how things went the last time I saw him. As annoyed as I was by his bluntness, he didn't deserve my bringing up what is still a painful subject for him. Besides, the old bachelor doesn't have anyone to "drop by" on a Christmas day. I could leave the chicken in the truck and take it to him instead. Maybe even the candy. Jimmy doesn't need any candy. He needs a diet.

The Nova up on blocks on the front lawn is crowned with the three inches of snow we had earlier in the week. It has been in that spot now for a quarter of a century, a monument of sorts. Jimmy's car is cleaned off and backed neatly into the turnout. There are tire tracks of varying widths in the gritty snow, like various vehicles have pulled in and backed out. They pulled up close enough to the front door that it couldn't have been drivers who missed the turn to the estates and used the driveway to turn around. It doesn't mean anything, but I'm enough of a cop still to stop and look at those tread marks, determine that they are from two different vehicles, and that neither one was Jimmy's Honda. I file that thought away for future reference. It makes me feel, briefly, like a cop.

I pull the bag with the stuff off the front seat, think about my idea of going by Deke's, and take the cold chicken out, putting it on the seat. Then I look and see the dog sitting there, ears alert to my actions. I can't leave the dog and the chicken in the same vehicle. Nor can I leave the candy instead. Chocolate is toxic to dogs. "This should be interesting." I open the rear door and invite the dog to go with me into Bull's.

It is every bit as depressing as I thought it would be. The place even still has the same sour odor of unclean beds, dirty wet towels, and overfilled garbage pails as I remember from my childhood. I never brought friends home, afraid and embarrassed at what they might think of me if they saw the inside of my house. As a kid, I was painfully aware that the "bachelor pad" of my father and older brother was actually a grotesque pit. But, as a kid, I also never did anything about it. Instead, I spent as much time out of my house as I could reasonably carry off. I hung out with friends, or made my way to Deke's place to help him feed his cows; sometimes I got only as far as Polly's. I put a lot of miles on my bike. As I walk through that storm door-free front door and take a whiff of the interior fug, I am cast back into my youth.

"When Mom gets home, she's gonna be pretty mad. We should at least get the dishes done. I can do the laundry; she showed me how." Cooper stands with his small fists planted on his skinny hips, facing his father. He has to look up to see the man's eyes, which are obscured by shaggy hair flopping down into them. His father sways slightly, as if there's a breeze in the kitchen.

"Waste of time. Throw the suckers out. I'll buy more. Better yet, we'll eat on paper plates from now on. No dishes to wash." Bull chortles, a gurgling sound in the back of his throat, like he needs to hawk and spit. "We'll live like bachelors. All pizza and football. That's how we Harrison men will live from now on."

"Bull, we can't do that. When Mom gets home, she's going to be disgusted with us." Cooper feels an urge to shove his father, to see if he can knock him over, to see if he's full of hot air.

Bull pulls out a chair and sits down, so that he and Cooper are now eye-to-eye. He shoves the hair out of his eyes and Cooper sees something in them that frightens him. They're rimmed in red, the whites crazed with blood vessels. He's seen his father's bloodshot eyes many times before, but this time there's a scrim over them, and it seems like his father's pale gray eyes are underwater. As if they're floating beneath the surface. Drowning. "You know she's not coming back, don't you?"

"Bull, she always does. She will this time, too." Cooper knows that his mother didn't run away this time, didn't leave them deliberately, but had an accident. That's what Bull said, that she had an accident and the Nova hit a tree. But, it wasn't a bad accident; there's just a crimp in the hood, and the cracked windshield. He can see that for himself; the car's back in the yard. It doesn't look that bad. Fixable. But Mom's in the hospital; that's where they took her three days ago. They won't let the boys in. They're too young, Bull says. Too young to be visitors.

"I'll wash if you'll dry." Cooper thinks that he's making a deal. If they can get the house cleaned up, Mom will come home. She's holding out on them cause she knows they've trashed the house in her absence.

Cooper runs the hot water, stacks the pots with dried-on tomato soup or canned chili, the plates with greasy slicks, and the forks with hardened food stuck between the tines. He squeezes in too much liquid soap, splashes hot, soapy water onto the floor. Bull stands beside him, grubby dish towel in his hands. Cooper bangs the pots and runs the water hard so that he can't hear his father's sobs.

Bull is kneeling beside the needle-challenged Christmas tree, trying to find the socket to plug it in. I'm a little afraid that the whole thing will go up like a torch if he manages to get the lights on, but it doesn't, and it is, surprisingly, kind of pretty. He hoists himself back to his feet, claps his hands together like he's accomplished hard labor. "Want some Christmas cheer?" He ambles into the kitchen. "Got hot cider. Not much kick, but it tastes good."

I take the paper cup with the mulled cider. He's been a little heavy-handed with the nutmeg, but it's not bad. The yellow dog has followed Bull into the kitchen, has been following Bull around since we got here. It amazes me, because he never follows me around. But I suspect that Bull has been feeding the dog crap from the array he's put out on the table—peanuts, a bowl of chips, salsa, a plate of pepperoni disks, hacked-off cheddar cheese, and crackers. "So, where's Jimmy?" I make a cracker sandwich out of the pepperoni and cheese. I've been in the house for six minutes and no sign of my brother.

"Jimmy? Oh, he's seeing a pal, but he'll be back in a minute."

"His car's here." Jimmy isn't exactly the type to take a walk.

"Guy picked him up."

"What guy? Who does he hang out with?" Hang out, like a teenager.

"How should I know?

"He dealin' again?" I hear myself slipping into the sloppy language of my youth.

Bull fixes his gimlet eye on me. "It's Christmas, for Christ's sake. Give it a rest, won't you?"

"All right." I catch him slipping the dog a slice of pepperoni. The dog takes it from Bull's hand as gently as a lapdog would. As concerned as this once-starved creature is about food, he does have good manners. He's going to make some family a real nice dog. I wonder when the Barkwell Kennels people will be back from their vacation. Wonder what they've done with their dogs while they're away. Wonder if maybe someone is taking care of things and might have access to records. I feed the dog a slice myself and go back into the living room. My plan to do a drop-in has been derailed, since Bull tells me he's got a frozen lasagna heating up. I guess I can't really bail on him if he's done that. Besides, I don't want to miss a chance to see my big brother.

The house is one of those uncharming antique places that are hard to heat. The living spaces are chopped up into small square rooms of practical purpose: kitchen, bedrooms, sitting room. The room that might have started out as a birthing room—the house is that old—is a bedroom, mine when I lived here. There is a second floor filled with the remnants of our forefathers which is closed off by a door at the top of the stairs to keep the heat from being lost upstairs. As Bull goes in to check on the lasagna, I take a little walk around the house. The first thing I notice is the padlock on Jimmy's bedroom door. There's also a padlock on the cupboard beneath the stairs to the unused second floor. When I was growing up here, there wasn't even a Schlage lock on the front door. My cop radar is pinging.

The wash of headlights through the front window alerts me to Jimmy's return. I am standing at the foot of the stairs, my elbow casually resting on the age-blackened newel post. The yellow dog has wandered into the room, his ears lifted and his nose pointed toward the front door. As my big brother pushes open the heavy door, the headlights are in my eyes, so I can't see the vehicle behind him, but I do notice that they're that sodium-style, a curving pattern of small bright lights, suggesting the eyes of a predator. Suggesting an expensive car like the one that backed out of here the other night and turned into Poor Farm Estates. Jimmy is bathed in that harsh bluish light. The dog growls.

"Hey, Coop, how the hell are you?" Jimmy slams the front door and grabs me in a headlock, throws a mock punch at my face.

Again, the yellow dog growls, a throaty warning. He's got his eyes on Jimmy, the first dominant gesture I've ever seen him make. His ears are flattened against the side of his lowered head and he growls a third time. His whole body is stiff, his tail straight out behind him.

"What the . . . " Jimmy releases me and for a sick moment I think he's going to kick him.

"Don't touch him." I push between them. I'm not under any illusion that the dog is protecting me. As soon as I speak, the dog moves behind me, trembling visibly, head lowered, tail tucked as if embarrassed at his own temerity, waiting for punishment. He begins panting, emitting a barely audible wheeze.

Jimmy scares him. Jimmy scares me a little. I'm not afraid of him, but I am afraid of the man he's become. Yeah, you might say that it was inevitable, but it still shocks me to see just how hardened he is. It isn't just the prison time, or his choice of career. I've known plenty of parolees and career criminals who had more than a flicker of humanity left in them. With Jimmy, it's an evolution that began a long time ago. There is a deadness in his eyes. He is capable of kicking this dog, and enjoying it. "Back off, Jimmy."

"Put him outside. I don't want no dog wandering around in here."

"He's not a sniffer dog, so I guess you don't have anything to worry about."

"What's that supposed to mean?"

"Means whatever you want it to." I put my hand on the dog and feel him trembling. He shrinks away from my hand and I know that I've lost ground with him.

Bull comes in. "Knock it off. Both of you. It's freakin' Christmas." He's got a dish towel over his shoulder, a can of Coke in one hand. "Come on, dog. I got something for you."

The yellow dog slips out from behind me and follows Bull into the kitchen.

"Why all the locks, Jimmy? What are you hiding?"

My brother stares at me for a deathless moment. "Keepin' Bull out of my booze. That's all. Nothing for *you* to worry about."

32

The lasagna is a little cold in the center, but Bull sets it on the table and they each hack off a block, eating without speaking. As soon as Cooper finishes his, he gets up and clears his place like a good boy. He snaps his fingers at the dog, who is pressed against the back door, as if hoping someone will let him escape. "Thanks for dinner. I've got to be going."

"Wait, Coop. I got presents." Bull shoves his plate to the middle of the table, tries not to notice the look on Cooper's face, like he's afraid this Christmas family reunion will never end.

In the sitting room, Bull hands Cooper a wrapped box, embellished with two stick-on bows, one red, one green, and gives another box to Jimmy, who sets it beside his chair. Cooper gives Bull an unwrapped carton of Camels and a gift bag with snowflakes all over it, then hands Jimmy a wrapped box. He isn't going to think about the fact that Jimmy hasn't bothered with presents. Jimmy's a busy guy. He doesn't have to buy presents for his father anymore. He's too old for that sort of nonsense. He's sitting there in that chair, both feet planted flat on the floor, fidgeting with a hangnail, preoccupied.

When Cooper was a little kid, it was tradition for him to open his presents first because he was the youngest. This time, he tells Bull to open his first. He's pleased with the gifts from his second son, says that they're real thoughtful. He puts on the hat and models the gloves. "Thanks, Coop, they're perfect."

Jimmy shakes his box of chocolates and says. "So much for Weight Watchers." Bull wonders if Jimmy is saying this for effect because he thinks that Cooper has noticed the food scale sitting out on the cluttered counter and suspects what that scale might really be for. Bull's never seen Jimmy weigh any food.

"I think that you can allow yourself one a day. That won't push the scale over." Cooper glances in the direction of the kitchen, where the scale is.

"Open yours." Bull has cracked open the cigarette carton. "Go on." He pulls out a fresh pack, taps it against his knee.

Cooper pokes a finger under the tape and pulls away the wrapping. Bull remembers when it was almost as exiting for him on Christmas morning as it was for the boys. That exquisite moment just before they opened the boxes, when you hoped that you'd been a good Santa. That nanosecond before you saw the disappointment that the Nintendo was used or the sneakers weren't Air Jordans, but a Kmart knockoff.

Cooper opens the box and looks up. "Hey, thanks, Bull. That's nice." He holds up the tie. It's a paisley design, greens and blues and yellows.

"I figured you could use it; you know, a man can always use a tie."

"It's great. I'm sure I'll have an opportunity to wear it." Cooper carefully returns the tie to the box, folds the tissue back over it.

"Like maybe New Year's Eve, like if you go to a nightclub or something." Bull is scrambling to figure out how to justify this gift, but Cooper eases him.

"Exactly what I was thinking."

"Jimmy, open yours."

Bull has picked out a tie with tiny fleurs-de-lis in yellow against a blue background for Jimmy.

"Oh good. A tie." Jimmy dangles the tie in the air, then drapes it over his neck. "Perfect for meetings with my parole officer."

Bull makes himself laugh; he's learning to treat a lot of what Jimmy says as if he's playing him. Kidding around. As if the son who has come to live with him—uninvited—is just joking around. That half of what he says or demands is him being deadpan funny. Not abuse.

"You guys can swap 'em if you want." Bull hadn't labeled either box, just handed them to his sons randomly. Like everything else in his life, random always seems to work best. Planning and thinking ahead are for other people. One day at a time—that's all he can cope with.

Cooper makes his good-byes, calls the dog, and is gone. Jimmy is in the kitchen, microwaving a second helping of the oily lasagna, the tie still draped around his neck. Bull taps a Camel out of the new pack, pats his pockets for his little green Bic lighter. He lights up and Jimmy swings around. "Outside with that. I don't want any more of your secondhand smoke"

"My house."

"You can kill yourself with those things, but not me."

"Nothing worse than a reformed smoker." Bull jets a stream of smoke in Jimmy's direction. "Holier than thou."

"Want me to crack out the Jack Daniel's? I got some in my room. Finish yourself off properly."

"I'm touched by your concern." Cigarette between his fingers, Bull points at Jimmy. "You got the end of that tie in your plate."

After the warmth of the house, the air outside is cold but nice. Bull stands there, looking at the stars, smoking one cigarette and then another. He can't seem to get it off his mind; just behind a locked door is his former best friend, Jack Daniel's. Glancing through the kitchen window, Bull sees Jimmy, the bottle in his hand. This is Christmas; surely there'd be no harm in a finger or two. A little cel-ebration. Leave it to Jimmy to poke him with the pointy end of the stick of temptation.

He sucks down another lungful of smoke, exhales into the night sky. He's gone this long without it. He can keep going.

Bull goes over to the Nova, brushes the last of the snow off the roof with the side of his hand.

33

It's not that late when I leave Bull's, so I head over to Deke's. The old man is happy enough to get the chicken, calling me "real thoughtful," but I think that he would have been happier with the candy. He doesn't say anything about our argument, and neither do I. We're New England men; we don't have to say "water under the bridge" to know that it is forgotten.

What is weird, though, is the dog. We're inside the house for a few minutes when the dog starts up again with his fearful trembling, eyes glazed, tongue hanging out, panting in the decidedly under-heated house. At first, I think he's having a seizure, but then I figure it out. This was exactly how he reacted to Jimmy. He'd already let Deke pat him on the head, so I know it isn't fear of this male human that is causing his panic. I glimpse Deke's shotgun by the back door. It's an old one, his father's gun. Now his gun. Right there.

"Can I look at your gun?"

Deke gives me a puzzled look; this gun has been in this house since I was a kid. He picks it up and hands it to me, at which moment the dog literally cries out—a yowl so plaintive that I feel cruel for instigating it. Deke's sleeping collie lifts her head from her paws and gets to her feet, shakes, and goes over to where the yellow dog has pressed himself against the back door. She gives him a nuzzle, as if to say, *You're okay.* He visibly relaxes.

"I think maybe he's gun-shy." Deke kindly takes the gun away from me, putting it in a closet, out of sight of the dog.

The power of a dog's olfactory sensors is astounding. It isn't out of the ordinary for a dog to know the scent of a firearm, especially one that's been fired. Argos could ferret out a handgun on a perp even before we frisked him. But having a dog react with a fear association is pretty odd. Unless you knew that he'd been shot. Dogs aren't necessarily tuned in to cause and effect, but this pup clearly understands the relationship between the scent of a gun and the hurt of a gunshot wound. And now I have a hunch why, far from his usual stranger/danger cower, the dog overreacted toward my brother with fear aggression. Carrying a concealed weapon is a big no-no when you're a parolee, and so I have something else to add to my growing list of suspicions about my dear brother. I have no doubt in my mind that Jimmy was carrying somewhere on his person.

There are two sides to the equation of drug dealing: the dealer and the buyer. If Jimmy is back in business, then who are his buyers? The third player is the supplier, the one who provides the merchandise in quantity to the dealer. My question about Jimmy isn't whether he's back in the business, but at what level. Is he supplying small-time dealers, or is he selling the stuff himself to stupid college kids who want to ace physics exams with the help of speed, or bored housewives nostalgic for their hippie youth and looking for an ounce of weed? And, who's bankrolling him? He certainly didn't come out of prison with a savings account.

I have to stop doing this, thinking like a cop. I'm not a cop. Not anymore. As far as I know, there's no law against keeping a food scale on a kitchen counter. There's no law against locks on doors. I don't have enough hard evidence to get a search warrant, even if I had the authority to ask for one. Even if it walks like a duck and quacks like a duck, you still need to be an officer of the law to convince a judge to issue a search warrant. But I do have Lev Parker. Maybe tomorrow I'll drop into Lev's office and put a bug in his ear. Lev is a good cop and I bet that Jimmy is already on his radar, but I can add a little inside information—the locked doors, the possible concealed weapon—and maybe get Jimmy on Lev's to-do list. How's that for brotherly love?

"Jimmy stop it. Stop it." The smaller of the two Harrison boys is crying, bloodied, on the ground and his older brother won't stop pummeling him. Cooper has no idea why his brother is beating him up after accusing him of a theft he didn't commit. No one touched his precious stash of pot. Cooper didn't even know Jimmy had it. But Jimmy has lashed out and accused Cooper because he's the only one who's ever followed Jimmy into the shed. But that was months ago, and he didn't see anything more than Jimmy firing up a cigarette. A cigarette. Nothing that Cooper would ever be interested in. He hates them, how they make his house stink, how they make his father's breath foul.

"You stole it. Either give it back or give me the money." Jimmy punctuates each word with an open-handed slap against the side of his brother's face. At thirteen, he outweighs his brother by twenty pounds.

Cooper is pinned, crushed by his brother's weight and fury. "I didn't take anything. I didn't."

Suddenly, a massive hand has Jimmy by the collar, lifting him up and off of his brother. Cooper gets to his knees, gasping, crying like a baby.

"What the hell are you doing to your brother?" Bull shakes Jimmy. "You trying to kill him?"

"He stole from me."

"So what? That's what brothers do. I stole from mine, and I may have smacked him, but I sure didn't beat the crap out of him. Cooper, go to the house."

Cooper is rooted to the spot, still crying.

"What do you think he stole, Jimmy?"

Jimmy is dead silent. He's nearly as tall as Bull, and he straightens himself so that the distance between their eyes is only a matter of inches. "Maybe it wasn't Coop. Maybe it was you."

With singular clarity, Cooper understands that this time Jimmy has it right.

Bull starts to laugh. "I'm saving your ass, boy. You're too young for that stuff."

"I don't use it, Bull."

"I see. Cooper, I told you to go back in the house."

Cooper stays, fascinated.

"How much you pay for it?"

"Less than I'll earn selling it."

"I want a cut."

"No."

"Ain't negotiable."

Jimmy has lost entirely the aspect of boyhood as he jabs a finger into his father's chest. "Mom sure would love to know you're using again. What was it she said the last time? Oh, yeah, that she'd leave your sorry ass forever if she found out you were back on drugs."

"She never meant pot. Besides, you tell her, and she'll flush it. You'll get nothing."

Jimmy contemplates this. "All right. No more than five percent."

"Ten."

"And you tell Cooper to keep his mouth shut."

"You hear that, Coop? This is our secret. Now go get washed."

In the house, Mona finds Cooper in the bathroom, bloody washcloth in his hands. She wants to know what happened. "Nothing. Me and Jimmy got into a fight."

"About what?"

"Nothing."

"Sure doesn't look like nothing to me." Mona takes the washcloth, rinses it, and gently cleans Cooper's face.

He won't tell her. He knows that if she ever leaves Bull again, she'll leave them all behind. Jimmy is too much for her, and Cooper knows it. He hears her crying when she thinks that no one's at home, frustrated by yet another call from the school, or a complaining neighbor. The "Bad Seed," that's what she calls her elder child. "Damien." "Rosemary's Baby." She has lots of names for her elder son, who, for reasons she cannot fathom, has taken all of the worst of both of them and become something wholly frightening.

If it wasn't for Jimmy, maybe they'd be a happy family. His father could stop drinking for real without the stress of a juvenile delinquent in the house. His mother could relax, not keep waiting for the next bad thing to happen.

I've struck out with the dog today. Two fear-inducing incidents in one day has proved too much for him. We leave Deke's and I practically have to drag him into the truck. Like a wrong-headed horse on the end of a lead line, he bucks and kicks and almost wriggles out of his collar. I lift him into the truck and slam the door. I'm exhausted. This day, which started out so peacefully, has gone south. I should drop him off at the shelter, give us both a night away from each other, but the shelter is out of my way and I just want to go home.

And so I drive back to my isolated cabin, one unhappy dog in the backseat, my stomach rebelling against the glob of undercooked lasagna sitting in it, and all sense of the Christmas spirit dissolved away.

34

Bull asked Jimmy to give him a ride to work, it had been raining all night and more rain was predicted. Jimmy wouldn't leave the house to give his father a ride to work because he said he had "friends" coming over and he didn't know when they'd show up. As if real friends wouldn't sit and wait for him. Such crap. As he was pedaling his Raleigh bicycle down the shoulder of Route 114, an approaching car hit a massive puddle and the spray hit Bull with full force, soaking his jacket and pants. Having dicked around waiting for Jimmy to offer him a ride, Bull was already late to work, no time to turn around and get dry clothes on. So he spent the day in the lumberyard, wet and cold. Try though he might, he couldn't talk the boss into finding him an inside job today, and he had spent the last eight hours in varying degrees of wet and cold, culminating in the long bike ride home along poorly drained roads, once again being hit with the backwash of cars passing him. He knew he should quit that friggin' job. He'd quit better jobs for less reason.

Now he's home, and even if he's changed into ratty sweats, he's still shivering with the kind of deep internal cold that can be heated up only by one thing. Bull knows that Jimmy has a bottle of Jack in his room. He brings it out now and again when he's in a mood, teasing his old man with it. "Want some? Oh, right. You're a teetotaler now. Bottoms up." He always was a little prick. Even as a kid. He used to tease Cooper unmercifully, giving him a Matchbox car that the kid coveted and then taking it away. Later, as they got older, he stole Coop's homework and burned it up or threw it into the toilet. Kid stuff. Wasn't happy till he got Cooper crying.

That lock wouldn't really keep him out. A Phillips-head screwdriver would fix the problem, and then he could put it back, with Jimmy none the wiser. Just a swallow. Just enough to get the old internal combustion going. A finger. Two at most. Bull stands at the kitchen junk drawer, his hand on the pull. Sure, there's got to be a screwdriver in there. Everything finds its way into this drawer. One of Mona's pet peeves. "Can't you ever put your tools back where they belong and not in my kitchen drawer?" she'd say. She had a lot of pet peeves, like putting dirty clothes in the hamper, not on the bedroom floor; never driving the boys when he'd been drinking, which was a hard one, because he was always drinking in those days.

He tries hard not to think about it, what happened. Just accept it. That's what they say. Accept what you can, change what you can, and know the difference. Bull's a little tired of having to hold up everything he does or thinks against a saying. He yanks open the drawer and, sure enough, underneath the crazy salad of string and bottle openers, broken crayons, dry Sharpie markers, spatulas, and paper clips, there is a screwdriver. A nice Stanley. Probably the one Jimmy used to install those locks in the first place.

The Nova is facing the road. He's been meaning to get the brake fluid into it for a couple of weeks now. When you step on the brakes, the pedal goes almost to the floor. He's pretty sure it's just low on fluid. Nothing more serious. No big deal, not really. He'll pick up some brake fluid at the gas station next time he gets gas. But he forgets. Mona's car is fine except for that low tire. Cars. Jeez, always something to worry about. No big deal, either. She's plenty capable of putting air in her own tire.

The school has called and Mona has flown out of here like her tail is on fire, equally angry that she's going to be late for work again and angry that her elder son has committed yet another schoolboy crime. She's left Bull in the kitchen, his head in his hands, completely incapable of handling this latest incident with his son. "Don't come," she'd said. "It's worse when you come." Not mere bullying this time, but the principal has accused Jimmy of nearly drowning a fourth grader. Not just shaking him down for his lunch money but then sticking his head in a toilet. Bull sits at the kitchen table, protesting: "If they had a separate junior high in this town, he wouldn't be picking on little kids for their lunch money." Mona tells Bull that he's missing the point. He always misses the point. Something has to be done about Jimmy, before he kills someone. Can you imagine a mother saying that about her kid? Bull gets to his feet, fighting to get his balance. It's ten-thirty in the morning and he's well into his daily drunk. He's unemployed again, and Mona's job as a medical receptionist is the only thing keeping her head up as she hands food stamps over to the cashier in the grocery store. "He'll be fine," he says. As he always says when the subject of Jimmy's increasingly antisocial behavior is the only topic Mona is chewing on.

Then she asks the one question he's been hoping she won't. "How do you suppose Jimmy came by that new PlayStation? The one he thinks I don't know he has? Stolen? Or paid for? How, Bull? Fourth grader's lunch money? I don't think so. And I think you do know. This has got to stop, Bull. I can't take it anymore."

Mona didn't slam the door when she left the house to meet with the principal. She'd gently shut the front door, the click of the latch echoing in the suddenly silent house. The sound of finality. Bull leaned one sweaty palm against the windowpane to watch her drive away, thinking that she shouldn't have taken the Nova.

Six months after Mona's death, Jimmy did his first turn in juvie, not quite fourteen years old.

The sizzle of sleet smacking against the kitchen window snaps Bull out of his reverie. He has the screwdriver in his hand and he's staring at it as if it's a mystery how it came to be there.

35

It's Friday night and I don't have a date. Max isn't coming home from his week at Tufts until tomorrow and Natalie is picking up a new rehab project.

Rather than spend yet another night with only the company of a dog who keeps himself to himself, I head out to the Lakeside Tavern, dog safely in the backseat. I can't afford to lose any more running shoes. It really is time to incarcerate my canine roommate, but I don't. I've got Jenny on the case, building up a nice Facebook presence for him, and she tells me that, given his pathological shyness, the more home time he can get, the better it will be. I suggest she offer him accommodations, but she demurs. Can't. Boyfriend is allergic. Yeah, right.

The calendar has tripped over into a new year, and the Barkwell people are still away. I've filled their answering machine, so I don't even get the recorded beep anymore. They have a fairly amateurish Web site, loads of pictures of cute puppies interacting with cute toddlers, but it's very static, no e-mail-contact button. I'm just a hair short of driving up there to wait it out on their front step.

The yellow dog settles himself down on the foam dog bed I've placed on my backseat. I bought it because I'm sick of dog hair all over my truck. He does seem to like it, and I know that it keeps him warm. I've tossed an old blanket over him just so that I won't be accused of leaving a dog out in the cold. Food, water, shelter—the basic tenets of good pet keeping. Not that I'm keeping him.

The Lakeside is bustling, so I head to the bar and squeeze myself in to stand between two guys perched on tall stools; nod to my left, nod to my right. The bartender knows me well enough that he brings over an IPA without my having to order it. I don't know if that's scary or an endearing example of life in a small town. I'm thirsty, so I go with the latter. The best part about standing at the bar is the fact that with your back to the room, you might not see people you don't want to see. You don't watch the door; you don't have to greet every person who walks by your table. In effect, it's perfect privacy. My left-hand neighbor isn't chatty; his eyes are fixed on the closed-captioned evening news. The guy to my right has a girl on his other side and he's playing one of those little wooden pegboard games with her, taking every chance he can to touch some part of her body. Sweet. Sort of. Or creepy. I don't know. I can't see her face, so I don't know if she's lapping up the attention or ready to slug him. I stand ready if she should choose to protest his attentions. These are the thoughts that are bouncing around in my mind when I hear a familiar voice and a meaty hand claps me on the back hard enough that I knock my beer over.

Bull, fully shit-faced. My father, fallen gloriously off the wagon.

I shovel Bull into the front seat of the truck. The yellow dog gets up and pokes his nose over the seat back, sniffs Bull's cheek, and then retreats to his bed. Bull stinks so badly of booze that even the dog has turned up his nose. I have no idea how he got himself to the Lakeside. I don't see his bike, and the bartender was pretty quick to say he hadn't served him. I have one idea—other than that he was hitchhiking and some sap picked him up—and that's Jimmy.

"Bull, what the hell happened?"

"Nothin'." He's got that belligerent tone I associate with his mid-drunk state. Early, you can hardly tell he's been drinking. Late, and he's soppy and your best friend. Somewhere between the extremes, Bull's latent anger begins to show.

I look over at him. In the quick dash of light from a streetlamp, I can see that he looks like he's been smacked around.

"Did you fall?"

He doesn't answer right away. Then: "Yeah. I fell."

"Off your bike."

"I guess."

"Did Jimmy hit you?"

Bull closes his eyes and they sink beneath the swollen flesh of his cheeks.

"Is he at the house?"

"I don't know. I guess." There is something else in his tone now. He's afraid I'm going to take him back there, to his own house. He's squeezing his hands together, fingers intertwined into a prayerful fist. For some reason, I notice that he's still wearing his wedding ring, a thin gold band that has embedded itself into his finger.

"What happened? What did Jimmy do?" I can't keep the anger out of my voice, the simmering rage that I have toward this brother of mine who is at the heart of all the bad things that ever happened to my family.

"Shut up, Cooper. Just please shut up."

Behind me, the dog whines.

I have no choice but to take Bull home with me. I half-carry, half-drag him out of the truck, forgetting for the moment that the dog is loose, free to walk off and back into the woods. But he doesn't. He follows us in and watches from the safety of his basket as I drop Bull onto my couch in an inelegant maneuver that nearly takes me off my feet. He outweighs me significantly and I certainly don't have the upper-body strength I used to when part of my daily routine was weight lifting in the precinct gym. Bull is either instantly asleep or unconscious. He's breathing, so I leave him there. Funny, but all I want right now is a beer. The one I didn't get, courtesy of my father's drunken greeting. I'm not sure I even paid for it. Great, let's add drink and dash to the list of sins of the Harrisons of Harmony Farms.

I grab a cold one out of my fridge, go out on the porch, and sit in one of the two plastic chairs my landlord has thoughtfully provided, slowly drinking my beer. By the time it's gone and I'm chilled to the bone, I've calmed down, made a plan. Bull can stay tonight, and tomorrow I'll get him to see that he needs to get Jimmy out. Now. Better yet, I'll try to talk him into pressing charges against Jimmy for assault. Parental abuse, for God's sake. Even as I consider that lovely thought, I know that there is no way I could ever get Bull to turn on Jimmy. He never has, and he never will. Jimmy is like his blind spot. I remember it so well, Bull defending Jimmy over and over. No matter what the infraction, it was always someone else's fault.

I push the door open and am blown away to see the yellow dog nestled in beside Bull on the couch, stretched out full length beside the snoring man, his head cradled in the crook of Bull's arm. He rolls his brown eyes toward me, and the very tip of his tail thumps against the cushion, as if to say, *It's okay. This is where I'm supposed to be. He'll be fine.*

Bull is standing in my kitchen, a quart of milk up to his nose to see if it's gone off. He's made a pot of coffee and the table is set for breakfast. He looks at me, smiles his patented big baby grin, and says good morning. I've been awake most of the night, fretting over him, and here he is, none the worse for wear except for the bruise on his left cheek and the dull shiner above it. I look around for the dog.

"He's been out."

"Okay. You walked him?"

"No. He went out; then he came back in."

Guess I shouldn't worry any more about his taking off. That's progress of a sort. I take the mug of coffee Bull hands me, sit at the table. He's fussing over scrambled eggs and I'm cast back into a time when he was the chief cook and bottle washer of the family. We didn't eat at McDonald's, at least not every night. Bull may have been half in the bag, but he always put a home-cooked meal on the table. I don't think I ever gave it a thought. Hot dogs and hamburgers, spaghetti, meat loaf—basic stuff. And something he called "slumgullion"—hamburger and stewed tomatoes with elbow macaroni. I get a craving for it as I sit at my own table, a grown man.

"Bull, are you going to tell me what happened?"

"When?"

"I don't know. Let's start with last night and work backward. What happened?"

"I went where I shouldn't have." Bull pulls the other chair out and sits heavily, props his elbows on the table and cradles his coffee mug. "End of story."

"And Jimmy caught you."

He nods.

"And smacked you around."

"I fell."

The eggs are starting to smoke a little and I jump up to rescue them. The dog has come into the room, takes a lap at his water. Bull pats his knee and the dog joins him on that side of the table. I look at the back of my father's head and am filled with despair. A first cousin to the kind of despair I felt in those first dark days after I lost Argos.

"Why, Bull? Why now? You've been sober for years."

"No, son. I've been sober for about eight hours."

"Will you start again, staying sober?"

"I can't say."

"Will you at least try?"

"You can't ask that, Coop."

"Maybe not, but I can ask what pushed you off the wagon this time." I spoon eggs onto his plate, onto mine. Grab the already-cold toast out of the toaster.

Bull gets up to get the ketchup out of the refrigerator, shakes a puddle of the stuff onto his plate, and tucks into his breakfast. He sips his coffee, looks at me, then sets his plate on the floor for the dog. "I can't tell you why I went off. I don't rightly know. Sometimes the trigger isn't obvious. I was cold, tired. Didn't think to call my sponsor. Was thinking about things I haven't thought about for a while."

"What kind of things?"

"Just things." Bull doesn't look at me, a classic avoidance technique used by liars. I didn't do a lot of questioning in interview rooms; my job—our job—was to catch them, not interrogate them. But on more than one occasion, I did question a felon, maybe even threatened him with the dog if I didn't like the answers he was giving me. Except for Jimmy, who can look you in the eye and tell you the most outrageous lie, most liars can't look you in the eye. They don't even know they're doing it, looking away. It's instinct.

I snatch up Bull's plate from the floor, drop it in the sink. I school myself to remain patient, like Natalie working with a stubborn horse. Never show anger. I think that it's important to know why Bull drank, because my own instincts suggest that Jimmy is behind it. So I don't face Bull when I ask the same question in a different way. A leading question. "So, why were you so cold?"

Bull has the dog's head in his hands and he's playing with his muzzle. The dog's tail swings back and forth in a languid sweep. His eyes are closed.

"Got wet going to work; boss kept me out in the yard all day. I was freezin' when I got home."

"Couldn't you have grabbed a ride with Jimmy?"

Silence.

I run the hot water, squeeze in too much liquid. "He's too busy?"

"Yeah. Something like that." Bull runs his hands down the length of the dog, scratches at the base of his tail.

"What else does he have in his room, Bull? You notice anything?"

"I was fixed on that bottle. There it was, sitting there in the middle of his bureau like it had my name on it."

"I think that it probably did." I wouldn't put it past Jimmy to entrap Bull this way. Just for fun. And if that was the case, then why did he get violent with Bull? Why did he smack him? Dump him at the Lakeside? He'd do that only if he was angry, and he'd most likely been angry because Bull did more than swipe that bottle. "When did he hit you?"

"Who said he did?"

"That shiner."

Bull touches his eye. "I told you, Coop, I fell."

"Can't you at least be honest with me? Jimmy hit you and it wasn't just for taking that bottle." I'm fast losing any advantage I have; losing my temper. "Bull. He needs to get out of your house. I can help you. You don't have to let him stay there."

Bull gives me a baleful look, slowly shakes his head. "But then I'd be alone."

36

Polly Schaeffer sits in front of me, her usual caftan abandoned in deference to the polar vortex we're enduring this winter. She's in a full-length faux-fur coat, equally faux Russian soldier-style hat. The warmth from the office has steamed up her glasses and she pulls them off, looking at me with myopic intensity. Ever since Roger spirited away her cat collection, Polly has been a ghost of her former self. She's lost her sparkle, her smile. I really think that what her son did was pretty reprehensible, even if understandable on one level. But he could have left her one or two. I'm hoping that I can cheer her up.

Jenny has tendered her notice. Just before we left work on Friday, she came up to me, handed me an actual resignation letter, and then burst into tears.

Like a good boss, I read the letter, folded it, and put it back in the envelope. She's got another job. She's taking what she does here and going to a big nonprofit shelter in New York State. "That's great, Jen, really great. They're lucky to get you." I'm not the world's most demonstrative man, and I knew that I was perilously close to overstepping the boss/employee boundary, but, what the hell, I got up from my desk and gave her a big hug. She pulled herself together and we had one of those clumsy laughs that people whose connection is about to be severed enjoy.

She's the one who suggested Polly as a replacement. "She's got a lot of love in her just wasting away. She knows her way around a kennel."

"She'll want to take them all home."

"She'll need boundaries, sure. But you're good at boundaries."

"Polly, would you be interested in a job?" I ask her now.

Polly has enough self-respect to act like she's weighing the pros and cons of the offer that I've made her. "I'm a little *mature* for a lot of heavy lifting."

"No heavy lifting."

"I won't watch you put them down."

"I don't put them down. Part of your job is to find them homes."

"What hours? I have my shows that I like."

The finance committee is going to be very pleased with me. I give her several hours less than what Jenny worked, and offer her a step-one salary, which is a tick above minimum wage. The town is going to be saving a little money. Go me.

Which makes me think about my own future. My audiologist has given me the good news about my hearing. The tinnitus is nearly gone, and although I'll never hear well out of my left ear, I made the thirty decibel or better benchmark. The rest of me is back in form. The running and the wood chopping, the lifting of cages and canines has brought me back into shape. In other words, for the first time in a year, I'm fit for duty. At least physically.

I've left the yellow dog with Bull at my cabin. I offered to drive him to work, but apparently Monday is his day off. Neither was he in a hurry to go back to his own house. I kept my mouth shut. He spent the weekend with me, and it didn't suck. Sober, he's a pretty good cribbage player. We walked the perimeter of Bartlett's Pond, the dog with us. For the first time, I dared to let the dog off the leash and was gratified to have him chug along with us, sniffing and peeing, crushing the new ice beginning to form at the water's edge as he waded in, lapping at the cold pond water.

"I was glad when you didn't go into the service." Bull said this apropos of nothing. "Glad you didn't follow in the old man's footsteps."

I could hardly tell him that there was no way I'd ever consider following in his footsteps, but civility kept my mouth shut. So I just asked why he was thinking of that.

"I don't know. I guess because sometimes I think that what happened to you was a little bit like what happened to me. Over there."

"Vietnam?"

"Yeah."

"How so?"

"Sudden death. It haunts you. Nothing clean about it. You wonder why you survived and other guys didn't."

I was speechless.

"I heard you last night." Bull patted his leg and the yellow dog left the edge of the pond.

"Heard me what?"

"You know. Dreaming."

"Yeah. I was." I snatched a stick up from the ground, flung it into the pond. "Does it ever get better?"

"For some, I guess. Not so much for me."

I wanted to ask him if he thought I'd ever recover. But I was afraid of the answer.

Jimmy called to ask if I knew where Bull was, as if he didn't have anything to do with his absence. I played it straight, as if he actually didn't. "He's a little banged up. I told him he could stay here."

"Good. Keep him."

"Hey, Jimmy?"

"Yeah?"

"What are you selling?"

Jimmy didn't even bother to tell me to go fuck myself, just hung up.

I took Bull's house key with me when I left the cabin this morning. I slipped it out of his jacket pocket and kind of forgot to mention it to him. I think I'll just stop by the house and get him some clean clothes. He could use some clean clothes.

An emergency call keeps me from going home at lunchtime. Bull doesn't have his cell phone, so there's no way I can call and tell him I won't be back when I said I would. What the heck, he's probably forgotten that I said I'd be home at noontime. I feel kind of bad about that. The call takes me out to the highway, where a dog has been sighted wandering along the breakdown lane. I'm dreading what I might find, but the gods are with me and I slip in behind him as he trots south. He's a fairly sizable mutt, what I would call a collie-shepherd cross, but for all I know, he may be some kind of designer dog. He's all business, ignoring the backwash of semis and cars merging onto the highway. I set my flashers and get out, catch pole in one hand, liver treats in the other. "Hey, bud." I guess my experience of trying to catch the yellow dog has jaded me, so I am completely surprised when he turns around and walks right up to me, takes the treats, lets me slip a noose over his furry neck and walk him to the truck. That's how it's supposed to be done. Even better, he's got a tag.

Two hours later, I'm still at the office, waiting for Mugsy's owner to show up, and I'm starving. Jenny offers to go get me something, but I decline. I'll deal with Mugsy and then I'll call it an early day. I fill up on yet another cup of coffee. Mugsy's owner isn't going to get the easygoing Cooper Harrison.

By five o'clock, Mugsy's gone home with his grateful family, adorable little kids hanging off his neck and the dad sheepish with relief. I don't even fine them. They're too damn cute to be angry with.

The temperature has dropped considerably from this morning, which started off in the twenties. I hope that Bull hasn't set my cabin on fire stoking the woodstove. Speaking of Bull, I think that maybe now's a good time to take a run past his place on my way home. Any luck at all and Jimmy will be elsewhere and I can, well, I can fetch my poor old dad some clean duds. A legitimate errand even if Jimmy is there. I put my hand in my jacket pocket to make sure that the house key on its plastic fob is handy.

As I pull out of the parking lot, my phone rings. I can't see the display, so I'm flying blind when I push the Bluetooth on. It's Natalie.

"Cooper, how are you?"

"Fine. You?" I recalculate my route to include the scenic drive along the lake, give myself more time. "Did you get that rehab horse?"

"I did. He's a wreck. Worst case of rain rot I've ever seen, and his feet are so overgrown that he can barely walk. I'm sitting here waiting for my farrier and I was just thinking that I hadn't talked with you for a while." There is something in her voice: a weariness I've never heard before.

"Natalie, is everything okay?"

"Sure. "It's just . . . "

"What, Natalie?"

"You ever just want to quit?"

"Yeah. Every day." I'm halfway around the lake. "But I didn't set out to be an ACO, so that's sort of understandable. What's going on with you?"

"I spent my morning breaking ice on the tanks and then trying to get an electrician here to figure out why the heaters keep blowing the circuit breaker. That's the kind of thing that sometimes gets me to wondering why I'm doing this. Is it worth it? To save, what, four animals? There were three others at this place, just as bad as this one, and because I haven't got the room, I can't save them."

"I know. Sometimes it just sucks." I get brave. "Want me to come by?"

"I wish you would. How about you bring dinner? Something easy."

I think that's about the best offer I've had in a long time.

As I had hoped, Jimmy's car is gone. I pull in, boldly parking the truck in front of the house. If Jimmy comes home, he'll have no doubt that I'm there and he'll be a trifle concerned at what I may have discovered. Maybe it will be enough to give him a little hint that his operation, whatever it might be, would be better served elsewhere. I walk around to the back door, past the up-on-blocks Nova.

Inside, I quickly grab a plastic bag and fill it with Bull's stuff just in case; if Jimmy does show up, I'll have my prop handy. While in the kitchen, I yank open the fridge and help myself to some leftover pizza. Then I get to work.

This would be so much easier if I had Argos. I have to stop thinking like that, I know. But it's true. Although, technically, he was a tracker, a dog trained as a sniffer would be able to pinpoint the location of Jimmy's stash without my having to resort to screwdrivers and guesswork. My guess is that Jimmy has a bunch of red herrings in this house. That is, these padlocks aren't all securing his merchandise. He's probably got one, maybe two hiding places. I mean, who would be so obvious as to put up padlocks like big red arrows saying: Something's hidden in here! I think that he's been playing with Bull's head. However, I know, I just know, that he's got something stashed in this house, and that's why it would be great to have a drug-sniffing dog with me. Save a heck of a lot of time.

I have to go with the obvious first, Jimmy's room. The hasp and padlock are on the floor; no doubt Jimmy found Bull in flagrante delicto. So the door's wide open, and I boldly enter Jimmy's room, experiencing a subtle flashback to when we were kids and he'd pound me for so much as appearing at his door. It really hasn't changed much. No Arrowsmith posters on the walls anymore, but it still wears the same faded brown-and-white-patterned wallpaper, which is at least three generations old. It still smells like unwashed boy. I don't bother with poking around in the bureau drawers. If he's got something in here, it's beneath the floorboards or in the wall. These antique houses are good for loose floorboards, and Prohibition encouraged the art of hidden cubbies. I step, rock, feeling for a subtle give in the floor, then move the bed, do the same. I slide the bureau away from the wall, knock, listening with my better ear for any hollowness. Jimmy's been hiding drugs in the house since he was a kid; I just have to think like him. Think where he might feel secure leaving his stock. It has to be someplace both secure and handy. Giving up on his room, I decide to check out the closet under the stairs. I pick up the screwdriver from where Bull left it on the floor.

There's no light in the cupboard, and I left my flashlight out in the truck. I can't imagine that there's a working flashlight in this house, but I scurry around to the logical places one might be kept. I locate one, but I'm not surprised to find the batteries dead. I'm running out of time. It's getting dark and I have no idea when Jimmy will come back. Pushing aside coats and boots, I feel around as best I can in that small closet before I screw the hasp back in place.

I've got the plastic bag with Bull's change of clothes and a toothbrush. I take one more circuit of the downstairs, hoping for that aha moment. Nothing. I grab another slice of cold pizza. And then I remember something.

As with a certain subset of rural home owners, ours was a family that never threw anything out. Not string or paper bags, not buttons or Christmas boxes. A Yankee heritage writ large on the back porch, where a doorless refrigerator and a baby carriage still reside long after they reached the limit of their usefulness. In the kitchen, too heavy to move out to the porch, is the aged cast-iron range that my maternal ancestors used, and what was at one time the only source of heat for the house. Tucked up beside it, its successor, a seventies-era white Westinghouse electric stove. The old range has devolved into a kind of handy countertop, piled with pots and pans, a cookbook, magazines, empty salt and pepper shakers. Once, when the electricity went out, I remember Bull firing it up again. There was just enough kerosene left in the glass jug that fed into the burners to get it going so we could have a hot meal. That was okay, but the house was freezing, so Bull then loaded the firebox up with scraps of two-by-fours. Within minutes, the kitchen was filled with smoke. The long-unused chimney was backed up with bird nests and the detritus of years of leaf fall. We survived that, but it was clear, that we should never use that range again, not for cooking and certainly not for heat.

Which makes it the perfect hiding place.

There are two things that a drug dealer generally carries: the drugs and the cash. I open the left-hand oven door, then the right. No drugs. Then I lift the burner plates off the top, reach in. Nothing. Then I smile, tapping the sheet-metal pipe that leads from the back of the range to the chimney. I should hear a hollow ping. I don't. It's more like the sound you get when you knock on a solid wall. Carefully, I pull the stovepipe out of the wall, put my hand in, and touch a brick, and another. Not clay bricks, but bricks of pure heroin. I've been around drug busts enough to know that what my dear brother has stashed away in our childhood home is a freakin' mother lode of heroin. I pull one package out. The trade has its own standards; in my hand is a package of neat little white powder–filled baggies, like the kind jewelers use, banded together and then wrapped into neat bundles. It's hard to say how many bricks are tucked into the stovepipe, but it doesn't really matter. I've seen the evidence with my own eyes. It could be ten bricks or fifty. Thousands or hundreds of thousands of dollars in street value. Plenty to send my brother back to jail for a very long time.

After slipping one tiny Baggie out from one bundle and putting it into the inside pocket of my jacket, I carefully tuck the package back into the stovepipe, then reattach the pipe to the hole in the wall. Then I open the cast-iron door to the old firebox. And there's the cash. Like the heroin, all sorted into neat packages of various denominations, none less than fifty. And there are a lot of them. Makes one wonder why Jimmy is driving a banged-up old Honda. He's got enough here to buy himself a Lexus. I close the door, throw the heavy latch back into place. Or maybe his handler has the Lexus. Again I have to wonder where Jimmy is in the food chain.

I don't have time to ponder this existential question, as the front door opens and Jimmy comes in.

"What are you doing here?" He tosses his keys onto the kitchen table, goes to the fridge, grabs a bottle of water. He's good; I have to give him that. Not once do his eyes go to the old range. He gives off virtually no "tell."

"Just collecting some stuff for Bull." I hold up the plastic grocery bag, take a bite of the old pizza. All perfectly natural.

"You going to keep him? Probably a good idea."

"Just one more night. And it's his house, Jimmy, not yours."

"Will be." He laughs, slugs back half the bottle of water. "Your turn to watch him. He really needs a keeper."

"Maybe so, but you're in his house."

"A couple more nights? Okay?"

"Why?"

Jimmy doesn't answer me. He sits and finishes the water, then shoots the empty bottle into the overflowing trash.

"You should recycle."

"Hardly the worst of my sins."

Jimmy is only a couple of years old than I am, but right now he looks like a middle-aged man, or a man with a really stressful job.

Even though he's been out for a while, he still has that prison pallor, that dull cast to the skin around his eyes and deep circles beneath them. A man who doesn't sleep well. Kind of like how I looked not that long ago, when I was sleepless. Comfortless. Kind of like I still sometimes do when I've had a bad night.

"You should get out of here. Find your own place. Why are you still here?"

"It's convenient. That all right with you?"

"Not if it means Bull is tossed out because you get mad at him."

"He snoops."

"He knew you had that bottle. Something tipped him over the edge. He doesn't care what you may keep in your little boyhood room; he just wanted—"

"I know what he wanted."

"What, Jimmy? What?"

"Same thing he always wants." He's speaking in riddles. Jimmy has always had this amazing ability to confound by a mix of prevarication and non sequitur.

"I think that the only thing Bull wants right now is to cling to his suddenly very new sobriety."

"Best place for that is with you."

"Maybe, but he wants to be home."

But then I'd be alone. I know that when my father said that, my response wasn't supposed to be silence, but an offer of hospitality.

"With you."

Jimmy bleats with laughter. "Me? You've been the son they were proud of. Why does he want to live with me?"

"Beats me."

He looks at me with those water-colored eyes. Dead eyes. Jimmy's eyes have been cold fish eyes for decades. I can't think if I've ever seen even a spark of happiness in them. Or joy, or humor that wasn't at someone else's expense, or anything other than malice. Anger. A nurtured anger. It's on the tip of my tongue to ask him, "What happened to you?" We were raised by the same inept parents, but we weren't abused. We were poor, and the town joke because of Bull, but we were clean and had food on the table. Life wasn't so much one of disappointment, as one of no expectations.

And then I think, Maybe I really don't want to know.

It's five miles, mostly uphill, so Cooper is sweating by the time he arrives at Deke's farm. He's going to ask Deke if he can live with him. It's been a bad couple of days and he just can't go home again. He needs a quiet, safe place to be. He'll do chores, anything. Feed the cows, muck the milking parlor. Collect eggs from the henhouse. Shoot, he'll vacuum and dust Deke's place, anything. Just let him stay. Bull won't miss him. He's got his hands full with Jimmy. Cooper just can't take the yelling anymore.

Deke is out back, tinkering with the tractor, pulling spark plugs out and looking at them in the bright sunlight. "What brings you here?"

Deke's collie goes up to Cooper, sniffs, waits for a pat. "Can I stay with you?" He kneels down, presses his cheek against the dog's skull. "Please."

Deke gets down from his perch to stand beside the boy. Puts a hand on the kid's shoulder and squeezes. "I got a cow about to calf. It's her first. I could use some help keeping an eye on her. Someone to let me know when the action starts."

Cooper spends the night in the barn, waking every hour or so to check on the cow, who doesn't calve that night, or the next. By the time she does, in the middle of the afternoon on the third day, Bull has come to fetch him. "Hey, son, I think it's time you left Deke alone. He's a busy man."

"I'm helping him."

"I know, son. You're a good help." Bull's hand on his shoulder is equally directional and affectionate.

"I've got to go. Bull thought I was coming back at noon, but I haven't gotten home yet."

"You tell him hello for me."

"Yeah, right. I'll tell him you can't wait for him to come home. Tomorrow. After work. I'm warning you: Put the rest of your booze in a better hiding place."

Jimmy gives me a smirk.

I think about the little baggie close to my heart and aim a forefinger at him. "See you around."

I get in my truck, figure I'd better get back to the cabin, see what Bull's been up to. Get him cleaned up and make some dinner. Feed the dog. Pretend like we're normal people. Not an off-the wagon drunk and an erstwhile cop with a drug dealer in the family. Tomorrow things will change. I'll take this lovely piece of evidence to Lev. Drop it on his desk like a cat drops a mouse on the kitchen floor. *You maybe want to get a search warrant now?*

I'll go to Nat's after I check on Bull and the dog. I feel a little twinge of excitement and I can't tell if it's because I'm about to see Natalie or because I'm finally about to nail Jimmy.

37

It's so dry in here. He's dying of thirst. Must be the heat of the woodstove, which Bull has stoked to the maximum of its safe limits. Freakin' cold front. He wasn't wearing all that much when he left home on Friday, just his hooded sweatshirt, so he's helped himself to one of Cooper's fleece vests. It doesn't zip over his belly, but it's a little extra layer. Now the cabin is so hot, he's stripped it and his flannel shirt off, opened the windows. Give him an oil furnace over wood any day.

Not a big fan of water, Bull opens the refrigerator to see if Cooper keeps any Coke. He shoves the bottles of Sam Adams to one side, then to the other. An open carton of orange juice. Four bottles of Sam. Carton of milk. Four bottles of Sam. Bull swigs the juice right from the carton, crushes it, and tosses it in the can. Still thirsty.

The yellow dog sits in the doorway, watching with a nonjudgmental look in his brown doggy eye, just hanging out. Coop won't miss one. Surely he doesn't keep track of the beer in his fridge. Bull peels a slice of American cheese off the pound, shares it with the dog. Still thirsty. Still four bottles of beer on the shelf. This strikes him as funny and Bull starts singing "Ninety-nine bottle of beer on the wall . . . " The dog gets up and climbs into his basket.

No TV. What's wrong with that boy? Probably no cable out here in the sticks, so why bother. On the other hand, Cooper must make enough to get one of those dishes. Bull's beginning to feel sorry that he didn't take up Coop's offer to take him home. Even if Jimmy does get mad at him when he finally goes back, he never said Bull should stay away forever. When Jimmy's mad, it's best to stay out of his way, but three days is probably long enough. Boy, was he mad. Maddest Bull's ever seen him, and that's saying a lot. He remembers those tantrums the boy threw as a three-year-old; they were epic. Feet banging, head banging. Making himself sick with screaming. Poor Mona, trying to rein in that kind of fury with her body, getting kicked, scratched.

Still thirsty. Still four bottles of Sam Adams in the refrigerator. Bull remembers a time when he could drink beer as if it were water, with about the same effect. Nothing. Nada. Peed a lot, that's about it. When he was a grunt in Nam, beer fulfilled all his liquid requirements. When he wanted a buzz—and that was pretty much all the time—he used more interesting, less liquid substances. And after coming home, miraculously in one piece—not like these kids today who survive their horrendous wounds because battlefield medicine is so good—those substances were the only thing that kept him sane. Sort of. A good blunt in the middle of the night when the dreams would replay his experiences was about the only thing that could calm him down. The smell of a burning roach filling his nostrils was the only thing to overwhelm the stench of burning flesh that lingered in his memory.

Long time ago. Lot of water under the bridge since then. Those poor kids soldiering in those Muslim countries don't even have the comfort of a glass of beer at the end of a mission. And they still have the scent of burned flesh in their noses.

"You want to go for a walk, dog? Coop said he'd be back for lunch. Let's hope he brings some Coke with him."

The yellow dog is immediately on his feet, nose pointed toward the door, tail wagging.

"Don't know why Coop's being so stubborn about you. You're a good dog. Guess there's just no room in his life for another dog. That K-9 partner of his left some mighty big footprints." Bull manages to zip up the too-small vest and they head out to circle the pond.

It's well past noon when they get back. No Cooper. Bull checks to see if somehow he's missed him, but there's no note. No change in the contents of the refrigerator. Still four bottles of beer. Bull needs to call his sponsor. The four bottles of beer are lying in wait for him, ready to trip him up a mere two, three days back into his sobriety. His sponsor will come and get him, but he needs to get to a phone to make that happen. How far is the main road? Not that far. For a man who bikes to work every day, a mile or two isn't that much. He can thumb a ride into town, maybe get dropped off at Cumbie's, the last place in Harmony Farms to have a pay phone. Bull fishes around in his pants pocket to see if there's a quarter. He finds two. Hopefully, that'll be enough. It makes him laugh, the idea that when he was a kid, phone calls were a dime. And he could fill the Nova with gas for about two bucks, three at most if it was bone-dry. Like he is now. What's one beer? It's not the same as indulging in his friends Jack and Jim. He never even feels the first glass of Jim Beam, just enjoys the bite on his tongue. By the second glass of Jack, if that's what he's drinking, there's only the smooth succor of warmth in his belly. By the next or the next, then he might be feeling a little . . . well, let's call it *content*. Beer hasn't got that power. Beer just goes down easy when you're thirsty. Which is what he is now. It'll take him an hour to get to Cumbie's, at the very least. Plenty of time for one beer to work through his system, even two.

Cooper's organized; Bull will give him that. Bottle opener is in the silverware drawer, right where you'd expect to find it.

When he pops the cap off the third beer, Bull is at the contentment stage. Life is all right. Maybe not good, but all right. Funny how beer usually does nothing for him. Must be that his resistance is low from being a teetotaler all this time. Bull gets up, amazed to feel the buzz. Amazed to have to reach for the back of the couch to steady himself. The yellow dog looks at him with this extraordinary look of concern. Who knew a dog could look like he thinks you're in trouble. "It's okay, dog. I'm okay."

It wasn't Jimmy's fault that he'd succumbed to temptation on Friday. That's one of the things he has to remember, that it's no one else's fault. It's his problem. He has to take ownership of it. Bull lines the three empties neatly on the counter, sticks his hand in his pocket again. Still has fifty cents. Still needs to call his sponsor.

"I gotta leave, boy. You wait here for Coop. I'll leave him a note." Cooper is certainly an organization freak, and he has a dry-erase board on the wall with a grocery list on it. His penmanship is precise, tiny. "Milk. Eggs. Bread. Dog food. Call dentist Tuesday. Truck insurance due 15th." Bull adds: "Thanks for everything." The three words are disproportionate, the *thanks* outweighs the preposition, and the *everything* peters away to lie up against the edge of the board.

It's getting colder, but Bull remembers to bank the woodstove. He sure wouldn't want Cooper to come home to a burned-down cabin. He's a good guest, so he fetches an armload of wood off the porch. It's a big armload, so he doesn't shut the door, letting the warm air out and the cold air in for the minute or so it takes him to set four splits around the base of the stove to warm them up. Bull pulls his hood up, heads out. It's a trudge, getting to the main road, and Bull keeps his head down and his hands shoved into his kangaroo pocket. The hood helps against the rising wind, even as it limits his peripheral vision. Eyes on the ground, one foot in front of the other, he's hoping that before long he'll hit pavement. The track is pretty easy to follow, although the subtle rise and fall of the terrain keeps catching at his feet. He stays upright; he's not that drunk. One foot in front of the other. Left, right, left. Just like the army.

Behind him is the yellow dog, happy to get another walk. Happy to follow.

It was pleasant, this second walk of the day. The yellow dog follows Bull as he moves along the two-track dirt road. The deepening cold lifts interesting scents up out of the ground, a rabbit, a vole. A coyote, the big male. The dog adds his own scent, obliterating the coyote's mark. The man he knows is called *Bull* keeps moving, muttering human language as he stumbles. His grumbling doesn't put the dog on alert; it's more like that muttery sound his mother once made. A comfortable complaint.

They reach the end of the track and Bull pauses. The dog sits behind him, patiently awaiting the next thing. He's getting a little hungry—which is to say, his normal state of being—and he thinks that going back would be a good idea. But Bull doesn't. So the dog follows, marking places where other dogs have walked along the verge of the paved road.

Cars go by, bending around the bulky form walking backward along the side of the road, his thumb out and his bleary eyes focused on the faces of the drivers who buzz by. Most don't slow; some do and then speed away.

The dog keeps to the bushes, keeping himself out of reach of strangers. Finally, one car stops completely, and Bull disappears into it.

The dog sits, neatly hidden by a screen of stunted junipers. Alone. Hungry. What's that? The sound of a small creature scurrying beneath the crispy layers of leaf fall? The dog drops his nose, finds the scent, and is at once a hunter. Feral. Gone.

38

When I get home, Bull and the dog are gone. At first, I think that maybe he's just gone to give the dog a walk, but then I notice the scrawled thank-you note on the dry-erase board. Okay, he's apparently walked out of here. But the dog? It seems that Bull has taken the dog with him. I don't even try to figure out why he took the dog, it's such a Bull kind of impulsive decision, but now I've got to go collect him. With Jimmy at the house, there's no way I'm going to trust the dog not to bolt at the sight of him.

It's so cold that I think maybe he went by the lone cab that serves Harmony Farms, he and the dog. Which I quickly realize would be impossible. No phone to call a cab. I can't figure Bull out, so I stop trying. In the words of youth: *whatever*.

I shower and dress in fresh clothes, suitable for an evening in, or an evening out. Text Natalie that I'm on my way. Happily, I get a text back suggesting I stop for pizza. At least this time it'll be warm.

The tiny Baggie is still in my inside coat pocket. I should put this someplace safe. There's a ceramic cookie jar in the shape of a pig on the counter. I never bother to go to the trouble to put cookies in it, so it's empty except for the cookie crumbs left in there by previous tenants. I drop the baggie in, put the pig's head back onto its shoulders. Which is when I notice the neatly lined up and very empty Sam Adams bottles. Oh, Bull.

My fault for leaving the beer in the fridge. His fault for drinking it. I take a deep breath. I just can't worry about him anymore. He's managed to walk out of here, and I didn't see him facedown along the side of the road, so I assume he also managed to hitch a ride. Which means I can spend my evening going from bar to bar until I find him, and, in a fairly accurate reenactment of my teenage years, pull him out, take him home, and sober him up. Or I can stick with my plans and leave him to his own devices. It's kind of a no-brainer. Besides, if he's got the dog with him, maybe he just went home. I'll drop by to retrieve the retriever after my dinner with Natalie.

I wash my hands, grab my keys, and I'm out the door.

The temperature has dropped even more, and as I drive along Lake Shore Drive I think that if this cold front keeps up, the ice may thicken up enough for ice-skating. At the very least, shallow Bartlett's Pond will freeze up and I may have a little more company than I'm used to in my remote location. When I was a kid, we played pickup hockey on Bartlett's Pond, as Lake Harmony was given over to ice fishing and the surface was never smooth enough. I was a pretty good hockey player in my youth and I coached a peewee team as my community volunteer service while I was working—part of the PALS program. I enjoyed it but felt bad for the kids who had never skated on natural ice, with its random clumps of vegetation sticking through to catch a skate, or detour a puck aimed for a teammate; to never learn to avoid the places that were too soft to skate on, cloudy instead of clear.

Rocco's isn't too busy, so I'm in and out in twenty. My text tone beeps—Natalie asking if I would mind picking up some milk at Cumberland Farms. She's so sorry to ask. I text back: *No problem*. And I smile, feeling like a, well, like a husband. It's really the mundane that defines a relationship, isn't it? Errands, chores. The tilt of a chin, a smile. Finding a favorite cookie in the cupboard. Cleaning the frost off a windshield without being asked. I am suddenly nostalgic for the ordinary, and I pull into Cumberland's parking lot with a mild surge of hope.

And there is Bull, leaning against the brick wall beneath the NO LOITERING sign, sucking hard on a cigarette, paper cup of coffee in one hand. No dog in sight.

"Bull, what are you doing here and where's the dog?" I ask when I get out of the truck. I have a horrible image of the dog dead by the side of the road.

He looks at me as if he has no idea who I am. He tosses the cigarette butt onto the ground, plants a big foot on it. "Dog?"

"The dog. The one you left my cabin with."

"I didn't take your dog."

I don't say, again, that he's not my dog. "He's not at the cabin. Did you let him out?"

Bull leans back against the brick wall. I can smell the fumes from where I stand. He's not drinking coffee out of that cup. "I left, but I didn't take your dog."

"You need to go home. Now." I am so pissed. I've got two pizzas rapidly cooling in my truck. I've got plans. I've got a life. But now I have to bundle Bull into my truck, drive him home, find some explanation to give Natalie as to why I'm going to be late. And find the dog. Again. I know. It's not the end of the world. But it is frustrating. If I hadn't spent most of my boyhood doing exactly this, I might be a little more patient, more understanding. But I did spend my youth pulling Bull out of bars, walking him home or, when I got my license, driving him home to sober up. Making sure he didn't choke on his own vomit. Making sure he had aspirin and water by his bed so that when he woke up with his daily hangover, he'd have relief. And then I caught up with my friends, or got to practice, late again. That boyhood resentment simmers so close to the surface.

"Get in the truck."

"No. I'm waiting for someone."

"Get in the truck, Bull."

"Coop, it's okay. I know what I did, and my guy's coming for me." He puts one hand against my chest, pushing me away.

His guy? Then I get it. "Your sponsor?"

"My guy."

"Why don't you wait inside. It's cold out here." I have visions of Bull freezing solid to the bricks, despite the infusion of alcohol.

"Kid behind the counter doesn't like it when I do that."

I yank open the heavy glass and metal door, go in, and grab a gallon of 2 percent milk. As I pay, I catch the kid's eye. "That old man out there?"

"Yeah, what about him?"

"Let him stay inside till his ride comes."

"Can't. He's loitering." He hands me my change. "Besides, he's drunk, and we can't have that in here. Makes the other customers nervous."

"You want a man frozen to death on your premises? That ought to make customers really nervous." I shove a ten-dollar bill at him, "That's enough for him to be a customer." I grab the milk and go back outside.

Bull sees me coming, waves me away. "I told you, he'll be here any minute."

"Go in. You've got ten dollars' worth of time in there. So go in. Get a real coffee."

"Coop, I didn't lose your dog." He looks genuine; he looks sad. "I wouldn't be that careless."

"I know." Intentionally, I think, *intentionally* careless about anything.

By now it's dark, and although it makes no sense to start looking for the dog now, I have to. I hate thinking of him outside on a night like this, whether of his own volition or by accident. I call Natalie before I leave the parking lot, suggesting that I drop the food and milk off, then take a slow turn along the roads that lead to my cabin. I'm hoping that she'll volunteer to go with me.

The truth is, things had kind of gone south when I called Natalie to wish her a Happy New Year, which is why I was so pleased to have gotten her call today. We keep doing this, this strange, cautious dance. I think it was when I mentioned that I wasn't going to renew my contract with the town but that I also wasn't going to apply for reinstatement on the K-9 unit. It was New Year's Day, what else does one talk about except resolutions?

"My resolution is to be out of this job at the end of the fiscal year," I'd told her.

"What will you do? Go back to law enforcement?"

"Possibly. But not the K-9 unit."

"Why not? It's what you love."

"Loved." End of story.

The pizzas are nearly cold when I get to Natalie's, but we each eat a slice before heading out. Natalie climbs into the cab of my truck, reminding me that the dog's bigger now, has a layer of good retriever fat that will help keep him warm. He's experienced out there. That will help.

"I don't know. I hope so." I still believe that Bull, in some careless, inconsiderate, alcohol-blunted way, has somehow lost the dog. But I didn't tell Natalie that. I glossed it over, saying that my father must have left the door open. I certainly didn't tell her about his headlong pitch off the wagon. Some things aren't for public consumption. I just said that Bull had left the cabin and the dog had disappeared.

I take a left out of her driveway. We don't say much, our eyes focused on the road ahead of us, the scrubby verge beside us. I risk a glance in her direction. She looks tired. I recall the despair in her voice earlier today. The frustration. The fact that she reached out. "I'm glad that you called me. I was wondering if you were mad at me."

"No. Yes. Maybe."

"And what are you now?"

"Better."

"If I can ask, what, exactly, did I do that set you off?"

"It's about being honest. Open."

"How have I not been *open* with you?" If my hands weren't occupied with steering, I might have used air quotes over the word. Instead, I grip the wheel. What is so magical about telling every detail, every truth, to a woman?

To my complete surprise, she laughs. "Oh, yeah. You're about as open as a locked door."

"You know the basics—reluctant return of the native; divorced." I take a breath. "My loss."

"I wish you'd tell me about that." Natalie lays her hand on my leg, just above the knee. Has anyone ever acknowledged the power of that not wholly sexual feminine gesture? It's the hand of support. Like the supportive hand on the back from a teammate after a heartbreaker, or the linking of arms that young girls do: *I'm here.*

And so I tell her the whole story.

"I wasn't supposed to fall in love with Argos. By doing so, I was breaking the tacit rules about being a K-9 handler. The dog was supposed to be a tool, like the firearm and the Mace and the handcuffs on my belt. But I did fall in love with him, and his loss crushed me. It wasn't just the tinnitus in my left ear or the dull pain in my back that prevented me from getting another canine; it was the fear of enduring another loss. The relationship between Argos and me was more than the sum of its parts, irreplaceable. He'd saved me, but I couldn't save him. I don't mean pulling me out of a burning building, which he never did; or savaging a man about to fire at me, which he did do, twice. But Argos came into my life at a time when I was unmoored, uncertain, and unfocused. "

He'd do anything Cooper asked. Anything. At his master's command, Argos would streak like a demon, elegant jaws slashing at the air until he tackled his target, taking him down, his jaws slashing at flailing arms. Moving at the speed of a jackal, moving so fast, he appeared elongated, ears flattened, one long furious dragon of a dog.

Cooper was his boss. His commander. His master. Argos looked to him with the devotion and loyalty and trust that defined his legendary breed. One-man dog. One-dog man. Cooper was smitten. He had never had any creature so entirely his. So entirely certain of his infallibility. When Argos was beside him, Cooper caught the admiring eyes of passersby; the approval of strangers who welcomed them, who knew that they were there for their safety, their protection. They were equally goodwill ambassadors and feared. Feared by the felons and fugitives, the drug dealers and convenience-store robbers. If Argos and Cooper were on the trail, there was no hiding. From Argos. From his exquisite nose.

So late one night, a night so deep into winter cold that it seemed like nothing could survive outside, Cooper and Argos got called into work. Reluctantly, Cooper crawled out of his bed, where his wife slept on barely disturbed. He pulled on layers of clothing, long johns, winter pants, two pairs of socks, cotton undershirt, uniform shirt, fleece vest, and heavy jacket. Argos would be fine as he was, his double-thick coat more than enough to withstand the elements. It was a quiet night, no wind to speak of.

This would be an easy collar. All they had to do was pick up the guy's scent and follow him. Although there was no snow on the ground, the cold weather would help Argos track him. There would be no place to hide from Argos's superior nose, unless their quarry had snagged a ride, and then his scent would dead-end. But the reports were that he'd beaten a path into an old, run-down neighborhood. This was a bad guy; this was a guy they all wanted to see brought to justice.

Argos cast around for the scent, sorting it out from the muddle of fellow cops, reporters, bystanders, and within seconds he struck it. It was so cold that it almost hurt to breathe in the air, and made it hard for Cooper to keep up with the dog, who plunged ahead, oblivious to the penetrating cold, happy to be working. Cooper had seen some football routes that were less complicated than the path this fugitive had taken. Up one street, down the next, through an alley, over a hedge. The fugitive must have figured there'd be a dog on his heels. Argos planted his forefeet on the lids of garbage cans, sniffing the empty air for the invisible trail the suspect had left behind, a trail of skin cells and effluvia.

Finally, Cooper and the dog came to a stop outside a small two-family house. No lights, no barrels set out front for tomorrow's trash collection. The screen door was ripped off its hinges and Cooper could see the jagged edges of broken glass in the windows. But there was something very live about the silent, dark, abandoned-looking place. In the cold stillness of the midnight air a subtle sense that a door had just shut, or maybe a tattered shade hanging in a blank window had moved. It was as if the house were breathing. Or holding its breath. Cooper stepped away from the pool of light cast by the one working streetlight on this rough street. Despite the wool scarf wrapped around it, he felt a chill run up the back of his neck.

Cooper radioed their position to the unit. Argos growled, then barked. The fugitive was out the back door, and Cooper instantly decided that they didn't have time for backup, that their quarry would be gone before a squad car could turn the corner. He took out his weapon. "Police!"

For months, the city had been plagued by a nutcase mad bomber. He'd call and say that he'd set up bombs on bridges or in tunnels, or in trash cans in highly trafficked areas. Lots of K-9 hours had been lost searching for the bombs he claimed to have planted, only to have him call back and say that he had planted a real bomb somewhere else. The city was on high alert. Not enough time had passed since the Boston Marathon bombing, and this nutcase was being taken very seriously. His fake bombs were all but real, saving one element or another, so it was clear that he knew how to make a bomb, and unclear why he kept tormenting the city with his series of fakes.

And now they had him, Cooper and Argos, had him corned like the vermin he was. In the dim light of a faulty streetlight, Cooper could see that their fugitive was dressed entirely in black, from the top of his head to the balaclava over his face, his midsection bulky and his legs spindly. He looked like a spider.

It should have been a pretty easy collar. Cooper had him cornered. He had the dog. He had backup coming any minute. He was so anxious to make this arrest that he felt as if he were vibrating. All he had to do was pull the trigger.

And now I'm almost to the end of my story when I will articulate what I have not spoken out loud to anyone. I pause for a moment. Natalie waits, letting me find the words.

"So I shouted, 'Put up your hands!' I leveled my weapon, gripped, as I'd been trained, in two hands. Even so, I felt the adrenaline pulse my aim out of true. I had him in my sights, within range, within protocol. He put his arms out as asked. But then, in a confident, almost casual motion, one hand went in toward his chest.

"I should have shot him, but instead I released the dog. I sent Argos into the arms of a suicide bomber. I sent him to his death. That dog had given me everything and I failed him entirely. I sent him in."

I've long since pulled the truck over to the side of the road. I'm quivering exactly like I was on that other cold January night. My heart is beating with the same tympanic volume.

Natalie's hand gently squeezes my leg. But she stays quiet, and I know that she's trying to find the words to excuse me.

"When I was interviewed after the fact, I told my superiors that I was not confident that I would have hit him. What I implied was that I thought my dog was fast enough that he would down him before he pulled the detonator."

It comes out of me then, the truth that has lodged in my soul like a tumor. "The truth is, I hesitated. I'd never shot to kill before. It was my fault. If I had . . . " I let the sentence hang.

Natalie takes me in her arms and rocks me, patting my back and telling me that it's really all right, to let it out. I try to say that I shouldn't be giving in, that I should be well past the weeping stage, but then I realize that she's quietly weeping, too. I don't know if it's for me, my story of loss, or for her own. It doesn't really matter. She pulls a crumpled tissue out of her jacket pocket and dabs at her eyes, then hands it to me. "Aren't we a pair?" She gives that little laugh that follows a meltdown, and, after a moment, I do, too.

The barn doors are closed, the horses all snug in their stalls, wrapped in their blankets, sipping water from heated buckets and munching the extra hay that will help keep them warm on this very cold night. I've put my inexpert electrical knowledge to work and gotten her tank heaters going again. We haven't found the dog and have come back to her place defeated. It's late, so I don't stay much longer, just long enough to eat a couple of slices of reheated pizza. She knows the worst of me now, but she doesn't flinch. I say good night and promise to let her know as soon as I find the dog. I love that she is so optimistic, saying that I will find the dog.

I have one final truth to share with this woman who loves animals and hasn't condemned me for losing mine; I tell her how Argos saved me. He'd provided me with something that I could love unconditionally without fear of its being taken away from me. He was wholly mine.

The stars are brilliant, diamond specks in the inky sky—just like the night that haunts me. But this night, the deadweight of my grief is gone. Lifted away. Someone has understood the depth of my grief, hasn't mocked it or told me I'll get over it. I should get over it. I must get over it.

It's cold and brilliant and so very clear. And there, waiting for me on the cabin porch, is the yellow dog.

39

His sponsor had sat with Bull for hours, until the soporific effects of the booze had been countered with the buzz of endless cups of coffee. They had talked, and then not talked. Over and over, Bull was reminded that every day was a new start and that he didn't need to think about why he'd succumbed to temptation, only think about not doing it again. His sponsor is someone Bull has known a long time, who has had some of the same troubles as himself, maybe not a dead wife, but a divorce. Vietnam. Maybe not a son quite like Jimmy, but a daughter who got herself in the family way at age sixteen. Everybody has troubles. When his sponsor dropped him off at the Poor Farm Road house, Bull thanked him, truly appreciative of the guy's efforts, a little maudlin at the kindness. He felt sober, and cheered.

"Thought you were staying at Coop's." Jimmy is sitting in the living room, dressed in a bathrobe, bare feet stuck in slippers, flipping channels. A new bottle of Jack Daniel's sits on the low end table.

"I left. Got homesick."

"Join me?" He puts his hand on the bottle. "Good stuff."

"Please don't, Jimmy."

"Hey, Bull, I'm just joking with you. I'm not sharing." Jimmy settles on a nature program.

Bull sits on the other end of the couch. "Coop doesn't have a TV."

Jimmy looks at his father, chuckles. "He always was an odd one."

"Still is."

40

L ev Parker stares at the baggie that I've dropped on his desk. The little rectangle filled with white is in stark contrast to the inky black of his professionally uncluttered blotter.

"Think that's enough for a search warrant?"

"Probably."

"Okay."

"The thing is, Jimmy's only one guy."

"With a shitload of heroin stashed in the stovepipe."

"Cooper, we've got the county's drug task force working on this."

"So? I've just dropped fifty dollars' worth of evidence in your hands."

"And we're grateful."

"But?"

"We want them all. We can bust Jimmy, but then the whole operation disappears out from under us."

"Unless he talks."

"Cooper, he never has before. Why would he now?"

Lev is right. Even as a little kid, Jimmy never ratted out a friend.

As a juvenile, he took six months in juvenile hall rather than give up his Fagin. As an adult, he spent twelve years without parole and never breathed a word against his partners. I could never tell if it was fear of retribution or a curious and misplaced loyalty.

"I've done what I can. It's up to you."

"Hey, thanks, Cooper. It will help. When the time comes. In the meantime . . . "

"I know. I'll pretend like we're the fucking Cleavers."

"Something like that."

Okay, I'm disappointed. Maybe it's colossally unbrotherly, but I spent far too many years of my professional career working to put men like my brother behind bars. I've seen up close and personal the devastating effects of what these bastards peddle. And I'm seeing what he's doing to Bull. The drug task force is a great idea, except that it's more than likely Bull will end up on the receiving end of an arrest warrant. Knowingly harboring drugs and drug activity—that should be good for a long sojourn in prison, and not county jail this time. Bull may be able to carry off playing dumb with a lot of folks, but not those guys. He may piss me off, but I really don't want the old man sent to prison.

I maybe shut Lev's door a little aggressively, but I really don't care.

Polly is grinning at me when I get back to the shelter. "You've got a message!"

She's adjusted to her role as assistant ACO with a vengeance. The place is spit-polish clean; the ancient Mr. Coffee has been discarded and a new Krups coffeemaker that she bought with her first week's pay sits in pride of place, usually with a plate of homemade cookies beside it. The cat room boasts a carpet-covered multiplatform tree, and I never once have to complain about the stink of the litter boxes. As part of her self-defined job description, she's been fielding all my calls instead of letting the answering machine do the hard work. Now she hands me a pink *While You Were Out* slip. "Barkwell Kennels. Mr. Stinson. They'll be at home all day," it says.

"Well, I'll be a son of a bitch."

"Cooper. Language."

I'd like to, but I don't sweep her up and swing her in my arms.

There is only one dog in residence today, the yellow dog. Polly doesn't keep him kenneled while she's here. He is flopped down in the cat room, apparently at home with felines. They ignore him. "Hey, bud, we're going to find you your lost owner today. What do you think of that?"

He gets to his feet, shakes, ambles over. For once, I give him a good solid pat. My determination to find the perpetrator who shot this dog hasn't diminished, but my certainty that his missing owner is the culprit fluctuates. At this point, I'm just hoping that the owner is a nice lady who will be glad to have him back. In my heart of hearts, I know that it will be well nigh impossible to prove abuse. But one thing is for certain: I'll be keeping an eye on whoever his owner is.

I grab a chocolate-chip cookie off the plate, gently close my office door, put my feet up on the desk, and dial the number for Barkwell Kennels, which by this time I have memorized. I am finally rewarded with a human voice. I quickly identify myself and tell an abbreviated version of the story, give the kennel owner the microchip number. Mr. Stinson tells me to hold on for a minute, and I hear him moving papers around. "Yeah, here it is. That number was assigned to a pup we sold to a guy named Boykin. How'd he get to you?"

"Boykin? Are you sure?"

"Yeah. Donald Boykin, Harmony Farms."

Bad year for dogs.

Cynthia Mann and Donald Boykin do not seem the type of people to leave a lost dog unreported. More like the type of folks who would launch a massive search party, post pictures, advertise a reward well out of proportion to the value of the dog. I take another look at the list of Labradors registered in the last year. Neither a Boykin nor a Mann registered a dog at all, and I know that their deceased spaniel should come up in the registry—if she was licensed. A ten-buck dog license. It's not like they can claim hardship. And, as our first selectman, it behooves Cynthia not to be a scofflaw where her dogs are concerned. I go back another year and find the spaniel. I'll give them a pass; it's pretty easy to forget to get an annual dog license, especially given the busy lives they must lead.

It just niggles at me, the fact that they never reported this dog missing. Then I wonder if he was never lost. Adolescent dogs can be pains in the neck. Maybe this yellow dog didn't fit into their busy lifestyle and they gave him away and whoever had him did the damage. Well, I can conjecture all day long; it really doesn't matter. What matters is returning this dog, who is nibbling at something Polly is hand-feeding him. I pick up the phone and punch in the number for the Mann/Boykin residence.

The female voice on the other end of the line bears the same Eastern European accent as the housekeeper at the old Callahan place. "Stacia speaking."

I identify myself and she waits until I state my business.

"We don't have any dog."

"No, I know. I've found a dog that belongs to Mr. Boykin."

"He doesn't have a dog."

"Stacia. Did he have a dog?"

There is a pause. "Yes."

"A Labrador?"

"I don't know. The black-and-white one was hit by a car. I don't know what she was."

"I know that. This is a yellow dog, big. A hunting dog."

Another hesitation. I don't think it has anything to do with English as a second language. "

"When will Mr. Boykin be home?"

"He's on a business trip. Home tomorrow night."

"Tell him I have his dog."

"Yes, sir."

Cynthia Mann doesn't keep regular office hours as selectman, but I've seen her often enough in the town hall around midafternoon, sometime between her ladies-who-lunch date and her afternoon yoga. I pop the yellow dog into the town's SUV and head over. The place is quiet on this Friday afternoon, sleepy almost. I nod to the tax collector, steal a handful of M&Ms from the town clerk's jar. "Cynthia around?"

"Just missed her. I think she said something about going down to Boston. She was dressed to kill, if you know what I mean." In Harmony Farms, any woman spotted wearing panty hose is considered dressed up. "Some big charity event."

"Thanks, Judy. If she should call in, ask her to call me." I have no real expectation that Cynthia will interrupt her philanthropic do-gooding to call the local dogcatcher.

That's about all I can do right now about the critter lounging in the back of the town's Suburban. I guess I'll have to suffer one more night with my roomie.

It is so cold tonight that I begin to wonder how long I can stay in this barely insulated cabin. Even with the Jøtul burning hot, the rest of the place is numbing. I have to leave the bathroom faucet dripping to ensure that the pipes don't freeze, which makes me realize that my hearing is way better, because the *drip drip drip* is driving me crazy. It's almost enough to make me invite the dog into my bed, a one-dog night. But I don't. Instead, I get a mercy call from Natalie.

I don't hesitate, just grab a toothbrush and the dog and head to Second Hope.

41

Mike and Dave are in the house when Bull gets home. Jimmy's pals. All three of them are sitting around the kitchen table, like they're looking for a fourth for a game of poker, except that there are no cards, no chips on the table. The little piles that are in front of them aren't real nickels.

"What are you doing home?" Jimmy casually places his hands over the bags in front of him, then looks at his friends, who do the same, like kids trying to hide something. They *are* trying to hide something.

"I live here?" Bull gives them a smile, hands palms-up like a cartoon character's.

"Jimmy, I thought you locked the door." One of them, Dave or Mike, mutters. Bull doesn't remember who is who, just the pair of them, like conjoined twins MikeandDave. "I told you this wasn't a good idea."

"You're home a little early." Jimmy's voice is not conversational.

"Yeah. About that."

It was only a matter of time. He was sick of that job anyway. Outside in all weathers, splinters and breathing in sawdust.

"You should go lie down. In your room."

"I'm a little old to be sent to my room." Bull blinkers his eyes with the flats of his hands. "I'm not around, I don't see anything, but I'm thirsty and I'm going to my own fridge."

"I mean it." Jimmy gets to his feet, motioning to his comrades to stay put, that he's got this.

"Jimmy," the other one says. Dave or Mike. "Leave him alone. He's your father."

"He's a pain in the ass."

One of them leans back in his chair. "Hey, Bull, you want to make some money?"

"Supplement my unemployment?"

"Yeah. Something like that. You want to keep your boy happy? Keep Jimmy safe? Do us a favor and I'll make it worth your while."

"Dave, this is not a good idea." Jimmy sits back down. It's weird to see Jimmy in a subordinate position, but clearly he is the low man on this three-man totem pole.

"Would you be interested in taking a package—oh, let's say of books—meeting a guy who's a great reader?"

"You want me to be your mule?"

"I wouldn't call it that. Our bike-delivery guy."

"No."

"Let me put it to you another way. You know a little too much not to be involved. Either work with us or . . . well, I don't think you'd much like the alternative."

"Dave, please. He's not reliable. He'll be fine. I can keep him under control." Jimmy's voice is pitched a little higher than usual. "Come on, Dave. You can't be serious."

It's Dave. That's who this one is. The bigger one. The one with the clean hands. The other guy has prison tats all over his. Mike.

Bull pulls a bottle of water out of the refrigerator. It's not what he wants. He wants a real drink. Something that will muffle the tension that is building here, something to blame when he makes the wrong decision. He knows that Jimmy is going to lose this argument. Jimmy needs to be smarter than that. These guys aren't friends; they're thugs. He takes a swig of the water. Drug dealers. Bull knows that if he doesn't take Dave's offer, take the bait, bad things will happen, not just to him but to Jimmy, too. Some kids admire basketball players or astronauts. Jimmy always admired the fugitives on *America's Most Wanted*. Bull can see him for what he is, a punk trying to be a player.

"I'll do it. How much you offering?"

Cooper has taken the afternoon off to take his old man down to the Social Security office in Leominster. Bull is grateful but nervous. He's afraid that his former law-enforcement officer son will somehow sniff out the big secret that Mike and Dave and Jimmy have forced on him, that he has gone from being willfully ignorant to complicit in their business. He's clean-shaven and freshly showered, old but fresh chinos on, a frayed-at-the-cuffs button-down shirt. His parka still bears the fragrance of lumber, but it's the only winter coat he has, since he never did find the other one. He's wearing the Christmas hat and gloves, but he's still cold, even in Coop's nice truck.

They've signed Bull up for Social Security. See if he can live on that. He's enjoying this, being able to say that he's retired instead of unemployed, retired instead of up and quit. Coop's idea. Smart kid.

"You think I should retire to Florida?"

"Yeah, why not. You can live cheaper, that's for sure."

"I'd miss my friends."

Cooper is kind enough not to point out that Bull doesn't really have any honest-to-God friends. Lots of acquaintances, but that's hardly a reason to stay put. Especially if things get tense with Mike and Dave and Jimmy.

"I'd miss you." Bull says this without looking at Cooper, not wanting to see his reaction. Waits a beat, two. No response. He's not going to ask if Coop would miss him, too.

"I'd come visit. Maybe take a vacation down there. Fish a little."

Bull looks out the window, smiling.

When they get back to 179 Poor Farm Road, Jimmy's car is gone, and Bull relaxes a little. He doesn't want Cooper to ask about Jimmy, or, worse, want to go in while he's there. Jimmy has made it clear that shouldn't happen again.

Cooper pulls up beside the derelict Nova, doesn't make noise about going inside. Between them, the dog reaches over the seat back, noses Bull in the ear. Bull reaches back, pats him, and climbs out of the truck. "Hey, thanks, Coop. I appreciate the help."

"No problem."

"See you."

"Hey, Bull. Can I ask you a question?"

"Shoot."

"Why do you still have that car?" He nods in the direction of the Nova. "It's not like you were ever going to restore it."

Bull walks around to stand between Cooper's open truck window and the rusted-out car. He runs a hand over the roof, crusty with tree litter and ice. "I don't know."

"It's been over twenty-five years, Bull."

"It reminds me."

"Of what?"

"Of consequences."

"The consequences of Jimmy's behavior? It didn't help, did it?"

Bull has always known that on some level everyone blamed Jimmy for the accident. If he hadn't been in trouble, Mona wouldn't have driven away, lost control of the car, and crashed into that massive oak at the bottom of the hill. But that wasn't really fair. And it's not fair that Bull has never tried to correct the error. "No. Mine. Didn't you ever know that she hit that tree because the brakes went? That I hadn't put brake fluid in? That if I'd gotten air in her tire, she wouldn't have even taken the Nova."

"Does Jimmy know this?"

"I don't know."

"Bull, you are a piece of work." Cooper closes his window, backs out of the driveway, then stops, pulls back in, and lowers his window again. "I'm sorry, Bull. That was rotten." He didn't look at Bull as he said that, but now he turns his face to look directly at his father. "I know what consequences feel like."

42

A bitterly cold night spent in a centrally heated house did wonders for my spirits and everything for my self-esteem as Natalie, now that I'd let her into my confidence, my trust, welcomed
me into hers. We split a bottle of wine and talked. She talked about
Marcus and I talked about Argos. She told me about the special
challenges of being in an interracial marriage, I told her about the
challenges of being the town drunk's kid. And then we stopped
talking. Our dogs nested together in Betty's bed and Natalie and I
nested in hers. We spent the weekend being as lazy as people responsible for the care and well-being of animals can ever be. We bundled
into long johns and polar fleeces to feed horses and muck stalls,
peeling off layers as the work heated us up. I made us chili and
Natalie baked corn bread. I was as happy as I had been in a very
long time.

Then Monday afternoon, Bull laid his revelation on me. It was
my own fault; I shouldn't have asked why he had kept that hulk for
so many years. I don't know why it's bothered me that he has, but
now it's going to bother me more, now that I know he holds himself

to blame. And, of course, he is to blame. But that doesn't take the responsibility for what happened off of Jimmy. It was still his action that set everything into motion. At least to my mind.

Well, I can't dwell on it. That's what Nat said when I called her. "Cooper, it doesn't change a thing. But you've got to feel sorry for him."

"Who, Bull or Jimmy?"

"Both of them." A beat. "All of you."

The Eastern European housekeeper at the Mann/Boykin residence is polite but emphatic that neither sir nor madam are available. I glance at the yellow dog, at this moment flat on his back while Polly scratches his belly. "How long have you worked for the family?"

"Six years."

"And you have no recollection of a yellow Labrador retriever being there?"

"A yellow dog?"

"Yes."

I can almost hear the wheels spinning, the internal debate. What mystifies me is the prevarication about such a simple question. Did the Mann/Boykin family ever have a yellow dog? Yes. No. Simple. What's the big deal? There is something decidedly stinky about this. This is not a language barrier. This is someone protecting her job. I think about the kitten that Polly "found" wandering on the old Callahan property, and how happy that housekeeper was to get her back. Maybe there's something in Balkan DNA that is careless when it comes to other people's pets.

I sigh. No point alienating the woman. "When do you expect them?"

"I will give them the message."

"Please do."

The dog heaves his own sigh—this one of contentment.

"Cooper, why don't you try Cynthia on her cell phone?" Polly pushes herself upright, leans on the edge of the desk to get to her feet.

I stick out my hand to help. "I would if I had her number."

"I do."

Why am I not surprised that Polly Schaeffer, recovering animal hoarder, would have the first selectman's cell number?

Polly whips out a recent-vintage iPhone, scrolls down her contacts list, and hands me the phone. I read off the number as I dial it from the shelter's landline.

I'm about to wonder if Cynthia doesn't take "unknown caller" calls, when I get the automated voice-mail message. I leave my name, both numbers, cell and office, but hesitate to tell her that I have her dog. Given her recent loss, that could be cruel. I do add that I've left messages at her residence, the implication being that I'm going to keep doing so until she or Donald Boykin get around to calling me. I'm not going away.

Time for a ride-along. I snap my fingers at the dog, who no longer bolts when I do. He lets me clip the leash to his collar and willingly accompanies me out the door and into the Suburban. We've come a long way. But it's time for this dog to go home.

I wend my slow way around town. It's warmed up a little, and folks are venturing out, doing those errands that they've put off while the extravagantly cold weather made the simplest chores painful to accomplish. I can't say that I'm actively looking for Cynthia, but she's ubiquitous in this town, so it wouldn't be unusual to spot her Volvo with the oval Euro-style window decal: HARFAR, Cynthia's latest bid to put Harmony Farms on the tourism trail. So far, she's the only one sporting it. I roll past the yoga studio and the Country Market, circle around the town hall parking lot. Nada.

A dogfight at the dog park pulls me off task and I give up my quest for the moment, but that's all right, as I plan to drop by the Mann/Boykin residence on my way home. I've been too patient. Besides, at this point it will look odd for me to hang on to this dog when I know where he lives. I really don't have to wait for them to come and collect him. The housekeeper with the faulty memory can just hang on to him till "sir and madam" get home.

I've dealt with the dog incident at the dog park, a fight I'd characterize more as a kerfuffle. No blood drawn, and the pair now gamboling about the park like old pals. It's the owners I have to separate. I suggest that they, both fairly new to dog parenting, learn to identify true aggressive behavior as opposed to posturing. Almost as soon as I return to my SUV, my cell phone barks. Glory hallelujah, it's Donald Boykin.

"My housekeeper said that you wanted to speak to me?"

"Yeah. I have your dog."

"I don't have a dog. You brought our dog home—in a plastic bag."

"A yellow Labrador. He's chipped and Mr. Stinson at Barkwell Kennels said that the number corresponds to a dog you purchased from him in October."

There is enough of a silence that I think that the call has been dropped. "Mr. Boykin? Is Stinson mistaken?" My tone of voice doesn't suggest that I'm giving him an out. It suggests that he damn well better not lie to me. It's a shadow of my former professional voice, but it does the trick.

"Where is it?"

"With me. I'll drop him off."

"No. Not necessary. I'll come to you."

The day had started out overcast, but now I have to fish around for my sunglasses as the midday sun sparkles off the melting snow. The yellow dog puts his head over the back of my seat, his breath tickling my cheek. I give him a pat on his boxy head. "You ready to finally go home, big boy?"

To my surprise, my voice catches a little.

I'm at my desk with a ham and cheese sandwich and a can of V-8 juice when I get an unexpected visit from Chief Lev Parker. He looks equally businesslike and uncomfortable. "I'm just saying, as a friend, you should maybe take your father someplace for a couple of days."

The yellow dog takes one look at the uniformed policeman with the service weapon on his hip and heads into the kennel room, where he sequesters himself with the shinbone I picked up for him at the Country Market.

"I assume that, as an officer of the law, you won't tell me why." I say that, but he really doesn't have to say more. Given his *suggestion*, it's a no-brainer that the drug task force is about to swoop down on my brother and whoever it is he plays with.

"Right."

I take it as a sign of professional respect that Lev is willing to stick his neck out this way—a tacit appreciation for the help that I've given him. I feel pretty good. "I guess I could take a couple of days off. Take him out of town."

"It's for the best, Cooper. And anything he might want to talk about might help in the long run."

If Bull informs on Jimmy and his friends, he might save himself. But I know that he won't do that.

I toss the remains of my sandwich.

He's here. He's here. He's here. The never-forgotten scent of human anger, human temper floats through the building. A particular human's anger and temper. The dog whimpers, a long, drawn-out, anguished whine, and then bolts out the kennel door to the run, where he can go only six feet before coming to the wire. He presses himself against it, as if he can squeeze through the wire diamonds. He begins a frantic digging, scraping toenails against the concrete until they bleed. His trembling threatens to shake him off his feet. He pants, tongue lolling, salivating, sides heaving. It is as afraid as he's ever been. *The man is here.*

❦

Polly appears at my doorway, "Mr. Boykin is here."

I stand to invite the town's leading philanthropist into my small, dim office. Donald Boykin doesn't look like one of those six-foot power brokers with a full head of white hair, a white shirt, and a power tie. He's smallish, almost dainty, balding, wearing fashionable eyeglasses. His suit is well tailored, charcoal gray, and his shirt is crisp and light blue. He's wearing a tie that could almost be called whimsical, with tiny multicolored staplers floating on a field of yellow. His footwear is clearly of the expensive designer variety, but it's soiled now with the gritty slush of the shelter parking lot. Nonetheless, he exudes the authority of one who draws a bonus-inflated seven-figure salary.

"Thank you for coming down. I would have been happy to drop him off." I offer Boykin a seat. He looks like he wants to dust it off before he sits, but he doesn't. He does that thing with his trousers, pinching the fabric at his thighs and lifting it as he sits, a gesture I haven't seen in years, at least not since polyester was introduced.

"Mr. Boykin, let's talk about your dog."

"Well, the thing is, I don't have a dog."

"Microchip says otherwise."

He thinks about this for a moment. "My assistant once purchased a hunting dog for my use. It failed as a hunting dog."

"Last fall?"

"Yes."

"Okay. So what happened to him?"

His eyes are milky blue behind the round lenses. He has a little tick; one eyelid blinks faster than the other. I can't decide if this is a "tell," or not. He's not the nervous type, or maybe it's more accurate to say that he isn't the type to show nerves. "Nothing. I sent it back and fired my assistant."

"Seems a bit harsh."

"Not at all." Boykin pats his knees. "Well, enough said. I suppose I have to take it."

I ask Polly to fetch the yellow dog. It all seems anticlimactic; after months of wondering about this dog's origins, I have his owner, but not his story.

Polly is taking a very long time. Finally, she shows up at the door to my office, empty-handed and flushed. "He won't come out."

I could chalk it up to the yellow dog's usual stranger/danger behavior. He's been cowering in his cell since Lev Parker was here. But the dog will do anything for Polly.

"Give us a minute, will you, Polly?" I get up and shut my door. With all my heart, I wish that I had a one-way mirror and a colleague behind it. "Just to clarify, you sent the dog back. To where? Barkwell didn't have him."

Do I detect a slight flush above that razor-sharp collar? "I found him another owner."

"So you—I'm sorry—your assistant bought an untrained dog; then you found out it didn't know what to do."

"Something like that."

"And when he wouldn't perform, you got mad."

"No." He clears his throat, considers his next words. "I would characterize it more as being embarrassed. I was hunting, for the first time in decades, with my immediate superior and a very important client. I had sunk a lot of money and time into this junket, the best liquor, the best cigars, the best blind, the best weapons, and the best guide. And this craven dog ruined the day."

"So you shot him."

"No. Never." He looks genuinely shocked. "I would never."

"Who did?"

"We're men who don't tolerate disobedience. Insubordination. We fire whole departments for underperforming. But we don't shoot dogs."

"The way I see it, you literally fired this dog. He was found with bird shot embedded in his hip."

Boykin begins to lose his mild-manneredness. He begins to get angry. "I told you. No one shot that dog. Why do you keep saying that?"

"But you were embarrassed, so maybe you kicked him? His X-rays showed multiple fractures of his ribs. Maybe hit him with your gun stock?"

He says nothing, picks a fleck of something off his lapel, then slides his hand into his inside pocket. "How much do you want?" His checkbook is one of those impressive ones, long and thick.

"We'll get to fines and medical reimbursement in a moment."

"No, I mean, what do you need here? New kennels, computers? Dog food?"

"I'm sorry, I don't understand." Is he bribing me?

"How about you? Is there something on your wish list? Everyone has a wish list."

He *is* bribing me. The first selectman's husband is bribing an officer of the law. It makes my head spin.

"This is inappropriate. Put that away, Mr. Boykin. You don't want that kind of trouble."

Boykin gets to his feet. I can see now that despite the daintiness, he is a formidable man. I'm sure that his staff quakes every time he speaks. He abandons the effort to bribe me. "I can make your life pretty miserable. Give me the fucking dog or enjoy the consequences."

"I've already done miserable. There's hardly anything you can do to improve on it."

"I can have you dismissed."

"I appreciate the favor, but I'm not sure that you can."

Behind him is Polly, who has the yellow dog on the end of a slip-knot leash, and he's straining hard to be anywhere but here. She's got both hands on the leash and is even redder in the face than she was before.

Boykin puts his hand out, fully expecting that Polly will place the leash in it.

43

The hard freeze of the past week has finally let up and a warm front brought rain instead of snow last night. Now the snow that was on the ground has turned to slush, making it a sloppy bike ride. The backpack shifts a little, making Bull's already-awkward pedal up the hill harder. Cars pass him; a jogger waves cordially as she sprints up and over the rise and out of sight. Bull huffs. He's really got to quit smoking. Over the rise is a short path through the state-owned land that leads to a rest stop off the highway. This is Bull's destination. He's to meet a guy there. The rest stop has no facilities; it's just a turnout for weary motorists, a place to catch a few z's, eat a quick picnic, pee behind a tree, or walk a restless dog. He's to wait for a silver car, New York plates. One guy. He's not to approach the car, but wait. Wait for the guy to wave him over to the car. That's what Jimmy said: "Just wait."

This is the part that scares Bull. Like being on patrol in Nam, that feeling that tonight might be your night. That some grunt would sneeze or fart and bring the Vietcong down on them. That a trip line would plunge you facedown into death. Bull tells himself this is different. It's broad daylight; he's just meeting a guy, handing him something he's driven a long way to get. He's just the messenger, just the grunt. Jimmy was so clear this morning when he lifted the backpack onto Bull's shoulders. "Don't do anything to screw this up. Don't get curious; don't say anything. Hand this over and get out of there."

There is a high chain-link fence bordering the perimeter of the rest stop. Bull supposes it's meant to keep hunters from using it as a convenient parking lot. He doesn't see any break in it, no easy place to gain access to the turnout. He's too fat and old to climb over it. It seems to him that Jimmy would have known that there was no easy way to do what it is he wants Bull to do. Unless he walks a half a mile to get around it, this fence is going to make things very difficult. What if the silver car shows up while he's looking for a way around? The only other thing to do is stand here, wait for the car, and then throw the back pack over the top of the fence. Bull leans his back against a tree to wait.

This is his third time running the errand, or, as he likes to think of it, simply doing a favor for a friend. His son's friend.

The first time, he almost blew it. Bull was sitting in a McDonald's on the highway, where Dave had dropped him off. Lo and behold, who should show up but Deke Wilkins. Bull ducked his head behind a post, but Deke, on his way out of the men's room, spotted him. "Bull Harrison, what the hell you doing here?"

"Could say the same to you."

"Dentist. Getting to the age where the teeth are worn-out and the bladder won't hold the twenty miles down to the dentist's office."

"Too much coffee. That's my problem."

"Yeah. You with someone? Got a ride?"

"I do. It's fine." Bull wasn't given much to praying, but he did right then. Prayed first that Deke wouldn't decide to sit down and then that he'd be gone before Bull's contact showed up. On the bench seat beside him was the blue backpack like the kids use. Once the contact showed up, Bull was to go to the men's room and forget the pack on the seat, then head outside and light a cigarette. Although he had no idea what his contact looked like, Bull had been told that the person would signal him to leave by dropping his wallet.

Deke lingered long enough that Bull fretted that his contact had come and gone and that he'd screwed things up. Mike and Dave have made it clear that failure was, as they say, not an option.

"You don't want to be late for your appointment, do you, Deke?"

"I'm all right. I always allow enough time for a stop."

"You don't worry about traffic jams?"

"That's why I always make a midday appointment."

A big black guy in a do-rag stood in line at the counter. He fumbled with his wallet but didn't drop it. Another guy came up to him and said something; they laughed, grabbed the food, and walked out. Bull took a breath.

"Well, I'd better get on the road." Deke buttoned his coat. "You sure you're okay?"

"Fine. Nice seein' you, Deke."

"Been seeing quite of bit of Cooper these days. You know he's been courting that horse-rescue lady?"

"No shit?" Bull had to smile. "That boy keeps things so close to the vest. Maybe a little romance will keep him in town."

"I don't think that's the best thing for him."

"Maybe not. He did love being a cop." Bull felt himself cringe at the word *cop*. Great. What if the contact heard him? "See you, Deke."

Deke finally left, and the next customer in line at the counter did drop his wallet. Bull scrambled out of the booth and fairly ran to the men's room.

An hour goes by. A blue Toyota pulls in, then a white van. Another hour and three black cars in a row come in for a pause in their travels. But no silver car with New York plates. Bull has alternated between pacing the length of the fence like some kind of zoo animal and leaning against a tree, because the ground is too wet to sit on. He's shrugged off the backpack, put it back on, and then taken it off again, relieving his back of the deadweight of the contents. Another hour goes by. He really needs to sit down. It occurs to Bull that maybe the backpack would be a good-enough seat. He's certainly not going to crush the contents, whether it's money or dope, and it's a good sturdy nylon backpack, impervious to the wet. He takes the pack off, sets it gently on the ground, and lowers himself with the help of a handy limb. That's better. Now he's hungry. Jimmy never said how long he should wait. Screw this. He'll call Jimmy and see if he should call it a day. Bull punches his hands into his jacket pockets, looking for his cell phone, hoists himself up, pokes around each of the pockets in his jeans. Nada. He could have sworn that it was in his back pocket, but it's not there. Frustrated, Bull kicks the backpack, which meets his toe with a clunking sound, like there really are books in it.

44

Boykin puts out his hand in that entitled manner of the 1 percent. Polly, clearly confused, puts the leash in it, at which point the dog bolts with enough propulsion that Boykin loses the leash and nearly goes to his knees. I grab his bespoke jacket and keep him upright.

"That dog sure doesn't seem to like you."

"It doesn't really know me. I had possession of it for less than a day."

It is probably my imagination that this dog, who freaks out at the presence of any stranger, is reacting to Boykin with even more panic than usual. I know that I'm reading my own developing dislike for Boykin as proof enough that he has had some part in creating the problem. He's certainly proven himself a bully. As a professional, I can't allow myself to do that. It's facts, not fantasy, that build cases. I have no proof that Boykin did anything more violent than fire his luckless assistant.

But I have one more arrow in my quiver. "You said you had a guide? Who?"

"One of those Haynes men. I can't remember which one."

"Is there any chance your solution was to give the dog to him?"

"He expressed some interest and offered to train him."

"Right then and there?"

Boykin's eyes dart to the left, and I've got his "tell."

"Did Mr. Haynes *discipline* the dog?"

Boykin does look at me now. "Not in front of me."

"Mr. Boykin, if you will tell me the truth, I'll be willing to overlook your indiscretions regarding my wish list and my continued employment." I guide him gently back into my office. "And I'll take the dog off your hands."

Four men and a dog leave the brand-new Range Rover in a safe parking space at the trailhead. It's barely dawn and three of the men are a little hungover from the previous evening's manly bonding over oysters and rare Scotch whiskey. The fourth man is silent, refusing the proffered "hair of the dog" and the Cuban cigar the others are tucking into multipocketed camo vests for the anticipated celebration they'll have once they've bagged their limit of ducks.

The dog, a pedigreed yellow Labrador, is delighted to be outside, and the scents and sights have his tail wagging in a metronomic side-to-side beat. He is young, just an adolescent, and this is all new to him. The sharp odor emanating from the pores of these strangers, the dull chemical scent of the guns is curious, if a little repulsive. Nonetheless, he shows himself eager to join the game, whatever it is. The fourth man, the one who has the scent of dog permeated throughout his clothing—there is another kind of aura about him, one that keeps the dog from approaching him.

The group finally sets off along a path that leads to water. The fourth man is the leader, and the three others follow silently, one of them holding the leash that is attached to the dog's fluorescent orange collar. He jerks the leash periodically, as if trying to tell the dog that he's in charge, that he's the alpha. The dog knows better, knows instinctively that this man is indeed subservient to all the others. He hears it in the way the man speaks to the others. There is a little of the puppy in him, licking the chops of the older, wiser dogs. The adolescent Lab is a submissive pup himself, always ready to take a lesson from an elder. Having this in common, he shoves his cold black nose into the palm of the man holding the leash and is rewarded with a smack. "Quit that."

He's never been struck before, and it startles him into ducking away from the man. He's immediately yanked back to the man's side.

They reach the blind and Len Haynes positions each of the other men in a row, shows them how to keep from shooting one another's brains out accidentally, and then takes the dog's leash, ties him to a ring screwed into the side of the flimsy wall before ensconcing himself behind the blind to take a nap.

The pond is quiet, not a duck in sight. An hour drags by, then another. The sun strikes the placid pond, revealing its shimmering emptiness. Donald Boykin is thinking that maybe this junket was a bad idea. Cynthia didn't like the concept of a boys' weekend at her house, despite the net worth those boys represent, and fled to New York. She also emphatically insisted that he not invest in a dog for a one-off duck hunt. They have a perfectly nice dog and they do not need another. Boykin has no intention of keeping the dog; he isn't defying his wife entirely, but will flip him like a penny stock. The worrying thing is that unless they bag a duck soon, this thousand-dollar mutt is never going to prove his worth in front of two men whose opinion is critical to him and his future with the corporation.

Haynes appears at the blind's opening. Is that an amused smile, or has the man got a bellyache? Haynes lifts a duck call to his lips and sounds it twice.

"Can't get a real duck, maybe we'll shoot this guy. After all, if it sounds like a duck . . ." This from the client. Boykin and his boss, Jonathan Wiley, laugh with desperate appreciation.

Boykin is unaware that he was holding his breath, but he lets it out at the sound of a real duck answering the fake one. The hunters hunker down, the dog somehow caught against them and the short wall of the blind. Len blows on the wooden duck call again. It's a good one, one he bought from that bearded cracker family on television. "That ought to do it."

Sure enough, from the far side of the small pond floats a pair of ducks, effortlessly gliding toward the sound of their phony fellows. Boykin has no idea if they're Mallards or Black Ducks or Muscovy or Daffy. He doesn't want to be the one to shoot first; that honor goes to his guests. But neither one fires. "Go ahead," he whispers. "It's your shot."

Len Haynes, leaning into the side opening of the blind, serves the three would-be hunters with a look that inspires all three to fire at once.

At the explosion of three shotgun barrels blasting over his head, the dog howls. He tries to bolt from the blind, but the fixed leash snaps him back. Wiley fires his second barrel and the dog tries to bury himself under Boykin's legs. Upended by the terrified dog, Boykin kicks out, his booted heels colliding with the dog's ribs. Another yelp.

"I got it!" The client is pointing wildly at the dead duck. Get the dog to retrieve it."

Boykin hauls himself to his feet, unties the dog's leash from the ring, and pulls him outside to the pond edge. Whatever is the command? Fetch? He tries it, but the dog continues his violent shaking, panting and bucking at the end of the leash, so much so that Boykin is afraid to let him go for fear he'll bolt into the surrounding wilderness. "Go get the damned duck." Boykin shoves the dog into the water, points madly.

There is the sound of laughter behind him, Haynes's ugly chuckle. "Looks like that dog won't hunt."

"Haynes. You get him out there." Boykin is furious. How dare this yokel laugh at him? Here, in front of Wiley and the client? At this moment, it is more infuriating than embarrassing. He'll teach him to laugh. "Get the dog out there or go get it yourself. I'm paying you enough."

"I ain't your dog. Get it yourself. Ain't deep." Haynes pockets the duck call, turns on his heel, and walks away.

Boykin immediately regrets paying Haynes the thousand bucks in advance. Highway robbery at that. Thousand bucks for a dog that won't hunt and a thousand bucks to have this moron walk them six hundred feet to a pond that has only two ducks.

"He's got you, Boykin. Never thought I'd see you bested by a hick." Wiley pulls a flask out of his vest. "And a dog." He offers the flask to the client.

Boykin knows that he should laugh, make the joke his own, but he is humiliated. Wiley doesn't offer him the flask.

In the center of Bartlett's Pond, the corpse of a Black Duck floats, motionless in the still water.

"I admit that I was upset with the dog's performance, and when Haynes said he'd take him, it seemed like the best thing for everyone. I was out the cost of the dog, but I didn't care at that point. As I said, I hadn't hunted in years and this was a one-off to impress the client. I didn't need the dog, didn't want it. Haynes did."

With the help of Boykin's testimony, and according to the Massachusetts General Laws, I have Len Haynes on the following violation: "to subject, cause or procure an animal to be tortured or tormented; to be cruelly killed, beaten or mutilated." In this state, those are felonies.

I've called dispatch to request that a patrol car meet me at the Haynes's place in an hour. In the meantime, I'll go pick up Bull.

The deep cold of the past couple of weeks has moderated and the day feels almost balmy. The snow left over after the last storm is nothing but gray slush along the side of the road or gritty mounds in parking lots. The kids have forsaken Bartlett's Pond, leaving behind a net and a lone hockey stick.

I'm in no hurry to collect Bull, but it's already been more than half a day, and Lev was pretty clear that sooner rather than later would be better in getting Bull out of the way. Although I want to bust Len Haynes, it's more important that I do as Lev has asked. Besides, Haynes isn't going anywhere.

I've called Bull's cell phone, but it's going right to voice mail. The only thing left is to run by the house on Poor Farm Road and see if

I can make it look like the most natural thing in the world to drop by and invite him to stay with me. If Jimmy is there, I won't stop. I won't jeopardize the operation by acting out of character. I'll figure something else out.

I'm in luck: Jimmy's car is gone; the only vehicle in the yard is the ancient Nova. I bang on the front door, but no one answers. I rattle the knob and am surprised to find that it's not locked, so I push in, call Bull's name. No answer. I'm not getting a good feeling about this. Just in case, I do a quick search through the house for him. His bedroom looks tossed, but it always does. Jimmy's bedroom door is wide open and, unlike Bull's, his room is fairly neat—no piles of clothes, no cocked-open bureau drawers, the closet door shut tight. A pair of nice oxford-style shoes are, heels out, under the made bed. I walk down the hall to the bathroom. A single toothbrush dangles from the porcelain holder, one disposable razor with beard filings lodged in between the blades, lies on the counter, along with a can of Barbasol shave cream. I happen to know that Jimmy likes Gillette. I also happen to know—after all, he's my brother—that Jimmy takes blood-pressure medication. The only medication in the medicine cabinet is an ancient bottle of Phillips' milk of magnesia and a five-hundred-count bottle of extra-strength Tylenol.

Back in the kitchen, I give the stovepipe a rap with my knuckles. It clangs with a hollow ping. I open the firebox door and find nothing inside by ancient ashes. Jimmy's gone. Bull's gone. And the evidence is gone. Either the drug task force has finally swept in or Jimmy's on the run. I don't know if Bull is with him or if he has been left dead in some ditch by Jimmy's cronies.

I shut the front door behind me and lean on the rusted-out Nova as I call Harmony Farms's chief of police. Either Lev's going to be pissed that the DTF missed Jimmy or he'll tell me that my brother and father are in custody. I'm hoping that's the case. I can bail Bull out, get a good lawyer. I've got a little money from the sale of the condo Gayle and I owned.

Lev is understandably pissed off about my news, but he gathers his professionalism to his breast and thanks me for the info. Then tells me, "You ought to go find your father."

"Yeah, I will. Hey, I asked for a squad car. I've got to do an animal-cruelty arrest today. That going to be okay?" In other words: Will your boys be too busy to help me out?

"I'm sure it'll be fine. Good luck."

If it were the bad old days, I'd start with the local watering holes, checking into each one until I found Bull. But as far as I know, he's stayed sober since that weekend he spent with me. Without drinking and without a job, he's got nowhere to be. Nowhere to go. *And* not answering his phone.

There are bike tracks leading out of the driveway and down Poor Farm Road. I put my truck in park and climb out to see if I can determine which direction Bull might have gone. There is just enough slush to take a print, but more than enough dry pavement that he wouldn't have had to pedal through it, so the trail ends at the stop sign. If he turned left, he was heading for the village of Harmony Farms. A right turn and I have no idea where he might have gone except for a jaunt around the lake. Hardly likely. I take the left and drive like I'm hunting a lost dog, slowly and with my flashers going.

I'm not seeing any sign of Bull. He's not at Cumbie's, his go-to hangout, dragging on a cigarette and slurping coffee, so I pull into a space in front of the market and go in, hoping that he's chewing the fat with Elvin, who's recently back from his Florida vacation. Bull's not there, but Deke is.

"You see Bull around?"

"Not today. Last time I saw him was at the McDonald's rest stop. I was going to the dentist, but he didn't say where he was going."

"Who was he with?" I don't know if the *who* or the *why* is the more important question, but I don't think Deke can supply either answer.

"Didn't say. Didn't see anyone. Seemed like he was preoccupied, though. Wasn't too chatty." We both know that Bull loves to beat his gums.

"When was that?"

"Gosh, must have been a week ago, my appointment was on the sixth."

Elvin pipes up. "He was in here yesterday. But you're right, Deke; he didn't seem himself. Came in, grabbed a Mountain Dew, paid, and left. Not a word out of him." Elvin hefts a tray of freshly ground beef. "Interesting, though, he paid with a fifty."

Oh boy.

"Thanks, guys. If he shows up, let him know I'd like a call from him."

Elvin and Deke nod in an eerily synchronous motion.

I have that hollow feeling you get when something is out of kilter, and although something is very wrong about Bull's appearance at a highway rest stop and his current absence, that's not what's causing it. My limbs feel light, and there is a slight current of vibration flowing through the veins in my hands. But if I'm trembling, it's not from worrying about Bull's whereabouts, but from an adrenaline punch. I'm pumped as I head out of town toward the Haynes's place. I'm going to deal with Len Haynes now.

I'm like a real cop; I've got the law on my side and penalties like jail time and whopping fines. It gets my blood flowing. It's a familiar feeling, this rush, and I wonder why I haven't missed it more. It's a nice safe reminder of the pleasures of law enforcement. Justice will be served. All my life I've wanted justice. To be unfairly equated with my reprobate brother, to be despised for being Bull's son—these were injustices that were only cured the first time I made an arrest.

Now I'm on my way to bring righteousness to bear on behalf of an animal who has suffered the injustice of abuse, and for the first time since I took this job, I'm pumped.

It's probably a mistake, but I've got the yellow dog in the truck with me.

45

H e should have known that something was going on. This was the first time Jimmy had set him up as courier. Before that, it was Mike who made the plans and gave him the loaded backpack and detailed instructions, and Dave who drove him to the site. Bull takes the time to read each title of the sixteen thick paperbacks stuffed in his pack, recognizing a couple of the authors, James Patterson, Dan Brown. He's heard of Jane Austen, but the type is really small and dense, nothing he'd want to read. Bull fishes around in the outside pockets of the pack, hunting for anything that might be what his contact will be looking for, hoping that Jimmy hasn't done what he thinks he has.

Bull lights a cigarette, takes a good drag, deep enough that there's hardly any exhaled plume. The hand that's holding the cigarette is shaking, and he's surprised to find tears in his eyes. It's pretty obvious Jimmy is in trouble, whether of his own making or as a result of someone else's bad planning, Bull doesn't know, but intuition tells him that Jimmy is doing something really stupid. If Jimmy has betrayed Mike and Dave and whoever it is they all work for, he's a dead man. Is Jimmy trying to protect him by sending him on a wild-goose chase of a drop that's never going to happen? Or just making a fool out of him?

Bull drops the cigarette onto the wet leaf mold beneath his feet, stomps on the butt, just to make sure it's extinguished. He shoulders the backpack and heads back to his bicycle. The wind has picked up, making the temperature feel colder than it is. The instinct that suggests Jimmy is in trouble works to keep Bull from simply riding toward home. If Jimmy wanted him away from the house so badly, he'd probably better stay away for a little while longer, long enough that whatever was going to happen already has.

Instead of pointing the Raleigh toward Poor Farm Road, Bull points north, the wind in his face, and sets course for the Lakeside Tavern.

46

It's been an hour and I'm sitting in the town's animal-control vehicle, pulled onto the side of the road in front of the Haynes brothers' stockade fence, right beneath the sign that warns me that I'm awfully close to private and well-defended property. I'm waiting for my cruiser to arrive so that I can take Len Haynes into custody. They're late. Although I have the authority to arrest, only a fool would do this alone. Len and Bob may be all wind when it comes to their views on the right to bear arms, but I don't want to be the test case. Although, as my job falls under the purview of the police department, I have the right to wear a weapon, I don't. I won't. I'm done with that.

Another six minutes tick by. No cruiser. I really don't want to let this go another day, and when Len Haynes's truck draws beside my idling SUV, I really have no choice but to address the issue and hope that my backup won't be much longer.

Len Haynes scrolls down his passenger window, his face wearing his most belligerent expression. Apparently, my pass for being Bull's son is over. "What do you want?"

"Got to talk to you about a dog."

"We talked about dogs. You saw that I did what you said about the kennels."

"This dog." I gesture beside me, where the yellow dog sits.

"What about him?"

I'm not going to have this conversation through car windows. "Pull in." I wait as Len drives up the incline into his ragged yard. I follow, parking my SUV right behind him. A ruckus of riotous barking comes from behind the shed. I get out of the vehicle, leaving the door open. The yellow dog remains where he is, his head cocked in mild interest at the cacophony from the unseen dogs.

Still no squad car. I zip up my jacket. The temperature is above freezing, but a sharp north wind has come up, reminding me that winter is far from over. "I need to ask you a couple of questions."

"You're entitled. I'm entitled to maybe not answer."

"You took a hunting party out last fall?"

"Couple of 'em."

"This one was with a local guy, Donald Boykin, and his coworkers."

"Don't know who they were. Some muckety-mucks with more money than brains, that's for sure." Len has modified his belligerent expression to something not quite as hostile. "Big fancy car, good guns, and a dog that wouldn't hunt. That the dog?"

"Why yes, it is. You recognize it?"

"Seen one yellow Lab, you've seen 'em all. Could be that dog, maybe not."

The dog is framed in the open door. He's sitting in my seat now, his ears perked, his expression alert.

No squad car yet and I have to assume at this point that there won't be one anytime soon. So I square my shoulders. If I don't carry a weapon, neither do I carry the tools for an arrest, but I'm going to take my chances and tell Mr. Haynes exactly why I'm here. If he's willing to come with me peacefully, great. If not, he can wait here for Lev's officers or become a fugitive. I don't really care. I'm that tired of the situation.

"Mr. Haynes, Mr. Boykin has come forward and accused you of willfully mistreating this dog." I begin to list the abuses Boykin told me that Haynes had committed. "And after kicking and beating him with a gun stock, you shot this dog."

Len Haynes is silent for a moment, and I can't help but think of myself as someone who has riled a grizzly. His color darkens and his eyes bulge, until I hope that he'll say something before he explodes. "Damned liar. He beat and shot the dog. His pals walked off and he had one more shell in his gun."

"His word against yours."

"I tell you one thing: If I'd'a shot that dog, I'da killed it."

"Were there witnesses?"

"Yeah, there was. Me. I was walking back to get him. His pals were already in the car and they all wanted to go home. I got back to the pond and there he was, screaming and waling on that dog."

Even with the aggrieved tone, I don't buy his story. "Why didn't you report him?"

"Why should I? His property. None of my business."

From the corner of my eye, I see the dog jump down from the seat, stretch, and shake himself. And then it hits me: The dog isn't afraid of Len Haynes. He was terrified of Boykin. He's not trembling, or panting, or running off. He's ignoring Len Haynes. Haynes is telling the truth.

The dog is a witness and he's just saved me from making a big mistake.

"I'm sorry, Len. Would you be willing to testify?"

Len's face slowly returns to a more normal color, but his hostile expression remains. He takes a good look at the yellow dog, and I can see that he's noted the scar on his hip. "Yeah, I will."

As I head back to the shelter to write my report, I continue my fruitless search for Bull.

47

The ice that looked so substantial from the shore creaks under his weight, but Jimmy keeps moving. He's struggling to walk against a stiff north wind. Each time the ice creaks, his heart, already beating hard from the exertion, jolts him with intimations of mortality. He hasn't been afraid before, but now he is. He had planned this all so perfectly: leave Harmony Farms and his coconspirators, his sad-sack father, his lawman brother, disappear forever on a fake passport and the proceeds of his deal with a rival dealer. The months of trying to keep Bull safe and Mike and Dave ignorant of his duplicity have been exhausting. He's just so tired.

When he left the Poor Farm Road house, all of the heroin and cash tucked neatly into a backpack similar to the one that Bull has been using for the small drops orchestrated by Mike and Dave, Jimmy decided to take the longer and more scenic route. He was to meet his man in a parking lot on the north side of the lake, at the man-made beach he and Cooper used to go to back when they were kids. No one would be there this time of year. The exchange would be swift and efficient and, like a movie cowboy, he'd drive off into the sunset. By this time tomorrow, he figured, he'd be sipping piña coladas in the Caymans.

Jimmy has planned for every contingency, but who could have planned on a deer? When the doe jumped into his lane, Jimmy jerked the wheel and the Honda skittered sideways, its front tires hitting a patch of black ice. Forgetting to turn in the direction of the skid, Jimmy overcorrected and the Honda ended up in the ditch. The seat belt kept Jimmy from bashing his head on the windshield, but he was momentarily stunned by the surprise of it. He sat there for a moment, collecting himself, then unbuckled and climbed out.

There was no hope of extricating this car without a tow truck. Before some do-gooder could pull up and offer help, Jimmy popped the trunk, shouldered the heavy backpack, and faced the expanse of the lake. The shortest distance between him and his destination, his future waiting for him on the opposite shore, was to go across it.

Now Jimmy pauses in his struggle across the ice and pulls out the cell phone he liberated from Bull's back pocket as he put the backpack filled with paperback books on his father's shoulders. He flips it open, sees that Cooper has called Bull several times. Cooper never calls. That bodes ill. Jimmy can never forget that Cooper is a cop. Oh, he may have demoted himself to ACO, but at heart, he's a suspicious, nosy, lousy cop. He thumbs in the memorized cell number of the man he is supposed to meet. "I had a little car trouble. I'm on foot." Jimmy hopes that his new best friend won't get nervous, think this is a trap of some kind. "I'm really sorry. I hit ice and my car went off the road. Yeah, I've got everything with me. Maybe you can give me a lift out of town?"

Jimmy never learned to swim. The most he'd ever do was paddle around near shore, clinging to a boogie board or an inner tube. He never imagined that one day he'd owe this lake for his escape, or owe it his life. Jimmy has forgotten the treachery of lake ice; he's forgotten about Stevie Bonner, who died when they were kids, crossing the ice on a dare. Or the ice fisherman from downstate who wasn't found until May. Or the heroic rescue performed by the brave passerby who hauled those two duck hunters out of the freezing water. He doesn't notice that there are no ice-fishing shacks arrayed at various distances along the deepest part of the lake because the ice is no longer sufficient to support them.

All he knows is that on that opposite shore lies his salvation, his way out of a life that has become fraught with blood pressure–elevating events. When Carlos approached him, on neutral ground, quietly, the germ of the idea of a new life began to take hold. Carlos has arranged everything, from the passport to the bank account in the Caymans. All he wants in return is the dope and the turf. Jimmy is putting his trust in him. He doesn't hate his own handler, but he knows that the boss will never let him go. He will always have the whip hand. It's been that way since he was a kid, just learning the business. Right from the get-go, the boss treated him like a son— pats on the cheek, an extra hundred for a good job. But the boss will never let him go, not even out of gratefulness that Jimmy never took the plea bargain, never gave him up to the authorities. "You're too good a man, Jimmy. I need you." End of conversation.

Jimmy's boots are beginning to weigh him down, each sticky step a battle against the burning ache in the small of his back and the increasing sharpness of the wind. The sky is mouse gray, the snow on the ice absorbing the color until it, too, is more gray than white. Where the snow has blown off the ice, it's a pale silver gray, just the color of his own eyes, and Cooper's. Cooper, who hates him so much. It's a tough thing to be hated by your only brother. What Cooper can't know is that he pretty much hates himself, too. That's why it's been so easy to follow the path of least resistance, to cling to a life that has been lived on the edges, in the world of big bucks and no conscience.

Jimmy takes another dogged step; he's halfway across now. The rest should be easy. The creaking is almost a comfort now, an accompaniment to each step, telling him that he's making progress, even if he feels like his frozen feet in their rubber boots are dead-weight. He can't tell what time it is by the dull gray of the sky; the winter sun is diffused behind the scrim. His hands are too cold to pull out the phone to check the time, his fingers too numb to press the tiny buttons to let Carlos know he's still coming. His gloves are wet from taking hard falls onto the ice. He thinks that he's been out here an hour, but it could be two hours, or maybe only fifteen min-utes. He needs to stop, catch his breath, rest for a minute, but he's terrified Carlos will leave, imagining that Jimmy has bailed. But he's got to stop, if only for a second. He turns in a slow circle to make sure there's no one out there to see him, a black figure against the gray-white scene.

Once when they were kids, way before Mona died, Bull brought them out here to the lake to fish. Somehow, Jimmy fell into the wa-ter, and he can still recall the terrifying moment when he thought he would drown. Bull's big hand grabbed him by the shirt, hauling him to his feet. "You're okay, boy," he said.

They'd all had a good laugh; the water was only waist-deep.

So, when the ice gives way beneath his feet, Jimmy plunges down-ward, hoping that it's only waist-deep.

48

I've put arresting Boykin on hold; my sense that Bull is in big trouble has only grown in the time I've spent trying to find him. I'm on my way to the Lakeside, my last hope. It's only by chance that I've come this way, the shore route. I'm actively looking for Bull, not Jimmy, but it's Jimmy's Honda I find wedged into the ditch. When I spot the vehicle, I pull up and climb out of my town SUV. I'm sure it's Jimmy's car, although one black Honda looks pretty much like another. I crawl inside, pop the glove compartment, and read the registration, which confirms that Jimmy's and my felon brother is around here somewhere. I examine the muddle of footprints, hoping to find two sets, but I'm able to discern only one type and size of clear tread. The trunk has been left wide open, gaping. It's empty.

The yellow dog has invited himself out of the SUV and has his nose pointed toward the lake. He barks, getting my attention. And then I see him, eking his way across the lake, a backpack against his shoulders, head down, persevering. Jimmy. Is he nuts? Walking across the lake? I have a small pair of binoculars in the Suburban and I reach in to get them. I have to be mistaken; this must be some fisherman checking a pole. This can't be my older brother, intent on reaching the other side of the lake, but it is. I lift the binoculars to see what he's heading for. The town beach. There's a car parked in the lot, an ordinary-enough car, midsize, American-made. Just the one car.

Jimmy pauses, bends from the waist, and I'm sure he's winded. He's in lousy condition and the ice has the consistency of sludge. Pulling himself upright, he makes a slow pirouette, and I figure that he's spotted me, because, he suddenly drops, like he thinks that he can hide from me. Then, with real horror, I realize that the ice has given way beneath him. I'm watching my brother die.

I frantically hit 911 and shout my stats to the communications center. Seconds are precious. The fire rescue team can't possibly get here fast enough. This is what I'm thinking as I grab my ice cleats out of the truck and tug them over my boots. Calling to Jimmy to hang on, I head out onto the ice.

My dreams are all too often the kind where I can't move fast enough, or at all. And that's just exactly how I feel right now. I'm really grateful that I at least have the legs and the lungs to run, even more grateful that I have my Yaktrax on and can make headway without falling. But I seem to be making no progress at all. I hear the crack of strained ice and hold up long enough to wonder what I'm doing out here, trying to save a brother whose whole life has been a cluster fuck.

The yellow dog moves ahead of me, cheerfully bounding in an erratic but forward direction, and I realize that he has some animal instinct about the safest route. I follow him, repeating uselessly "Find him, find him" at gasping intervals. I can't see Jimmy. I'm not even sure at this point if I'm heading in the right direction or will overshoot his location. Then I see a head, arms on the edge of the hole as he hauls himself up high enough that he can grab a breath. I drop flat to the surface of the ice, my emergency training kicking in. Just like a commando, I crawl toward my brother. The dog, seeing this new game, comes over to me, and I realize that he's putting me in danger by adding extra weight to the ice. "Sit. Stay."

God is with me, and he does.

I hear the sound of sirens in the distance. In the best of my dreams, backup docs arrive. But in the worst of my nightmares, it doesn't reach me in time. I can hear them, but I don't see the rescue vehicles, and the American-made car in the beach parking lot is gone. I press myself flatter and creep a little faster, digging the cleats of my Yaktrax in deeper, impelling myself forward. They're not going to get here in time. It's my rescue now.

"Cooper!" Jimmy's terrified face rises from the hole in the ice like a pale apparition. His dark hair is slicked back, his gray eyes filled with panic. "Get me!" His teeth are chattering, and ice crystals decorate his eyebrows.

"Don't waste breath; just try to relax. I'm getting there." I have nothing to work with, no ladder, no rope, nothing except my superior position of being on the ice and not in the water, and my upper-body strength. And I don't think that's enough. The best I can do, the very best, is to hang on to him until help arrives.

I stretch out my right hand. "Take it, Jimmy. Take it."

The dog is barking. It could be encouragement, or it could be warning. I don't know. I'm in that zone where my only focus is on reaching my quarry. "Reach for me, Jimmy. Reach." I stretch out my arms as far as I can and waggle my fingers, as if I'm coaxing a baby to walk. Finally, I feel his icy hand in mine, and suddenly I'm in the water, too. The ice has caved in and I'm sinking under the weight of my clothes and my brother, who has panicked and is working against me, pushing me deeper under the water. I duck his flailing arms, grabbing for the best purchase on him, the backpack, which is adding to the saturated weight of him.

I start to pull on the straps, but he starts screaming. "No. I can't." His face is a mask of sheer panic; he's equally afraid of the water and losing the damned backpack. "I can't." With that, he kicks and twists around, dunking me back under the water.

I shove him aside, kick myself to the surface, and launch myself as far as I can to grasp at the bumpy ice. The dog is barking furiously. Clinging tenuously to the fast-failing edge of solid ice, I look up, to see the impossible image of Bull Harrison riding his bicycle across the surface of the lake, the yellow dog racing to meet him.

"Stop!" I think that I'm yelling, but I'm not sure. He's got to stop.

I'm underwater again.

"Stay calm! Stay calm! I'm coming!" Bull Harrison drops his bike on the ice. Over his shoulder is the orange life ring that he's grabbed from the on-shore lifeguard stand. Attached to the ring is a twelve-foot line. Not a lot, but enough if he can get closer.

Bull had biked past the Lakeside Tavern. Kept his eyes on the road in front of him and kept going, finally arriving at the private pier at Upper Lake Estates. Warm from his uphill and downhill exertion, he'd been mulling over his situation, when he caught sight of two men out on the ice. At first, he thought they were a couple of nutcases skating on the soft ice. Then, to his horror, Bull figured out who the two men on the ice were, and what was happening.

Both his sons are in the water. Two boys he loves, even though they haven't been model children. Maybe they even, in their own fashion, love him back. Jimmy sent him on a wild-goose chase, sixteen paperback books loaded into the backpack instead of drugs. Cooper brought him home night after night, paid that clerk to let him stay inside Cumbie's. That's love. Sure it is.

The bike skitters away and Bull drops to his knees, makes his prayer to the Higher Power: *Let me save them and I'll stay sober forever.*

Don't let me lose both of them. Bull skates the life ring toward the open water, clings to the end of the line with both hands, keeping his sons afloat.

The yellow dog hunkers down beside Bull.

In the distance, drawing nearer but not close enough, sirens.

Two heads rise above the water; one hand finds the life ring. Cooper embraces his brother around the neck with one arm, furiously treading water to keep Jimmy's face up. There's no way Bull has the strength to pull them both up. Jimmy is barely conscious now, a deadweight, and Cooper is weakening fast in the cold water. "Give me some slack," he calls out to his father, and is rewarded with enough looseness that he thinks he can fit the ring over his brother's shoulders. But he can't. The backpack is in the way. Cooper's hands are almost too numb to work, but he manages to slide one strap off, then the other. The heavy pack disappears to the bottom of the lake. He still can't maneuver the ring over Jimmy, so Cooper links his arm through it, grasping Jimmy's coat collar in his other hand.

"Dad! Don't let go!"

The slack tightens, but they remain in the water. Cooper knows he's got to get out, help Bull on the other end of the line. But he can't. He can't feel anything anymore. Not fear, or adrenaline. He knows that he's giving in to hypothermia, but he kind of doesn't care. He hangs on to Jimmy's inert form, his treading water slowing down, his grip on Jimmy's jacket frozen into permanence. Cooper realizes that his brother is dead. His pale gray eyes are glazed over; all the fight in him is gone.

The yellow dog is barking furiously. Funny, he sounds just like Argos. That deep, proud, challenging bark. It's a comfort, that sound.

49

I have little memory of when the fire department pulled me out of the water. I remember that they wrapped one of those metallic space blankets over my shoulders. Jimmy's, too. Even though I knew that he was dead, they worked on him in the ambulance, where I lay beside him, and in the ER, where they took him behind a different curtain. With utter clarity, I heard the order from the attending doc: "Call it. Sixteen ten hours."

I am tethered to an IV drip, so maybe it's the warm saline coursing too fast into my veins, thawing me, but the warm fluid leaks out of my tear ducts.

A few minutes later, Bull comes into the unit, his Fu Manchu mustache still sparkling with droplets of lake water, his eyes red. "He's dead, Coop. Your brother's dead." He collapses into the side chair, covers his face in those great big mitts of his.

I pull my free hand out from under the heated blanket they've swaddled me in. I pull his hands away from his face. "I know, Dad. I'm so sorry." There is something else I need to say to him. "Thank you for trying to save us. You did all you could."

He squeezes my hand. "We both did."

The warm blanket begins to cool and the nurse comes in to replace it with a newly heated one. Bull keeps my hand in his. I'm just so sleepy.

We don't say much more. What is there to say? And then I think of something and startle myself awake. "Where's the dog?"

"Polly's got him. He's fine. Do you know, he pulled on the rope with me. Not like it was a game, but like he knew I needed the help. Planted his hind legs in and gripped that line with all his strength so we could keep it tight. Without him, I might not have been able to do it."

It sounds like something my Argos would have done.

I fall asleep, and when I wake again, Lev Parker is here and Bull is gone.

He's out of uniform and looks a lot like that kid I used to hang out with, my old teammate. He's wearing an untucked polo shirt, and I can see that he's a little thicker around the middle. His hair is prematurely shot through with gray, but he's still got the taut jaw with the five o'clock shadow he's battled since he hit puberty. "How you doing, Coop?"

"Guess I'm okay." I push myself upright. "Yeah, I'm okay."

"I'm sorry about Jimmy." He's not looking at me when he says it. "But I'm really glad you made it." He does look at me then. I see an old fondness, like he's just remembered that we were once friends.

"Tell me something, Lev."

He's on his feet, a tattered ball cap with our high school logo on it clutched in his hand. "If I can."

"Why didn't the drug task force act sooner? Why the delay when you had the proof on your desk? Proof that I gave you."

Lev Parker is a man of consummate integrity and devotion to his job. I watch the inner debate ride across his face as he weighs how much the truth will cost. We are in a public place, despite the privacy curtains. I can hear the relentless beeping of medical machinery, the incessant ringing of telephones at the nurses' station, and the squeak of rubber-soled shoes on the linoleum of the treatment rooms. Finally, Lev reaches a decision. He sits down in the side chair, pulling it up close to the edge of my bed. He leans in. "It was a mistake. Bad timing. The DTF was supposed to sweep in tomorrow because our inside man said that they would all be there for a meeting, everyone, including the ringleader. It was our opportunity to get them all."

"But he ran instead. Jimmy bolted."

"Looks like it."

"You think he got wind of it, the raid?"

"I don't know." I can see in his eyes that this failure is going to haunt my old friend for a while. He sits back, pats his knees like he's getting ready to leave, then leans forward again. "I hear you're planning on bringing Donald Boykin in."

"That's right."

"Can I ask you not to do it that way? I'll call him and have him come down to the station."

"Why?"

"His wife is our first selectman."

"That's hardly a reason. Are you suggesting that we can do this under the public radar?"

"Yes."

"It won't stay under the radar. It can't."

"It'll be more dignified for a man of his stature in the community."

"Dignified? Do you know what he did to that dog?" The warm saline drip is finished and the cold seeps back into my body. The heated blanket is barely warm. I am shivering again. "How does dressing well and handing out money here and there absolve you of cruelty? Do you know what he does to his employees? Fires them if they screw up. That's it, no mercy. And when this dog failed to perform, he beat him. Then, when the dog managed to get loose, he shot him. And you want me to treat Boykin with dignity?"

"Settle down, Cooper." Lev's voice isn't calming, but commanding. "I sincerely hope that you have the proof you need to make this stick, because if you don't, well, I don't need to tell you what will happen."

The implication is clear: One of us will be out of a job, most likely me. And that's just fine. "I've got a witness."

"Haynes?"

"Yes. You read my report." I don't tell him that the dog himself is a witness, although I've said something to that effect in my hastily written report: "Reactive in Boykin's presence."

"I did. And, Cooper, it's Len's word against Boykin's." Meaning, the redneck versus the philanthropist. Old Harmony Farms versus the new.

"That may be, but if I have to, I'll subpoena his boss."

"I won't tell you not to do what you have to; just be careful. That's all I'm asking. Really think about it."

The shivering is becoming uncontrollable; my teeth are chattering. I need more warm saline; I need another blanket.

Lev stands up, pats my shoulder. "You take care now."

A nurse starts a new saline drip, brings a freshly warmed blanket, and I doze off again, waking only when I feel the weight of another body slide in next to mine, the sweet weight of Natalie's arm over my side. Her cheek rests against my back. I am warm finally, well and truly warm.

I'm discharged from the ER just before midnight and Natalie drives Bull and me home to the Poor Farm Road house. The yellow dog is there waiting for us, courtesy of Polly Schaeffer. He greets Bull like a returning hero, all bounce and wag. I desperately want to go home with Natalie, but I can't leave Bull alone now. Even if I'm still numb to it, Bull has lost one of his sons. Natalie fries up some eggs and bacon for us, sees that we eat, and then strips and changes Jimmy's bed so that I have a place to sleep. I don't think that I can sleep anymore, but I do, and when I dream, it's of my mother. Her face floats under the water, her crystal gray eyes open and looking into mine.

When I woke this morning to bright sunshine, the yellow dog was staring at me, his muzzle planted on the edge of the bed, his brown eyes clear and bright. I'm not going to think about how much that reminded me of the way Argos would wake me in the morning. I'm not going to let myself slide backward into that abyss of grief. This is another dog, one who's finally healed from his wounds. Polly thinks she has a foster home for him, so he'll be out of my life soon. I'll put all of this to rest, happy enough with a successful outcome. That will have to do.

Bull is in the kitchen, making the day's first pot of coffee. I let him pour me a cup, then climb into my still-damp clothes. I have business to attend to—Mr. Donald Boykin to arrest.

Polly picks me up and drives me to where I'd left the SUV yesterday, pulled off the road behind Jimmy's abandoned Honda. The Honda is gone, impounded no doubt, and the Suburban is alone.

"Are you sure you don't need my help?" Polly would dearly love to accompany me to this event, but I'm not going to let her talk me into taking her along. I've called once again for a cruiser, and this time I'm assured that one will meet me at the Boykin residence. The dispatcher tells me that there was a bad accident out on the highway yesterday, hence the failure of my backup to arrive at the Haynes's.

Upper Lake Estates at Harmony Farms is lovely on this bright morning. The artfully winding road is impeccably clear of slush, and the only snow left is a gritty pile lodged near the maintenance build-ing. From the top of the highest point in the neighborhood, I can see Lake Harmony, opaque with the dull pewter of its softened, treach-erous ice.

Suburban moms are out in force, ferrying their kids to music les-sons, dance lessons, hockey lessons, Saturday play dates. I'm passed by a phalanx of mom cars, all big, all with highest safety ratings, all tricked out with those little family stick-figure decals representing parents, children, and the family dog. I spot one HARFAR Euro decal on a Mercedes SUV. Good for Cynthia: They're catching on.

I glance in my rearview mirror and spot the cruiser slowly fol-lowing me. Good. Now I just have to hope that Donald Boykin will be at home on this lovely Saturday morning. I signal and pull into the circular drive belonging to the town's first couple. Unlike the last time I was here, bearing the body of their deceased spaniel, I have not called ahead, so no one greets me in the front yard.

The cruiser pulls in behind me and, much to my surprise, it's Lev Parker who gets out. My first reaction is that he's going to try again to convince me not to do the job I am here to do, but he doesn't. "Officer Harrison, I've got your back." He gets in step beside me and together we walk up to the front door.

"Thank you, Chief. I appreciate it."

The housekeeper is a lot prettier than I had imagined. Twenties, blond, Slavic cheekbones. She doesn't wear a uniform, just a simple outfit of khaki trousers and white polo shirt. She takes one look at the town's chief of police and steps back, flushing. Probably in her country, the appearance of a police officer on your front step isn't a good thing. "Can I help you?"

We ask for Boykin and she invites us into the foyer, where we wait in silence for Donald Boykin.

I have failed before, in small ways and in large. I failed as a hus-band. Long before Gayle declared me unredeemable, I wasn't a good husband, a loving husband. I failed certainly as a son, estranging myself from my only parent out of a decades old resentment, a child-ish grudge. And I failed as a cop, failed my K-9 partner and thus lost him. My failures have brought me here to this moment, a dog warden; an unarmed, two-bit quasi–police officer.

On that deeply cold night, when the yellow dog and Cooper are invited to stay with Natalie, they are cozy on her sofa, a handmade afghan covering their legs, while the dogs are nested together in Betty's round bed. Natalie links her fingers with Cooper's. He playfully holds their hands up, examining the way that they look, ten fingers interlocked, hers neatly coupled with his.

"Marcus would do that; he loved the degree of difference in our skin."

Cooper gently extricates her hand from his. "I'm sorry."

"Why? You shouldn't be sorry to trigger a memory from time to time. I'm not going to not talk about him. He was a part of my life. But that doesn't mean that my life is fixed in amber. I don't mean my life; I mean my feelings. Just because I will always love Marcus, that doesn't mean that I can't move on. That I can't have a future."

I will not fail now. "Donald Boykin, you are under arrest for sub-jecting an animal to be beaten and attempting to kill said animal."

I am a cop once more.

Epilogue

Three Months Later

I swear, this is the last time I'm going to bring the Bollens' miniature donkey back to his donkey-stubborn parents. Cutie-Pie is placidly strolling beside me down Main Street, carrot by carrot, as I hold them out for him, encouraging each hard-won step one at a time. A pair of tourists dressed in hideous floral shorts stop and ask if they can snap our picture. I put on my best duty face and stop short of telling them where they can put their iPhones. I'm pretty sure they take our picture from behind anyway. But it really is the last time I'm doing this. Cutie-Pie will become the problem of the next ACO for Harmony Farms. Next week, I'm back on the job.

I pull into the driveway of the Poor Farm house. The yellow dog hops out of the truck, his tail swashbuckling behind him, bounding over to Bull, who's sitting in a lawn chair, smoking and sipping Mountain Dew.

"I've got a favor to ask, Bull. A kind of permanent favor."

"Shoot."

"Can you keep him for me?" I point to the dog, who is sitting by Bull's side, looking up at him with adoring eyes.

"You got it." Bull bends over and ruffles the dog's fur between his shoulders.

"I mean permanently."

I'm heading downstate to train with my new dog. Lev Parker has secured some grant money and I'll be back soon enough to take up my new position in the Harmony Farms police department as the resident K-9 unit. He says he got the idea when the DTF had to borrow a sniffer dog from another community to finally bust the drug ring, which was enough to convince Lev Parker that a dog on the force will be a useful thing. If they'd had a dog in the first place . . . Well, as they say, hindsight is 20/20.

Bull lifts his rumpled-paper-bag face to me, grins, and nods furiously. "Sure, sure. I'd love to have him."

I'll be back in a few weeks, but I've given up the Bartlett's Pond camp. We're moving in with Natalie; me and my new K-9. I've been assigned, at my request, a Labrador. A black one. Her name is Zeena.

"Hey, what'd you do with the Nova?" I've just noticed the empty rectangle of barren dirt, bare from decades under the car.

"Got it hauled away. The guy gave me a hundred bucks for scrap." Bull pushes himself to his feet. "Hey, you gonna name this dog before you go?"

I turn and look at him, the yellow dog pressing himself against Bull's side. "You do it, Dad."

I walk away quickly, not wanting to see the pleasure writ so large in my father's big baby face. Not wanting him to see me misty-eyed.

Acknowledgments

When I count my blessings, Jennifer Enderlin, Andrea Cirillo, and Annelise Robey are top of the list. None of this could have happened without the support, guidance, and belief in the work that this trio provides me. I am honored and humbled to be one of your authors.

I am also blessed with the fantastic team at JRA: Don W. Cleary and Don Cleary, Christina Prestia, Julianne Tinari, Michael Conroy, Danielle Sickles, Peggy Boulos Smith, Liz Van Buren, and of course, Jane Rotrosen Berkey. Much gratitude to the savvy, smart, and dedicated folks at St. Martin's Press, who take care of the nuts and bolts of getting a book from mind to market, including Ervin Serrano, who has given this book yet another of his amazing covers. Thank you Jeanne-Marie Hudson and Joan Higgins, Sara Goodman, Chris Holder, John Murphy, Kerry Nordling, Sally Richardson, Anne Marie Tallberg, Stephanie Davis, Caitlin Dareff, and Lisa Davis—and Carol Edwards, who has, on more than one occasion, saved me from myself. Thanks also to the wonderful folks at Macmillan who bring the written word to the voiced, Brant

Janeway, Samantha Beerman, Mary Beth Roche, and Robert Allen.

For insights into the work of a small town ACO, I am indebted to Barbara Prada, Animal Control Officer and Inspector of Animals in Edgartown, Massachusetts.

Finally, I am grateful for the loving support of my family, friends, and legions of readers. I do it for you.

A Man of His Own

Dedicated to the men and women of the United States armed forces and to their brave military dogs past and present.

And to my grandchildren, Claire and Will

Every dog should have a man of his own. There is nothing like a well-behaved person around the house to spread the dog's blanket for him, or bring him his supper when he comes home man-tired at night.

—Corey Ford

Part One

1938–1945

Prologue

His mother had sheltered him in the nest she'd made in a crawl space under the sagging weight of an old tavern tucked just off the main street of the city, which hadn't yet begun to recover from the Depression. She'd fed him first from her teats, all eight his alone as the only survivor of her brood of five, then from her mouth as she left him for short periods and scavenged for scraps, which she would share with him even as she withered from a decent-size purebred German shepherd to a scabbed scarecrow.

The puppy would never know her history, only that his mother had managed to survive long enough as a stray by falling upon instincts hard-coded in her blood—find shelter, find food, and trust no one—so that when she failed to return to their alleyway nest, he was almost capable of surviving on his own. Almost. What he didn't know about her was that at an earlier time in her life she'd been a show dog. Somewhere miles away, blue ribbons and a silver cup graced a dusty shelf. Not a runaway, but a throwaway when the neighbor's mongrel jumped the backyard breeder's fence.

He stayed in the nest, venturing out only to do his business, lap a little at a puddle of yesterday's rainwater. But his belly began to grumble. Sometimes it had taken her a very long time to return to the nest, so he made do with sucking on the end of his tail, comforting himself, one ear cocked toward the entrance to the blind alley. She'd be back. She always came back. He had no way to know how much time had elapsed except by the extraordinary hunger that refused to be satisfied with tail sucking, and his thirst, which was no longer satisfied because the puddle had dried up during the warmth of the day. Hours passed into days and the puppy knew only that his mother was still absent, and without her, he had no strength. What he longed for was to feel her body wrapped around his, to awaken to find her licking him ears to tail, to snuggle up against her warm body and let himself drift into deep sleep.

A noise. The puppy lifted his head, sniffed. A man had come into the narrow alley. His mother had always shied away from people, so he kept himself very still. When the human boldly urinated not three feet from where the pup hid, the odor of it filled the youngster with information. This person was male; this human being had eaten meat and wasn't thirsty. He couldn't help himself—the odor of food wafting out of the skin of this overwarm being drew him to his legs. He didn't consider revealing himself to the human; he just wanted to breathe in the tempting odor, as if by inhaling the scent of pastrami or ham, he'd be filled.

The rain came down and splashed into the hollows gouged out of the worn bricks. The sound of the soft late-summer rain and the earthy scent of refreshed soil confused the puppy. He ran his tongue against the rough brick, where a thin layer of moisture trickled toward him. There was no relief in it, only the torment of dissatisfaction. From the splintered access to his mother's carefully chosen nest site, he could see where the puddle he'd licked dry was re-forming. Nearly crazed with thirst, the puppy forgot his mother's rules and dashed out from beneath the building to lap at the new-formed puddle in an ecstasy of relief. And that's when his future was revised.

The sudden insult of big feet against his washboard ribs made him yelp, but something kept him from running back to the shelter of the crawl space. As a dog, a youngster just newly weaned, he didn't have the experience to nip or protest, and being swept up in strong human hands had a calming effect on him. Here was contact. Here was touch. Soft vocalizations unlike his mother's voice, but with her intent. *Hey there, little guy.* As soothing as her heartbeat.

The puppy made a token protest, and with a wisdom far beyond his mere eight weeks of life, he chose to accept this human's touch; this man's bond.

Chapter One

The men's room stinks so badly that Rick walks past it and out the open back door of the tavern. He's in an alley, a brick wall conveniently placed, so that he conducts his business in privacy. Today was the last day of play for the Waterbury Comets, and Frederick "Rick" Stanton has just spilled his good news to his teammates. Despite the C-league Comets' losing season, he's pitched well, and in the spring he'll report to the minor-league AA team, the Hartford Bees. It was surprisingly hard to say, and he was a little embarrassed to have gotten choked up, especially when they all raised their beer mugs and toasted his good luck.

He's finally going to be able to say good-bye to cobbled-together amateur teams, and all his years of hard work, from sand lot to high school to playing in college, have paid off. Sacrificing steady employment in a respectable profession like his father's, banking or accounting, in favor of menial jobs he has no compunction about leaving when practice starts up has been worth it.

Still, he'll miss these guys, the oldest among them the catcher,

"Foggy" Phil Dexter; the youngest, a kid of sixteen who cheerfully takes all their good-natured abuse, lugging most of the equipment, always riding stuck between two bigger players, fetching for the rest of them, and enduring persistent razzing about the state of his virginity.

Finishing up, Rick feels the first drops of rain on his bare head. Those few drops are quickly followed by a complete cloudburst, but he stays where he is. It's hot inside, and the cool rain feels good. Rick raises his face to the sky and opens his mouth, taking in the taste of fresh rain. "I'm the luckiest man on earth," he says to the sky, and in that moment, he's pretty certain that he is. Well, he should get back in. Eat another couple sandwiches, toss back one more beer; laugh at a few more tired jokes. The season is over and no curfew tonight.

Thoroughly soaked now, Rick turns around and trips over something, nearly pitching headlong onto the brick pavers. That something yelps.

It's a puppy, and rather than running away after being tripped over, it stays put, and for a hard moment, Rick thinks he may have accidentally killed it with his big feet. In the weak light of the open back door, Rick sees the glint of life in its eyes. "Whoa, fella. Where'd you come from?" Rick squats down and the wet and trembling puppy inserts itself between his knees as if seeking shelter. It sits and rests its muzzle on Rick's leg. As quickly as the cloudburst started, it fades away, the rivulets trickling down the side of the wall, pooling in the interstices between the bricks. "Where're your people, little guy?"

The puppy shakes, spraying Rick with a thousand droplets. Rick scoops it up and heads back into the tavern. In the light, he can see it's a boy, silvery in color, with a darker saddle across narrow shoulders and along ribs that poke out like the bones of a chicken. His ears flop over at entirely different angles, as if they belong to two different puppies. Probably a German shepherd, or at least mostly shepherd. The bartender doesn't say anything when Rick comes in carrying a puppy, so Rick holds him up. "He yours?" The barkeep shakes his head no.

The barkeep's wife swings a new pitcher onto the table and considers the dog on Rick's lap. "Probably got dumped out back. You found him, you keep him. Don't leave him here."

The puppy has settled neatly on Rick's lap, gently taking the bits of meat Rick offers without nipping those important fingers with his sharp teeth. He can't keep a dog; he's living in a boardinghouse. In nine months, he'll be at training camp. In a year, with luck, he'll be pitching for the majors.

"Got to name him if you're keeping him." Dan Lister, their manager, spreads a gob of mustard on his third corned beef sandwich. "How 'bout Spot?"

"Too common. Besides, he doesn't seem to have any spots, and who said anything about me keeping him?" Rick fingers another tiny bite of sandwich into the puppy's mouth.

"Lucky." Foggy has slumped in his chair, so that his chin is barely above the edge of the table.

"Well, he is a lucky dog if one of you bums keeps him." Rick holds the wriggling fur ball up as if offering the puppy for auction.

"Darby?" This from the kid.

"Darby?"

"I had a dog named Darby. My dad's Irish. It's how they say Derby over there. Darby was a real good dog, never left my father's side all the time he was sick with tuberculosis. We even let him come to the funeral."

The group grows silent. No one had known that the kid was a half orphan.

"Maybe I'll call him Rin Tin Tin. He looks like he might be

shepherd." Rick scratches the puppy under the chin. "What do you think? You gonna grow up to be some kind of movie star hero dog?" The puppy yawns, drops his head, and is instantly asleep. Rick realizes what he's just said. If he names this puppy, how will he ever drop him back in the alley? It's not even fair to keep the dog on his lap, to allow the little thing to accept a few minutes of comfort, let him think that humans are trustworthy. The party will break up soon, and what then? Abandon the tyke to the elements? His first trust in humans to do right by him destroyed, and maybe he'll never trust another human being again. Rick can feel the puppy's beating heart in the palm of his pitching hand. The fluff of baby fur feels like the softest mink of his mother's fur stole as Rick strokes him, lifting the spatula-shaped paws and feeling the thick bones of a puppy with the potential to become a large dog. If he's not hit by a car or starved to death.

Dan Lister pushes away from the table. "I'm done in. Go to bed, gentlemen. I bid you farewell. Keep healthy and see you"—he looks at Rick—"most of you, in the spring." The manager presses both hands on the table, suggesting that he's more sober than he is.

The bartender hands Rick a length of string for a leash, but Rick carries the ten pounds of soft fur in his arms. Foggy is bumbling into chairs and tables while trying to find the front door. "Come on, Phil, throw an arm over my shoulder."

Foggy Phil Dexter gladly slings his arm over Rick's neck and leans into him. "You'll be great. Bees need a good curveball pitcher." His breath is rank with beer and pastrami, but Rick doesn't mind. Phil's been a good friend and taught him a lot about the game. "By God, you'll be in the majors in a year."

"Your mouth to God's ear." Rick bears the weight of the

man and the small burden of the puppy as they walk the few blocks to their boardinghouse.

Everything that he's done has been fed by his lifelong ambition to play for the majors. Rick has never wanted anything else in his life. As a kid, he asked Santa for gloves and balls and bats; as a teen, he paid his own way to baseball camp, using the money he earned from a paper route. He never learned to sail, letting his father practically adopt the next-door neighbor's kid to crew for him. Tomorrow, he'll head down to his parents' Greenwich home. He wonders if, when he gives them his good news, his extraordinary and long-awaited news, they'll finally respond with some pride and enthusiasm.

The puppy in his hand wriggles himself up and under Rick's chin. Well, so what if they don't. He's a grown man, he's stuck to his plan, and now, at very nearly the last minute, at age twenty-seven, he's finally there. Almost. He doesn't want to be the world's oldest rookie when he finally gets the call to major-league baseball.

Maybe this will be the last winter keeping fit by any means possible while substitute teaching or doing temporary work at a busy accounting firm. In eight months, he'll be back in training, a hardball in his hand, sensitive fingers feeling for the seams, the magic of that perfect throw. The future spools out in front of him: a winning season with the minor-league Bees, then getting the call to the majors. His first appearance in the National League. Rick sees himself doffing his ball cap and waving at cheering fans. He's paid his dues, by God. Forfeited job security and Mary Ann Koble, who didn't want to be a ballplayer's wife.

The puppy yawns, burrows his tail end deeper into the crook of Rick's arm. Why not keep him? He could be a mascot. A lucky charm. A companion on all those miles of roadwork.

There is a church along the way, more beautiful than any other building on this defeated main street; its all-white marble facade glows softly in the newly rain-freshened air. Picked out in gold leaf on the pediment are Latin words: *Gloriam Deo Pax In Terra*.

"Pax. Peace." Rick looks at the puppy in his arms, now sleeping with utter trust in the man carrying him. It's started raining again, a warm drizzle that makes the wet pavement shimmer beneath the sparse streetlamps. "I'm the luckiest man on earth."

Pax. The puppy in Rick's arms suddenly wakes. He reaches up with his baby muzzle and his long pink tongue comes out to lick Rick's nose. Pax.

Chapter Two

I just didn't see myself a farmer's wife. No insult intended to all my friends who found satisfaction in it, but I just couldn't. I was, at heart, a town girl, even if the town was little Mount Joy, Iowa, population insignificant, city limits something like six blocks firmly built on the banks of the Mississippi River. It wasn't that I didn't want marriage; of course I did. And kids. But I wanted something else for them besides the grinding work of feeding America. I wanted something more for myself than being sentenced to cooking three meals a day seven days a week for insatiable farmhands. Pickling and canning and putting up. Putting up green beans and tomatoes. Putting up with bad harvests and droughts and too much rain and corn borers. I was a town girl, but the domestic realities of my farm-bred girlfriends made an impression on me.

Thus I was flirting with old maidhood, a ripe nineteen years old, my only significant accomplishment the high school diploma my mother had framed and hanging in the den. My high school chums were getting married one after the other, but I was determined that my knight in shining armor wasn't going to be one of the local boys, most of whom had already adopted the high seat of the combine as their throne and were deep in the family cornfields. Their chief currency was the half acre set aside for a new house, or the addition Daddy would put on the old one to accommodate the anticipated bounty of babies. More fodder, I thought, for the machine of agriculture. That's not what I wanted for my kids. I wanted for them what I wanted for myself, an indefinable *more*.

When I try to unravel the skein of circumstance that led me to meet Rick Stanton, I have to look to my cousin Sid. Cousins through our mothers, we were playmates, and then he grew into a boy, and I wasn't much interested in playing army or being forced into the damsel in distress role for Sid and his buddies to rescue on their imaginary chargers, wielding not so imaginary sticks as lances and swords. One unfortunate kid got his eye poked real good, as his imaginary knight's visor was a little porous, and the neighborhood mothers put a stop to stick play for a time.

The one thing Sid and I continued to enjoy together was baseball. We'd sit in our parlor, or his family's, the big cathedral radio on, our dads in their undershirts, sneaking Pabst Blue Ribbon beers past our mothers. We listened to the games of the St. Louis Cardinals, as close to a home team as those of us in Mount Joy, Iowa, had. We might have rooted for the Cubs, but my family had turned its back on the Chicago team a generation ago.

Sid sided with me even when I refused perfectly nice Buster Novack. Buster's family were good people, good farmers, but sown into the earth like the corn they raised. Life with Buster would mean respectability and church suppers, raising a nice family to farm the same acres as his grandfather farmed. The biggest excitement the daily corn futures. One day the same as the next. The truth was, I burned for something else. Something beyond watching a slender and good-looking Buster Novak take on a farmer's bulk. Maybe someday I'd regret a missed chance at an ordinary life, but right then it seemed more like a death sentence. So I told Buster no, thank you, and mystified my parents.

But Sid sided with me, and then told me I needed to get the heck out of Mount Joy, that the pickins were too poor for a girl of my standards. "You won't find a prince in this pack of paupers, Francesca. You've got to go farther afield." Sid, having reversed our pioneer heritage, was living in what we simply called the East, Boston to be exact, a graduate of Bryant College, in Rhode Island, and making a good living as an accountant for a shipping firm. He had become exotic. And when he invited me to visit him there—the East—I did. I packed enough so that, unbeknownst to my parents, should an opportunity arise, I could stay. I don't know exactly what I thought might comprise an opportunity, but I knew that should one arise, I'd recognize it. And I did.

So there it is, a friendly cousin, a girl on her first big trip, and a mutual love of baseball. Sid took me to Nickerson Field, traveling the whole way from his digs in Dorchester by subway, which for this country girl was almost as exciting as the train ride east had been, the shopgirls and the businessmen straphanging, looking bored, not the least bit uncomfortable as bodies bumped up against those of perfect strangers, as if this was all so ordinary.

Sid bought me a hot dog and a Coca-Cola, even though I'd asked for a beer. The Braves were playing the Cardinals and Sid and I were in hog heaven. Our seats were perfect, just a few rows back from the bull pen, where the relief pitchers played catch with catchers, legs extended in a balletic arc, the hardballs whizzing into the mitts with satisfying smacks. It would be so romantic to say that our eyes met, or that one look and I knew he was the one, but the truth is, I didn't notice Rick Stanton in the bull pen because he wasn't one of the pitchers warming up. He was acting as one of the catchers. So it wasn't until the game began and the relief pitchers all settled down to watch the action, rumps in white trousers lined up side by side on the wooden bench like pigeons on a wire, that this catcher unfolded himself into a tall, thin man, unburdened himself of the chest protector and mask, and, for reasons neither he nor I ever understood, looked up at me. And I waved.

It still goes back to Sid. Consulting his program, he identified this dark blond, tousle-haired ballplayer with the strong jaw and Roman nose as Rick Stanton, recently brought up from the Eastern League's Hartford Bees. A curveball pitcher with a decent win-loss history in the minors. He wasn't scheduled to play today, unless the game went south and the three other pitchers on staff that day were tossed out. I was rooting for the Cardinals, so I hoped that maybe I'd get to see Stanton play for that reason alone.

He didn't and the Braves won, but I admit that I hadn't paid much attention to the game itself. Every few minutes, I glanced back down to where Rick was fence hanging, a study of concentration on the game. Every now and then, he'd lift his cap, run a hand through his hair, and glance back at me. I couldn't tell then, from that distance, that his eyes were the richest hue of blue I'd ever seen. The kind of blue that seems to have a light behind it, like an Iowa sky on certain fall days. By the ninth inning, we were smiling at each other, and when the game was over, he jumped the fence and made his way up the steps to where I was trapped beside Sid in our row. Rick stood in the emptied-out seats just below me, which put us almost eye-to-eye.

"My name is Rick Stanton and thank you for coming to the ball game." Wisely, he put his hand out to Sid first. Later on, I asked him how he knew that Sid wasn't my beau; after all, he might have looked like a piker horning in on someone's girl like that, maybe even gotten himself decked. It was simple, he said; Sid was a good-looking guy, but you were smiling at me, not him.

Sid stepped aside and let me out of the row. "Sid Crawford, and this is my cousin, Francesca Bell. Good game, but I have to tell you she's a Cardinals fan." With that, my cousin excused himself to go to the men's room and left me with the man who would become my husband.

The moment is crystallized in my mind, but I remember it as if I'm looking down on these two young people. I see the girl, dressed in a summer skirt that lifts slightly in the breeze. I see this ballplayer, all long legs and arms outfitted in his baggy white uniform, the number 65 on his back. He has his hat in his left hand, gripping the curved bill. He reaches out with his right and takes the girl's hand in his. There is a frisson, a jolt, as if they are both charged with positive and negative ions, two forces meant to join up. It was the first time in my life I'd felt physical attraction, and the longer he kept my hand in his, the stronger the sensation. I leaned forward slightly, breathing in the scent of his skin, my eyes closed. I don't know what possessed me. Or, maybe it's more reasonable to say, I didn't know then. I just knew that Rick Stanton was what I'd been waiting for.

. . .

Our courtship seemed so fraught with complication: I lived in Iowa; he traveled all summer. The only thing to do seemed to be to get married right away, set up a home in the Boston area, based on his optimistic hope that he wouldn't be traded for a few years. But the thing I had the most trepidation about wasn't Rick, or leaving home, or setting up what might prove to be temporary housekeeping in a strange city. It was Pax.

"I want you to meet someone." What girl ever hears those words with enthusiasm? Usually, it's a doting mother who will assume you're not good enough for her boy, or a bad-boy pal who will resent you taking his drinking buddy away. In this case, it was Rick's eighty-five-pound spoiled-rotten German shepherd cross. And I knew right away that although I could certainly work my way into a mother's good graces, or charm a drinking buddy into brotherly devotion, with Pax, I had to earn his permission to be important to his man. We were rivals for Rick's heart.

Chapter Three

Pax didn't like to share Rick with anyone, but he especially disliked it when Rick would bring home females. On the one hand, as a male, he certainly understood Rick doing so, but women made Pax nervous. Mostly because he made them nervous. However, usually this was only a very short interruption in the life that they enjoyed. Being a lucky dog, Pax went everywhere with Rick, and he especially loved going to the ballpark, where the other men would slip him treats and act as if he were one of the team. Recently, Rick had started leaving Pax home alone for days at a time, a teenage boy coming to walk and feed him. "Got to hit the road, pal. This organization won't let you come." Pax liked the boy well enough, but he sulked and refused to engage with the kid. No amount of stick throwing or walks around the block would soften the dog's attitude. Rick was his person, and only for Rick was he going to act the puppy.

When the suitcase came out of the closet, it meant that Rick was going to disappear for a while, and then return happy or grouchy. Pax would greet him like a long-lost hero no matter what mood Rick came home in, and he had the knack of moving Rick out of the doldrums by simply reminding his man that he was there and ready for some playtime. For Rick, he'd flop onto his back, four legs waving in the air, all dignity abandoned.

In the winter, it was much better; then he and Rick spent most of the day together, working out at the gym and doing roadwork. They ran; they visited Shanahan's Bar and Grill, where the proprietor, a guy Pax thought of as Meatman but Rick called Dickie, would dole out chunks of raw beef as if he thought Rick didn't see him do it. Pax liked their first-floor apartment, where he had taught himself to open the back door; he loved that, especially when the neighbor's cat got cocky and walked along the perimeter. Rick liked it because then Pax could let himself out into the fenced-in yard. As Rick liked to say, win-win.

In the year that Pax had lived with Rick, Pax had only ever shared Rick with the stray teammates he'd invite back after games for a sandwich and beer, or the pals that would crash here at odd times when passing through town. That was fine; no one expected anything more of him than a polite deference. Once in a while, Rick would bring a female around, but they never stayed long.

Everything changed when Rick brought Francesca home. "I want you to meet someone." The dog didn't understand the words, but he understood the vocabulary of love. This woman wasn't going to disappear like all the rest. The pheromones spurted off them like fireworks, filling the dog's highly analytical nose with the truth long before the people themselves got it. These two were destined to be mates.

The woman reached to pat him on the head, as if he was some ordinary affection-starved cur. The indignity of her invading his space made him duck away, as if her touch would hurt. But he didn't growl. The tension in Rick was enough to put Pax in a state of readiness, but Pax didn't stiffen into his guard posture. Slowly, he sniffed the woman's still-outstretched hand and then took an olfactory tour of her whole person, ending with her knees. She let him sniff the most interesting part of her without shrieking as many females did when he arrived at that oh-so-revealing human spot, usually with a quick defensive shove against his skull. This one remained as aloof as he was, and that was fine. This one didn't try to force friendship on Pax, and that was one thing in her favor. So many of the females made that simpering cooing sound when introduced to him; this one spoke to him in a friendly, meeting-of-equals tone. Instead of keeping his wolf eyes on her as she and Rick sat side by side on the couch, Pax lay down on the rug at their feet and heaved a sigh. Instinct suggested that this new woman was about to be made a part of their pack.

Chapter Four

Besotted wasn't the right word. Or *bedazzled* or *smitten* or *be-witched*. Well, maybe *smitten* came close. Struck as if by light-ning. Rick put his hand in Francesca's and knew that if she ever let go, he'd die. She was so young, almost ten years his junior, but they were equals in all else. Her sense of humor, her way of charming even the great Mr. Stengel. The smile that meant she was purely happy. The way she brushed back her blond curls just before she kissed him. She barely came up to his shoulder, but he felt as if she lifted him.

It was like being in a play or a movie; everything felt accel-erated by the fact of her impending departure back to Mount Joy. They skipped the testing ground of going to the picture show, followed by a late-night snack at a diner, where they could talk about the movie if other conversation failed them. Instead, Rick moved ahead in the usual dating schedule. He didn't have the luxury of time to wait for what was typically his third or fourth date treat, so he took Francesca to dinner at the Ritz for their first outing. They held hands, fingers en-twined. They had everything to say and nothing. The harpist lent an ethereal air to the moment, her gentle music speaking out loud what was going on in his heart. How could this be? Rick had certainly dated, even loved once—his impatient fiancée Mary Ann—but this was different. For so long his plans had been formulated around his career, every decision weighed against its effect on that single-minded goal. Sitting across from this girl with her midwestern, matter-of-fact, down-to-earth, speak-her-mind confidence, Rick found himself fitting Francesca neatly into his life. He saw his future so clearly: Francesca, the house, the dog, the blond curly-haired kids.

"She's swell, isn't she, Paxy?" Rick and Pax have just put Francesca on the train back to Sid's place so that she can get ready for their date tonight. She's been to the ballpark every day, meeting him at the players' entrance after he's showered following a game or practice. He counts his lucky stars that this is a home week, no travel. He won't let himself imagine if he'd had to climb on the team bus and maybe never seen her again. Or lost the momentum that they have been building to all week. They've jumped the T and gone all over the city, to the Museum of Fine Arts and to the Isabella Stewart Gardner Museum, shopping at Downtown Crossing, but mostly strolling through the Public Garden and the Common, Pax between them and happy to be included in their adventures. After dinner, they go to clubs and dance until Rick knows his manager is going to be mightily distressed with him, out so late on a game night, but it hasn't affected his game. If anything, this new-love euphoria has made him indomitable. Called in for the last inning this afternoon, Rick struck out all three batters facing him in thirteen pitches.

They have accelerated from hand holding to kissing. He made himself go slow, not meaning to test her willingness, nor frighten her away, but she nearly frightened him with her response. It was as if she'd been waiting for him all her life. He won't let himself take advantage of that enthusiasm; he's a gentleman and he respects the proprieties. He forces himself to remember that she's a small-town girl, and a young one at that, and he won't send her home in any way less perfect than she arrived in Boston.

Rick can't let himself think about what the end of the week will mean. Francesca will go back to Iowa. His travel schedule doesn't include Mount Joy. He's not a free man until after the season ends, and that seems like an eternity. For the first time in his life, baseball seems secondary.

"How long does it take, do you think, for a man to be certain about what he should do about a woman?"

Pax cocks his head, opens his mouth slightly, and makes that little *humpf humpf* noise that Rick interprets as conversation.

"What's that you say? Marry her, right?"

Woof.

"I think you're onto something." Rick thumps Pax's ribs, ruffles his fur, and kisses him on the nose. "Sounds crazy, but that's the answer."

Pax leans against the leash, his nose plowing the way to a new scent laid in against a telephone pole. He lifts his leg. Obviously, there's nothing more to say.

Rick has never felt so sure about anything—except baseball—in his life. Francesca isn't the first girl he's met at the ballpark, but he is certain that she will be the last.

Chapter Five

My last night in Boston, our last night together, Rick took me to Norumbega Park on the Charles River in Aburndale to dance at the Totem Pole Ballroom. One of the area's premier night spots, "the most beautiful ballroom in America," the Totem Pole featured the best big bands and popular singers in the world. That night, we danced to the music of Benny Goodman. For a small-town Iowa girl, this was a magical evening. Made more magical by the feel of Rick's arms around me, the grace with which this long, tall ballplayer danced. Even in Mount Joy, we knew the new dances, and before long Rick and I were the center of attention as he flung me up into the air, my full skirt belling around my legs. We laughed and gasped for breath, and when the photographer came to us to take our picture, I was certain that he wasn't going to need a flashbulb, we were so lit from within. He captured us so perfectly, that anonymous on-staff photog. A lovely couple, starry-eyed with fresh love. Our future written in our smiles.

Exhausted, we finally flopped down on one of the settees arranged around the dance floor. When I rested my cheek against him, I came up against something hard in his jacket pocket. "What's that?"

"Oh, this?" Rick reached in, and I expected him to pull out a pack of cigarettes, because that's what it felt like. "A little something I'm hoping that you'll like." Then he dropped the kidding tone and slipped his arm out from under my head. Rick got down on one knee, and I thought that my heart would explode. "I know this is really rushing things, but I have never been so certain of anything—or anyone—in my life. Will you do me the honor of becoming my wife?"

One week to the day since we had met. And I had no reservations about saying yes.

And then I was on the train, heading home to Iowa. Sid, God bless him, hadn't said a word as I slipped into his second-floor flat at five in the morning, only yawned and started the coffee.

"Is he downstairs?"

"Yes. Asleep in the car."

"Go get him."

I ran downstairs as quietly as I could, so as to not disturb the neighbors, but Rick was gone. Of course, he had to get home to Pax. He'd be back in a couple of hours to take me to South Station, when we would have what we hoped was the only separation we would endure in our lives together. A few days on the road for the team wasn't going to have the same weight.

Pax and Rick picked me up, the dog relegated to the backseat but leaning his big head over the front seat, so that I could feel his whiskers against my cheek. Impulsively, I kissed that muzzle. Pax sniffed my cheek in return. "I'll miss Pax, too, you know. It isn't just you." I think saying that made Rick almost as happy as my wearing his ring.

I was such a baby, quietly weeping most of the way to New York, where I changed trains for the Chicago leg of my journey, dabbing my eyes with a sodden handkerchief, as if I had the least concept of what true absence was. I wallowed in the sweet agony of separation from my beloved. As I wearily climbed aboard the final connection home, I tortured myself with wondering if absence would make his heart fonder, or would he wake up in a week and wonder what the heck he'd gotten himself into? Rick promised a letter a day, a telegram a week, a phone call every other. Would his letters begin to thin out; would the telegrams seem more ominous than loving? Would he forget to call?

A telegram was waiting for me when I finally arrived back in Mount Joy. "MISS YOU MORE THAN WORDS CAN SAY STOP CAN'T WAIT TO HEAR YOUR VOICE STOP WILL CALL THIS EVENING AT 8 STOP ALL MY LOVE RS"

The dark tunnel of doubt opened to a bright new day.

Rick and I tied the knot in mid-October, not four months after that day in the ballpark. As soon as the season was over, Braves foundering in seventh place, Rick took the train for Mount Joy and I introduced my fiancé to my astounded parents. He knew Casey Stengel. That was enough to win over my father. He was well-bred, and that was enough for Mother. It might have looked a bit like a shotgun wedding, but it wasn't. "Marry in haste, repent at leisure" might be a well-founded adage, but we laughed at the thought that if we hadn't married, we might have ended up with my father's shotgun pointed at Rick's back. After all, Saint Paul did suggest that it was better to marry than to burn, and we burned for each other. That's the best way I can describe it. But I was an Iowa girl and he was a gentleman, and marriage was the only acceptable route.

My two best girlfriends, Gertie Fenster and Patty Olafson, stood up for me, and my older brother Arnie acted as best man, with Sid as his groomsman. At Rick's insistence, Pax performed ring bearer duties, wearing a black bow tie around his neck, the rings tied to it with blue ribbon. I was just glad he hadn't wanted the dog as best man. The guests threw rice for luck and I wept for joy.

We stayed in the Elyria Hotel in downtown Mount Joy. Our window overlooked the mighty Mississippi, but I'm not sure either one of us ever looked out at the view.

As much as I liked the big dog, to Rick, Pax was his baby. Pax was Rick's blind spot. He didn't see anything wrong with the dog following him around from room to room, so that anywhere Rick was, there was Pax. Even in our bedroom. Basking in afterglow, I'd look over and there would be Pax, the patient voyeur. At least Pax didn't get up *on* the bed, but I couldn't ignore the weight of his muzzle as he studied Rick's face for any damage I might have caused. Eventually, he'd humpf and flop down into his basket, clearly dissatisfied with my remaining in Rick's (in Pax's view) bed.

I began to feel like I hadn't passed some test, that I wasn't worthy of Rick. Those amber eyes would fix on me as I rubbed Rick's shoulders, sore from his day of hard practice, or sat in his lap as we canoodled while listening to the radio. Pax would lay with his head between his paws and sigh, exactly like my mother might do when one of us disappointed her. A hand-to-God sort of sigh. Rick thought I was nuts.

"He loves you."

"Does not."

"What makes you say that? Look, he's sitting right beside you."

"The better to keep me separate from you. He's between us, Rick." I wasn't sure if I was speaking metaphorically or literally at that moment, although Pax did always keep himself in the middle. We sat on the couch and the dog sat on the floor, his big head resting in between us.

"That's just so we can both pet him."

"What happens when we have a baby? How will he be?" As much as we knew that we wanted children, we were giving ourselves at least a year of marriage. The only advice my mother gave me on the eve of my wedding night was that if I relaxed, it wouldn't be so bad. The best advice I got was from the shortstop's wife, who knew a female doctor with a modern outlook on birth control and an admiration for Margaret Sanger.

"He'll devote himself to our babies. He has a massive capacity to love."

The very first thing I learned about being married to a professional ballplayer, was that I had to keep his state of mind in perfect equilibrium. Numbers were everything. In those days, there was no designated hitter, so Rick batted and pitched. He was a better pitcher, and no one expected him to be a great batter, but he still believed in his earned run average like it was tea leaves forecasting our future. Which, I suppose, it was. Those numbers dictated our lives. Good ones, and we got to stay put. Sinking ones, and who knew where we might end up. Bad ones, and his career might be over. Rick loved being a ballplayer; it was his first love, and I understood its importance in his concept of himself. Being a ballplayer *defined* Rick. So I swallowed my annoyance with having a big, shedding, slightly sloppy, all-boy dog in our one-bedroom apartment and molded myself into the best ballplayer's wife in the league. Supportive, pennant-waving, consoling, and laudatory.

Right after spring training, Rick started traveling two or three days a week; our honeymoon winter was over. Pax and I were left alone together.

It was rocky at first. The big dog didn't want to take orders from me, so I found myself cajoling rather than ordering: "Come on, Pax, let's go outside." "Come on, Pax, there's a good boy, don't get on my couch." Even though Rick expected me to, I certainly didn't walk Pax as much as he did. Just like the dog, I loved those evening walks with Rick, when we'd go hand in hand, talking about our days, or our future. But when Rick was on the road, I'd take Pax once around the block, me towing him along or being towed by the dog, depending on where his nose took him, and then head home to listen to the game on the radio, or wait for Rick's late-night phone call from a pay phone somewhere far away.

Rick was in Baltimore, and the heat in Brighton certainly rivaled that of Maryland. Hot, sticky, the only relief coming in those early hours before dawn, when the wind might shift a little and drag some of the cooler ocean air off Boston Harbor and inland enough to reach our stifling first-floor bedroom with its single window and no cross ventilation. Now, as a midwesterner, I knew heat. Our corn-raising community was unbowed by routinely high temperatures in summer; every woman carried a fan and a capsule of smelling salts in her purse to church. But this sticky, wet, humid heat was intolerable to me. The only cool place at night was on the front porch, so in the middle of the night, desperate and wide awake, I placed a thick collection of wedding-present blankets down on the deck of our first-floor porch and hoped that no one passing by in the predawn—the milkman, for instance—would notice a grown woman stretched out on the porch in a mysteriously glowing white nightie. Because of the arrangement of our front door and that of our neighbors', who, in their second- and third-floor flats, were more likely to be catching the thin breeze, I worried a little that Pax might dash down the steps. I gave him the first command I'd ever tried: "Stay." He looked at me with a dog's version of "Make me" but stayed, lying flat on his side against the short end of the porch railing. His soft panting put me to sleep.

I shivered, smiled at the sensation, then woke fully, to see the dog standing over me, head lowered, teeth bared. I fought the urge to push him away, freezing in place like a rabbit hoping the fox doesn't see it. Then I realized that Pax wasn't baring his teeth at me, but at the man who was urinating loudly into the hydrangea bushes planted against the porch. Pax's dewlaps twitched over his bared teeth. A growl percolated deep in his throat. I touched him, trying to tell him that it was all right, not particularly pleasant, but harmless. The growl went from barely audible to ferocious, and the man literally ran off half-cocked. Pax leaped over the railing, and the frightened drunk ran for his life.

"Pax! Come!" I had no real hope that he would, and I pictured this poor unfortunate guy with the seat of his pants torn out. Perhaps worse. Pax was fast; Pax was in high dudgeon. But he surprised me and returned to my side in three strides. If a dog's face can express "Wasn't that fun?" Pax's did. His long muzzle split wide and his long tongue lolling, he rolled his eyes up to me, and in them I saw that a sea change in our relationship had occurred. He'd protected me; ergo, I was now part of his responsibility. I hugged him then, and he took it as if it meant something to him, tail sweeping the porch floor. After all, it was possible that the drunk, seeing a woman in such a vulnerable position, had had more ominous plans post-urination and Pax had known that. Who knows? All I knew was that Pax had protected me whether or not it was really necessary. He'd done his duty by me.

We sat there a long time after that, Pax leaning his big body against mine as we sat on the porch steps. I kept an arm around him. The first bird sent out notice that the sun would make its appearance soon. Slowly, the night paled, and I heard the clop of the milkman's horse from down the narrow side street. I needed to get into the house before anyone saw me like that, dressed in my honeymoon negligee. "Come on, Pax. Let's put the coffee on." Before I could push myself up off the step, Pax did something that stopped me. He gently pressed his muzzle under my chin, just like Rick sometimes did to raise my face to his. Then he licked my cheek. Even though I didn't assign any human qualities to animals like, well, like Rick, I understood completely that I had been accepted. We'd always be rivals for Rick's attention, but at least now we could be friends.

Chapter Six

The frightening rumblings coming from Europe were only mildly concerning until the mandate came down in September 1940 that every man between the ages of twenty-one and thirty-six needed to get himself registered for the draft. If the invasion of Poland hadn't prompted this belated Selective Service Act, the bombing of London had. Every day, the news worsened and the newsreels portrayed a sickening disaster seemingly without end.

Rick and Francesca went together, hand in hand, Pax tagging along, as if registering for a peacetime draft was a lark, an excuse to get out in the fresh air and stroll the city streets. The worst, and Francesca agreed, was that his number would come up in the Selective Service's lottery and he might have to spend twelve months in the service. It would take a year out of his professional life, but maybe he could still play ball or coach on whatever base he might find himself. Francesca teased that maybe he could plead conscientious objector status, as playing for the Braves was, after all, his religion. Rick wasn't about to let Francesca know how terrified he was that he'd be drafted. Not because he didn't want to serve, but the fact was that a missed season was much more than just not playing. He was twenty-nine now, and it wasn't getting any easier to keep up with the younger guys. His arm was still good, but he was soaking it longer and longer. Not to play, even if doing some playground-level pitching, meant that he might never make it as starting pitcher. He was so close. Rick really loathed the idea of a setback.

Besides, this was the year when they were going to have a baby. Maybe Francesca was already pregnant. With a renewed contract with the Braves in hand, life was certain enough that they'd commenced trying. Trying. That sounded so, well, self-less. What they'd been getting up to could hardly have been called anything but self-indulgent. Francesca had been knit-ting up a storm, booties and caps, buntings and crib blankets, all given away to the other team wives and to their neighbor, who was in her seventh pregnancy. Yesterday, Francesca had shyly handed him a little capelet in the palest green, nearly white, satin ribbon threaded through the eyelets. "This one's for ours."

He took her heart-shaped face in his big hands and studied her amber-flecked green eyes and the way that her eyebrows arched over them, sooty lashes oddly dark against the fairness of her skin and hair. This was the face he held most dear. The look of hope, anticipation, and love all given away to him. How could he imagine leaving her for longer than a road trip?

By April, Rick's number still hadn't been called, and he'd packed up for spring training. By July, he was promoted to relief pitcher. By September, the season was over, and if the Braves had fin-ished a lowly seventh in the standings, Rick had gone home nonetheless confident that the upcoming baseball season of 1942 would be his year as a starting pitcher for the Boston Braves.

"What if Roosevelt changes his mind. What if he decides we should go to war?" Francesca took the newspaper out of Rick's hands and crumpled it up, throwing it to the floor, as if she wasn't the one who would have to retrieve it. It seemed like the headlines only ever spoke of the increasing possibility the president would succumb to the pleas of Churchill to throw the weight and power of the United States at Hitler's rapacious drive toward world domination. The political cartoons, the editorials, the talk on the street all pointed in one direction: the inevitable involvement of the United States in this global disaster.

"Sweetheart, we can't worry about it. We can only worry about the things we have control over."

"Like what?"

"Mmm, my batting average perhaps?" Rick pulled Francesca down onto his lap and smooched her, one eye on the big dog, who would very quickly come up with some distraction, like asking to go out, or for new water in his already half-full bowl, or dropping his rubber ball on their combined laps, begging them to stop and play with him.

"You get to worry about that, not me."

Pax had suddenly found some latent retriever in his heritage and scooped up the crumpled ball of newspaper, gently placing it in Francesca's hands.

"It'll never happen" was the consensus of opinion in the clubhouse and the street corner and at the Totem Pole Ballroom, where they went to dance on gameless nights, always claiming the same settee where Rick had proposed. "Roosevelt will keep us out. If your number hasn't been called by now, it probably won't be." Whistling in the dark.

By the end of November, Rick finally got word that the coming spring he'd be in the starting rotation. He'd finally be a starting pitcher.

"Maybe a move is in order. You know, to a place of our own, where Pax can run around and the kids—"

"Kids? Plural already?" They were lying in bed, fingers linked, still vibrating from their exertions.

"Yes. The kids can have a swing set and you'll never have to worry about men urinating in your hydrangeas. Some neighborhood with a good school, a house with a big yard. The neighbors will say, 'A ballplayer lives in that house, the one with the lily beds and rosebushes. The one with the beautiful wife and handsome dog.' It'll be the house where all the neighborhood kids congregate."

"Three bedrooms and a den?"

"Four bedrooms. And a two-car garage."

"Two cars?"

"Don't worry, I'll teach you to drive."

It all sounded perfect, even if the gods of conception had been stingy with success. The doctor they'd consulted could find no reason they shouldn't conceive. "Relax and give it time," he'd said.

On December 7, the Japanese bombed Pearl Harbor and all the best hopes for staying out of the war were blasted away, along with Rick's dream of starting for the Boston Braves and their more private dream of a baby.

Chapter Seven

It isn't that Keller isn't grateful—in a way—to his great-uncle for having taken him in when he did. If the old man hadn't shown up that snowy winter day two years ago, Keller would have spent the rest of his youth behind the wrought-iron fence of the Meadowbrook School for Boys. Orphaned, passed around from relation to relation, none of whom during those dark days of the Depression could afford another mouth to feed. A scuffle with the truant officer had landed Keller in reform school. He'd been living with Aunt Martha and Uncle Bud and their four kids, and they were visibly relieved to hand Keller over to the state, the burden of his presence in their overcrowded Revere flat nullifying any shame in doing so. Without a willing guardian, he went in, at age nine, without hope of release before age eighteen.

At Meadowbrook, Keller was fed, clothed, educated in reading and ciphering; taught the rudiments of the carpentry and print trades and some of the more useful talents of lock picking and theft from his fellow inmates. There were friendlier boys, and there were enemies and bullies. Boys from whom it was all right to bum a cigarette and boys you'd never turn your back on. There were clear rules, clear punishments meted out by teachers and staff and by the concrete hierarchy within the community of the boys themselves.

No praise, but then, he didn't expect praise, so he never minded its absence. There was no affection, but then, he was unused to affection. As close as Keller got to tenderness was when he'd slip away and visit the groundskeeper's dog, Laddy. The dog, purportedly meant to guard the groundskeeper's cottage, would wriggle with pleasure at Keller's appearance, gobble down the crusts or bits of half-chewed gristle, and then flop himself across Keller's lap to soak up a belly rub. The touch of the mongrel's soft pink tongue against his cheek was as close to love as Keller had known since the last time his mother kissed his cheek. A time so long out of mind, he could barely conjure up her face in his memory.

Clayton Britt drove Keller home from Meadowbrook in his ancient Ford truck, the bed filled with fishing nets and lobster pots. Every sideways glance at the boy sitting beside him on the rump-sprung seat bore the avid look of a man getting himself some free labor. Clayton was his dead father's uncle, Keller's great-uncle, and before he showed up in the superintendant's office, not someone Keller had ever heard of. Keller didn't like the greedy look in his uncle's eye. Clayton looked at him not like a long-lost and welcome relative, but as a potential slave, his ice blue eyes apprising Keller's man-size height and the size of his biceps. As they left the grounds of the reform school, Keller had bluntly asked, "How come I've never heard of you?"

"Don't know. Your mother's people never got on with mine."

"Then how did you know about me?"

"You're kin, boy. I'm the only kin you have that'll take you. Be happy I'm giving you a home."

Home is Hawke's Cove, a Jimmy Durante schnoz-shaped peninsula jutting out from the New England coast. Crossing the short causeway that attaches the village to the mainland, Keller gets his first sight of the eponymous cove, a deep natural harbor along which the village clings. The winter sun strikes blinding sparkles off the water and two fishing boats are iced in and coated with a frill of frozen spray.

Clayton doesn't stop, but passes through the village and deep into the center of the peninsula, eventually turning onto a washboard dirt road that leads to Keller's new home on French's Cove Road. The house is a four-square shingled fisherman's shack, two rooms down and two rooms up, with only the heat from the parlor woodstove to warm the place subjected to the relentless draft pushing through the uninsulated bead-board walls. Meadowbrook may have been a prison, and his sleeping arrangement a dormitory filled with forty-nine other sleeping, farting, stinking boys, but at least he was warm. Behind the house, a yard littered with the detritus of a coastal fisherman's life: nets, lines, mushroom anchors, a skiff belly-up on sawhorses. Below the bluff, the scallop curve of French's Cove, with two moorings and a short pier proclaiming Clayton's ownership of this slice of beach. On the moorings are a squared-off lobster boat also used for scalloping, and a small dragger. Neither vessel has a name.

Living with Clayton means lobstering in all weathers, standing hip-deep in the cove in leaky waders while a seven-knot wind blows in his face as he rakes for quahogs; or trawling for bottom fish and slicing himself on scales, hooks, and the sharp, savage teeth of menhaden-crazed bluefish. Life with Clayton means never being able to completely wash off the odor of marine life.

The only thing that makes this life bearable is the fact that Keller has been able to attend the local high school. He's had enough English classes to understand the term *ironic*. Being truant from school was what landed him in Meadowbrook; but being allowed to get his diploma is what will free him from Clayton. Once that piece of paper is in hand, he's out of here, and for that he can thank Miss Jacobs.

It was almost the end of March that first winter with Clayton when an official-looking envelope came in the mail. Clayton held it up to the kitchen light as if he could read through the envelope and discard it without opening it. "What in the heck is this?"

Keller had already become used to his uncle's rhetorical questions and kept his attention on a pot on the stove, giving the chowder in it a gentle stir. Clayton slit the envelope with his filleting knife, extracting a single sheet of paper, which he held aloft as he patted his pockets for his reading glasses. Glasses settled, he read the letter, then dropped it on the table. He folded his glasses and replaced them in his shirt pocket. Keller could feel the air being sucked out of the room as Clayton slowly turned to him. "You finish eighth grade, boy?"

"Yes."

"Get a certificate?"

"No. But that's as far as anyone goes at Meadowbrook."

"You sixteen yet?"

"Yes."

"Says here you need to go to school, but you don't." Subject closed, Clayton crumpled the letter and tossed it in the firebox of the range. "I didn't take you in just to send you off la-di-da. You can read and cipher, that's enough."

Clayton was right: An eighth-grade education was enough, and Keller shrugged off the idea as wishful thinking. Until Miss Jacobs showed up at their back door, tiny and trim in a shirtwaist dress, white hair permed into submission and the look of eagles in her eye.

"Clayton Britt, this boy needs to attend school."

"He's of age to quit."

"Does he want to?"

"I have the say in this house." Clayton stood in the doorway, his bulk keeping the high school English teacher standing outside.

Keller was behind Clayton, looking over his shoulder, and she looked right at him past the old man. "Step out here, son."

"No. You come in." Clayton doesn't hold the door open for Miss Jacobs, merely moves aside to let her in.

She didn't come up to either of their shoulders, but her bearing was pure authority. "Keller, what do you want to do?"

In all his memory, no one had ever asked Keller what *he* wanted, and as much as he knew Clayton would make his life miserable for it, he answered with his heart. "I want to finish school. I do."

"Clayton, this boy is entitled to an education. You cannot deprive him of that. I won't let you."

"What's it to you?"

Miss Jacobs lifted her chin, as if Clayton were one of her unruly boys and she was about to bring the switch down on him. "Don't be rude to me. I won't have it from you. Not you, Clayton Britt."

The pair stared at each other, and Keller realized that they were long-term adversaries, that between them there smoldered a history.

"See that this boy is in class on Monday. Keller, please dress appropriately. Bring your own pencil."

Before Miss Jacobs had stepped off the porch, Clayton slammed the front door, spun around, and slapped Keller. "Why'd you say that? For what you're doing, you don't need no education and you know it. Just looking for ways to dodge work. Lazy bastard."

But Clayton never attempted to prevent Keller from going to school.

There is no love between them, no affection, nothing more than any two men working together might share, an occasional laugh, a curse at the weather, griping about the lousy price the fish market pays for the fluke they spend four days offshore trawling for. If Clayton is taciturn, Keller is quiet. Clayton reads the evening paper spread over the kitchen table while Keller reads a schoolbook. They do not converse. They coexist. Most of the time.

It's Saturday night and Clayton has cracked open his Prohibition-era bootleg bottle of Canadian Club. They lost a lobster trap today when Keller lost his grip on the chain and it slid out of the pulley and into twenty feet of dark December water. A tire on the old truck is too thin to hold air and the spare is shot. Clayton sits at the kitchen table and tosses back a third shot. Keller sits opposite, keeping his eyes on his plate of cod.

Not for the first time, Keller wishes that the old man would let him get a dog. It seems to him that Hawke's Cove is filled with dogs. Dogs that sit patiently in cars as their masters conduct the business of the day; the fish market dog, called Flounder, which Stan Long claims is so smart, he could spell if he wanted to, but chooses not to. The big Newfoundland that goes out to sea on the fishing boat *Jane Anne*. The newspaper boy's dog, which follows him around from porch to doorstep on his route.

A dog would give him an excuse to walk out of the house; a dog would side with him against the old man's rants. A dog would listen as Keller whispered out his loneliness. A dog might fill that hollowed-out space.

But Clayton has said no. He doesn't need any other mouths to feed.

"You're a piece of work, you are. Losin' that pot. What kind of fool are you?" Clayton's indulgence in the whiskey most often follows days like this, when too much has gone wrong. Then Keller becomes an easy target for blame. "Kindness of my heart. I took you in. What's my thanks? Cost me a trap. Can't remember to put air in the tire. Like you was trying to make me mad." He goes from gruff to just plain mean. "You got plans to inherit this place? You just forget it, boy. I'd rather see this place go to the devil than to you."

"I don't want it. What gives you that idea? You keep me here like slave labor. Why would I want it?" Keller shoves the plate aside. He stinks of fish; he can't get the taste out of his mouth.

"I see you coveting it. Just like your mother. You come from nothing, boy. Your mother was a cheap whore."

"Don't."

"Tricked my nephew into marriage. Know how? Got herself in the family way. With you."

"You don't know that."

"Got her clutches on him, white trash."

"And just what do you think you are? A fisherman. High-and-mighty? Think your shit don't stink?"

Clayton pushes himself out of his chair, stands waiting for balance, as if he's at the helm of his workboat. Keller watches his hands. Sometimes when Clayton gets into the Canadian Club, he likes to take a swing at him. Keller has no difficulty deflecting the wild swings, and some latent decency always prevents him from decking the old man, as much as the feel of that jaw against his own hard fist would go a long way in righting some of the indignities he's suffered out of the old man's mouth.

Clayton wobbles and Keller grapples with him, waltzing him into the parlor and down into his chair, where the old man falls asleep. Sometimes the sight of that mean old man, drunken sleeper's drool drizzling into his two-day-old scruff, his outrageous slanders about a mother Keller has little memory of, is enough to burn his eyes with unspent tears.

Sunday has always been the only day that Clayton Britt doesn't go out on the water, adhering to some vestigial notion of a Sabbath, despite never having entered the precincts of a church. In the same fashion, Clayton calls lunch on Sunday "dinner," and he usually cooks the only beef the two will eat in a week, the rest of their meals consisting of salted, boiled, fried, or raw seafood culled from their catches. Short lobsters, a dozen littlenecks. And, always, boiled potatoes.

Nothing is said about last night. Clayton got himself up out of his chair long after Keller had gone upstairs to his lumpy and cold bed. Keller wants to finish high school, but sometimes he thinks that he should just up and go. Stuff a laundry bag with his few possessions and light out. He'll be eighteen soon, the age when the state would have set him free from Mead-owbrook if Clayton hadn't intervened. But if he can hold on, that diploma will be worth it.

This December Sunday, there's a football game on the radio and the two settle in after lunch to listen to it, Clayton in the one easy chair in the room, Keller on the braided rug on the floor, rather than in the spindle-back chair, which is the only other chair in the sparse room, its skirted chintz cushion oddly feminine in this intensely masculine house. The woodstove smokes a little and Keller gets up to rearrange the logs. Outside, the midafternoon winter sun is already weakening into an early dark.

Seconds before the game is to start, the broadcast is interrupted. Keller and Clayton lean toward the radio, trying to make sense of the rushed and repeated bulletin: "President Roosevelt has announced that the Japanese have attacked Pearl Harbor from the air."

Regular programming resumes, but Clayton shuts it off, his gnarled hand lingering on the peak of the radio. He coughs, then scratches at the stubble on his cheek. He looks at Keller. "Guess that you'll be leaving."

"Yes, sir." Keller looks away; he doesn't want the old man to see the happiness on his face, the relief and the hope. His life sentence has been commuted. The attack on the naval station at Pearl Harbor was surely horrific, but by it, Keller is set free.

As Keller Nicholson figures it, Pearl Harbor is about the best thing that could have happened to him, although he'll never say that out loud. The national outrage at the loss of life and the subsequent call to arms certainly is greater than his private joy at having a rock solid reason to leave his great-uncle

Clayton's house. Patriotism and duty to God and country. Even Clayton can't argue with that.

Keller doesn't wait to be called up. He isn't going to take a chance that the lottery will deal him a losing number, and there is no way he to going to miss out on this chance to extricate himself from Clayton Britt's life; no way, as a strapping young man, is he going to miss the excitement of going to war. As dire as the world situation is, he and many of his peers worry that they may miss it, that the war will be over before they can get into it. Four of the boys from last year's winning high school basketball team have joined up already and three boys, seniors this year and already eighteen, have talked their way out of finishing school and into boot camp.

The day after his eighteenth birthday, Keller strips out of his overalls and pulls on his only nondungaree trousers. He brushes the dirt off his shoes with a bucket brush and digs the dirt out from under his nails with the ice pick. If Clayton won't let him take the truck, he plans to walk the five miles to Great Harbor, or he'll hitchhike to the recruitment center that has been set up in the empty storefront beside the A&P. Someone heading from Hawke's Cove into Great Harbor will stop and give him a ride. No shame in sticking out a thumb.

Keller strops his straight razor and lathers his face with the bar of Ivory soap, shaving for the second time that day.

"You going somewhere?" Clayton leans against the bathroom doorjamb. Keller can see him reflected in the mirror, the old man's expression inscrutable. There is no way to see past the weathered skin into the man's thoughts. His eyes, ice blue and framed by crow's-feet earned by a lifetime on the water, study Keller with detachment. As if Keller means nothing to him, and his departure doesn't mean a season of hard solo work.

Keller rinses his razor, wiping it carefully on the towel

hanging around his neck. "Recruitment center. I'm joining up." Keller sets the straight razor down on the edge of the sink and reaches for his shirt. "I'd like to take the truck. I'll be back in an hour." He buttons his shirt and jams the tail of it into his waistband. "Two at most."

Clayton doesn't move, doesn't answer. Standing in thick wool socks, his rubber boots left standing by the back door, Clayton is just a little bit shorter than Keller, or maybe it's just that Keller feels bigger, taller; his resolve to join up has pushed him from boy to man. He has nothing more to fear from this old man.

Clayton moves away from the bathroom door to let Keller pass. "I'll take you myself."

Is it his imagination, or is there a little pride in the old man's voice?

Miss Jacobs came to see Keller before he left for boot camp. She looked so small and vulnerable, standing there in Clayton's sitting room; feminine in a way that he'd never noticed before. The raptor eyes and the hands that gripped a pointer like a lance were softened with a weary resignation. Even before he'd enlisted, she'd tried hard to get him to wait, to finish his last few months in high school, get that diploma, then sign up. But Keller no longer saw that bit of paper as his only method of emancipation. Now he had the army.

Keller asked Miss Jacobs to sit down, and she perched on the edge of the spindle-back chair, feet aligned, hands clasped together as if she was about to recite poetry. Sitting there in that unadorned parlor, looking every inch the schoolmistress she was, Miss Jacobs looked up from her clasped hands and directly at him, and Keller could see that she believed that she had saved him from ignorance, only to have him die a soldier. She reached into her handbag and extracted a book. "I'd like you to have this. It belonged to my father."

Keller took the copy of Malory's *Morte d'Arthur* from her, opened it, and read the inscription. "To Alfred Jacobs upon his successful matriculation. 1892." Beneath those words was another inscription: "To Keller Nicholson as he begins the journey of a lifetime. Best wishes and good fortune, Miss (Ruth) Jacobs. 1942."

"Thank you, Miss Jacobs. I'll always treasure this." Urged on by an unaccustomed grace, Keller kissed her cheek, and was surprised to find it wet. "You've been so kind to me. I don't know why. But I'll never forget you."

Clayton drives Keller to the train depot in Great Harbor, where he is to catch the early-morning Portland to Boston run. Leaving the truck running, Clayton gets out with Keller, hands him the small valise Keller bought himself with the little money Clayton has given him over the years. In it just some clean underwear and his shaving kit. The book from Miss Jacobs. He has nothing else.

"That's it, then." Almost as an afterthought, Clayton offers him a hand, and Keller accepts it. Two work-hardened palms meet for the first and last time.

"I guess it would be right to say thank you. For taking me in."

"Yeah. Well, good luck." Clayton turns quickly and walks away, as if Keller isn't leaving him and his hardscrabble life behind forever. As if this journey is of no consequence, that his only blood relation isn't going to war.

"You, too." Keller is rooted to the sidewalk, watching the

old man's back. It isn't affection or gratitude that he feels, but relief. Excitement. This is a ticking off of a phase in his life—like living with his mother's siblings until that became living in the reform school and that became living with Clayton. It's over and done with and now a whole new and completely self-chosen phase is about to commence. Keller feels like yelling: Yahoo!

Then, with a little hitch of reluctance, Clayton pauses, turns. "You know that you can come back."

"I do." But I won't, he thinks. This door is closing and a brave new one is opening up.

The Portland to Boston train puts Keller Nicholson into South Station half a day early for his connection to New York. After that, another eighteen hours to Fort Bragg. This is his first train trip, and Keller soaks it in, the novelty not yet worn off by the time he gets to South Station, and he's looking forward to the next leg of his journey. He has a few hours to explore what he can of Boston, and he roams happily up to the Common, window-shopping at Jordan Marsh along the way and eating a hot dog from a street vendor. The stiff breeze coming off Boston Harbor barely gets Keller's attention. He isn't far enough from home to sense a difference in the air. It's all too familiar, sea air chilled by a constant breeze. North Carolina is going to be a lot different. And from there, well, who knows what exotic places he may be in. Keller is back at South Station in plenty of time for his train. The crowd has grown, lots of uniforms, but many more, like him, still nominal civilians but wearing that excited, terrified look of new recruits. Keller feels like he's part of a club, and he is amazed at how there is no mistaking the other members. Maybe it's the families surrounding them, or the wives and girlfriends all "bearing up" under the circumstances. A guy just heading to New York on business wouldn't have a mother clinging to his sleeve and dabbing her eyes with a hankie. He wonders then if *he's* readily identifiable as a recruit. He has no one frightened for him, or proud of him. No one making him promise to write. He stands alone, his back against the wall. Keller thumbs through the first pages of the Malory, his attention on the bustle around him, but grateful for the shield of the book, giving him the appearance of a man calmly making the journey of a lifetime.

Keller jockeys for position in the line queuing up to board the Boston to Penn Station train. Ahead of him is an odd trio, a man and woman and a big handsome dog. Nice-looking dog. Shepherd maybe? A tarnished silver with black points. Keller has never had a dog, but he likes them. When the fellow hugs the dog and then his wife, Keller smiles, thinking that the guy has his priorities straight, but then he sees the anguish on the human faces and regrets his impish thought. A moment later, the dog is pushing people aside as the young woman gripping his leash follows like a blind person. Later, on the train, Keller keeps thinking about that image: the man and woman and dog and how separate and devoted the couple were to each other. In the midst of this crush, they had carved out a niche of privacy, guarded by the dog. In another moment, he's sound asleep and the image and the thought fade away.

Chapter Eight

It wasn't like Pearl Harbor happened and then Rick left. We had a couple of months of what I thought of as a grace period while the military got around to calling him up, and then he had a date for his induction, which gave us four more weeks before he'd depart for Fort Dix. We had time, but we wasted a lot of it anticipating the final moments. We played out the scene in our minds so often that when it finally happened, it was with an extraordinary sense of déjà vu. We should have spent the grace period walking Pax along the Charles, eating in restaurants we couldn't afford, laughing at mindless radio programs, and dancing at the Totem Pole. But instead, we clung to each other and made promises we couldn't hope to live up to. He promised to come back and pick up where we'd left off. I promised not to worry about him. We debated the wisdom of trying now for a baby. Rick even suggested that we sit down with a pad of paper with a line drawn down the center, heading the left column "Pro" and the right one "Con." As if he thought we were analyzing the concept of moving to a new house or buying a new car. I knew already what the biggest pro was—giving Rick something to hope for—and the biggest con—my becoming a widow with a small child.

"Maybe the fact that we haven't conceived is God's way of—"

"Oh, Rick, please don't say that it's God's plan."

"Okay. Maybe fate has intervened."

I blushed with the secret I had been holding so close to my heart, waiting until I was absolutely certain before getting Rick's hopes up. I was late. For the first time ever. We were inveterate calendar watchers now, and I counted four days. Four days of growing significance. And in six, he would leave.

In my mind, the real question was whether to get his hopes up and dash them in a letter, or surprise him in a letter by saying that our hopes had finally been fulfilled. One more day, I thought. I'll tell him in one more day. And then another just to be sure. A whisper in his ear the morning he leaves. I couldn't wait to see the beaming grin on his face.

Without jealousy, I let Rick go out alone with Pax on their evening constitutionals. Where I had always enjoyed the walk, now I understood on some level that these two buddies, man and dog, needed a little female-free time. Rick somehow had to explain to Pax that this wasn't a road trip, that this was something entirely different. This time, there might be months or even, God forbid, years before they'd be together again. I wept a little thinking how impossible it was to explain to a dog that you weren't abandoning him, that you hadn't forgotten him, that you were just the unwilling pawn in circumstances out of your control.

South Station. There was an icy breeze slicing across the tracks, so we went inside to wait. No one looking at the stiff-jawed man and the puffy-eyed woman said anything about the presence of the dog. In our obsessive playing out of this scene, we'd forgotten that the place would be crowded with other servicemen and their families. Somehow I think that we both saw this farewell taking place in a cocoon of privacy. Instead, the defiant smiles and unattended children running around shrieking so that the place echoed with their voices, didn't fade into the background like in some movie, but stood out as proof that what Rick was doing, and what I was enduring, was universal and unavoidable. We were not alone.

As if he understood that this wasn't an ordinary departure, Pax pressed himself up close to Rick, leaving silver dog hairs on his charcoal gray dress pants. We laughed, that awful strained laughter of people on the verge of tears. I brushed the hairs off Rick's leg, but they slipped off my glove and drifted back.

"Leave them." Rick held my hand, and I realized that he would spend the train ride picking those hairs off. I knew that he superstitiously put a few of Pax's hairs in his baseball cap for luck; maybe he'd do the same with these loose hairs clinging to his pant leg, collecting them, maybe even dropping a few in his wallet to remind him of this other family member he was leaving behind.

Waiting was interminable and, conversely, the departure was all too soon. When you have said all that you can say, the silence enfolds you and you cast about, searching for that last important reminder or anecdote, until there is only empty space in your head and your heart is screaming for relief. And then the whistle blows and suddenly all these men scurry away, last kisses and hugs, last admonitions to be careful. Last I love yous.

Rick knelt on the platform and put his arms around Pax.

I don't know what he said to him, but the dog licked his face, something he rarely did, and watched intently as Rick handed me the leash, as if the dog knew that there was a changing of the guard, that I was now the person in charge.

Then Rick took me in his arms in a way that he would never do again in quite the same way. He kissed me with a passion that I would never quite know again.

We didn't say anything else. No unnecessary reminders to write, no useless pleas to stay safe. The last thing Rick said to me was, "Don't stay. Don't stand out here in the cold and wave when I won't be able to see you. Take Pax for a walk. I want to think of you and him playing on the Common as if it's an ordinary day. Not here."

By now, the mass of enlisted men was funneling itself into the train; faces appeared at the windows as men jockeyed for position. Windows opened; heads and arms stuck out. I was nearly knocked down by the seemingly unending number of families that rushed the platform. Wives and children, mothers and sisters, little brothers looking jealous, fathers discretely touching eyes with handkerchiefs and maybe remembering their own departures twenty-some years before, leaving for another war. Everyone wanting a last look, a last word.

In the end, I didn't say anything. That morning, I had awakened with the thick rumblings of an impending period. Maybe it was for the best. Maybe this meant that Rick would come home to me, and our children would come easily after that. But it still felt like I'd said two good-byes—one to my husband and the other to the last chance we'd have to have a baby.

Pax rumbled in his throat, not a growl, but a warning to anyone pushing too close. I had to get him out of there. Rick was right. There was no way he'd catch sight of me surrounded as I was by taller, wider people all vying for that last look. I tried to fight my way out, but my "Excuse me" and "Pardon me" went unheard by a crowd aware only of its own farewells.

Suddenly, Pax barked, loud and full of warning. The masses parted, startled by the deep voice of the dog. Like Moses parting the Red Sea. I couldn't wait to tell Rick how his dog had taken charge of the situation. And with that random thought, the magnitude of what was happening washed over me. Rick was being sucked into the vortex of this new American reality of war. I wouldn't tell him this anecdote, but write it in the first of the thousand letters that I would pen for the duration. I shook back the wash of dread and told myself that I would write to him that night and tell him about how Pax had moved aside the crowd. I would tell him that we'd played on the Common and that we'd had leftover meat loaf for dinner. I wouldn't write down on that scrap of paper that Pax had had to guide me out of South Station because I was blinded by tears, doubly grieving Rick's departure and the thickly flowing evidence of our failure, once again, to conceive.

Chapter Nine

It felt wrong, this departure. The tension emanating from his people had put Pax on the alert. Pax understood that Rick was going away; it happened with enough regularity that he no longer worried about it. Rick always came back. And Francesca was good company while they waited for his return. But this time, for a long while before the actual moment of departure, this human pair had been exuding an indefinable vibration. Not grief, or hope, or happiness, or tension, or despair, but some amalgam of all of those. It was hard on his sensitive nerves, trying to sort out what exactly was wrong. Then the three of them went to that noisy, crowded place, and Francesca shuddered all night afterward, despite Pax keeping his eyes on her and his head on her waist, standing all night beside the bed without sleeping while she trembled. She was afraid, and he couldn't find out what the source of that fear was. He'd left her side only long enough to patrol the apartment, corner to corner, door to door, and nothing, absolutely nothing, seemed threatening.

There was always a rhythm to Rick's absences, and Pax

could sense which day would be the day he'd be home. Sometimes it was what Francesca cooked. A roast with its meat juices sizzling in the oven meant that Rick would be home. Sometimes it was that she whistled softly as she changed their bed, stripping off the more interesting-smelling sheets and putting on crisp ironed ones that would take a night to acquire the comforting scent of his people's bodies. A third indicator that their little pack was about to be returned to normal was the scent that Francesca spritzed on herself. Pax couldn't understand this need to disguise her willingness to mate, but humans did a lot of things that puzzled the dog.

Even for an animal with no sense of the passing of time, Pax knew that Rick had been gone a long while. No roast in the oven; sheets changed, but no whistling. No perfume clouding Francesca's proper scent. The slowness with which Francesca moved around the apartment. Drifting. Settling the new black curtains more exactly against the sills. Wandering into the kitchen but making no move to feed herself. More and more, Pax kept to her side, something he never did when Rick was there.

As she drifts from room to room, Pax follows, his cold black nose an inch from her hand, so that when she sighs and reaches back, she knows that he's there, ready to take on her worry. Sometimes she presses her cheek against his skull and whispers, but of all the words she says, there is only one word he knows, *Rick,* spoken over and over. When she does that, Pax closes his eyes, vaguely recalling the feel of his mother's body covering his and trembling with fear.

Chapter Ten

I think that many of us went into this war thinking that it would be over fairly quickly. Or that's what we told ourselves, because it was inconceivable that our men would be gone for so long. It had been half a year since Rick shipped out, bound for the battlefields of Europe.

We had a brief reunion when Rick got leave just before shipping out. He couldn't get back to Boston, so Pax and I piled into our 1936 Plymouth and drove all the way to New Jersey. As we started out, my hands gripped the steering wheel like vises, and I was more than convinced that my inexperience behind the wheel was going to be the death of us. Rick had taught me how to drive in those last few weeks before he left for boot camp, but I rarely took the car out. By the time I reached Fort Dix, I drove with one hand casually on the wheel and the other elbow resting on the open window. I'd become a driver.

I don't remember much of that reunion, just that it was a worse good-bye than that at South Station. Then he'd still been in civilian dress; now he stood there, crisp and stiff and unbearably handsome in his khaki uniform, his very scent unfamiliar. We had two days, and I don't think we saw the outside of our hotel except for taking Pax out. Rick made me leave him instead of him leaving me. I drove off in that Plymouth, Pax with his head hanging out the passenger window, me in danger of a wreck because of the tears. Rick briskly walked away from us in the opposite direction so that I wouldn't remember him with any other expression but a smile.

With so many of the men gone, the Fore River Shipyard had begun hiring women to fill in the holes in the line. My pal Connie Mills tried to chivy me into going in to see if I could be of use. Connie was married to one of the catchers, a player who hadn't waited for the Selective Service Act, but joined up the day after Pearl Harbor. "Do it with me. We can wear overalls and not worry about our hair. We can't keep sitting around; we need to do our bit."

"Doing our bit" was the constant refrain. A serviceman was doing his bit; civilians who collected scrap metal and saved bacon grease were doing theirs. We were inculcated with the idea that we were all responsible for the outcome of this conflict and we all felt a personal responsibility. Beyond victory gardens and blackout curtains, the American way was to make every personal decision based on the war. We learned to do without, a lesson learned from our parents, who had survived the Depression and handed down to us their experience to serve a new purpose. We took great pride in drinking our tea without sugar and learning to like margarine. We debated every use of the car and saved our gas-ration coupons like misers. Self was secondary to winning the war and sacrifice was honor.

"I'll give it some thought."

"Francesca, you're just moping around here. It isn't healthy. I know you're still a honeymooner, but, honey, you need to get out."

"I'm not a honeymooner, not anymore."

"You're a honeymooner until you have kids."

I know that Connie couldn't have meant to hurt me, but her words were like little slaps. I had to forgive her, though, because she could have no idea how hard we'd been trying to become parents, and that we weren't deliberately prolonging our honeymoon.

We were sitting at my kitchen table, Pax beneath it in what I called "his cave." Even as I swallowed Connie's words, I felt the weight of his paw on my foot, reminding me he was there.

"I have Pax. We have Pax."

Connie patted my hand. "Sweetheart, Pax is not a child."

But he was to me. He needed me. How could I leave him all day? Fore River was in Quincy, a long train ride from our little apartment in Brighton. Green Line to the Red. It would be highly irresponsible to leave the dog alone for what could be ten hours a day. He'd go mad. "No, I can't go that far every day."

"Then find something closer. Francesca, we all have to do something. Think of it as helping our boys over there with what we're doing here."

She made a good case. Connie was fired up, and I knew that she wouldn't let me be until I found some war work to do. And, truthfully, I was ready to do something. My little bit of volunteering with the other wives for the local children's hospital was good, but Connie was right: I needed to be a part of the war effort. Everyone I knew was doing something. Back in Mount Joy, my pal Gertie was taking a nursing course, and Patty was in charge of the blood drives for the whole county.

And both of them were now wives and mothers, as Connie suggested; it wasn't like I had kids at home to take care of to fill my time. Only Pax.

The wire factory had geared up for the war, along with so many other peacetime businesses, and was running three shifts to bend wire into the war machine. Second and third shifts paid best, but I was content with first. After all, we had savings and I had Rick's army pay, which wasn't nearly as much as his baseball salary, but enough to support me, so I left the better-paying jobs for those who really needed them. Best of all was that it was within walking distance from home. I could be home in minutes and often went home at lunchtime to let Pax out.

We were a noisy crew, the bane of the one male floor supervisor, who had to put up with our jokes and gossip and insistence on popular music in the break room. The puke green walls of the break room were plastered in what in another country might have been called "propaganda posters," but we looked on them as patriotic reminders of our importance in the war effort: BUY WAR BONDS; LOOSE LIPS SINK SHIPS; DON'T TELL SECRETS ON THE PHONE; DO THE JOB HE LEFT BEHIND; and other variations on the perpetual theme of winning the war and the continued responsibility of every citizen to remain alert and focused on the effort. I found myself studying the images of European peasants huddled against ominous threats and, my favorite, the one of the sinister-looking man sniffing around for secrets.

The morning *Globe* was filled mostly with news of the war and the noble work being done on the home front. It cheered me in some way to read of the galvanized spirit of my adopted community and my country in the communal effort to defeat the Axis powers and return the world to sanity.

Rick had been overseas for almost six months. His letters had begun to thin out, not as if the effort of writing was too much, but because the relentless bounce between periods of insufferable boredom and hours, days, or even weeks of adrenaline-charged action was telling on him. How could he continue to write jolly, flirtatious V-mail letters when all around him the world was coming apart at the seams? It's pretty difficult to keep up a facade of optimism when you are mired in the mud of the battlefield. I'd get them in bundles, six or seven letters herded together from the various places where he'd had the opportunity to post them, and their sameness was blatant as I read them one after another. Eventually, I didn't even need to sort them in date order; the messages were the same: He missed me. He missed Pax. He was all right. They were hunkered down in fairly comfortable circumstances, or they were on the move. He got to be so careful, there were almost no censor's marks on his single sheet of V-mail. If he'd gotten my letters, he might reply to a question, or offer advice, or comment on something I'd gossiped about. His letters were mostly out of sync with mine, and I might wait a few weeks before I opened a letter that would answer a question I'd forgotten I'd asked. "I miss you. I miss Pax. I miss spring training. I miss home." Those were the salient facts; that was his litany. And I wrote back that I missed him, and that Pax was fine and missed him, too. I told him to take heart, stay safe. We'd all be reunited soon, I said.

But I was not waiting out the war in some safe harbor; I was part of it. We were all part of it. Even just being in that break room, my hands toughened up from the work I was doing, made me feel proud that I was a part of the war effort. Who would have thought that I could enjoy the satisfaction of running a machine, of producing a product that would directly affect the war? I didn't have enough backyard for a victory garden, but I had sewn blackout curtains for every room in the apartment. Because I walked to work, I was saving those gas-ration coupons for the day when Rick would be discharged and I'd drive to the ends of the earth to get him. When the neighborhood kids came to the door, I turned over the day's washed-out tin cans so that they could be turned into tomorrow's tanks. I helped with the St. Alban's Ladies Guild jumble sale, the proceeds going to a fund for displaced children. It was always the thought of those European orphans that pierced my heart, little children whose parents were dead, whole families gone, with no way to explain it to tiny victims. In my dark moments, I wondered if the parents of those orphans would have preferred that they'd never been born than to have them suffer the horrors of invasion, bombardment, and abandonment.

Yes, we were all doing our part. So the day that I opened the *Ladies' Home Journal* and saw the full-page ad for Dogs for Defense, I didn't quickly turn the page.

WANTED: WAR DOGS FOR DOGS FOR DEFENSE/ENLIST YOUR DOG NOW, the headline read.

The ad made a persuasive appeal:. . . *there's a real job today for dogs that can meet the requirements for service with the United States Armed Forces! There are duties that the K-9 Corps can perform even better than men . . . sentry duty, pack work, messenger and communication service and sledge work are but a few of the jobs many dogs are already doing for their country.*

I read every word, my glance returning after each paragraph to the illustration of a dog that looked a lot like Pax. Pax fit the bill: *Dogs may be purebred or crossbred, must not be less than twenty inches at the shoulder, not storm shy or noise shy, not less than 1 year or more than 5 years old.* Pax was a big dog, he was a little under four years old, and he'd never made a sound during thunderstorms. I'd walked him all over Boston and he took in stride the cacophony of the city streets. He defended me against drunks urinating on hydrangea bushes. He was aloof but affable, never vicious. He had heart.

The promise: *Your dog will be well-trained, well-fed, and well-cared for while he's serving Uncle Sam.*

Purina Dog Chow, the very same I fed to Pax, was the sponsor for this ad run by the American Kennel Club's Dogs for Defense volunteer board.

My break was over, so I returned the magazine to the shelf of reading material we girls had brought for the communal room. Leaning into the small mirror hanging just next to the exit—something the female staff had requested for the once exclusively male break room—I dabbed on a fresh coat of lipstick. I may have been wearing denim overalls and had my hair pulled up out of my hard-won pageboy hairdo into a bobby-pinned pile of curls hidden by a kerchief to keep the dust and dirt out, but we all clung to our emblem of femininity—bright red lipstick. As I blotted my lips with a square of tissue, I saw behind me, reflected in the rectangle of mirror, a new poster: GIVE DOGS AND DOLLARS TO DOGS FOR DEFENSE . . . TRAINING SENTRY DOGS TO HELP OUR SOLDIERS.

I went back to the shelf and picked up the magazine, flipped the pages back to the Dogs for Defense advertisement, and ripped it out. I folded it and put it in my locker.

Everyone should do his bit.

I put the kettle on and opened up the box of cookies I'd baked for Rick. I'd used the last of our sugar ration to make them.

I had pressed my thumbprint into some of the cookies so that he'd see some physical manifestation of me. In a few, I had pressed three knuckles in an attempt to represent Pax's paw print.

Lately, I'd noticed that a number of the neighborhood dogs had vanished. The big setter and the beagle no longer came up to their fences to bark as Pax and I walked by. On our way around the block that evening, we bumped into Mrs. Tingley, as we often did on Pax's after-work constitutional. She was alone, her collie, one of Pax's favorite playmates, absent from her side.

"Where's Lady?" I stopped, hauling Pax closer to me so that I could chat.

Mrs. Tingley, a middle-aged woman who had sent three sons to war, didn't answer right away, and suddenly I worried that some horrible news had come to her. Her face began to crumple, but then she pulled herself together. "We donated her, you see. To the Dogs for Defense program. She's going to be a messenger dog or a scout."

"Dogs for Defense. I've seen the ads."

"She's doing her bit. Just like my boys."

"Don't you miss her?"

Mrs. Tingley looked down at Pax, then up at me, and smiled. "I do. But not as much as I miss my boys. Dogs like Lady will help get them all home sooner. I believe that. You should think about donating Pax. He'd be perfect. Besides, they'll send him home to you as soon as the war's over."

"I couldn't. How could I?"

"How can you not?"

The funny thing about becoming aware of something you've never noticed before is how suddenly you see it everywhere.

Now that I was aware of the Dogs for Defense program, everywhere I turned, there it was. The vanishing dogs. The posters, the ads, the newspaper stories featuring little kids handing a leash over to handsome military types. "We'll see that he gets home. He's doing his bit. You can be proud." Public-service announcements featured Rin Tin Tin as a recruiter for the K-9 Corp, and the newsreels showed the grainy images of dogs running, jumping, taking down well-padded targets, tails wagging, praised by smiling, pride-filled handlers. Saving soldiers' lives. Everywhere. And everywhere I went with Pax, the more I imagined that everyone we passed was thinking, There's a big strong dog. He should be doing his bit. As if this were a different war, I half-expected him to be handed a white feather.

No. I had made my mind up: Pax wasn't going anywhere. I needed him too much. He was my connection to Rick, my only companion, my entertainer, and my silent partner in the darkness of my worst thoughts. If I could have kept Rick out of it, I would have. I couldn't, but I sure could keep our dog home.

And yet, in that box of gingersnaps and lemon wafers I included not only a silly love note but the Dogs for Defense advertisement I'd torn out of the *Ladies' Home Journal*. I think that I wanted Rick to know that I hadn't succumbed to pressure. I think that I wanted him to agree with me. Or make the decision for me.

Chapter Eleven

Rick Stanton shakes off the catcher's sign. This batter is better than he looks and a fastball thrown to him has the potential to tie up this game. As it is, they're losing the light and it won't be long before the game is called because of darkness. Rick winds up, kicks, and launches a curveball.

"Strike three!" Pvt. Al Hooper joyfully signals his sergeant out. With good grace, Sergeant Phillips hands the bat to the next batter and doesn't argue that, from his perspective, it had looked like a ball on the outside left corner. Only on the playing field does the strata of rank become moot. And only rarely do they get to carve a playing field out of the battlefield. Once the game is won or darkness beats them to it, rank will be restored and Phillips will be back to making the calls.

Rick tosses the baseball gently up and down. The Boston Braves had sent him a box of balls and a carton of bats almost nine months ago. Through near-constant movement of their battalion, barrages, and battles, his platoon had lost most of the donated equipment. They are down to two balls and one bat. He'd joked that maybe they should start using grenades for batting practice, hitting toward the outfield of enemy territory. They all joke. They all play this bizarre form of pickup baseball for one reason only: It keeps their minds off the next day. It isn't enough to have survived until today. There is always tomorrow and it is tomorrow that they worry about. You know you've made it today. But, will your number be up during the next advance, the next ambush, the next time the enemy fires its big guns in your direction? Baseball, sometimes played in a tiny market square or in some farmer's abandoned field a few yards behind the artillery, is something they can do and forget for nine amateur innings why they are playing on foreign soil in a danger zone. And that tomorrow may not be your day.

If they are hunkered down in a small town or village, sometimes children will show up to watch. Eyes peek over windowsills, followed by a slow emerging from gaping doorways; the gradual building of an audience who watches the game in an unnerving silence. Nonetheless, these kids often surprise Rick with their knowledge of this quintessentially American game. Or, maybe it's just that kids have an innate understanding of how games are played. They watch as intently as genuine fans while the Americans, stripped down to undershirts, helmet liners instead of baseball caps, swing and miss, catch flyballs, run the bases—generally mess kits loaned for the duration of the game—sliding headfirst into home plate, which, by invented tradition, is always the helmet of the highest-ranking officer playing the game. They watch, and sometimes Rick will call a kid over and put him in the game. Ragged children, skinny in a way a child should never be, a wariness and timidity in their eyes that looks permanent. A tiny miracle may take place when he calls a kid over, stands him beside a mess kit, and gestures in crazy sign language that he should catch the ball and tag the runner out. Sometimes, not always, that one kid will lose the wariness in his eyes, and a little sparkle will show. One little moment of pleasure, of *play* in a life spent scrambling for survival. That was how they've lost most of the balls—Rick gives them to the kids in exchange for a smile. He thinks of his own unborn children. He'll teach them how to play the game and about these kids and how much the game of baseball meant to them.

This time, there are no children watching. They end the game before dark with a quick one-two-three last inning, chalking up a two-to-one victory for Rick's team. It isn't all that different from winning on the legitimate ball field, handshakes and backslaps, easy laughter, good-natured ribbing of the losing team. All that's missing is a tavern and a cold beer. All that's missing is the life he left behind. Most days, it is possible to keep his perspective. This carnival of noise and destruction and blindly following orders is his here and now. Francesca and Pax and playing baseball live in a very special compartment in his brain, a place that he lingers over only during those rare moments when he isn't fully engaged in the hard work that war forces on him. To dwell on what is a very different plane from the one he currently inhabits is like thinking of sex while pitching a no-hitter. To think of home and his life and how much he misses it is hazardous. It's a losing proposition.

Yesterday, the battalion had gotten mail for the first time in a couple of weeks. Rick had each one of Francesca's letters bundled together in the bottom of his pack, and during the stretches when they didn't receive mail, he'd extricate the bundle and read two or three randomly pulled out of the pile. He used to keep the letters in his field jacket pocket, but the bundle had become too thick to carry there, where it weighed against his breast, pulling him to one side.

So, like all his comrades, Rick stood in the crowd and waited to hear his name called by the quartermaster, the anticipation of a letter or two like a taste in his mouth.

"Stanton!"

"Here, sir."

The quartermaster deftly snapped a bundle of letters into the air, where it sailed precisely to where Rick stood.

"You ever want to pitch, you let me know." Rick tucked the bundle into his jacket.

"I got a hell of a fastball, Stanton; you don't want to hit against me." He rooted around a little more in the mailbag. "Wait, you've got a package." The quartermaster lofted a small brown paper-wrapped box to Rick.

Rick read each of the stockpiled letters from Francesca in date order, each one decorated at the bottom with her XX's and OO's and a messy paw print from Pax. Her letters, like his, had taken on a certain rhythm. The weather, a greeting from her parents via their monthly phone call, a snippet of gossip about neighbors or one of the players who had remained behind; a report on her day at the factory. A funny story about Pax. Pax sending his love.

The box held cookies, bashed mostly into crumbs by the time it reached him. Among the remnants was an envelope. Rick licked the tip of his finger and picked the crumbs off the envelope, savoring the bite of ginger as he tasted what his wife had tried to do for him.

Dearest Rick,
Sweets for my sweet. Pax did his own paw prints. Honestly.
With all my love, your own,
Francesca

His sticky fingers found the slick magazine paper and he pulled out the enclosed advertisement. Rick had seen one, a war dog. Just the sight of a well-made American dog, so unlike the scrawny, fearful mutts that scurried away from them as they approached, too long feral to trust human beings, had made him more homesick than he'd ever been in all this time. The dog had been a casualty dog, put to use in the aftermath of a battle, locating the still-living wounded. All Rick wanted to do was pat the dog, but the soldier handler was clear: No one was allowed to do more than admire this working canine from a respectful distance. Rick's fingers had itched to feel fur beneath his hand, and the rebuff had sent him into a funk of missing Pax.

Rick held that creased piece of magazine paper in his hands, studying the photograph of the German shepherd and his proud young owner. He looked away and pressed a hand against his sternum. When the big guns thundered, it could feel like one's chest was collapsing from the percussion. Rick felt exactly as if his chest was being crushed. He crumpled the page, pitching it away from him as if it were a grenade. Lacking enough weight, the paper dropped well within the danger zone. He knew what Francesca was doing, even if she might not realize it. It wasn't that he couldn't see it; he really could. Pax, big, strong, smart, working as a scout or sentry, as a casualty dog or messenger. Rick retrieved the ad, smoothed it out, refolded it, and added it to the bundle at the bottom of his pack. A working dog. Smart and loyal, more than capable of doing the kind of work the War Department had developed. Rick could see Pax in the K-9 Corps. He just couldn't see anyone but himself being the dog's handler. They'd be an excellent team, he and Pax. They always had been, even before Francesca. From the time he'd scooped up the wet, thirsty, hungry puppy, Pax had belonged only to him. Anyone who had ever loved a dog wouldn't easily give up that dog to war; but war was their life now. If Pax could talk, would he say he'd rather be home sleeping under the kitchen table than be doing his bit?

Rick and his platoon are called into formation, the balls and bat are stowed away, the momentary respite from action is over, and by this time tomorrow, well, who can say what may be true tomorrow. He doesn't have time to write to his wife, to answer that unspoken, implied question. He's squandered that time with a pickup baseball game. The game had gone well, but for once it hadn't given him the usual release from his present. No matter how hard he had concentrated on his pitching or his hitting, the idea of his beloved Pax being sent into the same kind of daily danger he endured obstructed his focus.

As Rick climbs up into the already-moving troop carrier, a hand grabs his, hauling him over the tailgate and into the truck; the private who had been the umpire for their pickup baseball game grins at him. "That was a great game. We should challenge the Krauts to a baseball game; we'd be sure to beat their asses."

Two days later, Pvt. Al Hooper was dead. He'd walked off to the side of the road to take a piss, smack in front of three camouflaged Germans, who opened fire on him, killing the boy instantly.

A scout dog would have alerted the platoon to danger. That umpiring private would never have died. That night, Rick bummed a sheet of V-mail from a buddy.

Dearest,

I know that you weren't asking the question, but the answer is that Pax should do his bit, too. We should volunteer him for the Dogs for Defense program. It's the right thing to do. So, it's going to be up to you now to keep one more creature in your prayers.

Love,

Rick

P.S. Please tell Pax that I'll be looking for him.

Chapter Twelve

Dear Mrs. Stanton,
This is to advise that your German Shepherd Dog, Pax, has
been called into the K-9 Corps of the U.S. armed forces . . .

When the war is over and you have had an opportunity to
learn firsthand from the soldiers who have benefited by these
trained war dogs, you will realize what a splendid contribu-
tion you have made toward your country's welfare in time of
war.
Sincerely,
Forest M. Hall
Regional Director
Dogs for Defense

Receiving that letter had been tantamount to getting Rick's
induction letter. Hall's reassuring words of my future pride
and Pax's inevitable glory did nothing to assuage the lumpen
feeling that surrounded my heart. I shook off Connie's atta-
girl embrace; I didn't feel noble; I just felt sad. Pax didn't have
any choice in the matter. Like a draftee, he was just being told

what to do and would be sent away. Rick at least could write to me and let me know he was doing all right; Pax would disappear for the duration, and I believed that I might never know where he was. Europe or the Pacific, the Aleutians or stateside, protecting the coast with the Coast Guard. That last option was the one I prayed for. Like Rick had said, I now had to add Pax to my personal prayer list, along with my husband and brothers, cousin Sid, and all the players who had left the game, voluntarily or not, to be a part of the war.

The men came to collect Pax on an early-summer morning. I'd taken the last couple of days off from the factory, loath to lose any more time with my dog than I had to. We went for long walks, used up my precious gas ration to drive to the country, where he could run unrestrained. I'd talked to him, explaining over and over what was going on and where he was going and what he was going to be doing, and how proud we were of him, but I knew that he only heard the soft speech as soothing, not as explication. He had no sense of what was to come.

They came, and you might have thought I was a mother sending her baby into war, the way I failed to hold back my tears, the way I clung to that dog's neck so hard, he had to wriggle loose. Because I was so upset, he became upset and acted as if the two youngsters sent to collect him were a danger to me. He growled and snapped, until finally I had to order him into the wood and chicken-wire crate. And then he looked at me like I was punishing him. I'll never forget that look of confusion in those beautiful eyes. He didn't whine, though, as you might expect. Despite his confusion and upset, Pax never whined.

"He's a nice dog, ma'am." This boy in his grown-up's military uniform shut the cage door, locking it with a twist of the wing nut. "He'll be a good soldier."

My mouth went dry for a moment before a metallic taste of bile flooded it. Panic has a flavor. "Wait. I can't do this." I reached for the cage, but the kid gently blocked my hand.

"But, ma'am, you have done it. You can't back down now." No longer a boy, but a soldier, a man with orders and the authority to carry them out.

"One more minute."

He dropped his hand, but I could feel his eyes on me as I knelt in front of the door. "I won't open it, I promise, but could you step away, please?"

He did, far enough away that I was confident he couldn't overhear my whisper. I spoke so low that I was sure only Pax could hear me and that he'd understand these last sorrowful words. "I love you, you big silly boy. Come back to me. Come back with Rick."

They drove off, my dog in the bed of that military truck. In my hand was his simple leather collar, which had been replaced by his new military-issue one. I coiled the leather around my hand and went into my profoundly empty apartment. That night, as I lay sleepless in my marriage bed, I found myself listening for the sound of Pax's toenails on the bare floor, patrolling the place one last time before settling into his bed. Outside, a dog down the street barked. No other dog answered.

When Rick left for war, I was one among thousands of women enduring a wartime separation. I busied myself and found purpose in the factory. When Pax left, I had only the small comfort of a handful of other dog owners and had lost a good deal of what had kept me busy before. No evening walks, no rushing home at lunchtime, no use for the few scraps of leftovers I couldn't bring myself to eat. I picked up Pax's scattered toys and gnawed bones and his leash and put them all in his basket in the corner of our bedroom, there for when he came back. I kept his collar in my dresser drawer, in safe-keeping for when he'd need it again.

Chapter Thirteen

Pvt. Keller Nicholson can't believe his luck. His application to join the K-9 Corps was accepted and here he is at the Dog Training and Reception Center in Front Royal, Virginia. He might have exaggerated his experience with dogs, confidently claiming that he'd owned several, when the truth was the only dogs he had ever lived with were the beagle Aunt Biddie owned, which kept him warm as he slept on the lumpy couch on the screened-in porch that served as his room when he lived with her, and Laddy, the dog the groundskeeper at Meadowbrook kept tied to a doghouse.

When the chance to become a handler arose, it wasn't the thought of either of those dogs that crossed Keller's mind and set him on this course. It was the fleeting sight of that dog with the couple on the station platform in Boston. The way the man knelt to say good-bye, the genuine affection, and the way the dog guided the woman through the commotion. The people are vague figures in his memory, but the dog stands out. He'd like a dog like that.

The former remount facility has only just been converted

to its new purpose, training dogs to perform the services of scout, sentry, messenger, or casualty dogs. The din is deafening as the four-legged recruits voice their opinions in barks, bays, and howls.

The civilian dog trainer has given the six new human recruits to the K-9 Corps an overview of their training program. "From now on, you and you alone are responsible for the care and well-being of the dog that will be assigned to you. We'll teach you how to groom him, feed him, train him, and work with him. No one else handles your dog. No one else is allowed to so much as pet him. He must look to you for everything that he needs—from food to praise. This way, we build a team of two. Your life and his depend on his unquestioning allegiance to you."

Keller feels a little thrill pass through him, a tickle of excitement, not unlike those long-ago Christmas mornings when his parents were still alive. He follows along as the five other soldiers are paired with their charges. A boxer for the big Indianan; a farm collie for the kid from St. Louis; a nondescript brown dog for another, an Airedale for the fourth. The fifth recruit is paired with a stunning Irish setter. Keller thinks that he would be happy with any of these dogs, each one meeting and greeting the man who would become its partner with sniffs and a general willingness to be friends.

The other new handlers are left behind as the trainer and Keller continue on down the line, passing all sorts of dogs.

"Nicholson, I got one I'd like you to try. But he's a tough one. No one's been able to handle him since he arrived, and if you don't make a go of it with him, he's going back."

The trainer leads Keller away from the rows of doghouses

to a rectangle of high chain link with a doghouse in one corner and a very sullen-looking animal sitting in the exact middle of the confined space. At their approach, the dog's head lowers and his eyes narrow and fill with an unmistakable hostility. He looks to be mostly Shepherd, but some other influence is evident, his jaw a little wider than a true German shepherd's, his muzzle maybe more boxy.

"Why's he in a cage?"

"He's a biter."

"Isn't that sort of what we want in a war dog?"

"We want a discerning biter."

"What's his name?"

"Pax."

"Funny name for a vicious dog. My high school English teacher would call it 'ironic.'" Keller squats in front of the enclosure. "Here, Pax."

A low rumble emanates from the dog's throat, like distant thunder on a summer's day. The dog makes no move otherwise; his eyes are fixed on Keller. Even with the sturdy kennel door between him and the dog, he begins to feel an instinctive urge to back away slowly. Pushing the feeling down, Keller instead makes a little kissy sound as he snaps his fingers softly, poking them through the diamond-shaped chain links. Despite the fearsome behavior, this is a beautiful animal. He's the color of tarnished silver and his muzzle is etched in the same black as the saddle over his shoulders. His ears are like capital letter *A*'s. Inside one of them is a tattoo, marking him as the army's own. He uses his ears like radar to judge the sounds coming from the parade ground; but his predator eyes remain fixed on Keller's own. The dog's rumble deepens into a growl. He sounds more lion than dog. The black-rimmed lips curl back and the dog's teeth are exposed in a wolfish grin.

The civilian dog trainer puts a hand on Keller's shoulder. "I feel I should tell you that two other handlers have tried him."

"How far did they get?"

"Not far. He scared the bejesus out of both of them."

Keller meets the dog's stare with his own. He sees it, and he knows it: the hollow eyes of the disconnected, the abandoned. The anger of being powerless. Being ripped from the known and thrust into the unknown. He sees it. He knows it. You can survive only by keeping all others at bay. The other boys at Meadowbrook had eyes like these, wary and suspicious. Trust was a concept completely removed from their short lives. Fed, watered, clothed, educated, but not cared for. Even among themselves, the bully hierarchy defined respect and demanded tribute, but friendship was rare.

"You don't have to try him. It's just too bad to have to send back an animal with such potential."

"Look, give me a chance. A couple of days. I can't make any promises, but I'll give it a shot."

"Okay. You got it." The trainer claps Keller on the back. "I take it you've worked with dogs before?"

Keller shrugs. "Nah. I just, well, I just think he needs a fair chance."

What Keller can't say, and really doesn't fully understand, is that there is something in this dog that recollects his own journey. Not since the day when he was five and his parents were killed when the Portland-to-Boston train collided with their stalled car, not since the day his aunts had abandoned him to reform school, not since the day his great-uncle Clayton Britt took him out and put him to work on the boat, has Keller felt connected to any living creature. Until now. Reflected in the dog's dark eyes, Keller sees himself.

Keller sits outside of the dog's kennel, a half-empty bowl of dog food beside him, the dog's intended dinner. He's been stationed here, alternately sitting with his back against the links or facing the dog, or most of the day. He's kept up a patter of conversation, as if the dog might actually be listening. He hasn't told him anything important, just nattered on about sports or how hot it is or about the way the guys in his barracks remind him of being in his old dormitory at Meadowbrook, except that there are no bars on the windows. "You got bars, don't you?" Keller holds another chunk of meat in his fingers and thrusts them through the links as if he's trying to feed the bears at a zoo. This one drops a bare three inches from Keller. "Bars are pretty awful. If you don't want to be behind bars, you should be nice. At least nice to me." As he talks, he's been tossing bits of meat into the kennel, hoping to entice the dog to move toward him. It's as if the dog has some invisible force field around himself; he's only snatched the bits of meat that have landed within reach, and he hasn't looked the least bit grateful.

The dog, in a sphinxlike position, doesn't move, but his eyes go to the latest chunk of meat sitting beyond his force field, then back to Keller's face. He doesn't lick his lips, but he does pant. It is unmercifully hot, and Keller's uniform blouse is darkened with sweat. Without the mitigating sea breezes of his coastal upbringing, he really feels the heat and humidity. This Southern summer heat is oppressive for a boy from the more temperate clime of New England.

The only concession the dog makes to Keller's presence is allowing him to refill the water bowl with the hose aimed at it from the safety beyond the kennel. Anytime Keller has slipped open the latch, the dog has growled and retreated behind the doghouse, not like a dog in fear, but a dog who refuses to be near a human.

"I know that it's hard to trust a stranger. Hell, I don't trust people I know." Keller laughs, and for the first time the dog inches toward the piece of meat. "Your people, for some patriotic reason, decided that you needed to serve your country, and I believe that you will. But first you have to serve me."

The dog creeps another inch.

All Keller wants for today is that the dog not growl when he opens the kennel door. He's tried six times in the last six hours and he's almost ready to call it quits. His five fellow handlers have all had their first training session and he can see them out on the parade ground playing with their dogs. All he needs to say is "Give me another dog," and he can be out there with a canine companion who is willing to be his partner, instead of trying to be a lion tamer.

"Okay, Pax. Last time. I won't deny you your dinner, but it would be nice if you were a bit grateful for it." Keller flips the U-shaped latch. At the sound, the dog leaps to his feet, head low, ears back. "No, you're right. Why should you be grateful for something when you never asked to be in this situation. That's like me being grateful to Clayton Britt every time he put creamed cod on the table. He had to feed me, and I guess I have to feed you." With that, Keller swings the gate open and steps in, bowl of horse meat held out as a potential barrier should the dog actually attack.

Pax doesn't. He sits. He watches closely as Keller lowers the tin bowl. The bowl sits right at Keller's feet. In order to get his dinner, the dog must approach the man. Neither one moves. Then Keller moves the bowl closer to the dog with his foot. The dog steps a foot closer to the bowl.

"So, that's how it's going to be?" Keller pushes the bowl

halfway to the dog. The dog moves to halve the distance between himself and the tempting bowl of food. "Come on, Pax, come get your dinner. I sure want mine."

The dog isn't growling, and Keller takes this as a success. It's enough for today. He pushes the bowl directly under the dog's chin. By now, the sun-warmed meat is attracting flies and a bluebottle buzzes around the dog food in the bowl. Without even taking his eyes off Keller's face, the dog snaps and the fly disappears.

Chapter Fourteen

Pax was bewildered. Boxed, freighted, handled by strangers, then brought to this place of dogs to endure the relentless cacophony of the displaced. He had no idea what was happening, or why. All the dog knew was that he had no clear mandate, no orders. Francesca had clung to him and then ordered him into a crate. She'd asked and he'd willingly entered the crate, turned around, and watched quietly as a stranger fastened the door closed. The crate was lifted into the back of a truck and Pax couldn't see over the tailgate. Couldn't see that Francesca wasn't following. The rumble of the heavy engine obscured any sound that she might have been making, calling him back.

The crate went from truck to train, and back to a truck. The air was different here, warmer and filled with the scent of other dogs and men. Pax stood in his confinement and barked out a greeting. He was taken out of his crate and he wriggled with anticipation, so many men. Surely Rick was here; surely Francesca would appear to take his leash in her hand. A veterinarian examined him, patted him on the head, and handed the leash to yet another stranger. And then another stranger attached him to a doghouse and left him there with a full bowl. But neither Rick nor Francesca appeared.

During the long night, the cooler air dragging thousands of new scents to him, Pax lay awake and grieving. He understood it now: He'd been sent away. The only people he trusted had turned him out of the nest as if he were a weanling puppy being chased off by a newly pregnant mother.

The only recourse for his battered spirit was to resist. A growl, a show of teeth, a bite, and these unfamiliar men knew enough to back away. He would not capitulate. He would not wag his tail for that bowl of food; nor would he eat it if anyone watched. He would not submit to being touched and he snapped at the hand of the first person to try to touch him. Even without the sense of abandonment, Pax's nature wasn't open to strangers. He'd tolerated Rick's pals, always polite, but always aloof. Francesca had been the only other human to penetrate that singular devotion. Rick was gone and now she had sent him away, and these strangers thought that they could lay hands on him and make him do their will. Not once in his short life had Pax ever bitten anyone until he bit the arm of the second man to think he could dominate the unhappy dog. That's when they put him in this isolated kennel.

This third man came and simply waited for him. He sat beside the enclosure, talking quietly. He tossed bits of meat to him, but Pax disdained touching any that didn't fall close by. Wounded in spirit, the dog would not be seen accepting his gifts. He growled when the man stood and defiantly opened the gate to the kennel. Pax showed his teeth and the man gave him the win when he stepped back out of the enclosure. The man came back and did it again, and again Pax growled to warn him away. The man knew that he had the upper hand, however, because he still held the food bowl in his hands. The bits that had landed beside Pax were not enough to satisfy his hunger. The man sat back down, and the two considered each other, the wires of the cage separating them.

Pax lay still on the hard ground and studied this man sitting purposefully in front of him. Their eyes flicked over each other's forms, the dog reading the man's youth easily; the man comprehending the dog's simmering rage. The dog locked eyes with the man and recognized that he, too, was a solitary creature, not given to connection. When the man didn't look away, the dog knew that they were equals. The man, like the dog, would not submit. When he came into the enclosure one more time, the bowl held out like an offering, a thin suggestion of caution came from his skin, and Pax admired that. The man wasn't afraid of the dog, but he respected him. Pax let him push the bowl to him, although he didn't eat until this patient man walked away.

The next day, it was just the same. A bowl of breakfast, fresh and still smelling like food and not carrion. The heat that reflected off his coat drove him to pant, his jaws wide, tasting the scent of the man's sweat, a scent that was working its way into the dog's thoughts. It told the story of what he'd eaten, and that he'd had beer the night before. Pax breathed in deeply; the familiar odor reminded him of Rick, who always poured a little beer into a saucer for him. He loved the grainy taste, like eating some kinds of good grass. Rick had been gone for a long time. The scent of the beer on this persistent man's skin made Pax long for the companionship of those hot summer nights when Rick would come home after a game and tell Pax all about it.

Pax had protected Francesca, and acknowledged her as his responsibility, but while Rick was there, his heart was always his. Man and dog. A dignified and purposeful relationship of equals. But Rick was gone and Pax had no way of knowing if he'd ever come back. So much time had passed, and with it the expectation of reunion, that Pax had thrown his heart into Francesca's care. Taking care of her and being loved by her. And then she, too, was gone. Like his mother so many years ago, vanished.

Here was this new man, cautious and patient, not reaching out to touch, respectful and smelling delicately of last night's beer. As long as the dog had been isolated in this hot, humid, strange kennel, he hadn't slept deeply enough to be rested. Like his wolf antecedents, he was on a perpetual high alert, ready to defend himself, a captive. But an unlikely relaxation came over him on the third day of this man's unwanted companionship. Pax fell into a deep sleep, his body shaded by the doghouse, his sense of being threatened gone for the short time he slept.

Waking abruptly, he knew that the man was still there. He raised his head, sniffed the air to gather in the man's now-familiar scent, and, satisfied, allowed himself to go back to sleep.

Chapter Fifteen

"We've got a lot more dogs. No sense wasting any more time with that one." The civilian trainer's name is Rod Barlow and he's been working with dogs, as he puts it, his whole life. A sturdy fifty or so, he says that he's encountered dogs like Pax before and if their people don't want him back, the best recourse is to put them down. In this case, though, sending the dog home is the best option, and his donor has made it clear that if he fails, he goes home. Lots of dogs have bombed out of the program; Pax is just the first to bomb out because of aggression.

"One more day, I promise. I won't waste any more time. Just give me that." Keller doesn't know why he's being so stubborn about this. It's not like the dog is giving him any notion of a breakthrough; and, in all his life, Keller has certainly never been one to embrace personal challenges. Meadowbrook taught him about finding the easy way out. Clayton taught him that hard work does hurt. Besides, he's falling behind his cohorts, as they have already mastered teaching their dogs to sit, heel, and come. At this rate, even if he gets Pax to cooperate, they'll end up in the next group and his new pals will be as-signed and gone.

Pax doesn't know that he's about to get sent home. He has no sense of failure, so why should Keller care? His buddies are already teasing him about his stubborn belief that the big shep-herd will make a great war dog.

Keller stands in front of the fence with Pax's breakfast bowl. He's already decided that he's not going to spend the day waiting for this mess of horse meat and kibble to stink. He's going to go in, feed the dog, and if he growls, Keller will call it quits.

"Okay, Pax. Here's your breakfast. I'm coming in and you're going to let me." Keller lifts the U-shaped latch and steps into the kennel as if he expects a happy greeting, not a bite. He doesn't move slowly, just deliberately. He sets the bowl down and picks up the empty water bowl. "You must be pretty thirsty. Hang on." He refills the water bowl and places it be-side the untouched food bowl. All this time, the dog has been standing, A-frame ears at attention, panting softly, but not growling. Keller doesn't move away from the food and water. "You want it, you gotta get past me."

There is a slight shift in the air, a barely discernible breeze that touches the back of Keller's neck, evaporating the line of early-morning sweat trickling down into his collar, and he shivers. The dog raises his nose to the air. Keller squats, snaps his fingers. The dog eyes him, and for a moment Keller feels like prey, until the dog's big ears fold back gently and the "at atten-tion" look recedes into "at ease." "Good boy. Come on, Pax."

Keller stretches out his fingers and the dog stretches out his nose. The soft, hot breath of the dog travels up his hand and along his arm to the elbow, then to his crotch. He tells himself,

This is how dogs behave; don't move. Pax continues his olfactory investigation against Keller's bent knees and, finally, to his neck and then his face. Keller's thighs are screaming at this point and he goes to his knees. He keeps both hands open and to his sides. He makes no move to touch the dog.

Suddenly, it seems like the dog is satisfied with Keller, as if he's passed some canine test of character and the dog has decided that he is sufficiently harmless. The dog walks past Keller to his food, which he bolts, then empties the water bowl. Keller stays on his knees, remaining at the dog's eye level. It isn't enough to feed the dog; he needs to leash him and take him out of the kennel. He needs the dog to be willing to be touched.

"This is your last chance, Pax. You'll get a dishonorable discharge if you don't cooperate with me. You don't want that, do you? Sent home in shame? You've got too much pride for that, don't you? I know what it's like for your family not to want you. I know how mean people can be. I do. So I know how hard this must be. No one can tell you that you're more valuable to the U.S. government than you are to your family. Maybe they didn't want you anyway, and this is a better option than some others. Maybe you scare them, too. I don't know. Maybe you were a burden to them. Are they poor? Are you yet another mouth to feed? The army will keep you fed; I can promise you that. I'm still eating a lot of chipped beef, but I can't complain. I'm still getting a lot of orders and sleeping in a roomful of men again, but I'm not complaining. At least I get a paycheck. At least I get some respect. You will, too. You work with me, boy, and we'll be top dogs in this outfit. You and me against the Nazis." He keeps talking and the dog begins to visibly relax.

"Did you have a cruel master? Someone who put the viciousness into you with a beating? That happens. I've seen that, too. Too many blows with the strap doesn't teach a boy to be good; it teaches him to hate."

Pax is still standing, but now he's standing beside Keller. Keller offers his right hand again to the dog. Pax sniffs, then lowers his head; his eyes turn away, and Keller takes that as permission. He scratches under the dog's chin, then runs his hand up to his skull. He strokes the ears down to his neck. Beneath his hand, the dog tenses up; Keller can feel the muscles in his shoulders harden. He pulls his hand away. The dog swings his big head up and sniffs Keller's face again. It takes a lot of nerve to remain perfectly still this close to the dog's teeth, but Keller knows that he has to pass some kind of test with this animal, and showing fear won't help him.

Pax sits in front of Keller. There is no longer any feral hostility in Pax's expression. He is panting, and it looks more like grinning than a hostile show of teeth. Suddenly, he yawns, a great gaping and wholly benign action. Keller reaches out again, and this time the dog raises one big paw and sets it in Keller's hand. The dog sighs, a sound less of capitulation than of relief.

Keller has never been in love, but he's pretty sure it can't hold a candle to the feeling he has as he and his one-man dog work together. Now that he's accepted Keller—and only Keller—as his leader, the dog responds to training with a joyous enthusiasm, as if it's all a game. They breeze through the basic obedience exercises: sit, heel, down, stay. They quickly catch up to Keller's pals, and he and Pax are now fully engaged in the training that will eventually determine their assignments: scout, casualty dog, messenger, or sentry.

Pax can scale walls, crawl on his belly as if under fire, sniff out a hidden "enemy," and stay put like a sculpture when asked. One of the two most difficult and make-or-break accomplishments is to ride happily in the back of the troop truck, which, surprisingly, several of the farm-raised dogs have failed. That seemingly ordinary test is frightening to them because they've never before been given the opportunity to do it. Pax bounds into the truck and acts like he expects to drive.

The second, and even more critical, test is to stand under small-arms fire without flinching. This one, Keller has worried most about, but here again, Pax stands his ground and tolerates the noise of a sergeant firing beside them, even as he folds his ears back. His expression is one of dislike, but not fear.

Pax can leap a three-foot hurdle as if he's got a springboard under him and scale a seven-foot solid wall like a champ. Keller puts him into an off-leash long down and walks away. After a time, he signals to the dog to come. Just as the dog hits the midway point, Keller abruptly signals a new command and the dog instantly flattens himself against the ground. As if he's under fire, Pax crawls to where Keller squats waiting for him.

Rod Barlow nods at Keller. "Good work."

Keller finds himself flushed with pleasure. *Good work.* It's as if a craving has been satisfied. A craving he was unaware of having. He keeps his head down as he praises his dog. *Good work.*

Keller hasn't written to Clayton at all since he left for induction, has never planned to write to the old man. And certainly he hasn't received any letters from his uncle. But he's filled with the helium of praise and he needs to share it. No, he won't write to Clayton, but there is someone else he can share this unexpected happiness with.

Dear Miss Jacobs,
I am well and I hope that you are, too. I want to let you know that I'm on my way overseas soon. I am a dog handler in the K-9 Corps and my dog is named Pax (which I remember you teaching me means "peace".) We're assigned to be scouts, which means we'll make sure that the way is safe ahead for our troops. Because I did so well, they asked me if I'd stay on here as an instructor, but I said no thanks. I can't imagine not being with Pax after all the training we've done together. I trained him and I want to be with him over there. Pax is a big dog, mostly German shepherd, and really handsome. We work really well together and it's not like work at all, but fun. You'd be surprised at what we can do. He's the best thing to have happened to me. If you saw him, you'd understand.

Keller isn't quite sure how to end this very first letter he's ever written.

Not much else to say. Keep well and don't let those rowdy students give you trouble. They'll have to deal with me if they do. Your friend, Keller Nicholson

He examines the page for handwriting flaws and, finding none, folds the page and slips it into an envelope and addresses it to Miss Ruth Jacobs, care of the high school. It seems too impertinent to send it to her house in Hawke's Cove, although he knows where she lives—in a small house with blue shutters and a well-trimmed hedge. Slipping the letter into his pocket,

Keller nudges Pax, who's sleeping the sleep of the well exercised. "Go for a walk?"

Before the last word is out of Keller's mouth, the dog is on his feet and waiting for the command to heel, ready for anything.

Chapter Sixteen

Pax is off leash, his flat leather working collar is fastened on, and his attention is riveted to the woods opposite. He is telling them in no uncertain terms that the enemy is there. Keller flags his squad and they take cover behind pines and oaks. There is no sound, and Pax understands that this means the enemy is aware of them, too. Everyone is keeping deathly still.

At Keller's signal, Pax has flattened himself against the ground and is about ten feet in front of Keller and the platoon. His ears are pricked and his nose works the air. He hears what the men cannot, the susurration of living breath in nervous men. He can smell what they cannot, the sweat of unwashed and exhausted men. Pax can tell, too, just how many of the enemy lie behind the trees on the opposite side of the rough circle of woodlot. If he could, he'd tell them there are only five to your seven, and one of those is wounded. But he's capable only of warning his platoon, not comforting them.

Their platoon leader signals for his six men to split up, half to circle to the left, the other three, Keller included, to move to the right of the woodlot. Keller nods and then signals to Pax to slowly move back to his side. Like his feral ancestors, Pax understands the exercise. To him, this is his pack. They are hunting. Race memory excites the dog, but his human training keeps him in complete focus on his man, his pack leader, just as, in the wild, he'd be focused on the alpha dog, unquestioning of his leader's orders. They are circling their prey, trapping it within the confines of their numbers. Pax becomes rigid, his very skin tense with the need for soundless movement, his muscles hardened with the exertion of moving like liquid. In moments, he is back at Keller's side; only the slight touch of his nose against Keller's hand breaks the discipline of the hunt.

Pax has become a dog with purpose. As much as living with Rick and Francesca had been rewarding, and comfortable, this life with Keller has hardened him into what his nature meant for him to be. A hunter. A guardian. A pack member with a job. Even when his feet are sore from the miles of hard terrain, his belly growling in anticipation of a battle-delayed dinner, his thirst barely slaked with the shared contents of Keller's canteen lapped out of his helmet, Pax is happy. Bivouacked in bombed-out cellars, or in the field, or against the crumbled walls of a village, Pax presses his long body against Keller's, settling his muzzle against his partner's neck, keeping them both warm. Like littermates, they play and eat and sleep and work in constant companionship, excluding all others. Their exclusivity suits Pax; he has only Keller to worry about. The others may surround them, and Keller interacts with them in their human language, but touch and comfort and food and grooming come only from Keller.

Pax loves his work, his purpose, and he has come to love Keller for giving it to him.

Now Pax alerts his pack to the presence of the enemy. The game is on.

Chapter Seventeen

It's been more than a year, but Keller has lost track of time. It seems like he and Pax have been together forever, been in this war all their lives. They've seen action in Italy and in Morocco. Now they're back in Italy as the rumblings of a major offensive can be felt. They've come a long way since those first few months, when he and Pax were viewed with suspicion at best and considered a waste of space and supplies at worst. Until Pax alerted him to the sniper barely visible in the bell tower of a village church. The dog's clear warning got the squad out of harm's way, and Big Sully, the most vocal skeptic regarding the usefulness of a war dog, took the sniper out.

After that, Keller and Pax were welcomed any time they showed up, ready to make the way safe for the squad or the platoon or the division. Everyone wanted to pet Pax, or feed him scraps, but Keller and the authority vested in him by the K-9 Corps strictly forbade such overtures. Pax is a one-man dog, he told them. One man's partner. His.

. . .

Another night patrol. Each patrol has the same purpose—to seek out the hidden enemy and get him before he can get them, and there is a certain rhythm to it, a dance of hide-and-seek. The dog is in his point position a few feet in front of Keller. The rest of the squad is fanned out behind the man and dog. As always, they are aware of the intensity of their task and the certainty that they will succeed.

They move, knowing that every step they take is fraught with the potential to reveal their presence to the enemy before they can locate him. For those who have been in this squad for more than a day, they are certain that the dog will give them the edge over that unseen enemy. He is their good-luck charm, their guardian angel. A quarter mile, a half, and the dog will freeze; no statue was ever as immobile and yet so expressive. Like a bird dog, he'll point out the machine-gun nest or the sniper. They'll protect their flank, fire, lob a grenade or two. Maybe take a prisoner, maybe simply pull the fallen enemies' Nazi-version of dog tags from beneath blood-saturated shirts and put them into slack-jawed mouths. Someone will come and claim these dead. Then, the signal to the platoon that the way is safe. Pax has made the way safe. They have become complacent.

The first shots ring out over their heads. The next round comes closer and the members of Keller's platoon fire their weapons toward the covert, where the Nazis lean around the trunks of pine trees and fire back at them. The veiled moon breaks free of its gauzy web and casts a silvery light down on the woodlot, filtering through the trees and giving shape to the dozen men engaged in this skirmish for possession of land none of them wants.

A bullet whizzes past Keller's ear and splits the thin sapling behind him. Even before his mind can register the nearness of that bullet, Keller is on his belly, crawling through the pine needles in the direction that every sensible bone in his body is telling him is wrong. Pax is beside him, slinking silently along the pine needle–strewn ground. Keller fires again, aiming at shapes, at the firefly flicker of rifle fire. He knows that every time he discharges his weapon, he, too, is betraying his position. The cross fire intensifies.

Keller is hit; the violence of the bullet throws him backward. He fights the pain and the insult; fights against panic. He is face up in the pine needles. Pax is beside him, whining and grasping at Keller's tunic with his teeth as if he could pull him to his feet. Voices fill the night, loud now, orders shouted in two languages; more gunfire and then the crash of boots pounding through the woods—whether running away or chasing, he can't know.

Keller stares up at a patch of starry sky no bigger than a handkerchief, visible between the trees. He misses the clear open sky above the cove, the stars and the constellations pinned to the velvet of a pure winter night. Pax stands over him, panting, growling. Keller feels the blood seeping out, touches the place with one hand and holds it up to the unfiltered moonlight. Pax licks that hand. Pain blurs his senses, blinding him to everything but the white-hot pain. He feels himself losing consciousness and fights it. He's got to make sure, make sure of something, but he can't recall what it is. Is he late for school? Is he out on the water, his boat wallowing against a beam sea? Is he impaled on the spear-point finial of the wrought-iron fence surrounding Meadowbrook?

Keller hears voices coming closer, thick with the incomprehensible speech of the enemy. His dog growls, a throaty savage sound, feral. Pax's blood lullaby. But the voices don't move away; they grow louder, closer. The growl becomes a snarl. Keller struggles to open his eyes, struggles to his knees and claws the ground for his rifle. He sways a little, and his rifle feels ten times heavier than it did. He can't quite get the muzzle up to point it at the Kraut who is coming at him, a trick of the moonlight making the blade edge of the German's fixed bayonet glint.

With a sound more roar than growl, Pax flies through the air.

Keller can close his eyes; his dog will keep him safe. The velvet darkness of oblivion takes Keller away.

"Pax? Where's my dog?"

"Nicholson, just take it easy."

"Where is he?"

The medic is fiddling around with a syringe, tapping it with a dirt-rimmed fingernail.

"Is he all right? Was he hurt?"

"I have no idea." The medic presses a fresh compress on the bullet hole in Keller's left shoulder.

"He won't eat. He's trained not to take food from anyone."

"That's not my problem. My problem is that I've got to evac you to a field hospital and I don't have room on the transport."

"Not without Pax."

"Without Pax."

Keller struggles against the soporific and lovely effects of the morphine that the medic has just injected into his arm. "Get him. Please."

The medic doesn't respond, and as the arms of Morpheus descend, Keller whispers Pax's name over and over, terrified that the medic is lying to him.

Chapter Eighteen

The hot scent of his partner's blood explodes in Pax's nostrils; the scent of being quarry, not hunter. As the shooter charges, bayonet fixed, Pax vaults from a standstill and knocks the German to the ground. He is trained to hold a prisoner in any fashion he can, and he holds this one down with the weight of his body and the tensile strength of his jaw, ignoring the man's screams and flailing. He overpowers this sinner, expecting that Keller will point his weapon and call him off. He doesn't, and the mingle of human voices in the woods grow closer, angrier, louder, and gunfire spits from every direction. Pax ignores it and keeps his jaw locked on the fallen enemy's arm, penetrating through the wool to the skin, muscle, and bone. He bears down; this is the man who hurt Keller.

So consumed in defending his partner, Pax doesn't hear the sound of the shot, doesn't feel the penetration of the first bullet. The second shot takes him down.

Chapter Nineteen

Keller opens his eyes, to see Big Sully looking down at him. Roger Sullivan, late of South Boston, is the one guy Keller knows will tell him the truth about Pax. "Is he dead?"

"See for yourself."

Keller is suddenly beneath a mound of wriggling dog. Sully helps hoist Keller upright so that he's neither crushed beneath the weight of the dog nor his shoulder wound reopened by the vigorous reunion. "Pax. Pax. What did they do to you, boy?" A slightly grungy white bandage is wrapped around the dog's middle and a thin line of missing fur mars the perfection of his skull.

"Bastards shot him, but he was moving so fast, they only grazed him. You should see what he did to them. When we got there, they were gabbling like they'd found themselves faced with a werewolf. Practically asked us to take them prisoner."

Keller recognizes bullshit when he hears it, but he's grateful to Sully for lying to him. "Thanks for taking care of him."

"Medics did a good job. He's a grunt like the rest of us, but nothing but the best for him." Sully is quiet for a moment, his usual glibness put away. He looks tired, as they all do. Maybe even a little discouraged. "Look, we lost Carson. Almost lost you."

"I'm sorry about Carson. He was a good kid."

Sully runs a hand down the length of the dog's back. Keller doesn't say anything; for sure, Sully deserves to break the rules. "Nicholson, your dog saved you. That Kraut would have finished you off if Pax hadn't attacked him. He's a lucky dog, but so are you."

Sully gives Pax one more forbidden pat and leaves Keller and his dog to rest.

"If anything had happened to you . . ." Keller cannot complete the whispered thought. His relief in having Pax here, alive and hogging the cot, brings hot tears to his eyes. Keller hasn't wept since he was a little boy, not since his first night at Meadowbrook, a thrown-away child, alone and confused.

This dog is his family. And the only other thing as frightening to Keller as having Pax killed, is the fact that, at the end of this endless war, Pax will go home to his real family. And Keller will be, once again, all alone.

Chapter Twenty

"I had your baseball card. Still do if my mom hasn't chucked out all my stuff." The private is a skinny kid from Lowell, all freckles and brown hair so thin that his scalp shows through his buzz cut as if he didn't have any hair at all.

"This war goes on much longer, that may be the only base-ball card with my picture on it, so you'd better hope she hasn't thrown it out. It'll be a rare one." Rick runs a cleaning cloth over the barrel of his carbine, a gesture faintly reminiscent of rubbing pine tar on his bat. The wind is picking up the higher up they go in the mountains and he's glad that it's summer, not winter; that's for the mountain troops, not him. Rick is squad leader, and it's his job to get this bunch of kids up and over the mountain to join their armored division as it collects these strung-out groups of five or six infantrymen slowly making their way along the narrow mountain trail. Some-times the trail takes them into the woods; sometimes it leads them up toward the sky. Sometimes, like now, it meanders along a series of ledges, wide enough for only one at a time to pass. Above them, already ensconced, the German army. At midday, Rick could hear the sound of artillery bouncing off the other side of the mountain, the vertical assault beginning.

"You had good stats that last summer you played." The kid is still chattering about ancient history. He won't admit it, but Rick is flattered by the kid's interest. Baseball was a lifetime ago. He's even lost track of how the Braves are doing, struggling to field a decent team with old-timers and the increasingly rare player with a high draft number and no qualms about not enlisting. Sometimes Rick wonders if he's still got it, his arm. He's muscled up, that's for sure, but does he still have the distance? The ability to put a small spherical object into an invisible box exactly where he wants it? It took years to develop that skill, and now it's been years since he's really used it, the little intersquad pickup games notwithstanding. He never throws his good stuff at amateurs; that would be like throwing a smokin' fastball at a Little Leaguer.

"Okay, everybody up. Let's move." Rick puts an end to the conversation.

The ledge trail is like a ruffle along the bald side of the Italian mountain, dipping in and out as the contour of the hillside folds in on itself, then bells outward. There is a stark beauty to the view, looking down on the green of vegetation, up at the azure sky. Lone pine trees cling to the hillside, tenacious and scrawny.

When they finally meet up with their division, Rick is hoping that he'll find a few letters waiting for him from Francesca. No, he knows that he will; she's a faithful correspondent. Through her letters, he feels like he is there for every little bit of her day, from her distaste for chicory coffee to the gossip at the wire factory. He knows that, so far, her cousin Sid is all right, and her brothers, too. She has no news for him about Pax. Pax has been in this war for more than a year, almost two. The only thing they know is that if anything had happened to him, they would have been informed. So, as he writes in his letters back, no news is good news. Their dog is doing his duty, his bit. Secretly, Rick wonders how long before this streak of good luck will run out for those Francesca loves. Five loved ones in a war is not good odds. What talisman does she keep in order that they remain safe? As a ballplayer, Rick has seen plenty of superstitions acted out before every game: the same socks, turning three times around before leaving the locker room, never letting a wife say "good luck" before a game. His own game-day nod to Lady Luck was to slip a few dog hairs into his cap. Whatever other superstitious belief she might have, Rick knows that for Francesca, it's mostly just prayer.

The trail rises and falls, rises again. The rocky hillside becomes sheer cliff, a hardened wall they keep to their right as the trail once again puts them on a narrow ledge. Rick wants to hurry his men through this all-too-exposed place.

It's the skinny kid from Lowell who falls first, victim to a clean shot from the precipice above them. The rest hit the ground, crab-crawling their way to the relative safety of the rock wall, keeping arms and legs close so that the Germans have nothing to aim at from above. Rick cranes his neck to see what their options are. The next squad will arrive in no less than half an hour. To retreat from this narrow ledge will open them up as targets as surely as moving ahead would. They are pinned down.

Rick fingers a grenade dangling from his belt, unclips it. The rock face is maybe thirty feet high and angles back slightly. Baseball is geometry. He's fired a ground-ball hit to the pitcher farther than that to get the double play. Slowly, Rick, keeping his back to the rock face, stands up. He has the grenade in his hand, and he tosses it gently, as if waiting for the catcher's signs. He briefly wishes that he were a left-handed pitcher; this toss would be easier if he were. But he's not. He's a strong righty, accurate and unhittable. Rick pulls the pin, steps away from the rock face, and fires the grenade, putting just enough arc in it that the explosive should curve right into the Germans.

Instead of diving back against the safety of the wall, Rick waits, watching in horror as the grenade, subject to the immutable laws of gravity, falls back toward him, where it will blow them all off this ledge.

As if he's watching a flyball coming his way, Rick instinctively reaches up to catch it.

Part Two

1946–1947

Chapter Twenty-one

"Come in." I held back the screen door to let Keller Nicholson and our dog, Pax, into our house. I felt nearly faint with relief at the sight of him, the dog. Our dog. Even before Keller Nicholson had gotten out of the mud-spattered car he and Pax arrived in, I was out of the house and down the walk to pull the passenger door open and release Pax into my arms.

When Pax didn't jump out, but looked to Nicholson for orders, I felt wounded. Snubbed.

"It's okay, Pax. At ease, boy." And with that, Pax bowled into me, licking my face and wagging his tail so hard, he nearly took himself off his feet.

"Ma'am, before we go in, there's something I'd like to say." He didn't step one foot over the sill, although Pax straddled it, forelegs in the house, hind legs still beside Keller.

"Rick has been waiting. He's been waiting for this dog a long, long time. Please come in."

"Mrs. Stanton, I want to keep him. I can't imagine life without him."

That froze me to my spot. How dare he say such a thing to me? "I guess that you'll have to try."

The litany of our prayers to keep them safe were intoned with fervent belief Sunday after Sunday, and still our boys died, or came back, like Rick, wounded, changed forever, their spirits crushed.

They found me at the wire factory, those crisply uniformed harbingers of disaster. Bright young men, charged with the unforgiveable duty of informing family members of their soldier's change of status from unharmed and alive to wounded or lost or dead. As if, in the formality of their words and posture, you might respond less emotionally to the news that your husband, who once wanted only to play ball in the big leagues, is now grievously wounded and simply to survive will be as close as he will ever get to living his dream; that your response will be contained by the choreographed manner in which these boys dressed as men have regretfully informed you that your life is never going to be the same.

My supervisor didn't send anyone for me; he came himself, taking me back to his office, where the soldiers waited, their white-gloved hands behind their backs, their caps tucked precisely under their arms; the weight of their duty not bowing them, but keeping them upright. Mr. Towne had also beckoned my pal Barbara, who shared a spot on the line with me. Maybe he felt that I needed to have a woman there. That I would behave with womanly weakness.

Seeing them, expecting the worst, it didn't quite penetrate when, instead of informing me of Rick's death, they told me he was wounded, and suddenly not in Europe, but in England. I think that Mr. Towne caught me as my knees buckled and slid a chair beneath me. "Rick is in England; that's wonderful news. He's out of it." I started to laugh. Whatever had happened, he'd be fine. He was in England. He was alive. These crisp young men had said so.

Barbara finally got my attention, shaking me out of my hysterical euphoria. "Francesca, he's seriously wounded. You understand that, don't you?"

"I just know that he's still alive."

Barbara took my hands in hers. Her nails were freshly painted, a bright bloodred, at complete odds with our factory work. "They've given you a telephone number. They don't know any more than what they've told you; you need to make that call."

The two soldiers bearing bad tidings were clearly waiting for some sort of civilian dismissal from me. Mr. Towne kept a hand under my elbow and I stood up. "Thank you."

The pair made a stiff about-face, one fell in behind the other, and they left the office, moving on to deliver more bad news to other families whose lives would be forever changed.

Keller Nicholson leaned his back against the screen door, keeping it open, neither entering my house nor leaving it. The dog was sniffing the air, his tail beating a rhythm against the copper screening. He danced on his front legs. He knew that beyond the hallway of this new house lay his man, the man who had always been Pax's one true master.

I hadn't told Rick that Pax was coming home until I was absolutely certain. I had no desire to get his fractured hopes up, only to find out that Pax hadn't survived, or, maybe worse, hadn't been able to be rehabilitated from war dog back to pet dog. If that had been the case, I think I would have gone to wherever they had taken him and stolen him back. If he'd changed from the loving, tractable dog we'd known three years ago into something else, something the army called "unsuitable for home placement," I would still have wanted him for Rick. Rick had lost so much, I just couldn't bear it if the dog was lost to him, too. With every week that went by postwar when Pax's status was unknown, Rick lost ground in his own rehabilitation. And then, after an eternity that was reminiscent of the eternity I'd waited for Rick to come home, we got word that Pax was safe and doing well in the retraining program. He could come home. It was the first genuine smile I'd had from Rick since the day he was returned to me.

"Let him go."

Keller bent and unclipped the leash from Pax's collar. The dog stayed where he was. He was still connected to his handler, unused to thinking for himself.

"Send him."

"Pax, go ahead." Keller's words held no command in them. They might have been nonsense syllables, meaningless drivel.

Pax looked at Keller, as if he, too, hadn't understood the softly spoken words. He wanted clarification. In that almost human desire for clarity, I could see how close these two must have been in the battlefield, dependent one upon the other for their lives. One misunderstanding and everything would go horribly wrong. The dog eyed Keller and waited for some better instruction. Even as his eyes studied Keller, his nose twitched, and I could see that the distraction of what he surely knew lay at the end of this short hallway was tantalizing him. So close to his beloved Rick, one command away from reunion.

"Pax. Go to him."

The dog's trot was soundless along the runner that led from the front door to the room that Rick occupied. Keller and I didn't follow, but waited in an awkward silence, which I finally broke. "Come meet him."

Chapter Twenty-two

Pax ambled down the corridor to a room where the door was not quite shut. He nosed it open, already certain that behind that door was the person he'd once been adhered to. It had been a long time ago, and the memory of that person was as faded as the dreams that he'd dreamed when opportunity gave him a chance to enter deepest sleep. But the scent had remained imprinted in his memory. A scent he would never have forgotten and one that he would have been able to discern among a thousand others. Keller was his present, and the bond he had with him was soldier-deep. If he had once trusted Rick with his daily requirement of food and exercise and play and affection, with Keller he had survived when others had not. It had been an atavistic existence, surviving by wit and by clan. Pax had acknowledged Keller as leader; Keller had depended on Pax to hunt and to defend.

This recognizable skin scent was overshadowed but not obscured by the other odors of this human body, urine and seeping fluids. A rotting that informed the dog that this human, this scent that he remembered in the same way he remembered his mother's, was not exactly like the man he had longed for until Keller came into his life. And then Rick spoke and all the strangeness fell away. Saying his name like breathing a prayer out loud: *Pax.* Out of this mouth, the word that had been the first word Pax had ever recognized for its true value sounded so different to his sensitive ears. It was as if, when identified by Rick's "Pax," he was a different creature from the one that Keller called Pax. Gentleness and play versus the serious business of war.

The big dog instinctively knew better than to throw himself into the arms of the man in the chair. He sat, then quietly lowered his head to Rick's lap. One hand stroked his head. The other, truncated and bound in a white gauze sleeve, lingered over the dog's head. The dog sighed. He didn't have the capacity to wonder how it was that, after all this time, after being sent away, after being befriended and given a purpose, after months in constant danger and after being solely Keller's own, he was here, in this strange house, with his head in the lap of his once and beloved master.

Rick was weeping into his fur, and Pax didn't know what to do to help. He'd never known Rick to be unhappy. His entire experience of Rick was one of optimism and joy. This casualty—for that's what he smelled like to a dog who had spent a lot of time behind the front lines of the battlefield—confused him, and he had only one option. He pressed himself deeper into Rick's lap, until only his hind legs remained on the floor. He whined, a guttural assurance that whatever it was, he would fix it. He would make it stop. The hand gripped the nape of the dog's neck, and Pax was filled with grief for his long-gone mother, who held him just so. Finally, Rick lifted his head and batted the tears away. "Good dog, Pax. You have no idea how much I've missed you. My good dog. Thank God you made it."

Words instead of tears were a good thing. Pax pushed himself off Rick and sat, his tail still swishing against the floor, his jaws open with the excitement of reunion, and his eyes on Rick's face. His ears, though, were turned back, listening for Keller.

Chapter Twenty-three

Keller really doesn't want to meet this Rick Stanton, this other claimant to Pax's loyalty. It was easier for him to have no face to imagine, no wheelchair-bound casualty of the same war he and Pax had emerged from intact. After nearly half a year in Germany with the occupation forces, Keller and Pax had finally accumulated the points needed for redeployment back to the United States. Keller had taken the dog to the re-training center and convinced the authorities that he should be the one to work with Pax. His excellent record of dog handling, and the earlier recommendation that he stay at the Front Royal Dog Training and Reception Center as a trainer worked in his favor and he was granted his wish. Besides his own dog, Keller was assigned to work with other dogs there for rehabilitation. Lots of playtime, lots of long, sauntering walks, no full-body crawl, no hunting down the enemy, no small-arms fire, no aggression against strangers. Keller was amazed at how these animals adapted to new circumstances, as if able to compartmentalize everything they had learned earlier. Better than some veterans he knew, who woke in the night in a sweat and had no tolerance for noise.

Keller had expected that the hardest thing for Pax would be to accept being touched or handled by others, to revert from being his one-man-dog to a dog it was safe for anyone to be around. He was a little disappointed at how easily Pax slid from war dog to pet. If Pax had retained his hostility to strangers, he might have been rejected for rehoming. And it would have been so easy to take him for himself. But Pax, surprisingly, seemed to understand that the threats and dangers he'd been trained to locate no longer existed. The edict came down: His people wanted him and he was rehabilitated. Discharged with honor from the U.S. Army, Pax needed to go home.

When Francesca had written that it would be impossible to leave her husband to collect the dog, Keller, on the verge of his own honorable discharge, volunteered to deliver the dog to the Stantons. Lucky for Keller, Rod Barlow was still involved, and he got the CO to agree to let Keller make the trip, highly unusual as it was. The CO was no fool; he knew that Keller was too attached to this Dogs For Defense volunteer. "Go, but don't think for one minute that they'll change their minds."

"I won't. I don't." But he'd rehearsed his plea aloud all the way from the retraining center. *I really think that the best thing for this dog is to remain with me. I'm thinking about joining the police force, and he'd make a great police dog. He's too well trained to be a pet dog again. He needs stimulation. He needs. I need. I can't let him go.*

Every mile of the journey from Virginia to Massachusetts, Keller fought against the temptation to simply change routes and disappear into the vast country that he and his comrades had defended. Only feeble honor kept Keller from doing it.

"Come meet my husband." Francesca steps into the hallway and Keller, empty leash in his hand, has no other choice but to go into the house and follow her down the corridor to the room where Pax has gone, his nose and ears homing in on his target precisely like they honed in on the enemy.

The room has been converted from a den into a hospital room. The drapes look less like something meant for a quiet retreat and more like a remnant of the blackout rules, heavy and drawn against the late-afternoon sun. On one wall, built-in shelving above a cupboard holds a set of encyclopedias and a tattered dictionary, but the rest of the room is furnished with the antiseptic materiel of illness and barren of homely comfort. Stateside, Keller has visited many a wounded friend, and this room smells as if it is inside a VA hospital, not inside a modest home in a neighborhood in peacetime America.

"Sir." Keller extends his hand and then balks, impulsively throwing up a salute as if belatedly realizing that Stanton's battlefield promotion was to staff sergeant. He feels foolish; both of them are civilians now, all honors and ranks behind them. The salute was meant only to compensate for the fact that Rick Stanton wouldn't be shaking hands ever again.

Stanton says nothing. Not looking at either Keller or his wife, he is focused entirely on the dog.

"Darling, Corporal Nicholson brought Pax back to us." Francesca's tone is cajoling, and Keller feels slightly embarrassed for her. Stanton continues to ignore them both.

The room is so still that Keller can hear the tinny sound of a radio playing in another house and, from a tree in the backyard, a raucous jay warning off a crow.

"Sir, I asked your wife—"

"Don't." Her tone isn't cajoling now; it is razor-sharp and

a warning. She shifts her shoulders back, deflecting his attempt to ask that her husband give up the only thing he loves.

Which means that he is the one who must give up Pax.

Rick Stanton finally looks at him. "Nicholson. Thank you."

"He's one in a million, sir." He's going to be unmanned if he doesn't leave this room right now. He needs to turn around and walk out of this house and get into the secondhand car he's bought with his savings and drive away. He needs to figure out what to do with the rest of his life. But Keller remains where he is, waiting for dismissal. Waiting for the moment when he'll have the strength to leave behind the only creature that he's ever loved, and that, he's certain, has ever loved him. A bitterness fills his mouth like a suffocating lump, forcing him to swallow, leaving him speechless. Only once has he ever felt this kind of pain, and to equate the death of one's parents with the return of a dog to its rightful owners seems wrongheaded, but that's how Keller feels. His parents are shadowy figures, remembered only vaguely; this dog has been by his side every moment for three years. What they have endured together isn't something that time will diminish. Privation, danger, terror, and courage. These will not fade.

"Corporal Nicholson, can I offer you something? A cup of coffee? You must be hungry; it's well after lunchtime." Francesca puts a hand on his arm, gives it a slight tug. She wants him out of here before he can say anything more.

"We ate on the road. We're fine." *We*.

"All right. Thank you again," she says, the hostess ready for the party to end.

"The thing is, he's my dog." The words come, flavored by the bitterness he feels.

Pax lifts his head from Rick's lap. He casts a sideways glance at Keller, then back to Francesca. His tail is no longer wagging. Rick's hand slips to hold the dog's collar, as if he's afraid Keller will order the dog away and the dog will go. But Keller has no stomach for a heartless demonstration of loyalty that he and Pax would inflict on this couple. And, right now, he's not sure that Pax would obey him. The dog looks like he's found heaven in Rick Stanton's immobile lap.

Francesca suddenly puts herself between Keller and Stanton. Her green eyes fix on him, her hand rises, and she points a finger at him. "No. Pax is our dog. Rick's dog. That was the agreement. We are very grateful to you for keeping him safe, but you need to leave."

"Wait." Rick pushes himself against the back of the wheelchair, sitting fully upright. For the first time, Keller notices that one side of his face bears the smooth scars of healed burns. His right ear is twisted, as if it had partially melted. "Fran, would you mind leaving us alone for a moment?"

She drops her hand, and her shoulders shift again. She steps away. "Fine. I'll be in the kitchen."

Stanton lets go of the dog's collar. "Why don't you take Pax out? As you say, it was a long trip, and I'm sure he needs to go. Right, Nicholson?"

Keller nods.

"Pax, come."

All three wait to see if the dog will obey her. The dog looks from man to man.

"Go ahead, Pax." Rick and Keller speak together and the dog follows Francesca out of the room.

Chapter Twenty-four

Sometimes, in the last few seconds of sleep, when the night's dreamscape still feels real, Rick Stanton can forget that he is no longer the man whose waking dreams had come very close to being fulfilled. He wakes always to the truth that his once-within-grasp dreams are now and forever reduced to memories. Memories of almost succeeding. Of not quite. Close but forever just out of reach.

Not just the dream of pitching in the majors but all the rest of what he had wanted—expected—to achieve in his life. He made it to the majors, and would have been in the starting rotation the spring after the war. He married a beautiful woman, and he would have treated her to a good life, a life of travel, a nice house, and a family. Rick Stanton wakes up to the reality that he is useless as a man, a provider, and a burden on this woman who never lets him see her struggle to cope. He is more or less locked up in this tiny room, living out his life, calling out to her to help him with the most humbling of tasks. She has become his nurse. She smiles and tells him jokes, and tries so hard to pretend that she's happy. In return, he has become *difficult.* Snappish. Frustrated by the effort of the simplest of tasks, he has turned gratitude for her help into resentment. She pulls his blanket up and he shoves it away. She strokes his hair back and he looks away from her. Rick wishes that she would storm out on him, allow him the dignity of getting angry with him. Her patience is wearing on his.

Getting Pax back has been the chief goal they've shared, besides keeping nonhealing wounds clean. Having him here was their holy grail, if only to have something else to think about besides his schedule at the VA hospital or whether it was finally time for another pain pill. They'd been made to wait, and the wait had become the ballast keeping their rocky boat from capsizing. "When Pax gets home," they said to each other, implying that things would improve. There was never any finish to that phrase, no complementing fantasy of a sudden return to health, or magic moment when they would look over the dog's beloved head and smile at each other like they used to. "When Pax gets home" was sufficient unto itself as the dog spent additional months in occupied Germany, while he was in the retraining center, while they waited for someone to bring their dog home.

Keller Nicholson has brought Pax home and, with him, an attachment that is so obvious, Rick can nearly smell it. They should never have let Pax's army handler bring him home. It isn't doing anyone any good. Not Nicholson, not Pax, and certainly not them. Like so many who come to visit, Keller looks past Rick and fixes his gaze on the thick drapes, or the shelf of encyclopedias. Anywhere but at him. Rick is glad that he insisted that Francesca get him up and into his wheelchair. It's bad enough being helpless, but being in that bed just exacerbates the impression that he's an invalid. Which he is, but not one who can't grasp at a last shred of self-esteem when another man is present. A fellow veteran. A subordinate, a mere corporal to his battle-won staff sergeant's stripes. "Sit down, Corporal."

There is a kitchen chair that serves as the guest chair in this tiny room filled with the paraphernalia of his physical needs. It's modern tubular steel, with a padded vinyl seat and back in a hideous turquoise-and-orange pattern that defies definition. There is a little tear in the vinyl and a fluff of stuffing pokes out. Keller pulls the chair away from the wall and sits opposite Rick. Now he is looking directly at him, and Rick looks for the pity that most visitors can't hide. To his surprise, Rick doesn't identify pity in those deep-set brown eyes; he sees something else entirely. Keller looks at Rick not with pity or sympathy, but with anger.

"I want him. He's been with me a long time. We're a team. He's not a pet any longer." The brown eyes widen and the pupils dilate until the brown is occluded by the black. His mouth is a tense line, his hands fisted on his knees. "I'll pay you for him."

It is so refreshing that Rick nearly laughs. Finally, someone who won't mince around just because he's a one-armed paraplegic former ballplayer. "Well, you can't have him. And there's no amount of money in the world that could buy him from me."

Keller gets to his feet so suddenly that the chair tips over with a crash. "I owe him my life. I can't just leave him behind."

"Nicholson, we know he means a lot to you, but you have to understand what he means to me." In the world of his pre-waking dreams, Rick often runs. He feels the air on his face and he feels the dirt beneath his feet. He doesn't know if he's running from or toward something. Right now, seeing this other man's distress, Rick wishes uselessly for the ability to run away from this scene. "You think that you need him, but *I* need him. I've had everything taken; he's what's left."

There is no change in Keller's expression, no softening into empathy, no lessening of the anger. "The only good thing I've ever had in my life is this dog. I don't have a wife, or a home, a family, a job. He's it, my life."

Rick knows that if Francesca hears the crash of chair against floor, she'll be back in the room in moments. He doesn't want her in here, and he doesn't want Pax in here, either, until they settle this. He doesn't want to see the dog choose Keller. Even while the dog's head was in his lap, Rick was painfully aware that he didn't have the dog's full attention and that when Keller entered the room, the dog relaxed, a softening of the excited tension in his shoulders, a lighter sigh.

Rick shifts a little in his chair. The place above where his spinal cord was severed is sore and he's afraid that Francesca is going to have to tend yet another break in his fragile skin. He needs to be lifted back into bed, to be rolled over so that she can salve it. "You have no job? No home to go to?"

"No, sir." Keller bends to pick up the kitchen chair. He sets it carefully back against the wall where he'd found it. He won't be detoured from his determination to win this argument by niceties. "But he'll have a home, you can be sure."

"Then what are your plans?"

Rick can see him thinking about his response, weighing the merits of telling the truth against a plain civil lie. "The thing is, I plan to keep this dog, maybe go into police work. It would be a crime to waste his talents."

Rick recognizes the challenge in Keller's blunt statement. He's challenging Rick to fight for this dog. A flicker of some vestigial machismo surges in Rick, the urge to take this subordinate and shake him, shake him until he understands that he's never going to take Pax from him. He feels like he can stand up and grab Keller and beat him to the ground, and he's boundlessly grateful for the redirection of his simmering anger and resentment. It's good to feel mad with someone besides himself.

"Not possible. I won't let him go."

Keller smooths the brim of his new hat, puts his hand on the doorknob. If he chooses to walk out, call the dog, and disappear, there really isn't anything Rick can do to stop him except cry "thief!" If Pax obeys Nicholson, heeds his orders, then Rick thinks that his heart, already crushed with the heaped losses of career and hope, will break.

He shifts in his chair again, the sore spot pulsing. Last night, when Francesca tried to shift him from the chair to the bed, she slipped, cracking her knee against the metal bed frame. She smiled and mocked herself, stubbornly refusing to admit that caring for him is difficult. That she isn't up to the task, that a five-foot-two-inch, hundred-pound woman is capable of lifting a six-foot-something man. "Look, Nicholson, my wife needs help. With me."

"I'm sorry to hear that." Keller lifts his hat to his head. He's said what he plans, and in the next minute he'll walk out that door and call the dog and the dog will go with him.

"Wait. Hear me out. I have an idea that might work for all of us."

Chapter Twenty-five

After Rick was shipped stateside, we spent nearly a year in Washington, D.C., while Rick was in the Walter Reed General Hospital there. Once he was discharged, we decided that we wanted to go back to the Boston area. There was a good VA hospital there for him to continue with his therapies and we both felt like it was home. It was the place we'd met and married and dreamed our big dreams. During those long months at Walter Reed, we focused entirely on getting Rick healed and rehabilitated enough so that I could bring him home. Bringing him home was goal enough; all our other prewar pipe dreams had gone up in smoke.

My cousin Sid—who'd made it back safe and sound and very nearly untouched by a war spent in England—found us a single-family house to rent in Quincy, not far from the shore at Squantum. I think he imagined that I'd be able to wheel Rick along the shore drive to enjoy the view of the Boston Harbor islands and eat takeout from Ray's Clam Shack like a normal couple. Of course that didn't happen. Our days were housebound, my only excursions to the grocery store and his to the hospital, where it seemed like he was continually being admitted because I had a hard time keeping up with the bedsores and the wound that just wouldn't heal where his arm, his pitching arm, had been blown away.

The house came with a one-car garage, conjoined to the main building by a glassed-in breezeway. Passing from the house to the garage always felt like being underwater as the light filtered through the glass blocks. The doorways weren't wide enough to get Rick and his chair through, so he ended up having to endure all weathers as I loaded him into the car from the front walk. We didn't have a ramp, either, so my biggest challenge was to ease him down the three steps, as if his wheelchair were a giant baby carriage, then anchor my weight against the forward motion of the chair as it rolled down the slope to the sidewalk. My fear was that someday I'd lose control and he'd go careering into the side of the car or, worse, into the street and oncoming traffic.

When Keller Nicholson brought Pax home to us, we'd been in that rental house a little more than six months. Rick had been hospitalized about five times in that period, and the little house didn't look appreciably more lived in than it had the day we moved into it. Rick was in what had been the den, and I slept upstairs in the larger of the two bedrooms. The second one, the one that still had nursery wallpaper from the previous tenants, I used to store everything I hadn't had time to unpack; most of our life together was contained in cardboard boxes with labels that described how life had been: *Wedding Presents, Photo Albums, Baseball Equipment.*

In another life, I'd have washed that charming babyish wallpaper and planned where to put a crib. I hated that room, a reminder of the end of our first, best goal.

In all that time, Rick had never told me what happened and

I believed that he couldn't remember. It wasn't unusual, after all. Traumatic amnesia. All I knew was that in the ambush, all of his men were lost, Rick the only survivor.

Rick kept Keller in his room, leaving me to fiddle around in the kitchen, craning to hear their voices, wondering what could be going on. Pax panted and paced the hallway from Rick's room to where I stood, useless, in the kitchen, too late for lunch, too early for dinner. The dog looked at me with a clear concern and all I could do was pat him and mutter words meant to soothe him. "It's all right, big guy. It's good to have you back. Will you be happy here? Did you miss us? Can you go back to being our dog?" My questions left my mouth unattached to any thought. "Will you miss him?" Him, Keller.

Finally, Keller appeared in the archway. He still had that military bearing about him, shoulders back, chin lifted, hands rigidly at his sides, the right one clutching the brim of his hat. I looked at his face for the first time, really looked at him, at the angular planes of his face and the aquiline nose suggesting an old Yankee heritage. What I saw was a man moving into the next stage of his life. His mouth was drawn into a military scowl, but his eyes, a deep muddy brown, glinted with enough hope that I felt my own burn.

Pax immediately went to him and sat at his left knee. I never saw a signal. Keller made no overt sign, but without hesitation the dog planted himself where he belonged. I saw the truth clearly now: This dog had formed an attachment as deep as an attachment between lovers. No part of Keller touched the dog, but the connection was as visible to me as if they'd been chained to each other. I wanted to hate him, and yet I couldn't. I understood him.

"What are we going to do?" I whispered, as if I thought myself alone in the room.

"Mr. Stanton wants to talk to you." Keller moved aside, the dog gracefully moving with him. I pushed past them to go to Rick, my hand reaching deep into my apron pocket to find a handkerchief. I was already in tears.

I expected to find Rick hunched down and devastated, and every inch of me pulsed to comfort him; but instead, he was sitting in his chair, straight and confident, his good arm crossed over his bad one. Without preamble, he laid out his idea. Keller Nicholson would stay on as Rick's aide. Room and board, and a small weekly salary in exchange for lifting and dressing and bathing and all the tasks that made up my day. In exchange for Pax.

"Franny, it's up to you. It'll take the physical burden off of you, but I know that having another person in the house means more work for you in other areas. But he's big, he's capable, and he's rootless."

"And we avoid having to argue about Pax."

Rick nodded. "Yeah. At least for a while. It'll give us all a chance to adjust."

A stranger in my house. We knew nothing about him except that Pax was a big fan. I felt like we were trusting a dog as a reference for an employee, a star boarder, an interloper.

"I haven't struggled. I haven't complained. I *want* to take care of you."

Rick reached out his hand and grasped mine. "I know you do."

I pressed the crumpled handkerchief up to my eyes. He hadn't touched me in a long time, and the feel of the soft skin of his palm against my more work-worn hand was too warm and I worried about a new infection starting. I'd forgotten how warm a kind hand can be.

"We give him a month." He squeezed my hand and let go.

"All right."

And so Keller Nicholson came into our lives and nothing was ever the same again.

Chapter Twenty-six

As it goes, it's not as bad as it might be. The garage is fairly well ventilated and the roll-out cot isn't the worst thing Keller has ever slept on. It's better than sleeping on the lumpy couch on the enclosed porch at his aunt Biddie's house, and certainly more private than Meadowbrook or a barracks. They've given him a three-drawer bureau with an attached mirror and an old-fashioned pitcher and bowl. He's got bathroom privileges, but he prefers to shave in the garage rather than take up time and make a mess in the house bathroom. His second-floor bedroom at Clayton's was smaller and, like this garage, unheated. He's on trial, he knows, and heat in the garage is the least of his concerns. If this situation doesn't pan out, well, Keller doesn't like to think of what might happen if it doesn't.

No, the accommodations aren't bad, but all the same Keller feels a lot like he did as a kid, living in someone else's house, on someone else's terms. Not exactly welcome, not exactly family, not exactly friend. At least he gets a paycheck and his free time is his own. The job is physically demanding, and at night he aches in places he never has before, not even after hauling pots and nets and gear from boat to shore. Not even after sleeping in a foxhole dug out of the rocky soil. The struggle to get Rick from bed to bath to chair and back again is a challenge even for someone as used to hard work as Keller is. Mrs. Stanton suggested that he visit the VA to get some pointers on how to lift a body, and maybe he will one day.

Pax spends most of his time in what Keller thinks of as Rick's sickroom. He's not sick, at least not in the sense of enduring a disease, but it is clear that this room has become his whole world, that to venture out of it is a labor-intensive struggle to get the clumsy wheelchair over the sill and through a door that barely accommodates its width. Leaving the house is worse, requiring Keller to throw his weight counter to the weight of the man and chair and roll it down step by step. He thinks it would almost be easier if he lifted Rick out of the chair and carried him, but Rick balks at that, the indignity of it. So, for most of the day Pax sits with him, his head on Rick's lap, eyes closed as Rick strokes his head over and over. Sometimes Keller hears him talking to the dog, whispering words that are meant for the dog's ears only. The dog patiently takes these confidences in and never reveals what they are.

But every night, Keller is quietly joined in the garage by his dog. He never orders Pax to come, but in the hour after Rick has been put to bed and Mrs. Stanton has gone upstairs to her room, the dog, having surveyed the property and deemed it safe, comes through the half-open door to crawl into Keller's narrow cot. Stretched side by side, they both drift into sleep.

"I don't see any shoes." Keller has gotten Rick up, toileted, shaved, and into a short-sleeved shirt and loose trousers.

"No point in shoes."

"You still have feet. You need something on them."

"Why? It's not like I'm walking out of here."

Keller abandons the search for shoes, kneels down in front of Rick, and slides on a pair of open-back slippers. The left one falls off. He puts it back on. "All set. How 'bout we get you into the kitchen for breakfast?"

"Just have Francesca bring it in here."

"She's set the table."

Rick says nothing.

Pax bangs the den door open with his head and Rick finally smiles. "Hey, big boy." The dog bounds in, tail swinging. He plants his head in Rick's lap, eyes up, ears up, doing his morning greeting routine. The dog fills up a lot of the space in the tiny room and Keller has more than once had to rescue pill bottles and teacups swept off the low tray table beside Rick's chair.

Keller leaves to tell Francesca that she needs to set up the breakfast tray again. He's batting zero as far as getting Rick to leave his room. He tries every morning, and every morning Rick ignores him or gets mad. "I didn't hire you to pester me. I'm comfortable and it's not worth the struggle. I'm in the way. Leave me alone."

"I don't know why you keep trying." Francesca has already set up the tray with juice, toast, scrambled eggs cooling off too quickly. She picks it up. "Grab some eggs for yourself. The coffee's ready." She gracefully swings the tray up like an experienced diner waitress and disappears down the hall.

There is one place set. Francesca's used plate and fork are in the sink. Keller pours himself some coffee and helps himself to the rest of the eggs. He doesn't sit, but leans against the counter, forking cold eggs into his mouth and sloshing black coffee after them. He can hear her voice, but not distinctly. It always sounds the same to him, like she's mollifying a child. She doesn't treat Rick like a man anymore; she treats him, in Keller's opinion, like a truculent ten-year-old.

This is a house with very little thought given to decor. Keller knows that they moved here hastily. She's told him how it was. After months of waiting, Rick's discharge from the hospital seemingly happened overnight. Francesca has been so consumed with caring for Rick that she's done little to make this small house homey. Furniture, sure; curtains, yes. But only a picture or two on the walls. One picture in particular tells him more of their story than he's been able to figure out from the bits of conversation he's had with either of the Stantons. Rick in a baseball uniform, in mid pitch, his back leg kicked, his pitching hand just unfurling across his chest. It's telling, he thinks, that this photograph is in a room where Rick never goes.

Keller has fashioned a clothes rack in one corner and his uniform and fatigues hang there, at the ready for his one-weekend-a-month service in the Army Reserves. This will be the first time he'll be away from the Stantons, and the first time since boot camp that he won't have his dog by his side. It's just a weekend, and not far away, just down on the Cape at Camp Edwards. It's been a bit of a surprise, how guilty he feels. Having just gotten the Stantons to where they are comfortable in having him around to do all the physical work and now leaving her to struggle with it for two nights. Guilty because he's really looking forward to being among healthy, fit men, even if it's only to drive a truck from one base to another in simulated maneuvers. Rick wears on him.

The other night, Keller brought up the subject of baseball, like any two guys sitting in a room might do. "What do you think of the Red Sox's chances this year?"

"I don't. I don't think of that at all and I'd prefer it if you wouldn't talk about it."

Rick slammed the door on that topic, which frankly leaves very little for the two of them to talk about during those uncomfortable moments while Keller bathes Rick or lifts him from chair to toilet. War talk isn't anything either of them wants to discuss, and, without the masculine conversational safety net of sports talk, that only leaves Pax.

She's not much better. At least calling her "Missus" has worn off. She's got a couple of years on him, like she might have been a senior when he was a sophomore, just about that much. Caring for her husband has prematurely aged her. Not in appearance, except for the dusky circles beneath her eyes, but in spirit. Maybe it's just that being married to an older guy, you can't be a kid. Keller was never a kid, either, but he's pretty sure that Francesca has become this way, not been raised to it. He understands Francesca's seriousness, and, coupled with the weight of her burden, her gravity.

But it's not a bad situation. After all, he's still got Pax.

Chapter Twenty-seven

Rick! Keller! Francesca! All together, sometimes even in the same room. To Pax, it feels like all the uneven places in his life have smoothed out. It's as if everything that had gone before was leading to this. Early life with Rick. The Rick-less time with Francesca. The exciting time with Keller when he had a job with commands instead of a job, like now, where he is allowed to perform tasks of his own invention. He is busy all the time. Mostly, he keeps Rick company. This isn't the Rick of old; this is a sedentary Rick. He never throws balls or sticks or leashes him to run along the streets. He no longer takes him to the park, or along the Charles River to walk for miles and miles. If Rick no longer requires active company, he more than requires inactive companionship. Pax gives himself over to this new dynamic. As long as he is nearby, within reach of Rick's hand, he is on duty. If Rick is in his bed, Pax lies alongside him, even when Francesca makes him get down. If Rick is in his chair, Pax sits with him. He waits while Rick goes into that place where he doesn't move, doesn't speak, breathing only shallowly. Pax has figured out that if he nudges Rick, or drops a heavy paw on his lap, Rick will emerge from this fugue state. *Good boy.* Job well done.

It might have been a joy to have both of his men in the same room, but there is this thread of tension that corrupts the perfection of it. He goes from one to the other, as if to tell them that he isn't divided between them, but is holding them together. But they don't understand. Francesca doesn't understand, either, and sometimes all Pax wants is to leave all three of them behind and spend a solitary hour in the backyard, waiting for the squirrel that lives in the cherry tree to come within reach.

At night, without orders, Pax divides his time unequally, finding Keller a better bunk mate. After all, they had kept each other warm during those long, harsh months of cold and commotion. Sleeping outside or under the precarious shelter of broken buildings; huddled together with backs against stone walls. Keller's body spooning his, each taking a turn enjoying deep sleep.

Not once has Keller ever ordered him aside for a mate, locking him out of their shared sleeping quarters, like Rick has. Even though Rick and Francesca now sleep in separate places, Pax still prefers his wartime buddy's warmth to stretching out beside either of the other two. Not that Francesca would ever let him on her bed.

But, on occasion, Pax leaves Keller, his acute ears hearing some small anguish coming from Rick. Then he goes back to Rick's room, places his cold nose against his first man's cheek, and waits for the grasp of his unsteady hand to tell Pax that he is helping. That he is doing a good job.

Chapter Twenty-eight

I extracted a straw, inserted it carefully between the floating lumps of vanilla ice cream and deep into the soda. I took a deep draw of the concoction and then caught a look at myself in the soda fountain's mirror. Foolish, girlish, I gave myself a pinup girl wink and took another sip. I'd had my hair cut, and it fanned my face in effortless curls. Unlike so many others, I never had to submit to the heat and stench of a permanent. My fair hair was always curly enough to avoid chemical interference and responsive enough to obey ordinary rollers and bobby pins. Maybelline carmine red banded the straw where my lips pressed. My indulgence. My vanity. Hair done and lips painted, I could have been any wife going home to a husband who would appreciate that she was taking care of herself. For all the good it did me.

This was luxury. An hour without guilt because Keller would give Rick his lunch and then bring out the chess set. Miraculously, he had managed to get Rick to play the game with him, when all other attempts at the distraction of cribbage or poker or rummy had failed. Maybe because it was something easily played one-handed.

In any event, Keller's presence had given me the opportunity of an afternoon to myself. If I'd had any friends, I'd have gone visiting or talked one of them into going out to lunch. Living as we did, in near isolation in a town where we knew no one, hadn't bothered me at first. But once Keller was there and I was allowed some guiltless free time, I began to miss the easy companionship of the other baseball wives. But it had been too long, a lot of the players had changed, and the truth was, I didn't live that life anymore. I didn't want to gossip about who might be traded, or whose wife was pregnant. Especially who was pregnant.

I might have called on Clarissa, Sid's wife, but to be honest, I hadn't taken to Clarissa. She was nice enough, but I didn't have the urge to pull her into my confidences. He'd married a Boston Brahmin Vassar girl and I wasn't her kettle of fish, either. We smiled at each other at our occasional family dinners, but we'd never be the kind of friends who chatted for hours on the phone.

I wrote often to my high school pal Gertie, now Mrs. Donald Richmond, proud doyenne of five hundred acres six miles beyond Mount Joy's town limits and mother to three little boys. Gertie's life was full of farm talk—crops, cows, and corn prices—and kids. I had nothing to offer but medical updates. I had half a dozen stock sentences and I alternated them so that it didn't look like I was writing the same letter over and over: *Rick is doing well this week. We had a good visit with the VA docs. We had a little setback with his catheter, but all is well now. The leaves are turning beautifully. We've had three big snowstorms in the past two weeks. The summer is proving to be rainy.* Blah, blah, blah. Life's just peachy.

My erstwhile boyfriend Buster Novak had been killed in action in the Pacific. I confess that sometimes I wondered what it might have been like had I accepted him. After all, my life hadn't turned out a whole lot different from that of farmwife. My daily concerns, with the exception of corn prices, pretty much came to the same thing as any farm wife dealt with: feeding my men, keeping the household running, looking out for the windstorms that blew through my existence every time Rick succumbed to a depression that never quite lifted. The adventure and culture and *excitement* were long gone, subsumed by the daily struggle to survive.

When Keller appeared with Pax, that gave me something interesting to tell Gertie. "Rick is really happy to have Pax back. Nicholson is such a big help. He's taken over all the heavy lifting for me. It's made such a difference." I was one gush away from making it sound like Keller was a willing participant in the Stanton drama, instead of a man who was there because we'd held his beloved Pax hostage. A little variation on the wisdom of Solomon. Everybody wins, right?

Corporal Nicholson. Keller. Shy guy. Rarely spoke until spoken to, which was difficult for me because I found myself shy around this perfect stranger in my house. If he'd been one of those easy sorts of guys, like Rick's former teammates, all full of jokes and playfulness, it would have been easier for me. But Keller was quiet and respectful and clearly trying hard to keep himself out of my way. Once a week, he asked if he might use the bathtub. Once a week, he asked if he might use my washer. I told him I'd do his laundry, and he blushed, as if the thought of my handling his BVDs was humiliating. Frankly, I was just as happy to have him take care of his own washing for exactly the same reason. It was just too *intimate* between male and female strangers.

"I can't have you do that for me. I'm fully capable of doing my own laundry, and you've got enough to do without my becoming a burden to you."

"Mr. Nicholson. Keller, you've taken a burden off me." The minute I said it, I regretted it. I sounded like I thought my husband was a burden. I'd meant the physical burden. "I don't mean it like that."

"I know what you mean." He lifted his army duffel bag full of dirty clothes up onto his shoulder. "Thank you."

I didn't know if he meant for the compliment or the use of my Maytag.

Our days passed into something resembling a routine, and I realized one afternoon as I handed Keller a stack of folded towels and shooed him upstairs to the linen closet that I had overcome my initial unease with having a strange man in my house. What helped was that I had begun to see him not as a full-fledged grown-up, but as a younger brother. Like my younger brother, Kenny. Kenny was a tease and a pest and a disappointment because, if I'd been destined to have a younger sibling—effectively pushing me into middle-child status—I'd wanted a sister. Like Keller, Kenny was eighteen when he joined the service. He survived the Aleutians and came back just as pesty and teasing as ever, although it was only in letters and during the quick hello he was afforded during the once-a-month phone call my parents made. "Hey, Knucklehead, you still bossy as ever?"

"You still being a brat?" My riposte was never as clever as I wanted it to be. I'd lost a little of my edge.

I didn't know if Keller had come back from the war the same as he had been or whether he'd been changed by it. He had no relatives, he said, so he had no experience of being a younger brother, pesty or not, but that's how I saw him, or, rather, how I chose to see him—well, not the pesty part. Keller was as considerate as anyone could want. But I chose to look at him as a kid brother. Keeping him at a safe remove, but a couple of degrees up from employee.

"Keller, I was going to sit in the living room and listen to the news," I said one night. "Would you like to join me?" Typically, Keller retreated to his garage space as soon as he'd gotten Rick into bed for the night. Usually, I sat with Rick until he shooed me off to bed, but on this night he'd wanted to read and sent me out of his room early.

"Sure." His dark brown hair had grown out of its military clip since his obligatory Reserve weekend. Since then, he'd let it grow, and its poker straightness defied the Brylcreem he dabbed on it, falling against a natural center part and flopping across his brow like a little boy's. He shoved it back and it fell forward.

I resisted the urge to comb it to the side, like I did with Rick's when he, too, let his hair grow out of his summertime clip, when the three or four curls on the back of his head would appear and I would tease them into life with my fingers and then he would tease me into life. "How about I make us a bowl of popcorn? I think that there's a variety show after the news."

The living room held only a three-cushion couch and a wing-back armchair that had belonged to my grandmother and that my parents had shipped to us as an anniversary gift the fall before Pearl Harbor. When I brought the popcorn into the living room, Keller had already warmed up the radio and was sitting in the armchair. Pax was on the rug, stretched out full length, so that his head was under the coffee table. I stepped over him so that I could sit on the end of the couch closest to

Keller and we could easily share the popcorn, over which I'd generously drizzled real butter—a luxury even then.

The minute I set down the bowl, Pax popped up, his amber eyes on the bounty. "No begging, you."

"When he was in the service, he was taught never to take food from anyone but me." Keller grabbed a handful of popcorn. "Now look at him."

I did and saw that the velvety black of the fur on his muzzle was fading with the onset of gray hairs. Even the sooty tips of his A-frame ears were threaded through with this immutable sign that our dog, our baby, was growing older. Rick had found Pax in 38, a tiny puppy. Our dog was almost eight years old. Still fit, still lively, but no longer young.

We'd been married almost seven years. By this time, we might have had two kids, maybe three. Sometimes lying awake in my solitary bed, I thought of those never-conceived children and felt hollowed out, dried up, and no longer young.

I finished my ice cream soda and reapplied my Maybelline carmine red lipstick. A thin paper napkin sufficed as a blotter. Time to go home, time to go back and see if Rick had trounced Keller once again at chess.

Chapter Twenty-nine

Keller is standing outside the glass-block breezeway, contemplating the angle of doorsill and ground.

"You look like you're solving a puzzle." Francesca comes up beside Keller. She's been out for the afternoon and he notices the fresh haircut. She looks nice. She looks relaxed. "I am. I'd like to build a ramp here. You know, to get the wheelchair out of the house easier." The wheelchair, not the man. "I can build one for the other side, too, so that he can get out to the backyard."

"It would help. Do you think you can do it?"

"I'm sure that I can do it. It's a matter of geometry. But, listen, I also want to widen the doorways, get rid of the sills. So he can wheel himself out of his room." Even though Keller suggests this, he wonders if Rick will ever leave his room. Being around Rick reminds Keller of the World War I veterans sitting outside the nursing home in Great Harbor, slumped in their wheelchairs, heads down, Sometimes they hadn't been seriously wounded, but their spirits were shattered. Their outward wounds had healed, but their spirits never would. Rick is like them, staring at the wall day after day, refusing to be grateful that he is back home. Frankly, it kind of pisses Keller off. It stinks, being crippled, but at least he made it out alive.

Bucky Carson didn't make it out, killed in the same action where Keller and Pax were both wounded. Neither did Dick Adams, and Keller still feels that sharp, disbelieving grief whenever he thinks of this particular death. Dick and his war dog, Rudy, both gone in an instant.

"I just don't know if the landlord will go for it. He might not be keen on making that kind of dramatic change to his structure. Maybe just the ramp for now."

Francesca slings her handbag up over her arm and goes into the house through the open breezeway door. Her shadow drifts over the thick glass blocks like an undersea creature. Keller thinks that he'll go in and check on Rick, see if he wants anything—except another game of chess. One humiliation a day is enough for Keller. After that, maybe he'll go to the lumberyard and get started on the materials for the ramp. He closes the breezeway door behind him and enters the kitchen. Francesca is there, still in her light coat, her handbag open on the table, its contents spilled out.

"Keller?" Francesca starts shoving the coin purse and checkbook and comb and lipstick back into her bag.

"Ma'am?"

"It's good you're here." She snaps the handbag shut and walks out of the kitchen.

He feels himself flush. He's not sure how to respond. No one has ever said that to him before.

"I'm glad to be of help." But she's in the hallway and his words fall into empty air.

Then she's back. Her coat and bag put away, she reaches for an apron. As she does, she steps closer to Keller. One hand keeps him from backing away. "Keller." She's more than a head shorter than he is, so she lifts herself up on her toes and leans toward his ear. "He's very glad you're here. He might not say it, but he is." Her breath is close to his ear—she doesn't want Rick to know she's talking about him—but the effect of her soft whisper against Keller's cheek incites in him the urge to place his hand on her waist and press his cheek against hers. She smells of laundry soap and fresh air.

Once when on patrol, Keller and Pax had come upon a small farmhouse, a crowded clothesline strung out behind it into the rare spring sunshine. The woman who lived there boldly walked out her door and left it open, as if to invite inspection. Pax was unconcerned as they walked the perimeter, so they left the yard quickly. But before they did, Keller, weeks from his last bath or clean uniform, walked between the lines of drying sheets and shirts, inhaling the idea of being clean and freshly clothed. Just like having a loving family, the concept seemed unattainable.

Keller swallows and closes his eyes. "I know he is. And I'm very glad to be here."

Keller uses the bathroom before he goes in to check on Rick. He needs a moment; he can't go into that room with the feel of Francesca's hand on his arm still there; with the desire to touch her back still evident in the pink of his cheek.

Pax is flopped on the bare floor, stretched out full length, taking up most of the space not already taken up with bed and tables and wheelchair. His head is beside the wheelchair; his tail is under the hospital bed. The room is stuffy and the dog is softly panting. He raises his head when Keller comes in, and Keller can hear the *flop-flop* of his tail against the hardwood floor beneath the bed. The tail bangs against a spring with a little chiming sound. Rick's lap blanket is on the floor, and Keller bends to pick it up. Rick doesn't like to sit without something across his knees; he's always cold, even in this closed-up room. "You should have called me." Keller settles the blanket back in place.

"It's all right. I can't keep you running back and forth like some deranged butler."

"I don't mind."

Pax extricates himself from under the bed and sits with the two men, his fond eyes addressing first one and then the other. His muzzle cracks open in a wide pant like a smile. He is perhaps the happiest creature Keller knows. Hours on patrol, or enduring endless hours of barrage as the big guns went off in near-ceaseless repetition, and the dog happily settled wherever Keller was. And now he was happily settled between the two of them. Keller thinks that the dog is bound to be bored. His life for the past three years had been one of work. Good work, important work. The only restlessness Keller sees is late at night, when the dog wants to patrol the perimeter of the tiny fenced-in yard. He isn't satisfied to do it by himself like a regular dog; he noses Keller into line and the pair of them walk around the yard. If Keller doesn't adhere to the dog's sense of performance, he gets a look as if to say, *You're asking for it, grunt. Fall in!*

Pax is like a retiree, a warhorse put out to pasture. Except that he's taken on the role of companion with the same dedication as he did scout. And then Keller is struck with an idea.

"You know, maybe we can teach Pax how to pick things up for you."

They practice with medicine bottles and chess pieces. Rick knocks something off his tray and Keller points at it. They've decided on the command "Pick it up" slurred together: "Pickitup." As used as he is to learning tasks, the dog figures it out in less than six tries. Proud of himself, he waits impatiently for Rick to drop something else. And Keller finds himself proud, too, not only of the dog but of himself for coming up with the idea. He loves it, this ability to communicate ideas between species. The moment when the dog looks at him with complete comprehension. As if they *are* speaking a common language.

It was like that in the war. Sometimes it spooked Keller, how well the dog understood him.

Chapter Thirty

"You're going to have to be clumsy every ten minutes to keep him happy."

"I don't see that as much of a problem." Rick says this without irony. He's infernally clumsy, and he still hasn't, after all this time, figured out that he has only one hand. He keeps instinctively reaching with his absent right hand, frustrating himself and his occupational therapists. Relearning how to do everything with the wrong hand has been difficult. He still fears soup, although forking the pieces of meat that Francesca has kindly precut for him has become easier if he thinks of the British fashion of left-handed eating and tips his fork with tines down. He doesn't say so, but Rick longs to be able to cut up his own meat. What a simple lost talent. His missing fingers itch to take up the knife and slice off a big thick piece of ham from a picnic shoulder. Sometimes he thinks he misses being able to do that more than getting up out of this chair and walking out the door. But not as much as feeling the smooth surface of a baseball, reading its individual personality in the stitching, the weight of it balanced tenderly in the palm of his hand before he settles it into position for a curve or a sinker or a fastball.

No amount of success with a fork in his left hand can compensate him.

Even with the windows closed, Rick hears the sound of sawing and hammering. Keller is building him a ramp so that it will be easier to get from the house to the hospital. Keller doesn't say exactly that; he just says it'll be handy, a quick slide right to the door of the car. No more teeth-jarring thumping down steps, no more humiliating reminders of his helplessness. Keller thinks that if it's easier to leave the house, Rick will. Except that he can't think of any place he might be taken other than the hospital. No other reason to struggle to get into the car. No place he wants to go.

"What do you think of this?" Francesca twirls into the room like a debutante. She's wearing a new dress, very fitted at the waist, and a lot longer than the dresses she wore before he went to war. The sleeves are a little puffy, trimmed with a white band. It's a blue-and-white print. She looks very pleased with herself, and it's so nice to see a genuine smile on her face.

"Very nice. You've been shopping?" Lately, with Keller there, Francesca has been going off almost every day, and she doesn't always tell him where she's going. It's like she's slipping out, a teenage girl secretly meeting a boy on the corner, hoping her parents don't notice that she's gone.

"No, silly. I made it." She gathers up the skirt, examines the hemstitching, tut-tuts. "See, I'm uneven here."

"It looks very nice, and you could have fooled me. Looks like something you'd pick up at Jordan Marsh."

Francesca twirls again, obviously enjoying the swish of a

full skirt. Her trajectory puts her beside him and she plants a kiss on the good side of his face. "Keller's almost done with the ramp. What say we get out of here tonight and get some dinner out?"

"And then what? Go dancing?"

"If you'd like." She doesn't hear his sarcasm, or she's ignoring it.

"No. I don't think I'm ready for that. For going out."

"Rick. This isn't good for you. It's time to—"

"Time to what, Francesca? Time to do what, exactly?" He turns his face away from her.

"Time to get on with your life. You're doing much better. I know what your occupational therapist told you. He told you that you need to get out, and you do."

"He's not the one who will be subjected to the pity stares." There, he's said it. The festering notion that he will be unable to abide being looked at with pity. He doesn't want the pity of those who came back from the war whole, or the "there but for the grace of God" pity of those who never went, to the curious stares of the rude and the innocent fear of monsters in the eyes of children.

"That's in your head, Rick. Yes, people may give you a look; that's natural. But they understand and maybe even admire you." She touches his unblemished cheek with her hand. "I admire you."

"Please don't." Even Rick doesn't know if he means that she shouldn't say any more or that she should stop touching him. Her touch is a taunt, a reminder of his other disability.

"Okay. So, I'll just go change and get lunch started." Francesca has gotten so good at keeping her voice modulated. She never lets him see her hurt or mad or frustrated. She tips the door half-closed on her way out.

Rick puts his face in his hand, so sorry, so very sorry for being the man he has become.

A cold, wet nose pokes through his fingers. Pax seems intent on spreading Rick's fingers wide enough that he can then give him a consoling lick on the nose. Rick leans his forehead against the dog's brow. "Pax, what would I do without you?"

Pax has nothing to say about that. He settles beside Rick, gives his front paws a freshening up.

One of Rick's slippers has come off. He's just noticed. "Pax, pickitup." He points to the footwear. Pax seems overjoyed to perform this small request and retrieves the slipper as if it were a rabbit dashing away. No Labrador had ever retrieved something as exuberantly or as gently. Now all he has to do is teach the dog how to put it on his foot. Rick takes the slipper out of the dog's mouth and praises him, as Keller instructed, with a scratch on the chest. It seems such a little recognition of the vast service the dog performs, but Pax seems pleased. It's true that the dog seemed to come to life as Keller was teaching him to pick up the things that Rick knocked to the floor, that his canine enthusiasm for learning is unbounded. He's a dog with a brain, and one that revels in performing his tasks. How did that happen? Before, Rick had a hard time getting him not to pull on the leash. Francesca could barely control him. All that energy had been funneled into the war machine and out had come this obedient, talented dog. But Pax's attachment to Keller is still jarring, still capable of creating a spurt of jealousy that makes Rick have to turn his face away from this guy who has proved to be such a godsend. Pax will spend all day with him in this room, but if Keller comes to walk him, the dog literally leaps up with joy. A kid going out for recess couldn't show more excitement. Is it the exercise or the time with his other master that incites it?

And yet, although Rick knows that the dog sleeps in the garage with Keller, if he wakes in the night, he finds the dog with him, as if he's been there all along.

As has become their habit at lunchtime, the three of them cram into Rick's room. Francesca has changed out of her new dress and is back in her workaday housedress. She moves the rolling over-bed table into the middle of the room to accommodate Rick's wheelchair and two kitchen chairs, and places a plate of egg salad sandwiches on it so that they can all reach.

Keller comes in with a bandage around his left forefinger. "Stupid mistake. Thought my finger was a nail."

Lucky for him he has his right hand and it doesn't impair his ability to eat his sandwich.

"Any requests for dinner?" Francesca touches up the edge of a sandwich with her finger and puts it in Rick's hand. As she licks the extra mayo from her finger, an image of her in bed flashes through Rick's mind, until he slams the lid on it.

"I have an idea. You suggested going out, so why don't you and Keller go?"

"No. I don't think that would be a good idea."

Keller is shaking his head as if the idea is apostasy. He is adhering to some protocol of his own invention.

"It's fine. You two both need a break. Go get some fried clams. Bring some back for me."

"What if . . ."

Rick puts his half-eaten sandwich down, takes Francesca's hand. "Nothing is going to happen for the hour it may take you to eat dinner. You're not leaving me in danger. Besides, I have Pax. He'll keep me company."

Francesca and Keller look at each other with almost the same expression of skepticism. Or, is it something else, a nervous shyness? Like two adolescents. Two wallflowers suddenly forced to dance? Rick realizes that he has no idea what kind of relationship these two have with each other. She speaks of him only in terms of how much he's helping. Keller never speaks of Francesca except to say she's in the kitchen or running an errand. It's obvious to him now, the way they seem to exist only on the periphery of each other. Coworkers, not companions. He doesn't know why that bothers him. It seems like they should be better friends than that. It means that Keller may yet be an imposition on Francesca even while he's giving her enough freedom to go get her hair done.

"I mean it. You both deserve a break."

Keller slips a crust to Pax. "I could do with a clam plate. It's been a long time since I've eaten clams."

"We'd only be gone a little while."

Rick can't tell if Francesca says that like a decision, or if she's trying to convince herself he can be left alone even for an hour. Has he become that much of a child that he can't be left? Life has become such an if/then equation. If they had had a baby before he went to war, would he then have come back infantilized? If he had died, would she then have been able to move on with her life instead of being trapped here with him? If he had come back whole, would the unspoken fact of their earlier failure to conceive been finally addressed? Maybe, if there had been no war, they would have conceived. It's a stretch to blame God for not giving them a child when they'd had the opportunity, but sometimes Rick does. And then he thinks that it's probably for the best. How would Francesca have coped with an active child's needs and those of a needy husband?

Keller points to the remaining half sandwich. "Anyone?"

"I can make more; I have more egg salad made up." Francesca looks ready to jump out of her chair.

"No. I'm done." Rick sets his unfinished half back on his plate.

Keller finishes the sandwich in two bites. He starts to wipe his mouth on the back of his hand but stops himself and uses his napkin. "I should get back to work." He grabs the back of the extra kitchen chair and leaves Francesca and Rick alone.

Pax looks after Keller but remains where he is, at Rick's side, patiently waiting for another crust. Rick hands him the rest of his sandwich.

"I think that maybe it's a good night for lamb chops. The butcher has them on special."

"Francesca, go out. Take Keller and go out.

"Rick, I feel a little awkward about . . ."

"It's not a date, Fran, it's a little break from cooking."

There is a faint tinge to her pale cheeks, not quite a blush, not quite embarrassment. It's as if she's been thinking about Keller and has been called out on it. Either she's uncomfortable with him or she's not. "All right. You're right." She stands up, gathers the plates into a stack. "But just be sure I'd rather be going out with you and that I'm going to keep pestering you until you say yes."

"I need time, Francesca. I need more time."

"You can have all the time you need, but you have to promise me that you'll try." She drops a kiss on the top of his head. "Promise?"

"Yes." The word has the sooty taste of a lie.

Chapter Thirty-one

If he had the capacity to put into words what he feels, Pax would think himself a lucky dog. If being safe and warm and well fed is one part of what a dog needs and wants, having the companionship and affection of his best people is three-quarters of perfect. One friend to be with as he dozes in the narrow patch of sunlight that ekes its way between the former blackout curtains in the small Rick-smelling room. The same friend to ask him for favors like picking up dropped things. Another friend to keep his training sharp, heeling, fetching, sniffing out potential threats to the home. Sit, stay, and even, when out in the woods, scaling barriers. Finally, the woman who gives him the best of the belly rubs, her fingers equipped for deep scratching and an instinct for the right places.

Yes, Pax is a lucky dog indeed and his sense of well-being tempers his still-youthful energies. He's been through the toughest of times—separation from those he loved, a time of re-quired aggression and wariness—and come out mild-mannered and willing to accept this triumvirate of masters.

There is only one thing that puzzles him: why these three

don't seem to be as content as he is. They are like a small pack lacking a leader. He's tried to step into that role, but their humanness limits their comprehension. He's taking as good care of them as he can, but they still insist on a separateness from one another. They don't snap at one another, and if they are jockeying for position in the pack, it's too subtle for him to detect. Instead, there is this *deference*. Keller was admirably alpha when they were a pack of two. But his position in this group is unclear. Francesca, as a female, is a likely candidate, but she, too, refuses to take the lead. If he had to, Pax might give Rick the leadership, but his ability to hunt or protect or mate is clearly compromised, and that should remove him from the head of the pack. So Pax watches out for all of them, not entirely comfortable in his role, finding it hard to interpret from day to day exactly what it is these three humans want from one another. At least he knows what they want from him. To be there for each of them.

Yes, he's a lucky dog.

Chapter Thirty-two

I think that it's still there, Ray's Clam Shack. Across Quincy Shore Drive from the beach, back in those days they served food fried in a deep fat fryer filled with liquefied Crisco, a maxed-out cholesterol feast and absolutely divine. I was a kid from the Midwest. Fresh seafood was a treat, and that fried mess of clams and french fries and tartar sauce was exotic to me. Keller insisted we get clams with bellies, suggesting that clam strips were akin to eating margarine instead of butter—just not good enough. I admit that it took a bit for me to get used to the taste and feel of the contents of a clam belly, but once I did, I never went back to the untutored Midwesterner's version of clams.

Even though the place was only a few blocks from home, we took my car. Partly because Rick's take-out dinner would be cold if we walked it home and mostly because neither one of us was interested in prolonging this excursion, leaving Rick home alone and potentially helpless. What if something happened? That sentence should be in all caps. Pax was there, at the ready to retrieve anything Rick could point to. Keller had refined the dog's mission to include getting Rick's sweater, which lay at the foot of his bed, or dragging his lap robe up and over his knees. Should the evening paper arrive when we weren't around, the dog would push his way out the front door and take it in to Rick, this last without a command or, to the best of our knowledge, anyone training him to do it. We still hadn't seen him open the front door to get back in. But, with all that, the dog couldn't dial a phone or put out a fire. Worst-case scenarios plagued me.

The other reason I thought we should take the car was because we were still very shy with each other and this whim of Rick's was best accomplished quickly. Without the third party of Rick, or even Pax, we were only a little better than foreign dignitaries without a common language.

We took our dinner to the beach, finding an empty bench to sit on side-by-side, the greasy bags between us. And we talked, as parents of young children do, of our two common interests. Rick and Pax. How funny Pax was with that squeaky toy hanging out of his mouth. How much better we both thought Rick was using his left hand.

Conversation petered out and we sat back to admire the view of the Boston Harbor islands.

Keller scuffed his feet in the sand. "This is lousy sand."

"What do you mean?"

"Kind of, well, kind of city sand."

I laughed. "You're a beach sand connoisseur?"

"Sort of. Spent a lot of time standing in it."

"Where?"

"Little place called Hawke's Cove. Up north of here. I lived for a while with my great-uncle." Keller lifted a whole clam dipped in a coating of tartar sauce to his mouth, chewed. "He's a commercial fisherman, mostly close to shore."

"That must have been nice, being on the water."

Keller didn't say anything for a moment, then shook his head. "It wasn't vacation. It was hard work."

There was no nostalgia in his voice, as there might have been with a lot of men. Even hard work has its nostalgic quality—a pride of purpose, of accomplishment. With Keller, it sounded more like he had survived something. He didn't elaborate then; only later did I learn about his virtual slave labor and understand that he had indeed survived something.

"Is that where you learned to eat clams with bellies?"

Keller gave me one of his infrequent smiles, and for the first time I saw that he had a really nice smile and wished that maybe he'd use it more. "That and how to make a mean chowder." He pronounced it in that quintessentially New England manner: *chowda*. "I'll make it some night if you want."

"Rick would love that. It was always what he ordered when we went out." And then I remembered that Rick avoided using a spoon. "Well, maybe not yet."

Keller knew what I meant. "He will. I promise."

The scenery recaptured our attention. A small boat was powering its way toward one of the islands, and I couldn't imagine what reason it might have for such a journey. As far as I knew, there were no inhabitants on the tuft of island that the boat was headed toward.

"That's a lobster boat; he's out checking traps. He's probably got them set where there're rocks. Lobsters like cover." *Lobstas.*

"Another thing your uncle taught you?" I crumpled up my empty cardboard clam boat and shoved it in the paper bag.

"Yeah." Keller followed suit, and grabbed both empty bags. We needed to pick up the order for Rick. "Can I ask you something?"

"Sure."

"Rick was a ballplayer, right?"

"Yes."

"So, why won't he let me bring in a radio so we can listen to the games? You'd think that he'd want to keep up."

Hadn't Keller noticed the fact that Rick left the sports section unread? I chalked up his insensitivity to youthful callowness. Of course, he wasn't a youth and it wasn't callowness. Eventually, I figured out that his bluntness had more to do with his upbringing, or lack thereof. "It's too painful. He was slated to become a starting pitcher with the Boston Braves, but instead he went to war and lost his dream."

"I'm sorry. I shouldn't have said anything."

"If you want to listen to the games, feel free. But don't think that you're going to get him to."

"I thought that if he'd listen to the radio, he might, I don't know, start to feel better."

"By being reminded of the loss of the thing that meant the most to him?"

"Look, he's in there all by himself, staring at the wall. Unless you're in there, or I'm making him play chess, he's probably *only* thinking of his loss."

The thing Keller couldn't know is that I understood Rick exceedingly well, including his aversion to the topic of sports. For a long time, I felt the same aversion every time one of my ballpark acquaintances or a friendly neighbor down the block announced that she was pregnant, something that was happening postwar with startling regularity. Or I stood next to a mother with a pram beside her in the butcher shop, watching out of the corner of my eye while she tucked the baby in more securely and smiled down with that Madonna smile all women are capable of. I tossed out the baby pictures my Iowa girlfriends kindly sent to me, inviting me to share in their joy.

Maybe making Rick listen to ball games *was* a good idea. After all, I was a little better now, having a new focus forced upon me with Rick's challenges, so that the sight of a pregnant woman on the street corner no longer made me avert my eyes. And there were so many of them. It was as if the world had gone procreation crazy in order to make up for the staggering losses of war.

"At least now he's got Pax. And you. Before it was . . ." I couldn't go on. I couldn't admit that those months of being Rick's only caregiver had been anything other than a privilege.

"Just you. Yes, it's a good thing that I'm here to help. And it's really good that Pax can at least get him to smile once in a while. But, Francesca, it isn't enough."

I was done with this conversation. I know he hadn't meant to, but he was making me feel like I had somehow failed Rick by not making him listen to baseball on the radio, forcibly reminding him that life and baseball had moved on without him. Well, they also recommended rubbing dogs' noses in their messes to punish them. "Let's go get the order and go home."

"I'm sorry. I didn't mean to stir up trouble."

"It's not like I don't see what's wrong, Keller. You never knew him as the man I married. He was charming and funny and sexy and full of life. He was *full of life.*" I hated the way my voice broke. I hadn't cried in a long time, not since I realized that tears really never relieved. They just pushed my thoughts inward, until I felt sorry for myself.

"The war took that from him, didn't it? I get it. But he's got the whole rest of his life to live, and if he can't even leave his room, what kind of a life is it going to be? For him, and for you."

The little lobster boat had moved out of sight around the curve of the island. A pair of seagulls had landed close by, attracted by our impromptu picnic. I had nothing to toss to them. We had eaten every bite. "Do you plan to stay on?"

"Do you want me to?"

"We do, but the question is, do you want to stay?" It came to me that Keller was done with taking care of a man who hadn't come through the war in the same way he had, with his limbs intact and his spirit undiminished. He didn't answer right away, and I could feel my heart hammering at the fear he would say good-bye and leave me once again alone with my husband.

"I do."

I didn't know I'd been holding my breath until I released it. "Oh, good. Good."

"But it's not enough." A coincidence of words, or had this been what he'd meant earlier about it not being enough?

"We can't pay any more, honestly." It was a pittance, eked out of Rick's benefits. We were feeding Keller, and providing a place to sleep. Even living with us, he had expenses—a car, clothing, and so on. Here he was at the beginning of his postwar life, living like a Victorian servant.

"No. That's not what I mean. I'm thinking of taking advantage of the GI Bill and going to college in the fall. I can do both, go to school and help out with Rick. If I can stay on with you, I mean."

"Of course you can." I almost giggled in relief. He'd stay. I felt reprieved and I knew that Rick would be pleased, even if he didn't say so.

Keller tossed the bags into a trash can and we dashed across the street, back to where Rick's dinner was waiting to be picked up. I don't know why, but we dashed hand in hand.

Chapter Thirty-three

"Pax, pickitup." Rick points to a medicine bottle sitting on the edge of the bedside table. It holds his painkillers—fifty little white pills guaranteed to take the edge off his continuing pain, if not cure it.

Pax watches Rick's gesture, identifies the target, and goes to the table. He lifts the bottle gently, glances back at Rick to confirm that he has the right object, and then brings it to him.

"Good boy." Rick scratches the dog's chest, then runs his hand over his head. "Really good boy."

Unscrewing the cap with his teeth, Rick shakes out two of the pills. He slips the morphine into the pocket of his sweater. Now his problem is how to put the vial back on the nightstand so that neither his wife nor Keller will notice. He is stockpiling, week by week, a dose of morphine he hopes will put an end to this nonsense. He's tired, really tired, and he could just take everything that's in this vial now, but he doesn't. He doesn't want it to look like a suicide. There, that's the word. *Suicide*. Death by personal choice. A death that would disqualify Francesca from his life insurance. One of these nights after

Keller gets him settled into bed and Francesca has kissed him good night, he'll swallow his purloined hoard of morphine pills, send Pax out of the room, and fall asleep for all time, putting an end to this half-life.

But right now his problem is how to get the little bottle back to where Keller left it. Rick is facing in the wrong direction. After the laborious morning routine of getting him out of bed and cleaned up, Keller always leaves him facing the door. They've been working on a new command, one invented to give Rick a little more freedom of movement within his room. Folded up on the tray table is a terry-cloth towel. He grasps it and shakes it toward the dog. "Pax, pull me."

Pax loves this new game and cheerfully mouths the end of the already-shredded towel.

"Pull me," Rick repeats.

With Pax's teeth gripping the towel and his weight sunk into his back legs, Rick keeps a resistance on the other end like a game of tug-of-war, until the chair slowly revolves and Rick is facing the bed instead of the door.

Perfect. Except that the space between the hospital bed and the wall is too narrow to navigate in the chair. He needs to get the dog to replace the vial, or at least get it onto the table. "Here, Pax."

Pax is at the ready, his tail swishing across the bare floor in anticipation of further usefulness. Rick gets the dog to take the bottle in his mouth. "I have no idea what to ask, so let's try: 'Put it down.'" Pax happily holds the vial and wags his tail, but his eyes are pure doubt. "Okay, whole new command for you. Pax, put it." He points to the table, but the dog puts the bottle in his lap. "Good boy." Rick has the dog take the object back and then touches the edge of his bed. "Put it." The dog puts it in his hand. "No. On the bed." This is stupid. He doesn't have Keller's innate ability to communicate with this animal. He doesn't have the right words or the right tone of voice. Like everything else in his life, he can no longer make it work.

Rick hears the connecting door between the kitchen and the breezeway open and then the sound of drawers opening and shutting. The smell of fried food precedes Keller and Francesca down the hall. In the half a minute it takes Francesca to gather a plate and napkin, Rick has to figure out what to do with the vial. Reflexively, he underhands it toward the bedside table. It bounces with a glass-on-wood clang and hits the bed. Rick wishes he'd used a curve.

"Is everything all right?" Francesca is behind him. "What happened?"

"Nothing." Rick hopes she's referring to the fact that he's facing away from the door. "Pax and I are just working on our commands. He's turned me around. So, what did you bring me?" Francesca turns him back around and gestures to the dog to leave the room. "Pax, out." The dog bolts out, as if he's been held captive. Francesca settles a dish towel across Rick's chest, tucking one end of it under his useless arm. He feels like a child and he peevishly pulls it off. "No utensils necessary for this dinner; you don't need to put a bib on me. I won't get sloppy."

He hates it when he speaks to her like that. But, honestly, the mothering thing is beginning to wear thin. She treats him like, well, like an invalid. At least Nicholson has the good grace to *ask* if he needs something done before assuming he wants it.

Francesca lifts a cardboard boat of whole-belly clams out of the bag. "Keller's going to stay with us. He told me so tonight."

"I thought it was our decision, not his."

Francesca looks stunned, then mad. It's a new expression for her, and he's perversely pleased with himself for inciting a wholesome emotion for once. "I said he could. It's what we want, isn't it?"

"As long as you're still okay with it. I know this hasn't been easy."

"It's all right. It's fine."

Rick sees that it is. This having a stranger in their midst has moved from odd to ordinary. "So where is he?"

Francesca looks away from him, her chin tilted a little, and Rick remembers how it once felt to take that chin in his hand and lower it so that their lips met. "He's listening to the baseball game."

"Oh." Of course he is. It's August and the season is building toward the World Series.

"He wants to know why you never listen."

"What did you tell him?"

"The truth. It's too hard for you." Now she looks back at him and the sadness in her eyes is more painful to him than his physical hurts; it splinters him. He has six pills in his sweater pocket. He needs to find a better place to keep them, but there is nowhere in this room that isn't touched by the two other people in this house. No privacy.

Chapter Thirty-four

Keller has arranged things so that part of the garage looks like a bedroom—the cot, the bureau, and mirror—and part looks like a sitting room. He has a radio plugged in on what doubles as his workbench and he can listen to the baseball games that Rick refuses to listen to. Keller rescued an easy chair from a neighbor's curbside trash and he's positioned it with an up-ended ammo crate for a footstool so that he can comfortably drink a beer and listen to the game or read a few pages of *Le Morte d'Arthur* under the light from his new pole lamp. With his first paycheck, he sprang for the radio and lamp, and in a couple of weeks he'll find himself a rug remnant so that when cooler weather comes, he won't be walking on cement. In his whole life, Keller has never before enjoyed having a place of his own, the privacy of an empty room. He'd been in isolation, sure, but that wasn't solitude; that was punishment. A windowless room at the top of the third floor in the administration building, no light, no food, no blanket. This is privacy. No one to interfere with him, no one to bully him.

His experience of women hasn't been one of maternal care

and kindness; his aunts were resentful of his extra mouth and the extra work, more quick to slap him than to praise him. He learned to keep out of the way, stay in the corner, not ask for more. Matron Willis at Meadowbrook looked the part of a kindly lady, a bit overstuffed, never seen without her apron, loose bun twisted on the top of her head; however, she was anything but. She and her husband, whom the boys called "Willie Whiskers" behind his back due to his walrus mustache, were the houseparents of his dormitory at Meadowbrook. Fifty truants and thieves, miscreants and the dispossessed lived in each of the four buildings charmingly called "cottages" by the founders of Meadowbrook School for Boys. There was nothing parental about their oversight. Matronly Matron Willis had a quick hand with the wooden spoon, and more than one boy was deafened by a blow to his ear with it. The boys were treated essentially as prisoners, and corporeal punishment, or being locked up in isolation, was the rule of the day.

Francesca takes care of him, making sure that he gets enough to eat, and that if he has a favorite, she cooks it. She brings him clean sheets every Monday. She seems happy to do it, even though he's said he is fully capable of washing his own sheets. It makes her seem like a landlady, as if this is a boardinghouse, except that they're paying him to be here. He's stopped her from actually making up his bed. He makes sure he joins her in the backyard when she's bringing in the sun-dried clothes. He carries the basket in for her.

Keller never entirely closes the door between his space and the breezeway, and at least for now, while it's still warm, the house door is also kept open so that he can be summoned at a word. The open doors don't diminish his sense of happy solitude, but it's nice to be within call of people who seem to want him to be there.

Pax comes in, tail wagging gently. "Hey, bud. Time for a walk?"

Roof.

"I'll take that as a yes." Keller ties the undone laces of his shoes. As he does every night, he heads down to the beach so that he can throw sticks for the dog. Tonight, the simple exercise of heeling off leash is the only reminder of their war work. The dog sticks like glue to his left leg, sitting as Keller waits at the curb for traffic to pass; never allowing himself to be distracted by the admiring glances of passersby. They pass Ray's Clam Shack on their route and Keller thinks about what he told Francesca about wanting to take advantage of the GI Bill and go to college.

Keller pulls a thick stick out from under a set of cement steps leading down to the beach from the sidewalk promenade. It's a particularly good one and he keeps it hidden so that they have it every time they walk to Squantum. He puts Pax in a sit-stay and then flings the stick as far as he can into the water. "Get it." The dog bounds after the stick, snags it, and crashes through the shallow water back to Keller. Imagine how much the dog would enjoy the cove below Clayton's house. Keller shakes off the thought. This city beach is just fine, thank you. The idea of going back to Clayton's house still has the power, after all this time, to squeeze his heart with dread.

The truth is, he hadn't really thought about going to college; it wasn't something that had ever been suggested to him as a goal. Not even Miss Jacobs had ever suggested that he apply, probably because she knew Clayton would never approve of such a lofty ambition. She was lucky to get him to allow Keller to finish high school. Keller can hear Clayton's voice in his ear, as if the old man were standing behind him: *Don't be getting above yourself, boy. Fisherman don't need no college.*

Francesca had beamed at him, asked him what he might want to study, *encouraged* this crazy out-of-the-blue idea. Saying it, that he wanted to go to college, wasn't anything more than a ploy to ensure that he can stay where he is, here with Pax. The money is scant, true. But the alternative would mean that he'd have to fight over Pax with the two people he's come to feel responsible for. He can't do it to them or to himself. Or to Pax. The dog is so content. All the months they spent during the war, and yet he never saw the dog's tail wag so much as it does now. Oh, there were times when a mission was accomplished and everyone could relax and the big dog would get a little silly. But they were never 100 percent safe, and so, never 100 percent relaxed. Neither one of them slept a full night until now, although Keller knows that Pax makes the rounds from room to room a couple of times a night. Still, it's a homefront kind of patrol. No real threats.

Francesca's reaction to his plan had been so genuine, as if she'd been worried that he might leave them. He's become necessary and welcome. Keller suddenly blushes at the thought of his grabbing Francesca's hand to run across the street last night. There wasn't even any traffic bearing down on them. It was impulsive, and the memory of it judders through him. Her hand wasn't as smooth as he had imagined. Her fingers linked through his were stronger than he might have expected from such a little woman.

"Pax, get it!" He whips the long stick as hard as he can. It tumbles end over end, and the rocketing dog is nearly there when it hits the sand.

She hadn't pulled it away in horror; she'd laughed and run

with him like they were little kids. Maybe they looked like sister and brother. Keller finds himself smiling at the soft-headed idea. She's so small and fair, and he's not. No one would take them for siblings.

Funny, Rick's insistence that they go out to dinner last night. It wasn't so much that he wanted them to leave him alone, but more like he hoped they'd work a little on improving their own association. He was right. Even in that short time alone—without the buffer of Rick or the dog—a little of the reserve that Keller and Francesca keep between them was sanded off.

It's getting dark so early these waning days of summer. Looking away from the glow of Boston in the night sky, he sees a sprinkling of stars has emerged. Keller can pick out Sirius, the dog star, always at the heel of his master, Orion.

Pax bounds up to Keller, shaking the stick as if it's a living creature whose neck he wants to break.

"Leave it."

The dog places the heavy stick at Keller's feet.

"Time's up, Pax. Let's head home."

Home.

Chapter Thirty-five

His two men confer and now Pax is being taught something new to do for Rick. All of his new accomplishments take place in this space. It's quite a change from the field work that he and Keller had done, long runs, lots of energy burned off, the flinty scent of danger overhanging every action. In comparison, these new accomplishments are really pretty tame. With Keller, he was part of a hunting pack. Lead dog, his followers flanking the prey and then taking it down for him. Here, he is domestic, nest building without a mate. *Pickitup. Pull me.* And now a two-part exercise: *Take it. Put it.* The men use a rubber ball as the training object, so he takes it in his mouth and then moves to a spot that Rick points to with his forefinger. Keller has taught him that *Put it* means to carefully put the object in the spot that he thinks Rick wants him to. It's not an easy task. Sometimes it's really hard to determine where Rick is pointing. He's dropped the ball on the floor, on the bed, on the table and had to go retrieve it when it bounced away and under the hospital bed. Crawling under the lowered metal frame isn't an easy thing for the big dog to do and makes him think of his war experience, crawling on his belly beneath rifle fire. Rick gets impatient and says *no no no no* a lot. Finally, Pax masters the nuances of Rick's gestures and has a perfect run of placing the object on the table when Rick points to it, on the bed, and, yes, on the floor as directed. Then they try other objects, like the little bottle.

Keller is pleased with him, but Rick keeps asking him to repeat the same exercise long after Keller has left the room. It has gone beyond mere practice and is sliding out of the realm of a game. Rick's repetition of the series of commands to retrieve an object, give him the object, take the object, and then put it where Rick indicates has taken on the same intensity as those exercises with Keller as the big guns thundered over their heads and the men around them depended on them to secure the way. Rick's aura suggests life and death even though the object isn't to locate an enemy hidden in a thicket, but to bring him a glass vial.

Rick's praise goes beyond a mere touch. Pax doesn't understand his words, but he knows that the tone of Rick's voice means that he is extraordinary.

Chapter Thirty-six

We had a ramp, thanks to Keller. He'd also appealed to my landlord, played the veteran card, I think, and had gotten grudging permission to widen the doorways and remove the sills to accommodate Rick's chair. A few days of noisy carpentry and Rick was, in our minds at least, set free. In his mind, it made no difference. He wouldn't budge.

"It's a beautiful day, and you haven't been outside since your last doctor's appointment. Come on, we'll go for a ride, maybe get some ice cream."

He looked at me as if I was treating him like a child. Which I was.

"I'm fine in here. You go."

"Keller's made this possible for you. At least come out into the yard. You haven't seen my lilies." My tone had tensed up, so that I wasn't so much cajoling as badgering.

Keller glanced at me and I could see the warning to be patient. It was hard. I'd been patient with Rick for months. More than a year. Would I be damned if I got a little impatient now and then? No one understood better than I did the magnitude of his loss, but it was my loss, too. It was, in my mind, the way life was now, and no amount of hiding in a darkened sickroom was going to change that. He needed to accept that things weren't going to go back to the way they had been. I didn't want him to spend the rest of his days like this, a self-incarcerated captive.

"Pax will keep me company. No need for you two to sit inside on such a nice day."

"Rick. Please."

My husband looked at me with a dull stare. Even his eyes had changed since the war. Eyes I'd once said were the blue of a Delft tile were now the color of distant shadows. He no longer looked at me with bright eyes, with happiness and anticipation, with humor or mischievousness. With desire. The war not only had taken his arm and left him wheelchair-bound but had also stolen his spirit.

"Okay. That's fine. But I'm opening these goddamned curtains." I pushed his chair aside and yanked open the dark drapes that kept his tiny room in a state of perpetual gloom. Sunlight burst in, revealing dirty streaks on the windowpane. I unlocked the double-hung window and raised it. Fresh late-August air, bearing the faintest tinge of a sea breeze, pushed into the room, ruffling Rick's hair. He looked like an underworld creature exposed to the light of day, squinting against the sudden brightness.

I'll never forget it, what Pax did then. He picked up the rubber ball that they used for training and poked it into Rick's left hand. Reflexively, Rick took it, and I could see the habit of squeezing a ball hadn't been amputated with his pitching arm. Pax stood back and barked as if to get Rick to throw the ball. Which he did, in an awkward throw, as if trying to rid himself of a nasty object. He threw the rubber ball right out the window and, to our amazement, the dog leaped out after it. In seconds, he was back in the house, ball in mouth and dancing on happy front feet, as if to say, *Do it again!* And Rick did.

"It would be easier on him if you went out in the backyard with him." Keller kept one hand on the back of Rick's chair. He'd come running at the sound of our excited voices, skidding into Rick's room as if he thought we were on fire. "He'd love it if you would."

The dog came pounding back into the room, nails skittering on the hardwood floor, ball clutched in his jaws, tail beating from side to side. He'd let himself in through the open breezeway door, open because we had hoped that we'd be wheeling Rick out of the house for his inaugural ride down the new ramp. Pax then took it in his head to tease Rick, to play a little game of keep away with him, making him reach for the ball, stretch a little.

"Gimme that, you mutt!" Why was it that the only time my husband seemed amused was with this dog?

Pax pranced around, shaking the ball like prey. His tail swept a metal washbasin off the bedside table, and the stainless steel clanged against the bare floor. In the next moment, he knocked the pile of magazines off as well, the *National Geographics* flopping to the floor like dead fish.

"I think he's telling you something, Rick." Keller grasped the handles on the back of Rick's chair and swung him around so that he could back him out of the room. Rick made a token protest, but Keller ignored it and kept going. "You'd better get outside with him before he wrecks this room any more."

And so we four rolled out of that sickroom and through the kitchen and out the newly widened door to slide Rick down the ramp Keller had built to give him access to the backyard. Pax led the way, the rubber ball firmly between his teeth.

I know now that Pax had been a hero during the war. I didn't know the story then; that would come later, as Keller and I became better acquainted. It was still too early to have begun asking those questions, questions about his service, about his experience. Keller's and Pax's, I mean. But that August afternoon, that dog became a bona fide hero in my eyes. He'd done what we hadn't been able to do, break Rick out of his self-imposed confinement.

Rick and the dog stayed outside until even Pax was exhausted from the game. Rick kept tossing the ball for him, and I sat on the back steps, watching. I might have cried a little. With every throw, it became more like a pitch. Slow underhand became an overhand toss, evolved to a slider, a curve. A sinker. No fastball, but I think that was more because our small yard wouldn't accommodate a long throw. As it was, Pax twice scaled the back fence to retrieve an inaccurate throw. With each pitch of his left arm, Rick's right stump rose in an echo.

Chapter Thirty-seven

Sometimes Rick wakes up in the night, or out of a diurnal doze, thinking that he's late for practice. It is so real, so immediate, that he imagines that his legs twitch and his right fingers are flexing. His heart beats, pumping blood through his veins as if he's been running bases. Then the fear of being late for practice—he's been late too many times; they'll fine him—transforms itself into the greater fear that his reality won't dissolve like a bad dream.

Francesca is so good to him, but even he can see that her patience is wearing thin. She wants him to accept his new dynamic and return to being the man she fell in love with. She's told him, whispered it into his good ear. "You're still the man I love. I fell in love with you for you, not because you're a ballplayer. That's like saying I only love you for your pitching. I'd have fallen in love with you even if you were a pipe fitter." She nuzzled him on the cheek, the wrong side, the side with the skin grafts, the side that feels invisible, as he has no feeling in it. "Whatever that is." She'd been in here an hour ago, coyly sitting on his lap, as if she might expect a response. He is loath to wrap the remains of his right arm around her in a quasi-hug. She kissed him, wanting something from him he cannot give. Rick wants desperately to desire his wife.

And the only thing he could say was, "I *was* a ballplayer. It was the only thing I ever wanted to be." He keeps beating the same dead horse. He knows it and there doesn't seem to be any way to prevent himself, to pretend that he's getting over it, to put on a brave face, to convince himself that he'll be fine. Instead, he's begun to snap at every suggestion that he accept this turn of events. He's a war hero, she says. Francesca doesn't know that, far from being a hero, he was simply a fool.

She slid off his lap and asked him what he might want for dinner, chicken or hamburgers. The minx replaced by the hausfrau.

It's nearly dark already. Francesca has replaced the blackout curtains with new white ones that allow the room to fill with daylight when Keller tilts the venetian blinds open every morning. Rick can watch the passage of time by the way the sunlight circles the perimeter of the room. Sometimes the metal blinds rattle in the late-afternoon breeze, chiming like a halyard on a flagpole and setting his teeth on edge. Rick can't maneuver his chair close enough to the window to close them, and he wants Keller to train the dog to pull the cord to raise them so that they stop clanging.

"Interesting idea, but you know that you can always ask me to do it. That's what I'm here for." Keller has finished bathing him and now carefully adjusts the pajama top so that the long right sleeve is pinned back and won't get tangled in the humiliating side rail of the bed. They're afraid that he'll roll out of bed like some little kid. You have to be able to flip yourself

184 • Susan Wilson

to roll out of a bed. You can't flip out if half of you is dead-weight.

"It would be nice not to have to depend on you. Or Francesca. Pax is so smart, and he likes working with me." The list of tasks that the dog can now perform to ease Rick's immobility has grown. He can now fetch a long list of items by name. It's as if he's memorizing vocabulary. He's conquered the "Get it/Put it series of commands, and when Rick is enduring the sharp phantom pains in his missing arm, Pax stands rock steady as he clings to the dog's nape. When the memory of pain eases, Pax licks Rick's nose, as if to say, *That's that, then.*

"Just try."

"Okay. Let me figure out how to do it. I'll come up with something."

Pax is sitting, watching, his golden-brown eyes following Keller's every movement; he's licking his lips in anticipation of the next thing that will happen—the nightly walk. Keller will disappear for an hour with the dog, and it is then that Rick feels most betrayed. Even if Francesca comes in with her knitting or mending and they turn on the radio to listen to the news or a broadcast from Symphony Hall, he doesn't relax until he hears the slam of the door and the dog comes back in to spend the rest of the evening with him. It isn't so much the fact that Keller gets to *walk* the dog; it's more that the dog is so happy to go with him. It's foolish to be jealous of Pax's attachment to Keller, but he is anyway. Pax was his dog, his rescued puppy, the boon companion of those happy, ignorant days before the war. Even before Francesca. How this dog can smile every time Keller reappears, really smile, a great happy canine chuckle coming out of his mouth, his eyes lit up, doing his puppyish happy dance, which once belonged only to him but is now being danced for this other man? Even if Keller has only been gone half an hour. What kind of experience forged this bond?

"What did you and Pax do, during the war, I mean?" Rick puts his hand out to stop Keller from sliding the chair to the bedside. "Scout, right?"

"Yeah. We were part of the advance team tasked with clearing out the enemy."

Rick slides his hand down the dog's side. Beneath his fingers he can feel a nub of scar tissue. "How did he get this?" It isn't so much a question as a demand. As if Keller failed somehow to protect the dog while Pax was in his care.

"He took a bullet. He was fine." Keller has his eyes on the dog, a liar's avoidance.

Rick takes a deep breath. "And what happened to you?"

"Are we trading war stories now?" Keller grabs the wheelchair and muscles it over to the bed. It's after ten o'clock, clearly past Rick's bedtime.

"Yeah. Don't you think it's about time?"

"Nothing like what happened to you. Is that what you want me to say?"

Rick feels a hot blush rise on the good side of his face, and he absently wonders if both sides of his cheeks turn red or whether the smooth, shiny new skin stays waxy. "I just want to know what happened to my dog."

"Our platoon came under fire."

"And he was out front?"

"We were. In the woods, pretty deep forest. We'd spread out; Pax and I were on point position, as always. He did his job. He alerted us, real quiet, real accurate, and we got down. The Krauts didn't know we had a dog, so they aimed high. We kept moving forward and, I don't know, all hell broke loose. I got hit. Keller drops a hand on the dog's head. "He defended me."

Rick hears the catch in Keller's voice. "Go on."

"Last thing I remembered was him giving it to some Kraut. A day later, I woke up in a field hospital, absolutely panic-stricken, wondering where he was. What had happened to my dog."

"My dog."

"Your dog." Keller takes his hand off Pax, aligns the chair, and removes the arm so he can lift Rick into the bed. "He's one lucky dog. He was all right. My buddy Sully got him tended to right away. If they passed out medals to dogs, he'd have gotten the Purple Heart."

"Did you?"

"Yeah. Would rather have gotten a promotion."

"He saved your life."

"He did." Keller settles the blankets, docks the wheelchair in the far corner, out of the way. "You want the light on for a while?"

"Leave it on. I may read."

Pax, as he does every night at this time, gets into the basket that they've put in Rick's room for him. He licks his nether parts, yawns, stands up, circles three times, and curls up. Rick knows that as soon as the dog senses he's asleep, he'll leave that cozy spot and search out Keller. Keller, whose life he saved.

Chapter Thirty-eight

Keller tries to be as considerate as he can be regarding Francesca and Rick's privacy. He doesn't eat supper with them unless asked. He takes his plate into his garage bedroom instead of eating alone at the kitchen table. He doesn't want them to feel like they have to invite him to join them in the tight confines of Rick's room, and if he's sitting in the next room, it's just too awkward for all of them. He's a third wheel, for sure, but he's not complaining. If Rick ever decides to come out of his room to eat, that may change. Three at a kitchen table is different. Still, he's aware that he needs to allow them husband and wife time, time when they can feel unobserved, uninhibited. That's another good reason to take long evening walks with Pax. Keller has signed up for an English class at Quincy College, so that will give them three afternoons a week without the presence of a star boarder in their house. Keller tries not to think about what kind of physical relationship Rick and Francesca may have. It's none of his business. Besides, they've been married a long time, so maybe it's not quite as important as it might have been. As important as it would be to him.

Betty Ann Carlin was his first. A quiet girl in his math class, completely unaware that she was very pretty behind those truly ugly spectacles. Clayton didn't hold with a social life, so he and Betty Ann said they were staying after for extra help and instead took long walks along the beach, finding themselves nestled into the concavity of low dunes. Maybe if there hadn't been a war, he'd have ended up marrying her; probably would have had to, the way they were going at it in the shelter of that cold sand. She never wrote to him, not even a Dear John.

Then there was the occasional war-destitute Italian girl willing to trade sexual favors for cigarettes and chocolate bars. Stateside, discharged and living with the Stantons, it's been a long time, and Keller is finding himself thinking all too often of sex. He's hoping that maybe he'll meet a nice coed willing to take a chance on an older man. At twenty-three, he's likely to be five years older than most of his incoming freshman classmates. Most of his fellow GIs will be attending the night classes, but with his odd little job, day classes make more sense. Rick needs him here at night to help him get ready for bed, to be available.

Sometimes it's hard to remember that Francesca isn't that much older than he is. Maybe it's part of being married to a man so much older; more likely, it's the life they have ended up with that has forced an early maturity on her—the weight of it.

Lately, he and Francesca have found a nice balance, no longer shy with each other, more relaxed and working smoothly together. He reaches for the dishes in the cupboard before she asks; she tosses him the can opener before he's got his hand on the dog food can. Once he has Rick settled for the night and she's been in to say good night to him, sometimes, not always, but some evenings when the weather is nice, they slip out onto the back stoop to share a lager and smoke a cigarette. They talk of other things besides Rick—light conversation about the news or the nosy neighbor who is perplexed by their living situation; whether Francesca should look into one of those freezer plans; if he should take an accounting course or test the collegiate waters with English literature. He's told her a bit about his past; she's talked about life in a small Iowa town and coming to the big city to find love.

Francesca taps at the open garage door. "I'm going to walk down to the market. Is there anything you need?" The weather has turned a bit cooler and she's wearing a sweater set he's never seen before. It fits so well that it makes him look away.

"How's Rick?" Keller closes his book, ready to do whatever might need doing.

"Fine. Pax is keeping him company. He said to tell you not to go in." She brushes a fleck from the front of her sweater.

Something about that little unconscious brushing stirs him. "Do you want me to go for you? Stay here and relax, put your feet up."

Francesca shakes her head no. "What, and read a French novel and eat bonbons?"

"If that's what you want to do, sure."

She taps a knuckle on the doorjamb. "Do you want to come?"

"I can carry the bags."

"And help me figure out what to have for dinner. I'm fresh out of ideas."

Keller has never eaten so well. Having gone from Depression-era make-do to institutional food to bachelor cooking and back to the institutional food of the army, he finds that home-cooked is something that amazes him pretty much every day, and when beef stew cycles back into the menu, he's as happy to see it as the very first time she made it. Roast chicken, pot roast, all manner of Iowa country-girl fare. And she seems to do it all effortlessly. Every single day.

"I tell you what. I'll cook tonight." Keller grabs his jacket. "The chowder I promised."

He is rewarded with her smile. A simple gift of a smile. The heady feeling of making Francesca happy travels through Keller's body. He's never made anyone happy before. He follows her out of the house, a silly grin on his face, and all he wants is to do it again.

"We should let Rick know we're both out of the house." The smile is gone. The weight that keeps Francesca grounded is recharged. The slight alleviation of that weight has evaporated in an instant. It is constant, this inelastic attachment of her responsibility to Rick.

"I'll go in and talk with him. If he needs me to, I'll stay. I can give you a list of what I'll need to make chowder." Magically, the smile comes back. He's taking a task off her shoulders and all he wants is to keep doing that.

Rick doesn't want him, waves him out of the room. Pax whines a little, knowing by Keller's body language that *outside* is going to happen. But he doesn't move from his place beside Rick. Keller unkindly thinks that it's because Rick has his hand on the dog's collar, but he knows that Pax won't leave Rick's side during the day unless one of them orders him to. It's uncanny, this attachment. On the day that he arrived here with Pax on the end of his official K-9 Corps leash, Keller would have bet the farm that Pax would have chosen him over Rick. Now he's not so sure. Francesca buckled on Pax's old civilian collar, and that old expression "A dog can't serve two masters" is proved wrong every day. Pax has figured out a way to do it. And it's been both challenging and fun to train him to be of use to Rick. The issue with the venetian blinds was fixed when Keller attached the rubber ball to the cord. Now all Pax has to do is grab the ball and pull. The blinds go up. A quick jab to the right and they lock in place. That was the hardest part of the exercise, and after a number of crash landings, he finally got it right.

"We won't be long."

"Take your time, Kel. Pax is here." Rick tugs gently on the dog's nape, and Pax seems to grin.

"Are you sure . . ."

"Keller, knock it off. I can be trusted to stay put and not get into trouble. My catheter is clear; my chair is positioned right; you've talked me into the radio, so I can listen to WBZ news. I've had lunch, dessert, and I can reach this week's *Life* magazine. Go out. Take Francesca and, for God's sake, forget the store. Take her to the picture show." Rick shifts his weight in the chair, half-lifting himself with his good left arm. "If the house catches fire, Pax will call it in."

Keller throws his hands up in the universal sign of surrender. "Okay, okay."

"And Keller. I mean it. She needs some fun. I know she doesn't have any girlfriends around here, so you're it. Show her some fun, and I don't mean just this afternoon."

"He's fine."

"What did he say?" She's put a hat on, a little lozenge of a thing that nestles among her curls. "Out with it."

"He'd like me to make sure you have some fun. More fun than going to the grocery store. Like seeing a film."

She doesn't say anything for a moment, then gathers her handbag and shakes her head. "He's being generous. He can't be left for that long."

Keller shuts the door behind them. "Francesca, he thinks we treat him like a baby. And you're what we called in the war 'collateral damage.' He knows that you are as trapped by that wheelchair as he is."

"I'm his wife. I want to be with him."

"He knows that. But, don't you see, maybe all this attention is overwhelming. Too much of a good thing."

Francesca spins around to face Keller. "A good thing? It's all we're ever going to have."

Keller shoves his hands into his jacket pockets. "I'm sorry. I've said too much. It's none of my business, except that he was adamant that I get you out of the house and show you some fun. That's all. You're all he has and he wants you to be happy." Keller doesn't offer his arm to Francesca; he keeps three feet away as they walk down the cracked sidewalk.

"That ship sailed, my friend. My happiness and his. All we can do now is take care of each other." Abruptly, Francesca turns around and goes back to the house. Keller is left standing on the sidewalk, his hands in his pockets, wishing that he'd kept his mouth shut.

Chapter Thirty-nine

Pax rests his chin on Rick's knees. He waits patiently until he senses Rick's heartbeat slowing down. Some days they go through this exercise eighteen times, except, of course, the dog has no sense of counting. He just knows that Rick's blood pressure is up and that the only way it will go down is if he stands or sits next to him, on his left side, as if aligning himself in a proper *heel*, and places his head in the man's lap. To an outside observer, it would look like simple human/dog affection. No human could possibly detect the curative effect that the dog has on the man. Rick cannot feel the weight of the dog's head in his lap, but he always knows when it's there, even if his eyes are squeezed shut and his good hand is wiping away the tears that threaten his dignity.

Nothing hurts; everything hurts. Pax always knows when this psychic pain occurs. He is instantly at the ready, and he will go so far as to drape his long front legs over Rick's dead ones and press his body against the man's chest until he gets the response he wants, the embrace of both arms. Hunching over, Rick will lay his cheek against Pax's skull, his breath tickling the dog's ears. Pax will stay motionless until Rick shucks off the spell of phantom pain and panic. Then he'll jump down from Rick's lap and grab a ball or a squeaky toy and transform himself from merciful spirit to mischievous sprite.

Eyes bright, he'll tease Rick with the object until Rick gives the order to put it in his lap. With the bedroom door fully open, Rick can throw the ball or the toy down the hall. Lately, he's managed to pitch it far enough that he bangs the front door. The big dog skitters down the hallway, rucking up the carpet runner into a roller coaster, catches the ball or the rubber mouse on the rebound, and runs back to Rick. It's his reward for doing his job. Pax has come to do his job very well.

Chapter Forty

We'd settled into a good routine, Rick and Keller and I. And Pax. Pax was a godsend. Keller did all the heavy work, and I was given the freedom to act like a normal housewife, planning meals and changing the curtains with the change of season. I think that Rick was showing improvement. During the late summer and early fall, we got him out into the backyard a few times, or I should say that Pax did. He'd tease with the rubber ball, poking it at Rick until Rick finally took it and tossed it. If Pax teased enough, Rick might allow us to get him outside and he'd throw the ball for the dog like he had on that first evening. But the weather turned colder and I didn't want to risk letting Rick go outside and sit. He was so delicate in so many ways. Prone to infections. Every day that went by when he didn't show symptoms of a bladder infection or a wound infection or a cold coming on was a good one.

Keller started school, testing the waters with a class in English literature. He had that book, the one about King Arthur that he'd kept on his nightstand as long as he'd been living with us, and it turned out that *Le Morte d'Arthur* was part of the syllabus for that class. I'd never read it, so, because he had a paperback edition from the college bookstore, Keller offered to lend his hardcover copy to me so that we could talk about it and help get him ready for the class discussion. The first thing I noticed was the inscription on the flyleaf: *To Keller Nicholson as he begins the journey of a lifetime.* Miss Jacobs. Keller was so closedmouthed about his past, whereas I found myself talking about mine, telling him about life in a small Iowa town, about my friends and what high jinks we used to get up to. Things like lighting May baskets filled with horse manure on fire and putting them on the front porch of the school principal's house, then running like mad, so we never actually got to see the look on her face. Picking all the new lilies in Mr. Bernardsen's garden and taking them home to appalled mothers. Keller had no such anecdotes, as if he'd passed through his early life, arriving fully formed on the shores of World War II. He chuckled at my exploits but never shared any of his own.

"So, who's Miss Jacobs?" I asked one day.

"My high school English teacher."

"You must have been pretty smart in school to earn this."

"I was. Smart enough."

It was like pulling teeth. "Was this a graduation present?"

"No. She gave it to me the day before I left for induction." He looked at me with what I'd come to recognize as his "Ask me no questions and I'll tell you no lies look, but not before I saw a flicker of memory soften his eyes. Whoever she was, Miss Jacobs meant something to Keller Nicholson.

Keller finally made that chowder that he promised. I took some in to Rick, knowing full well that the challenge of eating left-handed with a spoon was going to be hard. Keller, as usual, didn't join us for dinner. "Gotta study." A good new excuse for him to keep to himself, allowing us a privacy we didn't really need.

As dignified as Pax was, he was a terrible beggar and sat watching us, me on one side of the tray table, Rick on the other, the dog's eyes following every mouthful. "Go lie down." I wasn't usually the one to order the dog around, but that night I wanted no distraction for Rick. Pax gave me one of his "You've broken my heart" looks, but he went to his basket. I tied a tea towel around Rick's neck, set another one in his lap. He might not have been able to feel it, but hot chowder in his lap would have been very bad.

Rick didn't say anything, just stared into the shallow bowl filled with Keller's beautiful traditional New England clam chowder. Not thick. A thin cream broth with chunks of potato and clams. He'd bought the clams and shucked them himself, disdaining to buy minced clams.

"Try it." I took a mouthful. "It's really good."

"I can't. Give it to the dog."

"I will not." I set my spoon down and took his, dipping it into his bowl. "Here." I offered it to his mouth like a mother offers a spoonful of baby food to a child.

Like a child, he screwed up his mouth and turned away. "I'm not a baby. Stop treating me like one."

"Then pick up your own spoon and eat your dinner." I don't know why I got so mad then. It wasn't a particularly unusual refusal on Rick's part. It was just that Keller had made this chowder, made it because I said Rick liked it. Rick was being rude. I was glad that Keller wasn't in the room to hear him, but it would be hard to lie to Keller and tell him that Rick had gobbled it down. "Stop being a baby. You've got to learn to use your left hand sometime, and this chowder is worth it." I set his spoon beside his bowl, took up my own, and commenced eating the rest of my dinner.

Rick sat there, the soup spoon at a right angle to his full bowl. I'd inadvertently put it on the right side. I grabbed it and put it on the left side of the bowl, handle toward him.

"You don't have to hold it correctly. Remember that's what the occupational therapist said. Just grip it. Lean in, and eat this damned chowder."

Keeping my eyes on my own dinner, I didn't watch as he lifted the spoon left-handed, clubbing it in his hand like a little kid struggling with his manners. He dipped it, catching a little in the bowl of the spoon. Somewhere between the bowl and his mouth, the spoon tipped and the mouthful of chowder went right down the front of him. Slowly, Rick set the spoon down, pulled the tea towel from his neck, and placed it carefully over the still-full bowl. "I'm done."

Rick refused to try, so I gathered up those bowls, nesting my empty one beneath his full one. I grabbed the napkins and spoons and the waxed paper–sealed rectangle of pilot crackers and fled that room, my head roaring with the unspoken. Chowder slopped over the edges of the bowl, dotting my path from sickroom to kitchen. I didn't care. I stalked into the kitchen, the brightness glaring down from the ceiling light after the evening dimness of Rick's room. I was shaking, and that inner vibration of anger thrummed so intently that the chowder left in Rick's bowl trembled like a lake in an earthquake. A dollop crested the edge and ran down my wrist. It was cold, but I reacted as if I'd been scalded, and slammed the bowls from our wedding china hard into the porcelain sink, and I was glad at the destruction. Shards and chowder flew, spattering the window over the sink and the floor and the counters. One shard struck me on the cheek.

"Are you all right?" Keller was beside me, pulling me away from the sink. A towel dangled from the back of a chair, and he grabbed it, dabbing it gently against my cheek. "What happened? Did you slip?" He sat me down on that chair and knelt to examine me for more damage.

"He wouldn't eat it." I was crying, and the words came out in individual bursts.

"Oh, Francesca. Don't take it so hard." Keller turned my face toward his. "It's all right."

"No, it's not. Don't you see, Keller, he's just not trying."

Keller pulled me to my feet and, I don't know if it was instinct or impulse, but he held me in a hug. A hug is such a simple thing, and yet can mean so much . . . affection, sympathy, joy. I felt the length of his strong, healthy, complete body next to mine and gave in to the urge to lay my head against his chest. I hadn't been held by a man in such a long time except for Sid's cousinly embrace or my father's paternal one. This was both and neither. I look back now and imagine that he rocked me a little, but I'm not sure that he did. I put my arms around him and felt an equal contentment in the relaxation of his shoulders and back muscles. It would only hit me later, when I knew more of his story, that Keller had not had a hug himself in many a year. Maybe most of his life. I don't remember how long we stood like that, under the glare of the overhead light, chowder and china all over the place, maybe twenty seconds, maybe an hour. My arms around him, his around me. I could feel his breathing slow. In and out, in and out, until my agitated respiration finally matched his.

Finally, we did let go of each other, laughing a little in that embarrassed giggle of humans who have given into temptation, filing the moment away under things never to speak of. Keller got a mug out of the cupboard and filled it with chowder from the pot still warm on the stove. He buttered two pilot crackers and walked Rick's dinner down to him.

I should have thought of that. A mug. So simple an answer for a man not converting to left-handedness easily. If I had, that evening's meal would have been so ordinary. Things would not have been set in motion. Even now, I don't regret it. Even now, I remember how good it felt to be held.

Chapter Forty-one

They've gone out. After dinner, which Keller thoughtfully put in a mug so that he could handle chowder—which was really good; Francesca was right—Keller came back in and asked if he would be all right till ten o'clock or so, when they would be back from the picture show. "I will. Go. Have a great time and be sure to buy her a box of popcorn. She loves it."

Keller didn't respond, just made sure that anything he might need for the hour and a half that he would be alone was at hand. "Pax, you stay, keep Rick company." It was such an unnecessary command in Rick's opinion, and annoying. Like Pax would ever have to be *ordered* to stay with him.

It feels surprisingly good to be alone. Completely alone. Like the first time he was left home alone when he was nine years old and his mother had an altar guild meeting and his father was at work. A litany of "don'ts" and a list of "dos." He spent the afternoon poking around his parents' closet, looking for clues to their life before him. He found a shoe box of letters, but they were mushy and he didn't read them all; a pair of shoes from the last century, old-fashioned and surely too tiny for his mother's feet; a mink stole he didn't know his mother owned.

"Pax, get it." Rick points to the vial of morphine on his bedside table. Just sitting there, just out of reach. He's been asking for morphine every night and then palming the pill so that he can add it to his growing collection. The pain is real, and sometimes he retrieves the hidden pill because he can't sleep without it. Hide three, take one. It's a box step he's losing ground on. "Pax, get it." Rick has to repeat the order because the dog is unclear about the target. "Vial."

Cocking his head, Pax picks up the vial in his jaws as tenderly as a retriever picks up a duck. He brings it to Rick, placing it in his hand. "Good boy." Rick inserts the vial's screw top between his teeth, but Keller has it screwed on so tight that he's afraid he's going to chip a tooth. He then wedges the vial between his useless leg and the side of the chair, but the glass is slippery and turns with each twist, offering no purchase against the threads of the cap. There's a damp washcloth in the stainless-steel bowl he uses to wash up in the morning. "Pax, get it." Rick points to the cloth dangling over the edge of the bowl, and miraculously Pax cottons on to his meaning instantly, snagging the cloth in his teeth and carrying it over to Rick. Wrapped in the damp cloth, the bottle stays put and Rick finally gets the cap off. After all this, he extracts two tabs to make up for the effort. And he immediately drops them both on the floor.

The two little pills bounce twice and scatter like mice.

"Shit."

Pax cocks his head and then scratches vigorously at his side. He gets up and sniffs at the pills.

"Get it." Rick whispers the command, uncertain whether or not he really wants the dog to put morphine pills in his mouth.

Pax's sniffing pushes one of the pills into the middle of the floor, visible to anyone coming in the door. Rick maneuvers his wheelchair a little left. Maybe he can roll over the pill and crush it. It'll look like a little talcum powder carelessly spilled, instead of a clue revealing his exit strategy. The other pill has rolled under the bed; nothing to be done about that.

By now, he has squirreled away fifteen morphine pills. He really doesn't know how many it might take to, as Shakespeare once suggested, shuffle off this mortal coil, but he's guessing it's closer to twenty-five. Every one counts. Losing these two will set him back. In the quiet of the late afternoon, when he is just waking from a nap, before he needs Keller to come in and help him up, he sometimes hears the low rumble of two people in ordinary conversation. They talk back and forth, their words mostly indistinct. A little laughter. Rick tamps down the spurt of useless jealousy and makes himself be glad that Francesca has someone to make her laugh, even a little. He knows that he behaved abominably tonight. She's only trying to help him.

Francesca deserves so much more out of life than being chained to a man like him. She tries so hard. Kissing him. Putting her hands on him as if she expects the mere power of her touch will fool the demons and put life back into his desire. He's tried. The only unwounded thing left to him is his imagination, and when he pictures her as she came to him so often, seductive and beautiful and innocent and mercurial, nothing. Not even frustration. Dead to the world. The images that inflicted near-pubescent physical agony on him as a grown man are only images now. Pretty pictures. Not a eunuch. Not a gelding. Intact but impotent. Not a flutter. They had hoped, of course, that even insensate, he could still—what was the word the doctors used? *Perform*. Do his duty.

They should have tried harder, back when he was waiting

to go to war, tried to have a child then. How utterly egotistical and naïve they were to think that they had all the time in the world. That having his child and then losing him would have been a bad idea. Who could have ever predicted that, with him, she was saddled with both: a perpetual child, a helpless man.

"Pax, grab it." Rick holds out the knotted rope he now uses with Pax to move the chair around. Francesca jokes that they should get the dog a harness, like a sled dog would wear, and let him pull Rick down the street. Pax takes the knot in his mouth and helps Rick aim toward the renegade pill until the wheelchair tire hovers close to it. Rick hesitates. The loss of this addition to his collection is too dear, so he leans forward, stretches out his good arm. His own legs block his reach. Rick lifts his left leg over his right, clearing a path. In trying to reach it, his fingers accidentally move the pill just far enough that he can't pick it up and he can't move his chair any closer. "Pax. Good boy. I just need you to get it a little closer to me." Rick points to the pill but can't come up with a command that might make the dog actually push the pill closer. "Get it?"

It's as if the dog is contemplating what to do. Does he understand what Rick wants? He looks at Rick with those wise amber eyes, flooded now with the darker dilation of his pupils in the evening-dim room. He looks at the object, the target Rick aims his finger toward. There is a moment of stasis, of complete quiet, when even the street sounds fade into silence. Rick can hear his own breathing and the soft puzzled sound the dog is making. *What what what?*

"Get it."

Using the tiny teeth between his long wolfish incisors, Pax delicately lifts the tiny object up from the floor. His lips close over it and for a moment Rick panics. What if he swallows it? Would human-grade morphine kill a dog Pax's size? "Give it!"

Pax's dewlaps curl up in a comic mask of distaste as he drops the slightly wet ball of compounded morphine into Rick's open hand.

The slam of the front door startles Rick and he nearly loses the pill. Quickly, he hands the vial to Pax with the whispered command "Put it." The dog is his ally. The dog does what he needs, then helps Rick spin the chair back around, so that when Francesca appears in the bedroom doorway, he's right where she left him, Pax's head on his dead knees.

"How was the show?"

Chapter Forty-two

Pax doesn't like it when the three humans are in separate places. Some herd-dog instinct survives in him and he's only really happy when the three of them find themselves together. However, that isn't the usual dynamic, and the dog has had to content himself with dividing his time unequally. He knows that his primary function now is to stay with Rick. That's a role he loves and is proud to have. He delights in being able to carry out Rick's requests and it is his best task ever to absorb Rick's darkness into his fur. But he really likes it when he can pester Rick into going outside and throwing the ball for him like he used to. The ball doesn't go as far as it did long ago, when they'd play in the park and Pax might have to run half the length of the field to get the ball, but it is the only time Rick seems like the old Rick. If, in the old days, Pax might take the ball and run away, playing his version of keep away while Rick chased him, laughing and cursing, he knows better than that now and is willing to return the ball to Rick with dependable speed. Throw, catch, return, over and over, until Rick hands the ball to Francesca and Keller wheels him back into the house. Pax is never ready to quit the game, and he tries not to let his disappointment show. He trails along, hoping that maybe Keller will pick up the game later.

The good news is that Francesca and Keller seem willing to be in the same room together a lot more now. It's easier, not having to go from living room to garage all afternoon long while Francesca irons and Keller reads. Now they sit together, reading and talking, in the living room while Rick naps in his room. Pax settles on the braided rug and dozes, listening to their low voices. He doesn't understand one word, but the soft human vocalizations lull him. Francesca's voice has lost some of the tautness he'd grown used to hearing. Keller is using his voice more. They vocalize like crooning littermates, and Pax enjoys the sound of effortless companionship. He's one of them, Keller's sock-covered toes scratching at his belly, Francesca's fingertips finding the nirvana place at the base of his tail. *Good boy, Pax.* They smile over him, pleased with him. He's keeping everyone happy.

He *is* a good boy and life is sweet.

Chapter Forty-three

Keller chalks up that spontaneous hug to the emotion of the moment. She was upset, and he just wanted her to feel better. He tells himself that it wasn't any more significant than had Francesca been his sister. Or cousin. Except that he's never had a sister, or had any desire to touch either of his female cousins, who lodge in his memory as tormentors, not pals.

If it meant only a quick dash of human kindness, why are they assiduously avoiding physical contact now? If her hand bumps his in passing the salt, she apologizes. If he accidently grazes her with his arm as he is reaching for a screwdriver out of the utensil drawer, he backs away like he's been scalded. If it meant nothing, why does he think about it all the time? The feel of her cheek against his chest, the way she sank into him, as if climbing into a life raft. How good it felt to have his arms around another human being. It wakes him up at night.

After a warm early fall, the weather has turned more seasonable, and even with two extra army blankets over him and the dog's warmth, it's getting pretty hard to imagine staying in the garage bedroom much longer. At the very least, they'll have to start closing the connecting doors to keep the cold out of the house, and that will make it difficult to hear Rick if he needs Keller in the night, and Pax will have to chose one place or the other to sleep. They haven't talked about it yet, but they'll have to. Not counting the den, which has been made over into Rick's sickroom, the house has only two bedrooms, both on the second floor.

The thing is, Keller hates giving up the privacy, or the illusion of privacy, that the garage apartment offers. If he moves into the spare bedroom, there will be no separating himself from the Stantons. Even retreating to an upstairs bedroom to read or do homework won't give him the psychological break that going into his "apartment" lends.

But it's not just a loss of privacy that makes moving into the house an uncomfortable idea. After all, he's said good night to her any number of times and watched her mount the stairs to bed. Greeted her as she comes down in the morning, housecoat tied neatly around her waist but her curls tousled and her cheeks rosy like a child's. If she's slept well, he can see it in her clear eyes; equally, a restless night and he can read in the shadows beneath her eyes the thoughts that have kept her awake. Once, she greeted him exactly as she does Rick: "Good morning, sunshine." She blushed at her mistake, but throughout the day he kept smiling at having been so greeted.

Keller just can't imagine being across the landing from her all night long. It's just too intimate. It just doesn't seem—what's the word?—*proper* for him, as a single man, to be sleeping across the hall from his landlady. Sleeping, or not sleeping, a mere two yards apart.

Landlady. Keller laughs at his choice of word. What is she really? His boss? No. Rick's wife. He would be sleeping in close proximity to Rick's wife. What would the neighbors think?

"What do you say, Pax? Will the neighbors talk if they think I'm sleeping on the same floor as a married woman? Will you chaperone us?" Pax just shakes from nose to tail, stretches fore and aft, and utters nothing useful.

Maybe he'll go to the hardware store down on Hancock Street tomorrow and see if they have any space heaters he'd feel safe using. During the worst of the winter months, when the woodstove in the parlor was inadequate to the task, Clayton would haul out a cylindrical kerosene heater and fire it up. Keller remembers sleeping with one eye open on those nights, the noxious fumes of the burning kerosene leaving a bad taste on his tongue, and the fear of burning to death in the night.

It's easier to think of tomorrow's errands than it is his task of tonight. It's decidedly the oddest request that Rick has made of him, and he's still not certain how to handle it. Francesca kicked about it, too, but in the end Rick, as always, made a good case. It's their anniversary, the Stantons. And Rick wants Keller to take Francesca out to dinner and to the Totem Pole Ballroom out in Auburndale. "Be my surrogate."

Keller had to look the word up. *Surrogate*, meaning "replacement." A willing replacement.

"It's what I would be doing, and why should Francesca be denied a little fun just because I can't do it?"

"I don't dance." That seemed the most reasonable way to refuse. "I mean, not since they forced us to learn the box step in gym class."

"Francesca is a wonderful dancer; she'll help you out."

"Rick, don't do this." Francesca twisted a tea towel in her hands, and the smile on her face failed to suggest that she thought he was teasing, that Rick was having them on.

"Honey, come on. It'll be fun."

Keller put his oar in. "Rick, you take her. I'll drive you there. We can go early, get a good seat for you close to the floor."

"And do the jitterbug with her? No. I want her to dance and I want you to take her."

Rick keeps doing this, throwing them together, as if their eating at the Clam Shack or taking a walk or going to a picture show somehow *entertains* him.

"But, Rick, it's *our* anniversary. I want to spend it with you." Francesca had that tension in her voice again. The tension of not saying what she wants to.

Keller left the room; this was just too marital for him. Later, she came to him, smiling, shaking her head, as if Rick were a naughty little boy getting his way. "Have you ever been to the Totem Pole? We used to love to go. Good music. And, Kel, we don't have to dance if it makes you uncomfortable."

Keller wondered if she meant dancing in general, or just dancing with her might make him uncomfortable.

"Francesca, we can do whatever you'd like to do."

"I think I'd like to go." At once, Francesca looks young, girlish.

"Then we'll go." He points at her, smiles. "As long as you don't ask me to tango."

"You kids look beautiful." Rick shifts in his wheelchair. "Where's the corsage?" Keller hands him the box with the flower in it, ordered, exactly as Rick wanted—pink and blue chrysanthemums with a white ribbon. Rick gets the box open, but they all realize at the same time that there is no way he can pin it on his wife. Keller awkwardly fashions the arrangement to Francesca's dress. It flops and she unpins it, walks to the hallway mirror, and fixes it for herself. "They're beautiful.

Thank you." She doesn't look at either of them, so it's hard to tell whom she is thanking.

In order to make this less like a date and more like a night of bowling, they've had dinner already. Before he took his plate into his room, Keller got Rick out of his and to the dining room table, where he had put two place settings, a little bouquet of fall flowers in the center to mark the special occasion of their anniversary and Rick's grudging willingness to sit at the table. Rick insisted that he not be put to bed, that he'd be up waiting for them with Pax. He and Pax would listen to the live broadcast from the Totem Pole on the radio. He'd be fine, he insisted.

By the time Keller and Francesca arrive at Norumbega Park, the Totem Pole Ballroom is crowded and the dance floor swarming with people dancing to a small combo warming the crowd up for the next act. Black tuxedos and gowns in jewel-like colors blur and spin below them. Keller is dressed in his only pair of good trousers, black merino wool, his only dress shirt, and a tie borrowed from Rick. His jacket is borrowed, too. He's never owned a suit, never before felt the need, but here he stands with Francesca, in the dress that she made herself. She'd chosen the material well, with an eye toward what's fashionable, and she looks every bit as sophisticated as anyone else on that dance floor in the bell-shaped skirt and narrow belted waist of her blue-and-white dress. He offers his arm and they descend to find an empty seat.

"Can I get you something? A martini, maybe?" A martini sounds as sophisticated as she looks, he thinks.

Francesca tilts her head, nibbles her lower lip. He can see the thought process behind her eyes. Should she relax enough to say yes? Should they keep this as simply fulfilling a bizarre whim of Rick's? "Sure. Why not."

It takes nearly fifteen minutes to get through the pack lined up at the bar, and then he loses some of the expensive drink as he maneuvers his way through the crowd back to where Francesca waits, her gaze on the dancing couples, a smile on her face, as if she knows she needs to look like she's having a good time. But Keller recognizes that wan smile as one she so often wears when Rick has been difficult. "Here you go. What's the expression? Mud in your eye?" He wants to get that wan smile off her face and replace it with a genuine one.

"Something like that. I'm afraid I've never been one of the toast-giving crowd."

"Me, either. Seems like something they only do in the movies." Keller sips the martini, fishes out the olive, is uncertain if he's supposed to eat it, puts it back in, leaning the tiny sword that skewers it against the rim of the glass.

They watch the crowd in silence for a bit. It seems obvious to Keller that he should ask her to dance. They can't keep sitting here all evening drinking expensive drinks, ignoring the intent of being in such a place; it's not the sort of place where you go simply to sit and drink martinis. Rick is listening to the WNBC broadcast and will grill them later, want to know what music they danced to. "I have to live vicariously now. Do it for me." That's what he said as they went out the door.

Keller starts to speak, when Francesca sets her drink down and says. "So, tell me, how do you know so much about carpentry? You were a fisherman, right? Before the war?"

Maybe it's the unaccustomed martini, or maybe it's the music surrounding this conversation; maybe it's the fact that, in asking him about himself, Francesca has laid a hand on his arm, just above his wrist. Whatever it is, he is drawn into telling her the truth. "I went to reform school when I was nine. I learned carpentry there." He sits back, pulls his arm away, and waits for her reaction.

"Nine. Oh my, what could you have possibly done to get sent to reform school at that age?" She doesn't look at him with distaste, but curiosity, maybe even a skeptical amusement, as if she doesn't believe him.

"Truancy. Well, I decked a truant officer and the state took that as a sign of my delinquent nature."

"That seems very harsh."

"In a lot of ways, it was better than getting passed around from relative to relative who didn't want me. I got three squares a day and clothing that mostly fit. And a trade."

"But you were smart. I saw the inscription on your book that your teacher wrote. She thought a lot of you."

"Miss Jacobs? Yeah, she did. But that was when I was living with Clayton. He claimed me when I was sixteen. Put me to work."

They sit quietly, letting the old war tunes work a little nostalgia on them. Keller tosses back the rest of his martini. "Hey, we're here to dance, not reminisce."

Chapter Forty-four

The radio is tuned into WNBC's local affiliate. At nine o'clock, live music from the Totem Pole Ballroom begins. The announcer introduces the band, no one Rick has ever heard of, and the guest singer, also no one Rick has ever heard of. No Dinah Shore or Dorsey Brothers. But the music is nice and they play a lot of tunes he remembers from when he and Francesca thought a good night out on the town was when they went someplace and danced. For a little Iowa girl, Francesca knew how to do all the modern dances—jitterbug, Lindy hop, and even the East Coast swing. She was fun to sweep off the floor in his showboating exuberance, swinging her up feet-first toward the ceiling. Keller may take her out on the floor, maybe even now as the band plays a Duke Ellington song, but Rick doubts he'll have any of those moves. Too bad. Francesca deserves to have a great partner on the dance floor.

Pax stands up and shakes himself, shoves his nose beneath Rick's resting hand so that Rick can give him a good ear scratch. It's well past the point in the evening when Rick is put to bed, if only to lie there awake. Long hours in the chair, longer hours in the bed. The band finishes up "Cottontail" with a flourish, and the sound of applause fills the airwaves. The band leader introduces the next song, and a bouncy tune Rick doesn't recognize comes out of the boxy radio. His fingers begin to tap out the rhythm on the dog's skull, gentle six-eight taps, as if he's playing drums. Pax wags his tail and laughs his doggy laugh. Rick dances his fingers up and down the dog's long back and Pax motors his back leg as if he's being tickled. The music changes to a swing rhythm and Rick rocks from side to side, patting the new beat on his paralyzed knees. He can hear it but not feel the slap. He slaps his face on the bad side. A different sound than hitting terry-cloth-covered dead knees. Sharp and snappy. He slaps his good cheek and says, "Ouch!" He does it again. Pax has stopped laughing and watches, his eyes on Rick, his nose working and his ears, determined to comprehend Rick's behavior. He's making the sound of violence but laughing at the same time. Puzzled, but convinced there is no danger, Pax sits facing Rick.

"Let's dance, big boy." Rick thrusts the knotted rope toward Pax. Obligingly, the dog grasps the end and tugs left, in the direction Rick is looking. Then Rick quickly looks right and the dog tugs him right. The wheelchair swings left, then right, but not in time with the music. Pax can move him only a foot or so in either direction. It's more a slow waltz than dancing to the thumping beat of the high-energy trumpet solo being played now.

The plaintive first notes from a clarinet take the place of the energetic piece and a slow and sensuous music fills the room. Whatever it is, the key provokes a musical nostalgia in Rick. Every rising note reminds him that he is not listening to this music with his wife on their anniversary; he's playing with his dog and his wife is maybe dancing to this very sweet and sensual music with another man. Dancing in the very place where he got down on one knee, just like in the movies, and asked her, their acquaintance barely a week old, to marry him. And she said yes. He has cheated Francesca of the life she deserved.

Every descending third in the clarinet solo reminds him of how much he loves her. And how often he treats her like a servant, an annoyance. "Pax, why do I do that?"

Pax has let go of the rope. He has no answers.

The radio is on the built-in shelves that house the encyclopedias and the dictionary. The glow from the tubes casts a candlelike warmth into that dark corner. The music has grown too much to bear, but no one has taught the dog how to turn the radio off. Whenever the band takes a break, in that few seconds before the band leader or the announcer or whoever he is introduces the next song, Rick can hear the crowd noises—applause, laughter, the clink of stemware against stemware. People having fun. Francesca and Keller, having fun. It's what he wanted, to give her a good time. Is that her voice he hears, laughing like she used to in the days when the Totem Pole was *their* place? Touching him just so, so that he knew when it was time to leave; to go home and continue the dance. How soon would she suggest to Keller that they leave? How soon before her fingertips graze the back of his neck?

He has got to shut this radio off. It's enough to have made them go; it's suddenly too much to listen to it. He's like a blind man imagining a elephant.

"Pax, pull me." Rick tosses the end of the knotted rope out to the dog as if he's throwing himself a lifeline. "Pull." The dog is so astute to his gestures that Rick has only to look at the radio to get the dog to aim for it. The dog has to back up. If he were wearing a harness, he could pull Rick by moving forward, a more natural and effective method. But, as it is, the big dog literally has to back himself into a corner in order to get Rick where he wants to go. Which means that he can only get him within a foot of his objective, because the dog's own body is in the way. "Good boy." Pax slips out from the alley made between Rick's chair and the shelves. Rick can get himself close enough now; his good left hand is enough to propel the chair forward that much more. Except that the radio isn't on the lower shelf. It's placed on the third; no one took the time to move the books, instead just setting up the radio in the most convenient place. Keller drilled a hole in the shelves so that the cord, attached to an extension cord, runs down the back of the unit and disappears behind the closed doors of the built-in cupboard that makes up the base. Rick's fingers don't quite reach to the knob. No one has ever thought that Rick might want to shut the goddamned thing off. It's become such a habit, this leaving him out of things, making sure he wants for nothing and, by doing so, turning him into a hopeless invalid.

Rick stretches as far as he can reach. The music continues to taunt him, louder, livelier, sexier. She looked so beautiful tonight. Keller's hands on her as he struggled with the corsage. Shy or desirous? Rick pushes his chair back a foot. Examines the geometry of his helplessness. In therapy, they want him to get to the point where he can push himself up, be of more help to those helping him. Rick grips the armrest and pushes himself toward the radio; he lifts himself half a foot, maybe more, and then is struck with the truth. If he lifts himself with his only hand, he has nothing to shut the radio off with. He starts to laugh, a dry, hacking, chest-deep sound that brings Pax to his side. Even the dog knows that there is no humor in the sound he's making.

If he can grasp the cord, maybe he can jerk the plug out.

The band leader introduces the guest singer, and suddenly the room is filled with the throaty crooning of a woman lamenting her lost boyfriend. She's lost him to another. It's pure blues, and tears spring to Rick's eyes. "Pax, let's try something else." Together, they position him so that he can grab the latch on the cupboard door. It sticks a little, but he gets it open. Inside the cupboard, replacing the games and puzzles of previous tenants, are the medical supplies that he uses—tubing and sponges, basins and bandages.

Rick has to reach across his dead legs in order to feel around inside the cupboard for the cord. He thinks of them as ballast, that they'll hold him steady in the chair as he reaches. Because he can't move them, or feel them, he's perfectly assured that they will stay put. Because they don't move, he can't quite reach far enough into the deep cupboard to touch the cord plugged into the hidden wall outlet. He needs to get a little lower, a little closer. He pushes his chair backward and leans forward, but he's blocked by the length of his unfeeling thighs. The electric cord is a tantalizing inch from his reaching fingers. Rick tries moving his legs apart, lifting one, then the other and placing them against the sides of the chair, but the wheelchair is too narrow and the best he can do is a mere five or six inches of freeboard. Even with that, bent nearly in two, the solid roof of the cupboard obstructs his getting any closer. Rick bangs his head on the edge. It's hopeless; he's stuck here listening to the music that his wife and his *caretaker* are no doubt dancing to. Keller's hands on her waist, she's reaching up to place her left on his broad shoulder, her right hand—he pictures it bare, not gloved—in Keller's, palm to palm, fingers linking at some point in the dance.

The lament is wrung out to the last note and the song is

over. She wasn't betrayed; she's betrayed her lover. She's done him wrong.

Rick tries one more time, lunging past his dead legs and reaching deep into the cupboard. The next thing he knows, he's facedown on the floor; the wheelchair has catapulted backward, where it knocks into the tray table, upending it with the force of its empty trajectory. Everything on the table flies off; his water glass smashes on the bare floor, his magazines scatter, and his empty coffee cup rolls out into the hallway.

Pax is there, standing over him as if he's a fallen soldier on the field. The dog is upset, and keeps pawing at him. "I'm okay, Pax. I'm okay." The dog doesn't seem convinced. He barks, paces, comes back, and settles only when Rick touches him. "Francesca is going to kill me." Pax must agree, because he lies down beside Rick and heaves a great sigh. His normally upright ears are flattened side to side like immature puppy ears. "Maybe you can get me rolled over. Let's try. It's going to be embarrassing enough for them to find me like this, but at least I can be looking up." Rick runs Pax through his lexicon of commands to get the dog to fetch the knotted rope, then use his weight as leverage so that Rick can flip over. On his back, Rick looks right into the cupboard and, finally, reaches the plug.

Chapter Forty-five

If I had been reluctant, and maybe even a little mad, about going to the Totem Pole with Keller on my seventh anniversary instead of with my husband, that reluctance finally gave way to a relaxed enjoyment that I hadn't expected. I admit it, it was *fun*. It was fun to be in the company of a crowd of happy people, to have a drink or two. To dress up and feel pretty and desirable. To dance. Being there was a reminder of what I had rejected poor Buster for.

Keller wasn't the best dancer, and my shoes took a beating, but he improved as the night went on and we got over the shyness of two wallflowers on a forced date and let the music and the momentum carry us. An hour. That's all we stayed, a hour, maybe an hour and a half. Just long enough to have some fun, a laugh or two. An hour when our strange confederacy faded and a new dynamic emerged. Not employee and employer, or caretaker and the cared for, but a couple of friends out for a night on the town. We didn't speak of Rick, at least not after we started dancing. For this golden hour, we weren't two of three; we were just the two of us.

"We should go." I don't remember which one of us whispered this first. Between us, I think we said it twice or three times. And each time the band would launch into another terrific song and we stayed on the dance floor. My second martini grew warm on our table, untouched. We'd sat down between sets, Keller stealing the olive out of my glass, biting it off the sword-shaped pick with a smile.

To tell the truth, I was a little shocked at Keller's admission that he'd spent seven years in a reform school. Truancy. Hardly armed robbery, but still. If my initial reluctance to have him live with us had been based on nothing more than a primitive fear of strangers, this confession underscored how instincts are sometimes valid. It's a good thing he hadn't mentioned it at first, or I would never have let him into our house. But now I knew him. I saw every day how he had risen above such a rough beginning. My own growing up had been so effortless. Oh, sure, filled with bumps of childhood and the foibles of adolescence, but I was secure and educated and loved. Keller was not. The little I had gleaned about his early life had chilled me. After he'd been orphaned and passed around from relative to relative, reform school and the harsh life with his great-uncle might have turned him into a monster incapable of kindness. Here was this perfectly nice man, and the only affection he'd ever had was from the dog we all loved. In some way I understood that, although I don't think I had articulated it to myself at that point. All I knew was that I was glad he was there, that he was a gentle man who had somehow become a part of our lives. Part of our family.

"We got engaged here." I had finished my second drink and suddenly it felt necessary for Keller to understand why this place had significance; that it wasn't just Rick's whim that had sent us there.

"He told me."

"We barely knew each other, but I was sure he was the one."

"How did you know?"

How to answer that question? "I just knew."

Keller didn't say anything, and I wondered if he was thinking that I regretted my choice.

"I love him. He's not the same, and everything we planned on has been changed, but that doesn't change how I feel. I just wish I could convince him of that."

"He knows it." Keller gently took my two hands in his. "He knows it."

Those big hands holding mine were so warm, heated up by the warmth of the ballroom and the dancing, maybe the alcohol. I left mine in his and closed my eyes. "The thing is, sometimes I wonder." I couldn't finish the thought. I couldn't say it.

"Wonder what?"

"No. It's a terrible thing to say. I just sometimes wonder if it would have been better . . ." I trusted this man sitting there, but not with my worst thoughts.

"If he'd been killed, would it have been better? Is that what keeps you awake?"

It was, and Keller's saying it out loud shocked me. A tear leaked out, threatening to spoil my mascara. "No. Not exactly." I scrambled to deny it.

"Francesca, it's a natural thought. It doesn't mean anything." He handed me his folded handkerchief. "You'd be a saint for not thinking something like that now and again. And, as much as I admire you, I'm thinking you're probably not really a saint."

That made me laugh and gave me the knees to get up and go to the ladies' room to collect myself. Maybe I wasn't a saint, but I was beginning to think that Keller Nicholson was. No, certainly not a saint. A reform school angel sent to me.

Keller offered to fetch the car and pick me up at the door, but I refused. We'd been gone longer than I had wanted, and suddenly I was filled with a need to get home, to make sure that we hadn't misjudged. Despite what Rick had said about our staying out nice and late and having a good time, with the music reduced to a muffled pulse behind the heavy closed doors of the ballroom, I was gripped with a guilty sense of having called Rick's bluff. I grasped Keller's arm and, ignoring how sore my feet were in their trampled peep-toe heels, I pushed us both along to where the car was parked, Rick on both our minds, although we didn't say so. We didn't have to.

I knew that something was wrong the moment we pulled up in front of the house. Pax was barking, his deep and alarming bark, the one Keller said he'd used when cornering an enemy. The tone of it rose into a wolfish descant. Keller was out of the car and in the house before I could even open my car door.

"I'm okay. I'm okay." Rick was flat on his back, his head half in the open cupboard, his useless legs at an awkward angle, and yet he kept insisting that he was fine. It took a couple of tries, but between us, Keller and I got him up and into his bed. His nose was bleeding and a fresh bruise was ripening on his cheek.

Keller dashed into the kitchen for ice.

"What happened?" I was gathering the shards of the broken water glass. Shards once again. My life seemed as though it was forever breaking into bits.

"Did either of you realize that I can't shut the goddamned radio off?"

Rick was all right I mean, as much all right as he could be. I knew that the humiliation of being on the floor when we got home was injury enough. Keller got him ready for bed and I went in to say good night. It was our anniversary, and the best I got from my husband was a dry kiss. He pulled back when I cupped his head in my hand and pressed my lips on his. "I'm tired. Goodnight," he said.

I tamped down a little flare of anger. It had been *his* idea for us to leave him. His insistence that we have some fun. His assurance that he could be left alone without harm. And the first thing he did was blame us for his stupid action. The anger was snuffed almost before I had a chance to recognize it. We'd left the radio on for him, thinking that in some way it meant he could be a part of our evening. The evening that should have been his and mine, not mine and Keller's. It struck me then that all the time we'd been dancing to the ballroom orchestra, he'd been listening. I blushed a little, a guilty blush that somehow he might have seen how close I let Keller hold me. And how nice it had felt. Maybe that's why he'd been so determined to shut the radio off, so that the image of his wife happy in the arms of another man would shut off.

"Happy anniversary." I swung the sickroom door half-closed. Rick didn't answer.

Keller waited for me in the kitchen. Even though we'd had most of two martinis that evening, he held out a bottle of lager to me and popped the cap off another. Pax was conspicuously absent. I think he was upset about what had happened, too, and maybe thought in his doggy way that he needed to stay close to Rick that night. It was more likely that Rick wasn't asleep, and Pax never left his side until he was. So we didn't stay in the kitchen, afraid, I suppose, that somehow Rick would over-hear us. And even worrying about what we might say that would upset him, upset me. Nonetheless, we drifted into the garage. Keller offered me his rescued easy chair and leaned back against the workbench. We didn't speak, just took mouth-fuls of the beer, studied the labels, our fingers, the ceiling. My adrenaline-charged heart rate slowed with each sip and, along with it, the conflicting emotions of anger and self-inflicted guilt. I rested the bottle against my forehead and sighed. I didn't feel teary, just done in.

"He's fine. It wasn't our fault." Keller squatted in front of me.

"Is that what you think?"

"I'll fix it so he can control the radio."

"You think you can fix everything, don't you?"

Keller didn't say anything, just swallowed the last of his beer and stood up. He'd shucked the jacket and tie and stood there in his white shirt, the cuffs folded back, revealing sur-prisingly fine-boned wrists. It was late, almost eleven-thirty. My beer had gone warm and flat, and I really didn't want the rest of it. But I wasn't ready to call it a night. To get up and go now would leave the last thing I'd said to Keller hanging in the air. "I'm sorry. I don't mean it like it came out. You're a godsend."

"It's all right, Francesca. Everything is all right."

That's what Keller said, but it wasn't true. Nothing was all right, and I couldn't believe that it ever would be. I think that that evening was when I finally came to terms with what the rest of my life was going to look like. Rick wasn't going to im-prove beyond where he was. It was always going to be a deli-cate balance of helping him without humiliating him.

Rick wasn't alone in the extent of his injuries. Hundreds upon thousands of other soldiers had returned as damaged as he had—or even more so. But Rick's soul had been injured along with his limbs, and that was something no amount of physical therapy or a state-of-the-art prosthetic device could improve on.

"We should call it a night." Keller took my unfinished bottle of beer and offered his other hand to help me out of the chair. "Things always look better in the morning."

The warm touch of his hand made me realize how chilly I was there in the garage. "It's cold in here. You should think about moving into the house."

"Not yet."

Chapter Forty-six

The letter from Miss Jacobs is waiting for him when he gets home from class. Keller sees it propped up on the hall table, resting benignly against the empty china vase, which is the sole object on the table other than the car keys and, occasionally, a random dog toy. Pax comes out of Rick's room to greet Keller, ready for a break from his duties. Keller can hear Francesca's voice coming from the room and the sound of a spoon against china, so he knows he has a moment to take the dog out. The postmark suggests that the letter has been some time in reaching him, having followed him from the retraining center to here, and he thinks that he should have thought to write her to let her know that he's working and in college. She's going to be pleased with him.

Keller slides the letter into his pocket and snaps his fingers at Pax. "Let's go." They head out into a blustery November afternoon. Leaves skitter in front of them as they walk down the sidewalk. Pax becomes puppyish and chases them as if they're little animals scurrying away. A stepped layer of cloud bank hovers in the northeast, reminding Keller of when his days were forecast by the sky. These are merely clouds.

Keller doesn't think of the letter again until he takes his supper into his garage room. Even before he gets a first mouthful of ham, his dinner is cold. He should have started the space heater earlier, but he hates leaving it untended. It may be time to swallow his reluctance to move into the house. Keller sets the cold plate aside and pulls out the letter.

My dear Keller,

I know your uncle Clayton hasn't heard from you, so I am compelled to put my oar in. Your uncle is not well. In fact, I think you could say that he is failing. He's suffered from a cough for months now, and, typically, is refusing to see a doctor. I'm no physician, but I'd guess he has pneumonia. He's still working, but Stan at the fish market says that he brings in only a half bushel of quahogs or a penny's worth of bottom fish. What I'm trying to say here is that he needs you, Keller. I know things weren't good between you, but you're all he has.

Keller carefully folds the letter without reading the rest.

"Keller, come into the kitchen and let me give you a new plate." Francesca leans into his doorway, wraps her arms around herself against the chill, and shakes her head. "Don't be stubborn. We're finished and I'll be doing up the dishes. Come in where it's warm."

Keller nods, picks up his unfinished plate, leaving the folded letter on the ammo box. The breezeway is cold, too, so that the warmth from the kitchen touches his skin like a blanket as he comes into the house. Francesca takes his cold plate and hands him a new one. Macaroni and cheese, ham and canned peas. There is a pat of butter melting on the peas. He unbuttons the heavy woolen army-surplus sweater he wears in his room.

"Keller, you need to move into the house. I can't have you freezing to death out there."

Discomfort has overcome any reluctance, and Keller nods. "I guess maybe it's time."

"We'll have to move your stuff up there, because I don't have a bedroom set for that room. I've just dumped a lot of stuff in it that I haven't had time to put away properly. You wouldn't believe that we've been in this house for so long and I still haven't really moved in. I just don't know what fills my hours."

Keller catches the glint in her eye, and laughs, pleased to see her good humor return after a long absence—since the night Rick fell out of his chair. Sometimes it seems to him that no matter what Francesca does, Rick has no true appreciation. She goes into that room all smiles and comes out looking upset, looking like she's trying hard not to let him know that she is. It makes him crazy. Rick should be kissing the ground she walks on for the way she's always there for him, and he treats her like . . . Keller reins in his thoughts. It's none of his business. Married couples aren't always lovey-dovey. He sure knows that from observing his aunts and their spouses and how they snapped and snarled at each other and called it marriage. Rick snaps, but he has every right to. Not at Francesca, but at his situation. Keller has to keep reminding himself of that. Over and over.

He has to remind himself that he has no idea what a marriage really looks like.

He's been upstairs now for more than a week. Empty, the bureau wasn't heavy, and Keller and Francesca managed to get it up the stairs with only one misstep. His army cot was easy enough for him to wrangle by himself. Francesca carried up one armload of clothing; he carried up another. The room is too small to afford him a sitting area, but he has commandeered a small table to use as a desk.

That first night, he lay awake, listening to the sounds of the house, listening to the creak of the floorboards as Francesca walked to her closet, to the click of her lamp being shut off. The pipes banged a little as the furnace kicked on. He'd left his door ajar, just enough that Pax could push his way into the small bedroom and climb in with him. Because the door stays open, he can hear it when Francesca leaves her bed to go downstairs to the bathroom in the middle of the night, and he lies there, half-dozing until he hears her return. Within a few nights, he's gotten used to being up here, accustomed to the sound of another warm, breathing person within calling distance.

Chapter Forty-seven

Pax approves of Keller's new sleeping situation. It is so much easier to keep track of all the inhabitants of the house when two of them are nearly side by side and the third just below them. He can sit at the top of the stairs and hear everything that is going on in the house. So Pax hears Keller's restless shifting on the army cot. He hears the sleepless sighs of Francesca and his acute ears pick up the barely audible sound of Rick's dry eyes blinking. Outside, the late-fall wind scurries the leaves against the rough surface of the sidewalk and moans through the naked branches of the oak tree in the front yard. Sometimes his hackles rise at these sounds, a purely involuntary response to the domestic unrest.

Eventually, they all sleep and he is free to climb in with Keller. But first Pax checks in with Rick, testing the air for any distress. Then Pax stands for a moment just outside of Francesca's firmly shut bedroom door. He never scratches for admittance, simply makes sure that the noises from within are those of a sleeping human. Satisfied, Pax pushes the other bedroom door open and noses Keller into moving over. Keller reaches for the dog in his sleep, spooning him like they once did in bombed-out cellars and foxholes. The dog heaves a sigh. Things are not quite as they had been. The routines are the same, his duties the same. But there is an undercurrent that the dog feels deep in his bones; like the scent of winter in the air, the season in this house is changing.

Chapter Forty-eight

They're going to make him leave his room for dinner. Rick is trying hard to not make a big fuss about it. After all, it is Thanksgiving, and the smells coming from the kitchen are a visceral reminder of much happier days. Francesca's cousin Sid and his rather snooty wife, Clarissa, are coming. Keller will make it an odd number at the table. Rick has sussed him out on whether the man *wants* to spend a national holiday "on the job," but Keller assured Rick that he'll be there to help. It was a bit awkward, but it had to be asked. "You'll eat with them, of course, won't you?" Rick knew that Keller usually ate by himself in his garage room. Now that he's moved upstairs to sleep, Rick really doesn't know where Keller is eating, just that he still keeps out of this room at dinnertime, leaving Francesca and him alone. As if they have something important to say to one another. As if they needed marital privacy.

"I'll eat with you." And then, as if what he just said might be misunderstood as giving Rick a free pass to stay in his room, Keller added, "In the dining room."

Keller is a good carpenter and the widening of the door into the dining room looks like it has always been a wheelchair-wide archway. The landlord will have no complaints that their tenancy ruined his property.

Sid Crawford comments on the changes as soon as he and his heavily pregnant wife come in the front door. "You know, you ought to see if the landlord would be interested in selling the place to you. I mean, with the GI Bill and all, you can get a low-cost mortgage and do whatever you want to the place."

"I don't think we've ever considered making this a permanent home," Francesca calls from the kitchen, showing off her powers of carrying on two conversations at the same time. "I think we want something bigger, don't you, Rick?" She's clearly thrilled to have him out of his room; with every sentence she speaks, she bounces her thoughts over to him, as if he is some guest needing inclusion in the conversation, not a man fully capable of putting in his two cents.

"We've really never talked about it. We're fine as we are." Rick sips from the glass of eggnog in his left hand. Francesca has been liberal with the rum.

"For now, maybe. But you have to admit it's a bit tight." Francesca is like a jack-in-the-box, popping her head out from the kitchen and then ducking back in. Or a turtle. Clarissa is in there with her, stirring or peeling something. She greeted Rick with a quick hello and shrugged off her mink into Keller's hands, as if he were a butler, then disappeared into the kitchen. Rick thinks the sight of him bothers her. Frankly, the sight of her bothers him, but he can't quite admit to himself that it's because she's expecting. If things had been different, that might have been Francesca, twice over. Unfair, uncalled for, and stupid, but that's the thought that teases in the back of his mind. How can Francesca stand to be around her?

It is a bit tight with four upright adults and a man in a wheelchair, plus a big dog hovering around, hoping that someone will forget that he's not allowed to be fed from the table. Already he's vacuumed up the spillage inevitable in the preparation of enough food for a platoon. Rick suddenly feels a strange wistfulness about the Thanksgivings he and his platoon endured. A can of C rations and a round of personal memories of Thanksgiving coming from the war-weary company. Not close enough to a USO station to get the better meal; and yet, those little stories of mom's fiasco with a pumpkin pie or dad's mishap with a carving knife, of the world's best stuffing and the biggest turkey in the land were as much a true Thanksgiving as any he'd ever had.

Keller is quiet; maybe he's thinking of his Thanksgivings past.

They've given Rick the head of the table. Tradition, or is it because that's the best place for his chair? Keller asked him earlier if he thought he might want to sit in a regular chair. The dining room chair with the arms is the one they call the 'captain's' chair, and, presumably, he might not fall out of that one, but the shift from wheelchair to dining room chair would be ugly, so Rick shook his head no. If Clarissa is discomforted by the sight of a man like him in a wheelchair, she'd be more uncomfortable watching the process of moving him from one place to another.

Francesca sits at the opposite end, the kitchen end. Keller, useful, to his right; Clarissa to his left, and Sid beside Clarissa, next to Francesca. Pax is remanded to a corner, but that doesn't stop him from watching everyone with the avidity of a hungry wolf. Francesca has outdone herself. The table looks wonderful, all their wedding china trotted out for the occasion, pieces he's never actually seen in use. New tablecloth, new napkins. Candles. In the bright sunlight of a pristine November day, they flicker pale and unnecessary but cheerful. The turkey is delivered ceremoniously and they fold their hands as they were taught to do in Sunday school for grace. Rick simply fists his existing hand and stares at it. No one says anything for a moment, and Rick suddenly realizes that they are waiting for him, as host, to intone the prayer. "For what we are about to receive may we be grateful." The gathering choruses a ready amen and the serving bowls begin to fly.

Like the master of the house, Keller removes the blessed bird and takes it back into the kitchen to carve it. Rick tries not to let the bitter reminder of his disability spoil this day. It would have been worse to have Sid do the honors. At least Keller doesn't act out of pity, but utility. Keller returns with two platters. One has whole slices of white and dark. One has small pieces of cut-up turkey. This one, he puts next to Rick's left hand.

The conversation wends its way around the topics of their Iowa family and friends, the rate of inflation, and the latest headlines. Keller is politely asked about his college class; Clarissa talks at length about her layette for the baby due next month, oblivious to Francesca's sudden disappearance into the kitchen on some trumped-up desire for more cranberry sauce.

Sid wants to buy a new car and is thinking of getting a Studebaker. What does Rick think of them?

"I always liked their line of personnel carriers." Rick has a dainty arrangement of meat and mashed potato firmly on the tines of his fork. Somehow he's managed to do it without thinking about it.

"Well, I'm thinking of something a little more, um, family-size."

"The Starlight?" Keller hasn't offered much until the subject of cars came up.

"I think so. I like the styling of the trunk. Lots of room for luggage."

"Sid thinks that we should drive out to Iowa for Christmas, but I think that it'll be too hard with a new baby." Clarissa rests her hand demonstratively on her belly.

"Babies are good travelers; after all, don't they sleep all the time."

"Sid, my darling cousin, I don't think you have any idea what babies do." Francesca gets up from the table to replenish the squash bowl. Keller follows her, empty platter in hand.

Rick gathers another forkful, but not quite as neatly, and the clump falls back to his plate.

"So, Rick, giving any thought to getting a new hand?"

"I'm sorry, what?"

"You know, a hook. A guy in my building has one. Uses it like a tool."

"Sid, we haven't thought about such things." Francesca is in the room, half-full squash bowl in her hand. "We're not ready."

"It's okay, Fran. No, Sid, no one has suggested that a *replacement* is an option." Rick sets his fork down carefully.

"I'm sorry. I shouldn't have said anything. I was just asking." Sid reaches for another dinner roll. "Just thought you might be thinking about it, that it might help to get you back on your feet."

"If you haven't noticed, a hook won't do that for me. Or, do you mean getting back into the ball game? I don't think a hook will help me do that, either." He's gobsmacked, more shocked than furious. Sid speaks of things he knows nothing about. If he thinks that Rick's life will ever go back to *normal* just because he's got a hook attached to the stump of his pitching arm, he's nuts.

"Mr. Stanton's wound isn't properly healed. A prosthesis isn't possible right now." Keller sets the turkey platter down in front of Sid. "When it is, I'm sure he'll be open to the idea."

"Keller, that's not your business, either." Rick pushes himself away from the table with his good hand. "I'm feeling a little tired. Would you please take me back to my room."

"Actually, I won't. There's a mince pie coming in here with your name on it." Keller's smile is supposed to make the whole exchange look like a comedy routine. Rick is left pushed away from the table, and he has to get himself back close enough to enjoy that pie.

Sid and Clarissa hung on long enough to finish their dessert before Clarissa claimed weariness and they left. Sid clapped Rick on the shoulder on the way out. "It will get better." In the interest of family harmony, Rick allowed that as a clichéd and weak apology for Sid's ignorance. "I know. Time."

"Well, that went well." Francesca leans against the closed front door and rolls her eyes heavenward.

Rick reaches out with his good hand and takes hers. "Yes, it did. It was terrific."

She smiles down on him, squeezes his fingers, and then heads into the dining room to repair the damage.

Rick digs deep in the little pouch they keep attached to his wheelchair for his pens and pencils and crossword puzzle books. Amazingly, he's adapted to left-handed writing fairly well. His fingers find the twenty little white pills in his collection, hidden in that handy little pouch.

Chapter Forty-nine

Sid's incredibly insensitive remark about the "hook" really fried me. Sid was always one of those guys who speaks first and thinks second. For such a smart guy, he could really put his foot in it. At the same time, he was right. We were taking Rick's recovery at his pace. Why wouldn't Sid think that Rick was ready for the next phase of his recovery? I hadn't confided in Sid that Rick wasn't making much progress, partly because I think that I really didn't see it that way. Nowadays, they call it "enabling." Back then, we were just trying our best. I was trying hard to focus on small improvements, and getting Rick into the dining room for Thanksgiving was a big one. And into the parlor for Christmas was the best present I got that year.

Our house was so tiny that Pax very nearly took the tree down with his tail twice. Rick's parents had come for the Christmas holiday, and because I couldn't offer them a bed, they ended up driving from Connecticut and back in the same day. Maybe we did need to think about a bigger place, a place of our own. This was a stopgap measure, and even with Keller's improvements, it was inadequate for the long term. What was scary was that I had no idea how we would pay for it, GI Bill or no. Even with Rick's benefits, we were just scraping by. I needed to go to work, or Rick needed to get better enough so that he could. It might not be baseball, but he had a degree in accounting, and you didn't need two arms and functioning legs for that. But you did need to leave your bedroom. You did need to feel good. The other alternative: go back to Iowa.

The suggestion had come from my father during his Christmas phone call. "We miss you; I wish that you could be here. Why don't you think about coming home?"

"We need the VA here, Dad."

"We have hospitals. We could set you two up on the first floor of the house."

I promised to think about it and hung up. Rick was already back in his room; Keller was doing the dishes. Pax came out of Rick's room and nuzzled me until I got up from the little chair beside the telephone. "What do you want, Paxy?"

He pushed his big head against my waist. I swear he had overheard my conversation and was offering me a hug. "What do you think? Want to go to Mount Joy?" I rested my cheek against his skull.

I leaned against the doorjamb and looked into the kitchen, where Keller was busy scrubbing the roasting pan. His back was to me, but I knew he could see my reflection in the window over the sink, because he raised one sudsy hand and waved. What would Keller do if we moved to Iowa? Would Keller even consider such a move? It would put back on the table the thing that we had, with our arrangement, taken off: whom Pax most belonged to.

"Need some help?" I asked.

"You've done the brunt of it today. Why don't you go relax?"

He flipped a dish towel over his shoulder and reached for the next pan. "Or take Pax out for a walk around the block. He's been in most of the day."

"I'll wait for you to be done. We can both take him." Rick wouldn't miss us, not for the fifteen minutes it would take to speed around the block in the cold. I went in and checked before we bundled up. My husband was sitting up in bed, a novel propped against the table over his bed, but his eyes were closed. I lifted the book, carefully sliding in the bookmark, and rolled the table aside. How could I ever have thought that he might one day be able to hold down a job when a day sitting up in his wheelchair knocked him out?

With the winter solstice past, there was a discernible light left in the sky as we walked out of the house. Pax was off leash, and he led us down the deserted street. Christmas tree lights sparkled in the front windows of every house we passed. Above our heads, a single star appeared, and Keller pointed it out.

"Star light, star bright . . ." I began the childhood rhyme, expecting Keller to join in. He didn't, and it was another reminder of the hard life he'd had as a kid. He didn't know about wishing on a star till I told him about it.

"Looks like I've been missing a lot of wishing opportunities."

"Guess you'd better make up for it now, before another star appears."

I was a little ahead of him, a footstep or so. The end of the block was a stone's throw away. I felt his hand in its thick glove touch my shoulder, and I paused. Pax, always aware of us, also paused, sniffed, decided all was well, and forged on ahead.

"Are you supposed to say your wish out loud?" Keller asked.

I was facing him now; the lingering light had gone and it was full dark, but the streetlight cast our shadows behind us. "No. Never. A wish spoken out loud will never come true."

"I see. Well then, I won't say it." It was the strangest thing, how he closed his eyes and held his breath as if he wasn't wishing, but praying. Then he opened his eyes and laughed out loud. "Okay. How long does it take? For a wish to come true?"

"Keller, it's just a silly tradition. I swear you're falling for it." I gave him a playful shove with both hands on his chest.

"I am. Falling." As if to neutralize his oddly plaintive remark, Keller grabbed me, playfully wrapping his arms around me and rocking me from side to side, as if he was going to toss me in a snowbank. I laughed and struggled to get loose. My younger brother, Kenny, might have finished the job, landing me in a snowbank and then rubbing my face in it for good measure. Keller just suddenly let me go and called Pax back to his side.

We walked back to the house, laughing like little kids, with Pax romping up and down the snow heaped along the edge of the sidewalk.

Chapter Fifty

Another letter from Miss Jacobs, and Keller knows that it won't bear good news. Good news will keep and bad news won't go away, so he leaves the unopened envelope in his back pocket, until he forgets that it's there. There is so much else to think about. Rick is running a low temperature. Just low enough that they decide to wait and see if he comes down with a cold, or if it will eventually rise high enough that the question of a new infection will come into play. There has been so much activity, so many people in the house, that Keller is fairly comfortable with the idea that Rick is just run down a little and open to the common cold—given his rather isolated existence, he has no resistance—and not something more sinister like a bladder infection.

"Just under one hundred. Let's see if we can knock it back with an aspirin." Keller tips a couple of Bayer into his hand and hands them to Rick.

"Where's Francesca?" Rick has that bleary look of someone who has just awakened from an unscheduled nap.

"You remember. She's off to Sid and Clarissa's to see the baby. They got back last night from their trip to Iowa."

"Right. What did they call it?"

"I don't know. I think it's a girl."

"Sid's probably a little disappointed."

"Why?" Keller hands Rick a glass of water freshly poured from the pitcher on his table.

"Not a boy. Doesn't every man want a boy?"

"I guess so. Never thought about it. Is that what you would want?"

Rick hands the glass back to Keller. "No. It wouldn't have mattered to me. Although I suppose I did imagine having a son. Someone I could teach to play ball."

Wouldn't have. Keller hears the past tense. "I played some in school. We had one teacher there who was a pretty good coach. Of course, they collected all the bats and counted them before we left the diamond."

"Were you any good?"

Keller straightens the sheet over Rick. "I could hit if the ball was thrown right at me. But we had one kid, big ugly guy, he could hit. Couldn't run worth a damn, but man he'd pound those balls right over the fence." Ralph Patterson. He hasn't thought of the man-size boy in a long time. School bully. Far and away too old to still be in reform school.

Keller is finished in Rick's room, but he wants to keep the subject of baseball going, to press on and see how long it takes Rick to close down. "The Little League team here in town had a pretty good season. Bet they'd love some attention from a former pro. You know that their field is at the end of the street."

At first, Rick doesn't say anything, and Keller figures he's pushed a little too far. "I don't think so. You don't learn anything from a fool."

"What?"

"A fool. A man who believes that he can strike out the enemy with a live grenade."

"You do remember, don't you?"

"Oh, I remember. Francesca doesn't think I do, but I do. Not everything, of course, but I have a very clear recollection of my colossal error. Hubris. Do you know that word?"

"Yes."

"We didn't have the advantage of a dog like Pax. So my squad was surprised by a machine-gun nest. Pinned us down on the edge of a cliff. They were above us, and we were sitting ducks, as they say. From our angle, we couldn't get a bead on them." Rick's fingers are flexing, catching the blanket, releasing it in an unconscious gesture.

Keller keeps still, as if he's afraid he'll spook Rick out of telling his story.

"I got the bright idea I could pitch a grenade up high enough that it would land in the middle of the nest. Absolutely confident in my right arm. High and fast. Really high. Almost ninety degrees high. Like standing at the pitcher's mound and hoping to hit the moon straight up." Rick pauses, gathers his words, and Keller understands that this is the first time Rick has ever told this story. It's like he's tasting it, feeling the words for how painful they might be. In a moment, he continues. "They told me I couldn't. I'd have to expose myself, and there was no way I could do that without standing straight up. I had a grenade in my hand. I remember juggling it in my fingertips, as if I were looking for the seam, like you do with a baseball. I figured I could find the right position, that sucker would sail. Knuckleball? Sidearm? I wasn't top at either of those, but I had a killer curve, and that's what I was going to throw. Literally pitching for our lives."

Pax utters a soft whine. He's left his basket and is standing between Keller and Rick. Pax has his eyes on Rick and he drops a big paw on Rick's blanket-covered leg. Keller reaches out to touch the dog but pulls back.

"I juggled that grenade, adjusted my grip. What I failed to realize, or take into account, was the fact that a true pitch requires the whole body. I was betting our lives on my arm. An arm is only as strong and accurate as the kick. Up against the rock wall, on that narrow ledge, I didn't have room to kick. I pulled the pin and threw the grenade as hard as I could. Gravity is a bitch. Fucking thing came right back down and I stood there like an outfielder, ready to catch it."

"Holy shit. You caught it?"

"I did."

Keller slips his hand into his pants pocket and feels the edge of the envelope and, not for the first time, he wonders if, had that first letter from Miss Jacobs reached him at the retraining center, would it have changed things? Despite his adamant promise to himself that he would never return to Clayton Britt's house, would he have gone if he'd known about Clayton's illness? Was there in him, postwar and undirected, a vestigial decency? After all, he'd had no other place to go at the time. No. It wouldn't have been an act of compassion for Clayton. If Keller had thought for a moment about it, it would have seemed like an answer to his desire to keep Pax. He might have left the retraining center with Pax in his car and disappeared north, not doing the right thing in bringing Pax here, never meeting Rick. Never knowing Francesca. Keller simply can't imagine not being here. It's as if his whole life has condensed down to this small house. Far from feeling trapped, he revels in the freedom. For the first time in his life, he is safe, well fed, and as close as he's ever come to living with a family. A real family.

Miss Jacobs was right: She was sticking her oar in. What does she know about it, about the way Clayton used him? What does he owe Clayton anyway? Why should he owe him anything? Didn't he pay for Clayton's guardianship in hard work? Clayton was a stage in his life, that's all. Something he's overcome. If Clayton hadn't claimed him, he might have ended up like Ralph. Unwanted, a man in a reform school.

The people he owes allegiance to are right here. This man needs him, and so does she. And he needs them. Keller never felt connected to Clayton, not like he does with these folks. It sends a little shock wave down his spine, this realization that he has never been happy before.

"Do you want me to find the latest *Life*? I think I left it upstairs," he says to Rick now.

"No. I'm just going to take a little nap."

"Again?"

"I'm just so tired." Rick does look tired, more gray than pale, dark circles beneath his eyes, and his skin looks rough and aged. He looks like an old man. This story has been hard to tell, and hard to hear. So many men died because of mistakes. Blown off the edge of the cliff, Rick may have lost his pitching arm and broken his spine, but he also lost his entire squad. Keller gets it now, Rick's despondency. His darkness.

Pax noses Rick's hand, which is draped over the side of the bed. Keller watches Rick's fingers find the dog's comfort spot, just the inside of his ear. Pax closes his eyes in ecstasy as Rick rubs the little whorl. Pax reaches with one paw and draws Rick's hand to his mouth and licks it with a gentle tongue.

"Hey, Keller?"

"Yeah?"

"Don't say anything to Francesca. Please."

"I won't."

Miss Jacobs's second letter can contain no good news, and Keller is pretty certain he knows what's in it. He hasn't written her back after her first letter, where she told him about Clayton's illness. He doesn't know how to say that he cannot, will not, go back to Hawke's Cove and take care of the old man. He just can't. Especially now. He has two other people to care for.

Dear Keller,

I wish that I had heard from you before I had to send this letter, but I haven't, so I don't know if you will be shocked to hear that your uncle passed away last night. He was stubborn to the end and wouldn't go to the hospital. But he wasn't alone. I was with him. You probably don't know that Clayton and I go back a long way. Or maybe you just never imagined that the schoolmarm and the fisherman might once have been young.

The funeral is Saturday. I hope that you'll attend. You were his only living family, Keller. He wasn't an easy man, God forgive me for speaking ill of the dead, but I am certain that he loved you.

Saturday. Tomorrow.

Out of the question. Rick isn't well, and there is no way Keller is going to leave him to Francesca. It's a four- or five-hour drive or a long train ride. He can't be gone all day. Anything might happen.

I am certain that he loved you.

Chapter Fifty-one

Pax didn't like it, not one little bit. Keller had gone away. It was different from the usual gone away, which generally meant that he was to keep guard over Rick until Keller came back. This time, Keller carried things that belonged to him out of the house. This was not good. Pax whined and paced from sickroom to front door, literally putting himself between Keller and the outside, as if Keller was about to step off a cliff.

"It's okay boy. I'll be back later." Keller ruffled up the dog's fur and thumped him on the ribs, but that didn't make Pax feel any more secure about this strange turn of events. Francesca patted Keller on the shoulder like she sometimes did him, but Pax didn't see praise in the touch, more like the way a mother dog pushes a pup away from the teat.

"We'll be fine, Kel. Don't worry about us. You need to be there."

Pax didn't understand Francesca's words, only that she was exuding a fear scent even as she was making those sounds that the humans communicated with. His comprehension of their vocabulary was much better than their understanding of his vocabulary, but he still didn't quite get what was going on.

"I'll be back in the door by nine tomorrow morning at the latest. Anything happens, you call Sid. Okay, promise me?"

The pair stared at each other, standing so close, Pax couldn't hope to fit between them. Francesca made that gesture of placing her lips against Keller's cheek. It wasn't quite like the submissive gesture of a supplicant to a pack leader, chop licking; and not quite charged enough to be a sexual overture, but there was a radiant warmth that exuded instantly from both of them that made him study their faces for a clue as to what it meant.

Keller squatted in front of him, stared Pax in the eye like the leader he was. "Watch out for them." These words, the dog understood.

From Rick's room came the nearly inaudible sound of a man's fingers brushing against the bedsheet. Pax knew even before the humans could detect it that Rick was warm. Not the warm of comfort, but the warm of illness. He could smell it on him, this illness. A faint but growing trace of infection deep within his body. Keller shut the front door and Pax trotted to his post, but he didn't curl up in his basket. He placed himself beside the bed, where Rick remained despite the sunrise. He rested his long muzzle on the bed and closed his eyes as Rick's agitated fingers found his ears.

Keller had left and taken his belongings.

Chapter Fifty-two

Rick and I had both sworn to Keller that I could get Rick up, but when I went in to him, he was asleep again. The dog, who had made such a fuss about Keller's leaving, was sitting there in his usual place beside the bed, and there was something in his posture—his attention—that chilled me. I put a hand on Rick's forehead. His eyes opened and he smiled at me, then waved me away. "Just let me sleep at little more. I'll call you when I'm ready to get up." I knew that getting up was a process for him, and for anyone helping him it was strenuous and a struggle against indignity for both parties. I'd done it alone for so long before Keller's arrival. Now, having had help for these past few months, I dreaded it, so I was just as happy to let him stay there.

I sat in the kitchen and drank a second cup of coffee. Keller's breakfast plate was still on the table, a film of egg yolk clashing with the white. He had been so torn about this funeral. I really didn't know why he told me about it; he could have just kept it to himself and not gone if it was that difficult a thing to do, but he'd told me that he'd received word his uncle—great-uncle—had died and he should do the proper thing and go up to Hawke's Cove to the funeral. He wanted me to ask him not to. He gave me every opportunity. "I don't have to go, Francesca. I really wasn't close to him."

"Keller, he was your family. It will look odd if you don't go."

"To whom?"

I smiled at the grammar. Keller was excelling in his English class. "To the lady who wrote to you. Miss Jacobs? The one who gave you the book, right?"

"So you're saying I have to take a day off so that I don't disappoint Miss Jacobs?"

"Or yourself. He might not have been easy, but . . ." There it was, my tendency to speak before thinking, and I stopped myself.

"He took me in. Ergo, I should be grateful?"

"I suppose." Standing over him, I poured him a little more coffee. He smelled of his shaving soap, of the castile shampoo that he used. His hair wasn't slicked back yet and I noticed a little whorl at the crown, like a little kid's. I resisted the urge to comb down the unruly cowlick with my fingers.

I'd seen the letter. Keller had shown it to me the night before, handing it to me at the top of the landing before we headed into our rooms. It made me a little sad, wistful in an odd way. The schoolmarm and the fisherman. Was there a romantic story of unrequited love in between the lines?

I set the percolator back on the stove. "We'll be fine. Go pay your respects." After all, what else could I have said? Don't leave me alone with my husband?

So he'd gone, and here I was, sitting at my kitchen table, wishing he hadn't. I had lost a buffer I hadn't known he'd been providing. A buffer between me and the hard reminders

of my husband's condition. When Rick hadn't called me before noon, I went in to wake him up, thinking that he simply
shouldn't be sleeping all this time. Pax was still frozen in that
alert pose. When I went in, he turned his head and looked at
me, and if a dog could ask for help, this one was.

Rick was burning up. I ran water into a bowl and placed
the wet, cold cloth on his head. This woke him up, and he
stared at me as if he didn't know me. I stripped off his blanket
and examined his catheter, then called the doctor.

We had been so careful, but in those days, we had only
those clumsy rubber gloves that required boiling. There was
no hope we could simulate sterile conditions in a made-over
den. I can't remember the doctor's name. Isn't that odd? He
must have visited us forty times, and to this day, I can't recall
anything except the fact that he always smelled like clove.
Like maybe he was chewing it to mask the odors his profession subjected him to. At any rate, this doc, whatever his name
was, shook his head when he came out of the room. "I'll call
the ambulance."

It wasn't the first time this had happened, so the sense of
the bottom falling out from under me was only mild. I knew
what to do, what to pack, how long it would take, and I projected myself ahead to the happy moment when Rick would
suddenly be better, alert and sorry that he'd caused so much
trouble. I wanted to get to that part right away. Keller had said
to call Sid, but there was nothing Sid could do, and, besides,
he was needed at home. Clarissa was a needy mother. Besides,
I didn't want Sid. I wanted Keller. I needed him to tell me it
was going to be all right, that things were under control.

Pax seemed to know exactly what was going on. He didn't
get in the way; he didn't whine. He watched from out of the
way, sitting on the staircase as the ambulance crew came in

with the stretcher. Maybe he'd seen this before, on the battle-field, the medics transporting the wounded to ambulances. I knew that Keller had been wounded. Had this dog witnessed him being lifted away?

I buttoned my coat and searched for my gloves. All that time, the dog sat still, patient and calm. All of a sudden, I realized that I was, too. That things *were* under control. I stroked his head from black nose to ears and kissed him. "Such a good boy."

Chapter Fifty-three

Keller has inadvertently taken the local, so his journey to Great Harbor is painfully slow, interrupted every few minutes with pauses at outlying stations along the route. The slowness of the journey is actually not a bad thing. He's in no rush to get there, to go through the motions of the funeral and the pretense of caring, but he'd make darn sure to get the express on the return trip. He'd called Miss Jacobs to let her know he'd be there but hadn't prolonged the conversation much beyond telling her which train he'd be on and that he'd get Great Harbor's only taxi to take him to the funeral home. No religion for Clayton Britt, not at this late date.

He's got a paper cup of coffee cooling in his hands and a cruller in a bag on his lap. Every now and again, he reaches into the bag and breaks off a piece of the cruller. He's being careful not to get crumbs on his suit. Rick's suit. He's wearing the striped tie of fashionable width that the Stantons gave him for Christmas. He runs his hand down it every now and again to make sure that it's still in place. Keller has his reading assignment beside him on the seat, but he can't make himself pick it up. He just watches out the window as the urban landscape begins to give way to country, but he isn't really paying attention to the scenery.

A funny thing happened a week ago and Keller is still thinking about it. He was out shoveling the walk when one of the neighbors ventured over. This was a guy he'd waved to a couple of times, a businessman who kept long hours, coming home after five and leaving just as Keller was taking Pax out for his morning walk at sunrise. Early train into town, late train home.

"Hey neighbor." It was a Saturday, and the guy was dressed like Keller, ready for chores. "Bob Tuthill. Insurance."

"Keller, Keller Nicholson." Keller jabbed the shovel into the snow, put out his hand. He didn't have a ready job title to toss back.

"Nice to have you folks in the neighborhood. Sorry I haven't been by before this, but you know how it is," Tuthill said.

"I believe that Francesca and Mrs. Tuthill know each other." Bob's wife was one of the few neighborhood ladies who occasionally dropped by for midmorning coffee with Francesca. "Lady time," he and Rick called it, and Keller would break out the chessboard and keep clear of the kitchen.

"Yeah, wives are good about those things. Always borrowing sugar. Right?"

"Right." Keller knew that he had a foolish grin on his face and that he should enlighten Tuthill, but for some reason he didn't, and he was relieved when Pax came bounding over, curious about the newcomer.

"Nice dog. Always like a big dog." Tuthill reached out to pat Pax, but one look at the dog's face and he pulled his hand away. "Say, that her dad or yours I see you wheeling around?"

Before Keller could answer, Tuthill jumped topics and asked

if Keller had a second shovel. The handle of his, it seemed, had snapped off.

There was something so lovely about Tuthill's mistake. He'd validated a barely concocted fantasy, that Keller and Francesca were a couple. A fantasy that Keller was ashamed of but nonetheless let rise out of empty moments; a fantasy he could never wish into reality. To do so would be to lose Rick. Despite the bumpy nature of their acquaintance, he and Rick had become friends of a sort.

Somewhere along the way, Keller has fallen asleep, the crumpled bag of cruller crumbs still gripped in his hand. The conductor shakes him awake. He can see the railway sign: GREAT HARBOR. Despite all his intentions never to come back, here he is. It seems like a hundred years since he boarded this train at this station and headed to war. He left here a boy, and now he's a grown man, a veteran of war, and, against all predictions, a college student. Despite the slow train, he's an hour early for the funeral, so he decides to walk. He's over the causeway bridge from Great Harbor in fifteen minutes and on the main street of Hawke's Cove in twenty.

Nothing has changed. He may have been gone for years, but Hawke's Cove has sat, like Brigadoon, in a time warp. The storefronts haven't changed, their businesses existing in some kind of stasis of moderate success, the hardware store, the grocery store, Linda's Restaurant. The only suggestion that it isn't still 1942 or 1938 or 1893 is the late-model Oldsmobile parked along the curb, all fins and chrome. There's Joe Green from the dairy, and the Sunderland boys—even in their sixties, the bachelor brothers have always been called the Sunderland boys. Neither of them looks a day older than the last time he saw them. Keller waves from across the street and they wave back without a moment's hesitation in figuring out who he is. Maybe he hasn't changed all that much. The feeling that he's returned to Hawke's Cove a grown man dissipates, until Keller thinks that maybe he's dreamed it all. Maybe he's still that ruddy-faced adolescent hauling lobster pots out of the cove with his great-uncle, who's heaping abuse on him because he's dropped a marlin spike overboard. Maybe it's all been a fever dream filled with the energy of war and the contentment of living in a small Cape-style house with his dog and the people who seem to care about him. And he's about to waken. Even dead, Clayton Britt has a power over him, the power to make him feel worthless.

The funeral home is an unimpressive square building that once held the livery stable. A white clapboard facade dresses it up, and a canvas canopy suggests that those who enter here should be humbled. Keller removes his fedora and hangs it on the hat rack by the door. He can hear voices, and he walks toward them. A small group is gathered in one of the viewing rooms. At the far end is a casket, and for the first time Keller realizes that he's going to have to look at his uncle. Somehow, he had overlooked that part of the American ritual. The last look. Keller had hoped that he'd had his last look at Clayton Britt that day at the Great Harbor railroad station. *You can come back, you know.*

"Keller, how nice to see you." Miss Jacobs has come up beside him as he stands flummoxed in the doorway of the viewing room. She takes his face in her hands and draws him down to her for a kiss on the cheek. "You look well."

"So do you." Miss Jacobs, like everything else in this town, hasn't changed. "You're still the most beautiful girl at the dance."

"Keller, when did you learn to flirt?" But she's not displeased; she blushes girlishly and takes him by the arm.

He wants to resist, but he knows that he must carry out this awkward task, so Keller lets Miss Jacobs lead him to the head of the short line of those paying their respects to a hard, cold, solitary fisherman.

It's as if the undertaker has played a joke on Clayton. If the man never smiled in life, the mortician has him smiling in death. Keller feels a little sick. This waxy smiling effigy of Clayton Britt is just plain ghoulish. Even the undertaker hasn't been able to disguise the work-worn hands serenely folded over Clayton's breast, the gnarly grayish knuckles, the blackened thumbnail, the cut alongside one finger from his last haul. Keller stares at those hands, recalling the only time he ever touched them, one of them—the handshake Clayton offered the day he left for war. No. Keller remembers that Clayton used both hands that day, covering Keller's right with his left, as close to an affectionate gesture as the man had ever made. *You can come back, you know.*

Keller finds himself staring blindly at those hands until Miss Jacobs nods toward the kneeler. He sinks down to offer an unpracticed prayer. He has no idea what thought to loft to a God he's never been introduced to, so he just closes his eyes and thinks, Go where you belong, old man. May God have mercy on your soul. He tries to think of Clayton, but Rick and Francesca come to mind instead, and he finds himself praying for them. All of them.

Hawke's Cove's cemetery occupies a rise and is filled with the bad-teeth remnants of ancient slate headstones cheek by jowl with more modern and durable granite ones. Even though the temperature hovers just above freezing, the sandy soil is no obstacle in Hawke's Cove for a winter funeral and the gravesite is ready to accept Clayton. Keller shoulders the casket along with three others, two of whom are employees of the funeral home. The other pallbearer is the fish market owner, Stan Long. He keeps patting Keller on the shoulder and muttering, "A shame. A real shame." Keller isn't quite sure what shame there is in an old man's dying. It wasn't as if Stan was a friend. Or at least Keller had never thought of him as Clayton's friend, but he supposes that, living in such a small place and having daily contact, qualifies a person as a friend, even if that friend was never once invited to darken the doors of Clayton's French's Cove Road house.

Keller is surprised at the number of folks who have turned out on a blustery January day for the funeral of a near hermit. They don't hang around long after the final words are said, climbing back into cars and trucks or walking down the hill to the collation Miss Jacobs has arranged at the new VFW hall. Free lunch. No one has sniffed into a handkerchief. Released from the solemnity inherent in a graveside service, the attendees quickly fall back into the normal pitches of chat and laughter. They've shaken his hand and patted his shoulder, done their duty, and are now happy to have an excuse to stay away another hour from work or household.

Two headstones away is a granite slab engraved with the name of a kid Keller went to school with. KILLED IN ACTION. Not far from where Keller had been in the war. There but for the Grace of God . . . He'd noticed a couple of other casualties of war, but this was a kid he'd played a little basketball with on those rare occasions when Clayton gave him a little off time after school. Days when, like today, it was too windy to go out on the water. Keller bets that the mourners surrounding those graves didn't so quickly cast off their grief.

The view from this hillside cemetery is astounding. Keller looks at it with a new appreciation, as if by Clayton's death, the scales have fallen from his eyes and he can see the beauty of his surroundings. His memories of this place are cast in black and gray, but today he sees Hawke's Cove in brilliant Technicolor.

Keller thinks that he'll just skip the collation and wander around the cemetery a little, see if there is anyone else he should be paying his respects to. Then, because it's early enough, he won't have to stay the night, but can head back to the station and catch the late train to Boston. Keller sucks in a deep breath; the salt air carries a hint of tomorrow's weather. Yeah, head back tonight. Don't take chances. It was hard enough leaving Francesca alone to care for Rick, but this low-grade temperature of his is worrisome. He'll get back late, well after midnight, but he won't wake anyone when he gets home. He has a key. Pax will greet him and they can have a little walk around the neighborhood. Pax was so distressed at his leaving, as if the dog thought he wasn't coming back.

A lift in the breeze licks his cheek, and Keller thinks of Francesca's lips against it just this morning. The soft breath as she kissed him. What discipline he'd shown in not turning that cheek to catch those lips against his. The breeze also speaks of the feel of her fingers on his other cheek, grazing it lightly.

Keller sets his hat on his head, tilts it just so. The grave diggers are patiently waiting at a remove to get to the second half of their job, closing the grave.

"Walk me down the hill, Keller." Miss Jacobs is standing beside him, and she takes his arm but doesn't let him turn away from the grave, the lowered coffin still glinting warmly in the thin January light. It is then that Keller realizes that Clayton's grave already has a headstone. That seems odd. How can a gravestone arrive before the tenant?

FLORENCE BRITT 1893–1919. BELOVED WIFE.

"Is that his mother? No, it can't be. The dates are wrong."

"No, Keller. Florence was my sister." Miss Jacobs leans over and dusts the top of the stone with her gloved hand. "I wanted the headstone to reflect that she was Florence Jacobs first. But he didn't seem to remember that fact."

"He was married?" Keller is incredulous. How could he not have known this?

"You didn't know?" Miss Jacobs doesn't sound surprised.

"He never said. You'd think he might have mentioned it."

"It near killed him, losing her." Miss Jacobs links her arm through Keller's. "Influenza."

"I simply cannot imagine him in love." Keller shakes his head.

"Oh, he was. Head over heels. Keller, you have to understand that Clayton was a much different man then. He had everything going for him. He was a confirmed bachelor, had inherited his family's property, was making a decent living for the times, dragging. Happy living life as it came to him. Then we came to town, two spinsters ready to teach school. Flo was my baby sister, and I always believed that she was too beautiful, too vivacious to resist, that spinsterhood for her was just a temporary state. Well, Clayton took one look and fell under her spell. He was everything my excitable sister needed, rock steady, loving, and kind."

Keller shakes his head again. This is a story about someone else, not his uncle.

"It was like, having discovered real happiness, then losing it, Clayton turned against all happiness. Like so many then, she got sick, and there was nothing that could be done. It was over in forty hours. Clayton just never regained his spirit. It wasn't that he grieved; it was that the grief poisoned him."

"She was my age."

"And he was twenty years older. I didn't like it, but he was as good a husband to her as I could have wanted. Maybe I was jealous of her. I've often wondered if I was. I didn't think so at the time; I was just being a cautious old bat. The problem was that he didn't have her for very long, six months, maybe. Seven. He went from being a honeymooner to a widower. They hadn't had enough life together for him to have anything but happy memories. And they haunted him, so he stopped."

"Stopped?"

"Thinking, feeling, living."

Why does that sound like Rick Stanton?

Keller doesn't know what to say. He closes his elbow against Miss Jacobs's arm and takes her back down the slope to the VFW. Keller tests the idea of losing someone you love and can only imagine Francesca, whom he does not truly have. Nonetheless, by that wholly imaginary circumstance can Keller understand the depth of feeling that Clayton had had once in his life, and how its loss turned him. He needs to get back. They need him.

"I'm going to keep going, Miss Jacobs. It was wonderful to see you."

"You'll get everything, you know. He died intestate, but the law will figure you for the heir."

Keller gently squeezes the old woman's fingers, which are encased in fine black lambskin gloves. "You have my address. Give it to the lawyers."

"Keller. You remind me of him."

"Don't say that." It frightens him, this idea that someday he could become that angry old man. That disappointment in love has that much power.

Chapter Fifty-four

I never heard him come in that night. I was in such a deep and dreamless sleep that even the sound of the front door opening in the night didn't waken me. I couldn't remember the last time I'd slept so well. Having Pax in the house assured me of my personal safety. Having no one else in the house to worry about lowered me into oblivion.

Rick was responding well to the penicillin and they said he would be home in a day or two. He'd sent me home from his bedside, with the help of a stern nurse. "Get some rest," he said. "I've got all the help here I need." The stern nurse handed me my coat.

I got home to a dark house, having left at midmorning and come home late into winter dusk. Thank God Pax was there, that there was another mouth to feed and a beating heart to hear. He kept me company during those hours when he would have been in with Rick. He didn't seem to be asking any questions, and I marveled that he seemed to be taking this odd turn of events—no men—in his stride. It was so cold that I cheated him out of the good walk Keller normally would have given him, going only as far as the end of the street before heading back into my empty house.

When I went up to bed that night, I stood in the doorway of the nursery-cum-storage-cum-bedroom that Keller occupied. His cot was made up, with the blankets pulled military tight, and not an object was out of plumb. Hairbrushes aligned side by side, toiletries that I hadn't convinced him to leave in the bathroom erect in their basket. I never trespassed in there. It wasn't like his garage space, with the sitting area and the open invitation to come and sit and talk out of earshot of Rick when we needed to. Or maybe just talk about his reading or the weather. An oasis. This room, tiny and spare, gave me back almost nothing of Keller. I crossed the sill and went to his bureau, picked up those brushes with the boar's bristles dyed by the oils of his Brylcreem. How he fought to keep that lock of hair disciplined, and how I longed to touch it.

I was alone in the house for the first time in a very long time. Neither man was there and so I had only myself to hide from. When Keller had come out of the bath the night before, I'd caught sight of him dashing, towel-wrapped, up the stairs, his clothes bundled under one arm, his bathrobe left upstairs by accident. Bare legs, bare shoulders still glistening from dampness. Slender waist and long back, his spine a darker concavity against the polished muscle of his back. I'd turned away before he saw me staring. Before I embarrassed him with the flicker of want that I felt in a place that had been dormant for so long.

I set his brushes down, caught sight of myself in his mirror, the reflection of his cot behind me. I walked out of the room, leaving his bedroom door wide open, leaving mine wide open, too. Every other night, the click of my latch had proclaimed our respectability. Pax didn't come upstairs right away;

I could hear him moving through every room of the downstairs, checking things, making sure that we were safe. As I fell asleep, I heard him come upstairs, satisfied all was well. For the first time ever, he came into my room and I invited him up on my bed. He curled up on the end, not lying next to me as he did with Rick during the day and Keller at night.

It was the sound of running water that finally woke me that next morning. A comforting sound, until I remembered that I was supposed to be alone. Pax, whose weight had held me down all night, was gone. Still, I didn't jump out of bed. The fact that Pax hadn't made any fuss was enough to settle my startled nerves and push me back into the pillow. It was obvious; Keller had come home. I stretched, yawned, and went right back to sleep.

"Hey, sleepyhead." Keller tapped lightly on my open bedroom door. "I've got coffee, if you're interested." He stood there in profile, as if trying not to look in.

"I'd love some." Before he moved away from the door, I threw off my covers and swung my feet over the side. I pulled my housecoat on over my nightdress and followed him downstairs. The house was chilly—I'd turned the heat down a little too far—but the kitchen was warm in the midmorning sun coming through the window. Pax lay in a patch of it, as if sunbathing. The sunlight burnished his silver-gray coast, making it look like mink.

"So, it wasn't a cold, then?"

"Bladder infection. Catheter was a little clogged or something. The doc admitted him."

"I wish I'd known, I never would have left."

"We managed. We've done it before." I didn't mean it to

sound like it did, a little mean or cavalier. "I mean, it wasn't the first time this has happened, so I knew what to expect." I didn't confide in him how frightening it was, no matter how often it happened. I didn't tell him that every time one of these infections occurred, it could mean months back in the VA hospital. This time, we'd caught it early. I thought of Pax sitting there, his steely posture and the look of alert concern he'd given me.

"The problem is that we have to wait for the visiting nurse to do the catheter. If we knew how, we could change it more often." Keller set a cup down in front of me.

"You don't want to get into that level of nursing. It's not meant for amateurs." That was Keller, always thinking he could fix things. One more task, one more challenge. "Some things are just best left to the professionals. Tell me about the funeral."

"Not much to tell. It was all right. More people showed up than I would have expected."

"Not unusual in a small town. In Mount Joy, everyone shows up at most funerals because it's considered a civic duty."

"I found out he was married."

I could tell that this bit of ancient history stuck in Keller's throat. He didn't say it like it was interesting or puzzling, but as if it somehow *bothered* him. Like Clayton had been holding back on him. So I asked the next logical questions. "Did he have kids?"

"No. She died in the influenza outbreak, just at the end of it. She was twenty years younger than he was. She was my age when she died." For a man who had seen the youth of the country dead on the battlefield, he sounded surprised that a young woman might perish from disease.

"That's so sad." So my intuition of unrequited love had been a little correct. Just a different lover and a different cause.

"I keep thinking how miserable an old codfish he was, and wondering how different it would have been had she lived. Miss Jacobs said that he loved her." Keller lifted his face and looked at me as he said this. *He loved her.* "I keep thinking how powerful love is. That losing it can change a person so deeply."

"Having it changes a person, too."

With Rick out of the room, we decided to give it a good cleaning. Armed to the teeth with the tools necessary, we dragged or wheeled out all of the furniture, stripped the books off the shelf, and took down the venetian blinds, which I soaked in the bathtub in ammonia water. Pax curled his lips up in a hilarious mask of distaste and retreated to the breezeway. We each took two walls and washed them down until the pale blue brightened like an old master's glory revealed. Keller scrubbed down the bed, removing the mattress and running a sponge all over the mechanism that raised and lowered it.

By four o'clock, all that was left untouched in the room was the wheelchair, and Keller decided that would best be handled out in the garage, where he could give it a good going-over without getting the mopped floor wet again. "I'll tighten up the bolts while I'm at it."

While he was occupied with the chair, I rooted around in the cellar for a couple of pictures we'd had hanging in our first apartment. I would put them up on the unadorned but sparkly clean walls. One was a landscape painted by a local Iowa amateur that my aunt and uncle had given us for our wedding and the other a view of the Public Garden we'd bought ourselves from a street vendor at Downtown Crossing. They were cheerful in an uncheerful space. The hospital bed was made up like a normal bed, with the spread tucked neatly under the single pillow. The books had been moved to the higher shelf and the radio was where it should have been all along; the table over the bed had been scrubbed clean and pushed out of the way for the moment; the bedside table had been neatened up, and I put a new lamp on it, swapping out the rather institutional one with a bedroom lamp abandoned in the basement. The sickroom looked almost, but not quite, like a real bedroom. But it didn't look right. I stood in the doorway, my rubber gloves still on, the bucket of dirty water at my feet, and I couldn't help but think that, without the wheelchair, it looked like we had expunged Rick. As if we didn't expect him back.

Chapter Fifty-five

Keller and I went to the hospital together for evening visiting hours. Except for the fact that Rick had a roommate, an old gent with a prostate—or "prostrate," as he kept calling it—problem, it could have been any evening with the three of us sitting around a small space filled with medical equipment. Rick was so much better, although they'd found another decubitus starting on his left flank. We tried so hard, and still we weren't able to keep his skin completely healthy.

When we arrived, Keller grasped the trapeze dangling over Rick's bed. "We should get one of these. Think how much it would help."

Rick ignored the suggestion. "How's my Pax?"

"Pax will come with us when we come spring you out of this place." Keller let go of the trapeze and it swung gently over Rick. "He's missed you."

"I miss him. You be sure to bring him."

I shouldn't have, but I couldn't help feeling like Rick missed that dog more than he missed me. I thought it was true. I wasn't jealous, not in any serious sense. I remembered so distinctly then the first time Rick had taken me to his place, Pax sitting there waiting for him, suspicious of me, and Rick's absolute confidence that I would love his dog as much as he did. Now all I wanted was for him to love me as much as he did the dog. That sounds petty and dramatic. I don't mean that he didn't love me as much, but the quality of the love he had for that dog was so much purer, less troubled. The dog had gone to war and come home unchanged. Neither of us could say that about ourselves.

Keller and I were exhausted from our day's labors, so weren't very talkative, and Rick noticed. "What's wrong?"

"Nothing, just really tired." I told him what we'd been doing.

"So, you cleaned everything, even the chair?"

Keller nodded. "Yeah. Even the wheelchair." He was sitting to my left, and out of the corner of my eye I saw him lean back and cross his arms. I don't know why Rick sounded like he was talking about something else, like the word *wheelchair* was a euphemism. Maybe I was just so tired, I was hearing things.

The man next to Rick was trying to get out of bed and that didn't look like a good idea to me, but before I could say anything, Keller got up to look for a nurse.

Rick watched him leave the room. "Good time for me to get out of the way, then, I guess. Early spring cleaning." I thought the topic had pretty much run out and I didn't understand Rick's combative tone. That wasn't my imagination.

"More like late fall. I never did give that room a proper going-over when we moved in."

"I'll try to plan my hospitalizations to be more convenient."

I was too tired to rise to his bait. "Actually, I could only do it because Keller was there to help me."

"As always."

"Just being useful, Rick." Keller was back in the room. "It's what you pay me for."

"Right. Just doing your job."

That was enough for me. "I think it's time to go. You're getting tired."

"And cranky?" Rick looked away, and he did look cranky, like a little boy kept inside while his friends go outside to play.

"Yeah. A little." I bent and kissed his forehead, just like you would with a cranky little boy. "I love you anyway."

He took my hand and held it tightly, almost too tight, pulling me a little closer. "Good." This time, we kissed like proper lovers, but I couldn't help but get the feeling that it was for Keller's benefit.

Chapter Fifty-six

Pax has inspected every room in the house. He's listened, sniffed, looked in every dark corner, taken a lick at a missed drip on the side of the stove, lapped at his water bowl, and stood over the heat register to enjoy the blast of heat. Like a good sentry at his post, Pax feels confident that this house is safe. Safe and empty. It is the first time in recent memory that the dog has been left all alone.

Pax eyes the living room sofa, leans against it a little, rubs his chops against the nubby fabric. One paw, then another, and suddenly he's aboard. From the height of the sofa, he can sit and look out the window unobstructed. The neighbor's cat pauses at the curb cut, stretches, and sits to wash her face, as if she knows he's looking at her and she is taunting him. He has no quarrel with cats, but he doesn't much like this feline's attitude of entitlement. He barks. One full-bodied *roof* and the cat stops her washing and blinks. Moves on, question-mark tail in the air. Insouciant, but warned.

The people in this house aren't where they belong, and the routine has been disrupted. But Pax has long since learned to cope with disruption, to be flexible and to be alert to what he needs to do. Right now, he needs to sit on this couch and wait for the sound of the car to return. Once he detects the singular sound of *their* car, he'll jump down from the couch. Not because he knows he isn't supposed to be on the couch, which he does, but because he always needs to greet them at the door; that's part of his job. And, if a dog can hope, he's hoping that all three of his people will be in that car.

But only Francesca and Keller got out of the car this day, and Pax knows better than to look behind them to see if somehow Rick has been left outside. He greets them with the same enthusiasm as he would have his missing Rick. They talk to him as if he's supposed to understand all their language. The only words he understands are *Rick* and *tomorrow*. Not *tomorrow* as a concept, but the word always means "later on, not now." Ergo, *Rick, not now.*

Chapter Fifty-seven

We had worked hard on that room together, enjoying an easy companionship over buckets of Spic and Span. The radio was on and we sang along with some of the popular songs. Keller had a serviceable voice and I wasn't too bad. We muffed the lyrics and laughed. A little water might have splashed, a sponge thrown playfully. We were like two kids on a snow day, released, however temporarily, from the burden of our daily routine. All right, I'll say it, released from the burden of my husband. We both loved him; I know that. And that's what made it all right for us to acknowledge that we were enjoying one day, maybe two, without his presence. His very paternal presence. His dark presence over the lightness in ourselves that we were holding down. We were still young. I sometimes forget that. Keller and I were still in our twenties.

We'd come back from visiting Rick in the hospital less cheery than when we had gone. Rick's grumpiness had put a damper on our spirits. We hadn't said much on the way home, Keller driving my car. *Our* car, I should say, even though Rick would never drive it. I sat in the passenger seat and stared out the window until I felt his hand in its thick winter glove touch mine. "It's all right, Francesca. He's all right." He gave my hand a little tug. How like Keller to read my thoughts. I'm not sure if I was grateful or a little afraid.

Back at the house, we sprang Pax from his solitary confinement and walked to the beach. Keller threw sticks for him and Pax bounded and raced, splashed in the freezing water and barked at us as if he were a puppy without manners. The Harbor islands looked like great dark humps in the dusk and the Boston skyline glittered in the cold air, jewel-like and competing with the stars just emerging. As we walked back, the brightness of postwar illumination paved our way home.

We'd left the lights on, so our house was as brightly lit as any we'd passed. Warm and welcoming. We stamped old snow and beach sand off our boots and left them in the breezeway. In unshod feet, we scampered over cold tiles into the warm kitchen. Keller fed Pax and I rummaged through the Frigidaire for something to cobble together for dinner. We sat at the same table and ate scrambled eggs and toast. Face-to-face, close enough that Keller reached across and tipped a flake of egg off my face. I spooned my leftovers onto his plate.

The three of us flopped on the living room couch to listen to the radio—a little railroad train of hips and shoulders, mine next to Keller's and Pax's next to his in an unprecedented lapse of training—Pax especially enjoyed Jack Paar's show. We stayed up well past our usual fall-into-bed hour. It was as if we didn't want to let the day end. As if neither of us could figure out the best way to say good night without calling attention to the fact that we were, for all intents and purposes, unchaperoned.

Pax jumped down and stretched fore and aft, then went to the front door for last call. Keller put on his jacket and out they went. I shut off the radio and the house was suddenly too silent. Without thinking, I headed into Rick's room, as I did every night. The sight of the empty bed jolted me back into the moment. My husband was in the hospital and I was alone with Keller.

Chapter Fifty-eight

It's an accident, this meeting on the stairs. She's heading down to use the bathroom; he's going up after taking Pax out for his late night walk. He should turn this way and she should turn that. Instead, as she is one step above him, they find themselves face-to-face, body-to-body. He can smell the faint mint of her favorite Lifesaver. She can, no doubt, breathe in the taste of his last cigarette. He touches the inside of her elbow. She touches his cheek. The moment lingers, as if, having made these experimental gestures, neither one has a way of making sense of them. Here is a question being asked, for which there is no answer. He traces his thumb against the soft surface of her skin. She fans her fingers against his stubbled cheek, holds it as if she is puzzled at the contours of his bones. He's surprised to see that her eyes aren't simply green, as he thought, but flecked with shards of amber.

At the foot of the stairs, the dog sits, his gaze upon them, but he is silent.

They need to invoke Rick.

"I'm going to make cocoa. Come down." Her hand is still on his cheek as she says this.

"I will." His hand is still on her tender skin.

The moment passes and they continue on their separate ways: She goes downstairs, pauses, looks back at him, doesn't smile. He goes to his room, where he shuts the door and sits on his cot. Is it possible that his fingers burn with the heat of her skin? Keller touches his lips with the hand that touched her so tenderly. He then touches the cheek where her hand had held it, holding him still so that their gazes matched. He doesn't go downstairs to sit across a kitchen table from her, an unwanted mug of hot chocolate held in a hand already heated by a want that transcends mere lust. By the time she finally comes upstairs, he is asleep.

Pax remains as he is, at the foot of the stairs, alert and panting gently.

His cheek was so different from Rick's—his day-old beard darker, the angles sharper. His deep brown eyes softened the longer he looked into mine. The brush of his thumb against my most sensitive skin had sent a radiating pulse down into my deepest parts. For months—no, years—I had been untouched. Rather, touched only in dim affection by my husband, who had lost the ability to want me. Touched by Keller only within the confines of this platonic ideal we were living by out of respect and common decency and the love we both held for Rick.

I heated the milk and got out two mugs, but I knew that he wouldn't come down. I was relieved, to tell the truth. It was as if there was a thin membrane between us, a membrane that separated us from each other and temptation. On those stairs, we had pushed against that membrane. And so it was fragile right now and there was a grave danger that it would burst at the merest provocation.

Chapter Fifty-nine

It is almost time for his afternoon walk when instead Pax is asked to get in Keller's car, something he loves to do, although this time he's made to sit in the back, not next to Keller as he most often does. Francesca sits there and he supposes that that's all right. Pax puts his head over the back of the front seat, in between Francesca and Keller. They are unusually quiet, but also unusually close, so he has to push a little to get his head in between them. She keeps adjusting her gloves; he keeps pulling on his earlobe, as if he's about to issue a thought, but then keeps silent. They are making him nervous.

Pax's canine eyes are inadequate for detail, but he recognizes that they are traveling along familiar roads for a time. Then they turn, heading in a direction he's never been before. When they park the car, Pax expects the command to stay, guard the vehicle against thieves. Instead, Keller asks him to get out and fall in. Francesca is on Keller's right side and Pax is at heel at his left. They march to the front door in almost military precision. Left, right, left.

Pax is aware of people standing on both sides of the

walkway leading to the entrance of this building that harbors odors that remind the dog of his new purpose. At the entrance, a man speaks to Keller, but Keller clearly doesn't see him as an obstacle, more like a subordinate, and keeps a firm touch on the leash. The door opens to them and Francesca and Keller, with Pax at his side, go in. Pax isn't certain about the tiny windowless room that moves, but he betrays no concern, although he sits in order to feel more secure. The door opens again and everything has changed. He takes one deep investigative breath and doesn't need any further guidance at this point. He knows where they're going and whom they are going to collect. He can hardly make himself stay at heel as they walk down the long corridor to where Rick waits.

Roo, roo. Pax forgets himself as he fairly leaps into Rick's lap. He wriggles like a puppy and has no shame.

"Good boy. Good boy."

All three of them say it: "Good boy, Pax." It's as if he's done something of a heroic nature, although Pax doesn't have any idea what it is. Still, it's good to be the object of praise, even for a dog that has never lacked for praise.

Chapter Sixty

Keller wheels Rick to the car, where the awkward business of getting from wheelchair to front seat will be enacted. Pax is close by to lend moral support and Francesca is bringing up the rear with a bagful of his belongings. There is always something noxious about personal items brought home from the hospital, and she'll be tossing everything into the washer as soon as they get home.

The little pouch that holds his crossword puzzle books and pencils, and the precious trove of little white pills, isn't attached to the wheelchair, and Rick scans Keller's face to see if there is any suspicion; if, in giving his chair a good cleaning, Keller has found the twenty-one little pills safely resting at the bottom of that cloth pouch, hiding like fish beneath the reef of a crossword puzzle book. Keller betrays no hint that he's found out Rick's secret. But there is a tension in his jaw, something that makes him look like a man with something on his mind.

Keller wedges him into the front seat and Francesca leans in to kiss him, as if she's staying behind, not climbing into the backseat with the dog. Her lips are warm despite the frigid air, as if she's held on to some of the warmth of the indoors. But she doesn't look at him.

It's on his bed, the little pouch. The crossword puzzle book is there, and a newly sharpened pencil. He can't help himself: He grabs it almost as soon as Keller wheels him into his room. He dips his fingertips in the pouch and closes his eyes. They're there. He'll count them later, just to make sure, but it feels right. He doesn't even care if Keller is watching, curious.

"Missed your crosswords so much?"

"It's pretty boring in there."

"I'd have brought them. Why didn't you ask?"

"Hey, no problem. I just thought of an answer I missed; I can complete one of the hard ones."

Keller still has that tense look.

"What's on your mind, Nicholson?" Get it out in the open, deal with the consequences.

"I need a little time."

"You're entitled. You never take a day off. I mean, for things other than funerals."

"No, just the afternoon. I have some stuff I have to do."

"Go. We're fine." Relief blunts any curiosity. If any man needs some downtime, surely Keller does.

"Okay. Thanks."

"Don't thank me. It's not like I'm not going to dock your paycheck." Rick smiles, broad and real. But Keller doesn't and that tense look migrates across his face.

"Tell Francesca I'll be back by dinnertime."

"Fine."

Keller stands in the widened doorway. "She's a good wife. Don't you ever forget it."

Rick nods, perplexed and a tiny bit annoyed. Keller has stepped a little over the line. Pushed himself a tiny bit too much. Of course Francesca is a good wife. What's his point? Rick slides his hand into the pouch and begins to count his pills. What if Keller found the morphine? Would he have told Francesca? Or would he just have put them back in the vial, which he'll keep out of both Rick's and Pax's reach? Honor among thieves? Honor between veterans of the same killing fields? *She's a good wife.* Are they teammates or are they rivals?

Chapter Sixty-one

"Don't make lunch for me. I'm going to go get gas in my car."
It's the best excuse he can come up with, but there's no way he
can stay in this house, smile over grilled cheese sandwiches,
and pretend that everything is all right. He just isn't that good
an actor.

"Eat first. It's all ready." Francesca is holding a plate with
four sandwiches stacked on it.

Keller grabs half a grilled cheese sandwich, bites into it, then
calls the dog. "Pax will go with me."

"He just had a ride."

Keller doesn't answer and he doesn't care if Francesca is
puzzled by him. He just needs to get out of this house. He
swallows the rest of the half sandwich, calls the dog, and pulls
his jacket out of the coat closet. "I won't be long. You and Rick
enjoy a quiet lunch. Have some time together."

"What's going on, Kel?"

"Nothing." He takes a shallow breath. "Nothing's wrong. I
just need some air." He won't look her in the eye. He doesn't

want to see if she believes him, or if the boat of their friendship is taking on water. *Nothing happened.*

Keller drives aimlessly, following Quincy Shore Drive for a mile or so, circling around Hough's Neck to get another view of the Harbor islands. The water is choppy today; cream-topped waves leave foam on the gritty shore. Pax sits beside him, as close as a girlfriend on the bench seat of the secondhand Ford. He stops for gas, throwing fifty cents' worth into the tank. He could just keep going. There's nothing at the house that he can't live without. No memorabilia, no souvenirs. Nothing he owns has sentimental value. Keller ruffles Pax's fur around his neck. "What do you say? Where would you like to go?"

Pax huffs, sneezes, but has little other comment.

"Someplace they couldn't find us. Someplace far enough away they couldn't come looking for you."

Keller checks his wallet. Every Friday, Francesca leaves an envelope on his bureau, as if handing him a paycheck would somehow remind him that he isn't a member of the family but what he really is, a paid employee. Slightly better than a boarder, not quite a friend. *Not anymore.* Thirty bucks. Enough to keep moving for a while. A little tremor of excitement tickles him under his rib cage. A bit like that tremble of anticipation as he left Hawke's Cove for the service. Then he'd had a destination, a plan, a destiny. Right now, he's rootless and as free as he's ever been in his life; he can point this car in any direction and just go. No wrought-iron fences keeping him in. No authority, whether Clayton's or the army's, telling him where to go and what to do. A break from this tension-wrought situation.

The idea of that freedom is enough to make Keller go a little too fast through these city streets, his right foot empowered by his thinking, until he slams on the brakes at a stoplight.

Pax is unseated by the sudden halt, and he bangs his muzzle on the dashboard.

"Sorry, fella, so sorry." Keller pats the dog and takes a deep breath. Something catches his eye; the handle of Francesca's purse peeks out from under the front seat, where she'd stashed it out of the way for the trip home from the hospital. The sight of that singularly Francesca-associated object puts paid to any notion of flight. He can't leave her, even if it would be the best thing. Oh, he could return the purse and gather his few possessions, give notice in a proper and professional way, and then leave. Nothing stopping him from doing that. And they would find another aide. Now that they know they can adjust to having the help, a properly trained aide would be better for them anyway. Someone who comes in without any strings attached. Without any strings growing stronger every day. Pax would stay in the car; they'd never realize he was gone until Keller was long gone.

In his life, Keller has had most everything stripped from him by circumstance. But he's not sure that he can strip Pax from Rick with the same harsh entitlement that his aunts had in stripping him of his freedom; or that Clayton had in using him as slave labor. *For your own good.* And unless he stays with Rick and Francesca, Pax will be stripped from him. And every day he'll be forced to tamp down this unforeseen and unwelcome desire for another man's wife. Which is the harder choice? Lose Pax or lose Francesca? Keller realizes that there is no choice. Leaving, he will lose both. In fact, the truth is, he has neither.

When the light turns green, Keller turns left, heading back to where Rick, in his perpetual gloom, sits in that room. And where Francesca waits, maybe a little worried about him instead of Rick for a change.

Chapter Sixty-two

Francesca has come in with lunch, but Rick can see that she's preoccupied. Three and a half sandwiches. For once, she doesn't come in smiling and full of chat for the sake of filling up the silence in that room. She talks, but her heart isn't in it. "Do you want another half? Do you want tea or coffee?" She doesn't realize just how well he knows her. Keller's absence is the gorilla in the room. Rick wonders if maybe they had a fight.

She'll just keep pretending that everything is hunky-dory. It is so wearing. Sometimes he thinks that Francesca is holding up his world on her back, and it plagues him that she won't admit that she's tired. On her most aggressively cheerful days, he thinks that he'd give his other arm for her to be honest with him, to rage against the shitty end of the stick she's holding. He's survived another bladder infection, but that only serves to pump up her shortsighted optimism that he's going to improve, that these things are just temporary setbacks. Get back in the game! She's like a fan who never gives up hope. A real fan overlooks bad games and cheers for the team no matter what. Francesca really needs to accept defeat.

But this time, Rick can see that Francesca's preoccupation isn't about him, and it's like he's being cheated. Why should she be so concerned about their *aide's* wanting a little break? So what if Keller didn't want to eat his lunch. Why should she even be thinking about it? He goes back to thinking that Keller and Francesca have had a disagreement. But when a man and a woman have a fight, there has to be a certain kind of intimacy to fuel it.

Rick bites a chunk out of his sandwich; doesn't answer Francesca's benign question about beverage. He hears only the high note of tension in her voice, as if she's being garroted with an unspoken question.

"He took Pax with him?" The grease from the sandwich coats his fingers.

"I guess so. Yes." Francesca hands him a napkin. "That's all right, isn't it?"

"He shouldn't be taking Pax if he's going out for any length of time. I need him."

"So does he." Francesca drops her unfinished sandwich on the plate. "Did he seem upset to you?"

"No. Just a man needing an afternoon off to clear his head." Really, why is she so concerned? Like a teenage girl worrying about the disposition of her crush. Rick shoves the rest of his sandwich into his mouth to stop it up before he says something he will regret.

"Are you done?"

It takes a second for Rick to realize she means done with lunch. "Yeah."

She removes the plate with the uneaten halves and leaves him as he is, sitting in that chair, facing the door, through which he seldom goes, the grease from his sandwich still on his fingers. Pax should be here to lick them off. Rick manages to turn his chair around so that he is facing the interior of his room. What sky he can see through the open blinds is opaque in the thin daylight, and the first sting of wet snow hits the pane.

It seems like hours pass before Rick finally hears the front door open. He closes his eyes with relief. Pax is back. Keller has brought him back. The big dog bounds into the room, his fur cold and sprinkled with hard balls of sleet. He shakes and sprays Rick with moisture, then commences licking Rick's fingers one by one, like a mother dog licks the ins and outs of her puppy. Careful, considered, and devoted. Done, the dog's tongue unfurls to lick his dewlaps and he settles his head in Rick's lap for an ear rub. Rick strokes deep into the ear, sliding his fingers up the length of it, moving the cilia. In the pearly winter light, a darker skin emerges within Pax's ear—his tattoo. The mark that designates him as a war dog, a dog who saw service. Who, like him, was wounded in action. Keller's loyal partner on the battlefield.

Not one of the men with whom he served in that doomed squad survived. Removed from the battlefield, Rick was also removed from his platoon. Languishing for months in the hospital, first in England and then here, Rick lost contact with anyone he served with. Some guys, he knows, cling to those associations, reluctant to give up the camaraderie, the mythical brotherhood of battle, but he doesn't. Nor is he willing to seek out any connection. Not after what happened, and the fact that he survived. "Survivor's guilt."—that's what the shrink called it the one time he met with one. *Don't beat yourself up. You tried. Wasn't your fault.* Oh my, how many platitudes have been lobbed at him by all and sundry. Doctors, nurses, the shrink, Francesca. But not Keller. Keller listened to his story, but he didn't attempt to absolve him.

Rick can't read the numbers written on the inside of his

dog's ear. The thick cilia obscure four of the digits; he'd have to shave the inside of the ear to read them. Pax whines a little; Rick is holding that ear too tightly. He lets go, pushes the dog off his lap.

The sound of sleet hitting the window. The room is a little cold and Rick shrugs more blanket up over his shoulder. As he does most every night, he has awakened suddenly and without a known disturbance. He hears the click of the dog's toenails coming down the stairs, Pax alert, as always, for his awakening. Usually, the dog is there before his eyes open, sensitive to Rick's coming awake even from a distance. But lately, Rick has awakened alone in this room, comforted only by the quick sound of those nails on hardwood.

The dog comes in and touches him with a cold nose, as if he's been outside. He wags his tail and does the doggy equivalent of tucking Rick in, resting his head in the crook between Rick's shoulder and chin. Rick knows that as soon as he drifts off, the dog will go away. Go back up to the bedroom Keller uses now that he's been invited into the house, a narrow landing width away from Francesca and the room she occupies alone, sleeping in their marriage bed, a room he's never seen but pictures exactly as the one they had in their first apartment.

Sometimes in the quiet of the deep night, when the street traffic is done and the furnace is satisfied with the temperature and shuts off, Rick thinks he can hear them. The creak of a floorboard. The sound of a bedspring complaining. Like someone has gotten up and moved to another bed. It's just house noises, he tells himself. But tonight he hears murmuring. In the middle of the night, they are close enough to whisper to each other.

Last night they were alone in this house.

Rick presses his ear against his pillow, covers his other ear with the stump of his pitching arm. But he still hears them. Whispers carry farther than the natural voice. He uncovers his ears and strains to listen for distinct words. There is only the rising and falling of tone, and a slight crescendo/decrescendo, as if the conversation were scored with musical notation.

Is it the wind singing through the naked pear tree in the backyard, or the water gurgling in the radiators? It must be the sound of windshield wipers on a lone car on the next block. The train whistle, a foghorn. The sound of his own blood squeezed through his heart? But no. It's voices above him. Whispering to each other. He's sure of it.

Chapter Sixty-three

Pax circles and paces, utterly aware of Rick's agitation. He won't go back upstairs again tonight because he knows that Rick will not fall back into deep sleep again. There is a peppery scent emanating from him, and the remnant sharp scent of the hospital, where they found him and brought him back here. Rubber and alcohol wipes, baby lotion and iodine. Pax wrinkles his nose at the odors but keeps his chin on Rick's bed so that Rick can touch him. Through those fingertips, the dog judges that Rick's racing heart is slowing, but the agitation has not diminished and the clutch of those fingers occasionally becomes painful.

It's like when Keller and he were on night patrol, both of them listening for the sounds of the enemy. Sounds weren't enough, and everything depended upon Pax's being able to distinguish the difference between the scent of German sweat and that of his people. As different as black and white to the dog. Sounds weren't always as distinctive. A German bullet dropped from a cold and clumsy hand sounded the same as an American bullet hitting the bare earth. In the fog, sounds from the east could sound like they were coming from the west. All muffled, blurred. But scent told the story, and the dog ensured his comrades their safe passage through tight boundaries. Rick's scent is as different from Keller's and Francesca's household scent as that of the Germans was from the Allies'.

Rick is listening, and so Pax listens. Outside are only the normal sounds of night creatures moving and cold drizzle pinging off the gutters. Inside, he hears the breathing of sleeping people, the tick of the kitchen clock. Because Rick is, Pax is also on alert, but he cannot fathom what he's supposed to be listening for. It makes him anxious, and he pants a little, paces, returns to Rick's side. They are both awake until a heralding bird announces the momentary arrival of dawn. It has stopped sleeting and the nocturnal creatures have slipped away. Between that early bird's reveille and the laggards' the moment of predawn is more silent than the entire night.

Overhead, a bedspring protests the shift of a body. A floorboard creaks. Very softly, Pax murmurs. Rick is finally asleep.

Chapter Sixty-four

I waited that whole afternoon, listening for Keller's return, half-expecting that he wouldn't come back, maybe more than half-hoping that he wouldn't. It was all too complicated. I loved my husband as much as I ever had, but the spiky passion that had pushed us into a quick marriage and then had elevated to grand heights during our failed baby-making attempts was withered and in danger of dying out entirely. Which was all right. Unnecessary, only a vestige left. Love between us was different now.

Keller's touch had reminded me of passion, that's all. I would not act on it. I didn't need it.

When he came home late that afternoon, the sun long down, the headlights of his car beaming briefly against the white wall of the living room as he pulled into the driveway, I kept out of the way. I heard Pax's nails skittering down the hall to Rick. I could smell the winter air seeping into the house through the breezeway as Keller passed from garage to kitchen. I stayed where I was, turning on the lamps, pulling the drapes. I felt him approach more than heard it. I threw my shoulders back and pasted a smile on my face. There is no avoiding someone who lives in your house. The membrane between us had to be retained. We hadn't broken it; neither could we try testing it again.

"I'm glad you're back. How about hot dogs for dinner tonight?"

Keller slid his jacket off his shoulders and reached into the hall closet for a hanger. For a tense moment, I thought he wouldn't speak to me, that he didn't understand that we had to move ahead, to maintain our alliance as Rick's cobbled-together family. "Sure. Beans, too?"

Such a funny topic for reconciliation. Hot dogs and beans.

"Oh, and I found this." Keller held out my purse. "It was under the front seat."

I took it from him. "How careless of me."

He headed in to check on Rick, leaving me in the hallway, my purse in my hand. I had to wonder, had my purse not been in his car, would he have come back?

Chapter Sixty-five

Francesca had given him new shoes for Christmas, a nice pair of cordovan oxfords like he used to wear on travel days. Rick had smiled and thanked her, then watched as she put them away in his closet to be forgotten. It was so Francesca, to have given him something that suggested he might someday be seen in public again. For his birthday, she'd given him new pants, a pair of everyday khakis like he used to wear on weekends. Something presumably to replace the stained and thin-in-the-seat pants he's maneuvered into every morning by Keller. Rick wonders if these pants will even fit him. She'd bought his usual size, thirty-four, out of habit, not allowing for the fact he no longer has muscle on those thighs. He's shrunk. The only muscle he seems to still have is the one in his left arm, pumped up from playing tug-of-war with the dog. It's the only muscle he's using, although the therapists keep after him to use as much as he can of his back and shoulders. Rick has used the weather as a good excuse not to bother going to physical therapy. Too cold. Too snowy. Too icy. Too windy. Too lazy. It's too much. Too much to keep asking Keller to wrangle him in and out of the car, in and out of chairs, in and out of buildings. Keller doesn't complain. They should give him a damned raise.

Now, along with the resurrected paintings, there is a new calendar on his wall, a Christmas gift from the hardware store that Keller patronizes, featuring an old-fashioned tractor on the top above the months. He doesn't know why Keller stuck that in here. Rick's not the Iowan. What does he care about tractors? What does he care about dates? The worst part is, no matter what month it is that, red riderless tractor sits in that same cornfield. They're up to March and still that cheerful tractor doesn't make any progress. The calendar is supposed to chart his progress. But that isn't moving forward, either.

Since his last hospital stay, Francesca and Keller have become determined that he not spend all day, every day, in this room. Francesca says, "It's time, Rick. It's just no good to be sitting here mostly alone for so much of the time."

"You need to get moving, bud," Keller adds.

They cite the bedsores and the chance of succumbing to pneumonia as reason enough to get moving.

It's like leaving the safety of a cave for the uncertainty of an open plain—darkness to light. The afternoon light in the west-facing living room bothers his eyes. The overhead light in the kitchen glares down. It exhausts him. On good days, Keller and Francesca pile him, all bundled up in wool coat, hat, and gloves, into the car and she drives him down Route 3 to "see the sights" while Keller goes to school. They pass through Hingham and Duxbury, admire the scenery and make wrong turns here and there, giving the outing the aura of an adventure. But they don't talk about much of anything. She repeatedly makes sure his numb legs are covered with the plaid picnic rug, as if he could feel the cold on them.

At night, he feels like a little kid made to sit at the grown-up table. Keller and Francesca sit on opposite sides and carry on conversations based primarily on gossip about the few neighbors Francesca has come to know and people Keller meets at college. Rick has nothing to contribute until they touch on current events, and then he can trot out opinions gleaned from the newspaper and the radio. He's become quite an expert on the rise of communism, but he knows nothing about his neighbors.

"Spring training starts next week." Keller helps himself to more mashed potatoes, as if he's oblivious to the challenge in that remark. Is he kidding? Bringing up a subject like that, as if Rick *cares*.

"Doesn't seem possible another year has flown by." Francesca is a party to this. She hands Keller the butter dish.

"Or at least another season. I've only got six weeks left in the semester." Keller slices off a pat of chilled butter. "I'll be out by early May." This semester, Keller has taken on a full course load, and he spends every minute that he's not tending Rick's needs with his head in a book.

Rick gestures for the butter. "Have you declared a major yet?" He's going to give the spring training remark a pass. Keller is a man, and men do pay attention to such things.

Keller leans over and cuts the butter for Rick, dropping the pat on his potato. "That's kind of like deciding what I want to be when I grow up." He laughs a little, then shrugs. "Believe it or not, and Francesca thinks this is a good idea, I'm thinking of education."

"A teacher." Rick presses his fork onto the solid bit of butter, squashing it into the mound of mashed potatoes. *Francesca thinks it's a good idea*. It's like he's the third wheel in this ménage. Keller and his wife are always having these little casual exchanges, just as if they were the married couple and he was the goddamned tenant. Catch up if you can with their private jokes and the showy finishing of each other's sentences. Try filling the holes in the dialogue that, for them, need no explanation. Keller hands her the butter *before* she asks. "Good for you to have a goal. A real career."

"Speaking of which . . ." Francesca sets her utensils down, folds her hands.

He remembers when she would cast her eyes down like this, when they were alone and he knew that the moment she raised her eyes to his, he'd be incapable of denying her anything.

"Rick, we think that maybe it's time for you to start thinking about what you might want to do." Francesca looks him in the eye.

" 'We'?" He lays his fork down on the side of his half-full plate. "Do? Do what?"

The little moue of annoyance is a new expression for her. "For a living."

"Well, as you say, spring training has started already, so I guess I'm too late for baseball."

"Good one, Rick." Does Keller actually believe he's joking? Does he think this conversation is going to end in guffaws?

"Sweetheart, there are things that you can do." It's like she's a lion tamer and *sweetheart* is her three-legged chair. She cracks the whip. "We need you to at least think about it." Again the *we*.

"How can I—"

"You have an accounting degree, right?" Keller's perfect right hand holds a fork suspended in mid-flight. His perfect left hand is clutched in a gentle fist and rests on the table.

"Yes." They're ganging up on him. He can't believe this.

"And how am I supposed to go to an office? Are you going to chauffeur me every day? And hang around so I can be helped to the bathroom? You know, to empty my bag?"

Rick feels Pax's nose bumping the sleeve-wrapped stump of his arm, lifting it as if he expects Rick to pet him with that invisible hand. He ignores it. A paw goes onto his leg and he's aware of that only because he can see what the dog is doing. The dog is breaking the house rules against approaching the table and no one says anything until the dog speaks: *Roof.* He might be asking Rick to settle down, calm down. He is asking and, in pushing himself against Rick, pushes Rick away from the table.

How easy it is for people who don't have disabilities to imagine that it's mind over matter to overcome them. How dare these two conspire against him; how could Francesca be consulting with Keller about things that should be only their concern, between husband and wife? It's none of Keller's business. Francesca's disloyalty brings a hot flush to Rick's face, but his anger is turned at Keller. Keller is overstepping himself. "Take me to my room. Now."

"Rick, we're just saying that you're in much better condition than you were even a month ago. It's time. Time for you to—"

"Keller, maybe it's time for you to shut up."

Chapter Sixty-six

Pax put himself in between them, his front end in Rick's lap, his tail end backed up to Keller's chair. He whined a little, an oddly plaintive sound in the silence that followed Rick's hard-sounding words, like a human growl warning off a challenger. His tail wagged slowly, like a dog that expects a beating and hopes a show of submission will prevent it. Ears back, nose down. This discord was agonizing. They had finally begun acting like a proper pack and Pax was sorely afraid that now the pack, his pack, was disintegrating. Only one male can be leader; the other must either submit, or leave.

He followed as Keller pushed Rick back to his room. Instead of settling Rick in, Keller turned and walked out, leaving Pax to decide where he should be. A soft snapping of fingers and Pax went to Rick, sitting down in front of him, ears still in the supplicant position, hoping that Rick's heartbeat would slow to normal and the blast of heated anxiety would lessen as he found Pax's ears.

"What do they want of me?" Soft whisper into an ear, a susurration that tickles him a bit. *"What does she want of me? I'm*

not the man she married. Is that what this means? Because I'm no longer a provider?" A ragged breath. *"They don't understand that I'm scared. Scared that I've lost everything."*

Rick's fingers dug deep into the nape of the dog's neck. Pax closed his eyes, infused with the primitive recollection of being safe in his mother's jaws. When she'd gripped him thus, she'd been moving him out of danger. Rick's grip suggested that there was some danger Pax could not glean through his usual senses. Some danger emanating from within Rick.

Pax could hear the tiny *tick-tick* of the pills bumping into one another as Rick groped into that bitter-smelling pouch at his side.

Chapter Sixty-seven

An official-looking envelope arrives, a string of lawyers' names emblazoned on the upper left-hand corner. Clayton's estate has been probated and Keller Nicholson is the sole heir. He now officially owns the house, the boats, the moorings, the pier, the acre of unkempt pasture, and the half-acre woodlot. Keller has never owned anything in his life but that secondhand Ford, so the idea of this, even something as shrouded in unpleasant memory as that house, is a novelty. Becoming the default owner of Clayton's holdings has had the unexpected effect of coloring Keller's worldview. He may be a boarder here, but elsewhere he's a man of property.

Mooring rental will pay the taxes. Clayton had redone the roof a couple of years ago, so the house is in pretty good shape. He doesn't have to see it, or even pick up the key from the lawyer. The foursquare two-story fisherman's house can sit and wait for him, for when he's ready. For when he knows what he should do.

. . .

Francesca bends over her tangled yarn and Rick yawns over a magazine. Keller has his textbook open to the chapter on the Romantic poets and is making notes. Pax is in the fetal position in his basket, twitching in some rabbit dream. Or maybe a night-patrol dream. Keller still has those. But now his nightmares are informed by Rick's story. Of explosions and falling through space. He dreams all too often of losing Pax, of not being able to find him. Or finding him in pieces. He wakes in a cold sweat from those nightmares, relieved beyond words to always find the dog still there, in one piece, hogging the narrow cot.

Keller closes his textbook and excuses himself from the domestic scene. The dog is instantly awake, ready to do whatever Keller asks. He waves Pax back. The dog belongs in this room with them. As if to underscore that, Rick speaks to the dog. "Pax, stay here."

Keller suppresses a flash of annoyance; it's as if some other handler has ordered his dog. As if his command needs seconding. But this isn't some other handler; this is Rick. Rick, who has every right to command Pax. Keller has successfully turned the scout dog into a useful tool; retraining not only has reverted the war dog to a safe family pet but has also turned Keller's canine partner into a lifeline for his once and future master. For Rick. Francesca is focused on her yarn; her mouth twitches as she struggles to untangle the rat's nest of blue worsted.

Rick has everything, Keller thinks. He leaves the room before he can blush at the selfish and unbelievably juvenile thought. He's jealous of a cripple.

He's got an army reserve weekend coming up and he's actually looking forward to it. He definitely needs a break from this stultifying atmosphere of domesticity. He's deeply tired.

A couple of days outside, obeying clear and emotionless orders, forgetting the quotidian tasks of caring for an inert and angry man, will go a long way in refreshing his own spirit. Since the abortive suggestion that Rick start thinking about what work he might take on, they've kept their silence on the subject, waiting, hoping, that Rick will come around. But the black thing that inhabits him hasn't lifted enough to make that possible. They have begun color-coding his days: Today he's a little blue—a gray day. Very black today. Pax has become their bellwether. When he gets Rick to throw a toy, engage in a persistent game of fetch, then they know it's a good day. It's mid-May, and the semester is a week from done. Warmer weather has meant that on the days that playing with the dog brightens Rick's mood to pink, Keller wheels him outside. But when the dog comes out of Rick's room with a squeaky toy hanging out of his mouth and teases Keller or Francesca into playing, they know that it's a bad day for Rick. He won't emerge from what Keller has dubbed his "Cave of Gloom," and everyone else will tiptoe around, as if afraid to disturb the black thing that draws him into himself.

Francesca has released the yarn from its Gordian knot. She smiles and begins to cast on. She is relentless in her knitting. Socks and scarves, sweaters and vests. Keller's bureau drawer is filled with her largess. They all itch. He itches to touch her. Their chaste adherence to a dual loyalty and honor doesn't mean he doesn't *think* about breaking this unspoken and mutually enforced prohibition. There are days when Rick is so intolerant of her, days when Keller wants nothing more than to take her away, show her how it is to be loved properly. And then he watches her eyes as she deflects Rick's antagonism, wholly absent of hurt. Keller can't overlook the other days, the ones when Rick's equilibrium is level and the two, husband

and wife, share a joke or a smile fraught with the secret code of marriage, which Keller can't begin to understand.

But then there are the other moments, when the three of them—and Pax—become something like a family. Keller doesn't imagine that he is their child or some hybrid husband and brother, but a valued member of a small family that has built a retaining wall out of necessity. And those are the days that most break his heart. If he desires Francesca, it is as a man desires the unattainable, with bittersweet longing. If he feels like a part of a cobbled-together family, that fulfills a greater and more gentle longing.

Keller heads through the breezeway into the garage, checks the hardware store thermometer on the wall. Fifty-eight degrees. Warm enough. Tomorrow he'll bring his stuff back down here, where he can get away from feeling like he's skating on thin ice; no relief from proximity. Pax pads in, sniffs the corners, and sits beside him. "Ready to move back down here?"

Roof.

"Me, too."

The envelope informing him that he's an heir takes up space on his workbench. He's left it there with Miss Jacobs's letters, as if they were tools or scrap wood. Keller rips a sheet of paper from his notebook.

Dear Miss Jacobs,
You were absolutely correct. I have the dubious distinction of being Clayton Britt's sole heir, with the attendant inheritance taxes. So, without looking for it, I have it all. Nonetheless, I won't be back anytime soon. I've got a good thing here, and my studies are going very well. You'd be impressed with my vastly improved vocabulary.

He asks her to keep an eye out for potential tenants. He could bank the income. Add to the little nest egg built on his mainly unspent pay from his active service. A little more money would help to keep things afloat here. The occupational therapist and the physical therapist agree with them that Rick is perfectly capable of working at an office job, but until he accepts that he's as healed as he's likely ever to be, a little silent contribution to the household expenses from Keller will help keep them on an even keel. Francesca never needs to know that he's paying for groceries or home improvements out of his own pocket.

I've got a good thing going here. That's an enigmatic statement for sure. There are days when he's perfectly happy, and others when he questions his sanity. What is really keeping him here? Pax nudges his writing hand as if to hurry him along. "Please think kindly of me and let me know how you are."

Maybe he should think about selling the house, but Keller balks at the idea. No, the house in Hawke's Cove will wait for him. For when he finally has had enough.

Chapter Sixty-eight

Lately he feels a stiffness in his hindquarters that he's never had before, not even in those few days after he'd been wounded and strangers had handled him until Keller came back from his own wounds. It's just a little harder to get up, and the basket is so much more comfortable than the floor, even if the square of light warms it up. Better yet is the couch, and he's been deliberately disobedient every chance he gets, having been encouraged into misbehavior by the couple of times Francesca and Keller have invited him up to sit between them as they listen to the noises coming from the box in the living room.

Nothing else is diminished. His hearing is just as acute, his eyesight what it has always been. And his nose, superior instrument that it is, still carries the stories to him on the air—the air in the house and the air outside. In the house, the air is thick with the story of his people. How they use their voices but say nothing. How they emit the olfactory aura of discontent. He sighs and yawns and settles his head or paws on each of them in turn. But they don't take as much comfort from him as they did. Keller disappears. Rick dismisses him. Francesca orders him out of the kitchen. Even those painful times when Rick clutches at his nape, sucking the stillness and comfort out of him, have changed. Less frequent, less successful. Almost as if Rick has chosen to suffer his fear and distress alone. Like a mother hiding her nest from other dogs, even perhaps her mate. A hidden den is easier to defend.

A walk to the beach with Keller usually gets the kinks out. Pax hears the breezeway door open and he looks to Rick to see if he can go greet Keller. Rick's eyes are down, as they often are, and his fingers are playing within that little pouch he has attached to his chair. The bag holds those tiny white pills that the dog can smell even through the thick duck cloth. They clatter together as Rick fingers them, audible enough to the dog, if not to anyone else.

Chapter Sixty-nine

Pax materializes at Rick's bedside. Rick has gotten himself into a sitting position, the undisturbed blankets still neatly across his lower half. His pillow is folded in half, propping him against the headboard of the hospital bed. He holds a glass in his remaining hand. On the canyon formed by his motionless legs is his collection of twenty-two little white pills. The twenty-second spheroid is today's victory. He's been counting them. The number never changes, never improves, never becomes a sure thing.

"I'm all right, Paxy. You can go back to bed." Rick sets the water glass down on the bedside table. "Just counting."

Pax sits, his amber eyes on the man. He yawns, releasing a tension he's picking up from Rick.

"You're just like him, you know. Always watching me." Rick makes a little pile out of his collection. He's a miser hoarding gold coins. "Are you wondering what I'm waiting for? Is that it? Should I be dramatic, or just efficient? Will they figure out my reason?"

Pax sets one paw on the edge of the bed, noses Rick's dead

leg as if trying to push him into getting up. It was what the dog once did, a hundred years ago, when they were both young and vigorous and had a wide-open future. When Rick would flop down on the sofa of his bachelor apartment to catch a few z's after practice, the puppy would poke at him with his nose, up and down his arm, into the back of his knee. *Get up! Play with me!* Rick mildly wonders if the dog really understands what is wrong with him, if he thinks that Rick is just being lazy. "I wish I could take you out, run you on the beach, race you home. I wish that almost more than anything else."

Francesca left the window open a little when she came in to bid him good night. A light breeze stirs the curtains, a spring zephyr reminding Rick of those taken-for-granted days of spring training. That very first practice, when the morning air was still cold but the sun promised an afternoon warmth that would have them stripping off their shirts by lunchtime. There was a taste to the air, as if excitement had a flavor. Now all he can taste is the metallic flavor of medication.

"You want something, don't you, Pax? You want me to jump up and play with you like Keller does?" Rick hates it that the dog's head cocks in an ever-so-cute fashion at the sound of Keller's name. "You like him better than me?"

In answer, Pax stands and shakes, as if Rick is asking him unanswerable questions. He sits again to stare at Rick. It's as if the dog will keep his eye on Rick all night long, making sure that the man doesn't do anything rash. He's a guardian and defender, a preventer of final acts. Rick points to the basket. "Go to bed, Pax. Now."

With an almost human reluctance, the dog peels himself away from Rick's bedside and goes to sit in his basket. But his eyes never leave Rick's face. He's looking at him with human eyes—Keller's eyes—that portray a deep concern. A trick of the bedside lamp, and the dog's eyes become Francesca's, filled with an ancient love. She still loves him; she does. Despite Rick's night terrors, his middle-of-the-night paranoia about Keller and Francesca, deep down he knows that whatever is growing between his wife and his caretaker, she still loves him. This tripartite living has cast them all into mutable roles. Husband, patient, wife, friend, sister, brother, stranger, caregiver, war veteran, war hero, fool. The only immutable quality is their love of Pax.

Rick digs deeper into the empty cloth pouch, his fingers searching for another morphine pill. Maybe he's missed one. He is so tired. His wife and his friend might blame him for leaving them behind, but he is more cursed than blamed for having survived when his buddies had not. The one irreconcilable, the one factor that transcends all the other reasons for ending this struggle, the one he might scrawl on a piece of notepaper laden with his awkward left-handed writing, is his colossal and unforgiveable screwup. Keller idly remarks about coaching Little League, as if Rick could ever again lead a group of boys. Boys just a little younger than the ones in his squad, slaughtered because he thought he could pitch his way out of the situation. Killed by his own grenade, or finished off by the laughing Germans. How can he ever confess the shame of that? Yet without that confession, how can he ever make Francesca understand the magnitude of his despair? He allows her to think it's his wounds that grieve him, and she allows that partial truth to be enough to account for his gloom. But maybe not enough for the desperate act he intends.

Keller will get it, the truth of why Rick has done this thing, and maybe he can leave Keller to tell Francesca the story of the grenade and Rick's hubris. If he hasn't already. Is there a code between them as there is between husband and wife—no outside secrets? Some code. Rick has hung on to his shameful secret, keeping it from Francesca and letting the sharp edges of guilt chisel away at his self-esteem. He doesn't know if he's more afraid that she'll forgive him for putting his squad in danger, and try and make him forget that it happened, or hate him for it, for not being the man she thought he was.

Pax is back at his bedside. His eyes are no longer asking questions; they are zeroed in on what his hand is doing, the gathering together of his delivery from the constant pain of failure. He lifts his eyes to Rick's, makes a tiny vocalization that sounds almost like the word *no*. Rick puts the pills, one by one, into the handy cloth bag, counting them yet again. There are still twenty-two.

Chapter Seventy

Pax dreams a running dream and his feet twitch and his chest compresses with silent barks. He's chasing a man through trees and grass, across streets and into the deepest woods imaginable. The dream scent is as potent an aggression aphrodisiac as any he encountered while performing his duties as a member of the K-9 Corps. This threat is only six feet in front of him; he just needs to put on more speed to catch his man. But something holds him back; some weight prevents him from that final burst of speed and energy. Frustrated, he yelps like a kicked puppy. And then he wakes up.

Keller's arm is what's holding him down; in sleep, he's flung it over the dog's body. A thin gray light is visible in the bedroom window, filling the frame with a new day being sung in by the first bird. Pax raises his head, listens, sniffs the air. *Something*.

Pax extricates himself from Keller's embrace and slips to the floor. His ears move back and forth, judging the outside sounds against the inside sounds. Birdsong. The milkman two streets over. Breathing. Keller's. He walks through the breezeway passage, stands still. Francesca's soft breathing. Two are sleeping deeply. One is not. Rick.

The fur between his shoulders rises and Pax lowers his head, centers his weight over his strong forelimbs. As did his hunting forebears, Pax moves in a slow, liquid motion through the house on noiseless pads, as alert to danger as he had ever been on patrol. *Something.*

Chapter Seventy-one

Rick has decided that twenty-two is enough. One makes him feel good. Two make him drowsy. Surely, now that he's half the man he used to be, twenty-two should be more than enough. The trick isn't to swallow them all at once, but parcel them out over fifteen minutes, not long enough to fall asleep before the deed is done, but long enough between pills that he won't throw them up. Oh yes. He's thought a lot about this.

The pills are lined up on his tray table like a row of ammunition. His bedside lamp is on, casting a cheery yellow warmth to the white tablets. He's said good night to everyone. Francesca didn't understand that his kiss good night was the final farewell; the lingering sweetness of her surprised response to his kiss is almost enough in itself to make him step back from this ledge. And when Keller popped his head in to say good night on his way to the garage, Rick smiled and maybe confused him a little when he said, "Good night. And thanks. For everything." Keller just said "Sleep well" and left. Rick heard the kitchen light snap off and the sound of the connecting door being opened.

The prompt to this being the night was so simple. Johnny Antonelli, at age eighteen, had become a starting pitcher for the Boston Braves. Eighteen. The age of cannon fodder not long ago. Kid would have been a schoolboy during the war. The age when your body seems invulnerable. At twenty-eight, Rick was already ten years older than Antonelli when he got what should have been his big break. And even then he was already icing a sore pitching arm after every practice. This kid can probably pitch a whole game and then go play tennis. Even if he had come back whole and been put back on the Braves roster, a kid like this would have shown up sooner or later and shoved Rick out. Traded probably, or rarely played. It seems so unfair. Rick knows that this is crazy thinking, but it's been enough to get him to empty out the pouch and line up the pills. Rick has assiduously avoided the sports page, refuses to listen to games, but even he heard about this player, this paragon. This upstart wearing his number.

The pills are lined up on the tray table. Pretty little things.

He just can't go on this way. The darkness always there, the weight of his sin; the sharp point of his professional disappointment. His utter failure as a husband, unable to give his wife a child.

Keller will take care of Francesca, take care of Pax. He, too, is wearing Rick's number.

Rick swallows the first pill. Pax is suddenly there, his eyes fixed on him with a stare that is a thin degree from hostile. He should have known the dog would be in as soon as he stirred from the sleep he'd been feigning. Rick has spent the night tallying up his grievances, weighing out his justification, letting the pain in his phantom limb keep him awake. He's not sure if he wants the dog to be there for this final sleep, to be a silent witness to his cowardice, because, yes, Rick knows that

322 • Susan Wilson

he's taking the coward's way out, but that's okay. Rather a dead coward than a live fool.

"Go to bed."

Instead of going to his basket, the dog stands beside Rick, chucks his nose under Rick's hand to get a pat. That first pill has relaxed him, the pain in his phantom limb throbbing with less intensity. Rick spends a long time stroking the dog, whispering things into his tattooed ear that he'll never say again. Telling him that he needs to be a good dog. "You're a lucky dog, Pax. You have good people to keep loving you."

Pax doesn't wriggle with pleasure; he stiffens instead, the same kind of immobility he displays when a squirrel comes along. The same kind of immobility that Keller speaks of when talking about Pax's years as an army scout dog. A dog for defense. The silent alert to danger. It's almost enough to make Rick look up to see if there is an intruder. The dog's body is rock solid with tension. His eyes aren't on some distant mark, but looking right at Rick. As if he is the intruder. He backs away and lowers his head, eyes fixed on Rick's. He growls, a soft inquiring sound.

"It's all right. Go to bed." The last thing Rick wants is for the dog to alert Keller.

Pax remains where he is.

"So be it." Rick reaches for a pill, picks up the glass, washes it down. Sets the glass down, reaches for another pill. The dog's nostrils twitch, as if he can smell it and is repulsed by the odor of the morphine. Rick takes another. And another. Ten go down. He's got to be careful; he's swallowed nearly half the glass of water that Keller has left for him should he get thirsty in the night. He's not sure he could manage to chew his way through the remaining collection of pills.

Rick sets the glass down to gather up the rest of the pills for

A Man of His Own • 323

one last swallow. As he does, Pax suddenly leaps up onto the bed, knocking the tray table over, scattering the remaining morphine pills to all four corners of the room. And he commences barking an alert, a warning as vital as any alarm he made during the war.

Rick doesn't hear the dog or feel the weight of him standing on his chest. Rick gives in to the weight of the morphine as it pulls him down and down.

Chapter Seventy-two

The dog's first bark puts Keller on his feet. A purposed bark, a warning and a threat. Pax barks and barks, and barks until Keller, barefoot and shivering in his boxers and T-shirt, is in Rick's room. Not for an instant does he interpret the barking as a sign that there's an intruder or a squirrel. The dog's meaning is as clear to him as if the animal is speaking to him in English. *Danger, danger.* The moment Keller steps into the room, the dog ceases his alert, jumps down from the bed.

Rick is sleeping peacefully. Impossible. Not with all this noise. Not with the eighty-five-pound dog on him, barking in his face. Keller feels as if he's stepped on a land mine; his gut twists and he can't remember to breathe. In seconds, Francesca will be down, grasping her tattered housecoat around herself, looking to him to solve this problem. He touches Rick's face with shaking fingers. Still warm. He feels for a wrist pulse, but his own pulse is beating so hard, he can't distinguish the difference.

"Rick, wake up!" Keller manhandles Rick's pajama front, lifting him and slapping his cheeks. "Wake up!" Where is

Francesca? Why isn't she here? Surely the noise has awakened her, too. He just can't figure out what's wrong. Rick was fine when they went to bed. *And thanks. For everything.* Rick's words now seem sinister. And then he sees it, a single white pill caught in the folds of the blanket. Morphine. "Oh shit."

Keller tries for a pulse in Rick's neck. Maybe there's something. Please let there be something. Rick can't do this to them.

It's what he wants, Keller thinks. He lowers Rick back to the pillow. Leave him. From some deep, impulsive place, an unspeakable thought snakes into his brain: Just let him go. Everyone will be better off. The thought is outrageous enough to freeze him into a moment of hesitation that might be seen as his not knowing what to do, not as if he's impaled on the sharp point of treason. He has to get to the phone, the new extension he had installed is on the other side of the bed, but he can't move. She would be free, he thinks.

"Rick!" Francesca appears exactly as he imagined, the threadbare housecoat sloppily tied with the frayed belt. What he hadn't seen in his mind's eye is the frantic reach of her hands, pushing him aside, as if she has a greater influence on this outcome. Keller grabs the telephone, vastly relieved to be shoved out of the way.

They are sitting in a small windowless room, more closet than something meant for anxious family members. The emergency room's waiting area had been overcrowded with people, as if there was a white sale going on in this cheerless place. Two for one! Stock up! A nurse, capped and starched into authority, had taken them out of the general waiting room to leave them here in this closet with its two hard chairs and tainted scent of used linen. Keller wonders if it's a room designated for the bereaved, for people who need to be out of the general population because of the weight of their particular emergency. Not a room for those bringing in vomiting drinking buddies or kids with broken bones or babies with a rash, a fever. This is a special room for those whose lives are about to be changed.

Francesca sits quietly, her gaze upon her clasped hands, a handkerchief woven between her fingers. He paces, a useless exercise in this ten-by-ten room—really more dramatic than meaningful. Around and around he goes, a prisoner in his cell. He's pacing out of habit; this place is so like the isolation room at Meadowbrook. Sentenced for crimes as varied as insolence or instigating a food fight, Keller spent his incarcerations in that room, walking a perfect square, north, south, east, and west. It was better than huddling on the bare floor and straining to hear the sound of someone coming to release him from his punishment.

"I just don't understand." Francesca is still keeping her eyes on her hands, as if by addressing her clenched fists she can say what's on her mind. "I don't understand."

Keller stops pacing; waits until she can articulate her thoughts.

"How could he do this to me?"

Keller tips the door to the tiny room closed, kneels beside Francesca, and gently holds her in his arms. "It's really complicated."

She leans her weight against him and he thinks that he can stay like that forever. She pulled on a simple housedress to come to the hospital, the one she had been wearing all day, his favorite, a pale yellow sprigged with tiny roses. He thinks she looks lovely, even with her curls uncombed in her haste to dress. Maybe especially. She looks young, vulnerable, and willing to let him contain her within the strength of his arms. Arms bulked up with the daily effort of lifting an inert man. These are the wrong thoughts to be having. His place is to comfort and console, not desire.

"Can I tell you something?"

He feels the vibration of her voice against his chest.

"Of course."

"Doesn't he know how much it would kill me if he died?" Francesca laughs a little. "How easily we use those words— *kill, die.* But it would. I would die if anything happened to him. Happens."

Suddenly, it's uncomfortable, this kneeling on the hard linoleum floor. Keller shifts, squats in front of her. His hands are on her arms, and he shakes her to make her look up, away from her hands, into his eyes. He can't help himself: He strokes away one of the more unruly curls, the one that lingers by the side of her mouth. He takes her face in his hands. "It's more than that, Francesca. I mean, his pain is more than his wounds." How hard it is to put into words the answer she needs. "Sometimes what happens on the battlefield is so awful that it's impossible to talk about, but it never leaves you."

She looks at him blankly, puzzled, but doesn't try to take her face away from his cupped hands. "What has he told you?" She unlinks her hands and places them on his, which cup her face. He can't tell if she means to pull his hands away or secure them there. She studies his eyes, desperate to understand what he means.

"It's what happened, the day he was wounded."

"They were attacked from above. It was only a miracle that he survived." She drops her hands.

"Rick thinks that it was his fault that everyone was killed." Keller wraps his arms around Francesca so that he doesn't have to look her in the eye when he tells her an abridged version of the story Rick told him. Keller feels like he's betraying a confidence, yet without this betrayal, Francesca will never understand the truth behind Rick's self-destructive act.

"He told *you* this?"

"Yes."

"And not me." Francesca's face is so close to his, he can feel the soft puffs of her agitated breathing on his cheek. "Why couldn't he tell me? Abruptly, she sits back, pulling away from his touch.

A knock on the door stops Keller from saying anything more. The capped and starched nurse leans in. "You can go in now."

Keller stands up and offers his hand to Francesca.

Hers is warm, a little damp. "I can go in by myself."

Keller steps back, letting Francesca go.

Chapter Seventy-three

I was gutted. Hollowed out. I looked down on my husband, who would not look at me. Was this the same man who had kept glancing up at me from the bull pen as I stood in the grandstand, cheering on the opposing team? The man who had smiled at me and I'd felt the electric charge of connection pass between us? I'd thought that we were two halves of the same whole. This was the man to whom I had committed my youth and my life, eyes wide open. The lover who had made me believe we knew each other so profoundly that we experienced everything as one. But we hadn't. And my husband, my dearest, hadn't trusted me with his shame, his self-condemnation. It was as if I didn't know this man at all.

When he had arrived at Walter Reed, grievously wounded and so damaged, I was sent by the head nurse into a ward filled with other wounded soldiers. The massive room was cluttered with traction rigs, stainless-steel trollies, and simple curtains on frames rolled between beds. The antiseptic stench was pervasive in that ward, I fought against putting my hand to my nose. Every bed contained a ghost wrapped with the dead white of gauzy bandages, hiding missing eyes and protecting burned faces. They all looked the same, the mummification rendering the wounded into grotesque Kewpie dolls.

But I'd unerringly walked directly to Rick's bed; the obscuring bandages unable to hide him from me. I'd known him out of all the disguised wounded. And now I looked at him, his scars so familiar that they no longer occurred to me, and I didn't know him at all.

They would transfer him to the VA hospital once he was stabilized, and Rick would have to remain there until the doctors were confident that he wouldn't try again.

They drive home in silence. What is there to say that isn't obscenely mundane or too useless? They will eat leftovers; they will not ask questions that begin with the word *why*. When they pull into the driveway, Keller shuts the engine off and doesn't move to get out.

Francesca pulls the door handle, swings open her door, but she stays seated. "You go in. I want to take a little walk by myself."

Keller nods, willing to let her clear her head, hoping that when she comes back, she'll let him know that she doesn't hold him in contempt for keeping Rick's confidence. He watches in the rearview mirror as Francesca starts down the sidewalk, the yellow of her sprigged dress too cheerful for the look of grief on her face. The warm day has turned gloomy; a heavy cloud lurks in the southeast.

Keller and Pax wait in the kitchen for Francesca to come home. He's pulled out the leftover pot roast and potatoes and is slowly reheating them on the stove. He stirs, listens, stirs some more. The first strike of rain hits the kitchen window.

"Come on, Pax. Let's find her." He shuts off the gas beneath the pot.

Keller wishes that he still had the flat leather service collar that told Pax he was on duty, but his words are enough to get the dog's attention. "Seek."

The dog doesn't bolt; he casts slowly along the edge of the driveway, down to the sidewalk, turns left, then right, adjudging the depth of Francesca's most recent scent against the one she might have left earlier in the day. It's raining harder, and Keller wonders if the scent will be washed away before the dog can locate her. He unfurls the umbrella he snatched from the hall closet and repeats his command: "Seek."

Pax drops his nose to the sidewalk and strikes the scent. They march off toward the beach, then take a sharp right, as if she'd changed her mind. The blocks aren't perfectly shaped, and she's left a trail of indecision and confusion. A blind alley, a narrow sidewalk with crumbling cement lifted by old trees and a decade of frost heaves. Back toward the beach. Keller despairs that they are going around in circles, like children playing around a tree. Catch me if you can. They come to a playground, where Pax breathes in the scent of her footprints impressed in the new mud forming at the swing set. Did she sit for a moment on these swings? Maybe lifted herself up like a girl again, allowing herself to feel the freedom of leaving the ground? Or just rocked gently back and forth?

Pax doesn't mistake this "seek" for a game. The distress rising out of the fast-diluted scent powers him forward. She is in trouble. She is lost. Keller, the most rock steady of partners, is close to panic. Something has happened, and even a dog knows that it has something to do with what happened in Rick's room. Rick is gone again and maybe Francesca has tried to find him. Humans have such inadequate noses. Why didn't she call on him to help? Now she's missing and it is becoming more challenging to discern the scent molecules that she's left behind in her wake as they get closer to the shoreline and the rain beats down harder. Keller's scent of worry almost obscures the faint tracery of her scent in the air. Pax pauses at the footprints, gathers a fresh sample of Francesca, and raises his head. She's not far. He can hear her.

Pax nearly pulls Keller off his feet as he charges across the busy shore drive to the Squantum Yacht Club pier.

Francesca is drenched, but she leans against the wooden rail of the pier as if she's standing there on a summer day, oblivious to the way her dress clings to her body. Even before he reaches her, Keller sees how violently she is shaking and he pulls off his shirt to cover her shoulders. "Come home, Francesca. Come home."

She leans into him and he can see that the shaking is less from the chill of a late-spring rain than from the emotions that have driven her out here, staring down to the flat muddy shingle at low tide fifteen feet below the narrow pier.

Pax, quarry located, stands at her knees and pushes himself against her so that she moves away from the rail.

Francesca offers no resistance as Keller wraps his arm around her and the three walk the most direct way back home. The umbrella over their heads affords the illusion of intimacy as they walk through this neighborhood. A shelter for their shared distress. Keller is the one shivering now, but he isn't cold. His muscles twitch with unexpressed tension.

· · ·

Keller carries her upstairs as if she's his bride. Francesca is impassive, but she closes her eyes as he towels her hair, her face, her neck; gives a little moan as he unbuttons her soaking dress and rubs her shoulders. He wraps the bath towel around her and makes her sit so that he can remove her shoes. He slides a hand underneath her slip to unlock the mystery of garters and carefully peels off her wet nylons. He holds her icy feet in his hands and, in a spontaneous and natural gesture, lowers his lips to kiss them.

She breathes in sharply, as if awakening from a dream. Francesca takes his wet hair in both hands and forces his head up. And she kisses him.

Chapter Seventy-four

At his insistence, Rick has been gotten out of bed and is sitting in the small hospital solarium. This wheelchair is hospital-issue and he feels as though he is higher up than usual. The orderly tucked an extra pillow behind him, so he's also more upright, as if one half of his body is at attention. He doesn't want Francesca to find him slumped and defeated. He wants her to believe that his attempt wasn't the act of a weak man, but of a decisive one. This is one failure for which he will take full responsibility, and for which he is sorry. Whether or not he is sorry for having tried or sorry for having failed will depend on the look on her face when she comes into this relentlessly sunny room.

The orderly has faced Rick toward the window, with its view of nothing more than the sky. There is no one else in the solarium with him, no obligation to make forced conversation, no contention for the better magazines. There is a clock on the wall, a pie-size Timex with an audible tick as the second hand moves in a persistent sweep around the face, counting off the minutes as Rick waits for Francesca. Official visiting hours don't start for an hour, but he expects her at any moment, although he can't say why he thinks Francesca will defy the rules.

Keller will bring her. He won't let her come alone. Keller, who has become so important to them—to him, to her. From a shy and nearly mute helper, Keller has been transformed into a friend. Nonetheless, Rick is hoping that for once Keller won't come along with Francesca. He really needs time alone with her, not like the hours they spend closeted in his room, but quality time. Time enough to say what he needs to say, tell her the truth about what happened in the Italian mountains; to beg her forgiveness. He can't do that with an audience. Keller may have a stake in this, but Rick has to rebuild his life with Francesca from the ground up.

Gradually, he'd been lifted out of his dreamless narcotic sleep into a dream-filled slumber in which he saw her fading away like a ghost, an ethereal revenant of the happy-go-lucky girl she was before his transformation from luckiest man on earth to this wreck of a man. As long as she's believed that he is a casualty of war, not of ego, she's been tied to him by a love that has been refined into admiration and devotion from the fire of passion. But if she knows the truth, how long will she want to be tied down to a vainglorious idiot? How strong is love when there is nothing more than marital duty framing it?

All too often lately he hears her laughing with Keller, hears that girlish trill that he no longer teases out of her. Keller makes Francesca happy. She deserves happiness.

Rick begins to cry. He doesn't want to lose Francesca; she is everything to him. His life. More important than any loss—limb, mobility, career, even Pax—losing her would kill him. But she has to know the truth. And that may drive her away.

· · ·

My husband heard me come into the solarium, the click of my heels on the linoleum loud in that otherwise-silent room. His back was to me, but he sat up straighter and I watched him raise his hand to wipe his face, so I knew that he had been weeping. Those tears broke my heart. Then I was at his side, kneeling, touching his hand, and fumbling in my purse for my handkerchief. "It's all right, my darling, it's all right."

"I have to tell you something."

"No. You don't. I know and it's all right."

"Keller told you?"

"Yes."

"It's my story to tell."

"He needed to help me understand why you . . . why you did what you did."

"Where is he?"

And that was when I began to cry.

I awoke that morning to meet the pure light of a spring day and the certainty that Keller had to go. We had not succumbed. I kissed him and tasted his desire like thirst rising up to be quenched. Like mine had been in those early days of Rick's courtship, when we resolved it was best to get married rather than burn, when *burn* to me meant with unsatisfied desire, not the fires of hell. With his kiss, Keller instigated the memory of that old unrequited passion; his mouth and fingers ignited the fire of my physical desire, which had been tamped down for so long by circumstance of war and wounds. I wanted him. As I had wanted my husband from the first.

And it was the thought of Rick that stopped me.

"No. We can't."

"Francesca." His voice was deep with the words pressing to get out. "I love you."

"Keller. No. You can't."

"I do." Keller Nicholson was an honorable man. A good man. He gently released me and kissed my cheek. "But you love Rick."

"Yes. No matter what's happened, or what he did, he's my husband."

Keller picked up his forgotten shirt from the floor. "I love him, too, Francesca. I do."

Rick would be gone for weeks, or even months. Keller no longer had a purpose in our house. We would be dancing around each other, alone except for the dog. It wasn't concern for what the neighbors might say. Not at all. After all, he could rent a room somewhere else for the duration. It was that I wasn't sure I had the moral fortitude to have Keller so close. He'd poured his heart out in those three little words and I didn't know if I was strong enough to resist temptation—and afraid that someday I might take what comfort he offered. I could never forsake Rick, so all that Keller would ever have of me would be far less than what he wanted. Keller could never have my love.

So I said the words that effectively broke everyone's heart. "Keller, it's time for you to go."

"Where's Keller? And Pax? What happened?" Rick hands Francesca back the handkerchief.

"I've asked him to leave. You're going to be away for a while and there's no reason for him to stick around."

Away. Rick appreciates Francesca's euphemism for being committed to the psychiatric ward of the VA hospital. He appreciates her sense of fair play for Keller. But there is something more at stake than Keller. "Fran, what about Pax?"

She bursts into tears again, this time gasping and inconsolable. "I don't know."

She is on her knees, her head in his lap, and he strokes her curls, not like he strokes Pax, for the comfort he gets from touching the dog, but in order to comfort his wife, who has effectively given the dog away.

Rick pulls Francesca into his lap, wraps his arms around her, and kisses her with all the passion of a capable man. There is something that she isn't telling him, and that's all right. In the end, he will never speak to her of his grievous mistake in the mountains in Italy and she will never speak of the real reason she has sent Keller away.

Rick holds his wife and is amazed at how good it feels.

Chapter Seventy-five

It doesn't take long to stuff his duffel bag. Fold up the cot. Find his textbooks, his *Morte d'Arthur*. Packed up in minutes, Keller tosses everything into the backseat of his car, leaving the lamp and the chair. Into the ammo box he shoves a few of the tools he's bought—a hand drill, a screwdriver, a hammer. He can't find his winter coat, then remembers hanging it in the hall closet. All the time Keller packs, Pax is at his side, worried, making little grumbling sounds in his throat.

He's made a grave mistake, a life-changing mistake, in touching her last night and now she wants him to leave. They no longer need him. With Rick away for an undetermined period, Keller is free to go. Free to go. That's what she said. Free. He's never felt less free in his life.

"I'm sorry for what happened. I won't let it happen again," he told her, ashamed at the pleading in his voice.

Francesca looked at him with weary eyes. "Keller, it's time."

"What will you tell Rick?"

"That it was time." She didn't offer him breakfast; she was leaving to see Rick. It was too early for visiting hours, but she needed to go. Unspoken but implied: Be gone when I get back.

Hurt has evolved into anger. Fine, he'll go, but he's goddamned going to take Pax with him. He's going to do what he should have done in the beginning, packed the dog into his car and kept moving. Avoided all this unhappiness. If this is love, who needs it? If this is what loving friends does for you, screw it.

Going through to the kitchen, Keller spots Pax's bowls. His leash is hanging on the breezeway doorknob. He snatches them up, puts the bowls in the ammo box and hangs the leash like a bandolier around his torso. In the hallway, his winter coat reclaimed, Keller sees Pax's squeaky mouse on the top of the hallway table. He shoves it in his pants pocket. Then he notices that the drawer in the hallway table is pulled out slightly askew. The June humidity is oppressive and the drawer in the hall table is stuck cockeyed and half-open. For some reason, this enrages him and he pounds it with the heel of his hand to set it straight. Nothing moves, so Keller gives it a good yank to pull it open. The whole drawer flies out of the table and everything in it falls to the floor. Sheets of ecru writing paper scatter, along with a fountain pen, pencils, and a boxful of paper clips. A date book embossed with 1942 falls open, facedown. Keller gathers the objects, and when he picks up the forgotten date book, three photographs fall out.

Francesca and Rick at the Totem Pole Ballroom, grinning into the camera. They both look so young, so happy. The second photograph is of Pax sitting on the top step of a porch, his long forelegs on the next step down. Even in this black-and-white photograph, his color is brighter, sharper than it is now.

Keller looks at the last photograph. Someone, maybe Sid, has taken a family portrait. Francesca and Rick stand side by side on the porch steps. It is winter and they are wearing dress coats, perhaps on their way out to some party. It is so strange to see Rick standing up. Keller is a little surprised to see how tall he is beside Francesca, as if she's shrunk. She's looking up at him, instead of him looking, as he does now, up at her. The look on her face is worried love. Pax stands between them, his eyes, too, on Rick.

Francesca and Rick and Pax. Keller flips the photograph over and reads the inscription: *On our way to the station. March 1942. Smiles fake.*

Out of the depths comes the memory of seeing that couple and their dog on the station platform. And then it hits him: Rick and Francesca were the couple he saw at South Station that cold winter afternoon when he, too, was on his way to war. He sees again the man embracing the dog before he does his wife, but now he is Rick and the woman is Francesca. He remembers the dog forcing the crowd away from her. Protective. Pax. The little family that would never include anyone else.

The truth isn't a mallet hitting Keller over the head. It is more insidious, a wraith of smoke burning up through his gut into his bloodstream. Whatever he and Pax have had, Pax was and always will be *their* dog.

He takes the black-and-white photograph of Pax and puts all the rest of it away in the drawer.

Chapter Seventy-six

Keller is gone and Pax knows deep in his heart that he won't be working with him again. There was something so different about this leave-taking. Not just the packing but the heavy aura of completion, too. Something was finished, over.

Pax waited for his praise: *good dog*. The scratch on the chest to indicate he had performed well. "Stay with them. They need you." Pax understood the *stay* as an order. The other words just brushed his ears, along with Keller's two hands, his forehead pressing against the dog's big skull. But it was an order and the dog will perform it to the best of his ability for the rest of his life. He has a purpose, a job. And two people who love him very much. A good life for a lucky dog.

Keller will fade, cast into Pax's dreams as the touch of a hand, the sound of a voice. The memory of war. A time of peace.

Part Three

2008

Chapter Seventy-seven

It shouldn't surprise him, to be contacted like this. It's not like he hasn't left a trail over the past fifty-odd years. Keller Nicholson may not have won the Pulitzer, but his plays have been performed to acclaim and his novels have received decent reviews. As a well-regarded professor of history, he's even been a regular talking head on the local NPR station when the topic is war, the essential ingredient in all his work: the effect of war on the human soul.

Even so, when Lila Stanton contacts him via his university e-mail, he is stunned. She says she wants to talk to him about her parents. Parents? Despite being an octogenarian, Keller lives in the twenty-first century and is facile with technology, so he quickly Googles this Lila Stanton. It's true: Francesca and Rick had, against all expectations, become parents after all. Checking her out on Facebook, he sees that Lila is distinctly Asian and middle-aged, so Keller assumes she was a Korean War orphan.

He served in that war, too. Not as a dog handler in combat, but as a dog trainer at Fort Riley, in Kansas, primarily training sentry dogs. Decent dogs. Good dogs. But none of them, like any of the dogs he's lived with since, as smart as Pax.

In her e-mail, this Lila is a little vague about her reasons for wanting to talk to him. Isn't he just a footnote in her family's life? A blip on their radar? Someone who lived with them for a short time, a full lifetime ago.

"I was hoping that it would be possible to visit you. I live in Boston and I thought that I might zip up to Hawke's Cove some afternoon and take you to lunch."

He wonders if she's just using this weak and ancient association to impose herself on him. She's probably got some manuscript she wants him to look at. Or wants to pick his brain about getting published. A memoir, that's what it is. *How I Went from Being a Korean War Orphan to an American Girl.*

He wishes she'd said something about Francesca.

Keller hits reply. "Fine. Give me a date. I'll make lunch."

Even before he can power down his laptop, a reply pops up. She wants to meet this Saturday, and she has something for him.

Keller drove away from the Stanton's North Quincy house that day, his belongings heaped up on the backseat, Pax's leash still bandolier-style around his body. Deeply sorry. Deeply hurt. Aching already for what he'd left behind. He drove past the hospital and thought about going in to say good-bye to Rick properly, but he kept going. He knew Francesca would be there, and he just couldn't do it. So he kept driving, blindly following a northerly route until the scenery began to look familiar and he realized that he'd done what he'd sworn he'd never do. He was back in Hawke's Cove.

He'd stood on the back steps, the key from the lawyer in his hand. The sun was just setting and the afterglow burnished the water beneath the bluff to a rosy glow. In the distance was the edge of the rest of the world. The place where he'd blown it. Ruined his own chance at happiness.

Inside, the house was damp and cold and smelled of dead mice. It was exactly as the old man had left it. No one had been in the house since his death; no one had cleared away the remnants of the man. The mice had consumed all the dried foods; all that was left of Clayton's last loaf of bread was the wrapper, chewed into fragments. A glass was upside down in the drainer and a single plate flanked it, sentinels to an old bachelor's life.

Upstairs, Keller pushed open the door to his uncle's bedroom. In all the time Keller had lived in this house with his great-uncle Clayton, he'd never set foot in the old man's room. On the otherwise-bare bureau, a photograph in a surprisingly ornate frame was propped against the fly-specked mirror. Keller picked it up. The old man himself, his arm linked with a pretty young woman in a diaphanous white dress, her wedding headpiece low on her brow in the fashion of a long-ago decade, a veil floating around her like a phantom. Keller studied the faces. If there was a resemblance in the doomed Florence to her older sister, Ruth Jacobs, he couldn't see it.

This Clayton is smiling, and his joy in the moment is projected beyond the flat dimensions of the foxed old photograph. A brief golden joy that will soon become the lead of grief. Keller sees himself in the streaky mirror and thinks that he looks like Clayton. The Clayton he knew, not this younger, better version of the man. He slipped the purloined snapshot of Pax out of his pocket and set it beside the wedding photo of Clayton and Florence.

·   ·   ·

Lila is due at any minute. He sent her the address and decided to let her find her way to him via GPS. He's nervous and hates that he is. He can't figure out why he should be nervous, but then he thinks, What if she asks me a question I can't answer? Worse, what if she tells me something I don't want to know? His chest feels tight with anxiety and he presses at it with his fingertips. He's lived a full life since then, a good-enough life. Resurrecting those buried memories of the happiest he'd ever been before meeting Margie and having the kids serves nothing. Remembering old grief, when the more recent loss of his wife is still painful, is just a useless exercise.

Suddenly, she's there knocking on his door, and Keller welcomes Francesca and Rick's only child into his house.

Chapter Seventy-eight

I couldn't bring myself to tell Keller Nicholson via e-mail that my mother had died. I know that sounds a bit odd; after all, she was in her eighties and had heart disease, and people in their generation can't possibly be surprised to hear of one another's passing, but it just didn't feel right to let him know that way. However, I was there on her behalf. She'd spoken of him so fondly over the years, as someone who had come into their lives when things were bad, when Dad was suffering from what we now know as PTSD. And, of course, no story of Keller could be told without stories of Pax. As a kid, I had the two of them inextricably linked in my mind, even though I knew that Keller had left them and that Pax remained with them for several more years.

"Pax our wonder dog."—that's what Mom called him. I swear that there were a thousand pictures of the dog—as many as of me as a three-year-old refugee from Korea. But none of this Keller Nicholson.

It wasn't until I was in grad school that I connected the Keller Nicholson of *Dogs of War* fame, the novel that was required reading in some high schools, and the Keller Nicholson of Pax and the time my parents lived in Quincy. They'd moved to Norwood the first year Dad joined WEEI's sportscasting team, having built a fully handicapped-accessible house on a fenced-in quarter-acre lot in the booming suburb. Dad had passed in 1985, but I'd only recently lost my mother.

"I brought this." We'd been talking, weeping a little, because I was riling up long-dormant feelings in him and more recent loss in me. I handed him a clasp envelope. "It was tucked in her dresser drawer with your name on it, so I know that she wanted you to have it."

Keller pressed his fingers against his chest, a soft gesture he'd been making all through our tomato soup and grilled cheese lunch. He didn't open the envelope right away, sort of just studied the handwriting on it, as if he couldn't read it clearly. When he finally did open it, the little brass clasp was so old that it broke as he bent it up, freeing the flap and revealing what my mother had left to him.

The leather of the dog collar was cracked with age and had been tightly coiled in that brown kraft envelope for so long that it looked like the inside of a nautilus shell. A dog tag dangled from the metal loop, a 1954 Norwood dog license, the same year they adopted me. On the broad surface of the leather collar itself was a brass nameplate with three letters stamped in bold Gothic type: PAX.

Keller made a soft sound, as if the air had been pushed out of him, but he was smiling. He held the dog collar in both hands like a holy relic, something sanctified. "Thank you for bringing this." And then he reached out and took my hand.

Chapter Seventy-nine

Lila has gone, leaving the dog collar there on his table. Keller keeps looking at it, even as he tidies up the remnants of lunch. He washes two glasses and two plates, wipes the cast-iron frying pan out. Funny how this middle-aged Korean woman reminded him of Francesca. Nurture will win out, he supposes. The grace of brushing away a hair from her cheek, the way she cocked her head to listen to him, all gestures reminiscent of her mother, absorbed by observation instead of born into her. A little of Rick, too. The way she pursed her lips before she smiled.

Lila could have sent the collar through the mail, and she certainly deserved better than the company of a weepy old man and a lunch of grilled cheese, but he was deeply grateful that she had been there, that she understood how important this artifact from a lifetime ago was to him. Not simply Pax's collar but also a message from Francesca. She had remembered him.

. . .

Keller takes the dog collar with him into the parlor, sets it in front of the latest family portrait in residence on the end table beside his La-Z-Boy. There's a new Ken Burns documentary on tonight, but he doesn't turn it on. The last light of day has faded, leaving the room in shadow, but he doesn't move to turn on the light. From beyond the open window comes the soft lap of cove water against a low-tide beach. A little wind is frisking the fading leaves of late summer. The faint aroma of skunk wafts on it; the little skunk family beneath the scallop shed must have been startled by something. Even with that, it's really quite perfect here. Clayton's ghost was long ago exorcised by a living and garrulous family.

Another ghost has been laid to rest, thanks to Lila. A ghost Keller has been carrying around with him since the day he left the Stantons' house. Not so much a ghost as a grain of sand buried in the oyster of his heart. Francesca had forgiven him. The grain of sand has become a pearl.

Keller Nicholson picks up the dog collar and holds it to his breast. Pax. He was a good dog, the best. Pax had never been without love, the love of his people.

One lucky dog.

Epilogue

The winter wind shakes the house, screaming over the water and through the windbreak of juniper trees. Over the roar of the day-old northeaster, Keller hears scratching at the back door. It is a delicate sound, like the very tips of a sapling's branches brushing against a screen. It deepens. No longer random, the scratching at the door is deliberate and purposeful. Insistent. Demanding. Keller pulls himself out of his chair, finds his slippers with his toes. The house is dark. Either he's forgotten to turn on the lights or the electricity is out. But Keller isn't hampered by the darkness; indeed, he sees his way clearly as he walks toward the sound.

Keller opens the back door. Now there is no wind, no cold air, no sleet, no sound at all. Pax is there, his tail wagging like mad, like it always does when Keller has been absent for a while.

"Well, there, Pax. Where've you been?" Keller kneels and wraps his arms around the dog, who raises his muzzle so that he can lick Keller's face. "I've missed you."

Pax shakes himself free and sits in front of Keller. He's

wearing his flat leather on-duty collar and his long canvas military lead is attached to it. He faces the empty distance beyond the open door, then swings his big head back to Keller, his eyes bright with expectation, his mouth open in a doggy grin. He barks once.

"Time to go?" Keller takes up the leash.

The dog stands and shakes himself again. Ready.

"Okay, Pax. Let's go."

Acknowledgments

This book would not be the book it has become without Andrea Cirillo and Annelise Robey, who have been my stalwart girl guides throughout the process. Their combined expertise and enthusiasm has been unflagging, and for that I am truly grateful. To the rest of the family at JRA: Peggy Gordijn, Don Cleary, Christina Prestia, Julianne Tinari, Michael Conroy, Danielle Sickles, and, of course, Jane Rotrosen Berkey, thank you for all you do.

Thanks, as always, to the team at St. Martin's Press, especially Jeanne-Marie Hudson and Joan Higgins, who understand the vast and changing world of publicity and social media, and cover artist Ervin Serrano, who has illustrated my imagination so beautifully. Thanks, too, to Caitlin Dareff, Sara Goodman, Chris Holder, John Murphy, Kerry Nordling, Sally Richardson, Matthew Shear, Anne Marie Tallberg, and a special shout-out to Carol Edwards, my brilliant copy editor. Thanks, too, to the folks at Macmillan Audio: Brant Janeway, Samantha Beerman, Mary Beth Roche, and Robert Allen.

A special note of deepest gratitude to Jennifer Enderlin, my editor extraordinaire, who knew that this book could be so much better and worked really hard with me to make that happen. Thank you for never giving up on me or on this book.

Of course, none of this would be as much fun without the love and support of my husband, kids, extended family, and friends. Thank you all.

Sources

Books

Downey, Fairfax, *Dogs for Defense: American Dogs in the Second World War, 1941–45*; by Direction and Authorization of the Trustees Dogs for Defense, Inc. (New York: Daniel P. Mc-Donald, 1955).

Erlanger, Arlene, *TM 10–396*—War Dogs (Washington, D.C.: GPO, 1943).

Rosenkrans, Robert, *U.S. Military War Dogs in World War II* (Atglen, PA: Schiffer, 2011).

Web Sites

www.thedailyjournal.com. "World War II History: Dogs for Defense."

www.militaryworkingdog.com. (The Military Working Dog" (Military Working Dog Foundation).

www.qmfound.com. "Quartermaster War Dog Program" (U.S. Army Quartermaster Foundation).

Video

Return to Norumbega: A History of Norumbega Park and the Totem Pole Ballroom. Bob Pollock. Produced by Joe Hunter. 2005. Remember Productions.

Suggested Reading

Luis Carlos Montalván, *Until Tuesday* (New York: Hyperion, 2011).

Susan Wilson is the author of many novels, including the bestselling *The Dog Who Danced* and *One Good Dog*. She lives on Martha's Vineyard. Visit her at www.susanwilsonwrites.com.